DUTY'S COST

DUTY'S COST

TED RUSS

Published by Chinook Publishing LLC.

First Edition: 2024

ISBN: 978-1-7343925-6-2

Cover design & interior formatting:

Mark Thomas / Coverness.com

He knows who he is.
This one is for him, and all those like him.

CHAPTER 1

Bound, gagged, and hooded in the trunk of the car, Val flexed his fingers. They were numb. Plastic zip ties also bit into his ankles.

I swear this asshole is hitting every pothole on purpose.

Val tried to shift his weight around to lessen the impacts, but it was futile. The car speeding through the dark city tossed him around like a loose bag of groceries.

How long have I been in the trunk of this car? An hour, maybe?

The smell of mildew and motor oil permeated his clothes.

His body slammed forward as the car came to an abrupt halt. Val heard the vehicle's doors open and felt the old car jostle and rise as the heavy men got out. One of them mumbled something in Russian that Val could not quite make out. The others laughed.

Feet scrapped on the ground around the rear of the car.

The trunk popped open.

Val heard the metallic click of the switchblade, and his body tensed, anticipating stabbing pain.

Instead, the bindings on his ankles fell away.

Hands grabbed him and hoisted him out of the trunk, setting him on his feet but maintaining a firm grip on his arms, which were still bound behind his back.

"Walk!" the gruff, familiar voice said as they pushed Val along.

He thought he heard water.

A voice from above called out in Chechen. More laughter from the group that forced him along.

They turned. Val tripped on something, but rough hands steadied him. They were walking up a creaky incline now. He was sure he heard water. Was it lapping at the side of a swimming pool?

A couple of quick direction changes.

The hands on his arms pushed him forward up another dozen steps.

"Stop," the voice commanded, as a firm hand met his chest.

The hands gripping his arms maintained their hold.

Val steadied his breathing. It was going to be an interrogation room or some kind of execution setup. Probably a drain on the floor to make for easy cleanup.

He took a deep breath.

Someone yanked the hood off his head.

Val blinked, eyes adjusting to the dim lighting, as a man behind him removed his gag.

He spat, trying to clean his tongue. The gag was a filthy rag that left grit in his mouth.

Surprised he was not dead yet, Val quickly scanned the area to get his bearings.

He was on the aft deck of a large yacht facing forward, standing in the middle of a teak-floored seating area, semicircular white sofas to each side. Two more levels rose above him as he looked forward, each one with a pair of armed men standing against railings looking down on him. A closed, reflective sliding glass door stood at Val's front, beneath the overhang of the upper decks.

He could see his reflection in the glass, surrounded by five mercenaries. Dressed in dark-green fatigues with no identifying insignia and armed with modified AK-74s, the mercenaries had taken Val hostage almost a week ago. He'd tired of their company quickly.

Val shook his head as a sickening recognition flowed through him – He'd been on this yacht before. Years ago.

The *Monarch* was a ship he'd never wanted to be on again.

One of the mercenaries, who had a swollen black eye, stepped forward and slid open the reflective glass door.

The open door revealed the yacht's expansive, well-appointed saloon, encompassing a formal dining area, a seating area, and a bar. A large dining table with chairs for ten stood directly in front of Val, just a few steps in from the open glass doors. Past the large dining table, a lone man sat at a small bistro table that had been placed in the middle of the seating area. Two empty chairs sat at the table with him.

The two mercenaries holding Val's arms pushed him forward, leaving the two other armed men out on the aft deck. The black-eyed mercenary followed, closing the sliding door behind them.

Val looked around the saloon as they walked the length of the long table. The floor was dark, polished hardwood. Wide windows sitting above knee-high bookcases ran the length of each wall with their curtains pulled shut. Books, globes, and expensive-looking knickknacks filled the shelves. Luxurious tufted leather reading chairs sat by the windows.

Past the lone man at the bistro table, a bartender dressed in a white shirt under a black vest and necktie stood behind a large carved wooden bar. He glanced at Val and then went back to cleaning glasses with a white cloth. Bottles of liquor sat on shelves in front of a mirrored wall behind the bartender. Four empty stools stood at the bar. Closed doors stood on either side of the bar, hinting at off-limits luxury behind them.

Val's escorts stopped him short of the bistro table.

He and the seated man took stock of each other.

The man wore a tailored black suit over an open-collared black shirt, his graying black hair swept back over his ears. The bottom half of his left ear was missing, as if the claws of an animal had torn it away. The man sat with his hands folded together on the red tablecloth that covered the small table.

Val wore jeans and a gray sweatshirt. His clothes were dirty, the same ones he'd been wearing for almost a week. His wavy dark brown hair, not quite as long as the seated man's, was just as gray.

Both men had the look of tired athletes. In their early fifties, bodies that had once been young and powerful were now weary and damaged. But despite the obvious fatigue and scar tissue, they were both still fit and had an air of lethality. Like what they had lost in youthful power and endurance, was more than made up for with experience and cunning.

The seated man smiled. "Hello, Val."

"Hello, Alexei."

"What happened to you, Zakir?" Alexei asked, switching to Russian and pointing at the man's blackened eye.

Zakir grunted and walked toward the table.

Alexei glanced at Val.

"Ah." Alexei smiled. "You and Val have gotten along well, I see."

"The only reason he is not dead is you ordered me not to kill him," Zakir growled, standing next to Val.

"Do not take it personally, Zakir. Val has punched me many times."

"This was all he had on him." Zakir wasn't interested in the current conversation. He handed Alexei a switchblade.

Alexei turned it over in his hand and smiled. It was a large one. A red number thirteen marked one side of the black wooden handle.

"You kept it," Alexei said in English. "All these years."

"Yes," Val said.

Alexei nodded with approval and placed the knife on the table. He motioned at the empty chair across from him.

Zakir pulled it out from under the table. The two men holding Val's arms shoved him into it. They maintained their grip on Val as Zakir cut the plastic flex-cuff that bound his wrists.

Val resisted the urge to groan in relief. He pulled his numb hands into his lap.

Alexei gestured at the three men looming over Val, telling them to step back. They hesitated, not trusting Val.

"Is okay." Alexei gestured with more insistence and glared at the men.

They nodded and backed away. Zakir and another mercenary sat at the bar, while the third walked to the dining area. He leaned back against the long table and rested his arms on the buttstock of his weapon, staring at Val.

Val and Alexei sat facing each other across the small table, the bar to one side, dining area to the other, armed mercenaries on both.

"You look good, my friend," Alexei said.

"So do you," Val said. "Except for the ear. What happened there?"

"Syria."

"Oh. I got my own version of that."

Val leaned his head forward and parted his hair with his hands to expose scar tissue on the top of his head.

Alexei nodded and smiled as he looked at the puffy pink skin.

Val raised his head and tried to read Alexei's face. Was that anger? Sadness? It didn't matter.

"I heard you had retired," Alexei said.

"I did."

"What is it like? To be retired?"

Val shrugged.

Alexei smiled and nodded. He looked like he was about to say something, but then thought better of it.

"What are you doing here?" Val asked. "I thought you might be busy in Kyiv or Crimea. Why Illichivsk?"

Alexei looked at Val for a moment without answering his question and then turned in his chair to motion at the bartender.

The bartender handed Zakir a bottle and two shot glasses. The mercenary brought them to the table and set them in front of Alexei and then returned to his barstool.

"Bourbon?" Val said. "Alexei, you shouldn't have."

"Only the best for my friend." Alexei grabbed the bottle and worked at its top. "Like the day we met. Do you remember?"

"Yes."

A squeak filled the quiet saloon as Alexei pulled the top off the bottle.

Alexei poured two tall shots of bourbon and slid one across the table to Val.

Val looked at the glass.

"How many of these do I get?"

"We'll see." Alexei didn't look Val in the eye. "When is over, is over."

Alexi reached behind his back and pulled out a pistol. He placed the pistol on the table next to the switchblade.

Val chuckled. "Thanks for that," he gestured at the weapon. "I wouldn't have been able to figure out where this was headed without all the theatrics."

"Is no theatrics. Is my obligation to a friend. I could have done this the hard way."

"Fine. Let's get started. You go first."

Alexei smiled and picked up his shot glass. "First toast. To Sydney."

"Fuck you," Val said in a quiet but angry voice.

"Okay, okay." Alexei laughed. "I am sorry. I did not realize you were still mad."

The mercenaries tensed, hands moving to their weapons, not sure what Val was going to do. He had a reputation.

Val realized he was leaning forward over the table, the pistol almost within reach. That wasn't his intent, though. He wanted to strangle Alexei, not shoot him.

"Is okay!" Alexei said to his men, still laughing. He looked left and then right, making eye contact with all of them. "Trust me. Is okay. That was my fault."

Keeping their eyes on Val, the mercenaries on both sides relaxed.

"Shit, Val." Alexei shook his head. "I am sorry. Sincerely."

Val leaned back in his chair and sat in silence as Alexei looked at him.

Alexei raised his glass again. "First toast."

Val was motionless. Glass of bourbon sitting in front of him.

"To Kosovo."

Alexei held his glass in the air, waiting.

Val sat like a statue.

The bartender paused, cleaning glasses. Zakir's head tilted. They both looked at Alexei's raised glass, and then at Val.

Val fought it, but a smile spread slowly across his face. His shoulders relaxed, and he shook his head.

"No," Val said. He lifted an arm from his lap to grab the bourbon. He moved slowly, concentrating so that his still numb fingers did not fumble and spill the drink as he raised it.

"To Colonel Ziora."

Alexei smiled a joyous, open-mouthed smile.

"Yes! To the colonel!"

They clinked their glasses together, and the two old spies downed their bourbon.

CHAPTER 2

27 July 1999

Kosovo

The C-17 shuddered and its nose pitched down as the pilot extended flaps and lined up for the final approach to runway three five of the Pristina International Airport. Val tightened his seat belt in the jump seat. He'd talked his way up front into the cockpit before they departed Dover Air Force Base yesterday by throwing around the few aviation terms he knew.

Val was able to do that a lot, talk people into things. His six-foot frame, confident posture, and strong jawline should've been off putting, the whole package just a little too much. But his warm smile and reassuring vibe always seemed to put people at ease.

Sitting behind and between the two pilots gave him a clear view of the airfield ahead. Even from many miles away, it was obvious that it was not a normal commercial airport. Numerous Russian antiaircraft and armored personnel carriers ringed the perimeter, weapon systems facing outward. Russian aircraft and tactical vehicles, parked beneath camouflage netting, lined the runway.

Val looked north past the airfield as the pilots started their landing checklist. It was a clear day, and the midmorning sun was high. From their altitude of three thousand feet, Val could see a wide, flat river valley stretching away to the north-northwest. It was the Kosovo field, where the Serbian army made a doomed stand against the invading Ottoman Empire in 1389.

Six hundred years later, almost to the day, the newly elected president of the Serbian Republic, Slobodan Milošević, gave a speech on the twenty-eighth of

June, 1989, commemorating the cataclysmic battle at the Gazimestan Monument, which now sits on the southern end of the Kosovo field. Milošević used the memory like a fulcrum to raise Serbian national fervor. It was not a heavy lift. The Yugoslav wars began soon after.

After a decade, with more than a hundred thousand dead, several million displaced, and ethnic cleansing on a scale not seen in Europe since the Second World War, NATO finally acted with resolve. Their ground occupation of Kosovo began more than six weeks ago, on the eleventh of June, 1999.

The Globemaster's fourteen landing gear wheels barked as they touched down on the runway. Val jerked forward into his restraining belts as the pilot laid on the thrust reversers. For such a huge aircraft, the C-17 could stop quickly. A handy capability when landing on austere runways around the world.

"Welcome to Kosovo," the pilot muttered as he cleaned up his configuration and taxied off the active. "The world's anus."

"How long are we here?" the copilot asked.

"Four hours."

"That's about four hours too long."

"How long did you say you were here?" The pilot turned in his chair to look back at Val.

"About six months," Val answered.

The pilot and copilot looked at each other and then laughed.

The airfield was an overloaded, chaotic hive of activity. NATO's Kosovo Force, or KFOR, had already surged to more than thirty thousand soldiers in-country, on its way to fifty thousand. The daunting logistical task of housing, feeding, equipping, and maintaining that force manifested itself at Pristina Airport as NATO and other military elements shoved everything they could through a constrained airborne pipe.

Val nearly fell out of the C-17 under the weight of his duffel. He put the bag on the ground and stretched. His back was tight from the long flight. The air was hot and carried pungent hints of jet fuel, irritating Val's nose. Not yet ready for the sweltering Balkan sun, he lingered beneath the aircraft's massive wing and looked around trying to absorb the activity.

This was not like the shiny NATO facilities he'd been stationed at during his tour in Germany as a tanker. Mud and grime covered everything, including the crumbling concrete of the airstrip. A single derelict building served as the terminal and headquarters.

Russian, French, British, Italian, German, and American soldiers were everywhere. Each group wore their own uniform, adding to the chaotic vibe. There were more than thirty partner nations involved in the peacekeeping operation. It looked to Val that all of them were represented on the airfield, each nation trying to exert influence on the strategic facility.

Like ants at a picnic, the sweating ground crews moved in focused streams, swarming onto the material and devouring it, breaking it down so that it could be ingested by a helicopter or a truck and taken out to units on the frontier. They were breaking chains on tied-down vehicles, forklifting pallets of ammunition, and moving large stacks of food and medical equipment. They attacked everything disgorged from the large cargo aircraft, clearing the airfield so that the cycle of arrivals and departures could continue unhindered.

Val left the shadow of the C-17 and moved toward the airfield staging area, dodging Humvees and forklifts along the way. Trucks were loading up there and taking US personnel to Camp Bondsteel, the largest US operating base in Kosovo, where all new personnel first reported in-country.

Val signed the convoy manifest and climbed into the back of one of the two-and-a-half-ton cargo trucks. The canvas sides of the truck had been rolled up to provide some ventilation but the air in back was stifling. An enormous pile of bags sat in the middle of the truck bed between the two inside-facing wooden benches. Val added his bag to the pile and sat down.

The convoy took about an hour and a half to travel the less than fifty kilometers to Bondsteel. Val sat quietly in the back, sweating through his uniform as he studied the Kosovan countryside. It was a filthy landscape of decay. Washed-out dirt roads, abandoned vehicles, trash, and dilapidated buildings. Dirty and tired pedestrians walked in the muck on the side of the road, their belongings on their backs.

Val grew tired of the dirty sameness of the passing war scape. He leaned his head back against one of the truck's wooden canopy supports and stared at the canvas top. Recalling his meeting with General Bryson only five days earlier, Val closed his eyes and shook his head.

Shit detail doesn't quite seem to cover it, sir.

CHAPTER 3

Five days before landing in Pristina, Val caught an early flight out of Monterey, California, where he'd just graduated from the Defense Language Institute's Russian program. Later that afternoon, he reported to Brigadier General Bryson at the Defense Intelligence Agency headquarters on Bolling Air Force Base in Washington, D.C.

General Bryon graduated from West Point in 1978 as an infantry officer. But after his first assignment in Italy, he was recruited into the precursor of the program Val now served in. Trained by the CIA in human intelligence tradecraft, Bryson had been running spies, or people who ran spies, for almost twenty years. A tall, fit man with a full head of hair that had gone silver, Bryson was a legend in the defense intelligence community. He'd gone up against the Russians in Berlin in the early eighties, worked with Delta Force during the invasion of Panama, deployed with Special Operations Command during Desert Storm, and, the rumors said, done a lot more. Rumors he never really denied. Thoughtful and profane, General Bryson inspired intense loyalty within the small US Army covert human intelligence community.

"Fucking finally," Bryson said. "You're here." He gestured at a conference table across the room without looking up from his desk. Val sat at it while the director closed the file he was reading and picked up a stack of notebooks. The director's assistant closed the door behind her as Bryson walked to the conference table and put the notebooks in front of Val.

"Congratulations on graduation." The general walked to his seat at the head of the conference table. "I hear you did well."

"Thank you, sir."

"And sorry to cancel your leave." There was no apology in the general's voice.

"It's okay, sir." Val pushed thoughts of Sydney and their plans out of his mind. The stars just never seemed to align for them. "Duty calls."

"It does, indeed, son." Bryson nodded. "Those are the hard copies of your briefing books. They're not to leave this building." The director pointed at several notebooks on the table. "They contain country background material and dossiers on all the key players and organizations you will work with and near in Kosovo. It's good work. You need to be intimately familiar with all of it before your departure."

"Roger that, sir." Val tried to conceal his surprise. He hadn't known what this meeting was about until that moment.

Why the hell am I going to Kosovo?

"Here is the soft copy." Bryson slid an encrypted jump drive across the table to Val. "That goes with you. Lose it, and your next duty station will be making little rocks out of big rocks at Fort Leavenworth."

"Understood, sir."

"I'm going to give you your mission now. Then you'll spend the next forty-eight hours squaring yourself away before getting on a C-17 to Pristina."

"Yes, sir."

"When the Russians seized the airfield at Pristina, they secured themselves a seat at the table in Kosovo," the director began. "We'd been stiff-arming and grin-fucking them until then, talking nice about playing well together, with no intention of giving them any meaningful influence.

"The Russians were pissed. And not just because they give a shit about the Serbs. They do. Sort of. But what they really don't like is the loss of the buffer state of Yugoslavia and NATO expansion eastward.

"So, while everyone at the UN was congratulating themselves on the passage of Resolution 1244, and NATO prepared to roll into Kosovo with all their pretty vehicles and starched uniforms lined up on the border, a ballsy two-star Russian general named Viktor Zavarzin led a small force of two hundred lightly armed paratroopers in an early-morning, lights-out, radio-silent dash in forty vehicles from Bosnia directly to the Pristina Airport.

"When the sun came up on the twelfth of June, NATO was still holding their dicks on the border while Zavarzin and his paratroopers were drinking beer on the runway."

Director Bryson smiled and shook his head. "Never forget, Rafter. No one plays a weak hand better than the Russians. No one."

Val nodded, seeing the grudging respect on Director Bryson's face.

"Well, it took more than a week to un-fuck the situation," the director continued. "The Secretary of Defense flew to Helsinki to meet with the Russian defense minister, and they finally got to an agreement that gave NATO access to the airfield.

"As a result, the Russians got to put a brigade with three combat battalions on the ground in Kosovo."

The general grimaced at his own comment.

"They sent their 13th Tactical Group under the command of Colonel Ziora," Bryson continued as he pushed a map of Kosovo that had been lying in front of him on the table toward Val.

"One battalion in our sector in Kamenica." He pointed at sectors on the map. "One in the German sector, and one in the French sector. Colonel Ziora and his brigade headquarters are in Kamenica. The Russian units are supposed to take orders from the KFOR chain of command while also remaining under Russian command and control.

"In exchange for giving Ivan a piece of the pie, NATO got control of flight planning, approach control, aerial port operations, and a bunch of other crap for Pristina. The Russians maintained responsibility for airfield security, ramp management, and other ground-operations-related bullshit."

Val looked at the director, wondering if he'd heard him correctly.

"Yeah." Bryson rolled his eyes. "I don't understand it either. It's a clusterfuck. But it got things moving again."

"So, we're stuck with those sneaky bastards on the ground with us, all over the country, up to god knows what. Making matters worse, at present, we don't have anybody qualified to embed and liaise with the Russians. Our officer in role at the moment, Captain Phillips, is a vanilla army tanker. General Stenson put him in the slot because Phillips is a good officer and it was a staffing requirement that didn't even exist until the Russians got themselves invited to the party at the last fucking minute. So, they shoved Phillips into the breech."

Director Bryson smiled at Val. "I'm pulling him out and shoving your ass in it."

Val blinked, getting his head around it.

"Your mission is to live and operate with the Russians, keep tabs on their bullshit, and report to myself and General Stenson, the American commander in theater."

Val nodded and said slowly, "So, I'm basically a babysitter?"

"Call it whatever you want, son."

"Sounds like babysitting to me. Not exactly what I thought I'd be doing as a Cobra Snare."

The Cobra Snare program was the Defense Intelligence Agency's own human intelligence arm. Operating under the cover of various DOD billets, it was a top-secret platform for recruiting and running foreign assets, the only component of DIA authorized to conduct cross-border and other high-level intelligence operations. It was a small team composed of all volunteers that had been recruited, assessed, selected, and trained at a high cost to the army. Val had just completed two years of training after being accepted into the program. This was not the sexy first assignment he'd been expecting.

But he only had himself to blame for that.

"Let's get this straight right now, son." Bryson pointed at Val. "You and I both know you're fucking lucky to be a Cobra Snare at this point after the stunt you pulled at the Farm. I went to bat for you, used up a few of my own big-ticket IOUs to keep you in the program. Don't make me regret it. At this moment, all I want to hear out of your wise ass mouth is, 'Sir, I understand.'"

Bryson stared at Val.

Val lowered his head slightly. "Sir, I understand."

Bryson didn't uncoil at all.

"I really do, sir," Val added, raising his head and squaring his shoulders to the angry general. "I appreciated it then, and I still do, and I won't let you down. Whatever you need me to do, I'll do it."

"Good." Bryson let appreciation creep into his voice.

The general leaned back in his chair and continued.

"General Stenson, a fine officer and a friend of mine, called me a week ago, asking for help. His vanilla army tanker isn't getting the job done. It's a vulnerability. He needs a Russian-speaking officer who is trained in intelligence fieldcraft and knows how the game works to go live with the Russians for a few months so they don't destabilize the fragile progress we have made to date. I told him he was in luck because I had just the officer for the job."

"And, yes," the general said with a big grin, "this is a shit detail."

Val couldn't help but grin back.

"How bad can it really be, sir?"

"You're about to find out." Bryson grinned again in a way that told Val it was going to be pretty bad.

"But, you go downrange and do good work? Then, when you get back, we'll talk about your next assignment. I have some good ideas, by the way. I look forward to sharing them with you."

"That sounds great, sir."

"Now go pack."

CHAPTER 4

The truck jerked to a stop at the Camp Bondsteel gate checkpoint around noon. Val looked around as the guard waved them through, noting the difference the US Army Corps of Engineers could make in just a little more than a month. The roads were freshly paved, and dozens of new one-story buildings were laid out in a neat grid. He saw a gym, a small PX, and a barbershop. Val knew it wouldn't be long before Burger King, Pizza Hut, and other American comforts were in place.

The US Army occupied Bondsteel when they first rolled into Kosovo and had been working to improve it daily. KBR and Halliburton were on-site on day one alongside the first troops. Now their engineers and surveyors crisscrossed the base in large SUVs as they plotted the grand development plan for what would become the United States' largest base in the Balkans for decades.

The deuce-and-a-half stopped, and Val hopped out. He walked a few paces away, dropped his bag, and took a deep breath. The sound of Chinook helicopters coming and going reverberated in the background as he turned slowly to take in the terrain. Bondsteel sat in a large basin in southeast Kosovo with rolling hills and mountains on all sides. Mount Ljuboten, standing almost 2,500 meters tall, was the most dramatic. About fifty kilometers away, it straddled the border of Kosovo and Macedonia, but loomed large over the base despite the distance. To Val, the place was like a dirtier version of Austria.

"Captain Rafter!" a voice called. "Captain Rafter, sir, is that you?"

"Roger that," Val answered as he turned to see a mismatched pair of American soldiers walking his way. One tall Black sergeant, the other a short white specialist. They both saluted Val as they approached.

"Good afternoon." Val returned the salute.

"I'm Sergeant Travis," the tall one said. "This is Specialist Zimmer." He pointed at the smiling, shorter soldier. "We're your terps, sir. Welcome to Kosovo."

"Thank you, Sergeant." Val smiled and shook their hands. "What's a 'terp'?"

"Interpreter team, sir." Zimmer lifted Val's bag from the ground and hoisted it on his back.

"Thank you, Zimmer," Val said. "But I can get that."

"Actually, sir, you need to jump through the in-processing hoops over there." Sergeant Travis pointed at one of the new buildings behind Val. "We'll take this to our Humvee and wait for you. Then we'll head down to the Russian sector."

"Got it. Thanks, guys."

Val moved through the in-processing tasks quickly, updating his will and other paperwork, and signing for his combat gear. At each station, the administrative soldiers made small talk and asked Val where he was bound for. Everyone in earshot gave him a *what the hell are you thinking?* look each time he answered, "The Russian sector." By the time he finished in-processing, he'd gotten this reaction a dozen times.

Thanks again for the shit detail, sir. Val silently invoked General Bryson as he walked back to the terps.

"So, the Russian sector doesn't have the best reputation up here." Val threw his gear in the back of their Humvee.

"Ha!" Zimmer laughed. "You got that right, sir."

"Don't let 'em scare you, sir," Travis said. "It ain't that bad."

Val hopped in the back seat, and Zimmer gunned the Humvee off Camp Bondsteel.

"Next stop, Kamenica!" Zimmer said, false enthusiasm dripping from his voice.

"When did you guys get to Kosovo?" Val asked.

"We rolled in with First Armored on day one," Sergeant Travis said. "Shit was crazy then."

"Shit is still crazy now," Zimmer said over his shoulder.

"True enough," Travis nodded. "But it seems to have cooled down a notch or two the last week or so. I mean, it's still chaos over here. But June was biblical."

"I think it's still crazy," Zimmer said to Val. "You'll see, sir. Every day the same shit—fight fires, disperse angry mobs, quell violence."

Sergeant Travis nodded in agreement. "Yes, sir. Every day at the end of our cycle, I go to the operations tent and check the totals for the day. Just to keep things in perspective."

"The totals?"

"Murders, arson, and vandalism."

"Sounds lovely." Val shook his head.

Zimmer and Travis laughed ruefully.

Half an hour later, they pulled up to a small American military compound. "Here we are, sir," Sergeant Travis said. "Your own little slice of heaven here in Kamenica."

They went through the checkpoint at the gate and pulled into the parking area of the two-acre American outpost. Most of the compound was taken up by twenty C-huts, shipping containers with cut-out windows and doors. They served as sleeping facilities, as well as the latrines and common shower areas. The rest of the compound was the operations center, which comprised two GP medium tents side by side on a permanent foundation. One tent served as the common operations center in which anyone was allowed, while the other was a classified communications facility. Access to the classified communications tent was restricted. Val would use this facility to send and receive reports and cables to and from the DIA and CIA.

"How many personnel are stationed here?" Val asked as they exited the Humvee.

"About a dozen, including yourself, sir," Travis answered. "The military intelligence detachment has eight soldiers commanded by a first lieutenant. Their mission is to observe and report on the Russians."

"Terrific." Val's mission was to develop relationships with the Russian leadership. He worried that living with a group of MI soldiers would make that more difficult.

"Don't worry, sir," Travis said, anticipating Val's concern. "I've been here since day one and have to say the Russians don't mind too much. They understand how the game is played. They're not friendly with the squirrels, by any means. But they don't hold them against us."

"Squirrels?"

"That's what we call the military intelligence geeks," Zimmer chimed in. "Because they're always sneaking around. Like squirrels."

Val laughed as he walked to the rear of the Humvee to grab his duffel. As he rounded the corner of the vehicle, he walked into a stern-looking, dark-haired, medium-size dog. She looked to Val like a shepherd mix. She wasn't growling. But she was about to.

"Lilly! He's cool." Zimmer pointed at Val. "That's Captain Rafter. He's with us."

Val held out his hand. Lilly took two tentative steps forward and sniffed it.

"She's with you guys?"

"Yes, sir," Zimmer said emphatically.

"Sort of," Travis said.

"What do you mean, 'sort of'?" Zimmer protested.

"She lives on the compound with about six other dogs," Travis continued, ignoring Zimmer. "She's the bravest. It's her pack. They'll slink out here once she decides you're okay."

"They're the best personal security detail you can ask for, sir," Zimmer said. "The best."

Lilly was still sniffing Val's hand. He kneeled in front of her and let her smell both. "Attagirl," he cooed. Still sniffing, she edged forward until she was smelling his chest.

"You like dogs, sir?" Travis said, now standing over his shoulder, watching the introduction.

"Yeah. Had one when I was growing up." As Val spoke, Lilly sniffed him thoroughly.

Lilly gave in. She lowered her head and pushed forward into Val's chest.

"There we go," Val said. "That's my girl." Lilly was pushing into Val with the top of her head as he rubbed behind her ears and on the back of her neck. She was lean and strong.

Val looked up as several other dogs appeared from under the C-huts. They surrounded him, sniffing madly to see who Lilly had just approved.

Travis smiled. "That usually takes a few days."

Zimmer nodded. "And he didn't even use bacon."

"Okay, sir," Sergeant Travis said. "I hate to break this up, but I was told to have you ready to meet with General Stenson at 1400 hours."

Val stood up. Lilly took the hint and darted off, her troops in tow.

"Lead on, Sergeant."

CHAPTER 5

27 July 1999

Kamenica, Kosovo

"**G**ood to meet you, Captain Rafter." General Stenson gestured at Val to sit down.

They were alone in the classified communications tent. There was a small planning table with four chairs in one corner. Val sat on one end, and the general sat on the other.

Val studied the general. He looked just as Val expected he would. Closely cropped hair framed a stern but thoughtful face with dark-gray eyes. The man had the well-proportioned look of a pentathlete and had moved efficiently through the room. Val had heard of Stenson before, and not just from Bryson. The general had made an army-wide name for himself in February 1991 as a tank battalion commander that tore up an Iraqi armored division in the Gulf War.

"I don't have too long here, Captain. I've got to be back on Bondsteel for an operations briefing at 1600 hours." The general placed his Kevlar helmet on the table in front of him.

"Let's talk about the 13th Tactical Group. I think they're good troops. And I think Ziora is a good commander. But the fact is, the Russian agenda isn't entirely in sync with ours. If they could destabilize this whole place again, they would. Furthermore, I can't make any sense of their true strength levels, and I keep hearing rumors of a lot of mischief on their part.

"Captain Phillips is a good officer," the general continued. "But he is a tanker. He's not trained in intelligence. He did a favor for me by taking this job, but I'm looking forward to having a true intelligence professional here.

"I need to know what Ziora and the 13th are up to. The truth is, I don't care about their drinking and whoring and knuckleheaded crap. But any destabilization activities or outright theft or falsification of records I want to know about. NATO is paying the Russians for their support. I want to ensure we're getting what we pay for. Hell, I need to get what we're paying for."

Val nodded as the general spoke.

"You will report directly to me. We may communicate through my deputy commander for operations, Colonel Rogers, from time to time when I'm busy. Just don't tell him anything classified. And if he calls to ask you something, it's for me. Answer it. Tell him what you can."

"Yes, sir."

"Now let's talk about General Order Number One."

General Order Number One was a blanket edict that covered every soldier in the American task force. It prohibited the consumption of alcohol at any time in Kosovo. It wasn't much liked by the Americans, and none of the other KFOR member nations put their officers and soldiers under such a restriction. For the Americans, though, it was a zero-tolerance environment. Officers or soldiers that violated General Order Number One were shipped back to Germany the next day and court-martialed.

"You're exempt," the general declared. "How is your alcohol tolerance?"

"Um…pretty good, sir," Val was surprised to be discussing his ability to consume alcohol with an army general.

"Well, however good you think it is, you're going to have to get better at it. Those bastards just drink a lot. I try to never visit Col Ziora on an empty stomach because I know when I walk in there, I'm not getting out without drinking half a bottle of vodka." Stenson grimaced. "Makes my head hurt just thinking about it.

"If you're going to fit in over there, you're going to have to hold your own. I'm serious."

Val nodded.

"And we need you to fit in over there," the general emphasized.

Val nodded again. "I will, sir."

"I know it sounds stupid, Captain, but it's a big deal to them." He pointed notionally over Val's shoulder in the direction of the Russians. "My sense is

Captain Phillips tried to avoid those situations. I think it negatively affected his ability to form relationships with the Russian senior leaders and, therefore, his ability to provide me with intelligence."

"I understand, sir."

"Excuse me, gentlemen." The general's aide, a captain, walked into their area. "Wheels up in five minutes, sir."

"Thank you." The general stood up.

They left the operations tent and walked out into the parking area. The general's Humvee was idling, and several officers and NCOs milled around, waiting for him. Lilly circled them at a distance, ensuring things didn't get out of hand.

At the sight of Val, Lilly came over to him at a trot. Val winked at her and petted her without breaking stride as they walked to the Humvee. She walked next to him.

"Been here a day, and you've already got a security detail, eh?" Stenson said to Val, noticing Lilly.

"I guess so, sir."

The general smiled at Lilly.

"She looks like a good one."

Stenson stopped at the Humvee. "Welcome aboard, Captain Rafter."

"Thank you, sir." Val saluted.

The general returned the salute and hopped into the back of the Humvee. His entourage jumped in after him, and the Humvee pulled out of the compound, headed for the helipad in the UNMIK facility.

The United Nations Mission in Kosovo's facility was next to the American compound, separated by a high-security fence. It was the UN's headquarters in the province and was a much bigger facility than the American compound. The UN had commandeered several buildings, the largest of which was a three-story municipal building. The facility had a large open field that was used as a helipad. Val could hear the general's Black Hawk helicopter start its engines on it as the Humvee pulled out.

Val sat down on the steps to his C-hut. Lilly came over and sat next to him and Val reached out to pet her. He was feeling fuzzy from the thirty-six hours of travel.

After a few minutes, Lilly's ears swiveled and her head tilted as the whine of the Black Hawk's twin turbine engines spooled. It was still early in the pacification mission. Nerves and flight tactics reflected this, and the helicopter pilot executed a high-performance takeoff that minimized vulnerability. The engines howled as the aircraft's flight path carried it directly over the American compound, Val, and Lilly.

"Easy, girl," Val said as the loud, dark helicopter, nose down and accelerating, beat a path over them.

Lilly, though, turned her head and gave Val a look that he took to mean, *You've been here half a day, and you're seriously giving me advice?*

Val sat on the steps with Lilly for a while after the helicopter was gone. Now that he was no longer traveling, his thoughts drifted to Sydney. A pang of loneliness ran through him. He reached out and scratched Lilly behind the ears.

Sydney was a CIA officer Val met during his training at the Farm before going to the Defense Language Institute. They had planned to meet up in Europe for two weeks in July after he graduated from his Russian class at DLI. He had a bunch of leave saved up, as did Sydney, who was on her first assignment with the agency in Moscow.

Instead, Val was sitting on dirty steps outside a worn-out C-hut in Kosovo with a stray dog. If he thought about it too long, his head would spin and he would feel sorry for himself.

"I'll see you tomorrow, girl," he said, standing up. Val stepped into his C-hut and was asleep minutes later.

Lilly sat outside the door for a minute and then rejoined her pack.

CHAPTER 6

"Sir, I really don't think that's a good idea," Val heard Sergeant Travis say to Captain Phillips. Val approached them, drinking a cup of unpleasant coffee from the machine in Sergeant Travis's quarters. It was late afternoon, and Val was still feeling the jet lag from his journey from California to Kosovo. He hoped the caffeine would sharpen him up for his meeting with the Russians.

Val met Captain Gene Phillips, the officer he was replacing, an hour earlier in the operations tent. Phillips was now standing at the front of a Humvee while Zimmer and Travis ate a late MRE lunch as they leaned against the vehicle's hood. They were shaking their heads at Phillips, who held a bottle of Jack Daniel's.

"What are you talking about, Travis?" Phillips argued. "Ziora loves American whiskey."

"Yeah, sir. He does," Travis said, mouth half full of MRE chili mac. "But you don't. And you know he's going to make you drink it with him."

"Guaranteed," Zimmer said.

"No. We won't stay that long," Phillips said. "It'll be fine. He loves this stuff."

"Very good, sir," Sergeant Travis said. Then, seeing Val approach, he said, "Let me open the back for you, sir."

Sergeant Travis met Val at the back of their hard-shell Humvee. He opened the rear hatch so Val could stow his tactical gear. Behind the open hard shell, he looked at Val and whispered, "This is going to be a disaster, sir."

Val remembered his conversation with General Stenson about the Russians, alcohol, and Captain Phillips.

"Anything I should do?" Val whispered back.

"Nothing you can do for the guy now, sir. Just enjoy the show," Travis said under his breath as he closed the hard shell.

Val nodded, feeling sorry for Phillips. They had only just met that morning. He seemed nice enough, but Val gathered he was stubborn and slow to take advice. It was clear that Phillips was looking forward to rotating back to the world he understood, US Army tanks.

The Russian base was directly across the street from the American compound. It consisted of several large municipal buildings that the Russians had commandeered from the Kosovars. The gate security guards waved the American Humvee through after a quick check and Val could tell that they knew Phillips and the terps. They parked in a visitor spot at the base of the largest building and walked inside.

"Captain Phillips!" Colonel Ziora boomed as they stepped into his office. "Always pleasure!" The colonel stood up from his desk and lumbered across his large office to shake their hands. Ziora was tall and had the shape of a fading lumberjack. His shoulders were broad and his arms were strong, but his belly was large, straining the buttons of his pressed camouflage top. The colonel's red nose and cheeks betrayed his constant drinking. Still, he was a large and solid soldier.

Val scanned the room as the colonel came toward them. Standing to the side of the colonel's desk was a Russian army major and captain. Val smiled at the major, who was shorter than the colonel. His black hair was long for an army officer, even for a Russian, and he wore it slicked back, accentuating his mafioso vibe Val. His uniform was more disheveled than the colonel's, and Val noticed his boots were filthy. He stared back at Val without expression. Val nodded at him. He didn't nod back.

Val's gaze shifted to the captain, who looked as if he'd stepped out of a Soviet World War II propaganda poster. He was impressive. Taller than Val, his body angled sharply from his shoulders to his narrow waist. His uniform was perfect. From his insignia, Val could see that he was airborne qualified and had trained as a sniper. He smiled at Val.

Colonel Ziora shook hands with Captain Phillips and the terps before turning to Val.

After sizing Val up for a long moment, the colonel looked over his shoulder at the Russian captain and said in Russian, "He might give you a run for your money in wrestling, Alexei."

Val smiled. He looked at Colonel Ziora and said in Russian, "Thank you, Colonel. But please do not make me wrestle today."

Ziora's eyes got wide.

Travis and Zimmer looked at Val in surprise. They hadn't known he could speak Russian.

"This is most excellent!" Colonel Ziora said in loud English, extending his hand to Val.

Val shook it, and the colonel yanked him in for a bear hug. "You will not have to wrestle today. But someday soon! Dimitri. Alexei. Come meet our new partner, the American Captain Rafter."

The pair walked quickly to Val.

"Pleased to meet you, Captain Rafter," the major said, without introducing himself.

"Likewise," Val said with a smile. He read the major's name tag: "Orlov."

"I am Alexei Volkov," said the captain. "I am the 13th Tactical Group executive officer. It's my pleasure to meet you, Captain Rafter." He and Val shook hands.

"It's very good to meet you, Captain Volkov," Val said in Russian. "I am looking forward to working together."

Captain Volkov nodded, answering in friendly English, "Please, call me Alexei."

"Thank you. And I hope you will call me Val."

"Colonel," Captain Phillips said. Val turned to look at him, realizing that the colonel had taken over the meeting, not waiting for introductions or ceremony.

Ziora turned from Val to Captain Phillips, who was now holding the bottle of Jack Daniel's. Sergeant Travis grimaced behind Phillips and locked eyes with Val as if to say, *Here we go.* Zimmer was smiling like he was about to observe a painful belly flop.

"Is this gift?" the colonel said, eyeing the bottle. "I am most touched, Captain Phillips."

"Yes, sir. I wanted to give you this gift as an expression of my gratitude for our partnership."

The colonel nodded as Phillips spoke. He then placed a hand over his heart and said, "You are true friend, Captain Phillips."

Is he getting emotional? Val wondered about the colonel.

"We must share this bottle," Ziora said.

"No, sir." Phillips shook his head. "This is my gift to you."

"Nonsense! Alexei!" Ziora turned to the Russian captain. "Please bring us some glasses."

Despair washed over Phillips's face as he realized his mistake. True to the Russian custom, Colonel Ziora was going to acknowledge the gift of alcohol with a celebratory drink with the person who'd brought the gift. Phillips' problem was the other Russian custom that dictates that once a bottle of alcohol is open, it's bad luck not to finish it. And talking tough over the hood of a Humvee on the American compound was one thing. Saying no to a forceful Russian colonel who loved to drink American whiskey was something else.

You poor son of a bitch. Val chuckled to himself.

The colonel took the bottle of Jack Daniel's from Phillips and ushered the group to the sitting area in his office. A sofa sat against the wall. A large coffee table was placed in front of it, and six drab upholstered chairs surrounded the table.

Alexei dropped eight glasses down on the table as the group took seats. Phillips and the terps sat on the sofa as Val took a seat in a chair. Alexei smiled at Val and sat in the chair next to him. He seemed to be in on the joke.

The colonel sat in the chair at the head of the table, and Major Orlov sat to his left. Colonel Ziora opened the bottle of Jack Daniel's. He poured everyone a full glass, put down the bottle, and held his shot glass aloft.

"To Captain Phillips, our partner in the glorious task of bringing peace to his war-torn Kosovo. *Na Zdorovie!*"

"*Na Zdorovie!*" the group cheered in unison before downing their shots. Phillips choked his down awkwardly.

The colonel leaned forward and reached for Phillips's empty glass.

"Oh. No, sir." Phillips was unable to get to the glass before the colonel's big hand grabbed it. "I really can't have another. I'm taking this blood pressure medication, you see, and the doc says I absolutely cannot mix it with alcohol."

"That's very bad." Colonel Ziora poured Phillips another shot. "I hope you get better soon." The colonel poured everyone another shot as Phillips stared at the full glass in front of him.

"And now a toast to our fallen comrades," the colonel said.

Keeping with custom, the rest of the room raised their glasses without speaking. There was a silent moment of hesitation, and then the shots were downed. Phillips took part, having no other honorable option.

"Well, this has been great, sir." Phillips tried to initiate his escape.

"Yes. It has been." the colonel grabbed the captain's glass again.

"Sir, really…" Phillips said as the colonel filled the other glasses.

The colonel raised his glass. "To the ladies!"

"To the ladies!" the room shouted. Everyone, including a dejected Phillips, downed their shot. The whiskey was warming the group up quickly, and the colonel refilled everyone's glass, starting with Phillips, who didn't protest this time.

Val looked at Major Orlov, who sat without expression, looking back at Val.

"To the improving health of Captain Phillips!" the colonel said, interrupting their staring contest.

Val joined in with the loud toast of *"Na Zdorovie!"* Russian for "to your health."

"Val, I want you to meet my company commanders. They are excited to meet you."

Val noted the colonel had referred to him by his first name. Something he hadn't done with Phillips.

"I'd like that, sir," Val answered in Russian.

"Alexei, would you ask the commanders to come in?"

"Yes, sir."

"But first, Alexei." The colonel lifted his glass. "To our new friend, Captain Val Rafter!"

The group raised their glasses and downed their shots. Alexei left the room as the colonel filled the glasses. Starting again with Phillips.

An hour later, the colonel's office was full of Russian officers. Val had been introduced to the 13th Tactical Group's entire chain of command. They were a friendly, boisterous group. Travis and Zimmer, along with Val, had matched the colonel shot for shot until the Jack Daniel's bottle was empty and Phillips had passed out on the sofa.

"Val!" Colonel Ziora yelled from across the room. "Have you ever had Beluga vodka?"

"No, sir!"

"I fix that for you now!" The colonel strode back to the seating area. He slammed the bottle down on the coffee table and looked at Phillips, who didn't move at all despite the loud noise.

The colonel shook his head at the sleeping American captain and pulled a large switchblade out of his boot. He looked at Val and smiled as he popped open the knife, making a loud *snikt*.

Travis suddenly appeared next to Phillips. The tall sergeant stood over the captain's head and smiled at the colonel.

"Relax, Sergeant Travis," the colonel said in Russian. "I just want a few mementos of my good friend, Captain Phillips. To remember him by."

Travis looked at Val as the colonel reached over and cut off Phillips' 1st Armored Division unit patch. Smiling at the large triangle patch for a moment, the colonel then reached down to cut off another.

Val gave Travis an *it's okay* nod. As far as Val was concerned, it was harmless and deserved. Phillips had been foolish.

Travis smiled but stood next to the colonel until he was done removing patches.

"You like?" the colonel asked, noticing Val staring at the knife.

"Yes. Never seen a knife quite like that."

The colonel folded the knife shut and handed it to Val. "Is one of my favorites."

Val admired the long black wood handle before pressing the button. The satisfying *snikt* passed through Val's hand as the large blade swung out and locked into place.

"Is twenty-five-centimeter blade," the colonel said as he arranged Phillips's name tape, jump wings, and 1st Armored Division patch on the coffee table.

Travis looked at Val with a smiling shake of the head and stepped back a few feet, confident that Phillips would not be further molested.

"He got it in Chechnya," Alexei said as the colonel poured more shots. "He has a collection of knives.

"Sometime, I will show you," Ziora said, handing Val a shot glass of vodka.

"I'd like that, sir." Val closed the knife and handed it back to the colonel.

"Good." Ziora winked at Val and raising his glass.

The shots flowed for the next hour. Val fought his inebriation as he worked the room, trying to connect with each of Ziora's senior officers. As he did so, he kept an eye on Major Orlov.

The flowing alcohol did nothing to mitigate the Russian major's quiet unpleasantness. Even when in small drinking groups, he appeared to Val to be in a bad mood or pretending. Russian officers in conversations with him never smiled. They enjoyed his presence even less than Val did.

Captain Alexei Volkov was a different story, though. He was clearly the informal leader of 13th Tactical. He was charismatic and exuded confidence. Wherever he went in the room, a group of officers would gather around him. Val hung with Alexei, who escorted him around the room, ridiculing the Russian officers in turn. The object of Alexei's loud ribbing would revel in the attention, belly laughing at the punch lines delivered at their expense. Val could see they loved Alexei.

"Val," the colonel boomed from his seat at the head of the coffee table. "Would you like to go to the best banya in Kosovo?"

The room erupted in a chant: "Banya! Banya! Banya!"

All Val could do was smile and nod, inciting a louder chant: "Banya! Banya! Banya!"

"Bring my vehicle around!" Ziora said in Russian, standing up.

"Sergeant Travis," Val called across the room.

"Yes, sir?" Travis said, walking over to him.

"You been to this banya?"

"No, sir. They have never invited us before."

"Okay. Call the squirrels. Have someone come grab Captain Phillips. I guess we're going to the banya."

Val and the terps followed Ziora, Alexei, and Orlov out of the building. The colonel's Waz was waiting at an idle, his driver at the wheel.

The Waz was used by the Soviet Union and the Warsaw Pact all over the world. Slightly larger than an American jeep, they're more rounded on the edges and can seat up to seven passengers. The two primary strengths of a Waz are its ability to drive in almost any terrain and the ease of repair. As a result, they're all of indeterminate age. But like the legendary AK-47 assault rifle, any slob can maintain one, and they have proliferated around the world.

"Okay," the colonel said loudly to his driver as they piled in. "We go to banya now!"

It was the only command the driver needed. He goosed the Waz and peeled out from the HQ building. The guards knew the drill and had already opened the vehicle gate. They saluted as the colonel and his entourage careened by.

The colonel turned around so that he could speak to Val, who sat in the second row with Alexei and Sergeant Travis. Zimmer was in the wayback on the floor.

"We go now to visit my armor company."

Val nodded but was confused. He hadn't seen any intelligence about Russian armor units being in-country. It surprised him to learn they had gotten tanks into Kosovo.

"They are very good unit," the colonel continued. "Great men! But they have no tanks!" The colonel let out a belly laugh and gave the driver a good-natured punch in the shoulder.

Alexei laughed as well and slapped Val on the back. Val laughed also. He knew it was not that funny, but no one was feeling any pain after the Jack Daniel's and vodka.

The armor company with no tanks was stationed down the road from Kamenica in an abandoned work compound of an inactive ore mine. Even for Kosovo, it was a grimy setting. But in true Russian fashion, the unit had made the best of things, and had constructed a beautiful wooden banya.

Banya, to Russians, is more than just a sauna. It's as respected an institution as the Orthodox Church. Wherever the Russian military goes, whether it be Africa or the Arctic, enterprising and homesick soldiers will devise a way to construct a banya.

The Waz skidded to a stop in the mine work compound, and everyone piled out of the vehicle.

"Music!" the colonel yelled in Russian as he began to strip. "Play the music!"

ABBA's "Dancing Queen" erupted from the compound's speakers. Val looked at Sergeant Travis.

"Yeah," Travis shrugged. "They love ABBA."

The colonel, now naked, handed Val a felt cap.

Val puzzled over it for a moment until Alexei, pulling his socks off, leaned in and told him, "Is for your head. It protects the hair from banya."

Minutes later, the colonel led the naked, felt-capped entourage into the banya.

"Wow," Val said.

"Impressive, yes?" The colonel smiled. "As I told you. Best banya in all of Kosovo."

The craftsmanship of the wooden sauna was impressive. It was a large space, with a two-level bench along each wall. In the middle of the room, there was a roughhewn oven structure with a chimney that rose out through the ceiling. Made of stone and mortar, the oven was the work of an artisan. And, at that moment, it was hot as hell.

"Where did you guys get all of this wood?" Val asked, gazing around at the walls.

"Oh. It was donation from some of the local Albanians."

Val understood the colonel's meaning.

Ziora led the group in the classic Russian banya cycle. They sat in the heat for about ten minutes until they had a good sweat going. Then, at the colonel's signal, they took turns beating each other with birch branches. This seemed to raise the temperature more than twenty degrees instantly. It was nearly unbearable. At that point, they would pour buckets of ice-cold water on their felt-covered heads and retreat to the waiting area outside to drink beer and allow their body temperatures to normalize.

Val sat between the colonel and Alexei each time in the banya. The major always sat at the other end and observed. On the third visit, the colonel's cheer was dampened.

"I am glad you are here, Val," the colonel said in Russian. "We all must cooperate in this terrible place."

Val nodded, noting the sudden change in mood.

"Do you know?" Ziora said in a low voice. "Last week, not even five kilometers from here, a Serbian family was gunned down in their car in front of a market."

Val shook his head. "Terrible."

"It was. Alexei was first to get there."

Val looked at Alexei, who stared straight ahead and said, "A mother. A father. A young boy. And two young girls. All full of bullets." Alexei looked at Val. "I was around the corner with a squad of soldiers. We heard the gunshots and drove there quickly. When we arrived, the driver's door was open, and the father lay on the ground in a pool of blood. He must have tried to get out of the car. But the worst part was the Albanian children in the windows looking down on the murder."

Alexei took a deep breath.

Val waited for him to continue.

"As we drove up, they were cheering from the windows. Giving the V sign and making a knife cut across their throats."

"Damn," Val said.

"Yes. They were seven years old at most. Cheering a family's murder."

Val looked at Travis and Zimmer, who nodded as if to say, *Like we told you, sir…this place is crazy.*

"As usual. we never found the gunmen who were responsible. And the townspeople had seen nothing."

Alexei's sad face turned back to the wall.

The colonel leaned into Val as if to whisper, but said in a normal voice, "It's the children that bother Alexei the most. He feels it very hard." The colonel put his fist against his heart. "I learned this about him in Chechnya."

Val nodded and looked at Alexei, who still stared at the wall. The Russian siege of Grozny in '94 and '95 had been ugly for both sides. Though it was not the Russian military's finest hour, the Chechens got the worst of it when the Russians unleashed the largest bombardment in Europe since World War II.

Val thought of his own experience in late 1994 and 1995. He and his friends were enjoying post–Cold War NATO and planning weekend ski trips.

"Val," the colonel said. "I will tell you the truth. The most scared I have ever been was in Afghanistan. The angriest I have been was in Chechnya. But the saddest I have ever been is here. In this place. This Kosovo. This is a very sad place." He put his arm around Val. "That is why we must work together. We must be partners."

After the group had enjoyed the banya for another hour, talking about life and expectations of their partnership, the colonel stood up suddenly.

"This is special day, Val. We will celebrate with a special treat from Moscow. Arrived just today." The colonel walked out of the banya to the waiting area.

As they followed the colonel, Val looked at Sergeant Travis, who shrugged and gave Val an *I have no idea* face.

After a few minutes, one of the colonel's aides appeared and handed him a rolled up newspaper. The colonel, like a proud fisherman, walked over to Val and opened the newspaper.

"This is a Russian delicacy, Val. Dried sturgeon. Very special. I get it occasionally from Moscow. Only to be shared with good friends. Will you have some with me?"

"Sir, I'd be honored."

"Very good friend!" the colonel yelled, as if Val might have refused him. Out of nowhere, the naked Russian colonel produced another, smaller switchblade. He popped it open and began serving pieces of dried fish.

For the next hour, they ate the dried sturgeon and drank more beers while doing another three rounds in the banya. Finally, after midnight, noticing that Sergeant Travis and Specialist Zimmer had fallen asleep in the corner of the outside area, the colonel said, "My friends, this has been a wonderful night. My driver will take you back to American compound." After they had all dressed, the colonel shook hands with the terps and gave Val a hug.

Alexei walked Val and the terps out to the Waz. The terps piled in the middle seat and fell instantly back asleep. Val opened the front passenger door and then turned to Alexei. "Thanks for the time tonight. I sincerely appreciate it."

A genuine smile spread across Alexei's face. "It was our pleasure, Val. I am very glad to be working together with an officer like you."

"Likewise."

They shook hands again, and Val climbed in. Twenty minutes later, the driver let them out at the gate to the American compound. The tired group made their way back to their sleeping quarters.

Lilly darted out of the darkness, running up to Val. He came to an unsteady halt as she sniffed his pant legs, deeply inhaling the smells of vodka, banya, and sturgeon. She looked at Val with a face approximating disapproval and drifted back into the shadows under the C-hut.

"Sorry, girl," Val called after her. "But, honestly, it's part of the job."

Val got up the few steps to his C-hut. He didn't brush his teeth or get out of his uniform. He collapsed onto his bed. His last conscious thought before falling asleep was: *That was an interesting day.*

CHAPTER 7

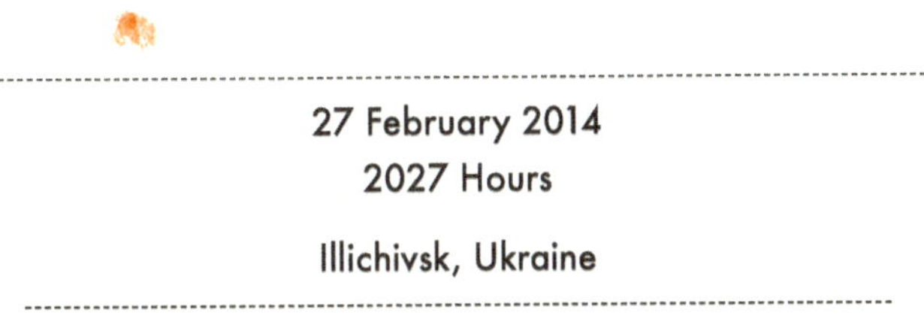

27 February 2014

2027 Hours

Illichivsk, Ukraine

"How is the old man?" Val asked Alexei as he put down his shot glass. "Do you know?"

"Yes!" Alexei nodded and gestured at Val with the bottle of bourbon.

Val leaned across the table with his glass, his hand only a foot from the pistol and switchblade. Zakir, leaning back against the bar, glared at Val and tapped a finger against the buttstock of his rifle, wearing a face that said, *Give me a reason.*

"He is doing very well," Alexei said, pouring Val another shot. "You know, his mission in Kosovo was viewed as big success in Moscow. He made a lot of important people happy. He is retired now. Has small dacha on lake about two hours outside of Moscow. Real postcard kind of place."

Val leaned back in his chair. Zakir rested against the bar.

"You know what?" Alexei said, excited. "I think I have picture." He pulled out his phone.

Val looked around while Alexei thumbed through images on his phone.

Curtains drawn so no one can observe us in here—not a great sign for me. And I count at least ten mercenaries, four in here with us if I include that bullshit bartender, two on the aft deck just outside the sliding glass door. And then the four I saw on upper levels as they brought me in. What I don't know is how many are behind those doors on either side of the bar.

Val rubbed his forehead.

I'm so fucked.

"Here it is!" Alexei handed his phone to Val. "See? The old man did fantastic."

Val looked at the photo and could not suppress his smile. It was picturesque. An old stone and wood cabin sat on a knoll overlooking a large lake. Rolling hills spread in every direction, and the lake's far shore was miles away. The rows of a small garden ran on one side of the house.

"Good for him," Val said with sincerity.

"Indeed, my friend. He was a lot smarter than you and I."

Val looked at Alexei and nodded.

Alexei shrugged as if to say, *We are doing our best.*

Val looked at Alexei for a long moment, and then asked him, "So, how long are we going to hang out on the bastard's yacht?"

Alexei's face hardened.

"Not so long."

Val downed his shot of bourbon.

Alexei did the same.

Without speaking, Alexei reached across the table and filled Val's glass again.

Alexei poured another shot for himself and then leaned back in his chair.

Val noted the warmth in his belly and cheeks. *Good. The last thing I want to do is face this bullshit sober.*

"Is busy night out there tonight," Alexei said in a knowing voice, gesturing past Val at the rest of Ukraine.

"I wouldn't know."

"Oh?" Alexei's eyebrows raised. "That is not like you."

"Well, it's hard to see shit when you're blindfolded and locked in the trunk of a car."

Alexei laughed.

And kept laughing.

Val tried to fight it, but when he heard a few laughs from the armed mercenary standing to his left in the dining area, Val smiled.

"You are so right!" Alexei said through his guffaws. "You can't see shit with a hood on your head locked in the trunk of the car!"

Val laughed.

"I mean, can you, guys?" Alexei gestured to the mercenaries on both sides.

The bartender tried to look busy.

The mercenaries smiled and shook their heads. "No, you can't see shit, boss," Zakir said in Russian. He covered his mouth with a large, meaty hand to hide his laughter.

"Damn it, Val," Alexei said, getting control of his breathing. "I have missed you so much."

Val caught his breath. He reached out and grabbed his shot glass, and then leaned back in his chair.

"I've missed you too, asshole."

And he meant it.

Alexei's eyes welled up.

Val watched a tear run down Alexei's cheek. *Sentimental fucking Russians.*

Alexei held out his shot glass. "To Kosovan skiing."

Val held up his glass. "To Lilly."

Alexei's head tilted at the name.

"Yes. To Lilly."

CHAPTER 8

September 1999

Kamenica, Kosovo

The BTR-80 is a Russian armored personnel carrier that traces its roots back to the Soviet Army's experiences in World War II. Designed with combined-arms operations in mind, BTRs enable commanders to deploy infantry with armor formations. The first version of the BTR entered service in 1959, and the Russians have been improving it ever since. Universally recognized as tough and adaptable vehicles, they have been widely exported and have seen action all over the world.

Manned by a crew of three, the BTR-80 can carry seven fully equipped infantrymen in its armored hull. Most configurations are equipped with a turret-mounted 14.5-millimeter heavy machine gun and a coaxial 7.62-millimeter machine gun. The fifteen-ton vehicle is 7.7 meters long, almost three meters wide, and rolls over almost anything in its path on eight enormous wheels. It was not designed for the narrow, cobblestoned streets of central Kamenica.

That didn't stop the 13th Tactical.

Val winced as the BTR-80 he was riding in sideswiped a civilian car with a grinding metal-on-metal ripping sound. The Russian troopers next to him belly laughed as a side panel from the old car flew into the air.

Val was in the second BTR of a four-vehicle convoy barreling through the small town at 1830 hours, as most Kamenicans were trying to enjoy dinner. The turbocharged, water-cooled V-8 diesel engines howled as they drove at high speed. Civilians dove out of the way. Val let out a sigh of relief that they had hurt no one as they emerged from the downtown area and burst onto an empty road. The first vehicle accelerated, and the three trails followed.

A couple of months into his deployment to Kosovo, Val was still not used to peacekeeping, Russian style.

This mission had started in the same way they all did. One of the squirrels came running to find Val.

"Sir, Captain Volkov called! He says they're rolling on a mission if you want to go."

"Roger that," Val yelled over his shoulder, already running for the door. "Log my departure."

"Yes, sir!"

Val had grabbed his gear and run toward the Russian compound, stopping to pound on the terps' C-hut as he went. Travis or Zimmer would always leap out, gear in hand, running after Val. Lilly typically intercepted Val before he made it off the American compound, and would escort him across the street to the Russian gate, where Val would finish donning his equipment as Lilly circled him, barking.

Whichever terp had responded would catch up to him there, and they would have just enough time to lock and load their weapons before the BTRs would come rolling off the base. One of the vehicle commanders, usually the second, would wave at Val as they slowed down at the gate. Val and the terp would jump through the crew hatch between the second and third wheel while Lilly barked at the giant Russian vehicles. She would then chase the convoy as far as she could, barking all the way, before turning back to wait for Val on the steps of his C-hut.

Once on board, Val would grab a headset, and the vehicle commander would give him a quick mission brief. The first time this happened, Val realized the Russians approached military operations differently than the US.

"There is conflict in the town of Střelice. We go break it up," the vehicle commander might say. And with that detailed plan, a platoon of heavily armed Russian soldiers in four armored vehicles would tear down the road, over fences, through front yards, across planted fields, and wherever else the lead vehicle was inspired to go to get to their destination.

The first time Val got those terse instructions in the back of the BTR-80, he leaned over to Sergeant Travis and said, "What the fuck?"

"Yeah," Travis yelled back over the howl of the vehicle's diesel engine. "They're not much into the five-paragraph operations order thing, sir."

The Russians also were not that into the "safety thing." Soldiers would ride on top of the BTRs, legs dangling off into the street as they hung on to a metal rung. None of them ever wore a seat belt. Even when riding in civilian cars. Val once asked Alexei to buckle up when they were driving to a meeting. Alexei refused. "I don't want to be trapped in the event of an accident," he said, stating the logic that Val heard from every Russian whenever he raised the topic of passenger restraints. This approach was ridiculous to Val, who had grown up in the US Army's over-the-top safety culture. To him, it gave the Russian missions a joyride-with-guns vibe that he alternated between smiling and cringing at.

Adding to the joyride vibe was the fact that, most of the time, the Russians were tipsy—or worse. The Russians were not bound by the American General Order Number One and, in fact, thought it silly. They typically drank before and during dinner, which was when most of the calls came.

And when the calls came, they answered.

The missions were varied: break up a minor riot, save an "Alb" from being killed, or prevent a group of Albs from setting fire to a Serb house. But almost every time involved dealing with pissed off crowds. Alexei always went on the missions that Val went on, having been assigned by Colonel Ziora to monitor the American officer. Val was glad his minder was Alexei rather than Orlov.

Val tried to go on at least two of these missions a week. After each one, he would accompany the platoon with Alexei to the Serbian restaurant around the corner from their compounds for a night of Serb barbecue, vodka, and storytelling. It was during these evenings that Val's fluency in Russian proved the most valuable. He was accepted as a comrade and learned many things.

The evening always started with *sto grammov*, or a hundred grams of vodka. Then the night was off and running like a turbo diesel BTR-80.

At dinner, Val heard stories of the Russians in Afghanistan, firefights in Chechnya, and tales of life in the Soviet and then the Russian army. He and Alexei would argue about the merits of their own military's approach to operations. Val, even though he secretly liked the BTR, would denigrate the Russian equipment and extol the virtues of the M1 Abrams main battle tank and the Bradley Fighting Vehicle. Alexei would feign outrage, making the men of the 13th nervous. Were they about to witness a headline-making fistfight between a NATO and a Russian officer? Finally, the two would let everyone off the hook, laughing and hugging like long-lost friends. It was never dull.

Once the group had their fill of seasoned Serbian meats, peppers, and potatoes, they would stumble back to the Russian compound. Lilly would join Val, intercepting the group before they went through the gates. Val always brought a small portion of leftover meat and would feed her as the night went on. Alexei would demand a few pieces so he could feed the dog as well. The Russian gate guards were soon familiar with Lilly and considered her to be Val's personal companion. As such, Lilly had full access to the Russian compound.

It was usually at this point that Orlov would join them. Val noticed that even the Russians kept their distance from the icy major. Orlov would spend the rest of the night on the periphery of the group, except for the times he would approach Val and attempt to engage in conversation.

"Your day was good one, Captain?" he would ask in halting English.

But the conversations never progressed beyond curt pleasantries.

They would spend the next few hours drinking and listening as the Russians passed a guitar around and took turns playing it. Val was stunned to find that every one of the Russian soldiers could pick up the instrument and play to the point that they, and many in the room, had tears in their eyes. He sensed how strongly they felt about their country, profession, and long, tragic history. All sang well, but sometimes the voice and guitar would combine in a way that compelled everyone to join in. Even Orlov. It might have been alcohol, but the old, sad military songs touched on truths and feelings that got to Val every time.

Sometimes Colonel Ziora would show up. When he did, Val knew that his night would be extended by a few hours. There was more drinking as the colonel commented on the most recent operation or world happenings. Within a few minutes, Val would know if they had been joined by what he and Alexei called "the happy colonel" or "the sad colonel."

The happy colonel told stories of his service in Afghanistan, Chechnya, and North Ossetia; the fine Russian soldiers he'd served with; and the enemy he believed to be common to Russia and the United States. "The radical Islamic elements, Val!" he would say. "Believe me!" the colonel would yell for emphasis before leaning into Val and saying in a serious voice, "Your country does not know it yet, but you must join us." Then he would smile and say to Alexei, "And they will, Alexei. You will see. They are our brothers!"

The sad colonel spoke of his time in the Soviet Red Army. "End of Soviet Union was great loss, Val," he would say with tears in his eyes. "Not just for me and my countrymen. But for the world!" The colonel's melancholy nostalgia would quickly turn to anger. "Is shameful that NATO would use the unrest in Yugoslavia to expand to the east. Unwarranted! Wrong!" he would say, glaring at Val. "Explain this to me, Val!" The first time it happened, Val got uncomfortable and started to look for the exit.

But Alexei intervened with a laugh, saying, "At least they sent us you, Val. He is good officer. Right, Colonel?"

"You're right, Alexei. There is brotherhood and there is politics." The colonel would turn his gaze from Alexei to Val. "And we're not talking politics here!"

Then, whether he was happy or sad, after a time, the colonel would stand up and spread his arms wide before saying loudly, "Banya!"

At the end of the evening, no matter how late, Val would stumble back to the American compound and go directly to the secure section of the operations tent. The squirrels learned to stay out of his drunk way as he tried to remember everything he'd learned that evening and to get it all into a coherent cable. The Farm had taught him memory techniques to enable him to hold on to important facts during long, often drunken, meetings. But it also emphasized: Write the cable as soon as you can. Intelligence is precious cargo. Don't rest until you have delivered it.

*

In addition to insinuating himself deeply into the operations and activities of the 13h Tactical, Val invested time in getting to know his way around Kamenica's local government. As an American officer living in Kamenica, everyone wanted to spend time with him. Val used that access to develop useful relationships while engaging in one of his favorite activities. Eating lunch.

There was no mess hall on the small American compound where Val lived. Each day, they got one warm meal transported to them in mermites, tough metal containers that used hot water to keep food warm. Most days, the one warm meal was a meager breakfast of powdered eggs and paper-thin, tasteless bacon. The small detachment then sustained itself for the rest of the day with MREs.

Val took note early on that lunch was often the main meal for Albanians. So, on many days, lunch became a time when Val indulged in warm food while developing working relationships. A win for Val, and, he liked to think, a win for America.

One of these lunch relationships was Zyph Hyka, the deputy mayor of Kamenica. Zyph struck Val rather like the nerd at the athletes' table. Unlike his boss and most of his colleagues in the municipal government, Zyph didn't sport a bushy mustache with the athletic-plus-belly body type. He also lacked Val's favorite Albanian attribute, a warm smile.

Zyph was skinny, pale, balding, and clean-shaven. He was intense, and always seemed nervous to Val, eyes darting around, scanning the area, whenever they spent time together.

"So, how did you end up in this job?" Val asked the first time Zyph agreed to get lunch with him. They were sitting in an Albanian restaurant around the corner from the municipal building. Smells of rosemary wafted around the table as Zyph spoke.

"I grew up in Kamenica," Zyph began. "I did well in school and got into a good college in Pristina. When I returned, I married my high school girlfriend. We had three children by the time Kosovo started to come apart. At that time, I had a successful accounting practice. It did not take long for the war to kill most of my family."

"Both of my parents, my two brothers and their families, and my aunt were killed in the span of a month. I have one surviving uncle and two surviving cousins left."

He paused and looked at Val as if he expected the American to explain why it had all happened. Val had heard stories like this many times already. They never got easier. He nodded respectfully.

"In March, my house and place of business were burned to the ground. I was afraid for my wife and children, who were, miraculously, still alive. So, I snuck them out of town in the middle of the night, and we walked to Macedonia."

"Why did you come back?" Val asked.

"Kamenica's mayor at the time, Erion Krasniqi, was a lifelong friend of our current mayor, Basha Lukas. In May, Erion's body was found in an alley, hands bound, shot twice in the back of the head. The city staff that hadn't already disappeared resigned and fled. The post of mayor was open until late June, when my friend Basha agreed to take the job. Looking for people he trusted, he reached out to me to join his staff."

Zyph looked at Val and shrugged. "My wife was against it, and I was scared. But a man must do what he can. So I returned."

The waitress appeared with their lunch, gjellë—a traditional Albanian stew of slow-cooked meat and vegetables—and a salad of tomatoes, cucumber, and feta. As Val came to realize, this "Shopska salad" was a cornerstone of every meal in Kosovo. He couldn't escape it. Which was fine because he liked it.

"And how is your family?" Val handed the platter of gjellë across the table to Zyph. "Still safe?"

"Yes. I miss them very much, and I hope someday it will be safe enough for them to rejoin me here. But, until then, I do what I must."

"And America will do what it must," Val said, wanting to reassure Zyph. "We'll be here as long as we have to. And soon, your family will be able to rejoin you. You'll see."

"I hope so, Val."

Val left that first lunch together with a new appreciation for the nerdy deputy mayor. There was a quiet, dignified strength to Zyph that Val could not say for sure he possessed himself.

CHAPTER 9

The weeks fell quickly into a repetitive operational rhythm for Val. He would wake up early and go for a jog with Lilly before spending a couple of hours in the secure tent with a coffee studying the most recent intelligence cables, Lilly at his feet. General Stenson usually touched base with Val to ask a question or two about his most recent intel report before 0800 hours.

On days he had time, Val would meet Zyph for lunch. On afternoons he was on the compound, he would prepare for evening missions with the 13th, or plan other intelligence-gathering activities across the country. Because of the time difference, he found General Bryson usually wanted his conversations late in Val's afternoons.

Val's schedule and clearance level were adjustments for the squirrels and Major Noreen, the Analysis Coordination Team leader. Noreen commanded Cooke's team of squirrels and several other small military intelligence outfits in Kosovo.

Because of the sensitive, top-secret nature of Val's Cobra Snare activities and the intelligence he had access to, no one could be in the secure section of the ops tent when Val was. This hadn't been the case with Captain Phillips, and the squirrels had gotten used to having the run of the secure section every day at all hours. Particularly Major Noreen, who used it as his office during his frequent visits to the compound.

This made for an awkward first meeting between him and Val.

Val was returning from a mission with the 13th Tactical. He was late for a secure call with Director Bryson and in a rush. Val ran into the secure section of the tent and found the major at the computer.

"Oh. Good afternoon, Major."

"Good morning. Captain Rafter, is it?"

"Yes, sir. You must be Major Noreen?"

"I am." The major walked over to shake hands with Val.

Despite being stationed in one of the shittiest locations in the world, there was not a speck of mud or dust on the major's uniform. As they shook hands, Val regarded Noreen's smart-guy smile and knew they would never see eye to eye on anything.

Val looked at his watch and said, "Sir, I'm sorry to do this, but I need to ask you to leave the secure area. I need to make a call."

The major's face stiffened.

"Excuse me, Captain?"

"I am late for a call with DIA, sir." Val walked to the computer and picked up Noreen's helmet and briefcase. He walked them back to the stunned major. "I need to get my TS drive out of the safe and get set up, and you can't be in here when I do that. I'm sorry to be abrupt, but I'm running late."

Val held the major's helmet and briefcase out, but the major didn't take them.

"This is my compound, Captain. I'll decide who uses what parts of it and when."

"Not if I'm here, sir. Again, I'm not trying to be rude, but I need to get set up, and you don't have the clearance to be in here while I do that." Val smiled and held the helmet and briefcase out again. He waited for an instant to let his words sink in, and then he went for the major's jugular.

"Or you and I can call General Stenson," Val said as politely as he could. "And he can clarify things for you."

Major Noreen's nostrils flared as he took stock of the tall captain in his secure area.

"Very well." He took his helmet and briefcase from Val. "Carry on, Captain. We'll talk later."

"Great." Val smiled. "I'll look forward to it."

The major avoided the secure area if Val was on the compound during his visits from then on, rather than endure being ejected by a junior officer again.

*

Val slowly pieced together an accurate picture of Russian military activities. They impressed him. The Russians looked at their participation in KFOR as a chance to serve alongside NATO and put their imprint on the resolution of a conflict they had a large stake in. But they also saw this as an opportunity to use the relationship for their benefit, both petty and large.

The Russians siphoned all the fuel out of the light sets and generators provided by KFOR and sold it on the black market. They ran protection rings for both Serbs and Albs, taking money on the side like mobsters from the local businesses to ensure they were protected.

The boldest move, though, was that the Russians claimed to have about 50 percent more soldiers in Kosovo than they actually did. KFOR paid the Russians $1,500 USD a month for each soldier they had serving in the region, up to the limit that had been agreed upon by KFOR. But for several reasons—the cost of flying soldiers over, the lack of trained "peacekeepers," competing requirements, and just flat-out criminal intent—they were never at full strength. Far from it.

Val confirmed that the Russians never had their maximum number of soldiers on the ground, though they claimed the maximum number in their monthly reports to KFOR. They were bilking NATO. The money flowed to the deployed Russian headquarters, commanded by Colonel Ziora. Val didn't know what happened to the money after it got to Ziora. But he suspected the colonel got to keep some of it before sending it on to his sponsors in Moscow.

Confirming the bogus troop counts kept Val hopping. He spent weeks crisscrossing Kosovo, popping in and out of the Russian sectors, often staying overnight with the Russian units in far-flung corners of the country. Even though he was fluent in Russian, he always took one of the terps with him on his observation missions.

Travis and Zimmer marveled at Val's energy. They got to alternate with each other on what they started referring to as "Rafter road trips." But Val went on every one.

One day in November, as they returned from a long and tiring observation trip, Sergeant Travis cursed as he turned the Humvee into the American compound. "Aw shit. Major Noreen."

Major Noreen stood outside the Operations tent with his arms crossed. Lieutenant Cooke stood next to him, looking at the ground. Cooke said something to the major, and Noreen glared at the Humvee as Travis turned off the engine.

Val got out of the Humvee and walked toward the tent, noting the Kevlar helmet fastened to Noreen's head accentuated the small diameter of the major's neck. Val thought about punching him as he walked by.

He saluted the major without speaking and tried to walk past him and Cooke into the ops tent.

"Just a moment, Captain Rafter," Noreen said, returning the salute.

"Sir, I'm returning from a mission and need to write up my reports."

"This won't take long. I want to speak with you about the dogs on this compound. They're a problem."

"There is no problem, sir."

"Oh, I believe there is, Captain. I don't want those animals on my compound."

"They're my dogs, sir," Val said, squaring up to the major. Lieutenant Cooke watched the confrontation, looking like he wanted to crawl under one of the Humvees and hide.

"They're part of my team," Val continued. "They're not your concern."

"Everything that happens on this compound is my concern, Captain. I'm ordering you to stop feeding and encouraging the dogs to loiter on the compound. Do you understand?"

Val was not in the mood. He couldn't stop himself.

"Sir, let's get a few things straight. You're responsible for this facility, but I own the mission. I'm the one who has to deliver on the intelligence." Val jabbed himself in the chest as he spoke. His anger surprised the major. Cooke's eyes were wide. "When I say something is part of the mission, then it's part of the mission. And those dogs are part of the fucking mission." Val stopped for a few heartbeats to let Major Noreen digest his words and aggression and then said, "And if I have a problem with mission support, then I'll make goddamn sure it's in my daily report to General Stenson."

Val paused again to let his message sink in. *I report to the commanding general. You report to a lieutenant colonel. Don't fuck with me.*

"The dogs are on my team. They provide security and early warning. If anyone fucks with them, they're fucking with my mission. Now, if you will excuse me, sir, I have to write up my intelligence report for General Stenson and DIA."

Val turned to leave. He knew he'd gone too far and expected to be called back as he walked away. He would have hammered a junior officer who spoke to him the way he'd just spoken to the major.

But Noreen didn't call him back.

CHAPTER 10

A few days after his run-in with Major Noreen, Val met Zyph for lunch at their usual place around the corner from the municipal building.

"What do you think of the 13th Tactical?" Zyph asked after they ordered and were waiting for their food.

Val looked at Zyph, but could not discern his motivation, so he answered him honestly.

"Better than I was expecting. What do you think of them?"

"I think they are the best and worst thing that could have happened to Kamenica," Zyph answered. "On the one hand, the soldiers have shown great heart and restraint. Ethnic Albanians are returning to Kosovo in ever more numbers, as you know. Not all have returned to take municipal office like me." Zyph smiled briefly before a sad look came over his face. "There has been retribution. Violence. Many have taken revenge on the Serbs. There have been murders."

Val thought about the colonel's story of the murdered Serbian family.

"The Russian troops are seen by many as having a Serbian agenda. They are protested and attacked almost everywhere they go. I expected them to be much rougher with us. But, in truth, for the most part, they have been measured and fair. They respond to protect Albanians as quickly as they do Serbs. In this, I have been pleasantly surprised."

"And on the other hand?" Val prompted Zyph.

"And on the other hand, something is not right. I believe they are working against us. I believe that one day we will regret letting them into our midst during this time of weakness." Zyph leaned forward and spoke to Val in a quieter voice. "There is an old Albanian proverb that says, 'The wolf loves the fog.'"

Zyph leaned back in his chair. "And the Russian wolf, I am afraid, loves the fog of war most of all."

The waitress appeared, setting down a large platter of lamb kebabs in the center of the table. She gave each of the men an empty plate and then left.

Val hesitated, still thinking about Zyph's comments.

"But it is very good to have America here," Zyph said. Then he added, smiling, "Especially you, Val."

CHAPTER 11

The next night, the 13th Tactical was called out on a mission right after dinner. Val had just finished a chili mac MRE when the call came. Val and Zimmer ran to the Russian compound, Lilly at their heels, and hopped on the second BTR. There were only two vehicles on this mission.

"Explosion in Korminjan," the vehicle commander told Val. "We respond."

Korminjan was a tiny satellite town of Kamenica, about fifteen minutes to the south.

Val and Zimmer hopped out of the BTR as soon as it pulled to a stop. Alexei exited the other vehicle and motioned to Val to catch up to him. They followed the Russian infantry squad as they jogged about fifty meters to a smoking vehicle.

The soldiers set up a security perimeter as the squad leader and Alexei advanced to the vehicle. Val motioned to Zimmer to stay on the perimeter and followed a few steps behind Alexei.

Alexei stopped short of the car and put his right hand to his forehead.

"Alexei!" Val called. "What is it?"

Alexei stared at the bloody scene in front of him. "Fucking animals," he said.

Val stepped next to Alexei and looked into the vehicle. A dead woman slumped on the steering wheel. The back half of her head was missing. Three dead children lay in a bloody tangle in the back seat. Some limbs were missing. Some were intertwined. One child was decapitated. Intestines spilled out of another. A small, severed arm was stuck in the rear window.

"Jesus," Val whispered. He looked away.

"Secure the site!" Alexei yelled in Russian. He'd composed himself. And he was angry.

"I want to talk to all the witnesses! Bring them to me!"

Two hours later, the site had been secured, and the bodies removed from the smoking vehicle. They lay under blankets twenty meters away.

Alexei sagged in a field chair behind one of the BTRs. Val had sat with him through the witness interviews. They had been worthless.

"It's a fucking terrible and familiar story, eh, Val?"

Val nodded. Alexei was darker than Val had ever seen him.

"A Serbian family stops at an intersection," Alexei said in a pained voice. "Two men approach, smash a rear window, and toss in two grenades. The explosion kills the mother and her three children. And, no… " Alexei shook his head slowly in sarcastic resignation, "no one could identify the attackers."

Alexei pulled out a package of cigarettes. He didn't smoke as much as the average Russian, most of whom would burn through dozens of cigarettes during their dinners and singing and banya. Alexei almost never smoked. But he did when he was sad or stressed.

Val didn't know what to say. He waited as Alexei lit up and took a long drag.

"Things are shifting, you know?" Alexei said to Val.

"How do you mean?"

"We came here in June to stop the Serbs from killing the Albs. But you can feel it shifting. The Albs are turning murderous now. And I cannot blame them. The Albs have been unemployed, shit on, and killed for years. Now, while we hold Serbia's arms behind his back, they take their chance to cut his neck."

He took another drag, bathing his face in the dim red light.

"You add to this the Albs' not-so-secret weapon, and you do not have to be a fucking genius to know what this country looks like in ten or twenty years."

It was well known that the Albanians were producing children at twice the rate of the Serbs. The Albanian population in Kosovo already outnumbered the Serbs. Many viewed the demographic growth rate as cementing their long-term advantage.

"So, why the hell are we here, Val?" Alexei asked, staring at his friend. "Why does it matter?"

Val sighed. "I don't know, Alexei. We're soldiers. We don't get to choose."

"I know," Alexei said, looking away from Val and back at the family lying dead under blankets.

No one went to the restaurant after they returned. Val tried to speak to Alexei, but he just shook his head and walked away into the Russian compound.

CHAPTER 12

Val woke up the next day feeling uneasy about Alexei. He shoveled down his breakfast in the secure section as he read the morning's cables. He then walked into the squirrels' operations center. "Lieutenant Cooke," Val said.

"Yes, sir?"

"Need you to do me a favor, please. I'm in a hurry. I've got a last-minute tasking from Pristina. It's in the American sector. I'd like Captain Volkov to accompany me. There may be some tactical learnings he'll need to pass on to Colonel Ziora. Would you call over there and request Volkov be here for a 0900 departure?"

"Roger that, sir."

"Thanks. I'll be getting my gear together. Call me if there are any issues."

A glum-faced Alexei got into Val's Humvee at 0903 hours outside the American compound.

Val was driving. He accelerated away as soon as Alexei's door was closed.

"Put on your seat belt," Val said.

"Fuck you." Alexei pulled the seat belt out from under him and let it fall to the side. "I am really not in the mood for bullshit, Val."

"Good," Val answered. "Neither am I."

Val didn't try to talk to his friend. He drove in silence.

After twenty minutes of southerly progress, in the opposite direction from Pristina, Alexei began to fidget. But he didn't give in.

Val smiled when Alexei crossed his arms and leaned his head back, making a show of going to sleep.

But when they pulled into a gas station an hour later in the small town of Pozharan, Alexei began to waver.

"I've got to piss," Val said, getting out of the Humvee. "You might want to also," he called over his shoulder to Alexei.

Alexei cursed in Russian as he jerked open the Humvee door and got out. He followed Val to the bathroom at a distance.

Alexei ignored Val's smile when he came out of the small restroom. Val walked back to the Humvee.

When Alexei returned, Val was already in the Humvee with the engine idling. Alexei opened his door and saw the can of beer on his seat. He grabbed it, got in, and closed the door without speaking. Val looked straight ahead. A Kosovan Peja beer sat open between his legs.

"Put on your seat belt," Val said.

"Fuck you."

Val turned back onto the main road and took a sip of his beer.

"What are you doing?" Alexei asked him.

"In America, we call this a 'road soda.'" Val smiled at Alexei. "It helps break up a long drive."

Alexei rolled his eyes at Val. He knew how uptight the American military was about drinking, and how much trouble Val could get into for this kind of behavior. Five minutes later, as Val drove with his eyes looking straight ahead, Alexei popped open his can and took a sip of beer. Val pretended not to notice.

Alexei still refused to ask where they were going, but he stopped fidgeting and relaxed as the terrain became more mountainous, and he opened his second beer.

"I better not," Val said when Alexei offered him another. "Secret to the road soda is to make it last. But you go ahead." Soon, the mountains were towering above them to their front.

After two and a half hours of driving, they pulled into the parking lot of the Brezovica ski resort. Brezovica sits on the northeastern edge of the eight-thousand-foot Šar Mountains, less than five miles from the border with Macedonia. Established in 1956, the ski resort enjoyed decades of momentum, culminating in the eighties, when Communist Party leadership from the Soviet Union, as well as young revelers from Belgrade and Skopje, mixed in après-ski that could go late into the night. Brezovica even served as a backup to Sarajevo for the 1984 Olympics.

But the Yugoslav wars and malaise that followed stunted the ski resort, as they had the rest of the country. The resort's infrastructure suffered from disrepair and lack of investment. The decrepit cinder-block buildings and malfunctioning ski lifts clung to the ideal north- and northwest-facing slopes. Still, the deep and pristine snow returned every year.

"What ridiculousness is this?" demanded Alexei when he got out of the Humvee and looked up at the towering ski resort. The colder-than-normal November had been good for the snowpack. Untouched snow covered the mountain.

"I thought you told me you enjoyed skiing?" Val asked as he looked around. The old resort hotel loomed behind him. It was six stories of dirty beige and looked like a mid-rise office building trying hard to be a hotel. Many of the windows were broken, and the restaurant structure that extended from the base of the hotel had burned at one point. Val looked to the right of the hotel and saw the base of one of the derelict ski lifts. Empty chairs, full of snow, hung from the cable.

"I love skiing," Alexei said slowly as he took in the sad, decrepit, snowy resort scape. "But this does not look like a place we can ski today."

"Bullshit," Val said, his back to Alexei. He waved at someone whom Alexei had not yet seen.

A group of small engines fired up in the distance. Val turned around and smiled at Alexei. "You're a size twelve shoe like me, right?"

"What?"

Three snowmobiles appeared from behind a cluster of trees, moving at high speed. They swooped down the snowbank on the far side of the hotel and drove up to Val and Alexei. The drivers wore camouflage overalls and matte-black motorcycle helmets. They each had an M16 cross slung over their backs, but they were not the normally issued weapons Alexei was used to seeing Americans carry. These had been modified.

The snowmobiles crunched to a stop. The lead driver took his helmet off.

"Val Rafter!" the American said with a smile as he dismounted his snowmobile. "You ready to go skiing, you son of a bitch?"

"Hell yes, Mark," Val answered, walking to Mark and giving him a hug. Mark popped the seat of his snowmobile up and grabbed two pairs of camouflage overalls, which he gave to Val.

Val walked over and gave one pair to Alexei and then started to put his on.

Alexei stood dumbfounded, the camouflage overalls in one hand and a beer in the other. It was just too far-fetched.

He looked at Val with a questioning face.

Val zipped up his overalls and walked over to Alexei. He leaned in, putting one hand on Alexei's shoulder, and said quietly, so the others could not hear, "We're skiing today, Alexei. Just you and me. Fuck Kosovo and the crazy-ass Serbs and Albs. Fuck the Russian army. Fuck the US Army. Fuck everyone. I think you and I have earned one day of fun. What do you say?"

Alexei smiled like Val had never seen before, and a tear broke free and ran down the Russian's face.

"I say yes, Val!" Alexei said in Russian. Alexei gave Val a bear hug and then yanked on the overalls.

Val walked over to the lead snowmobile. "Thanks, Mark. I can't tell you how much this means to me."

"No sweat. Any day out in the air on a mountain like this is a good day." Mark looked at Alexei for a moment and then asked, "Is he crying?"

"Yeah. They're like that. They get emotional."

"Cool."

Captain Mark Watson was an A Team leader in 10th Special Forces Group. He and Val met when Val was a tanker stationed in Germany.

10th Group had a long history of winter warfare specialization. Headquartered in Colorado Springs, the green berets honed their skills there when not on deployments throughout Europe and elsewhere. Captain Watson's team had been in and out of the former Yugoslav areas many times during the last three years. His current assignment was in the southwestern corner of the American sector, which included Brezovica. He and Val had been in touch via email since Val got in theater. When Val heard about the abandoned ski resort, he filed it away on his something-I-have-to-do-before-leaving-this-shithole list.

When Val saw the darkness in Alexei after the grenade attack killed the family in Korminjan, he thought it was a good time for a change of scenery. He contacted Mark, who was, of course, game to run them up the mountain on snowmobiles for half a day. Mark brought their Special Forces–issued ski boots and skis and the camouflaged overalls, gloves, and hats. The gear was not flashy. But it was perfect for that day.

Alexei and Val skied like madmen. They bombed down the mountain as fast as they could and then drank bourbon from a bottle that Captain Watson brought for them as they rode back to the top on the back of the snowmobiles. The snow was untouched except for their own tracks.

Alexei was a much better skier than Val. But Val made up for the skill deficit with a willingness to ski on the ragged edge of being out of control. The competition was on. They skied so aggressively that Captain Watson finally said to Val, "Can you guys tone it down just a little? The last thing I need is to have to call for a medevac. I could never explain it to KFOR."

The last run nearly gave Watson a heart attack. Alexei's and Val's legs were spent. They flew, barely in control, down Brezovica's super-G course. Alexei's tight and precise turns opened up a large early lead that Val clawed back against for most of the long, plummeting run. As they neared the bottom, Val accepted it was hopeless, and changed his tactics to a suicide mission. As they reached the bottom, he abandoned all caution and barreled into Alexei's legs. The result was a spectacular tangle of limbs and ejected skis. Watson shook his head at the laughing pair, relieved the day was over.

Alexei was in a much better mood on the drive back. He was talkative, which was good for Val, whose fatigue and alcohol consumption made him tired.

"Do you ever think about leaving the military, Val?" Alexei asked as they neared Kamenica.

"Sure. Don't you?"

"No. I don't know what else I would do."

Val smiled at the comment. Alexei took a sip of beer.

"You know, my father served in the army," Alexei said, looking out the window. "And my grandfather fought the Germans in World War Two."

Val nodded. It was the same with many of the Russian soldiers.

"Besides," Alexei continued, "I like the army."

"Yeah," Val agreed. "I guess I do too."

When they finally pulled up to the Russian compound, Alexei smiled at Val. "Today was the best day I ever had in the army, Val. Thank you."

"Me too, Alexei. I'm really glad it worked out."

Alexei nodded, and then his brow furrowed. "You are a crazy son of a bitch, Val. I hope that it never catches up with you." Then the smile came back to Alexei's face. He laughed and slapped Val on the back. "And if it ever does, I hope I am not there to see it!"

CHAPTER 13

The weather in late November turned cold and wet in Kamenica. The fireplace in Zyph's and Val's favorite lunch place, and in most houses, was blazing to fight the damp chill.

The petty strong-arming, NATO bilking, and black-market dealings by the 13th Tactical were as entertaining as ever to Val. He joked with General Bryson that logging his daily reports felt more like writing a cheesy organized crime novel than intelligence cables.

In early December, Val went on a mission with Alexei and the 13th Tactical that spanned three days.

"Come on, Val," Alexei said. "We go to northern Kamenica for show of force."

"A show of force?" Val asked with concern. The most docile of Russian patrols was brutish enough that the term "show of force" made Val nervous.

"Yes. The violence in the north of Kamenica has increased in the past few weeks. Ziora has asked me to take two platoons on a patrol through the northern towns so that they know we are still here and that we mean business."

Val nodded. Alexei picked up on the skepticism.

"I have heard there are two wonderful restaurants in the north," Alexei said in an inviting voice. "I promise you will not suffer."

"Fine. Let me pack my shit."

"Excellent! We leave first thing in the morning."

Val took Sergeant Travis with him on the uneventful mission. Word of the rolling enforcement preceded the Russian convoy on their route. By the time the Russian BTRs lumbered into each small town, all the local thugs were on their best behavior. Alexei and his infantry platoons would dismount and conduct patrols and searches, nonetheless. In several towns, they located Serbian and Alb males who were wanted by KFOR for acts of terrorism. In only one case did the suspect resist. Never a good idea when facing Russian infantry, particularly for Albanians. The Alb was medevaced to Pristina by helicopter.

Each night, Alexei and Val would try the best local restaurant. On the second night, Val said to Alexei, "This is an infamous day in American history."

"What day is this?" Alexei asked.

"December seventh. Fifty-eight years ago, on this day, the Japanese conducted a surprise attack on the United States, pulling us into the Second World War."

"Oh yes. Your Pearl Harbor." Alexei took a sip of wine. "We had been fighting for some time by then. Germany attacked us in June."

"I know. Surprising, after you guys had played so nice together in Europe, dividing up Poland like friends do."

"Don't be an ass," Alexei said with a smile.

Val raised his hands in a *don't shoot* gesture.

"You know, for many years, they trained us to expect a surprise attack from America on Christmas," Alexei said.

"What? That's ridiculous."

"No. It is your history. You are historical surprise attackers. Your general-president Washington led a surprise attack on Christmas. And there have been many other similar American holiday aggressions. In Russia, we try to learn fast and remember long."

Val laughed and raised his glass of wine, which Alexei clinked with his.

Late in the afternoon the next day, Alexei's BTR stopped in front of the American compound. Val and Sergeant Travis hopped out. Alexei followed, grabbing Val's rucksack. They walked past the gate guard into the American compound just as Major Noreen was coming out of the squirrels' tent. Val and Sergeant Travis saluted the major as they passed him. Noreen returned their salute with a strange smile and got into his waiting Humvee.

"That was a strange look he gave you," Alexei said as the major's Humvee pulled off the compound and drove off.

"Yeah," Val said, shaking his head. "He's a strange guy."

Val and Alexei walked together up to Val's C-hut.

"Okay, Val." Alexei placed the rucksack at the foot of the steps. "Thank you for accompanying us."

"It was my pleasure, Alexei," Val said, walking up the steps and unlocking his C-hut. "I will—"

Specialist Zimmer approached from behind Alexei. The look on his face scared Val.

Val's expression startled Alexei, and he turned to see what his friend was looking at.

"What is it, Zimmer?" Val asked. "What's wrong?"

The stricken American soldier stopped at the foot of the stairs. Zimmer could not look at Val.

"Speak up, Specialist," Sergeant Travis said, getting worried. "What's the problem?"

"The dogs, sir…"

At that instant, Val realized Lilly was not at his feet sniffing his uniform, trying to decipher where he'd been. And none of the rest of the pack was in sight.

"What! Where are they?"

"Major Noreen, sir," Zimmer said.

"Yeah. I just saw him leave," Val said. "What did he do?"

"I'm—I'm so sorry, sir. He wouldn't listen to me. Even the LT tried to make him stop. But he's a major, sir. There was nothing we could do."

"Where did he take them? Zimmer, get in the Humvee. We're going to get them." Val jumped down the stairs and yelled, "Lieutenant Cooke!"

Cooke came walking out of the headquarters tent, his face a knot of worry.

"Captain Rafter, sir," he said, saluting.

Val returned the salute as he said, "Where did Major Noreen take the dogs?"

Cooke looked at Zimmer in panic. "You didn't tell him?"

Zimmer just shook his head.

"Tell me what?" Val demanded.

"Sir, Major Noreen had the dogs destroyed."

Everyone looked at Val.

Several heartbeats passed. Val sat down on the bottom step to his C-hut and put his head in his hands.

"What does it mean to destroy dogs?" Alexei asked Sergeant Travis.

"Killed, sir," Travis answered in a whisper. "It means he had them killed."

"Who would do such a thing?" Alexei asked.

"Major Noreen."

"This major I just now saw? Why does he hate dogs?"

No one answered Alexei. All eyes were on Val.

Val stood up, looked at Zimmer, and said, "Give me the keys to the Humvee."

"Sir?"

"Give me the keys to the fucking Humvee!"

Val's anger made Zimmer take a few steps back. He was stunned into silence.

"Val," Alexei said. "What are you doing?"

"Specialist Zimmer!" Val yelled as he walked over to Zimmer. "Give me the goddamn keys!"

Zimmer reached into his pocket.

Sergeant Travis took a step toward Val. "Sir, I don't think—"

"At ease, sergeant!" Val shouted at Travis.

He snatched the keys from Zimmer and turned and walked toward the Humvee.

When Val was halfway to the vehicle, Alexei jogged over to catch up to him. He put his hand on the driver's door just as Val tried to open it.

"I'm sorry, Val. You cannot do this."

"Fuck you, Alexei." Val shoved the Russian captain.

Alexei stumbled backward a step but surged back in front of the door before Val could open it.

"I'm sorry, Val. But you are not thinking straight right now."

"Get out of the way," Val said. The American soldiers stood watching them.

"No," Alexei said. "I won't let you go after that major."

Val lunged at Alexei. The big Russian used Val's momentum to throw him to the side. Val slammed into the rear door. He screamed in rage and punched Alexei in the face. Alexei fell backward but stopped his fall by grabbing the vehicle's big front tire. He launched himself back at Val just as he got the front door open. Alexei struck the door in an explosive tackling motion.

The door came off its hinges. Alexei and the door knocked Val backward. Val landed on his back. Alexei and the door landed on Val.

Val screamed again. Unintelligible. Heartbroken.

"That's it, Val!" Alexei yelled as he tried to stay on top of the door and his friend. "Let it out!" Val tried to punch Alexei but could not reach him because of the Humvee door and the length of Alexei's arms.

By now, the gate guard and several of the squirrels gathered around the fighting men. No one moved to break them up, though. They sensed it was up to Alexei. He was the only thing between Val and rash actions he would regret.

Val kneed Alexei in the groin. Alexei barked in pain and lost his balance on the door. Val kicked again and then shoved Alexei to the side. The door prevented Alexei from getting a good grip on Val.

Alexei flung the door away in exasperation. It sailed through the air, nearly striking one of the squirrels.

Val lunged for the doorless front seat, but Alexei kicked Val's feet out from under him. Val stumbled, just stopping his fall with a two-handed grab on the steering wheel.

Alexei, wincing in pain, grabbed at Val's legs. Val kicked. But Alexei held on.

"Goddamn it!" Val screamed. "Let me go!"

"No!" Alexei crawled, hand over hand, up Val's body. "I will not!"

Val screamed again as he tried to pull himself into the vehicle. But the Russian was too strong and heavy. Alexei held him in a bear hug, long arms wrapped around his chest.

Val tried to hit Alexei to break his grip, but the Russian's chest-high squeeze restricted his ability to strike.

The men panted, frozen in an agonizing stalemate. Val could not get into the Humvee, and Alexei could not break Val's grip on the steering wheel.

Slowly, Alexei raised his right foot and placed it on the Humvee. Val saw the foot placed next to him and tried to get ready.

Alexei grunted as he pushed off the Humvee with his right leg. Val resisted for an instant, but then lost his grip. The two men flew from the Humvee and skidded across the gravel parking surface.

Alexei quickly repositioned himself on top of Val. He reset his grip and readied for the next round.

But Val was done. He lay gasping on the gravel.

Alexei was breathing heavily. "I'm so sorry, my friend… But I could not let you… chase the major… You were out of your mind… You would hurt him."

"I wasn't… going to… hurt him," Val's words came between pants. "I was… going to… kill him."

Alexei nodded. He rolled off Val onto his back.

"Either way," he said. "I am sure is not allowed in US Army… I am sorry to fight you…but I will not see you in trouble because of the cruelty of this major."

Val struggled to his feet, tears running down his face.

Alexei stood as well. "What is major's name?"

"Noreen," Val said before turning away and limping slowly toward his C-hut.

Alexei nodded, and the rest of the stunned Americans watched him limp back to the Russian base.

CHAPTER 14

"What is bothering you, Val?" Zyph asked as they sat in their usual restaurant. "You are not yourself today."

"Nothing. Just a few long days at work lately."

"I understand," Zyph said.

The waitress brought their lunch, qofte, a lamb meatball dish served over rice with a small Shopska salad alongside.

They ate in silence for a few minutes. Zyph dug in. Val took a few half-hearted bites.

"Val," Zyph said as he chewed on a large bite of meatball. "What is wrong?"

"It's nothing, really."

"Bullshit," Zyph said, surprising Val. The Albanian never cursed. "I have learned that Val Rafter is always hungry."

Zyph finished chewing, swallowed, and then wiped his mouth with his napkin. He put down the napkin and crossed his arms, looking at Val.

Val regarded the nerdy Albanian and smiled.

"If my friend will not eat," Zyph said, "neither will I."

Val sighed heavily and leaned forward, elbows on the table.

"Um… The truth is, Zyph, I feel ridiculous telling you this."

"Nonsense. You can tell me anything."

"It's just that you have lost so much."

Zyph uncrossed his arms.

"There was a stray dog," Val said. "Her name was Lilly. I got really attached to her. She was killed a few days ago, and…well, I miss her."

Val shook his head.

"And I feel absurd telling you, who have lost so much, about this. And, truthfully, I am surprised by how hard it has hit me. In this country, this fucking landscape of bottomless sadness…it is the death of this dog that has hit me the hardest."

Zyph nodded.

"I'm sorry," Val said, shrugging. "I feel ridiculous."

Zyph waved a hand in a dismissive gesture. "I understand. There is nothing to be sorry for."

Val leaned back in his chair.

"You know, Val," Zyph said. "There are people in town who have lost much more than me. Unfortunately, in Kosovo, there is always a bigger tragedy to be found. And I have felt this thing that you are feeling, this embarrassment at the depth of feeling for something that seems small compared to others, when they have endured so much more. I have learned it is all bullshit."

Val smiled at the second profanity he'd heard his friend utter. He liked this side of Zyph.

"Loss is loss, Val," Zyph said. "And I am sorry for yours."

*

Val sat on the steps to his C-hut and prepared himself. Major Noreen was scheduled to visit the compound for the first time since Lilly and her pack were killed about two weeks ago. Val was determined to neither give the major any satisfaction nor do anything stupid. He'd hoped to be on a mission with the 13th Tactical, but the entire battalion was engaged in their monthly base cleanup activity. Colonel Ziora mandated the practice, which involved every soldier and officer in the unit and touched every inch of their facility. The day of frenzied cleaning had inexplicably been rescheduled from later in the month to today.

Val could see three Russian flatbed utility trucks lined on the street across from the American compound to the right of the gate. The lead truck was loaded with half a dozen portable latrines. Judging by the difficulty the soldiers had loading them on the truck, Val could tell they were full. He grimaced at the thought.

As Val considered the volume of shit he was looking at, he spotted Alexei directing the work. Val smiled and stood up. He left the American compound and walked across the street.

"Wow, Alexei," Val said. "You must have really pissed off Colonel Ziora to get this duty."

"Not now, Val," Alexei said tersely.

"You know," Val said, ignoring his friend's irritation, "in the US Army, we would call this a shit detail."

Val laughed at his own joke. Alexei glared back at him and waved him off. Val noticed he was holding a small handheld radio.

A transmission came across Alexei's radio that Val could not quite hear. Alexei looked nervous to Val. "Everything okay, buddy?" Val asked.

"Val, please just leave me alone!" Alexei shooed Val away with his hands and then pointed at the American compound. "Go!"

"Fine. Jeez."

Val walked back to his C-hut and sat back down on the steps. From the top step, the gate to the American compound was to his left. Alexei and his cleanup crew were straight ahead on the other side of the security fence and across the street, and the road continued to Val's right.

Val didn't blame Alexei. He knew what it was like to manage soldiers doing dirty and boring tasks all day. But he was still a little miffed.

Val watched as Alexei held his handheld radio to his ear for a moment and then spoke into it. Alexei then barked an order at the soldiers on the Russian flatbed wrestling with a heavy portable latrine. They nodded and started tying ropes to the tops of the latrines.

Alexei called two soldiers to him and quickly gave them orders while pointing here and there. Val sat up, trying to decipher Alexei's darting hand motions. Alexei turned back to his radio.

One soldier ran and hopped into the cab of the lead flatbed. The other ran to the trail vehicle.

What the hell are they doing? Val was endlessly fascinated by the strange machinations of the Russian military.

The soldiers in the back of the lead flatbed finished tying ropes to the top of each latrine and hopped to the ground. Alexei said something to them. They nodded and grabbed the ropes, throwing them under the vehicle. Then they ran behind the shit-laden truck, where Val could not see them.

Alexei's radio chirped again, and he raised it to his ear.

The sound of a Humvee's diesel engine is burned into the brain stem of every American soldier. Val heard the familiar sound and looked to his right. He winced as he recognized Major Noreen's Humvee.

"Fuck me," Val mumbled before reminding himself of his goals. "No satisfaction and no confrontations, Val,"

The major's Humvee was about fifty meters from the compound entrance, following closely behind a Russian Waz.

The Waz was moving slowly, just in front of the Humvee.

Curiously slow.

The Waz passed the trail Russian flatbed with Noreen's Humvee just inches behind it. Val noticed the Waz was driving in the middle of the road, making it impossible for the Humvee to get around him, and he smiled, thinking how frustrated Noreen must be. Russians cared little for traffic laws or for consideration of other vehicles. Normally, this irritated Val. At the moment, he savored it.

The Waz crept past the lead flatbed and its load of full latrines. Then, when the major's Humvee was even with and just below the latrines, the Waz jerked to a stop.

As Major Noreen's driver hit the brakes and stopped inches from the Waz, the trail flatbed started up. It swerved out from behind the second flatbed and surged forward until it was just a couple of feet behind the major's Humvee.

The Russian truck driver honked impatiently.

The major's driver got out and shrugged at the truck behind him before walking to the Waz and motioning at the driver to roll down his window.

The Russian truck driver honked again. For a long time. Then he revved his engine. And then he honked again. It was an irritating racket.

It was more than Major Noreen could take. He got out of his vehicle.

The major was on the opposite side of his vehicle from Val, standing in between the Humvee and the latrine-laden flatbed, so all Val could see was his motionless head staring at the honking Russian truck. Val laughed at the chaos.

Then he gasped and stood up.

Val couldn't believe what he was seeing. The ropes tied to the tops of the latrines were tightening, pulling them toward the edge of the flatbed. Toward the major.

The latrines were starting to tip.

Val looked at Major Noreen. He was focused on the disrespectful, honking Russian truck.

Val looked at the honking truck behind the Humvee and then at the Waz. He spotted Alexei about twenty meters to the left of the Waz, radio in hand, gesturing in a yanking motion.

He looked back at the latrines. They were leaning over the unaware Major Noreen.

Val finally put it together as the latrines tilted past the point of no return.

Classic vehicle ambush.

As the latrines fell past horizontal, their doors opened, releasing their foul payload. Noreen was oblivious until the instant he was struck by more than a hundred gallons of urine and feces.

The Humvee took the weight of the falling latrines. But the impact burst the structurally weak containers.

Val heard the sickening sound of a large quantity of thick liquid hitting the ground, followed by continued splashing as the remains spilled out.

The major's driver was motionless, trying to grasp what was happening.

The Waz fired up and sped away onto the Russian base.

The flatbed stopped honking and backed up slowly to its spot behind the second vehicle.

Major Noreen crawled around to the front of his Humvee. He was soaked in piss and covered head to toe in shit. He struggled to his feet and, standing with his arms held out from his sides, let out a loud wail.

The American gate guard, as well as several of the squirrels who had heard the honking truck and come out to investigate, ran over to the major and began wiping muck from his tightly shut eyes. They guided the major toward the American compound.

Val looked to his left and across the street. Amid all the commotion, no one else but he noticed as Alexei, looking at Val, snapped to attention, rendered a salute, and yelled, "For Lilly!"

Val saluted back. Then, understanding now was not the time to run to Alexei, he put his hand over his heart in a gesture of thanks as tears ran down his cheeks.

Alexei nodded.

Then the Russian turned and waved at a squad of soldiers on the Russian base. They ran out and began the cleanup.

*

The latrine incident was the topic of much heated speculation for a week after it happened. Noreen had been medevaced by air back to Pristina that day for observation. The medical staff wanted to be sure that he hadn't ingested any human waste–borne pathogens. He was fine and was released the next day.

There was a general suspicion that the incident hadn't been entirely random. General Stenson even paid a visit to Colonel Ziora a few days later. Val had to sit in on the meeting in which the general asked the colonel, point blank, if it had been intentional. The colonel denied his men had any involvement and turned to Alexei, who also confirmed it was a regrettable but purely accidental incident. The colonel then called in the Waz driver and the work detail that had loaded and then dumped the shit on Major Noreen. Ziora asked them if their actions had been intentional, and Val translated their negative responses and long, earnest apologies to General Stenson.

The colonel then insisted the general join him for a few peacemaking shots of vodka, and Alexei winked at Val. An hour later, the two senior officers were slapping each other on the back and trading stories.

CHAPTER 15

Near the end of his tour, Val raised the topic of Zyph Hyka on one of his secure calls with General Bryson.

"Hyka? The mayor's aid?"

"Yes, sir. You haven't responded to my request to move forward with recruiting him. Just wanted to hear your thoughts on the matter directly."

Val had submitted a request for authorization to recruit Hyka as an asset a month prior. His reasoning was that Hyka was well-placed in the Kamenica government, with access to both KFOR and Russian contacts and initiatives, and had a promising civil career in front of him.

Furthermore, Hyka's patriotism and his innate need to be part of a cause he perceived to be bigger than himself provided a perfect ideological leverage point for Val to exploit. He could paint the picture of complete US alignment with Hyka's values for a better Kosovo, appeal to their common need to fight the forces of evil allied against them and convince Hyka that working with the US discreetly was a truly patriotic decision.

It was a classic development structure that would put the recruitment in a context that would appeal to the target. Over time, Hyka could develop into a high-placed asset in a region where the US was rebuilding its clandestine network.

"You won't like what I think, Rafter," Bryson said. "First off, Hyka needs more development. Not much, but at least a couple months so that we can validate him well enough to risk recruiting. And you're rotating back at the end of this month.

"Second, Hyka really should be a CIA asset. He's a civilian, for starters, and I can't even guarantee I'll have a Cobra Snare in-country after you rotate out. CIA, though, is strapping in over there. They'll be in-country for the long haul, and stability matters in running assets."

"Got it, sir. I understand."

"The work you have done with Hyka lays an excellent foundation. It will enable CIA to move quickly should they decide to follow up."

"Yes, sir," Val said, trying unsuccessfully not to let his disappointment seep into his voice.

"Damn, son," Bryson chuckled. "You sound like someone peed in your cornflakes."

Val laughed.

"You've done well on this assignment," Bryson said. "Giving us the decoder ring to the Russian bilking operation. You don't have to bag a new asset as well."

"Thank you, sir."

The general's praise made the rejection go down smoother.

*

Val spent most of his last weeks in Kosovo trying to nail down a comprehensive inventory of the 13th Tactical's unit numbers and illicit activities. It was a slow time operationally, the cold and snow of December dampening Kosovo's violent tendencies, so Val was able to focus on his notes and analysis. Though not a Cobra Snare, his replacement was a trained foreign areas officer. Val wanted to set the new guy up for success with a robust intel handoff.

Two nights before Val's departure date, Colonel Ziora threw a party for Val. It was held downtown in the large apartment that belonged to one of the UN police officers from Ukraine. Colonel Ziora had one of his infantry companies lock down two blocks around the apartment for security. Inside was an odd, drunken collection of nearly every nationality involved in the KFOR mission: Russians, Macedonians, Ukrainians, Bulgarians, Norwegians, French, Italians, and Brits.

A lot of ABBA and bad eighties club music blared throughout the apartment as everyone, dressed in different styles of uniforms, speaking different languages, danced their own version of bad club dancing. Alexei ensured each person contributed a celebratory toast and had their fill of vodka. The bad dancing, jokes, man hugs, man tears, and drunken vows of eternal friendship went late into the night.

The next day, Val rose with a terrible headache and promised himself he would go to bed early that night. His last in Kosovo.

After submitting his final reports and cables in the morning, Val met with Zyph for their goodbye lunch. Zyph was disappointed to be losing Val.

"It's gonna be fine, Zyph," Val said, reading the concern on his friend's face as they were finishing lunch.

"Perhaps. But I cannot help but worry. Both for Kosovo and myself. To have a new American officer that must learn everything again. The Russians will take advantage of this."

Val looked at Zyph and tried to exude confidence. "Zyph, listen to me. It's going to be fine. Like I've been telling you, we're here for the long haul."

Zyph nodded and tried to smile.

"Thank you, Val."

"Of course." Val silently hoped the CIA would follow through on Zyph's recruitment. And then not screw it up.

"I am glad to have met you, Val," Zyph said as they said goodbye outside their favorite lunch spot. "And hope to see you again someday."

"It's been my pleasure, Zyph. And I believe we'll meet again."

After lunch, Val packed his stuff and prepared for an early-morning departure. At 1800 there was a knock on his door.

It was Alexei.

"Are you ready, my friend?"

"Yes. But I'm not staying out late tonight, Alexei. I'm still hungover from yesterday, and I've got an early wake up in the morning."

"Nothing late, my friend. We just go for pizza."

"Okay, then."

The two men left the American compound and walked toward the city center. It was a cold evening, and they didn't speak. The moon was close to full, and there was a thin blanket of reflective snow covering everything, giving the night a soft glow.

"Peaceful night," Val remarked.

"Yes. Hard to tell is war zone."

They turned the corner, and to the right, Val saw an array of small lights strung up in a field. Several fifty-five-gallon drums holding large fires surrounded a table. Colonel Ziora sat at the table.

"Shit, Alexei," Val said with some irritation.

"It will not be a late night, Val. I promise. Last night was a good party. But it was not the proper goodbye for friends."

Val smiled. "Son of a bitch."

"Yes," Alexei agreed.

They walked a hundred meters through the thin snow to the table. It was warm in the middle of the burn barrels, and Val unzipped his jacket. The colonel stood and gave Val a hug, slapping him on the back several times.

"I'm going to miss you, Val. I put in a request with my good friend General Stenson to have your time in Kosovo extended, but he refused me!" The colonel feigned shock and insult.

"Well, I'm fucking glad he did, sir," Val said, smiling.

Ziora laughed.

Four Russian soldiers walked out of the shadow beyond the burn barrels. They each carried large trays of food. Various meats and salo, a type of fatback eaten by Russians to absorb vodka. Pickles, beet salad, and freshly baked bread rounded out the feast. They placed the food on the table and then each shook Val's hand and said, *"Proshchay, Kapitan,"* Russian for "Farewell, Captain."

"Sit, Val," Alexei said. "We have dinner together."

Val sat and lost track of time. He and the colonel and Alexei sat for hours, eating, drinking, and telling stories. The colonel yelled into the darkness, summoning a soldier whom he dispatched for a guitar. Soon, Alexei was playing the guitar, and the three men sang together. By then, Val had learned many of the lines. They sang of brotherhood, hardship, and loss.

Major Orlov walked into the lit area about two hours into the soiree.

"Ah!" the colonel said. "Major Orlov, it looked like you would not make it. Sit with us."

Val was in such a nostalgic mood, he didn't even mind the major joining. Orlov sat at the table across from Val and gave him the friendliest smile that he'd ever seen on the major. Val raised his glass, and the major met it with his.

"To your health, Captain Rafter," Orlov said.

"And yours, Major."

"And where do you go next, Captain?" Orlov asked. "Will you be back in the States?"

"No," Val answered, speaking more to Alexei. "I'll be attending a foreign affairs and security course at our Marshall Center in Garmisch, Germany."

Alexei smiled. "Near Austria, right?"

"Yes."

"Excellent skiing!" Alexei smiled wider.

"Yes!" Val said.

"I know this school," Major Orlov said. "I have heard that it is an excellent course. Congratulations to you."

"Thank you, Major."

After another hour of singing, drinking, and eating, the colonel stood up.

"Val, you have been a good friend to the 13th Tactical, to me, and to my officers." The colonel gestured around at Alexei and Orlov. "You became, very much, a part of my battalion." The colonel cleared his throat as emotion swelled within him.

"I therefore want to give you a gift to remember us, your friends, by." The colonel pulled a small package out of a pant cargo pocket and gave it to Val.

"Sir, you really didn't have to…"

"Open it!" the colonel yelled.

Val unwrapped the gift and held up the switchblade.

"It's the large one, Val," the colonel said. "From our first night."

"Yes." Val felt the swell of emotion within himself. "I recognize it."

Alexei winked at Ziora. "You see, sir! I told you he would love it."

Val turned the knife over in his hand and saw a red "13" carved and painted into the black wooden handle by one of the colonel's artisan soldiers.

"That is a special modification we made to it." Alexei placed his hand on Val's shoulder. "To help you not forget."

"Gentlemen," Val said, unashamed of his tears. "I will never forget."

*

Alexei walked Val back to the American compound well past midnight. "You see?" Alexei said as they reached the gate. "As I told you. Not a late night at all."

"Can't ever trust a Russian," Val said, smiling.

"No, Val." Alexei grinned. "You cannot."

Both men looked at their feet for a moment.

"Well, I guess this is goodbye," Alexei said.

"Yeah. I guess so."

"I am very glad you came to Kosovo, Val. You were a good friend to me. I have so many good memories. Our illegal ski trip is my favorite. You did that for me at just the right time."

"Don't kid yourself. That trip was as much for me as for you."

"Such a poor liar, you are," Alexei said.

Val shrugged. Then his smile faded, and he said, "And you saved me from going to jail for assaulting a superior officer."

"I think it would have been more than assault."

Val nodded. "He might have preferred it over what you did to him."

"For Lilly," Alexei said.

"For Lilly."

"I know we serve in different armies," Alexei said, "for different countries… but you are my brother."

"Get in here, brother," Val said.

They hugged and then turned away from each other.

"You're a crazy son of a bitch, Captain Val Rafter!" Alexei yelled at Val over his shoulder. "May it never catch up to you!"

Val saluted his friend and walked onto the American compound. Alexei walked through the gate and disappeared into the shadows of the Russian side.

CHAPTER 16

"**I** must say," Alexei said, putting his shot glass down on the table next to the pistol and switchblade. "I really appreciate you coming to Ukraine. Is good to see you."

"Fuck you," Val said.

"I am serious," Alexei said in a wounded voice.

"I am too."

One of the forward doors next to the bar opened, and a man wearing a dark suit walked into the saloon. The lack of reaction from the mercenaries told Val he was expected, or at least known. And that they felt in control of the situation and surroundings. They were not worried about surprises.

It wasn't only his clothing that set the newcomer apart from the mercenaries. He was also younger. Val estimated him to be in his late twenties.

The young man walked quickly to Alexei's side, avoiding eye contact with Val.

Alexei poured another shot for himself and then handed the bottle to Val with an apologetic face. He swiveled in his chair so that he could have a private conversation with the young man, who cupped his hand over his mouth and whispered.

Val poured bourbon into his glass and then set the bottle back in the middle of the table near the pistol.

His eyes lingered on the switchblade and firearm. It was enticing to think about grabbing the pistol and blasting his way off the *Monarch*. But he knew he would never make it. Instead, he winked at Zakir.

The bruised mercenary dragged a finger across his neck and smiled.

Alexei got agitated. He shook his head and pushed the young man away.

"Enough," Alexei said in Russian. "No more excuses. Simple task. Bring him here, as I told you. Now!"

The young man stood straight, his face pained by Alexei's rebuke. He hesitated, then thought better of it. He stole a long look at Val.

"Leave us!" Alexei barked.

"Yes, sir," the young man said before turning to leave.

Alexei swiveled back to the table, rolling his eyes. "I'm sorry. He is a little star-struck. You have a reputation, you know."

"I didn't know."

"You should know," Alexei said in a scolding voice.

"He works for you?" Val asked, wanting to change the subject. "The young one?"

"Yes. His name is Peskov." Alexei leaned across the table and said to Val in a confiding voice, "Does it seem like they get younger and more stupid every year?"

Val smiled.

"Maybe not for you guys," Alexei said. "With your global wars on terror, you have more battle-tested veterans. Combat clears out the dumb ones, right? And your big American budgets make everything much sexier. For us, is just us poor Russians just trying to keep the world safe for our people and our motherland."

"Yes." Val nodded in exaggerated agreement. "It's god's work you're doing, Alexei. Truly."

"I agree," Alexei said with a broad smile. "I tell my people this every day."

Val could not suppress his laughter.

Alexei nodded, glad to be on a happier subject.

"This is something I don't think I know about you, Val," Alexei said. "How did you get into this nasty business of ours?"

"Me? I was just a dumbass volunteer."

Alexei nodded, his face somber. "I was same. My grandfather served in World War Two. He was my hero, my whole family's hero. He fought against the Germans under Zhukov. In our neighborhood, people would sit around him listening to his stories for a long time. I always sit in front, at his feet. My father served in army also. A good officer. He retired as a colonel. So, for me…was natural."

Alexei rubbed his chin.

"The older I am, the more amazing it seems to me."

"What's that?" Val asked.

"How do our two countries never seem to run out of volunteers?"

"Yeah," Val said, shaking his head. "Their one true, inexhaustible resource."

"To dumbass volunteers," Alexei said.

Val clinked his glass against Alexei's, and they both threw back.

CHAPTER 17

10 July 1997

Ansbach, Germany

The train jostled to a stop at the platform in Ansbach, Germany. Val got up slowly, sore from almost twenty-four hours on the train, not to mention the ninety-six hours of drinking and dodging bulls in Pamplona. He gave his buddy an easy shove to wake him. Val reached up to grab his dirty backpack from the overhead luggage rack. They walked off the platform and through the train station in silence.

"You want a ride?" his buddy asked him when they reached the street corner.

"No, thanks. It's only half a mile to my flat. I'm going to stretch my legs."

"Suit yourself. See you at PT tomorrow." His buddy turned and walked to his car. Val walked through the town's old center.

Sunday afternoons were always quiet. None of the shops were open, and most folks were home getting ready for the workweek. Val rented a second-story flat from a German couple, the Fischers. They were older and had a son in his thirties who lived up north in Hamburg. They were a kind couple and doted on Val, having him down for dinner once a week. The Fischers also loved it when he used his ration card to give them two cartons of cigarettes each month with his rent check. Val expected them to invite him over tonight, eager to hear about his adventures in Spain.

Val was tired, though, and was thinking of excuses to avoid dinner as he walked to his building. He didn't notice the stranger standing in front of his door until he nearly bumped into him.

"Good afternoon, Captain Rafter," said the stranger.

"Good afternoon, sir," Val responded.

The man was dressed in civilian clothes, wearing jeans and a button-down shirt, and had a small leather satchel thrown over his shoulder. But Val could tell he was an American officer. "Who are you?"

"Lieutenant Colonel Frank Wilson."

"How do you know who I am?" Val asked as he shook the man's extended hand.

"I'd like to talk to you, Captain. Can we step inside?" He smiled and stepped away from the door to allow Val to get to the lock.

"Sure."

Val unlocked the door and led the colonel up the stairs to his flat. He threw his backpack on the floor and walked to the fridge.

"How was Spain?"

"Good," Val answered. "You want a beer, sir?"

"Yes, please."

Val grabbed two bottles of beer and handed one to the colonel as he walked past and out onto his porch. The colonel followed.

Val's porch overlooked the small backyard. Like most Germans, the Fischers loved to garden, and their backyard was a well-manicured collection of thriving herbs and vegetables. The porch hung on the east side of the building in cool shadow as the hot July sun set.

Val sat at the small table and gestured for the colonel to sit in the other chair.

"How did you know I was in Spain?" Val asked.

"Your battalion commander told me."

"How do you know Colonel Burton?"

"We went to West Point together."

Val chuckled.

"You went to Appalachian State, right?"

"Yes, sir."

"You were commissioned in '93?" the colonel asked. "Armor officer?"

"That's right."

"And you're stepping down from a successful company command in a few weeks?"

"Yes, sir."

"And you put in your paperwork?"

Val took a large swing of beer. *Oh, that's what this is about.*

"Look, sir. I appreciate the colonel asked you to come here and talk to me, but I've made my decision—"

The colonel interrupted him. "You've got it wrong. Burton didn't ask me to come here. And I know you're planning to get out. I'm not here to talk you out of it. I just want to present you with another option. What you do is totally up to you."

Val put down his beer and looked away from the colonel. He gazed across the green and rolling countryside of Germany for a moment before saying, "You gotta love the US Army. Almost half a million people under arms, and yet it feels like a gossipy high school."

"That's not all you hate about the army, though, is it?" the colonel asked, putting his own beer down.

Val turned his head and looked at the colonel.

"I can't say I hate the army, sir. But I'm ready to do something else."

"You're bored, right?"

"Yeah. I am."

The colonel nodded and took a swig of beer.

"Well, I may have another option for you that does not involve you getting out and trying to pretend you're a civilian."

Val's eyes narrowed at the comment.

The colonel smiled and reached into his bag. "First, I need you to sign this," he said as he pushed a piece of paper across the table to Val.

Val pulled the paper closer and read it. When he was done reading, he leaned back in his chair and looked at the colonel. "Is this for real, sir?"

"It is, Captain. That piece of paper states you understand that what I'm about to tell you is top secret and that if you speak of it afterward, regardless of what you decide to do, you will be punished under UCMJ for disclosure of classified information." The colonel pushed a pen across the table. "I promise you, if you breathe a word of this, I'll make sure you end up in Leavenworth." The colonel then leaned back in his chair. "Or you can simply not sign it, and I'll leave."

Val picked up the pen and signed the paper. The colonel smiled.

He took the paper and pen from Val and put them away. He then leaned forward and said, "The Defense Intelligence Agency runs its own small spy organization. We use the cover of various army assignments as a platform for recruiting and running foreign assets. We're a small team, less than fifty of us. And we're the only members of DIA authorized to conduct cross-border and other high-level intelligence operations. Extremely important, sensitive, and sometimes dangerous stuff."

The colonel took a swig of his beer. Val tried to look unimpressed by what he was hearing.

"The records of every officer involved in the program have been moved out from the purview of big army and are in a protected/access-only status," the colonel continued. "They have, effectively, disappeared. Were you to join, you'd also disappear. First you'd enter a clandestine training pipeline, which would culminate in you going to the Farm. Upon graduation, you'd serve around the world, often in an OPCON status for the CIA."

The colonel leaned back in his chair and let Val digest what he'd heard.

Val's mind raced as he eyed the colonel.

Is this for real?

"This is very much for real, Captain," the colonel said with a smile.

"Why are you asking me?"

"We look at promising young officers as they approach the window."

"Look at?"

"Review your performance. Get feedback from your commanders. Assess suitability for the program," Colonel Wilson said.

"Your commanders say a lot of things we like, Captain." He raised his hand and ticked off points with his fingers as he continued. "You're adaptable to new situations. You're comfortable in international settings. You attack problems in the absence of guidance."

The colonel dropped his hand and smiled. "You also have a reputation as a bit of a lone wolf, which can be good or bad. But we'll smoke that out."

"What did you mean by 'approach the window'?" Val asked.

"Integrating officers into the program is a trick shot. If you were to be accepted, your career timeline would drastically change. It would be reviewed and updated to strike a balance between building out your cover status—things like attaché training, language school, in-country foreign area officer assignments, and the necessary clandestine training you'd need to complete. It's a lot, and there is a narrow window of time to get someone into the program and get them trained without attracting unwanted attention."

Val sat silently for a moment. He and the colonel stared at each other. Finally, Val spoke.

"What would the next step be? When would I start?"

"Ha! There's the Rafter confidence I've heard about." The colonel stood and grabbed his satchel. "I'm not offering you a job, Rafter. I'm offering you a chance to try out. That's all."

He handed Val a business card. It read, "Field Support Office" and had a single phone number on it.

"Call that number if you want to give it a shot."

Val walked the colonel down the steps and out to his car. The colonel turned and held his hand out to Val.

"Good luck with it, Rafter."

Val shook the colonel's hand. "How do you know I'll try it?"

The colonel smiled and got in his car.

CHAPTER 18

"I'm Sydney," she said to him as she walked to the bar.

She'd circled it twice, looking for a good entry point to get a beer. There was not much of an opening here, but this guy stood out to her. And not because of his broad shoulders and charismatic smile, though they were nice. What pulled her in was the fact that he looked relaxed. Most of the others in the student recreation building, a.k.a. "the Bar," in Farm speak, were on edge. Their Farm class kicked off the next day, but he looked like he could have been going fishing in the morning. His relaxed energy was like a magnet. She wanted to be around him.

The Farm is the legendary CIA training facility the US government has never acknowledged. It's hidden on Camp Peary, a nine-thousand-acre military reservation near Williamsburg, Virginia, and started its life during World War II as a US Navy Seabee training base. Allen Dulles, the director of the Central Intelligence Agency from 1953 to 1961, established the Farm early in his tenure, and it has been the formative training crucible for generations of CIA, Defense, and other clandestine intelligence officers ever since.

"I'm Val," the guy at the bar answered.

"Good to meet you."

"You too," he said, smiling with his back against the bar. "You trying to get in here?"

"I am." She was suddenly glad she'd worn her skinny jeans and a tight black sweater. She'd debated, it being the first night and all. But she looked too good in them. With her face framed by wavy blond hair cut in a short bob falling just below her jawline, and dimples anchoring her smile on both sides, she was the picture of all-American girl-next-door beauty. She wanted to feel confident tonight. His eyes told her it was the right move.

Val stood and slid his stool a few inches to one side. He sat back on it and leaned over to make room for her.

"How is that?"

Sydney cocked her head at Val, surprised by his less-than-inviting response. "That's all the space you can spare me?"

"Ordinarily, I'd offer you my seat." Val raised his palms in apology. "I wish I could. But I'm kinda on duty."

Sydney was about to bemoan the death of chivalry when she saw the coin lacquered to the bar behind Val.

"Oh, I get it." Sydney pointed at the old unit coin. "You're sitting at the MOTC spot."

Years ago, military students attended a course at the Farm known as MOTC, or Military Officer Training Course. In those days, they had more of a "blue collar" paramilitary role and a separate curriculum from the more "white collar" CIA case officers who operated out of the embassy platform. The tension between the two communities is legendary, and stories of the old rivalry are favorites in the community.

No one knows who fixed the coin there, but its position at the prominent corner of the L-shaped bar offers the best vantage point of the entire SRB and the easiest access to the next drinks. It's a highly prized spot, and it's still considered the duty of the first military officer in the SRB each day to claim that seat, or to finagle their way into the chair if a nonmilitary student beat them to it. The military student is then duty bound to defend the spot until closing time, passing the throne only to another military student in times of crisis of the bladder.

"I am." He smiled. "But we can make it work. Get in here."

Val leaned farther to the other side and motioned Sydney in. She stepped forward, arm brushing against him as she leaned into the bar and waved at the bartender.

"Yeah," Val said, acknowledging the busy bar. "May take a while."

"Well, I hope you don't mind me crowding you for a few minutes?"

"Not at all."

Just then, the person on the other side of Sydney stood and walked away from the bar. Sydney pounced on the seat.

"Well done," Val said with an approving nod.

Sydney smiled and looked around, still getting her bearings.

About fifty feet behind her on the other side of the building, a group of students sat watching the large-screen TV. To her left, there were booths, and, in a side room, pool tables and dart boards, which were getting a lot of action. To her right, there were more room and tables and then an adjacent screened-in porch. The large bar, which could easily accommodate over thirty folks, was filling up. The inside of the SRB had the disconcerting feel of an adult summer camp. But, in reality, everyone was trying to get in one last relaxed evening before the start of training.

Sydney glanced over at Val. He sat with his arms crossed, leaning back against the bar with a detached air. Also, his drink was empty.

"You want a beer…um…soldier?" she asked.

"Sure."

"What's your rank, anyway?"

"Captain."

"Captain what?" Sydney asked, trying to get Val's last name.

"Captain Thorne." Val winked.

Thanks to former instructor Aldrich Ames, who provided the Russians the true first and last name of several hundred Farm students and cadre, Farm students are now only allowed to reveal their first name. Knowing or discussing a student's last name carried consequences. Everyone was, therefore, referred to by the last name of "Thorne." Non-official cover students went a step further and conducted their full Farm training "in pseudo," the intelligence community's term for using fabricated identities.

Sydney gave Val an approving nod and twisted in her seat to gesture at the bartender. Val snuck an appreciative look at her body.

"I saw that, you dog!" yelled a voice on the other side of Sydney. "Ma'am, I'm sorry to report that this man has harassed you."

Sydney turned and looked at Val with a huge grin on her face. Val lowered his head and rubbed his eyes. He recognized the voice.

"He's a dog, that one!" yelled Tony as he leaned forward on the bar so that Val could see him on the other side of Sydney. Tony was a second-generation Italian American with a tan complexion and a large body. He could have been a devastating womanizer had he not married his college sweetheart, to whom he was absolutely loyal. One would never have known his virtue by listening to him speak, though. It seemed all he thought about was sex, and he hadn't met a female form he was not compelled to ogle.

"You turned away to order a beer, and he undressed you in his imagination and did unspeakable things! Trust me. I know this guy!"

Val shook his head.

"You deny it?" Sydney gasped. "I'm hurt."

"Sydney, meet Tony," said Val with resignation.

Tony extended his hand to Sydney.

"Good to meet you. Are you a captain also?" Sydney asked, shaking his hand.

"What? Hell no! I work for a living!" Tony said with a smile.

Sydney looked at Val, confused.

"What Tony is saying is that he is a noncommissioned officer," Val explained.

"Staff Sergeant Tony Thorne," Tony said with a smile. "And you are?"

"Sydney. Pleasure to meet you."

The bartender returned with beers for Val and Sydney, and the three of them clinked their bottles together.

"So, what did you do in the army?" Sydney asked Val.

"I was a tanker."

"Tanker?"

"An armor officer."

Sydney looked at him with a blank expression. She had little knowledge of or experience with the military.

"You know what a tank is? Large metal thing with tracks and a big gun?"

"Yes," Sydney said flatly.

"Well, I was in a unit with a bunch of them."

"Sounds cool."

"It's not," Tony interjected. "Tankers are a bunch of pussies."

"Is that right?" Sydney turned her head to look at Tony. "And what were you?"

"Infantry. The one true branch."

"He just wanted to be in a job where he didn't have to think faster than he could walk," Val said.

Sydney laughed as Tony shoved his arm past her to extend Val the finger.

"What do you do in the infantry?" Sydney asked.

"Nothing special." Tony looked at his watch. "Oh shit. Sorry. I have to call the wife. Good meeting you, Syd. Later, Val."

"The name is Sydney," she corrected. But she was already talking to Tony's back as he hustled out of the SRB. She looked at Val.

"So, what does he really do in the army?"

Val shrugged.

"Uh-huh," she said skeptically. "How long have you guys known each other?"

"Nine weeks. We met at the military pre-course."

"Really? Seems like you've been friends a long time."

"We've got a common background in the army. And we spent a lot of time helping each other out over the past weeks."

Sydney nodded and turned her head to look back across the crowded SRB. As she scanned the room, the sound of greetings, new introductions, and clinking glasses filled her ears. If she hadn't known she was standing on the grounds of a secret US government training facility, she would have easily believed she was at a popular bar in a college town favored by the grad school crowd. But she felt out of place, doubting that she shared a common background with anyone in the crowded room.

Born into wealth and privilege in Connecticut, Sydney's parents were hotshot lawyers at a prominent New York City law firm. Affluent, focused, and distant, they lived a life of board room meetings, private jets, five-star hotels, and elaborate charity events while their only daughter was passed back and forth between nannies, private tutors, and tennis coaches. Craving warmth and love from her parents, Sydney found none. Instead, she learned she could get by on their attention, won only through achievement.

Surviving like this for years, Sydney's isolation and craving morphed into anger. Over time, she harnessed that anger, fueling a white-hot ambition and carving a path of athletic and academic achievement that landed her at Princeton. By the time she graduated, Sydney was ranked nationally in tennis and double majored in history and political science, the two undergraduate degrees her parents thought would best position her to follow them into law.

Her parents were ecstatic when, months before she was scheduled to graduate, Sydney was accepted into both Yale and Harvard Law Schools. Luxuriating in their daughter's accomplishment, so clearly derived from their good qualities, her mother and father engaged in spirited debates at dinner parties about where Sydney should go, entertaining and impressing their friends. Suddenly, Sydney was worth having around. Intelligent, beautiful, accomplished, and congruent with their world.

Sydney let it go on for the last months of school and then struck, revealing just before graduation that she'd applied to Georgetown University's Walsh School of International Relations. Her parents were dumbfounded.

They worked on her. How could she be serious? Had she given this enough consideration? Did she realize how disappointing this was? What in the world would she do with such a degree?

It was the most attention her parents had ever paid to her. And, despite knowing that it was focused solely on making her do what they wanted, making her fit, Sydney loved it.

For a while.

Then the anger took back over. Sydney crushed them, delivering her decision in a curt goodbye as she packed her car. She drove to Georgetown, determined to conquer. She would deliver the final blow to her mother and father by succeeding spectacularly at something they didn't know shit about and could not affect. They should've loved her.

Driven by her resolve to distance herself from her parents' world, and a fascination for international relations, Sydney continued to excel academically. She was drawn to and reveled in the complexity and scope of geopolitics, commerce, and languages. She spent her second year abroad, studying in London, Paris, and Berlin. Her parents tried to visit, but Sydney was a moving target. She had no time for them.

Anxiety settled over Sydney as she flew home from Europe with only a few weeks left to go before graduation. She was still weighing several job offers. They were all great opportunities, each one offering more money than she had ever expected to make in her chosen field. But she couldn't decide.

As the wheels of the 747 touched down on the runway at Dulles, Sydney realized she didn't want any of those jobs. They reminded her too much of her parents. Too corporate. Too narrow.

That was when it occurred to her. The Central Intelligence Agency.

Going to school in Georgetown, the State Department and intelligence communities were always in the mix and never far from mind. But she'd never considered it. Not really. Not until she was faced with paths that reminded her of her parents. Once she opened her mind to it, it seemed perfect, it seemed destiny. An opportunity to excel in a challenging and meaningful endeavor that would also be a rebellion against her parents' world.

She would join the CIA and, someday, run the place.

Almost a year to the day after landing back in the US, Sydney sat next to Val at the bar in the SRB on Camp Peary, nervous about starting her Farm training the next day.

But it was a good nervousness, an anxiety born of facing the unknown, of wanting to do well.

Sydney smiled, took a sip of beer, and looked around. It felt good to be here. It felt right.

"What side did you get?" Val asked her.

"Huh?" Sydney's mind snapped back to the SRB.

"Side," Val said louder, over the din. "What side are you assigned to?"

The students at the Farm were divided into four different "sides," named after the cardinal headings. Consisting of about sixty students, each side was further divided into smaller operational groups of ten to fifteen. Students went through most of the training in their small group.

"I'm in North Side."

"So are Tony and I," said Val.

"Really?"

Val smiled and nodded. Sydney reached toward Val with her beer. They tapped them together.

"To new friends," she said.

"To new friends."

CHAPTER 19

The Farm employed a crawl, walk, run rhythm as it taught the tradecraft necessary to being a successful case officer, and the volume of instruction accumulated quickly. The first graded practical test took place the second week. Each student had to navigate an embassy reception at which they needed to build rapport, elicit information, and set up a follow-on meeting with a foreign national.

The exercise forced them to demonstrate proficiency in all the relationship-building and manipulation concepts that were thrown at them over the past week. This was the class's introduction to the "blue sheets" the instructors used to score and critique the students. The blue sheets were dreaded from that day until graduation. Particularly by the North Side.

Mr. Wall, a thirty-year CIA veteran, was the senior instructor for North Side. A slightly overweight man with the washed-out gray complexion of a lifelong chain-smoker, Wall still retained the charisma and edge that made him a legendary clandestine service officer. The innumerable rumors of his exploits sounded like a greatest-hits list—Vietnam, Cambodia, Berlin, Moscow, Cuba, Chile. What was not the topic of speculation, however, was his approach toward training his side. The man was an infamous hard-ass. He ran three students out after the first graded practical exercise. The remaining students of North Side took notice.

Each day dragged on, but the weeks passed quickly. Val, Tony, and Sydney were assigned to the same small group and went through every task and challenge together. The first was a master class in surveillance detection routes.

The cardinal rule that underlies everything taught to clandestine intelligence officers is never drag surveillance to a meeting. Ever. The surveillance detection route is the primary method of living up to this obligation.

SDRs are fluid, situational tools. They can be executed on foot, in a vehicle, or in combination. They can take minutes or last days. They can be the product of months of planning, or be thrown together ad hoc by necessity. But all SDRs share a common architecture: routes with stops and changes in direction that seem "natural" to an observer but enable a case officer to determine whether, by whom, and by how many they're being surveilled.

Prior to operations, a case officer always familiarizes themselves with a new area. They look for good routes, cover stops, intrusion points, pickup locations, and blind spots. The goal is to feel comfortable driving around without a map and able to hit a scripted, predefined route, which to the observer looks as casual as a routine drive to work but hides covert activity or ingress to meeting an asset.

The students practiced SDRs ad nauseam. First by car, driving all over Fairfax County. Then by foot, which they practiced throughout DC while being pursued by vehicles, foot patrols, and stationary surveillance dressed incognito.

Because SDRs are the mission-critical tool of clandestine operators, training at the Farm drills the subject over and over and over. It was foundational, extensive, exhausting work. Students are sick of SDRs by the time they graduate. But they're damn good at them.

The training wasn't all fieldcraft, though. There were also the dreaded reporting protocols. It wasn't enough for a case officer to spot, assess, develop, and recruit agents. None of that matters if the intelligence does not make it back to Langley. And the way intelligence makes it back to Langley is via a reporting protocol that Tony, and most army intelligence types, found overly complex. Whereas the army tends to lump everything into one report, a practice Tony had gotten comfortable with in his years at Fort Belvoir, the CIA breaks things into two primary reports: an operations cable and an intelligence report.

The juggling of two different intel reporting languages is a constant gripe among DIA case officers running CIA assets. At the Farm, it was giving Tony fits.

"Damn it!" Tony would yell. "Why do they make this shit so fucking obtuse?"

It hadn't taken long for the three friends to establish a supportive routine to get through the infamous material. After dinner, Tony would come to Val's room. The supposed purpose of his visit was to review the day's material with Sydney and Val, but the session was more about helping Tony. He struggled with the extensive report-writing requirements.

"It's designed to protect sources and methods, Tony," Sydney would call from the corner of the room.

"I've got your sources and method right here," Tony would respond, grabbing his crotch.

Sydney called out key concepts and questions as Val coached Tony through report writing. After an hour or more of this, the trio would walk down to the SRB for a beer or to relax playing darts or shooting pool.

Tony would leave the SRB first. He called his wife every night at 8:30 p.m. Val and Sydney wouldn't stay much longer unless it was a Thursday. On those nights, they tended, like most students, to stay late and drink at the bar in the SRB.

When the bar really got going on those nights, many poor decisions were made. The Farm is full of type-A, witty, good-looking, and charismatic young people whose rigorous selection indexed strongly on their ability to influence others. The common crucible of their foundational clandestine training experience establishes a unique bond among them all. Hookups happened. And not just among the single.

Val and Sydney got close. It was on one of those early Thursday nights. They both had drunk a lot and were walking back to their dorms. It was late February, and they were bundled against the cold. At the fork in the path, Sydney reached over and tugged Val's hand out from his coat pocket. He squeezed her hand back as they stopped and faced each other.

Val put his hands on Sydney's hips and looked at her for a long time.

Then he dropped his hands and took a small step back.

"Terrible idea?" Sydney said.

"Yeah. Probably shouldn't while we're in the same unit, don't you think?"

"In the civilian world, we call it 'coworkers,'" she said with a slight roll of her eyes.

Val reached out and took her hand again. He leaned in and kissed her quickly on the cheek, then turned and walked to his quarters.

Sydney raised her hand to her face as she watched him leave, then slowly walked back to her own.

CHAPTER 20

"Congratulations, you've all made it to the last phase of Farm training. Station Phase."

It was the first week of June, and North Side sat tall in their seats in their large classroom. Mr. Wall stood motionless on the small stage as he briefed the class. He had been pushing North Side hard since day one and had run out more students than any other senior instructor.

"Station Phase is designed to accomplish three goals," Mr. Wall began.

"The first is to give each of you a crash course in how an agency station operates out of an embassy. It makes sure you're not a total idiot when you show up at your first posting.

"Second, it forces each of you to prove you have learned everything you need to know to be a clandestine operator. If you don't prove it, you won't graduate.

"Finally, and most importantly, this is our last chance to get rid of those of you who are not suited to our profession. If you cannot multitask, deal with stress, manage high-profile operations, think on your feet, or are otherwise undesirable, we designed Station Phase to smoke you out. And we'll make good use of it."

Mr. Wall paused for a moment to let his words sink in before gesturing to an assistant, who handed him a folder.

"You will each be assigned to a station team of eight to ten students. Each station team will have a primary instructor who will assign missions and monitor your performance. Your primary instructor will be assisted by the rest of the cadre, and you will, of course, be subject to surveillance at all times.

"Each station team will operate under the leadership of a chief of station, who is responsible for ensuring the station meets all of its objectives." A murmur rippled through the class. Sydney gave Val an excited jab of her elbow. "The cadre selected the chiefs of station based on class standings and performance to date. In a moment, I'll read the names of the station chiefs. If your name is called, please stand and move out into the hallway. There, you will find your team assignments, including primary instructor, posted on the wall."

The class watched as Mr. Wall opened the folder. Chief of station selections were a big deal. The selectees were always regarded by peers and cadre alike, as the most capable students in the class. Graduates of the Farm remembered for the rest of their careers who the chiefs of station were for their Station Phase.

"Samuel Thorne," Mr. Wall announced.

The class applauded as Sam, a former State Department officer with sandy-blond hair, stood up. Sam beamed as he returned high fives from classmates while he moved to the rear and out into the hallway.

Val shifted in his chair as the announcements went on and admitted to himself that he wanted his name to be called. He knew it was unlikely, given the number of sharp CIA students in the class, and the pervasive understanding that the chief of station experience was "wasted" on a military student. Bound for careers with DIA, the Army of Northern Virginia, and other units that no one had ever heard of, military students would never serve as a chief of station in the "real world." They would have to be very good to get one of the slots. Val really wanted it.

"Val Thorne," Mr. Wall announced.

Sydney let out a whoop as Val exhaled and stood up.

Across the room, Tony stood and yelled, "Hooah!"

"One of our military students," Mr. Wall said, shaking his head.

Val looked at Sydney. She smiled at him, clapping, and said loud enough for him alone to hear, "So arrogant already. You'll be intolerable now."

Val winked at her.

Sydney shook her head as Val walked to the aisle and to the rear of the room.

After the last name was called, Mr. Wall said to the rest of North Side, "Congratulations to our station chiefs. In less than twenty-four hours, they'll be sorry they got the job. And good luck to each of you. Station Phase begins in the morning. You're dismissed."

There was a loud buzz of conversation as North Side jumped out of their seats and headed to the hall. A combination of the challenge before them, the amount of work behind them, and the proximity of graduation had everyone excited.

There was jostling and shouting in the hall as students craned their necks to see the assignments and called to their buddies to announce teams. Tony and Sydney shook their heads as they stood in front of Val and the rest of Station Three.

"I'm protesting," Tony said. "How do I get out of this chickenshit outfit?"

"If you figure it out, let me know," Sydney said to him.

Val smiled and looked at the rest of his team. There were eight, including himself. In addition to Tony and Sydney, there were three men and two women. Val knew them only in passing from the past five months, but he was happy. They seemed solid.

"Sorry, guys," he said to the five. "Looks like we got saddled with the ass end of the class." He gestured at Tony and Sydney.

Tony shot Val the bird.

"Nonetheless. For my first official act as your station chief, I'd like to buy everyone a beer."

There were smiles all the way around the team as they walked across campus to the SRB.

*

Station Phase got old quickly.

The mission cadence was demanding. Val got to the station by 0600 hours to get a jump on reading the incoming intel reports and ops cables before the team started to roll in around 0630. He wanted to have a rough idea of what the tasks of the day were going to be so that he could huddle with his chief of operations the minute she walked in.

By 0800 hours, the team was running missions, and several would extend late into the night. The team would be jamming on their intel reports and ops cables by midnight and would not finish until 0300 hours. Val proofed everything before it was transmitted, and he and Sydney were always the last ones to leave the station each night. She refused to leave until he did.

The station was a classroom converted into a notional US embassy in the fictional country of Wilton. Maps of Wilton covered two walls, and tables with computer workstations were set up in rows. The class had been pretending to operate in Wilton for months now. The location had been ingrained so deeply by this point that, to Val, the letters "Williamsburg" on the large maps actually spelled "Wilton." It's strange what the Farm does to one's head.

As chief of station, Val decided who supported which mission and delegated tasks to his chief of operations, Sydney. She'd been a no-brainer for the role. Val respected her logical thought process and ability to maintain sight of strategic objectives during chaos. He also knew she ran a mean SDR and could pull her own mission load as well.

He assigned the role of collections management officer, or CMO, to Liam, a former manufacturing consultant. Liam was an efficient and clear writer and a meticulous fact-checker. This made him the lead report writer and final authority for all the ops cables and intel reports for the team. He and Val quickly developed a rhythm of writing and proofing each other.

Besides the collections management function, Liam provided a humorous counterbalance to Val's and Tony's hypermasculine military vibe. Liam was a quick-thinking, wiry, glasses-wearing young man from Chicago. He wasn't all brains and no bite, however. He'd advanced to the semifinals of the class's close-quarters-combat tournament. Turns out he could move as quickly as he could think.

By the third day, fatigue blanketed the team. Val could see it as each person walked into the station. It reminded him of Army Ranger School, the grinding two-month leadership crucible required of special operations soldiers and small combat unit leaders. They weren't as dirty or quite as sleepless, and were not conducting night patrols in a swamp, but Station Phase was still a hard suck. Val responded as he'd learned to in the army, by putting the age-old maxim, "Embrace the suck," to work. He stayed positive and made sure Tony did the same.

The team functioned well as they progressed through the mission profiles. The scenario involved running several agents to ascertain Wilton's true intentions regarding a neighboring country. There was a possibility Wilton may invade, and Val's station was tasked with providing the answer.

CHAPTER 21

"**I** had to abort," Tony said as he walked back into the classroom on the second-to-last night minutes before midnight.

"Shit," Liam responded, pushing back from his laptop.

"Yeah. I spotted the tail about halfway through my SDR." Tony took his jacket off and slumped into a chair.

SDRs give a case officer multiple tools to determine whether they were being tailed. If they were, the rules were simple. Act natural. Execute an abort route. Report back and wait for further orders. A case officer never, under any circumstances, tried to lose a tail because it confirms that they were up to something unusual and marks them as intelligence.

It's a great advantage, in fact, once a tail is discovered. The case officer could casually study the tail as they progressed along their abort route, getting a firm fix on their tail's appearance and surveillance techniques, informing their future SDRs.

"I got a good look at the guy, at least. He's burned now. I'll recognize him a mile away."

"That's good," Sydney said. "But we didn't get the information we needed."

Tony's mission had been to meet with a source that had information regarding the disposition of the Wiltonian military on the Washingtonian border. The failure to obtain the information resulted in a troubling mission assignment for the last night of Station Phase.

As soon as it hit the next day, around noon, Sydney and Val discussed it in front of the rest of the team.

"I don't like it," Val said.

"I don't either," Sydney agreed. "But it's the mission."

"Walk me through it again, Sydney?" Tony asked. "I'm hoping I missed something."

"It's not complicated. At 2100 hours tonight, there is a meet with a Washingtonian intelligence officer who has information regarding the Wilton Republican Guard's orders. They've been on training maneuvers on the border, as you guys know, and there is a concern that the training is an excuse to get them into position to cross the border."

Sydney gestured to the map as she spoke. "After the meet and information exchange, the instructions are to go with the Washingtonian intelligence officer to meet with another of his sources that has information on the Wiltonian Air Force's readiness."

"Where is the meet?" Liam asked.

"About twenty-five minutes away. Right outside of Williamsburg. The second meet is there also, but we don't know the specifics yet," Sydney answered before asking Val, "Who do you want to take this one?"

Val was shaking his head.

"What is it?" Tony asked.

The team looked at Val.

"It's a setup."

"I don't know what to tell you, Val," Sydney said. "It's the mission."

"Don't you think it's weird?" Val was still shaking his head. "If you're foreign intelligence, why would you ever take a US intel officer along to another meeting? Why disclose a relationship you don't have to?"

The Farm hammers the concept of compartmentalization into its students. Never expose anything you don't have to. A relationship. A piece of intelligence. A method. Anything. Only dole out the need-to-know. And be stingy with that.

"It doesn't make sense," Val said to no one. "Makes me wonder about the real purpose here."

"What option do we have, Val? This is the assigned mission."

Val knew where they were coming from. The training was set up to expose students to different scenarios. Sometimes that meant accepting a contrived element. He understood that. But this one was just too off.

"So, who's on this one?" Sydney asked.

"Me," Val said.

As COS, Val was expected to take a lighter load but still execute missions. But his voice signaled something else, and it got everyone's attention.

"What are you thinking, buddy?" Tony asked.

Sydney crossed her arms.

Liam's head tilted.

The rest of the team regarded Val skeptically.

Val smiled, anticipating the response he was about to get.

"I'm going to flip the script."

"Oh, really?" Sydney said.

"How?" asked Tony.

"After the first meet, when the foreign intel suggests we go to the next meet, I'm going to draw down on him and detain him."

Liam's eyes got wide.

Tony smiled, and Sydney lowered her head at the outlandish suggestion.

"I'm going to take him hostage and negotiate the acquisition of further intel." Val looked at his team. "I'm not going to the second meet."

The team digested the plan for a moment. Sydney spoke first. "Seriously, Val. Who do you want on this mission?"

Val ignored her question. "Sydney. As chief of operations, you'll be in charge here at the station while I'm downrange."

"Dude…" Tony started.

"Drop the bullshit, Val," Liam said.

"It's not bullshit. You guys know I'm right."

"You are right," Sydney said. "And, for the record, I agree with your assessment and think your proposal makes total sense. But it's too disruptive. The cadre will consider it a breach of training. We'll all be blue-sheeted out of the course. And that's if it goes well. If it goes poorly, I could see assault charges being filed against you."

"I agree. Your plan sounds extreme, Val," Liam said.

A few heads around the room nodded.

"They're right, buddy," Tony said. "It's a ballsy idea. But not one that would be rewarded here."

Val knew he was losing them.

"Okay. Fine. You guys are right." Val held up his hands in a surrender gesture. "Thanks for talking sense into me."

Later that night, as Val walked through the parking lot to his car to start his SDR to Williamsburg, Sydney called out to him.

"Val. Wait up."

Val stopped and turned as Sydney closed the distance.

"What's up?"

"Don't be an idiot tonight."

Val didn't try to argue. He shifted on his feet as he met her glare. "I'll call in when I'm on the way back." He turned to leave, but she grabbed his arm.

"Seriously. It won't go well," she said, maintaining her grip. "I know you hate all the romper room rules here, as you call them. But you're almost done. They picked you to be chief of station, for chrissake. Why do you have to turn everything into some kind of BASE-jumping, dick-measuring bullshit?"

"It's going to be fine, Sydney," was all he could think to say. "Trust me."

"Fuck you."

She let go of his arm.

He turned to walk to his car.

"It's also selfish, you know," she said to his back. "Your entire team is going to take shit for this. Hell, they may kick us all out."

He looked back. "They won't. Will you please trust me?"

But she was walking back to their station already.

*

After ninety minutes of SDR, Val sat in a corner booth in a bar in Williamsburg, speaking with his Washingtonian intelligence counterpart, who had introduced himself as Stan Barrow. The conversation was going well. The Washingtonians had a mole in the Wilton Republican Guard, and he was singing.

"What's the level of certainty around all of this?" Val asked when Barrow completed his report.

"One hundred percent."

Val raised his eyebrows.

"Seriously," Barrow responded. "Our guy is highly placed. He's got the access, and he has been in bed with us for years."

"All right, then. I'll type it up as soon as I get back tonight."

Barrow scanned the bar. "Good. So, you ready to move to the next one? Where did you park?"

The plan was for the Barrow to ride with Val and direct him to the next meeting.

"I'm about five blocks away in an alley," Val said.

"Are you kidding?"

"Sorry. It was the most suitable spot to be sure I was clean."

The agent nodded. "Okay, then." He stood up. "Let's go."

Val stood and led the way to his car. He was only partially honest about his site selection. Sure, terminating his route at an easily cleaned spot was important since you never wanted to park in front of a meeting site, and even a two-block walk to your vehicle added a layer of protection. Also important, though, was that it placed Val's vehicle in a blind alley, and he was about to try to pull off his risky maneuver.

As they neared the car, Val fell behind the officer by a step. He reached into his pocket and gripped the neon-green water pistol he'd purchased earlier in the day. It was a last-minute decision, but he wanted a prop in his hands when he made his move.

It was commonplace at the Farm for instructors to wave their arms and create scenarios that altered and constrained the student's reality as if they had come from Zeus himself. "You're on a plane traveling with a source over the ocean and have just received notification that enemy intel officers are waiting for you at your destination." Or, holding nothing in their hand: "This is a disc with proof of an illicit weapons program. You must get it out of this building despite being searched at the door. You have three minutes to hide it on your person. Go."

It wasn't clear that students had the same world-altering powers, but Val was going to try to use this method anyway to seize the initiative from Barrow. He hoped the neon-green squirt gun that he'd filled with ammunition would demonstrate his seriousness and commitment to the scenario.

His heart pounded as he drew the weapon and pointed it at the foreign intelligence officer.

Okay, Rafter. You're all in.

"Stop right there."

"Huh?" Barrow stopped and turned around. His eyes got wide when he saw the green squirt gun. Not in fear, though. He was amused.

Barrow couldn't stop grinning as he said, "What the hell is that?"

"This is a fully loaded US government–issued nine-millimeter semiautomatic pistol."

"Oh, it is?" His smile degraded as he realized something was happening.

"Yes. It is," Val said as he hit the button on his car key fob.

The trunk popped open, and the intel officer's remaining smile transitioned instantly to a scowl. "What the fuck are you doing, Val?" Barrow said, clearly breaking role by referring to Val by his true name.

Val knew shit just got serious. An instructor should *never* break role in a mission and refer to a student by their true first name.

Despite the seriousness of the true name reference, Val didn't take the bait. He was committed.

"My name is Heath Morgan," Val said, reasserting the scenario into reality. "I'm an intelligence officer of the US government, as you know. You, Stan Barrow, are my prisoner now, and I'm ordering you into that trunk."

"And my name is Lawson. I'm an instructor at the Farm, and you're a fucking student, and you're way out of bounds! This mission is over."

"Officer Barrow," Val said, taking a deep breath and a step forward. "I'm telling you for the last time. Get into the trunk or I'll shoot you where you stand." Barrow was a couple of inches shorter than him and not an athletic guy. Val now stood inches from him in his old wrestling stance with the squirt gun pointed between Barrow's eyes. "With this, um, nine-millimeter pistol."

Barrow stood motionless. Val could see that he was trying to compute what was happening and had gotten the message that Val was all in on the scenario.

Good. I have a window to bulldoze him.

"Look, I don't want to hurt you. But I'm not going to the next meeting, and you're going to answer some questions for me. Once we're done with that, I'll drop you off wherever you need to go."

Val gestured to the trunk, and to his surprise, Barrow stepped toward it.

"You're in so much fucking trouble," Barrlow mumbled to himself.

"I'll push down the rear seat so we can see each other," Val said as the instructor got into the trunk. Val hesitated before closing the lid. "At this time, I'm simulating tying your hands and legs together." Adding another layer of security to his scenario.

"Oh, for chrissake," Barrow said.

"Consider yourself tied up." Val closed the lid and ran around to the driver's side back seat. He opened the door and yanked down the seat back. Then he hopped into the driver's seat and turned to look at the rear of the car. The officer had put his head at the opening so that he could glare at Val. He pointed the green squirt gun at the intelligence officer.

"If you try to escape or do anything sudden, I will shoot you."

"Fuck you. You're so fucked. I'm so blue-sheeting your ass."

Val started the car and pulled off onto the main road.

"Where the hell are we going?" Barrow demanded.

"We're going to drive around until you tell me what I want to know."

"Fuck you," Barrow said as he kicked at the trunk lid. He'd decided he made a mistake and kicked the trunk lid several times. "Dammit!" he screamed.

"This can be over in five minutes if you cooperate."

"Fuck you!"

"I want to know who was waiting at the next meeting," Val said calmly. "What was going to happen? And what Washingtonia is up to."

"Fuck you!"

"Suit yourself. I'm headed to I-64 with a full tank of gas. I can drive all night." Val angled his rearview mirror so he could see Barrow's enraged face.

Ten minutes later, Val pulled onto I-64, pointed south. The intelligence officer hadn't spoken since his last explicative. "Come on," Val said. "Don't make me drive around all night."

"I'm not telling you shit."

Good. At least he is talking again.

"I told you. My name is Heath Morgan, an officer of the US government. Answer my three questions, and we're done. It's that easy."

"You're so fucked."

"That may be so," Val said in his most reasonable voice. "But you're in my trunk now. And I swear to you, I will not let you out until you tell me what I want to know. The quicker you tell me, the quicker you can get out and get started on getting me, Heath Morgan, fucked."

The agent was quiet. Val couldn't tell if he was dummying up again or mulling it over.

"I was taking you to Wiltonian intelligence."

I knew it.

"Go on."

"They're trying to ID the American intelligence assets in-country. They wanted me to bring you to a meeting to burn you so that they could PNG you out of Wilton."

PNG is short for "persona non grata." It's the worst thing that can happen to an intelligence officer. You're burned. Outed internationally as an intelligence officer and returned to your country, never to work as a field officer again. Sure, you can work at headquarters pushing paper, but you won't be posted to the field ever again, and if by some miracle you do make it overseas, you won't be hitting the streets, working fully undercover in the most ballsy of circumstances.

"Why are you working with them?"

"Because they are paying me. I'm a double agent. I'm a member of the Washingtonian Intelligence Force, but I work for Wilton."

"Does Wilton intend to invade?"

"Yes. As soon as they are able to blind your intelligence on the ground."

Val nodded to himself. *I might get kicked out. But I'm damn sure not coming back empty-handed.*

"Okay. I'm taking you back to Williamsburg."

"Fine."

Val drove back to a second secluded alley in Williamsburg that he'd scouted previously on one of his many area familiarization missions.

He pulled the car to a quick stop, hopped out, and popped the trunk. Barrow leapt out, red-faced.

He closed the distance to Val quickly and jabbed his finger in Val's chest, gritting his teeth only inches from Val's chin.

"My mission in life now is to get you fucking expelled, asshole."

Val kept his arms limp. Sensing that if he added any tension to the situation, fists would fly and he would be truly fucked. He nodded respectfully but bit his lip.

The officer cooled off by a couple of degrees. He took his finger out of Val's chest, turned, and walked off into the shadows. Grumbling the whole way.

Val exhaled.

Mission accomplished...I think.

*

Val pulled back onto Camp Peary after midnight. He parked his car and walked slowly back to the station, listing in his head all the key intelligence points he'd learned from Officer Barrow. The Farm hammers into students never to write anything down until they get to a secure area. Particularly not when in a foreign country. Being discovered with intelligence notes on your person is one of the quickest ways to get PNG'd, or worse.

Sydney and Tony were waiting for Val outside of the classroom building. Tony sat on the steps. Sydney stood behind him with her arms crossed.

"So," Tony said. "Were you an idiot tonight?"

Val stopped at the base of the steps in front of them. "Depends on how you define 'idiot.'"

"Need me to spell it out for you?" Sydney asked.

"Does it include disrupting a Wiltonian initiative to ID and compromise all US intelligence assets in-country before launching their attack on Washingtonia?"

"What?" Tony said, springing off the steps.

Sydney raised her eyebrows, but she waited for him to continue.

Val stepped by them into the building. "Come on, guys," he said with a smile. "Let's get started on the reports and cables."

Val and the team got to work. Val dictated to Sydney and Liam as they drew up the intel report and operations cables. As he walked through the operation for them, the rest of the team members shook their heads and gave each other high fives.

"Goddamn, Val," Tony said. "I can't believe it worked. You cracked this whole thing wide open."

Val smiled but noted Sydney didn't share the same level of enthusiasm. She got more pissed as the report-writing session went on.

Finally, shortly before 0300, they submitted their final cables.

"Thanks for the help, team," Val said. "I'm sure tomorrow is going to throw a few curveballs at us. Let's get some rest."

They filed out of the station as a team, their last night of Station Phase behind them. The next day, Saturday, they expected the exercise to wrap up around midday. Then they would have Sunday off before debriefs began on Monday. Val was the last out and locked the door.

"Look at them," Sydney said to Val as she slowed down behind the pack to let him catch up to her.

"Oh. You're speaking to me."

"It was killing you, wasn't it?" She smiled as she walked next to him.

"I hate it when you're mad at me. You know that."

"And I hate being mad at you. But, Jesus, Val! You can be so fucking selfish and arrogant."

Val stopped. Startled. "I thought we were making peace and doing the apology thing?" he said as his arms came up in a helpless palms-up shrug of defeat.

"We?" Sydney stopped and faced him with her hands on her hips.

"We what?" Val asked, sensing he'd just committed an error.

"*We* were about to do the apology thing?"

Val smiled.

"Well?" Sydney cocked her head.

"I'm sorry, Sydney."

Sydney studied him. "For what?"

"For being an arrogant, selfish asshole."

She was unconvinced. Almost six months down the rabbit hole of the Farm, she, like the rest of her classmates, had effectively earned a master's in psychology. And not the good kind. Not the kind that helps people. She now knew how to spot the weak points in someone's mental architecture. How to listen for their true motivations, problems, and interests. How to find imbalances and give them a little shove. The thing about Val that worried her was that he didn't need a shove.

"What?" Val asked, jerking her out of her thoughts.

Sydney said nothing.

"Come on. What are you thinking?"

"You're a mess, Val Rafter." Sydney broke Farm rules herself by referring to Val by his last name.. Though forbidden, friends often shared their last names as the Farm wore on. Beyond friendship, it was a sign of trust. Between her and Val, maybe more.

They hugged as they both chuckled.

"Please don't be mad at me, Sydney." Val squeezed her. "I hate it. And I really am sorry."

He gave her two pats on the back and released her.

She laughed ruefully.

"What?" he asked.

"I think you just bro-hugged me."

Val laughed in acknowledgment, and they walked back in silence to their separate quarters.

CHAPTER 22

al's alarm clock woke him at 0500 hours after he'd been asleep for an hour and a half. He groaned as he got out of bed and walked, lead-footed, to the bathroom.

Last day of Station Phase. Thank god.

The shower got him half awake. Two cups of coffee helped some more. The brisk walk through the dark Farm campus to the classroom station got his blood pumping. But it was the sight of a stone-faced Mr. Wall and gloating Lawson sitting at the planning table in his station room that jolted him fully awake. There was another man that Val didn't know sitting between them. Val knew he was cadre because he'd seen him around the Farm a few times, but never interacting with students. He was always speaking with Mr. Wall or another of the senior instructors.

"Good morning, Captain." Mr. Wall referred to Val by rank, a clear signal of formality and seriousness. "You fucking dumbass."

"Good morning, sir." Val stood in the open doorway.

"Close the door and sit down."

"Yes, sir."

Val sat across from the three men. Maps, spreadsheets and other documents lay haphazardly on the table between them.

"I think you and Lawson know each other," Mr. Wall said, not asking a question.

Val nodded at Lawson, who held his reserved smile.

"This is Mr. Hutton, my operations officer."

The other gentlemen glared at Val as he sat across the table from them.

"Lawson debriefed me and the rest of the cadre on your antics last night,"

Mr. Wall said. "I've read your station's intel report and operations cable. What I want to hear now is your justification for your actions. What was your thought process?"

Val hoped that the question meant he hadn't been kicked out yet as he started talking in the most reasonable-sounding voice he could muster. "When we received the mission for last night, I was troubled by the potential for compromise."

"What do you mean, 'compromise'?" Mr. Wall asked.

"Two sequential meetings like that were too risky. They presented multiple opportunities for our relationship to the Washingtonian intelligence officer, his identity, our identity, and whoever we were meeting at the second meet to be compromised. We had limited experience with the Washingtonian intelligence officer, Mr. Barrow, so I had no confidence in the accomplishment of that part of the mission. But the second meeting was a black hole. I had no background on the source we would meet with. He could have been a double agent, an idiot who dragged surveillance to the meeting, or simply not worth the risk."

The three men were expressionless as Val talked.

"We had sufficient resources to conduct two separate meetings that would have compartmentalized the risk of compromise, but Washingtonian intelligence had set it up to be sequential." Val paused for effect. "It violated too many of the principles we've been taught here."

"So, why did you not request that the meetings be de-linked?" Mr. Wall asked. "As three other station teams did?"

For the first time since he entered the room, Val's heart sank a little. *I'm fucked. There was an approved solution, and I missed it. Maybe I am an overaggressive, selfish asshole.*

But as his eyes swept over the three men, he caught Lawson's smug smile. *No. If I go down, I'm going down swinging.*

"I considered it, sir," Val said. "But decided that it would've been an opportunity missed."

"How so?"

"De-linking the meetings would've achieved the goal of compartmentalizing and reducing risk. But our mission was to determine the true intentions of the Wiltonians. My judgment was that the proposed mission was so..." Val struggled to find the right word, but after a few seconds, he plowed ahead, "fucked up, there was intelligence to be gained by exploiting it."

Hutton, between Lawson and Mr. Wall, crossed his arms but didn't drop his expressionless mask.

Mr. Wall stared at Val.

Val fidgeted in his chair.

Tony burst into the classroom with Liam and Sydney. They took a few steps before registering the presence of Val and his interrogators at the planning table. They came to an awkward halt, leaving the door ajar. Liam looked at the floor and swallowed hard as Tony looked back and forth from Val at one end of the table to Mr. Wall and his lieutenants on the other.

Sydney cleared her throat. "Good morning, Mr. Wall."

"Good morning, Miss Thorne." Wall didn't take his eyes off Val. "You're the chief of operations for this station, correct?"

"Yes, sir."

"You'll be the acting chief of station today. Captain Thorne has been recalled from Wilton and is on a plane back to Langley," Mr. Wall said, making it so with just his words.

Tony, Liam, and Sydney's heads swung in unison toward Val. He looked at them and smiled his best *no problem* smile.

Val and Sydney locked eyes. He couldn't tell if he saw concern or a told-you-so expression.

Sydney pivoted back to Mr. Wall. "Yes, sir."

"We need this room for a few more minutes," Mr. Wall said.

"Yes, sir."

They left quickly. As soon as the door shut behind them, Mr. Wall said, "Let's try that one again, Captain. Rather than de-link the two meetings, you chose to detain the Washingtonian intelligence officer, role-played by Lawson here."

"Yes, sir."

"And what was your reasoning for doing that?"

"I figured that one of two things was true. Either the Washingtonians were up to something, in which case, I might be able to turn the tables by surprising them and thereby gain valuable intelligence. Or they were not up to something and were just being stupid. In that case, they would simply be pissed off at us and know to never be stupid when planning operations with us again."

Val looked at Lawson and smiled. Lawson stared back.

Mr. Wall stopped writing and put down his pen. "I see. And you would've foregone the second meet?"

"No, sir. I'd have rescheduled it for the following night."

"What if that wasn't possible? You would've lost the opportunity."

"It was a risk, sir. But I thought the risk of a trap was more dangerous, and that this course of action gave us the best opportunity to gather mission-critical intelligence."

Mr. Wall didn't betray his thoughts. He looked at Val. "What are the rules regarding training scenarios?"

"Take all commands from the cadre." Val repeated the oft given instructions.

"What else do we tell you guys?"

"What the instructor says goes." Val began to get nervous.

"So, why did you disobey the cadre member?"

Fuck it. I'm committed now. The only way through this is straight ahead.

"I didn't disobey Lawson, sir."

"Oh, really?" Mr. Wall crossed his arms. "How do you figure?"

"The scenario was such a cock-up, you guys practically forced the students to change the mission. When you do that, you lose a little bit of control over what we're going to do. So, to be shocked when someone comes up with a response like I did is just a lack of foresight. And then to call time-out because you don't like what the student is telling you to do is…weak."

"When an instructor calls a time-out, it means time-out." Mr. Wall raised his voice.

"I'm not arguing that, sir. But Lawson got in the trunk! I never touched him or forced him to do that. I mean, for crying out loud, sir…I pointed a neon-green squirt gun at the guy, and he hopped in my trunk. So, if the instructor went along with the scenario," Val pointed at a fuming Lawson to emphasize his point, "how can you say I disobeyed him? And why the hell am I in trouble?"

Lawson's eyes got big in anger, and he opened his mouth to speak, but Mr. Wall cut him off by leaning forward and glaring at him.

Val stopped talking. He'd gone too far, and he knew it. He put his hands in his lap and took a deep breath.

Mr. Wall turned his head back to Val and nodded slightly, as if confirmed in his beliefs. "Anything else you want to add, Captain?"

"No, sir."

"Then I'm going to cut to the nut. What you did was bold and intuitive…but it was also arrogant and risky. The scenario might have had some problems. But we expect students to exercise good judgment at all times. In addition to your arrogance and poor judgment, I don't like the fact that you disobeyed one of my cadre. You don't get to pick which of your leadership you obey. Do they let you do that in the army?"

"No, sir."

"Didn't think so." The tired old spy sighed and stood up, surprising Lawson and Hutton. They jumped to their feet.

"You're done, Rafter," Mr. Wall said. "Expelled. Pack your shit and be ready to out-process first thing Monday morning."

Val looked at Mr. Wall and nodded slowly. His mind was racing as he tried to think of a good counterargument. But he'd already given his best. He had none left.

*

Later that night, Val sat at the MOTC barstool in the SRB accepting free drinks from his classmates. Sydney and Tony flanked him at the bar and tried to keep his spirits up.

"Look at it this way." Tony leaned into Val. "You're fucking famous."

"Yeah," Val answered. "The guy that famously got kicked out on the last day of Station Phase for being an idiot."

"Have they said anything to you since this morning?" Sydney asked.

"No. I went back to my room and packed my bags right after Wall told me to. Haven't heard shit since."

"I can't believe they kicked you out," Sydney mumbled.

"Come on, Sydney. You told me this would happen."

Sydney was about to respond when Liam stuck his head in between them. "Val, can I buy you a beer?"

"Sure, Liam." Val noted Liam seemed more than a little drunk.

Liam waved two fingers at the bartender. "Everyone is talking about you," Liam said to Val. "So ballsy! And no one likes Lawson, so it's like bonus points!" Liam slapped Val on the back.

The SRB was full and loud. Station Phase was over, and the class was celebrating. Nerves were still frayed as they faced the final grade-out on Monday by the instructors. The blue sheets would be cutting people's heads off for sure. But for now, it was enough to be done.

The bartender set two beers in front of Liam and Val.

"Here's to you, Val." Liam raised his glass. "You crazy son of a bitch!"

Val tipped his beer toward Liam and took a swig. "Thanks, Liam."

Liam eased back into the crowd. Sydney reached over and put her hand on Val's shoulder. She looked at him but said nothing. He nodded.

Val glanced around the SRB. He caught several people looking at him. It was true. Everyone was talking about it. Across the bar from Val sat two instructors. Station Phase was a long grind for the cadre as well, and it was clear they were also glad it was over. Without intending to, Val caught one of their eyes. The instructor smiled ruefully and raised his glass Val's way in a *Yeah, you're ballsy, but I wouldn't want to be you* manner. Val raised his glass to the instructor, took a swig, and told Sydney, "I need to get out of here."

"You okay?"

"I'm fine. I'm just tired of being the famous idiot." Val stood up. Tony gave him a silent wave good night.

On the walk back, Val wondered what he was supposed to do now as he passed in and out of the light of the tall lamps that lined the paths of the student housing area. *Do I call personnel command? What assignment can they give me that I'd even want now? What do I want to do now, anyway?*

"Val." Sydney was behind him.

He stopped and turned. "What's up?"

"I…um…just realized something." She walked up to him.

"We're not coworkers anymore." She took his hand and pulled him closer.

They kissed for a long time beneath one of the tall lamps. Finally, Val put his mouth to her ear. "My place or yours?"

"I don't care. But you have one minute to take me there."

They went to his.

CHAPTER 23

The four friends sat in one of the booths at the back of the Green Leafe Pub. Val, Tony, and Liam gnawed on large cheeseburgers, while Sydney ate her usual, the fish-and-chips.

Just a twenty-minute drive from Camp Peary, the Green Leafe Pub had become one of their favorite places to get away from the pressures of the Farm. It was a cozy, narrow space with a long bar on one side, some high-top tables that ran down the middle, and large booths on the other side. With good pub food and dozens of beers on tap, the Greene Leafe drew a lot of traffic from the College of William and Mary and greater Williamsburg. This gave the place a constant flow of what Tony called "nice scenery." But it was mostly just a comfortable, social spot where the four could spend a few hours and forget about their weird new profession.

"God, I'll miss these fish-and-chips," Sydney said, mouth full.

"Who knows if we'll ever be back here, huh?" Tony said. Hamburger in hand. Mouth also full.

Val swallowed. "I'm just glad to be here at all."

"Amen to that." Tony raised his beer.

Sydney gave Val, sitting next to her, a sidelong glance. "Lucky son of a bitch."

"It wasn't luck," Val protested. "It was justice!"

"Oh, it was luck." Liam's voice was muffled by his cheeseburger.

Luck or justice, it had been too close for Val's comfort. On Monday morning, as Val packed the last of his clothes, he was summoned by Mr. Wall.

Mr. Wall made Val wait outside his office for more than an hour before calling him in. The senior instructor sat behind his desk as Val stood nervously, waiting for him to speak.

"Sorry to make you wait, Captain," Mr. Wall finally began. "Have a seat."

Val sat in one of the chairs facing Mr. Wall's desk.

"I've been trying to come to terms with what I have to tell you," Mr. Wall said. "But it's clear to me that this is just going to be one of those things that will piss me off until the not-so-distant day I die.

"The fact is, a bunch of high-ranking defense intelligence assholes weighed in over the weekend, including the deputy DIA Director, Brigadier General Bryson. They're not as troubled by your behavior as I am. Since you're here on their dime and will be serving in their program, Director Tenant went with them."

Mr. Wall hesitated. His jaw worked as if he were chewing a tough piece of meat, then he cleared his throat.

"So, Captain, you're going to graduate."

Val tried not to show emotion as a wave of relief swept over him.

Mr. Wall stared at him as if frustrated with a puzzle, one with a confusing number of pieces left to set into place. He pulled open his desk's lap drawer and picked up a pack of cigarettes. He put one in his mouth and struck a match.

Val watched the flare of the match igniting. Mr. Wall tugged a few times on the cigarette to get it going and then shook the match to extinguish it before flicking it into the trash can.

Mr. Wall held Val's gaze for a moment and then took a long, deep drag from the cigarette. He exhaled, allowing the smoke to spill out the right side of his mouth. The pale cloud clung to his face.

"So, are we done here, sir?" Val asked.

Mr. Wall took another deep drag and expelled it to the right again. His eyes stayed locked on Val as the smoke mingled with the dissipating remnants of his previous exhalation.

This is getting old. Val glanced at the door.

"You know, human intelligence ultimately boils down to that sacred moment when it's just our officer in the room or car or wherever with their source," Mr. Wall said.

"Uh…yes, sir."

"There is no other witness to that interaction, to obtaining the intelligence. Think about it—most of what we do here at the Farm is focused on teaching you guys how to get to that meeting alone and unobserved. That's why we spend so much time beating SDRs into each of you. We're really good at that part, I think. Training a future intelligence officer to avoid, detect, and evade surveillance."

Val nodded.

Mr. Wall stared at him.

"Well, good chat, sir," Val said, standing from his chair. "I—"

"Sit your ass down, Captain. I have not excused you yet."

Val hesitated. Then, taking note of Mr. Wall's fierce expression, he sat back down.

This guy is pissed.

The end of Mr. Wall's cigarette glowed as he filled his lungs with smoke again. The haze around him thickened as he exhaled slowly.

"Yep. We're really good at making sure you guys are *capable* of getting to that sacred moment. Not as good at ensuring you're *worthy* of it."

Mr. Wall cocked his head.

"Do you know why that moment is sacred, Captain?"

"Yes, sir."

Of course, Val did. Mr. Wall had emphasized it often during the past six months of training.

"What makes it sacred is the reliance and trust we place in our intelligence officer in that moment." Mr. Wall said, ignoring Val's answer. "We count on that officer to be a professional, to report back accurately and completely. We rely on them to tell us exactly what they learn, without commentary, manipulation, or omission. Without agenda. And by 'we,' I mean everyone. The whole machine. The whole intelligence community and all of its customers. All the way up to the president."

Mr. Wall took another slow draw from his cigarette.

"I don't think you measure up to that crucial moment, Captain." He pointed at Val with the half-burned cigarette and let smoke pour out of his mouth. "You're not worthy of that sacred trust."

Val sat in silence, taking in Mr. Wall's words.

"There is something wrong with you. You have a worldview that you can't shake for some reason. You think you're right. Or, maybe, you have to be right. I don't know."

Lines appeared on Mr. Wall's forehead, and his chin tilted up slightly. He was quiet for a moment.

Val fidgeted in his chair. He was about to propose that he leave when Mr. Wall suddenly brought the cigarette back to his mouth and burned it down to the filter with one deep final draw.

"I don't know why you're like this, what made you this way," he said at a rapid clip, as if returning from a long delay and wanting to get on with things. Smoke drifted from his lips, adding to the haze hanging over his chair. "But what I do know, sure as I'm sitting here, is that there will be a time when you're alone in that sacred moment, and you're going to place your finger on the scale, assert your worldview, and manipulate the intelligence."

Mr. Wall leaned back in his chair and crossed his right leg over his left. He rubbed his cigarette butt out on his right shoe.

He looked up at Val as he threw the cigarette into the trash.

"And bad things are going to happen."

Val crossed his arms. "You seem pretty confident in your ability to predict the future, sir."

"It's my job, Captain. I'm fucking good at it."

"Well, I'm sorry you feel that way," Val said, figuring it was better than saying, *Go fuck yourself.* He just wanted to get out of the man's office without further graduation-risking confrontation.

"Me too. Because you were done, Rafter. Finished. My job is to flush out the unworthy, and I did my job."

Mr. Wall shrugged, defeated. "You got away with it this time. But the sad truth about our business is that everyone's luck always runs out. Always. If you don't get a handle on your arrogance and willingness to take chances, you're going to get someone killed. I promise you."

Val nodded and tried to give Mr. Wall an earnest *I'm really listening hard to your wisdom* expression.

"Shit." Mr. Wall shook his head sadly, seeing through Val's act. He opened the lap drawer and grabbed another cigarette.

"The other thing I've learned after thirty years as a spy is that people don't change." He looked at Val. "Please prove me wrong." He put the unlit cigarette in his mouth and slowly closed the lap drawer.

Mr. Wall picked up the matches. "Now get the hell out of my office."

The words still stung, even after a few beers in a booth in the Green Leafe Pub with his friends.

"How funny was that graduation ceremony?" Val tried to change the subject for himself.

"No kidding!" Sydney said. "Classic Farm, right?"

Graduation was held in one of the huge hangars on the Camp Peary airfield. This made it easy for CIA Director Tenant and other VIPs of the intelligence community to fly in with their unmarked planes and shuffle quickly into the cover of the building. After a speech in which the director told them they were the future of the nation's clandestine capabilities and applauded the class for their achievements, he shook each hand and gave them a diploma. The diplomas were also vintage Farm. Val had laughed out loud when he got off the stage and read the name: Val Thorne.

After the secret ceremony, the cadre walked among the students and took back all the diplomas. No takeaways that could identify anyone were allowed. Classic Farm.

After Val had given his diploma back, he turned to leave and walked right into Brigadier General Bryson, deputy director of the Defense Intelligence Agency. He didn't have a congratulatory look on his face.

"Rafter." The one-star general ignored the "Thorne" name tag on Val's uniform.

"Yes, sir."

"You aren't even fully qualified to go downrange yet, and I have had several meetings about you." The general stepped closer to Val as he spoke. "That sound like a good thing to you?"

"No, sir."

"Correct." The general looked Val over for a moment. "Well, there are several officers whom I respect that think you're worth a second chance. So, you've got one." The general stuck his finger in Val's chest. "But understand this: you owe me."

"Yes, sir."

The general withdrew his finger and turned to his aide, a nervous army captain who had been standing several steps behind the general. "When does my plane take off?"

"Sir, we're wheels up in twenty minutes."

"Good. I want to talk to the director. Go find him."

"Yes, sir." The major spun on his heel.

The general looked back at Val. "Alright, then, Rafter." He extended his right hand. "Don't let me hear your name again for a long while."

Val shook the general's hand. As he did, he thought he saw the slightest smile. But the general released the handshake and was gone in the crowd before he could be sure.

"Thank you, sir," Val said to his back.

Now, swallowing cheeseburger and beer in the Green Leafe Pub, Val's intent was that General Bryson never heard his name again. Ever.

"You haven't told us yet where you're going, Sydney," Liam said. "What assignment did you draw?"

Sydney finished chewing and wiped her mouth with a napkin. Tony and Liam looked at her, waiting, as she slowly grabbed her glass of beer and took a slow swallow. Val looked down at his lap.

Sydney replaced her glass and wiped her mouth slowly again as she alternated between looking at Tony and Liam, delaying her response.

"You got it, didn't you?" Liam said.

"For fuck's sake!" Tony said. "Tell us!"

"I told you she would get it." Liam nodded.

"Yes." She didn't resist the smile. It spread wide across her face.

"Moscow." She turned her eyes to Val. He smiled at her, his face full of pride and heartache. Val was happy for her. But her achievement confirmed what they had each known from the beginning. They would never have much time together. Under the table, she put her hand in his.

"Yes!" Tony startled the group at the high-top behind them. They turned to look. Tony mouthed, *Sorry.*

"I don't think the folks at the end of the bar heard you, Tony," Val said. "Could you shout again so they all notice and listen in to where the CIA is sending Officer Sydney Thorne?"

Tony gave Val a dismissive wave of the hand and looked at Sydney. "Congrats, Sydney. Are you excited?"

For the CIA students, Moscow was the pinnacle. Only a few of the top-rated students were assigned to the station there. Despite the fall of the Soviet Union, the Russians were still considered by intelligence and security experts as one of the United States' major strategic adversaries.

If anything, the fragmentation of their empire and resulting chaos had made the region and the actors more dangerous. The CIA still considered the GRU and the other branches of Russian intelligence as their main competition and chose their best to go up against them. There was no more hostile intelligence environment than Moscow, and Sydney had wanted the Moscow station from her first day.

"I am. Thanks. I still can't believe I got it, really."

"Oh bullshit," Tony said. "You had it in the bag from our first exercise. You're the best agency type in the class. Don't you forget it."

"Aw shucks, Tony."

Val smiled at her faux modesty. One of the things he liked about Sydney was her confidence. She was good, and she knew it. Val understood that.

"How about you, Liam?" Tony asked.

"Egypt."

Val nodded. "Congrats." He gave Liam a high five across the table. Liam had been gunning for the Middle East from day one. It was a sought-after theater that would involve extensive training in the Arabic language. Liam smiled in excitement.

"I've got to say," Tony said, "it was nice not to have to worry about the assignment thing." The agency students had to wait until the last day to get their assignments. They all piled into one of the large auditoriums and waited for their name to be called out. It was a public agony that Val and Tony were spared. "I'd hate to be one of those poor bastards who got counter-narcotics."

"Ugh," Val said, agreeing. For the most part, the bottom of the class pulled counter-narcotic assignments. No one wanted it. None of the hard chargers, at least. They all wanted the Near East, Central Eurasia, or Counterterrorism Divisions.

For Tony and Val, though, it was back to the army.

"When do you have to report back to Fort Belvoir?" Sydney asked Tony.

Months ago, Sydney's comment would have elicited an angry, evasive response from Tony. Unlike most Farm students who showed up with aspirations to join a top-secret corner of the US government carrying out sensitive and dangerous missions, Tony was already there. Stationed at Fort Belvoir, Virginia, Tony served in the Intelligence Support Activity. Nicknamed the Army of Northern Virginia and tracing its history back to the Iranian hostage crisis in 1980, the ISA was basically Special Operations Command's own little CIA. They ran spy rings, intelligence operations, and surveillance platforms for the military. Tony had been there for years and had only just now had time to get to the Farm.

Over the last few months, his friends had slowly pieced together where Tony was stationed and what he did. Though he never confirmed their suspicion, he stopped denying it. The close-knit group understood that for what it was—the sign of friendship and trust.

"Not for two weeks," he told Sydney. "Taking the wife out West for a well-deserved vacation."

Sydney smiled and nodded. Then she looked at Val.

"Where you headed next, Val?" Liam asked.

Val wiped cheeseburger grease from his mouth. "I'm headed to the defense attaché course first, then DLI for Russian language training."

The Defense Language Institute was in Monterey, California. It was a gorgeous setting for a demanding, immersive language training center.

"When will you actually get to Moscow?" Tony asked Sydney.

"Oh, not for about six months. I've got a couple of courses to get through first, including the hostile environment training course."

Tony and Val nodded with respect. The HETC was next-level stuff for the agency, like their version of Ranger School. It was a demanding graduate-level course in SDRs and other countersurveillance techniques that prepared a case officer for the challenge of operating in the highest-threat environments, like Moscow. In places like that or Beijing, a case officer had to assume they were being surveilled by multiple tails from the moment they left their flat or place of work. It was a grinding, stressful environment that demanded complete focus at all times.

"Well, that's great. You two will have plenty of time to bang each other more before you go to Moscow," Tony said matter-of-factly.

Sydney rolled her eyes as Val shook his head. Liam chuckled. The romance was known in their small group. It was approved of, and therefore worthy of the highest form of praise—ridicule.

"Oh, yeah!" Liam said. "We have something for you, Val." He gestured at Sydney. She released Tony from her reproving glare.

"Yes!" She reached under her seat and pulled out a wrapped gift.

"What's this?" Val said.

Sydney was beaming. Tony rubbed his hands together. Liam smiled.

"Seriously, guys," Val said. "I didn't know we were doing gifts."

"We're not doing gifts, you dork," Tony said. "This isn't a gift."

"Looks like one," Val said.

"Well, it's not." Sydney shook her head.

"It's more of an award," Liam said.

Tony leaned toward Sydney. "I'm actually not sure why we wrapped it like this, then. Makes it seem like a gift."

"Shut up for a minute, please," Sydney said to Tony. "Val." She turned to face him. "On behalf of your entire Station Phase team, the Farm, the agency, and indeed the entire country…"

"Oh, for fuck's sake…" Val said, strapping in for what was sure to be an embarrassment.

"…Tony and I would like to present you with this, um, gift…"

"So, it is a gift, then?" Tony said.

Sydney shot Tony a withering look.

"Good thing we wrapped it, is all I'm saying." Tony shrugged his shoulders in defense.

"Please shut up!" Sydney said as Val chuckled. He was going to miss his friends.

Sydney turned to Val and handed him the gift. "Fuck it. This is for you, asshole."

Val unwrapped the box and then opened it cautiously. When it was obvious that nothing was going to splatter on him, he pulled the top off. He laughed at the sight.

In the box lay a wooden plaque on which was mounted the neon-green water pistol he'd used to get the drop on Lawson. There was a small brass plaque mounted beneath the pistol. Val felt his face get warm as he read it: "To Val Thorne, Chief of Station, Wielder of the Green Squirt Gun, Master of the Trunk, Arrogant Asshole, and Good Friend. June 1998."

Val looked up at his friends.

"I think the arrogant asshole is getting emotional!" Tony said with pleasure.

Liam nodded.

Sydney smiled.

"Can I get a round of drinks for my friends?" Val yelled as he raised his hand.

CHAPTER 24

Val heard footsteps to his left, out on the aft decks of the *Monarch*. He scanned Alexei's face, who glanced to his right at the sliding glass door with expectation. Alexei's eyes narrowed and his jaw clenched. Val turned in his chair to look. The large mercenary leaning against the dining table glared at him.

Val noted the mercenary was much closer than he'd realized. If Val made a move, he would have only seconds before the burly armed man was on him.

Val could see, outside the sliding glass door, the young, suited Russian intelligence officer ascending the steps from the *Monarch*'s lower deck. A short, chunky man with wavy black hair walked behind him, followed by two mercenaries. Wearing jeans and a dark sweater, the shorter man had his arms crossed tensely in the chilly night air.

Anger and recognition flared within Val.

Alexei took his pistol from the table and returned it to the holster in the middle of his back as the intelligence officer slid open the glass door.

"Val," Alexei said as Peskov and the shorter man walked into the saloon area. "Control yourself. I have been more than kind, against my team's advice, and removed your bindings." Alexei reached across the table and slid the switchblade closer.

Val glanced back at Alexei. "Fuck you."

Val leapt out of his chair and knocked the shorter man to the floor with a punch to the side of his face. He tried to get his hands on the man's throat, but the big mercenary was already on him.

Alexei shook his head and poured himself another whiskey.

The shorter man scrambled away as the other mercenaries piled onto Val. One of them shoved Val's face against the floor as Zakir put a knee in Val's spine and bent his arms behind his back. The third mercenary restrained Val's legs.

Alexei watched as they zip-tied Val's hands behind his back and bound his ankles together. When they were done, the three mercenaries stepped away from Val, leaving him on the floor near the dining table. Alexei downed his shot of bourbon.

Val jerked his bound body around until he was lying on his side. He glared at the shorter man, who stood frozen in front of the small bistro table.

"I'm going to kill you, Burian," Val said to him.

"Oh, come on, Val. You take everything so personally." Alexei sighed heavily and looked at the bartender. "We need another glass."

The bartender nodded. He stepped out from behind the bar and handed a shot glass to Alexei.

"Burian," Alexei said. "Come sit with us."

One of the mercenaries stepped behind Burian.

Burian hesitated.

"Burian, relax," Alexei said in a hospitable voice. "You are among friends here. We are just going to talk. Please, sit down."

Alexei smiled and gestured at the chair.

Burian sat with Alexei, who poured him a shot of bourbon. Alexei reached across the table and poured bourbon into Val's glass as well.

"Turn him around so he can see us," Alexei said to the mercenary who had returned to his post by the dining table.

The mercenary grabbed Val by the ankles and spun him around so that he was lying on his slide with a view of Alexei and Burian, sitting above him at the table. Val could also see the young Russian intelligence officer, who had taken a seat at the bar.

Val studied Burian, who glanced nervously around the room. *He's scared. Something took him by surprise. And it wasn't just my stupidity.*

"I will tell you, Peskov," Alexei said to the young Russian intelligence officer, "you would not know it tonight, but the three of us here had some good times together. Very good times."

Peskov raised his eyebrows slightly at the comment. He looked at Val, bound on the floor, and at the Ukrainian, sweating at the table with Alexei.

"If you say so, sir." Peskov smirked.

Alexei raised his glass. He held it in the air until Burian raised his as well.

"Sit him up," Alexei said to the mercenary at the door as he gestured at Val.

The mercenary yanked Val up by the shoulders and propped him into a seated position, supporting him with a knee in his back.

"Peskov, help him with his drink." Alexei gestured at Val.

Peskov walked over to the table and picked up Val's shot glass.

"Next toast," Alexei said as Peskov walked over to Val. "To our time together in Germany."

Burian nodded.

"To Garmisch," Alexei said, making eye contact with Val.

Val, despite the pain of the bindings cutting his wrists and his fury at Burian, could not resist the smile that cracked his sweaty face. *Why not?*

Alexei grinned in response.

Burian fidgeted in his chair.

"To skiing," Val said with a resigned smile.

"Yes!" Alexei seemed to tear up. "To our skiing!"

Val opened his mouth and leaned his head back slightly.

"With respect, Peskov!" Alexei barked. "Do not spill on him."

Peskov carefully poured the bourbon into Val's mouth.

Alexei, satisfied with Peskov's service of Val, downed his whiskey. He waited for Burian to drink his and then set his own glass down. He looked at Val sadly. "That was good skiing."

CHAPTER 25

"This doesn't suck," Sydney said.

Val nodded, unable to speak with his mouth full of Gulaschsuppe.

Sydney smiled at him from across the long, narrow table. She closed her eyes and leaned back to absorb the midday sun, which hovered over the Garmisch ski area in a cloudless blue sky. She closed her eyes and tilted her head back. The light from the sun hammered through her eyelids, a bright-orange glow. It hurt her eyes. But the weather and operations tempo in Moscow had been tough on her over the past fifteen months, so she relished the sun's beating. And she wasn't the only one.

January and February had dumped near record snow on the Bavarian Alps before yielding to a warm March. Conditions on the mountain were excellent, and the slopes were crowded. Most of the skiers relaxing over food and drink on the outdoor patio of the Bayernhaus had stripped down to their T-shirts. Val and Sydney had done the same.

The Bayernhaus sat on the northeastern edge of the ski area at the top of one of the longest and lowest runs in the park. It was an easy cruiser that descended all the way down to the town of Garmisch-Partenkirchen. Val and Sydney were refueling on beer and food before their last run back down to town. Having spent most of the day carving up the slopes almost two thousand meters above them, their legs were tired, their faces were chapped, and they were happy.

Val couldn't help but steal a glance at Sydney. She was leaning back as far as she could manage, with nothing to rest against behind her.

"No, it doesn't," Val answered. "It's perfect."

Sydney nodded and leaned forward slowly as she opened her eyes.

Val raised his glass. "I'm really glad they sent you here." He smiled a crooked smile and extended his glass toward her.

"Me too." She clinked his glass. They both drained the last of their beers.

"Shall we?" Val gestured toward their skis propped up against each other at the edge of the patio.

"No," Sydney said, standing up.

She plodded around the table, snow crunching beneath her ski boots, and sat next to Val. She swiveled, lining herself up with the sun on the long bench before leaning back into his lap.

"I'm not done soaking up this delicious sun."

"Okay," Val said as she adjusted and squirmed until satisfied with her position and comfort. "Long as you want."

"Thanks," she answered in a soft voice.

Val looked at his empty beer glass but stifled the urge to get another one. He didn't have the heart to jostle Sydney.

Val looked north and down the mountain at the town of Garmisch-Partinkirchen. On the slopes on clear days like today, he felt like he was in a helicopter, hovering over the picturesque German town.

Garmisch-Partinkirchen is wedged into a valley that's less than a kilometer wide and runs southwest into Austria. The town sits on the northern edge of the Alps that rise north from Monaco and curl east, erupting along the borders of France, Italy, Germany, Switzerland, Austria, and Slovenia before settling back into the earth just north of Vienna at a bend in the Danube.

Val could make out the sprawling Marshall Center campus on the western edge of the town. He thought about his conversation with Deputy Director Bryson back in Virginia just two weeks ago.

The director had insisted on meeting with Val face-to-face before he flew to Europe.

"Great to see you, Captain Rafter," the director had said when Val walked into his office.

"Good to see you too, sir."

"Have a seat."

Val walked over to the director's sitting area. It seemed like a decade ago that he'd been here for his initial mission briefing before departing for Kosovo. But it had been less than a year.

"How was your leave?" The director sat down across the large coffee table from Val. He held a file in his hand.

"Good, sir. Thanks."

"What did you do?"

"Caught up with some family. Got some time with a few friends from the Farm."

Liam and Tony threw Val a days-long welcome-home party when he got back. They met him when his C-17 landed at Dover Air Force Base and didn't let go of him for seventy-two hours. By the time Val left Virginia for home in North Carolina, his liver was aching.

"Good. You earned it. Six months in Kosovo is a long haul. Are you ready for the Marshall Center?"

The George C. Marshall European Center for Security Studies was the answer to a dangerous security deficit exposed during the Russian coup attempt in 1991. As they watched that crisis unfold in Moscow, Western defense officials belatedly realized they needed much stronger security contacts within the emerging democracies of Eastern Europe and Eurasia. The coup in Russia failed, but the lesson struck home in the West—meaningful relationships with emerging defense organizations take years to build. The Marshall Center was officially established in November 1992 for this purpose.

Now the Marshall Center is a world-renowned international school bilaterally sponsored by the American and German governments and staffed by security professionals from ten partner nations. With its mission of educating, engaging, and empowering security professionals and partners, the prestigious school aims to help address regional, transnational, and global challenges. The center brings in around eight hundred students annually from over thirty countries throughout Europe and Eurasia for a variety of courses. The web of defense and security relationships that now exist across the world because of the Marshall Center is extensive.

The curriculum involves discussions of regional security, rule of law, principles of democracy, international institutions, and crisis resolution. It's a highly sought-after assignment for American Foreign Service officers, liaison officers, and defense attachés because it establishes relationships they can leverage for decades.

Not only would attendance cement Val's cover for the rest of his career, but the school was located in one of the most beautiful spots in the world with some of the best snow skiing in Europe.

"Yes, sir. I'm very excited."

"You should be. But I want you to go there with your eyes open and head on a swivel."

"Okay," Val said, not exactly sure what the deputy director meant.

"The Marshall Center operates as a partnership between the US European Command and the German Federal Ministry of Defense," Bryson continued. "The US pays most of the multimillion-dollar budget via European Command, which is also tasked with operating and overseeing the center."

Val nodded. He knew all this.

"You need to understand, Captain, that the geniuses at the Pentagon have placed a strict ban on intelligence recruitment activities at the Marshall Center."

"Are you kidding, sir?"

"I am not. And let me tell you, son, they're on a hair trigger about this. No spotting, no assessing, no developing, and sure as hell, no recruiting."

"Why not, sir?"

"Hard to believe, right?" Bryson shook his head. "You've got a highly concentrated and lucrative target environment there. Hundreds of young, up-and-coming leaders, with good placement and access, spending long periods of time away from their countries, socializing with international students and engaging in academic discussions that may evoke independent thoughts."

Val nodded in agreement.

"Well, DOD wants to protect the Marshall Center's integrity." Bryson emphasized the word "integrity," with a roll of the eyes.

Val exhaled in disbelief.

"I'm serious," the deputy director said. "This is a contentious topic between the military and intelligence bureaucracies. The director of national intelligence realizes how potentially lucrative the center could be. But DOD leaders are very cautious, and they're skeptical of the intelligence communities' aims, not to mention our methods. So, the ban stays. Even though such idealistic constraints do not encumber foreign governments and militaries. The Russians, Ukrainians and others come to the center to play. And they play hard."

General Bryson paused, letting what he'd just explained sink in.

"But don't even fucking think about it." The deputy director glared at Val, voice suddenly stern. "These are the bureaucratic equivalents of tectonic plates. You get off the reservation at the Marshall Center, and you will be crushed, buried, and forgotten."

"I get it, sir."

"You better," Bryson said, his voice maintaining its edge. "You get sideways there like you did at the Farm, and there will be nothing myself or the director can do for you."

"I understand."

"I want more than your understanding, Captain. I want your personal commitment."

"You've got it, sir."

"Good." Bryson leaned back in his chair. "With all that being said, there are two more matters I need to discuss with you."

Val tried not to look nervous. It had been strange for Bryson to call for a face-to-face meeting prior to his departure for Germany. He understood the ban on recruiting at the center and could see why the deputy director would want to lay down that law in person. Val was worried about what was coming next.

"This is the first." He handed Val the file he'd been holding. "I'm very sorry about this, son."

Val opened the file. It was a printed intelligence cable from the CIA's base in Pristina. Zyph Hyka was found dead in his apartment in Kamenica the day after Val left. His throat had been cut.

Val felt the blood rush to his face. He read it again. *Oh, Zyph! Oh shit!* Val kept staring at the report, anger and sadness welling inside him.

"Any reason to believe Hyka had enemies?"

"Only the standard ethnic enemies one has in that hellhole," Val said, anger creeping into his voice. "He was a good man. I don't think he was into anything criminal, if that's what you're implying, sir."

"I was not."

"Do you think the Russians did this?" Val asked, a feeling of guilt running through him like an icy chill.

General Bryson looked at Val for a moment.

"We don't know for certain," he finally said.

Val closed the file, looked at the general, and cleared his throat.

"Do we have any indication whether—"

"Stop it, son. This didn't happen because of you."

Val looked down at his feet. An awkward silence settled between them. Had Val's relationship doomed Zyph? Did Val push too hard?

"Like you said," Bryson continued, "that place is a hellhole. You helped make it better. Period."

Val took a deep breath and then looked up. He set the file on the table in front of him. "Thank you for telling me, sir."

"I thought you'd want to know. And the chief of base in Pristina is all over it. I'll let you know if they find out anything. You have my promise on that."

Val nodded.

"What's the other thing you wanted to discuss, sir?" he asked, wanting to keep the conversation moving so he could leave as soon as possible and digest the news about Zyph.

The director nodded, allowing Val to change the subject.

"NSA has intercepted Russian communications that mention you by name."

"What?"

"We've picked up chatter in which the Russians talk about you going to the Marshall European Center for Security Studies. They're bragging about the relationships they built with you while you were in Kosovo."

"Yeah," Val said, shaking his head, anger still seething in his voice. "They were a real charming bunch."

Bryson studied Val for a moment.

"They're sending an intelligence officer to the course," he finally said, looking at Val evenly.

"To what? Recruit me?"

"No." Bryson shook his head. "They're not that stupid. We know they recruit other nationalities there. But they wouldn't risk a high-level embarrassment like that."

The general shrugged as he kept talking.

"I don't always understand their motivations or what they're up to. Lately, it seems like their whole foreign policy has boiled down to kicking us in the jimmies whenever and however they can. Maybe it means nothing. Maybe they just want to stay in your face. All I know is, this new president of theirs, Putin, is going to be a problem. He's a KGB lifer. A true believer. He is going to be an aggressive son of a bitch."

Bryson leaned back in his chair. "And I think we're going to be dealing with him for a long time, unfortunately."

Val sat across from the deputy director and stewed.

"Are you angry?" Bryson asked him.

"Yes, sir."

"Good."

Bryson studied the young captain.

Val returned the stare.

"That's all I have, Captain. I wanted you to hear it all directly from me."

"I appreciate it, sir."

"Now, I want you to go to Germany." The general leaned forward. His voice conveyed more understanding and empathy than Val had ever heard from him. "I want you to study; burnish your cover as an army liaison officer; and have fun skiing, drinking, and goofing off there in Garmisch. You've earned it."

"Yes, sir." A smile cracked across Val's face.

The general nodded, and they both stood.

The deputy director held the door for Val. "Just remember, keep your head on a swivel."

After that send-off from General Bryson, Val was astonished when he ran into Sydney in the hallway of Building 101 on the Marshall Center campus.

Val's jaw dropped for an instant, but he quickly recovered.

He walked toward her as she was putting new textbooks into her backpack.

"Hello," Val said in a friendly voice.

Sydney hadn't seen Val approaching. But she didn't miss a beat. There were other people in the hallway.

"Hello?"

"I'm Captain Rafter." He held out his hand. Sydney shook it, the first time they had touched in more than a year and a half. "Welcome to the Marshall Center."

"Thank you, Captain Rafter. I'm Captain Brooke Monroe."

"Brooke," Val said with an eyebrow arched just enough for her to notice. "I'm Val."

"Nice to meet you, Val."

Val scanned the area. He gestured subtly toward the window. Sydney and he stepped out of the center of the hallway.

"If you're free tonight, Brooke," Val said in a low voice that only she could hear, "why not meet me at the Local Cure? It's an Irish pub. Just a few minutes down the road into Garmisch. Great beer and food."

"Sure. I'd like that."

"1900 hours?"

"Perfect."

"See you there."

Garmisch is, for the most part, a family-friendly European ski town. Most of its cobblestoned streets are quiet in the evenings. The Local Cure, though, went late into the night. An integral part of Garmisch's nightlife for decades, the pub had become home to the town's ski bums, misfits, and expats. It was a fun and welcoming scene.

Later that evening, Val and Sydney found a high-top table away from the crowd where the loud music would let them speak without too much concern about being overheard. They ordered beers and food, and then Val tore into her.

"What the hell is going on? You knew I was going to be here. I don't get so much as a courtesy heads-up? That's bullshit!"

Sydney listened to Val protest while she ate French fries.

"Your cover is you're an army captain? Are you fucking kidding me? No one is going to buy that. You're going to get figured out in a second."

Sydney rolled her eyes at the insult and chewed.

"Besides," Val said, leaning in across the table and speaking in a lower voice, despite the cover of the music. "This place is off-limits. There is a ban on any activity, especially recruiting. You guys know that."

Sydney washed her food down with a big swig of beer and then wiped her mouth with a napkin.

"You done?"

"For now," Val said, grabbing a beer and taking a long swallow.

"I think it's just precious that you guys at DIA like to say what's in and out of bounds. But little news flash for you…Vladimir Putin is for real. And by real, I mean real bad. So, at the agency anyway, we're not going to wait around for him to bend the US over and shove it up our ass. We're getting aggressive."

Val looked at Sydney for a long moment. "I fucking love that!" He leaned forward with a lusty smile. "Please tell me what you're up to."

"Sorry. Can't." Sydney took another swig of beer.

"Maybe I could help," Val said earnestly.

"Nope."

"Oh, come on!" Val pleaded. "I'm a fucking vault. I won't tell anyone."

"Listen to yourself," Sydney said with mock disgust.

Val leaned back in his chair with a harrumph.

Sydney took another sip of beer.

This was the moment the CIA had been concerned about. So concerned, in fact, that they had actually called the whole thing off, told Sydney her mission at the Marshall Center was scrubbed.

Sydney had done well in Moscow, notching her belt with a successful high-value recruitment that many had argued was too risky to attempt. But she'd nailed it. As a result, she was nominated for a follow-on mission at the Marshall Center. Another risky, high-value recruitment that would require her to be in pseudo.

The agency got to work backstopping her fake identity with their typical, nearly foolproof level of detail. Captain Brooke Monroe was an army captain who'd served two tours in Germany; graduated from Arizona State; grew up in Houston, Texas; and was born the same year as Val, 1971. The agency also scrubbed and re-scrubbed the attendee, faculty, and staff lists to ensure there was no possibility of anyone Sydney had ever been exposed to in true name in Moscow showing up and blowing her cover. This included students, instructors, temporary assignees, everyone that might be in her vicinity in Garmisch. The scrub was clean except for one name.

Val Rafter. A US Army captain that Sydney had gone through the Farm with. The clandestine operations leadership balked. They scrubbed the mission.

But Sydney argued with them for days, telling them she could handle Val. Days stretched into a week. Finally, she got them comfortable with it. Barely.

But this was the moment of truth. If she could not get Val to be cool, her mission would end. That was the deal.

Sydney looked around and then leaned toward Val.

"DOD doesn't know I'm CIA," she said in a serious voice. "Langley spent a lot of time making sure my paper trail is bulletproof. Then I almost didn't get this mission because of you. Because you were in this class. But I told them you were a professional, that you'd not blow my cover. Please don't make a liar out of me."

Val held Sydney's stare for a moment. He leaned forward, extending his glass.

"Your secret is safe with me. You know that."

Sydney smiled and clinked his glass.

"I do know that. And I appreciated the way you handled our run-in earlier. I think it's best we don't admit to knowing each other prior to getting here."

"I agree," Val said. "Dumb tankers like me don't get a lot of exposure to… What are you supposed to be, anyway?"

"Counter-proliferation liaison officer," Sydney said, chewing another bite of bratwurst.

Val rolled his eyes.

"Get over it," Sydney said.

Val chuckled. Then frowned. He looked at Sydney.

She caught his glance and their eyes locked. The cost of her mission fully sinking in with them both.

Sydney took a swallow of beer and looked around to make sure no one was watching. She took his hand and then leaned in to kiss him. Val put his hand to her cheek. They let the kiss last longer than was wise, their lips unwilling to part. It had been too long. They were unable to separate themselves.

"Another beer for you two?" the waitress asked in a happy New Zealander accent.

"No!" Sydney said, a little too loud and too suddenly, whipping her head from Val. His hand hung in the air for a moment, empty.

"Alrighty, then," the waitress said, unperturbed. She walked away into the noise and commotion of the Local Cure.

Sydney glanced left and right and then looked at Val.

"We can't…" she started to say, before looking down at the table.

"You sure?" Val said without conviction.

"We can't. This is too important. If I get this done, Val, it will be such a big deal. I'll be on my way. I just…" Her voice trailed off again, eyes still downcast.

"Hey," Val said.

Sydney looked up.

"I get it," he said. "You don't have to worry about me. Do what you have to do. Get it done."

Sydney smiled, relief spilling into her expression.

"Thank you." She started to reach for his hand.

She caught herself, bringing her hand back and putting it in her lap.

Val smiled.

"It's gonna be tough."

"Yes," she said. "Yes, it is. But when this course is over…"

"Ten weeks."

"Ten weeks," she repeated, nodding.

"It's a date."

"You're damn right it is," she said.

Now, two days later, sitting in the blazing sun on a bench in front of the Bayernhaus, Val looked down at Sydney's head in his lap and smiled. He was glad they had sent her to the Marshall Center, even if it inflamed feelings they could not act on, and even if he felt professional jealousy. He was glad to be nearer to her.

Val had forced Sydney out of his heart and mind when he was in Kosovo. He had to in order to focus on the job. When he rotated back to the States, he told himself that he wasn't back long enough to reach out. They wouldn't have any meaningful time together. He had to leave for Germany too soon.

And he planned on the women of Europe taking his mind off of her.

Now, seeing her again, being close again, he remembered how much he liked her, how much he respected her, and what a nice body she had. He was glad they would have some time together now, even if it couldn't be romantic.

"Why are you smiling?" Sydney asked him.

"Nothing."

"Seriously." Sydney held her hand up to shade her eyes from the insistent sun. "Tell me."

"Seriously, it was nothing. I'm just glad you're here."

"Me too."

Val and Sydney sat outside the Bayernhaus until they were sluggish from beer and sun. At three p.m., Sydney reluctantly stood and stretched.

Val watched as she arched her back and raised her arms while she faced the sun in her tight white T-shirt.

She caught him looking and smiled.

"I'm sorry," she said, now bending over in a leg stretch. "But I've got to get down the mountain."

She straightened and looked at Val.

"We've got that reception at 1800," she said, shoving her hair back into her red knit cap.

Val looked at his watch. "That's in three hours."

"Well, I need a shower, etcetera," she said, grabbing her jacket off the bench.

"That's a lot of etceteras. Besides, I still have half a beer."

"Stay and enjoy it." Sydney zipped up the jacket. She leaned over and buckled her ski boots.

Val looked at his beer and around the patio. The sun was brilliant, the sky was blue, and the snow was white. He felt an urge to go with her, but he didn't want to leave.

"You sure?"

"Of course," she said, nodding. "I would stay if I could."

"But you can." He patted the bench in invitation.

"Sorry. Brooke Monroe needs time to primp."

Val watched as Sydney clicked into her ski bindings. She turned and waved at him before poling away to the slope and accelerating out of sight.

Val took another swig of beer.

CHAPTER 26

Val walked into Wörner Hall on the Marshall Center campus. The informal class reception in one of the large meeting rooms had been going on for half an hour. A dour-faced female Department of the Army civilian sat at the welcoming table that had just a handful of name tags left on it.

"Oh," she said with a pinched smile as Val grabbed his name tag. "You made it, Captain Rafter."

Val winked at the lady and walked into the reception. He scanned the large room while he put on his name tag. Flags from each of the attending student nations stood around the room, which had been set up with an open bar and hors d'oeuvres.

The reception was an informal icebreaker for the incoming class and faculty, intended to give everyone a chance to get to know each other before classes began the next day. Multiple high-top tables stood next to large windows with views of the Alps, now doused in shadows as the sun set. Students from more than twenty countries mingled awkwardly with a dozen older faculty. Everyone tried to avoid the loaded topics hanging in the air.

Val smiled to himself at the sight of the Armenian and Azerbaijani students staring each other down from opposite sides of the room. The unresolved conflict of Nagorno-Karabakh obligated confrontation wherever it could be had, even over stuffed mushrooms and German beer.

A young man walked by, sporting early eighties, pressed, acid-washed jeans topped by a well-preserved Members Only jacket. An older gentleman in dark pants and an ill-matched dark sport coat followed him closely.

Belorussians.

They were infamous for their practice of never going anywhere alone. One was always older than the other and thought to be the "minder" who would keep tabs on his countryman to ensure they didn't speak against Belarus policy or socialize too much with other countries.

Val smiled. This was going to be fun.

He spotted Sydney across the room. Drink in one hand, leaned back in laughter amid three men, she looked as good as ever in jeans and a tight black turtleneck sweater. *Brooke!* he told himself. *Her name is Brooke Monroe! Don't screw this up.*

Val repeated her cover name to himself as he took a few steps in her direction and then stopped, stunned.

Alexei Volkov.

The Russian laughed with Sydney, his back to Val.

Val stood motionless, calibrating to the situation.

"They're sending an intelligence officer," he remembered General Bryson saying.

"Val!" Sydney said, waving. "There you are!"

Val unstuck himself. He walked toward Alexei and the group.

Alexei turned and spotted Val.

They locked eyes.

"Hello!" another of the men next to Sydney said to Val as he stepped up to the group. He leaned eagerly past Sydney and extended his hand. "I am Nicolae, is nice to meet you."

Val took his eyes off Alexei to acknowledge the greeting and shook the man's hand. Nicolae was the shortest one in the group, with closely cropped black hair, hazel eyes and a wide smile.

"Good to meet you," Val said, charmed by the glow of enthusiasm emanating from Nicolae.

"And I am Burian," the man on the other side of Alexei said. He was stocky with hair that was too long to be within the regulations of whichever military he served in. "From Ukraine," Burian added, answering Val's unspoken question.

"Good to meet you, also." Val shook Burian's hand. "I am—"

"Captain Val Rafter!" Alexei boomed, interrupting Val. "US Army!"

Nicolae looked at Alexei, startled by the tall Russian.

"Okay?" Sydney said slowly, mostly to herself, as Alexei, his eyes moistening, grasped Val by the shoulders.

Nicolae looked at Sydney, who shrugged to show she didn't know what was going on either.

Burian smiled at Alexei, seemingly familiar with his effusiveness.

"Don't!" Val put his hands on Alexei's chest to resist the Russian's hug. "No crying, you sentimental Russian bastard."

"Do not lecture me, Val!" Alexei said, a little too loud. "You crazy son of a bitch!"

Many heads in the room turned to see what the conflict was. A couple of nervous faculty members headed toward Val and Alexei. It was not uncommon for faculty to have to defuse altercations between students who could not leave their national identities and causes at the door.

"Get in here!" Val said, unable to resist anymore.

Alexei and Val hugged and slapped each other's backs while most of the room watched. The faculty member that had gotten closest to them, a US Marine colonel, hesitated, and then smiled at the sight. He turned away, chuckling, and waved off his colleagues. The colonel had been around and could spot brewing fisticuffs. It was clear there were none here.

Sydney, gobsmacked, stood in silence.

Burian chuckled.

Nicolae's eyes darted around the group, desperately trying to figure out what was going on. Russians and Americans hugging?

"It is so good to see you, brother!" Alexei said.

"Good to see you too," Val said. "And surprising. You didn't tell me you were coming to the Marshall Center."

Alexei's smile turned mischievous.

"Truthfully, I didn't know it. Honest truth. But when I heard you were going, I researched it and made my case very hard. What can I say? Sometimes we get lucky!"

That's bullshit.

"Well, I'm thrilled you're here," Val said.

"So you guys know each other?" Sydney asked.

"Know each other?" Alexei said. "No. We are brothers!"

Alexei grabbed Val in a bear hug again. Val didn't resist.

"Served together in Kosovo," Val managed to say to Sydney as he endured the large Russian's squeeze.

Sydney nodded.

"How do you two know each other?" Alexei asked, pointing between Val and Sydney.

"We didn't before getting here," Sydney said quickly. "I met Val as I was inprocessing."

"I see. So you two are not dating, then? Good for me, maybe?"

Alexei winked at Sydney.

"No. We are not dating, Alexei," Val said. "I'm all yours, big guy."

Alexei belly laughed, and again the room looked to see what the commotion was.

Nicolae and Val made eye contact.

"Nicolae, sorry to have interrupted your introduction," Val said. "But you know how Russians can be."

Nicolae nodded knowingly. "I do indeed."

"And where are you from?" Val asked.

"I am from Moldova," Nicolae said, avoiding eye contact with Alexei.

"Oh." Val glanced between he and Alexei.

"Is okay, Val," Alexei said. "Nicolae and I have already met."

The Russian put his long arm around the shoulder of Nicolae, who didn't recoil, but whose face betrayed his dislike.

"We are good friends!" Alexei said, giving Nicolae a squeeze and then releasing him.

"And you, Burian?" Val asked. "You know Alexei?"

"I do." Burian nodded and smiled. But he didn't elaborate.

Val looked at his watch and then around the room. The reception exuded all the excitement he normally associated with the US Army's mandatory, organized fun.

"Nicolae," Val said, even though he was addressing the entire group. "You up for getting out of here?"

"Getting out of here?"

"Head into town. Have a little more fun."

Nicolae looked around the room nervously as Sydney and Alexei nodded. Burian smiled as if he might not fully understand what was implied but liked the vibe.

"Um," Nicolae said. "But the event is not over?"

"Nicolae!" Alexei said. "You will learn, when this guy says, 'Let's go do something,' you go." Alexei pointed at Val. "Is always good time."

"Is that so?" Sydney asked, lacing her voice with a tinge of skepticism that only Val picked up on. "Then I'm game."

"I'm telling you," Alexei said, looking at Sydney but playfully punching Burian in the shoulder. "Always!"

Sydney gave Nicolae a subtle nod. He smiled.

"Okay," Nicolae said, warmed by the sense of inclusion. "Yes. I go with you."

"Great. Let's split up, so it's not so obvious a rejection of these guys," Val said. "We'll meet in the parking lot in five minutes."

"He always has plan!" Alexei said to Burian and Nicolae. "I love it."

The group split up and walked in different directions. Sydney walked with Val.

"So, that was awkward," she said.

"What?" Val asked as he grabbed a small plate and started stacking hors d'oeuvres on it. He and Sydney walked to the corner of the room, and he ate quickly.

"Nicolae fought the Russians in the Transnistrian conflict as a lieutenant. Was wounded pretty bad, I think."

"Oh shit," Val said, hesitating before putting a stuffed mushroom into his mouth.

"Yeah."

Transnistria was a breakaway region of Moldova with long historic ties to Russia and Ukraine. The Russian 14th Guards Army had been stationed at the Dniester River in Transnistria for decades. When the small region launched an effort to break away from Moldova, the 14th Army helped in many ways, both overt and covert. The conflict lasted from November 1990 to July 1992, ending in de facto independence for Transnistria. It was not a happy outcome for Moldova, which remained angry with Russia's intervention.

"I'll keep an eye on him," Val said.

"Yeah. Me too."

"What about that Ukrainian?"

"Burian? Dunno. Seems like a nice enough guy." Sydney said.

Val nodded as he chewed on a fried cheese stick.

"I'm going to sneak out," Sydney said. "See you there."

Val nodded, his mouth full. He stood in the corner, working through his stack of food. He'd almost cleaned his small plate when an older gentleman approached him.

"Captain Rafter?"

"Yes, sir," Val said, swallowing.

"I'm General Stokes," the man said, extending his hand.

"Oh," Val wiped his hand on his pants before shaking the general's hand. "Yes, sir. Good to meet you, sir."

Retired Lieutenant General Stokes was the director of the Marshall Center. He was a Rhodes Scholar who had fought as a platoon leader in Vietnam and then led a division in Desert Storm. Stokes served as the commanding general of US European Command before retiring and taking the job of director, traditionally given to a high-ranking American retiree with relevant experience.

Dressed in a blue blazer on top of a crisp white shirt and khakis, Stokes looked at Val with slate-gray eyes, hand in his pockets.

"Heard you were in Kosovo before joining us here at the center," he said to Val.

"Yes, sir."

"That must have been interesting."

"Yes, sir. It was."

"Third Armored Division here in Germany before that, right?"

"Yes, sir."

"And what did you do between Third AD and Kosovo?" Stokes asked.

"The defense liaison course, sir."

"Uh-huh." The director looked around the room and then took a step closer to Val. He leaned in and said, "Captain, I don't care if you're DIA, CIA, ISA, or some other TLA I haven't heard of. No fucking spy games at my course." Stone pulled his hand out of his pocket and counted off offenses as he prohibited them. "No spotting. No assessing. No developing. No recruiting." The director pointed at Val like he was pointing a pistol at his chest. "If I get wind of you crossing my red lines, you will be gone. And I mean gone from the army, not just the Marshall Center."

Val wanted to say, "Well, you've got at least one CIA and one Russian intelligence officer on the loose in your henhouse, tough guy," but he kept quiet.

Director Stone put his hand back in his pocket. "You got me, Captain?"

"Sir, I don't understand why you think—"

"Don't!" the director said in a voice that was not loud but carried force. "I review all attendee personnel files for every class. I've been around long enough to know how to spot you guys. So spare me the bullshit. All I want to hear from you is, 'I understand and will comply, sir.'"

"I understand and will comply, sir."

Stokes smiled.

"Great. I want to hear about Kosovo, Captain. I'll have my secretary set something up. Welcome to the Marshall Center."

Stone shook Val's hand again and walked back into the crowd.

Jesus, I need a drink.

*

Everyone stayed out late at the Local Cure that night. Other Marshall Center students showed up as the night went on. Val even spotted a couple of faculty members. It was a fun scene with loud music and flowing alcohol. Val watched Sydney chat up Alexei, who, of course, responded to the attention with his typical gusto. At one point, when Sydney had gone to the restroom, Alexei leaned into Val and said, "This Brooke is beautiful woman."

Burian nodded as Val fought the urge to say, "She's with me."

Sydney showed up a few minutes later and paired off with Alexei at one of the more private high-top tables in the corner. Val felt a twinge of jealousy and then remembered their secret. He chuckled.

So, while the director is watching my every move, Sydney will be flying under the radar, making mischief, and trying to recruit a Russian agent. I wonder if the CIA planned it that way?

"I review all attendee personal files." Val remembered what General Stokes had said at their earlier encounter. *Well, I guess you missed one, sir.*

Val smiled in grudging respect for the agency's ability to backstop a pseudo identity. They were pros.

"May I join you?" Nicolae said, approaching Val's table.

"Of course."

Nicolae smiled as he sat down. He looked at Val and opened his mouth to speak but was interrupted.

"Val!"

Nicolae and Val turned toward the booming voice across the bar. An older gentleman, dressed in jeans and a plaid flannel shirt over a tie-dyed T-shirt, approached their table.

"Hank!" Val said. "Good to see you!"

"Same to you, buddy." Hank slapped Val on the back.

"Nicolae, I want to introduce you to my good friend, the mayor of Garmisch. Hank Ballard."

Nicolae sprang from his seat.

"Is honor to meet you, sir!" Nicolae said earnestly, extending his hand to Hank.

Hank looked at Nicolae's hand, then at Val, then back to Nicolae.

Hank and Val laughed.

Nicolae dropped his hand, puzzled by their reaction.

"I'm sorry, Nicolae," Val said, stifling his chuckles. "It's just an expression. Hank isn't the real mayor of Garmisch. Far from it."

"Hey!" Hank said. "It's not so crazy."

"Actually, it's not," Val admitted.

"Good to meet you, Nick." Hank extended his hand.

"You also," Nicolae said.

"Hank has lived here for years," Val told Nicolae.

"Fifteen years," Hank said, smiling at Nicolae.

"He spent a few decades working for the army as a civilian. What did you retire at?"

"Doesn't matter," Hank said. "Where you from, Nick?"

"I am from Moldova. And is Nicolae, please."

"Welcome to Garmisch, Nick!" Hank said. "If you need anything while you're here, you let me know. Let me get you a beer."

Hank raised his hand. The bartender, despite being on the other side of the room and surrounded by a crush of people yelling at him for a drink, immediately poured a beer for Hank.

"No, thank you," Nicolae said. "First day of class tomorrow and—"

"Nonsense. Just one more. You too, Val."

Val looked at Nicolae and shrugged as if to say, *Just go with it.*

Nicolae took the cue.

"You have known each other a long time?" he asked the two Americans.

"Bout a week," Val said.

Hank nodded.

Val had met Hank at the gym. They'd struck up a conversation at the bench press and were fast friends before their workouts were over. Val recognized a Garmisch expert and fellow adventurer in Hank. One that he could learn a lot from. And Hank saw a younger version of himself.

Hank had risen quickly up the DOD civilian ranks until, at fifty, he was a GS-16 helping to set policy for US Army European Command. He knew he'd found his home in Garmisch, though. The mountains, hiking, skiing, and people soothed his questing like nowhere else in the world had. And he'd been to many places. So, when the army told him it was time to move again, he told them, no, thank you. Instead, Hank engineered a big demotion for himself, moving all the way down to GS-5 to maintain his post privileges and access to the PX and hospital. Now, he split time between handing out towels in the gym twenty hours a week and acting as the unofficial mayor of expat Garmisch.

When three more beers arrived at their table, Hank, Val, and Nicolae held their big mugs aloft. "To new friendships in the most beautiful place in the world, gentlemen."

They drank.

And those were not the last beers of the evening.

CHAPTER 27

The low-key academics and beautiful setting energized Val and Alexei. It didn't take them long to establish themselves as the informal leaders of the class. By the second week, they were regularly engaging in "lunch bombing runs." Running out of class at eleven a.m., they would hop into Val's car, which they had preloaded with all of their gear. They would race to the ski lift and see how many runs they could get in and still get back to class by one p.m. Val used his 13th Tactical switchblade to slice cheese and sausage, which they devoured as they rode the chairlift back up between runs. Their best was three high-speed runs.

It was a record they could never break. Val even drafted Hank's help. He would sit outside the academic building in his old pickup truck, engine running, ski equipment in the back. Val and Alexei would dash out and pile into the truck the moment class was dismissed. Hank raced across Garmisch and deposited the two at the steps of the ski lift. It didn't matter. The gondola just didn't go fast enough to get in more than three runs.

Val's technique improved, but Alexei was still a far better skier, besting Val on most days. Val was crazier, though, taking risks that often sent him careening off-piste.

Panting after the bruising runs, Val and Alexei would stumble back into the classroom at the last minute. Disapproving instructors learned to ignore the chuckles of respect from Nicolae and the other students. Sydney would just shake her head.

On the weekends, Val and Alexei organized their own "ski bar," which quickly became a well-attended favorite activity of the entire class. On Saturdays, when conditions were favorable, Val and Alexei rose early and hiked halfway up toward the Kreuzjoch peak in the Garmisch-Classic ski area to build an ice bar in a spot just off their favorite run. Laughing with a thermos full of coffee and Baileys, a drink Val introduced to Nicolae, Alexei, and Burian, they built and stocked the ice bar before the lifts opened.

By noon, the smell of grilling meat, sizzling under Hank's watchful eyes, would float up the slopes, as Kazaks, Uzbeks, Tajiks, and Kyrgyz tumbled down. They were the worst on the snow and resisted all coaching efforts from Val and Alexei. Their high-speed wipeouts and collisions with trees, barriers, and other skiers amused everyone, and somehow no one ever got hurt.

The rest of the group spent the day roaming all over the mountain. Nicolae was one of the better technical skiers, able to keep up with Alexei. Val usually came next, barely in control. Burian's skills on skis were poor. But his chunky, low center of gravity worked to his advantage. Always last, he rarely fell.

By the end of the day, dozens of students and even a few faculty would be dancing in ski boots around the ski bar to ABBA songs, which Alexei insisted on playing. When the sun got low and the radio batteries got weak, the group would help Val and Alexei break down the bar.

Near the end of the packing process, when the lifts had closed, people started edging away from the group and putting their skis on. The intermittent pop of ski bindings and soft groans as people snuck in subtle warm-up stretches were telltale signs. Val would feign concentration, giving special instructions to Nicolae on how to pack this or that fragile item into a backpack, and telling Burian to stop drinking and help pack up. But he was really watching the group out of the corner of his eye as they formed a starting line that spread across the slope.

Finally, after a wink of thanks to Nicolae, Val would grab his skis and walk to the center of the starting line, avoiding eye contact with everyone. He would twist and bend over, warming up his inebriated body and driving the group mad with anticipation. By now, Alexei was in a starting crouch, jamming his poles deep into the snow for purchase.

After popping into his skis, tightening his gloves, and lowering his goggles, Val would take one last look around, smile at his comrades of the mountain, and then scream, "Launch the fleet!"

With shouts of excitement and friendship, the drunken international menagerie plunged down the slope. Alexei led the group in a final, blazing, drunken run.

Val and Sydney never spoke about it, but Val kept his eye on her throughout the course, as she seemed to make good progress with Alexei. They spent a lot of time together, but Val kept the jealousy at bay by reminding himself, *It's just business.* He looked forward to the end of the course when class would disperse, and he and Sydney could finally spend time together. In the back of his mind, he also entertained thoughts of welcoming Alexei to the good guys. Maybe helping him settle down in America when his time spying for Sydney was over.

*

By late April, the snow had lost its grip on the mountains around Garmisch. The green alpine meadows thousands of feet above the town re-declared themselves and welcomed grazing herds of bell-wearing cows. Trails that had served as bombing runs for Val and Alexei now hosted lush grass and wildflowers. The mountaintop glaciers remained, as they always had, but the ski lifts closed.

The students began traveling outside of Garmisch, enjoying Europe in spring. Many came from much less wealthy, more rundown countries in Eastern Europe and Eurasia. The disparity of wealth and development shocked them. Even so, they reveled in their experiences.

Val and his group of friends went on hikes and road trips together almost every weekend. Sydney seemed to develop a sisterly concern for Nicolae, insisting on including the shy Moldovan in social activities and study groups. On weekends, when no one else could go, Val and Alexei would set off on their own.

On Friday afternoon in early May, as Val packed for the crew's weekend road trip, he got a phone call.

"Rafter, it's Bryson."

"Good afternoon, sir," Val said, wondering what was up. He hadn't spoken to the general since their meeting back in January.

"I'm in Stuttgart for meetings. I want to see you tomorrow evening."

Val hesitated. He was really looking forward to this weekend's road trip. It was to one of his favorite cities, and there were only two weeks left in the course. He was feeling the impending departure of his group of friends.

"You there, Rafter?"

"Yes, sir. Sorry. Just…it's just that…" Val's voice drifted as he realized his mistake.

"Oh, I'm sorry, Captain," Bryson said without a hint of an apology, "would it be an inconvenience?"

"No, sir," Val hurried to say.

"Because if it doesn't fit into your schedule…"

"No, sir. It's fine."

"It's 'fine'? Well, that's a relief. As long as it's fine with you, Captain."

"No…I mean, of course, sir. I just—"

"I'd hate to impose on you."

"I meant to—"

"Let me see if I can change my schedule around."

"Sir, that's really not—"

"Ruiz!" Bryson barked. Val shook his head, admonishing himself for being an idiot. He could hear that the general had dropped the phone from his mouth, and could picture Bryson's panicked aide, some hapless major, looking quickly at his boss.

"Sir?" Val heard a voice, distant from the phone in Bryson's hand.

"I may be inconveniencing Captain Rafter," the general said. Val's head and shoulders sagged. "Would you do me a favor and check with Special Operations Command Europe and see if we can move the schedule around to better accommodate the captain's…"

Bryson hesitated.

Val grimaced and squeezed his eyes shut as if waiting to be slapped in the face. *Here it comes.*

"Captain Rafter, what is it that Special Operations Command Europe will be accommodating?"

"Um…" Val knew it was futile to resist. *Just get it over with.* "Prague, sir. We had planned to go to Prague for the weekend."

"Why didn't you say so in the first place?" Bryson responded before dropping the phone and yelling across the room: "It's worse than I thought, Ruiz! We're talking Prague here. This man has a trip to Prague planned."

The general's aide didn't respond. Val could picture the major, relieved that there was not an actual emergency, looking at his boss and smiling with approval as Bryson tortured the impudent captain.

"Don't worry, Rafter," Bryson said in a falsely reassuring voice. "Major Ruiz thinks he can move some shit around, tell the special operations commander for Europe to come in on the weekend, so that you can go to Prague and play grab ass with your friends."

Val sighed to himself.

"Or here is another idea," Bryson continued as if the notion had just struck him. "It may be crazy, but you tell me what you think. Tomorrow, at 1800, you drag your ass from Garmisch and meet me for dinner at the Gasthaus Dorn, just to the south of Ulm. Major Ruiz will send you the address. What do you think of that, Captain?"

"Sir, I think that sounds great."

"Really? Are you sure?"

"Yes, sir."

"Well, that's great," the general said. Then, without bothering to lower the phone from his mouth, Bryson yelled, "Ruiz! Tell the SOC commander it's okay. Captain Rafter has found some flexibility in his schedule."

Val looked across the room at his half-packed bag.

"See you then, Captain," Bryson said. "And don't worry. Prague isn't going anywhere."

*

Ulm sits on the Danube River, almost a hundred kilometers to the southeast of Stuttgart. About a two-hour drive for Val, he'd left Garmisch around 3:30 in the afternoon to make sure he arrived on time. He didn't want to incite the general again with tardiness.

Gasthaus Dorn sat on a small hill overlooking the Iller river just before it flowed into the Danube on the southern outskirts of Ulm. A classic German gasthaus with rooms to rent, a dining area, and a small bar, the Dorn had been owned and run by the Dorn family for almost 150 years.

Val arrived about twenty minutes early. He walked into the dining area and smiled as he looked around. Decorated in the traditional, understated German style, the wood-paneled room was encircled with benches and tables. A shelf ran along the top of each wall, adorned with books, stuffed wild game, and beer steins. A dozen more tables filled the room, each covered with a dark-green tablecloth.

The place was already full, and Val didn't see a place for him and the general to sit.

The old man is going to be pissed. Val walked across the dining room to a set of French doors that appeared to lead outside.

Val stepped through the French doors and out onto a large patio with about a dozen more tables. The patio overlooked an enormous field that stretched away for hundreds of meters until falling away into the river. Plowed into deep rows, the dark river valley soil seemed to almost glisten in the afternoon sun. The slight breeze carried a pleasant hint of wet earth across the patio.

Each table on the patio was full. The murmur of conversation and the clinking of forks and knives hung in the air. Val thought again that the general was in for a disappointment. Hopefully, there was another restaurant nearby.

Then Val spotted him.

General Bryson sat at a table at the far edge of the patio next to the railing. It was the best table on the patio, with a clear view of the plowed field and the Iller river. The larger buildings of Ulm stood in the distance.

It was the first time Val had ever seen the general in civilian clothes. Dressed in blue jeans, a white polo, and a blue blazer, the man looked like a retired banker, not a modern-day military spymaster.

An older gentleman sat at the table across from the general. They were laughing together. And as Val approached, he noticed they were speaking German.

"Ah, Captain Rafter," Bryson said upon seeing him.

The older gentleman turned and then stood to greet Val, holding out his hand.

"Meet Herr Dorn," Bryson said to Val.

"Welcome," Herr Dorn said, smiling warmly and shaking Val's hand. "A friend of Herr Bryson's is a friend of ours."

"It's good to meet you too, sir. Thank you."

"Please." Herr Dorn gestured at the chair he had just vacated.

"Thank you."

"Something to drink, sir?"

"You know what to give him, Otto," Bryson said with a knowing smile. "I'm sure he has never had it before."

"Very good," Herr Dorn matched the general's smile before turning to leave.

Bryson nodded at Val.

"Good to see you. And thanks for making the time," Bryson said in a voice that sounded genuine.

"Glad to be here, sir. Thanks for inviting me."

Val was genuine as well. Now that he was sitting with Bryson, it felt good. Good to be face-to-face with his mentor again.

"This is one of my favorite places in Germany." Bryson looked out at the plowed field and then across the patio. "Started coming here often back when I was stationed in Berlin. I had a buddy in Stuttgart I'd come hang with whenever I could get off the island. He brought me here for the first time, and I have been coming here as often as operations and travel will allow ever since."

A faraway look came over the general as he did the math.

"For more than thirty years, I guess."

Herr Dorn reappeared with a bottle of beer and a cold mug.

"I had to use one of yours," Herr Dorn said to Bryson. "I guess is okay?"

"Yep. This young man is worth it."

Herr Dorn nodded, but gave Val an assessing glance as he set the mug down.

Val watched as he opened the bottle and poured.

The beer was the color of molasses, and dark-brown foam formed as it filled the glass. Herr Dorn held the bottle upside down over the glass mug for a long moment at the end, ensuring every bit had run out before nodding to the general.

"Thanks, Otto."

Herr Dorn nodded and departed, leaving the two men together. Val noticed that Bryson's mug was half full of the same dark beer.

"Otto and his family have been brewing beer for as long as they have run this place," Bryson said. "They do about four or five kinds. Their dark beer is, by far, the best and most well-known. It is renowned throughout Baden-Württemberg."

The general raised his mug.

"Prost," he said, offering the traditional German toast.

Val raised his mug and knocked it against Bryson's. The heavy glasses emitted a satisfying clunk.

"Prost, sir."

Val brought the mug to his nose and inhaled deeply. The pungent tobacco-like aroma swirled into his nose, accompanied by hints of malt and caramel.

Oh, this is going to be good.

Val felt the frothy head of the beer against his nose as he took an unhurried sip. He let the dark liquid linger in his mouth, savoring the perfect balance of malty sweetness, bitter hops, coffee, and dark fruit flavors before swallowing.

Val wiped the froth from his nose as he set the mug down and then looked across the table at Bryson.

"Damn, sir."

"Uh-huh," the general said, smiling.

They both took another large sip in silence. Val wiped beer froth from his nose again.

"Hardest beer to get in Germany," Bryson told him. "The family's brewing capacity is tiny, and they just don't give a damn. So, if you're not a longtime patron worthy enough to be on their coveted allocation list, you're shit out of luck."

"And you're on the allocation?"

"What do you think?"

Val chuckled and took another appreciative sip.

"You hungry?"

"Yes, sir."

"Good. Me too," Bryson said. He looked at Herr Dorn, who was standing next to the French doors, and gave a subtle wave. Dorn nodded and stepped through the doors. Bryson looked back at Val.

"I've already ordered for us, if that's okay with you."

"You're doing good so far, sir."

An hour and a half later, Val pushed back from the table.

"That's it, sir. I've done all I can do."

Bryson surveyed the empty dishes that had formerly held cordon bleu schnitzel, pork steak in a pepper cream sauce, sausage, sauerkraut, egg noodles, carrots, peas, and potatoes.

"I think we did well, son."

Val nodded and took the last sip from his second Dorn dunkle. He would have loved a third, but the two-hour drive back to Garmisch would be hard enough on so full a stomach. The sun had sunk below the horizon, and a calm twilight had settled over Ulm. The dark, linear shadows of the plowed field were expanding, swallowing the land.

It had been a nice evening. Too nice.

Surely, the general didn't invite me here just because he needed company. Val wondered what was coming.

He didn't have to wait long.

The general took the napkin from his lap, folded it, and laid it on his empty plate. He looked around, slowly scanning the entire patio before picking up his plate and setting it to the side. Bryson leaned forward, elbows on the table, and looked at Val.

"I have something to tell you, Rafter. And it's not good."

A pang of anxiety shot through Val. *Am I being reassigned? Kicked out of the program for some reason?* He leaned forward, mirroring the general's posture.

"I promised you I'd let you know if we learned what happened to Zyph Hyka."

The name hit Val like a slap. He hadn't thought of Zyph in months. The soothing atmosphere and activities of Garmisch had pushed his dead friend from his mind.

"Two weeks ago, a United Nations Police squad responded to a disturbance in a small town outside of Kamenica. A group of Serbian thugs were shaking down an Albanian shop, and the shopkeeper's neighbors called for help. The police were good troops. Swedish, I think. They rolled in and kicked ass, taking three of the Serbs into custody. They ran the standard ID and database searches, and one of the Serbs came up hot. Superhot. Turns out the guy was a well-known leader in the Serb underground militia and was wanted across Kosovo in connection with dozens of crimes, including murder.

"So, the Swedes run his name up the flagpole, and soon everybody wants a piece of the bastard. Luckily, our chief of base in Pristina got wind of what was going on and hurried down to Kamenica, where the Serb was being held. He convinced NATO that there may be a lot to learn from the guy and got authorization to make a trade. Maybe lessen the punishment in exchange for valuable information.

"The chief of base took his best interrogator into a cell with the Serbian, and they came out four hours later with a list of intelligence longer than your arm. The son of a bitch sang like a scared little bird."

Bryson paused. He glanced around the patio again.

"He confessed, among other things, to killing Zyph Hyka."

Val took a deep breath and let it out slowly.

"Well. I'm glad they got him."

Bryson looked at Val. His face tightened.

"He also said he was told to do it by the Russians. By an officer in the 13th Tactical Group."

Val blinked several times.

"Who? Which Russian told him to do it?"

"He didn't identify the Russian. Said he didn't know his name. Said all he knew was that he was a Russian officer that would give him jobs from time to time."

"Did he describe him at all? Tall? Fat? Anything?"

"No."

Val examined Bryon's face for a long moment.

"No description at all?" he asked.

"No."

"Well, did they fucking ask? Can we tell them to ask? Let me talk to the guy."

"No," the general said firmly.

"Why not?" Val's voice was rising. He glared at the general.

"Val!" Bryson said in a quiet but sharp voice. He leaned across the table. "I told you because I promised I would," Bryson growled. "Not so you could get involved. Now rein your shit in and don't make me think this was a mistake."

Val's face relaxed slightly. He took a few breaths, then nodded.

"I'm sorry, sir."

Bryson glared, then relaxed slightly.

"It's okay, son. This shit hurts. I know. That's why I wanted to talk in person."

Val leaned back in his chair.

"It really doesn't matter which Russian killed him, anyway," General Bryson said.

"It might."

CHAPTER 28

A week after meeting with General Bryson, Val and the rest of the class were knee deep in final academics. The last component of the course was a series of written exams, which tamped down student activities for a time, including among the group of friends. Val was glad for the diversion of academic stress and the excuse for less interaction with Alexei. He remained troubled by what General Bryson had told him about Zyph's murder. He'd almost convinced himself that it could not have been Alexei, that it had to have been Major Orlov. The realization that he could never be sure, though, anguished him. He didn't know what to do. So he tried to bury the disquiet beneath the stress of final exams.

One evening, as Val was studying alone in his quarters, someone knocked on his door.

"Brooke," Val said as he looked up and down the hallway. "What's up?"

"Can I come in?"

"Yeah, sure," Val said, standing to the side.

Sydney walked in quickly, a strained look on her face.

"You okay?" Val asked.

She walked into his small living room but didn't sit down.

"What's wrong?"

Sydney shook her head and paced back and forth.

"Sydney!"

She stopped pacing. "I'm in trouble."

"Okay. No problem. Tell me what's going on, and we'll fix it."

"I don't think it's fixable." Sydney shook her head.

"I bet it is. Tell me."

Sydney took a deep breath.

"I'm having an affair with Alexei. I'm going to disclose it to the agency. I'm going to list you as a witness."

Val stood motionless, looking back at Sydney.

"Say something," she said.

"Tell me that again."

"I'm having an affair with Alexei, Val," she said, her voice more apologetic this time.

Val nodded once. He took a few steps back until his legs bumped into a chair. He sat down and scratched his head. His eyebrows arched. They hovered for a moment and then sank into sharp angles over his eyes, which stared off into the distance.

Sydney paced again.

"But I thought…" Val said, shifting his stare to Sydney. "I thought… Wait, is that part of the development process with him?"

"No." Sydney shook her head.

"But he is your target, right?"

"No."

Val blinked.

"Then who the hell is?"

"I can't tell you that."

"But you can tell me you're fucking a Russian intelligence officer?"

"How do you know he is intelligence?" Anxiety almost stifled Sydney's voice. "He told me he was an infantry officer."

"Oh, for fuck's sake, Sydney." Val shook his head, anger creeping into his voice. "Everybody here is intelligence!"

"You don't know that."

"You're intelligence! I'm intelligence. You think we're the only ones?"

Sydney opened her mouth to speak, but nothing came out.

"I was with him for six months in Kosovo," Val grumbled. "Trust me, he is intelligence."

"Oh Jesus," Sydney said in a quiet voice.

Val leaned back in his chair.

Sydney sank onto the sofa and put her head in her hands.

"Well, shit," he muttered. "I thought you and I were…"

"What?" Sydney snapped, raising her head. "You thought you and I were what?"

Val sat up, startled by the anger in her voice. "I dunno." He shrugged. "A thing?"

"You thought we were a thing?" Sydney pointed back and forth between them.

"Um…gonna be a thing?"

"Going to be a thing?" Sydney shook her head in disbelief. "Then why the hell, if we were going to be a thing, would you let he and I…"

She hesitated.

"Fuck?" Val said, a sharp edge to his voice.

Sydney lunged off the sofa.

"Fuck you!" Sydney jabbed a finger at Val, inches from his face. "You don't get to judge me!"

"Whoa, Sydney! Easy. I'm not judging anyone here. But you've got to give me a few minutes to catch up with all this."

"Why would you let me and Alexei get involved if you wanted us to be together?" she asked, still leaning over him. "What kind of man does that?"

"What?" Val yelled. Now he was pissed off. "What kind of man?" Val jumped to his feet. Sydney stumbled backward onto the sofa. Val stood over her. Now he was the one pointing. "The kind of man that backs up a friend on a mission. That doesn't get in the way, even though it hurts to watch. The kind of man that respects the fucking job and why we're here!"

"Okay," Sydney said, her voice wavering.

Val lowered his hand and regained his composure. He sulked back to his chair and sat down.

They sat still, both staring at the floor.

"I'm so sorry, Val."

"Me too," Val said, not looking at her. "If I had known…"

"You know I couldn't tell you my target."

"You could have told me Alexei was *not* your target." Val leveled his eyes at Sydney.

Her eyes welled up, but she maintained her composure.

"I should've done that." she whispered.

Val rubbed his eyes and then looked at Sydney. He stood up, walked over to his kitchen, and returned with two shot glasses of whiskey. He gave one to Sydney and went back to his chair.

Val downed his whiskey.

Sydney did the same.

"You're not going to disclose shit," he said.

"What?"

"You're not going to disclose shit to the agency."

Val stood and walked over to Sydney and took her shot glass from her as she digested what he'd said. He refilled both glasses, returned hers to her hand, and sat back down.

"I have to disclose it."

"No, you don't." Val knocked back the whiskey. "Who else knows about this?"

"No one besides you. Except Alexei, of course."

Val grimaced.

Sydney drained her shot.

"Sydney, if you disclose this relationship, your career as a field agent is over. You'll be assigned to a desk, will probably never work overseas again, and will be under the microscope of the agency's counterintelligence assholes for the rest of your shitty career."

Val let that sink in before continuing.

"You're too valuable to the country in the field. They would not have sent you here on this mission if they didn't view you as a strong case officer. How is your mission going?"

"Really well, actually."

"Exactly." Val smiled briefly for the first time since Sydney came to his room. "You learn from this, move on, and we keep our fucking mouths shut. I think you're strong enough not to let this lapse in judgment affect your future decision-making. I'm not going to let you waste your career and potential positive impact on the agency's mission."

"I don't know," Sydney said. "I don't know if I can do that."

"Do what?"

"Not tell."

"You told me."

Sydney sat in silence.

"I wouldn't be suggesting this if I had any doubt," Val said. "If I wasn't committed."

Sydney thought for a long moment.

"What is it?" Val asked.

"What if Alexei tells his side?"

Val thought about it and then asked, "Do you think he is developing you?"

Sydney's shoulders sagged as if she were considering the possibility for the first time.

She was quiet for a moment.

Val waited.

"I really don't think so," Sydney finally said. She pointed at her head. "I'm rerunning every conversation we ever had. It just doesn't seem like development."

Val's eyes narrowed, considering her words.

"If it wasn't you, then who was it? I guarantee you he is developing someone for recruitment."

"I don't know," Sydney said. "But I don't think it's me."

"And even if it is you, so what? They make runs at Americans all the time. He got nowhere and has nothing to report back with. For all you know, he is sweating telling his own people as well."

Sydney's brow furrowed with worry.

"Get in front of it," Val said. "Tell him you're disclosing the relationship."

"But you said not to disclose it."

"That's right. But he won't know that. All he'll know is that he can't hold what happened over you because you have already told the folks that matter."

Sydney nodded slightly.

"You have to tell him in an innocent way," Val said. "Like you're so new to this international romance stuff, and this is what I said you should do. Like it's all such an adventure."

Sydney took a deep breath.

"Tell him it's what you told me to do?"

"Yes. He won't fuck with me."

Val got up and took her shot glass. He refilled them and then walked back in silence, letting her get her head around it.

Sydney nodded as Val put her shot glass in her hand.

"Then you're going to have to beat the poly," he said, standing over her.

US intelligence officers are subjected to regular polygraph tests, particularly after overseas assignments. Questions about contacts and relationships with foreign nationals are always thoroughly covered.

"Shit," she whispered to herself, looking into her whiskey.

"You can do it."

Val turned and walked back to his chair.

"I'm scared," she said before downing her whiskey.

"Don't be. If I didn't think you could do it, I would not be recommending this. I'd just be helping you fill out the disclosure paperwork. But you can do it. And it's the right thing to do."

"How in the world is this the right thing to do?"

"Preserving your career and the ability to make an impact is the right thing. Period."

"And you really think this will work?"

"I do. If you do one more thing."

"What's that?"

"End it," Val said. "End it with him for good. Tonight. If you let it go on, it will get messier and messier, and you'll be stuck with no way out."

"I can do that." Sydney nodded.

"Promise me."

"I promise. I'll end it."

They looked at each other until Sydney said, "Thank you."

Val didn't respond. He drank his shot of whiskey and looked at the floor.

"And I'm sorry, Val. So sorry."

*

Val tried to avoid Alexei for the last week of the course. The test schedule made it easy. Val would claim he was helping someone study or trying to get ready for the tests himself. When exam week was over, though, Val was out of excuses. It was mid-May, and Garmisch was getting warmer and greener as summer approached. Hikers replaced skiers in town, and the restaurants set their outside tables out in the sun. Alexei asked Val to meet him at the Local Cure for a few goodbye drinks. Alexei was leaving Germany the next morning.

"So, where do you go next, Val?"

It was a bright afternoon, and they were sitting outside to absorb the last of the sun, which would soon fall beneath the mountains to the west.

"I'm not sure yet. To be honest, I'm trying to get them to let me stay here for another six months or so."

"So you can ski?" Alexei's eyes lit up. "I am jealous!"

"We'll see if I can pull it off. I'm not optimistic."

Alexei watched as Val took a long sip of beer. He waited until Val had put his large glass beer mug back on the table before saying, "Val, may I ask you something?"

"Sure."

"Are you mad at me?"

"Am I mad at you?"

"Let's not play games, Val. Not after all we have been through together."

The sky blazed orange as the sun sank beneath the mountain peaks and a long shadow crept up the valley toward Garmisch and the Local Cure.

"This is because of Brooke," Alexei said.

Val stared at Alexei. He said nothing.

"She told me she told you about us," Alexei said with a pained face. "I wish she had not done that."

Shit, I told her to get in front of it and take away his leverage, but this is awkward.

Val nodded. "I bet you do."

"I do because I wanted to tell you myself. I wanted to tell you from the beginning. I think she did too."

"It's strange, then, isn't it? That neither of you did."

"Val, if I had known you had feelings for her, I would never have started anything," Alexei said, holding up his hands in a helpless gesture. "But you said nothing of this to me."

Because I thought she was developing you, asshole.

"And then, after she tells you, you avoid me," Alexei said with hurt in his voice. "Why not come to me? Tell me that you're angry. Two men, two friends, should be able to discuss such things."

"Discuss?"

"Yes," Alexei said, as if he were making progress.

Val shook his head and took a long swig of beer.

"I would come to you," Alexei said.

"Give me a break."

Val shook his head and took another long swig of beer.

"I would!"

"To discuss it?" Val put his mug down a little too hard. Beer sloshed over the top.

Alexei watched the beer run down Val's hand and spread across the long wooden table.

"Now that you mention it, there is something I'd like to discuss," Val said, eyes narrowing as he stared at Alexei. "How about we discuss Zyph Hyka?"

Alexei leaned back slightly.

"Zyph Hyka," Val said slowly.

Alexei sat motionless.

Val glared at Alexei.

The silence between them extended.

A look of sadness crept over Alexei's face.

"Val!" a voice came from the adjacent street. "Alexei!"

It was Burian. Val and Alexei looked at the ground as the Ukrainian walked up to their table.

"Beautiful evening, right, guys?" Burian said, oblivious to the tension between the two men. "May I join?"

Val stood up. He looked at Alexei for a heartbeat and then turned to Burian.

"Take my place, Burian. I have to leave."

"Okay, Val," Burian said, walking around the table. "You sure?"

"Yeah," Val said, as he turned away from Alexei. "I'm sure."

CHAPTER 29

"Nicolae, I can't thank you enough," Sydney said, pushing back from her laptop and the conference table. The last slide of a presentation beamed on the wall. The mountains loomed outside the window. "I could have never done this without you."

"It was my pleasure," Nicolae said. "Sincerely."

"I hope I didn't get you in too much trouble back home."

"Don't worry about that. I never take holiday. They owed me a couple of days, at the very least."

"And your wife?" Sydney asked, feigning hesitance. "At home alone with two young daughters. How did she take it? You staying to hike a few days with friends?"

"They may be a harder case." Nicolae chuckled.

"Oh no."

"No. This is not something to worry about," Nicolae shook his head. "I have gifts for her. For all the girls, for that matter. I have learned, with women, these go a long way to getting a man out of the hound's house."

Sydney laughed.

"I'm sorry. This was a bad thing to say about women. I joke, you know."

"It's okay. Really, it's. And it's actually true."

"Good," Nicolae said with relief.

"And I appreciate you not telling either your wife or your boss the real purpose of you staying."

Sydney had asked Nicolae to help her with an anti-proliferation presentation she told him she had to give to her boss shortly after she returned to the States. She told him it was highly sensitive and that he should not share his participation with anyone, including his family or boss.

It was a lie. There was no presentation assignment from her boss.

Sydney's ask was one of a series of development activities she had run on Nicolae. As a case officer prepares an asset for recruitment, they'll ask certain favors of the individual to both deepen the unique relationship the two share and to test the individual's willingness to go outside the normal range of their permissible activities. This process of creating "validation tests" is an important step in demonstrating the individual's suitability for recruitment, and a key component for receiving the green light from headquarters to move forward.

In Nicolae's case, his agreement not to discuss details of this relationship with his wife or workplace in Moldova, as insignificant as he thought it may be, was a continuation of little steps that Sydney hoped would prepare fertile ground for the coming conversation.

"But it's 'doghouse,'" Sydney said, still chuckling. "When you're in trouble, you're in the doghouse. Not the 'hound's house.'"

"Ah! Doghouse. Yes!" Nicolae said eagerly. He loved learning English idioms. "Thank you."

Sydney nodded. She stood and began to collect her things.

"I will be right back," Nicolae said. "I must walk the dog."

Nicolae smiled, proud of himself, and left for the latrine.

Thanks very much, Val, she thought as she shook her head. Val had taught Nicolae the American toilet slang during one of the long days at the ski bar.

She hated it. But Nicolae loved it. She didn't have the heart to tell him to quit.

Sydney looked at her watch. The thought of Val reminded her he was leaving today for a TDY assignment. He would be gone almost a month, missing her departure from Garmisch in a few days. She'd told him she would meet him at the train station to say goodbye. It was going to be tight. She had less than an hour to get there.

Sydney closed her laptop and took a deep breath.

Here we go.

Sydney's entire mission at the Marshall Center had led to this moment. The incident with Alexei had almost derailed it. If it weren't for Val, she would be back in the States right now, beginning her life as a pariah within the agency, or worse.

Instead, she was on the verge of a career-making achievement. If she could pull it off.

The CIA sent Sydney to the Marshall Center to develop and recruit Nicolae Muntenau.

Born in March 1969, Nicolae was an ethnic Moldovan and the son of a policeman and schoolteacher. Raised in the capital of Chişinău, Nicolae came of age at the end of the Cold War.

It was a tumultuous time for the small, landlocked country. Sandwiched between Romania and Ukraine, Moldova had struggled to protect its integrity since the fourteenth century. The collapse of the Soviet Union offered the hope of self-determination but doused the region in chaos.

In high school, Nicolae fell in love with Sasha, the daughter of struggling winemakers to the north of Chişinău. One year younger than Nicolae, Sasha fell for the earnest city boy. Nicolae graduated and followed his father into the police force while he waited for Sasha. He was eager to serve his country and to provide for his future bride. They married a few months after Sasha graduated in the fall of 1989.

In 1990, as the newlyweds started building a life together, Moldova declared its independence from the Soviet Union and held free elections. But the small state was not immune to the ethnic and historical riptides that were tearing the Soviet Union apart. On the eastern side of the Dniester River, the predominantly ethnic Russian and Ukrainian region of Moldova, called Transnistria, declared its own independence from Moldova.

Few people in the world would have known much about this argument over 1,607 remote and mountainous square miles between the Dniester River and the Ukrainian border. But in November 1990, as young Nicolae Muntenau kissed his wife goodbye and left Chişinău to lead a Moldovan police platoon in combat in the Transnistrian War, the CIA and others got very nervous.

The narrow strip of contested land was also home to the Soviet 14th Guards Army, its large equipment and weapons stores, and a cache of Soviet nuclear weapons. The world's post–Cold War arms control nightmare was beginning.

The 14th Guards Army backed their ethnic Russian and Ukrainian kin in the conflict, dooming Moldova's efforts to maintain sovereignty over its territory on the east side of the Dniester. By the time the small conflict ended, Nicolae had been wounded twice, and the breakaway government in Tiraspol, the self-declared capital of Transnistria, had maintained its de facto independence.

Moldova had not only lost face, but it had also lost control of most of its heavy industry. Punitive Russian sanctions after the conflict strangled Moldova's wine industry and severely disrupted the fledgling state's economy. Recovery would take almost a decade. Nonetheless, Moldova pressed forward with free market reform.

As Moldova continued its western trajectory, the CIA assessed the developing situation in the region. It was not good. Transnistria still had enough conventional weaponry and military equipment within its borders to outfit several armies. Ethnic and regional conflict, fomented and manipulated by international players, blanketed the remote, mountainous region in shadows. And the CIA had no assets in the area it could leverage.

Nicolae returned home to his wife after the cease-fire was declared in 1992. He'd gained a reputation as a fierce fighter and coolheaded small unit commander. His first daughter was born that fall.

A Moldovan patriot, Nicolae was excited by his country's democratic future and supported the difficult, but foundational, economic reforms. He was a believer. And, after he'd healed from his wounds, he continued his service as a junior member of the country's fledgling defense community.

Nicolae slowly developed a unique portfolio in the Moldovan government. After the war, while serving in government, he earned his college degree with a focus on international relations and security studies. Nicolae also celebrated the birth of his second daughter. As Moldova sought a peaceful resolution to its Transnistrian problem and worked to improve its relationships with Russia, Ukraine, and Romania, Nicolae's veteran pedigree, intelligence, and ability to form genuine relationships quickly established him as a valuable emissary.

In early 2000, before reporting to the Marshall Center, Nicolae was appointed to an important role in the Moldovan Ministry of Defense focused on counter-proliferation. With access to the most sensitive intelligence in the region; visibility into legitimate arms deals originating in Transnistria; and working relationships with Russian, Ukrainian, and Romanian counterparts, he was the kind of target that made the CIA's mouth water. When the agency learned he would be attending the course in Garmisch, they decided to run a play. And they picked Sydney to run it.

Sydney had proven her chops in Moscow, but this had been a stretch assignment. Ten weeks was a ridiculously short amount of time to develop an asset. But spared the time and effort of having to spot a potential asset, Sydney had gone to work on Nicolae from the moment she'd gotten to Garmisch. She thought he was ready but was shocked when Langley agreed. She almost wished they hadn't.

But this was exactly the kind of high-visibility recruitment she'd been positioning herself for over the course of her full, albeit short, career. The director himself had sat in on her pitch for permission to recruit.

I crushed that pitch, she thought, looking out at the mountains, *and I'm going to crush this one.*

"Beautiful, yes?"

Sydney turned to see Nicolae standing in the doorway.

"Yes. I'm going to miss it."

"Me too," Nicolae said, walking into the room. "Though, I will tell you, our Moldovan mountains are just as beautiful. Different in some ways. But just as beautiful."

"I'd love to see them someday."

"I would love for you to see them as well. Sasha and I and the girls could take you on some wonderful hikes."

"Someday, perhaps."

"Yes," Nicolae said. He gathered his things from the conference table and put them in his satchel.

Sydney walked over behind Nicolae and shut the door.

Nicolae turned at the noise. He smiled at Sydney.

"Are we not done?"

"I hope not," Sydney said as she walked back to the conference table and sat next to Nicolae. She gestured for him to sit as well.

"Nicolae, I want you to know how grateful I am for your help on this project," she began. "More than that, I'm really grateful for our friendship."

"I'm grateful too, Brooke."

"From the beginning," Sydney continued, "From the first day we met, I felt a strong alignment between you and me. Shared values. Shared visions of how the world could be. Shared passions for freedom and democracy. Shared professions, even. We both work in the defense and security organizations of our countries, trying to keep those values, visions, and passions safe from harm."

Nicolae nodded.

"And we have a shared understanding of the danger that confronts those things we love."

Sydney paused, giving time for her declarations of alignment and commonality to take hold.

Nicolae looked at her.

Sydney couldn't decide if she saw puzzlement on his face or not.

She charged ahead.

"I feel like I can really trust you, Nicolae. Can I?"

"Yes." Nicolae nodded. "I am your friend, Brooke. You can trust me."

"Good. And I think you trust me as well?"

"Yes. I do trust you."

"I hope so. Because I believe you and I can do important work together. Very important work."

Nicolae leaned back in his chair.

His radar just started screaming at him.

"You said we were friends, Nicolae," Sydney said. "You're right. We are friends. So, I have to tell you, I'm a US intelligence officer."

Nicolae sat motionless.

"I think you were starting to figure that out recently," Sydney said, complimenting him, hoping to get him to drop the expressionless mask his face had become.

Nothing.

Sydney got nervous.

"I want to work with you, Nicolae." Sydney leaned forward in her chair and looked him in the eye. "We both share grave concern for the Russian influence that has permeated the Moldovan government. This influence is a threat to the peaceful future of Moldova, and its partnership with the United States. Together, you and I can counter this threat."

This isn't going well, Sydney thought, trying not to let Nicolae's intense face throw off her rehearsed pitch.

"I want you and I to work closely together going forward so that we can make more progress towards the goals we are each working on independently now. I want us to work together to achieve the things that Moldova cannot accomplish on its own."

She paused, observing him closely.

Nicolae blinked rapidly a few times.

Need to start spelling it out for him.

"I would like you to gather certain pieces of information that can make a difference. That can make the difference you and I are both currently working on our own to achieve. I want us to work together. Starting now."

Sydney could tell that Nicolae's mind was racing. But he wasn't saying anything. She couldn't tell if he was close to saying yes or about to run out screaming.

She needed to know.

But she didn't want to push yet. It was a lot for a person to process. She knew that.

Better to play it cool with him, she thought as she slowly leaned back in her chair. *Don't push.*

Nicolae's brow furrowed.

"I do not understand. What do you mean, 'gather certain pieces of information'?"

"Things that we, the United States government, need to know or confirm in order to make the best decisions possible," Sydney said in her most nonchalant voice. "To take the best and most effective actions possible for the betterment of both our countries."

She waited half a moment before adding, "Things that we couldn't know or would not be able to confirm without your help."

"Help?"

"Without your access or relationships."

"Well, of course I will help you," Nicolae said, smiling nervously. "I helped you today. Have I not said I will help you in the future?"

"Yes. You have said that. And I appreciate it. But I want us to work together more closely, and confidentially. To do more together. To have a greater impact. And to do this, we need to have the kind of relationship where I can ask you to get information of value to both of us. Information that might be considered very sensitive by Moldova or its allies, but which will help to counter the Russian threat. The information and partnership I'm proposing would help achieve the aims you and I are so passionate about."

"Brooke, if you are making some kind of…" Nicolae hesitated, his eyes darted around the room. "If you are asking me to spy for you…I will not do this."

The sparring begins, Sydney thought, relieved for an instant before a wave of anxiety passed through her.

"Sparring" is an Agency term for the resistance and counterargument that a potential asset puts up when pitched. Sydney had been through it twice before in Moscow. It was the make-or-break phase of the pitch and was nerve-racking for the case officer. If it wasn't dealt with appropriately, the sparring could derail the whole pitch.

Nerve-racking as it was, though, most case officers welcomed it. It was a sign that their potential asset had a moral compass, a brain that assessed risk and necessity, and a deliberate decision-making process. An asset that offered no resistance when confronted with an invitation to betray their country was suspect. The one pitch Sydney had given that didn't encounter sparring hadn't felt right. The asset was too eager, too rudderless, and had flamed out within six months.

Sparring was so common that it was a training topic at the Farm, and case officers actively prepared for it. A successful sparring response is built on two components: the case officer's ability to make a strong argument for their aligned values and vision, and the potential asset's assessment of the case officer's professionalism and trustworthiness, as they are being asked to entrust that officer with their life.

In Moscow, Sydney had role-played before all her pitches. Getting in a room with a few other case officers or even analysts and letting them respond to the pitch, forcing Sydney to react in real time, was an invaluable exercise.

Unfortunately, on her own at the Marshall Center, this preparation technique was not available to Sydney. But she'd run through this conversation dozens of times in her head over the past week, war-gaming each point, trying to anticipate all the ways he might respond.

"I wouldn't call it spying, Nicolae."

"I will do whatever is in my power to help you, always. But it must be within the rules of my country," he said, shaking his head at the thought.

"Nicolae, I'd never ask you to do anything against your own country. I just might ask you to share information that others in your country may not want you to share. Because they don't have the same relationship you and I have. The same level of trust. Or the same shared goals."

Nicolae shook his head.

"I do not like this conversation."

"What don't you like about it? We're talking about all the things we could accomplish together."

"Why can't we continue to work together as official liaisons for our respective governments?" Nicolae said with a sudden excitement in his voice. "We can accomplish all of our goals in this way."

"Nicolae," Sydney said in a sobering tone. "Not everyone in your government is aligned with the goals of eliminating Russian influence and fighting corruption."

A deflated look came over Nicolae.

"Many people in Moldova are making a lot of money off your country's dilemmas and Transnistria's chaos and weapons stockpiles."

Nicolae nodded sadly.

"They will work against you and me. We can't let them win. We have to be smarter than them. More committed. Bolder."

Nicolae sat still and quiet, looking at the floor. Sydney let him stew for a moment before continuing.

"Nicolae, I want you to know that I thought long and hard about this. I would not ask you if I didn't trust you, and if I didn't think it was necessary and worth it. I'm proposing this next step for us for two reasons. The first is that we can do so much more together if we have the power of the US government fully behind us. And the second is, I can provide you so much more protection if the US government knows we are working together."

Nicolae looked at Sydney. She waited, but he said nothing. Still, she thought she could sense him weakening, warming to the concept.

"I value our partnership. I trust it. And I want us to work together, unfettered by what some corrupt bureaucrat in Chișinău thinks about what information should be shared or not.

"I want you and I to blow up the corruption in your region, not to be constrained by it. I want Moldova to regain control of Transnistria. And I want the Russians to leave. For good.

"Therefore, I think we need to be bold. Together."

"I will not betray Moldova," Nicolae said, pointing a finger at Sydney.

"Good! That is the furthest thing from my intent. I want to help Moldova."

Nicolae leaned back in his chair. His emotion seemed to have receded. But Sydney could see that his mind still raced. After a moment of silence, Nicolae said, "I am sorry Sydney, this is not just about me. I must think of my family. This is too risky. I will not do it."

It's time, Sydney thought. She had another card to play, one that she saved for this moment.

"Do you want Daria and Eniko to go to college in America?"

His chin raised slightly at the mention of his daughters. Eight and six years old, they were the center of his and Sasha's life, and Sydney knew it.

Sydney nodded and told him, "We could make that happen."

"How?"

"You're our friend, Nicolae. I told you, we won't be constrained."

She paused.

Nicolae's expression changed. His mind running a wholly different calculus now.

He wants to.

"And think of what we'll have accomplished in the next ten years," Sydney said, trying to keep the momentum. "When Daria is ready to go to college."

"Think of the Western, global perspective she and Eniko will get when they study in America at places like Harvard or Stanford."

Nicolae tried not to react to the biggest American brand names in education. But his eyes betrayed excitement.

Sydney turned to look out the window and let it hang in the air like that for a moment. The sun was getting lower, and the shadows were creeping up the mountains.

When she turned to look back at Nicolae, she could see the conflict in his face.

He is close.

"Nicolae."

He looked up from the table.

"I need to leave soon," she said. "And I'm sorry to do this to you, but I need to know. There will not be another chance at this. If I report back that you have declined, they will move on. Your opportunity will be lost. I told them you were the one who could truly make a difference. And that we could depend on you. But I need to know before I leave this room if we have an agreement."

"This is not something I can do lightly, Brooke!"

Nicolae stood up and walked to the window, his eyes fixed on the mountains.

Sydney wanted to press but made herself stay quiet. *Better to say nothing, to let him think, than say the wrong thing.*

Awkward seconds ticked by.

"Do you know what will happen to me if I am caught?" he finally asked, still facing the window.

Here we go.

The danger of spying on one's own country affects potential assets differently. Many never get past it and walk away from the pitch. As Sydney prepared her pitch for Nicolae, she planned for this objection.

"That won't happen, Nicolae," Sydney said definitively. "We won't let that happen."

He rubbed his eyes.

"Do you know what will happen, though?" he asked, without turning from the window.

Sydney didn't take the bait, she sat in silence.

"I will be executed. Shot as a traitor."

She stood up and walked over to Nicolae by the window. She put her hand on his shoulder and looked in his eyes as he turned his head toward her.

"I am not going to minimize the risk here, Nicolae. It is real. I know because risk is something I live with every day. But I live with it willingly because I believe the bigger purpose is worth it.

"I've put myself at risk by disclosing my true identity to you."

Taking her hand from his shoulder, Sydney shrugged and smiled at Nicolae. She looked out the window.

Can't rush. This has to be a slow pivot. Make him believe the risk is shared. That the purpose is also. And that it is worth it.

Sydney looked at the mountains, only the very tops were still bright in the glancing sunlight.

"I have to tell you, though," she continued, lowering her gaze to the shadows at the bottom of the mountains. "I find comfort in the fact that I don't bear the risk alone. I am part of a team. I have been scared at times, in some very close calls. But the team always came through for me. I want you to be part of that team.

"I feel like you already are, really. That is why I felt comfortable taking the risk of revealing myself to you. I feel like you would never let me down. And I promise we will never let you down."

Sydney looked at Nicolae. His face was pained. He stared out the window.

"You have to make your own decision," she said. "But for me, working on a team that is trying to do good is worth the risk.

Nicolae turned his head an met her gaze.

"And what would happen to my family? If I am found out. What would happen to them?"

This is good. He is not thinking about himself.

Don't hesitate.

"They would retain the full support of the United States of America," she said in a solid voice. "They would not just be safe. They would be looked after."

"You would get them to America?"

"Nicolae, I will never make a promise to you that I cannot keep. What I can tell you now is that they will be safe and looked after. Over time, as you and I prove your value, I can work on this part for you. I have no doubt that our contributions together will merit a special outcome for your family."

Sydney broke eye contact. She turned her head back toward the window to obscure her face. She did not want Nicolae to see any hint of her internal struggle.

She was not lying. Not really. But she was suggesting things she could not commit to. Not on her own. And she was planting a seed of hope she knew she would use to manipulate him going forward.

Sydney understood that Nicolae was a patriot and a family man. She carefully structured her pitch to leverage both. By casting it as an appeal to a common cause, she aligned it to his patriotism. And by planting visions of benefits to his family, she aligned it to his sense of duty as a father. This combination was compelling to Nicolae, and she knew it.

To see it working on a man she had come to know, like, and respect evoked a twinge of guilt she had not expected during her preparation.

This is what I am supposed to do.

This is my mission.

She swallowed the feeling and delivered the final blow.

"What is the risk of not doing it, Nicolae?" she asked, turning her body from the window to face him.

He looked at her, his expression pained.

"Because you are right," she said, stepping closer to him and lowering her voice. "There is risk on the path of us working together. But what if you don't accept? And you and I do not help to stave off the Russians?"

Pause. Let him catch up. Keep saying you and I.

Nicolae watched her turn and start back to the table.

Sydney spoke in a slow, ominous tone as she walked away from him.

"Because, as you and I know, they are coming. Whether it is simple meddling, covert operations, or open aggression, they are coming. What is the risk to your country then? Or to your family? Your daughters? What kind of future will they have in a Russian occupied Moldova?"

Nicolae almost flinched at the comment.

He rubbed his forehead as she started to collect her things and put them in her bag. She moved deliberately, signaling the final count down, grabbing one thing at a time and putting it away.

"And how will you feel when that happens?" Sydney asked, continuing to gather her things. "Knowing that you could have done more?"

Framed by the window, dark mountains loomed behind Nicolae. No sunlight reached them anymore. His silhouette stood motionless, rooted in place by the agonizing crossroads.

Sydney studied him in silence.

He needs one last push.

She placed the final folder in her briefcase and then walked back to him.

He watched her approach, still frozen in place.

Sydney took his hand and stood close to him.

"I know this is a lot," she said, holding his hand in both of hers and leaning in. She spoke almost in a whisper, inches from his ear, eyes locked on his, in the voice of a trusted confidant. "It is sudden and hard, and I wish there was another way. But there is not.

"Only you can make this decision. But, as your friend, I have to say…all I see is goodness here. It is good for your country. And it is good for your family. Doesn't that make it a good thing that we would do together?"

Nicolae's head leaned closer to hers.

"If I do this, Brooke…" he hesitated, his eyes searching hers for something.

Sydney's heart leapt, but she masked her face.

Yes, Nicolae! Yes! Do it…

"If I do this…I need your word. My family's safety and well-being come first. Always."

I've got him!

"You have my word, Nicolae. Your family will always be our first priority."

Nicolae took a deep breath and let it out slowly. Sydney felt him release the last of his resistance.

"Okay," he said, his voice low. "I will do it. I will work with you, Brooke."

Sydney embraced him.

He hugged her back.

"Thank you!" Sydney said, stepping back. She smiled, a hand on each of his shoulders. "Nicolae, we will do so much good together."

Nicolae was smiling, glad to have the conflict behind him. "I am excited too, Brooke. Very much so."

"Good. Now, there are a couple of formalities we must get out of the way," she said, turning and walking back to the table.

"Formalities?"

She dug a piece of paper out of her bag and motioned to him to join her at the table as she sat.

"It's the government, after all," Sydney said, rolling her eyes and placing the piece of paper on the table in front of him as he sat next to her.

"To get you the most possible resources and protection, I need your signature on an agreement."

"A signature?" Nicolae asked with incredulity. "Are you serious?"

"I am," Sydney said with a shrug.

And she was. Sydney could not decide if she thought it was ridiculous or not, but Langley always wanted a signature on some kind of agreement. The wording of the agreement didn't matter. Sydney had written the agreement for Nicolae as a consulting contract. It never mentioned Nicolae by name, referring instead to "the consultant." Likewise, it never mentioned the US government, only "the client." And the services were a meaningless jumble of corporate consultant speak. "Provide expertise" and "highlight areas of synergy" and, Sydney's favorite, "syndicate learnings across platforms." She wasn't even sure what the last one meant.

Sydney leaned over and signed on one of the signature lines. She smiled at Nicolae and handed him the pen.

"I just need you to sign here." She pointed at one of the signature lines.

The piece of paper in front of Nicolae carried no weight whatsoever within the US government. Presenting it to anyone anywhere would only get you laughed out of their office.

Except at Langley, which insisted case officers get such a signed document from every new asset at the pitch meeting. As ridiculous as the document was, Langley had learned long ago to respect the ritual. Getting the asset to take a pen in hand and sign something tapped into the ancient dynamics of agreement and commitment. It was, in a sense, their first post-recruitment validation test.

"Look, Nicolae," she said in an almost apologetic voice. "This document is actually really important. I have to get it back to headquarters so that they can start planning your support."

Nicolae hesitated. His *are you fucking serious* facial expression pained Sydney. This was the problem with the requirement. It gummed up the asset.

"It has my signature on it, Nicolae," she said in a coaching voice, putting her hand on his shoulder. "You don't need to sign yours. Just sign anything. You can sign, 'Mister X,' if you want. I'll make it work at headquarters."

Langley didn't love it when case officers employed Sydney's "just sign anything" technique. But it was a common practice among case officers, and Langley had learned to accept it.

Nicolae looked at Sydney.

She nodded.

"Let's do this," she said, smiling.

Nicolae signed: "Mister X." He put down the pen and nodded.

Sydney took the piece of paper and put it in her bag. She looked at her watch. Val's train left soon. She pushed his departure out of her mind. She had to stay focused.

"Okay, Nicolae. Listen carefully."

She paused and made eye contact. It was important that he retained this part.

"I know that this has been a very emotional meeting for both of us. But I need you to focus on the things I am about to tell you."

Nicolae nodded. "I am listening."

"You and I won't speak again for a few weeks. Zero contact. No email. No phone calls. No nothing. Similar to the way I asked you not to disclose our meeting today in any email or phone conversation, this is how we'll communicate going forward. We're going to arrange every meeting in advance and avoid any contact in between. This is for your protection, Nicolae. Do you understand?"

"Yes. I understand."

"Okay," Sydney said. "I'll be in Odesa in three weeks. I arrive on Wednesday the seventh of June and will leave on Sunday the eleventh. You and I will meet on Friday the ninth at this address at eight a.m. in Illichivsk."

Sydney didn't spell it out for Nicolae, but this would be his re-recruitment meeting and, as long as nothing went off the rails, a detailed asset training meeting to set the conditions for the clandestine relationship they had just begun. The follow-up meeting was another of Langley's best practices and always followed shortly after the main recruitment meeting. The agency found it was good to meet with a potential asset again quickly before their doubts or second thoughts got the better of them.

Best case, the meeting ended up being a very matter-of-fact session to repeat the high-level alignment and goals and establish the protocols and fieldcraft that the case officer and agent would use together. Worst case, it was a redo of the whole recruitment. The case officer faced the objections, sparring, and refusals all over again. Sydney was hoping this pitch would find fertile ground within Nicolae and their re-recruitment meeting in June would be smooth. Either way, she would be ready.

Sydney slid a slip of paper across the table.

"I need you to memorize it right now."

Nicolae looked at the address and then back at Sydney.

"You run your country's counter-proliferation program," Sydney said. "Illichivsk is one of the leakiest ports in the world for the arms black market."

Nicolae nodded.

"How often do you go there?" she asked him.

"At least once a month. I meet with Ukrainian counterparts to coordinate operations. We also run a joint port inspection program together."

"Perfect. So it will look completely routine for you to visit Illichivsk in June."

"Yes," Nicolae said.

"Come up with a reason."

"I will."

"Good," Sydney said, looking at her watch again. "Now. The address. Memorize it."

Nicolae looked at the piece of paper. The intense look on his face made Sydney smile. Despite being a world-weary veteran that had been wounded twice in combat, Nicolae could still give the air of an earnest college boy.

Sydney took a quiet, deep breath as Nicolae studied the address.

There was one more step. And it was usually the hardest.

"How are we doing?" she asked him.

"Good. Is memorized."

"Let's hear it."

"Fifty-five, Eighth Line, Illichivsk."

"When?"

"Eight a.m., Friday, the ninth of June."

"Good." Sydney nodded.

Nicolae smiled.

"I know this is not comfortable, Nicolae," Sydney said, ready to take on the next piece. "And I know it involves risk. And I appreciate it. Everyone I work with appreciates it. We want you to know you can trust us and that we value you. We don't expect you to do this for free."

Nicolae's eyes narrowed slightly.

"What do you mean?"

"I mean, we value you. We value the risks you're taking."

Sydney pulled an envelope out of her pocket. She tried to hand it to Nicolae.

"Brooke?" Nicolae said with reproach. "Are you trying to give me money?"

Sydney was at once relieved and daunted. In reality, one never wanted the asset to accept money easily the first time. It should, with a good person, grate against their conscience. Also, someone that took it too easily would be easy to lure away with more money. Or they might even already be taking it from someone else as well.

"I'm not giving you anything, Nicolae. The money is a resource to support the mission we're undertaking together."

"No," Nicolae said sternly, shaking his head. "As I told you. We are on same team. I do not need money."

"I know you don't need it. But we cannot expect you to take time away from your family to gather information without us providing support for whatever you may need."

Nicolae shook his head.

Had it been up to her, Sydney would have skipped the money at this stage. She was that sure that Nicolae was in, and she was confident she could get him to start taking money in the coming months. But the exchange of money with the asset was another foundational element cementing the relationship in the eyes of the CIA.

Not for blackmail. Unlike the Russian's love of kompromat as a means for securing the full compliance of their assets, the agency never did that. The money was not for overt leverage. It was another of the rituals of espionage the CIA had learned to respect and rely upon. They wanted the relationship to be as serious as possible to the asset, and for there to be no mistaking how important it was, what they'd entered into, or what the stakes were. It was the symbolic demonstration of an asset putting "skin in the game."

The best expression of that skin in spy games, after thousands of years, remained money.

Sydney knew HQ would not be happy if she didn't get Nicolae to take the money, and that it would impede her being able to expose Nicolae to more advanced tradecraft tools such as a covert communications protocol. The CIA would want additional validation before entrusting an asset with those sensitive resources.

Also, absent an exchange of money, Nicolae would not be the same high-quality, pristine scalp for her to parade victoriously around the agency. And she really wanted that.

Sydney looked at her watch. She was definitely going to miss Val's train now.

An hour later, having successfully concluded the seminal meeting, Sydney walked out of the Marshall Center's Plenary building and into the cool summer air of the Bavarian evening. Nicolae had left fifteen minutes earlier, with the agency's money in his pocket.

It was, by every measure, a successful recruitment.

Sydney tried to contain her excitement, cloaking her face in an expressionless mask. On the inside, though, she was doing somersaults.

She'd just successfully developed and recruited a high-priority asset in record time. And she'd done it right under the army's noses at their precious ivory tower, the "off-limits" Marshall Center. She wanted to pump her fists, to spike a football, something.

She didn't, though.

She walked deliberately back to her flat, trying not to think about missing Val's train.

*

Val swayed with the train as it made its way north out of the Alps toward Munich. The sun was high in the sky, illuminating the mountains to the left and right of the train and shimmering off the grass in the flat valley.

Val's mood was not as bright.

Val pulled out his cell phone and listened to Sydney's voice mail again.

"Stepping into a meeting where I can't have my phone on," she said in a hushed voice on the first message. "I'm sure you understand. It's going to be tight. But I should just make it to the train station before you leave. I really want to see you. Keeping my fingers crossed."

Val shook his head and listened to the next one.

"I'm so sorry. This thing went much longer than I expected. When we see each other again, I'll tell you about it and you will understand. I wish I could say more. But I can't. I miss you already. Call me tonight?"

Val put the phone down and closed his eyes. He could hear the excitement in her voice. Whatever it was, had gone well. Part of him was happy for her. But mostly, he was frustrated and hurt. He let his body sway gently side to side with the train until he dozed off.

CHAPTER 30

27 February 2014

2108 Hours

Illichivsk, Ukraine

The mercenary propping Val up stepped back to the dining table. Val slumped back to the floor.

Lying on his side, Val could see Alexei and Burian sitting at the table.

"Peskov," Alexei said, summoning the young intelligence officer with a gesture.

Peskov stepped over to Alexei, on the side opposite Burian. He leaned over, and Alexei spoke to him quietly behind a cupped hand. Peskov nodded and then left the room through one of the forward doors.

Val tried to move his fingers. They were numb. His wrists throbbed from the zip ties digging into his flesh.

"Alexei, if I promise to be good, can I return to my seat at the table?"

"No. Your promises are no good, my friend."

"How about cutting these wrist bindings off, then?" Val asked in the politest voice he could muster. "They really hurt."

"No. Is your own fault."

Val closed his eyes and tried to calm his breathing and focus past the throbbing pain. Every time his heart beat, he felt it in his wrists. He was a dead man, most likely. But if he was to have any chance of getting out of this, he needed to think clearly. And that meant he had to stop being distracted by numb fingers, throbbing wrists, and stinging ankles.

And Burian. He had to swallow the anger that rose at the sight of Burian. He had to think clearly.

Val opened his eyes and looked at Burian. The Ukrainian's forehead was glazed with a sheen of perspiration, and his eyes darted around nervously. One knee bobbed rapidly under the table, and his hands alternated between rubbing the tops of his thighs and fidgeting on the table.

Burian was terrified. He was not enjoying being here.

And where was "here"?

Since they flew into Odesa, Val hadn't been in the car all that long at any time, and given the size of the *Monarch*, Val reasoned they must be in Port Illichivsk.

At least they were still docked. *If we were moving, I'd be truly fucked.*

As long as we stay in port, I have a chance. Every spy satellite in the US fleet is focused on Ukraine right now. Port Illichivsk, like the rest of the country, must be under nearly continuous surveillance. Somehow, I need to draw attention to the Monarch.

A sudden pulse of vibration from below traveled through Val, still lying on his side on the deck. The growl of large pistons, suddenly spurred into motion, filled the air and then receded as they settled into a slow idle. Val felt their RPM throughout his body.

Fuck me. They fired up the engine.

Val heard a few shouts outside but nearby the ship and could picture the gangway being lifted and ropes cleared. He stole a glance at Alexei, who met his eyes with a smile and a shrug as if to say, *What the hell did you expect?*

Alexei grabbed the bourbon and poured himself and Burian another shot.

The vibrations emanating from below increased in frequency as pistons growled in a higher pitch. Val's weight shifted forward for an instant as the ship's power train dropped into reverse and inched the vessel aft.

"Val," Alexei held up the bottle. "May I toast her now?"

Val tilted aft as the *Monarch* dropped into forward gear, reversing its thrust.

"Sure." Val decided whiskey was better than dwelling on his fate.

Mercenary hands grabbed his shoulders again and lifted him to a seated position as Peskov returned to the room through one of the forward doors.

"Ah," Alexei said. "Better timing than usual, Peskov. Please help our American guest again with his toast."

Alexei filled Val's glass and set the bottle down.

Peskov returned to Val with the full shot glass. He pulled him up to a seated position and looked back at Alexei, waiting for his eccentric senior officer's direction.

"And remember, Peskov," Alexei said. "Respectfully. Do not spill."

Peskov nodded. If he felt the task beneath him or offensive, it didn't show.

Alexei raised his glass. He glared at Burian until the Ukrainian raised his. Peskov lifted a glass in the air for Val.

Alexei shifted his angry glare from Burian. His eyes softened, and he swallowed as his chin raised slightly.

"To Sydney."

"To Sydney," Val said, trying to embrace the name as it left his mouth. He wished he were with her.

He wished a lot of things.

Peskov gently poured the bourbon into Val's mouth.

Val swallowed slowly.

The *Monarch* moved away from the dock, making her way toward the Black Sea.

CHAPTER 31

30 August 2001

Garmisch-Partenkirchen, Germany

Val's cell phone rang around six that evening. He looked at it and grimaced. The number was blocked, but he had a good idea who it was. It was midday at DIA HQ. They knew he was supposed to be on leave this week but would not hesitate to call if they judged it necessary. If it was them, it would be a long conversation. One he wasn't in the mood for.

Val was hungry. He and Mina had spent the day hiking in the mountains around Garmisch and were now heading out to meet Hank at the Local Cure for beer and pub food. Or would be as soon as Mina was ready. He glanced at his bedroom door. He didn't hear the shower anymore, which was progress.

A marketing manager at BMW in Munich, Mina had come down to Garmisch to visit Val for a few days. They'd met earlier in the year on a train and had been spending time together as their schedules allowed. Val had been on a mission in Eastern Europe for most of August, and the two of them were enjoying the chance to reconnect.

Val's phone continued to ring.

Without a good excuse not to, he answered it.

"Rafter."

"Hello, Val."

Val sat up.

"Sydney?"

"Aww. He remembers me."

Val was quiet for a long moment.

"You there?"

"Yeah," Val said, standing from the sofa. "Sorry. Kinda surprised to hear from you, is all. Where are you?"

"Kyiv."

"How did you get this number?"

"The folks I work with know how to find a phone number."

Silence settled over the line again.

Val didn't know what to say.

He glanced at his bedroom door and then walked over to the balcony. He slid open the heavy glass door and stepped outside into the early-evening air. After graduation, Hank helped Val find a flat on the southwest side of Garmisch, off the beaten track in a neighborhood popular with expats. Val's balcony looked due west through fields and cow pastures at an unobstructed view of the mountains. It was beautiful and private, and Val loved it. Even the rich, bracing smell of the cow pastures.

"I'm sorry, Val," Sydney said.

He leaned against his balcony railing.

"I hate the way things ended in Garmisch," she said. "I hate that I didn't make it in time to see you off that night. I hate that we haven't talked in more than a year. And I hate that you're not in my life."

Val looked to the west at the Zugspitze, its jagged peak backlit by the setting sun.

Sydney waited, listening for some clue to tell her how he was reacting. Even just his breathing.

Val closed his eyes and rubbed his forehead.

The silence extended.

The balcony door slid open.

"*Fertig!*" Mina said, stepping out onto the balcony. "Sorry that took so long. Let's go eat."

She leaned in to kiss Val on the cheek, and he nearly dropped the phone. He clutched at it with both hands, barely saving it from impact with the hard tile floor of the balcony.

"Okay," Val said, straightening up. "Gimme just one minute here."

Mina glanced at the phone in his hand but smiled.

"Okay." She leaned in and kissed him again.

"But hurry, *bitte*." She stepped back inside, sliding the glass door closed behind her.

"Sorry about that," Val said once the door was shut.

"It's okay. That's all I wanted to say."

Sydney hung up.

Val held the phone to his ear for another moment, the things he wanted to say finally coming to mind. He looked at the phone.

"Shit," he mumbled, glaring at the unknown number.

*

A week later, Sydney's cell phone rang in the afternoon.

"Hello," she answered, after noting the unknown number.

"Hello, Sydney," Val said.

"How did you get this number?"

"The folks I work with know how to find a phone number."

"Uh-huh. I bet it was Liam."

Val smiled.

"Was it Liam?"

"You know I can't reveal a source, Sydney."

"Fucking Liam." Sydney sighed.

"I think he was always kind of sweet on you."

"Is he still in Egypt?"

"He is. And loving it."

"I bet he is. I bet he is kicking ass too."

"That is certain."

Silence fell over the line.

Val tried to picture her in Kyiv in late summer. He felt the silence on the line settle and thicken like it had last time. He charged into it.

"I'm sorry too, Sydney. I should've called you when I got to Munich that night. Hell, I should've called you back right then from the train. I thought about it. I'm sorry I didn't. I was just so raw. Mad about a lot of things, so when you didn't make it to the train station—"

"Val, I'm so sorry about that. I meant to. I hope you believe me when I say there was nothing I could do. It was just bad timing. I—"

"Hey, hey, hey," Val said, stopping her ramble. "It's okay. I was saying that I should've been more understanding. Not let my anger turn on you. You didn't deserve that. You were working. I get it."

"I should've said goodbye," she said. "I should've called soon after I left Garmisch. I should've done a lot of things differently. But I was so mad at myself. And scared about…"

She hesitated. She couldn't say it all on an unsecured line.

"Scared about what I was going to have to do," she said.

"I know. So, you're in Kyiv now? I guess you got through it?"

"I did," she said without pride.

Sydney leaned back in her chair and thought about the polygraph. They had tested her soon after she returned to Langley, before shipping out to Kyiv. She got through it using the method Val had explained to her and she then studied and practiced.

A mixture of art and science, the method involves devising a cover story that's related to but less severe than one's actual violation. Then defending it to the hilt.

You can't stop your body from responding during a polygraph. Even if you try to mentally disengage from the questions, physiological tells will give you away. The key is to have a well-rehearsed explanation for why you're showing signs of emotional duress, and to develop rapport with the polygrapher.

In Sydney's case, her violation was the failure to declare a foreign contact and relationship. A highly sensitive contact at that—a Russian intelligence officer. So, Sydney developed a story about how she had a passionate one-night stand with an Italian skier traveling through Garmisch. It was her first week at the Marshall Center, and they met at a bar called the Local Cure. She was very drunk and her memories of the night were fuzzy. But she remembered having sex on the balcony beneath the mountains. And had the sense it was very good.

He had a good time as well, and continued to text and call her for weeks, leaving long, pleading voice mails. She ignored his emotional appeals to see her again. But she didn't report them. She knew that this situation would have triggered the "close and continuous" reporting requirement, but she was just too embarrassed. She was not, after all, a one-night stand kind of lady.

During the polygraph, when her body responded to questions about foreign contacts, and the equipment detected biological signs of stressors that implied lying, Sydney disclosed the embarrassing tale of her brief Italian lover. She blushed and fidgeted as she related the story, acknowledging she should've reported it, but she was ashamed.

The polygrapher bought her story and assured her it was not a violation. He tested her again as required, and she triggered again. But at that point, she could see the end in sight. She played up the embarrassment and guilt again and pressed her cover story that she'd never had any other reportable foreign contacts in her life. The polygrapher was convinced. Who wouldn't be? She got through it.

"You like it there?" Val asked.

"Oh yes. Love it. And I think you'd love it."

"It's definitely on my list."

"And Garmisch? Fabulous as ever?"

"Yes."

"You still running around with Hank?"

"Chasing him, more like it. The guy is one of a kind. Hiking, skiing, biking… and every physical adventure leads to a little-known mountain hut where he drinks and tells stories for hours. So much fun. But he is going to kill me. They broke the mold with that guy."

"I can't believe you're still there."

"Well, I do travel a lot. But it's a great place to be stationed."

Sydney nodded, wanting to ask him more about what DIA had him doing, cursing the unsecure line again.

"Liam told me what you're up to over there," Val said. "Sounds great. And perfect for you."

"Did he? Damn it, Liam."

"Don't worry," Val said, not wanting to get his friend in trouble. "He just gave me the basics."

"Uh-huh."

Val smiled, feeling sorry for Liam when Sydney got a hold of him.

Liam had told him about Sydney scoring a high-profile weapons trafficking assignment in Kyiv. It was the kind of assignment that typically went to a more senior officer.

"She must have done something pretty special when you guys were at the Marshall Center," Liam had said. "I guess I figured you woulda known what it was?"

"No," Val told him. "I knew she was working on something. But didn't know the specifics."

"You talked to Tony lately?" Sydney asked, snapping Val back to the present.

"We talk every few weeks. And we've linked up a few times when he has passed through Europe for work. He's good. Same old Tony."

"That's good."

Silence settled on the line and left an ache on their hearts. Val spoke first.

"I want to come visit you, Sydney. Fuck this distance and telephone. Let's spend some time together."

"I'd like that, Val," she said without hesitation. He could hear her smile in her voice. "I'd like that a lot."

"I can get to Kyiv at the end of September, if that works for you?" he said, his smile just as big.

"I'd love that," she said, standing from her chair in excitement.

"Me too. Let's do it."

"Yes," she said. "Let's do it."

CHAPTER 32

Sydney knocked on the hotel room door.

There was a moment's hesitation as Nicolae confirmed it was her through the peephole.

He opened the door, and Sydney walked in quickly.

She took her jacket off as Nicolae locked the door.

"Hello, Sydney," Nicolae said as he took her jacket. "It's good to see you."

"It's good to see you, too."

They had been working together for more than a year now. The first few months were slow, as Langley threw validation tests at Sydney to run Nicolae through. She was frustrated. But he passed each one easily, and she knew it was just the time-honored process. A good asset was like a garden. It could not be rushed, and the early preparation would yield satisfying results if the gardener remained patient and methodical.

A few months ago, when she was posted to the embassy in Kyiv, Sydney revealed her true name to Nicolae. There were many practical reasons to do this, and he'd passed over a year of detailed vetting and validation. Sydney had been worried about Nicolae's reaction. How would he feel about her lying to him for that long? But, to her relief, he not only understood but also recognized the importance of the gesture. It heightened the sense of trust between the two of them.

Sydney was excited. She and Nicolae were gaining momentum in their relationship just as his career in the Moldovan defense and security apparatus was accelerating.

"We don't have long," Sydney said. "Do you have the file?"

"Of course."

He pulled a manila folder out of his briefcase and handed it to her.

"You even got photos?" she said, looking up from the file.

Nicolae smiled.

"Damn," Sydney muttered, looking back at the information in her hands. "The analysts are going to go batshit over this stuff. Good work."

Sydney shook her head. Nicolae continued to outperform even her expectations. She almost wanted to have an off-the-record conversation, teach him how to be slower and more strategic about how he gave the agency information. He could make more money that way and likely extend his usefulness.

He was making her look too good, though.

Sydney placed the file on the small table and gestured at Nicolae to sit down.

"Let's go through it quickly," she said.

Her cell phone buzzed.

Sydney looked at the number. It was the embassy. She hit ignore.

"Yes!" Nicolae said, sitting down next to her. "You will find this very interesting."

Her phone rang again. She hit ignore again.

Nicolae placed the papers and photos in a certain order as he prepared to give Sydney a quick briefing.

Her phone rang again.

"Damn it. I'm sorry, Nicolae."

"Is fine," he said, not taking his eyes off the table. "Answer it."

"Go ahead," she said into the phone, standing from the table and walking to the other side of the room.

"Need you back at the station ASAP," Garcia barked.

"What? I just got here."

Sydney thought about the tiring three-hour surveillance detection route she'd just executed to make sure she didn't drag surveillance to her meeting with Nicolae. She was damn well going to have a meeting after all that.

But Garcia was the chief of station in Kyiv, responsible for all CIA operations and personnel in-country.

"Just fucking get back, Sydney. Now."

"But sir—" Sydney protested. But Garcia had already hung up.

Sydney stared at her phone for an angry moment. Her anger flipped to anxiety, though, as she thought about the tone in Garcia's voice.

She'd never heard that before.

"Bad news?" Nicolae asked.

"I have to go."

"So soon?"

They had been planning this meeting for more than a month. Nicolae's role in the Moldovan government gave him cover to travel to Kyiv from time to time. This meeting was supposed to be a major download from him to Sydney. That she was abruptly leaving five minutes into their meeting was unsettling.

"Will you be coming back?" he asked.

"I'm honestly not sure, Nicolae," she said, grabbing her coat from the closet. She sensed the unease in his voice.

"Look," she said, putting on her coat. "I'm sure this is some administrative bullshit that has nothing to do with you and me."

She walked over and put her hand on his shoulder.

"Remember, I'm looking out for you. And I'm going to tell you if you ever need to worry."

Nicolae looked up from his chair at her and nodded.

"This is just part of working with the US government." She grimaced in frustration. "A lot of fucking reindeer games."

"Reindeer games?"

Sydney shook her head. "I'll explain next time." She took the file and closed the door behind her.

An hour later, she walked into the American embassy.

Sydney glanced around as she approached the security gate. There were more US Marines on the perimeter than usual.

"What's going on?" Sydney asked the sergeant at the gate while a marine checked her ID.

"You'll get briefed inside, ma'am," he said without looking at her. His eyes scanned the rooftops across the street.

The marine handed Sydney her ID and waved her by.

The military presence persisted in the lobby. As Sydney passed through the metal detector, she noted they were in full-body armor and carried more weapons than usual.

"What is Gunny putting you guys through today?" Sydney asked the marine guard checking her bag.

Master Gunnery Sergeant Williams commanded the seven US Marines assigned to provide security for the Ukrainian embassy. He had a reputation among his men for being a touch overeager, constantly volunteering them for additional duties and dreaming up training scenarios that often ended up screwing up their weekends.

The marine guard ignored her.

"She's clear," he said to his corporal, who nodded at Sydney and stepped past her to assess the next person in line.

Sydney shook her head as she took her bag back and started down the hallway. As she moved through the "front" of the embassy toward the small CIA operations area, she passed groups of people huddled around the several TVs that were mounted high on the walls. A few of the ambassador's staff were crying. Sydney jerked to a halt when she saw the images on the TV.

The World Trade Center towers were burning. Black smoke rose against a clear blue Manhattan sky.

Sydney took several steps forward until she was close to a cluster of staff workers. Sydney gaped as she tried to make sense of the sight. For a moment, it looked like there was only one tower.

"What happened to the other tower?" Sydney asked.

No one answered her.

"Please," she said, tapping on the shoulder of the young man in front of her. "What happened to the other tower?"

He turned over his shoulder to look at her.

"It collapsed," he said, in a whisper.

Sydney blinked. She tried to ask him how it happened, but she couldn't find the words.

"Airplane," the young man said in a quiet, heartbroken voice.

Sydney stood in silence behind the group of staffers and stared at the TV.

"Knox!"

Sydney spun toward the sound of the voice. Garcia was striding down the hall, coming from the ambassador's office.

"Where the hell have you been?" he asked her without breaking stride. Sydney fell behind him, and they both took the hallway toward the secure CIA area.

"I had my meet with Lightfoot today." Lightfoot was Nicolae's randomly assigned code name, used to protect his identity within the agency. "What the hell happened?"

"All we know right now is that commercial airplanes were hijacked and flown into both World Trade Center towers and the Pentagon."

"Jesus," Sydney muttered.

Garcia stopped at the door to the secure area to show the armed marine guard his ID. Sydney did the same, and the guard stepped to the side.

The small, secure operations center was jammed. Uniformed military and plain-clothed personnel crowded around the map-covered conference table in the middle of the room. The embassy's entire clandestine contingent, CIA and military, was in the room. People coming and going had to squeeze between the wall and chairs. Two large TVs hung on opposite ends of the long axis of the room. Each showed the same awful image of the remaining tower burning against the blue sky.

Colonel Mayfield, the defense attaché, stood across the table on the other side of the room beneath one of the TVs. He held an Iridium satellite phone to one ear and a STU headset to the other.

Mayfield was one of those old officers who gave the air of having seen it all. His camouflage uniform was "tabbed out," covered in the patches and insignias of exotic military courses from around the world. He'd led a Special Forces unit in the first Gulf War, was with the 82nd in Panama, and spent years in military intelligence in Europe during the Cold War. Everyone loved to listen to the colonel's stories, particularly Sydney. They always reminded her of Val.

Today, though, the old man's face was taut, and his eyes narrowed. He looked terrified.

That rattled Sydney more than the terrible images playing out on the TVs.

"All right, listen up!" Garcia nearly shouted to make himself heard. Conversations quieted and the rustling of papers stopped as all heads turned to look at the chief of station. Colonel Mayfield put down the sat phone but kept the secure telephone handset to his ear.

"The FAA is grounding all flights. There may be another hijacked aircraft. They're not sure. The—"

Gasps interrupted Garcia.

He looked at the TV in time to see the second tower collapse. Within seconds, only black smoke remained on the TV.

Quiet sobs filled the room. Garcia hesitated. A tear ran down Colonel Mayfield's face. Sydney clutched the back of the chair in front of her.

A moment later, Garcia spoke in a slow and even voice.

"We're on lockdown until further notice. No one leaves the embassy unless authorized by me. We've got one mission now, people. Figure out who the hell is responsible for this. Work every source, contact, friend, and enemy you have out there. We're going to figure out who is responsible, and then hell itself is going to rain down on them."

*

No one left the embassy for the next forty-eight hours.

Sydney spent that time either on the phone, in the restroom, or sleeping on the floor of the conference room that Garcia had set up as a rest area.

Minutes after the second tower fell, Garcia pulled Sydney into his office.

"I need you to pulse every source and contact you've got, Knox," he said, sitting down behind his desk.

Garcia was a thirty-year-plus company man. He joined during the height of the Cold War and served in just about every Communist capital before the great unraveling of the nineties. He was tired, didn't like the new world order, and planned to retire after this tour.

Garcia's wiry, short frame was dressed in baggy clothes. Most of his shirts bore ink stains on their pockets, and his thick hair was going gray. He gave the impression of an energetic, absent-minded professor. But Sydney knew Garcia had gone head-to-head with enemy counterintelligence officers all over the world, and personally briefed more than one US president.

Garcia had liked Sydney immediately when she reported to Kyiv. "Anyone that has done time in Moscow is okay in my book," he said as he reviewed her file with approval. "Far as I'm concerned, those pussies that work in Central Europe shouldn't even call themselves case officers."

He looked over the open file at her.

"Sorry," he said unapologetically.

"No need. I agree."

Sydney had made it her mission to learn everything she could from Garcia over the past year.

On September 11, 2001, though, he was the same as her and the rest of the world, trying to catch up.

"We need to know if Moscow is clean or not," Garcia said to her as they both looked at the TV in his office, watching black smoke rise into the Manhattan sky.

"You don't seriously think the Russians did this, do you? What's Langley saying?"

"Langley's like the rest of us." Garcia rubbed his eyes. "They don't know shit. And as far as the Russians go, no, I don't think this was Putin's doing. He is more aikido than karate. But I wouldn't put it past him to look the other way while some nasty shit was brewing in the southern republics or Transnistria or some other cesspool they allow to fester."

Sydney spoke briefly to Nicolae on the night of September 11. He used a burner phone in Ukraine, consistent with the protocols Sydney had prescribed for him.

"Is so sad what has happened, Sydney. Is terrible. I am so sorry."

"Thanks, Nicolae."

"I will do whatever you need me to do."

"Thank you. I knew I could count on you. The best thing you can do for me and for Moldova is help us determine if there was any link at all with anyone in Transnistria. Were these guys trained there? Did they get any help from there? Anything at all."

"I understand. If there is a connection, I will find it."

"I don't know what this means for our next meeting. Things are crazy right now. But I'll be in touch as soon as I can."

"I understand, Sydney. I will be fine. And I will be working on things here."

There was a pause on the line. Sydney was not sure what to say next.

"Sydney," Nicolae said softly. "Are you okay?"

"Yes. I'm okay. I have to go."

She hung up before Nicolae could say goodbye.

*

By the afternoon of the thirteenth, Sydney, like everyone else, still had learned nothing useful.

It was particularly frustrating for Sydney because, unlike other American Marshall Center graduates, she could not tap into any of the international relationships she'd formed there. Burian, for example, would have been an excellent source to talk to. He now worked in the Ukrainian equivalent of the Pentagon in Kyiv as a conventional military strategist. His vantage point and relationships could have helped provide a small bit of clarity and perspective. And, who knows, maybe even useful regional intelligence.

But Sydney had been in pseudo at the Marshall Center. Captain Brooke Monroe had ceased to exist the day she left Garmisch. And Sydney and Brooke could never be associated with each other. By anyone. Except Nicolae.

Intelligence officers have always faced this tradeoff when they execute missions under false identities. Being in pseudo confers a certain amount of freedom during the mission but takes away options in the future. The problem is you don't know what's being taken away until you need it. This dynamic is accentuated in the rich relationship building and networking environment the Marshall Center affords.

"Go home," Garcia finally told Sydney late in the day. "Get some sleep and come back at it with fresh eyes in the morning."

Sydney nodded. "What about you, sir? You look like shit. You need to rest too."

"When I'm dead, Knox," He lit another cigarette. "When I'm dead."

Sydney shook her head and left his office. She grabbed her coat and headed out of the embassy, noting as she did how sad and exhausted everyone looked. Even the marines in the lobby looked tired.

She stepped out of the embassy and took a left to head back to her flat. She walked two blocks in a daze.

"Brooke!" a familiar voice called.

She looked across the cobblestoned street and came to an abrupt halt.

No fucking way.

It was Alexei.

He stood on the other side of the street in jeans and a black T-shirt. Hands in his pockets.

Sydney froze.

Alexei smiled faintly and crossed the street.

He walked up to her and put his hands on her shoulders.

"I am so sorry," he said.

"What?" she managed to say, getting control of herself. "What are you doing here?"

"I was nearby when it happened. I thought I might find you here. I've been waiting outside for the past few hours."

"Nearby? But…"

"I know," he said, looking into her eyes. "I know we said we would not see each other, not contact each other. I just came to check on you. That is all. Is terrible what happened. I'm sorry if I startled you. I can leave you alone if you prefer."

"No," she said, leaning into his hands. "It's okay. I mean, it's good to see you. It's just been a long day."

"I know. Let's get you some food."

He turned, pulling her with one hand in his direction.

She didn't resist his tugging.

They walked down the street together.

It was a sunny Thursday afternoon in Kyiv. The cafes were filling up with early diners. Alexei and Sydney sat at an outside table at a small Italian restaurant she had been to before a few blocks from her flat.

They ordered food and a bottle of wine. Alexei poured her a glass and then himself before leaning back in his chair.

He looks good, she thought. *He always looks good.*

She shook her head.

What a huge mistake that would be.

"What is it?" he asked.

She tried to erase her smile before responding, "Nothing. I haven't slept in two days, so I'm a little punchy."

"Was mistake to come?"

"No," she said, more definitively than she meant to. "No. I'm really glad you came."

"Me too."

The waiter stepped up to their table. He placed a small pizza between them and gave Sydney her caprese salad.

"It's just unreal," Sydney said quietly as Alexei sliced the pizza and plated a piece for her.

"Is terrible." He nodded as he handing her the plate.

"All those people. Those people that jumped rather than burn."

Alexei shook his head.

Sydney stared at her pizza.

"Eat, Brooke. You need to eat."

She looked up at him.

"You're going to need your strength. Will be a long war for you, I fear."

"For me?"

"For your country, I mean."

He leaned across the table and pointed at her pizza.

"Eat!" he said firmly.

Sydney took a small bite. The warm, crispy margarita pizza tasted good.

"*Spasibo*," Alexei said.

Suddenly, Sydney was starving. She took another, bigger bite.

Alexei smiled.

"Fuckers," Sydney said after a few quiet bites of pizza.

"Pardon?"

"The people that did it." Sydney took a sip of wine. "They are gonna die. I promise you that."

"I do not doubt you."

She took another large bite.

Alexei watched her chew for a moment and then said, "But that will not end it. You are in it now. Take it from me. The Islamic extremists are many. And will never stop. You will have to kill them all."

Sydney leaned back in her chair. She knew he was right. She wondered what the future looked like now.

"To be honest, the only surprising thing to me is that it took this long," Alexei said.

"For what?"

"For them to attack you."

"We've been attacked before. We've been attacked plenty."

Alexei swallowed a bite of pizza before saying, "Okay, then. But this is the first time they draw real blood."

Sydney thought about that as Alexei followed the large bite with a large sip of wine.

He wiped his mouth and leaned back in his chair. "Is very good pizza here."

Sydney smiled. That was the side of Alexei she loved. The appetitive, sensory-driven side that loved to share experiences. She would miss it if she thought about it too much. She was glad when he asked her a question.

"How do you like Kyiv?"

"I love it. Might be my favorite city."

"Really?"

She nodded.

"Why?"

"Well, beyond its beauty? The history, the river, the people. All of it. I love it."

Alexei was smiling. "I agree with you. Is great place. You know they believe the city goes back more than fifteen hundred years? Is on an ancient trade route between Europe and Constantinople."

"I know." Sydney looked around at the city as it glowed in the evening sun. "In America, we have cities that are not even a hundred years old. This is just incredible."

"Many invaders have agreed with you," Alexei said. "Vikings, Mongols, Nazis... They have all left their mark on this city."

"I think that's one reason it's so beautiful, though. You can see all those influences as you walk around."

"What do they have you doing here?" Alexei asked, pouring Sydney more wine and refilling his glass.

She smiled.

Alexei shrugged to claim innocence. "Just making conversation."

Sydney chuckled. "Boring stuff. Import negotiations. Tax issues. Visa applications."

Alexei rolled his eyes and put his fingers to his head in a pistol motion. "Ugh."

"Yes. 'Ugh' is right, but it got me here to this wonderful place."

"We toast to that." Alexei raised his glass.

She clinked her glass to his, smiling as she took a sip.

Sydney had sought this assignment in Ukraine to continue her momentum within the agency as a burgeoning gray arms expert. She'd learned over the past year and a half just how much shit she'd put herself in the middle of.

Human history in Ukraine goes back more than thirty-two thousand years. Its location, sitting between Russia and Europe, with the Black Sea to its south, has made it key strategic terrain for just as long.

Absorbed by the Soviet Union after World War II, Ukraine regained its independence in 1991. It spent ten years progressing in fits and starts as it tried to plot a course between Russia, NATO, and the European Union. Now, in 2001, Ukraine was haltingly rounding the corner to democracy. But it found itself sitting between a cauldron of chaos and instability to the west, and a newly ambitious Russia to the east.

On Ukraine's western border, Transnistria still simmered between the Dniester River and Ukraine, not totally independent but not totally part of Moldova.

On Ukraine's east lay Russia and the southern republics of Ossetia, Chechnya, and Dagestan. Less than a day's drive from Kyiv, they seethed with Islamic fundamentalism and breakaway ambitions of their own.

"It's a fun time to be here," she said.

Alexei gave her a puzzled look.

"Not today, I mean. With all the shit that has happened," she added. "But in general. In Ukraine, I mean. It's an exciting time for them. As they find their way and strengthen their independence."

"Their independence?"

Sydney nodded as she took another sip of wine.

"Independence from who?"

"Oh god, Alexei." She realized too late what she'd walked into. "I'm tired. Give me a pass today?"

"Sure," he said, taking a deep breath. "Just remember, about a quarter of Ukrainians are ethnic Russians." He gestured around.

Sydney made a show of slumping back in her chair and swigging her wine.

"Do you not know of Kyivan Rus'? Russians were here over a thousand years ago. We were the founders, leaders and defenders of Ukraine even then."

Sydney gave Alexei an exaggerated nod and stretched her arms out, embracing the speech she'd heard many times before about several other regions.

"Millions of Russian soldiers died defending and liberating Kyiv from the Nazis. Khrushchev and Brezhnev themselves both fought here." He pointed at the ground as if jabbing a flag into it.

"Thanks for the pass," Sydney said to him, holding her hand up for the waiter.

Alexei took a large sip of wine.

The waiter stepped up to the table.

"*Perevirte, bud laska*," Sydney said, asking for the bill in Ukrainian.

"No," Alexei said, reaching across the table to take Sydney's hand.

She was startled. But didn't draw it back.

The waiter stood motionless, waiting for the resolution.

"I'm sorry," Alexei said with a pleading smile. "I stop."

Sydney hesitated.

Alexei looked at the waiter. "I prefer to pay the bill myself."

The waiter smiled and nodded.

"But please bring us another bottle of wine first."

"*Da, ser, srazu*," the waiter said, answering Alexei's English in Russian with a smile before turning away.

Alexei looked at Sydney with such a happy and startled face, it made her chuckle.

"You see?" He beamed. "I did not plan that!"

Sydney shook her head, also smiling.

"I promise you," Alexei insisted.

"All right, all right. Can we go back to our mellow catchup over wine now, please? Remember, I'm exhausted and you're here to comfort me."

"Yes, yes. Of course."

The waiter returned with a second bottle. They sat in silence for a few minutes, each sipping wine and watching passersby.

"Brooke," Alexei said, his voice low and serious. "I just want to say again how sorry I am about what has happened."

"Thanks, Alexei. I really appreciate it."

"And I want you to know, and ask you to let your people know, that we had nothing to do with it. We had no indications from anywhere that anything like this was being prepared for or was going to happen."

Sydney studied Alexei's face as he continued.

"And if there is anything we can do to help, in any way, I hope you will feel comfortable letting me know. Our two countries are in this together now."

She placed her glass on the table.

"Um… I really don't know what you mean by all that, but thank you, I guess."

Sydney hoped her voice didn't sound as anxious as she suddenly felt.

What the fuck? Her mind raced. *Why is he doing this? Am I burned?*

Alexei put his glass down and folded his hands together on the table.

"I think it would be a valid question to ask, whether this attack came from one of our more troubled southern republics," he said in a low voice. "I just want to emphasize that we don't see any indication of that. But we will be checking. We will let you know what we find, of course."

"Alexei," she said, trying not to show her agitation. "I'm sorry, but you're not making sense to me."

Sydney scanned the area. There were no obvious overwatchers, but the hair on the back of her neck stood up. It was the same feeling she got in Moscow when she suspected she was being followed.

"Sydney." Alexei paused for an instant after calling her by her true name. "Today, of all days, we can drop the pretending."

Shit. I'm burned.

"Is not hard, and you know this," Alexei said in a gentle voice, reading the alarm on her face. "We review all of your embassy personnel, just as you review all of ours. Strange to find you here under a different name from the one I knew in Garmisch. You need multiple names to do your import negotiations, tax issues, and visa applications? That's a tough business."

Alexei smiled.

Shit. Shit. Shit.

Sydney remembered why she'd been to this restaurant before. She'd been so fuzzy with fatigue when they had gotten here earlier, but now she realized she used the location for sensitive meetings.

Wake up, Knox! she scolded herself.

She looked at the small water fountain nearby. The sound of the water, only a few meters away from the outermost tables, prevented any electronic eavesdropping. She knew it well.

She looked back at Alexei, who winked, having tracked the direction of her glance.

Sydney got angry.

"Today, of all days, Alexei, I don't want to deal with this bullshit. You want to say something to me? Then come by the fucking embassy and take a number, asshole."

Sydney stood abruptly.

"I'm too tired for this. I'm going home. Goodbye."

Alexei stood as she did. He grabbed her hand, and, again, she didn't withdraw it.

"I understand," he said. "Most important to me is that you know how good it was to see you."

"You've got a funny way of showing it."

"Those were things I had to say. I have a job just like you have a job. That doesn't mean I don't also have feelings, Sydney. Feelings for you."

Sydney yanked her hand from his. She turned to pull her purse from the back of the chair.

Alexei stepped closer to her.

"Look around, Sydney." He gestured with his head toward the fountain. "I picked this place for a reason. No one can hear what we say to each other now. Not your country. Not mine."

Sydney looked at the fountain, then back to Alexei. He nodded, just enough that she alone could notice.

"I think about you," he whispered. "About us. All the time."

He put a hand on her waist and pulled her closer.

She allowed it and pressed her body against him.

They stood next to their table in an embrace. The waiter, who had seen them stand and started their way, turned and walked back to the kitchen.

CHAPTER 33

---

27 February 2014

2132 Hours

The Black Sea

Lying on the deck, Val could feel the gentle rise and drop of the ship as it moved through the water. The higher frequency growl from below reverberating through his body told Val they were cruising.

His wrists hurt.

He thought he could feel blood dripping off his hands from the tightly cinched bindings but couldn't be sure. His hands were numb.

I think we have been underway for almost twenty minutes, Val forced himself to calculate. *If we're going twenty knots, that would be somewhere between six and seven nautical miles. I think a nautical mile is a little longer than a statute mile, so… God, my wrists hurt.*

"Alexei," Val said.

Alexei looked down at Val.

Burian didn't.

"Please. My wrists are killing me. Can you please have them undo my wrists?"

Alexei nodded with empathy.

"Shortly." Alexei raised a finger as if to ask for Val's patience.

Alexei looked at his watch and then at Burian.

Burian, whose knee was still bouncing like a piston beneath the table, returned Alexei's glance. When Alexei said nothing, Burian ran his hand through his hair and looked down at the table.

Val caught Alexei glancing at Zakir. Alexei dipped his head in the slightest of nods toward the armed mercenary.

Burian missed it.

"Burian," Alexei said in a friendly voice. "Join me outside for chat, if you would."

"Okay."

Alexei stood and walked past Val to the aft sliding glass door. Val was on his side, facing forward, so he could not see Alexei but heard the door slide open and felt the cold air off the Black Sea spill into the dining room.

Burian stood and followed Alexei, avoiding eye contact with Val as he passed by.

The sliding glass door closed.

Val grunted as he tried to roll over so that he could look rearward.

"Oh, you wanna see?" Zakir taunted Val.

"Fuck you," Val mumbled, trying again to flop over so that he could look aft.

"Yeah, yeah." Zakir stood from his barstool and walked toward Val. "Always tough guy, you are."

Val sucked in his breath to prepare for a kick in the ribs.

But the mercenary reached down and grabbed Val by the knee and shoulder. "I help you, asshole." Zakir flipped Val over to face the sliding glass door. "But I don't think you will like."

Val looked past the legs of dining chairs through the glass at Alexei and Burian standing on the rear deck. Alexei pointed a pistol at Burian's head, who was on his knees begging.

A shot rang out and a flash lit the aft deck.

Burian's body slumped forward.

Zakir, standing over Val, chuckled and looked down at him. "You next, asshole."

Val heard one of the forward doors open and people walking in. Zakir opened the sliding glass door for a pair of mercenaries that walked past Val carrying a length of heavy chain. The two walked out onto the rear deck to Burian's body. Zakir followed them out. They wrapped Burian's legs in the chain as Alexei stepped back into the room.

Alexei shut the glass door behind him and walked past Val to the table. He picked up the 13th Tactical switchblade and then returned to Val to cut his bindings off. Alexei walked back to the table, sat down, and poured two shots of bourbon, leaving the switchblade in front of him on the table.

Val got up slowly. He stood, hands at his side, and watched the two mercenaries as they finished wrapping Burian's dead legs with the chain. When they were done, they lifted Burian's body and threw him overboard.

Zakir opened the sliding door and stepped back in. The two other mercenaries walked down the aft stairs, disappearing from view.

Zakir closed the sliding door and then walked back to the bar, winking at Val along the way.

"Val, have seat with me." Alexei gestured to one of the empty chairs.

Val turned slowly but didn't approach the table.

"Please, Val. You look like hell."

"Why did you do that?" Val asked matter-of-factly. "Why kill him?"

Alexei sighed heavily and leaned back in his chair.

"I have known Burian a long time, Val. I recruited him when we were all at the Marshall Center. We work together fifteen years…" Alexei's voice trailed off. He rubbed his eyes. "He talked too much, Burian did. So, he was a loose end I could not allow."

Alexei picked up the shot glass closest to him and downed it.

"I always do my duty, Val."

"Am I next?"

Alexei sighed again.

"Please, Val." Alexei gestured again at the chair as he refilled his shot glass.

Val walked over and sat down. He rested his hands on the table. Streaks of dried blood ran down his fingers, and his wrists were ringed with deep, angry gashes.

"To Burian." Alexei raised his glass. "He did his best."

"Fucking traitor."

Alexei shrugged at Val's comment and threw his bourbon back.

Val's fingers were numb, and he fumbled with his glass, spilling some whiskey. He lifted the glass by mashing both of his hands together around it. Shaking, and spilling more whiskey, he raised the glass to his lips and then said, "Fucking traitor," again before dumping the drink into his mouth.

Val lost his grip on the shot glass. It fell from his numb hands, bounced off the table, and skidded across the room under the long dining table.

"What is wrong?" Alexei asked. "Why so shaky? I know you have seen death before."

"My fingers are numb, asshole." Val held his bloody hands up for Alexei to see.

Alexei nodded as if just remembering an obvious fact. He swiveled in his chair to face the bartender. "Bring us a towel and warm water."

The bartender nodded, and moments later, placed a bowl of hot water between Val and Alexei. He handed Val a white towel and then returned to the bar.

Val dipped the hand towel into the bowl of hot water and rubbed one of his hands.

"How many times did you go to Iraq, Val?" Alexei asked as he watched Val massage his hands with the warm, wet towel.

"Three."

"And Afghanistan?"

"Two."

"Sydney went several times also?"

"Yeah." Val dipped the towel in the bowl. Clouds of dissolving dried blood swirled in the water. "Everybody goes at some point."

Val pulled the towel from the water and massaged his other hand with it.

"How many times have you been to Iraq?" Val lifted his eyes from his hands and stared at Alexei.

Alexei met Val's gaze for a long moment, then smiled and shrugged.

Val nodded ruefully.

Outside the sliding glass door, a mercenary mopped the deck, while the another sprayed it with a hose.

CHAPTER 34

"Attention to orders!" Val exclaimed. Three dozen special operators came to a decent imitation of attention. The gaggle of Delta commandos, SEALs, and Rangers stood in front of the headquarters building on Shark Base. It was late afternoon and the slanting sunlight reflected off the operator's sunglasses as the dark, slow water of the Euphrates River flowed behind them.

This was ordinarily a quiet time, just before mission briefings, that the soldiers would use to relax and center themselves before the night's violence. The brutal optempo in Ramadi and al-Anbar Province made it rare to find a group of special operators standing at attention this time of day. But their favorite army interpreter was being promoted, and none of them were going to miss it.

As Val read the orders aloud, one of his field control officers, a stocky sergeant first class from San Diego named Amos, removed Faisal's specialist rank and replaced it with sergeant's stripes.

"The secretary of the Army has reposed special trust and confidence in the patriotism, valor, fidelity and professional excellence of Omar Faisal," Val continued, speaking in a loud and measured cadence. Promotion to sergeant was a significant milestone for a soldier, elevating both rank and the weight of their responsibilities and influence. Omar had asked Val to read the promotion orders at this ceremony, and Val wanted to do it justice.

He glanced up from his script to sneak a look at Omar

Th sharp-witted twenty-five-year-old Iraqi American was fighting back tears as Amos pinned sergeant bars on his desert camos. Lean and athletic from a lifelong love of soccer, Omar stood straight and kept his watery eyes straight ahead.

On 9/11, Omar had just started his junior year at the City University of New York. He was in the city that day. After the towers fell, he walked out of Manhattan across the Brooklyn Bridge with thousands of others, through a thick haze of gray ash and dust.

Omar volunteered for the US Army the next day. The son of Iraqi immigrants, he was fluent in Arabic and was quickly selected for the interpreter track. He was in Afghanistan with the Rangers within a year. This was his first tour in Iraq. He had never visited his parents' homeland until he went there as a soldier.

"In view of these qualities and his demonstrated leadership abilities and dedicated service to the United States Army, he is therefore promoted from specialist to sergeant effective 28 November, 2006. Signed Colonel Wyatt, Task Force Commander."

Val smiled as cries of, "Hooah!" erupted from the normally reserved special operators.

Omar beamed as Val winked at him and shook his hand.

"Thanks for doing that, sir."

"The honor was mine, buddy," Val told him. "Thank you for including me."

Val took a step back, making way for the wave of congratulations. Back slaps and handshakes nearly smothered the well-liked buck sergeant.

Val smiled at the sight. He and Omar had grown close over the past months, going on countless missions together as American forces, along with their Iraqi partners, tried to win back al-Anbar. In addition to recruiting and running Iraqi sources, Val's Human Intelligence team led the battlefield interrogation of enemy combatants and exploitation of captured sensitive items. It was an essential role in the Joint Special Operations machine that churned 24/7 in Iraq.

With Val's team managing the human intelligence process on the objective, other elements of the task force could focus on security and prep for follow-on missions. There were many nights they went from target to target to target, repeatedly adjusting their plan and focus as Val's team gathered more intel from each mission. It kept the enemy off balance and on the run, but it was exhausting for the team.

As the Suni Awakening gained traction and fostered green shoots of stability, Val and his team were increasingly taking part in the task force's helicopter-borne missions to intercept foreign fighters crossing into Iraq out of Syria. During these operations, they were responsible for identifying, interrogating, and processing prisoners while integrating any intelligence provided by sources they were running out of Shark Base.

Amidst it all, Val came to think of Omar as a younger brother. A seasoned combat veteran, Omar was still quick to smile, and had a genuine and approachable nature that made him an effective interface with Iraqis, even under stressful circumstances. He could also be a wise ass, and his eyes hinted at his readiness to laugh at life's ridiculousness, even in adversity. This special mix of effectiveness and ability to "roll with it" made him a favorite of the special operators on Shark Base. So much so that Val had to monitor Omar closely, ensuring he did not burn himself out by going on too many missions.

"Major Santanna!" a voice called.

Val turned to see one of the operations officers walking towards him.

Val was in pseudo in Iraq. It was a precaution to protect him from revenge seeking al-Qaeda and other terrorist organizations. "Max Santanna" recruited and interacted with a lot of unsavory characters in theater. He had also killed many of them. It was assumed that some of the assets he dealt with were of temporary loyalty, if not outright double agents. The name Max was known by the enemy. An enemy who would, if possible, pursue him back to the United States for revenge. When they did, the trail would evaporate.

"You've got a call on the secure line in the Ops Center, sir."

"Thanks. I'll be right there."

Val took one last look at a happy Sergeant Omar Faisal before turning and following the captain into the task force headquarters.

Shark Base was part of the larger US facility in Ramadi about 110 kilometers west of Bagdad. It was home to a small but potent task force of SEALs, Rangers, Delta, and the CIA mounting aggressive operations against al-Qaeda. Shark had its own airstrip, beefed-up security, and the little extras that came with being part of Joint Special Operations Command. The rest of Ramadi housed a large conventional US Army unit and had all the indicators of a long-term US presence: a recreation center, a huge KBR-built and run mess hall, a coffee bar, and a shitty little strip mall.

Shark Base also featured three Saddam era palaces standing in a row only a hundred meters apart from each other on the edge of the Euphrates. US forces occupied the palaces during its initial invasion of Iraq, and the southernmost now served as headquarters for the task force and a large CIA contingent used another. The third palace was occupied by a large component of "White" SEALs, a rambunctious and highly capable bunch that often took on risky missions that supported the task force.

The commandeered palaces were strange to Val. Despite high ceilings and long hallways, the large buildings somehow always seemed dark and gloomy. The task force headquarters palace had a large, central great room where Val imagined decadent banquets being held during the good old days of Saddam Hussein. The task force had converted the cavernous room to their operations center. A single expansive video screen, over thirty feet wide, lined one wall. The screen was usually subdivided into different feeds from manned aircraft, drones, helmet cams, and other sources. It could also tap into the main JSOC feed from Balad.

Tables were set up in a horseshoe formation facing the wide screen and were always full of interagency personnel working at computers. The cycle never ended. Analyze the last mission. Prepare for the next. Sometimes multiple times a night. Bleary-eyed, sleep deprived, and hailing from every corner of the Joint Special Operations community, there were usually at least three dozen people in the operations center.

When big missions got going, twice that number would cram into the large room. Usually, Val was outside the wire, taking part in those missions. But on the few times he was in the Ops Center in a support role, he would glance around the large room and chuckle at the thought of the palace's previous owner. What would he think at the sight of all these Americans in his palace great room taking part in a different kind of banquet?

A banquet of violence.

Val followed the captain to the corner of the Ops Center and took the secure telephone handset.

"This is Major Santanna."

"The old man went for it!" Tony said with excitement.

"Bullshit!"

"No bullshit! He wants a briefing tomorrow."

Val smiled and pumped a fist.

"If I get to Shark, can you get us a ride to Balad?" Tony asked.

"Yep. For sure."

"Here we go, partner. See you tomorrow."

"Roger that!"

Val hung up the phone and smiled again. He and Tony had been working on this one for a while.

CHAPTER 35

Val snapped awake when the helicopter lurched to the right. His hands tightened on the M4 rifle between his legs.

He glanced quickly at Tony, sitting across from him in the MH-47G. He was still asleep.

The door gunners on each side of the aircraft were leaning out of their stations, scanning for hostiles, but not shooting at anything—always a good sign.

The pilot was starting their approach to Balad Air Base and had put the Chinook into a steep, corkscrewing descent to minimize their exposure to small arms and rocket-propelled grenades. Standard operating procedure.

Val leaned back in the nylon webbing seat and rubbed his eyes. He'd been in Iraq for almost six months now and had been "reversed out" that entire time, working only at night, even when he was not running missions outside of the wire. It was strange to be up and moving about in the mid-day sun like this. But when the commander of Joint Special Operations Command Iraq called you in from the frontier for a meeting, you came on his schedule.

Val adjusted his legs to get more comfortable. As he did, he woke the prisoner at his feet.

The first time Val saw prisoners on board his JSOC aircraft, he was uncomfortable. But that was five years ago, on his first tour in Afghanistan shortly after 9/11. He was used to it now. Always hooded and usually in shower shoes, they were restrained and chained to the floor of the aircraft. They sat, heads down, with green chem lights tied to their heads and arms. A musty smell wafted up and down the aircraft, as most of them hadn't showered in a long time.

The Chinook carrying Val and Tony was full. There were several large pallets of cargo secured to the floor and numerous military personnel and contractors. So, as often happened, the prisoners leaned against the soldiers' legs as they tried to get comfortable.

The aircraft's engines suddenly spun down, and the sound of the rotors changed as the pilot dumped power. The sudden acceleration in their descent woke Tony.

Val smiled. Some people woke up in a combat zone ready to fight, their eyes sweeping the environment and hands clenching their weapons. Not Tony. He was slow to wake no matter where he was, and it took him a couple minutes to get his bearings, even from a quick catnap. His yawns and stretches always amused Val.

Once the aircraft was on the ground, Val and Tony walked off the aft ramp with the rest of the passengers while the military police kept weapons trained on the prisoners. Across the tarmac, a Predator drone taxied toward the runway for takeoff.

Val and Tony squinted as their eyes adjusted from the shadowed Chinook cabin to the intense afternoon sun.

Balad was a joint base wrapped around a large airfield shared between conventional units and JSOC. About forty miles north of Baghdad, Balad was captured early in the invasion of Iraq in 2003 and had become a critical facility in the war effort as the main headquarters for the Joint Special Operations Command in Iraq.

Val and Tony walked toward the joint operations center, passing between rows of heavily armed black helicopters and several unique civilian aircraft. Like everything else at JSOC on Balad, the aircraft on the ramp was a cocktail of interagency kick-ass. The 160th, Air Force 24th Special Tactics Squadron, CIA Special Activities and others all had equipment there.

Val and Tony showed their badges and cleared their weapons in the outer security tent, leaving their M4s in the weapons rack but keeping their sidearms. They walked into the huge tent structure of the joint operations center.

The epicenter of the JOC was the cavernous main tent. Smaller tents and passageways radiated out from the main tent, providing meeting rooms and office facilities for all the participating JSOC and supporting elements: CIA, NSA, NGA, British SAS, Australian special forces, and the JSOC commander's joint staff.

Val and Tony had been in the JOC many times in the past months and navigated quickly through the labyrinth of fabric walls to the main room.

"Do you have to piss?" Tony asked Val. "I really gotta piss."

"No. I'll wait here for you."

"Okay." Tony turned back toward the door they came in.

Val set down his satchel, leaned back against the wall, and took in the activity in the JOC. He was a seasoned combat veteran, but he still found what went on in the JOC to be impressive. Everything here was on a much bigger scale than what they had at Shark Base.

There were four semicircular rows of desks set up on rising platforms facing a long wall of six thirty-foot-tall video displays. Each screen showed a different operation that was taking place, or the intelligence, surveillance, and reconnaissance drone feed on a target being tracked.

Every time Val came to Balad for a briefing, he would take time to sit and watch the activity in the JOC. Clusters of personnel seated at the rows of desks talked in hushed tones as the mission they were supporting played out in front of them. Val would look around and think about the staggering level of effort represented in the room. Each screen showed not only the live update of a mission but also, to Val, conveyed a backstory of someone's life's work.

He would look at a screen that showed a lone civilian vehicle driving down a desert road and think about the hours that someone at Langley or in JSOC had put in to get that drone to prioritize that particular vehicle. Or he'd watch the overhead footage of the four-man Delta team stealthily working its way through a village in the middle of the night—and think of all the trials each operator had to go through in their career just to make it into Delta. Or he'd view the images of a helicopter extracting a SEAL team from a rooftop and think about the selection process to become a Night Stalker—realizing there was probably almost a hundred years of aviation experience in that one aircraft.

Val shook his head. All this effort by folks that could probably have done anything they set their mind to in life. But they chose this.

Val leaned forward when he realized all the screens were focused on the same mission.

That didn't happen a lot.

There was a small team on the roof of a building and another team in the street attempting to breach the ground floor. Their actions indicated they were taking fire.

There was a group of NCOs seated and taking notes at the last row of tables in front of Val. He leaned forward and asked them what was going on.

"A Blue team in heavy contact, sir," one of the NCOs said, using the JSOC code word for the SEALs. "They had to assault in daylight right on the X, and now they're in some shit."

Val shook his head and stepped back.

"On the X" meant the team was dropped right on top of the objective rather than approaching it in stealth from a few kilometers away. A necessary tactic when there was a decent chance of the target fleeing or there was not a good way in, but always the operators' last choice. Inserting on the X was a loud, unambiguous commitment of force, laying all your cards down on the table at the outset of an operation. Val had been one of those cards on a few occasions. It was never a pleasant experience.

The fact the SEALs had to do it during daylight hours made it worse.

Val rubbed his forehead as he noted the dense urban area they were fighting in.

"What's up?" Tony asked, stepping to Val's side.

"They put a blue team right on the X," Val said over his shoulder. "Now they're in heavy contact."

Tony grunted.

The SEALs pulled back, trying to break contact. Whoever their target was would get away today. The question now was how to get the SEALs out.

"There's the old man," Tony said.

Val turned to look as the JSOC commander, Lieutenant General McStone, walked in quietly with his operations officer and XO close behind. He took a seat in the middle of the room and stared intently at the screens.

General McStone was a mustang, a commissioned officer that started out as an enlisted man. He was also a career special operator. When he was enlisted, he served in one of the Ranger battalions. As a junior officer, he made it into Special Forces and commanded an A Team before being selected to join Delta. McStone was tall and lanky with the look of a country boy that could punch above his weight. The general had been in command of JSOC in Iraq for almost two years now and had fine-tuned the complex organization into a well-synchronized killing machine.

Still…shit happened. And when it did, when he had a group of soldiers in trouble, the general usually came to the JOC to watch. His presence tended to hush the room more than normal.

Val and Tony had been in narrow scrapes in Iraq more than once. Val wondered if a concerned McStone had sat in here when he and Tony were slugging their way out of a small house or barreling down a narrow road in an up-armored Humvee. One thing was certain—outside of the wire in contact with the enemy, Val never felt all the eyes in the JOC on him. He just felt alone.

Val watched as the blue team pulled back from their objective. They hunkered down a block away and increased their rate of fire. Radio calls went back and forth from the team and their commander as they tried to get air support. Within minutes, an F-16 put a laser-guided bomb on the target house.

"Jesus," Tony whispered as the screen went white from the explosion.

"Must have been a two-thousand-pounder," Val said under his breath.

"On one fucking stone hut."

As the drone footage regained clarity, it was clear that the house had collapsed. Only smoking rubble and a few secondary fires remained. Several of the small structures around the crater were partially destroyed and burning.

The blue team reported they were no longer taking incoming fire.

"Not gonna get a lot of intelligence outta that," Tony said.

Within a few minutes, reports of civilian casualties came over the radio. The atmosphere in the JOC got even more tense.

Val looked at Tony but said nothing.

Tony shook his head.

Blue had a reputation in JSOC of going in heavier than other operators, of causing quite a bit of collateral damage that you usually didn't see from the other organizations.

"I'm going to find a quiet spot to review my notes," Val said. "This isn't helping my concentration."

"Yeah, do that. Don't want you to fuck this up."

Val left the JOC and walked down one of the radiating, tented hallways looking for an empty desk he could use. His briefing with McStone was in about half an hour, and he wanted to review his notes one more time.

He was hoping he was in the National Geospatial-Intelligence Agency area. They built all the mapping and documentation for targets and were typically geeky, agreeable folks. They wouldn't mind him squatting at a desk. He walked into a small conference room set up with workstations. Three people in civilian clothes were looking at a map on the wall. An empty desk sat in the corner.

"Excuse me," Val said, to get their attention. "You guys mind if I sit at that desk for a few minutes? Have a briefing with the old man in half an hour. Just want to review my notes."

The three people turned to face him. Two men and one woman dressed in the standard outfit for deployed nonmilitary personnel: khaki cargo pants and sand-colored button-ups.

The woman was Sydney Knox.

"Sure, Major," said one of the men.

Val stared at Sydney.

Sydney stared back.

The two other men looked back and forth between them. Val and Sydney wore the same expression with wide, surprised eyes.

The awkward silence extended.

"You okay?" one of the men asked Sydney.

"Yes." A smile broke across Sydney's flushed face. "I know this major, is all. We go back."

The two men shrugged and turned back to their map.

Sydney gestured at the table in the corner and started walking toward it. Val followed slowly.

Her desert operations clothing was baggy and unrevealing. Still, Val felt a familiar ache, long suppressed. Much of it was because he'd been living in a war zone for a while, focused on operating and living. He wasn't prepared for the sudden flood of attraction.

Part of it, though, was Sydney and all the old feelings.

All of it was the last thing he needed right now.

"What are you doing here?" he asked with more edge to his voice than he intended.

"Good to see you too."

"I—I didn't…" Val stammered and then shook his head. "I haven't heard from you in five fucking years."

"Yes. And your letters have just been piling up on my nightstand."

"I've been fighting a war, you know."

"Yeah?" Sydney looked at herself and then around the room. "A lot of us have. You want a medal?"

"That's not what I meant."

Sydney took a deep breath. "Put your shit down. Let's talk."

Val nodded and stepped forward to the table. He peeled off his large, heavy satchel and laid it on the desk.

"It's Max," he said in a quiet voice. "Max Santanna."

Sydney nodded to show she understood and glanced furtively at her agency colleagues.

The two men were engrossed in a conversation in front of their map.

"Santanna?" she said quietly to Val. "Coulda been worse, maybe?" she added with a smile.

Val was in no mood.

"We were going to meet in Kyiv. Then I don't hear from you for five years?"

"Again… I never heard from you either."

"I was deployed. I was in Afghanistan a few weeks after 9/11."

"Deployed with no phone, no email, no postal service for five years?"

"I called you a couple times."

"Yes. Twice. From strip clubs in Germany," Sydney said, her voice now also sharp. "Not a voice mail that makes a girl leap for her phone."

She crossed her arms.

"Oh, for chrissake. I was headed back to the sandbox and blowing off steam." They glared at each other.

"The point is, I was thinking about you," Val said, breaking the standoff. "I just thought you would've reached out at some point."

Sydney uncrossed her arms.

"Look, it's been a shitty five years for just about everyone in the country. It's good to see you."

Val noted the door swinging shut on something in her statement, but he took the peace offering.

"You too."

"And a major now?"

Val shrugged.

"I think they're giving gold oak leaf clusters to anyone that can fog a mirror these days."

"Where are you stationed?"

"Over on Shark Base."

"I know it," Sydney said with a nod.

"What about you?"

Sydney gestured at the room.

"You're looking at it. I'm part of the counterterrorist fusion cell. Been here about two months."

"Holy shit!" Tony boomed, startling both Val and Sydney. Tony stood in the doorway, his mouth gaping with a wide smile, hands already stretched out toward Sydney.

The other two CIA officers glared at Tony, disapproving of the interruption and noise in their area.

He ignored them.

"Get over here!" he bellowed, avoiding her name on purpose, in case she was in pseudo.

He was on her. Lifting her feet off the floor in a bear hug.

Sydney hugged him back.

"Vinnie," he whispered his pseudo in her ear.

"Vinnie!" she said with excitement. "What are you doing here?"

"What I'm always doing." He placed her back on the ground and stepped back. "Trying to keep this dumbass alive and out of trouble."

Tony gestured at Val.

Sydney laughed. "God, it's good to see you."

"So good! Most of the crew is back together, eh, Max?"

"I guess," Val grumbled. "I didn't get the same greeting you got, though. That's for sure."

"Yeah?" Tony said, undeterred. "Well, that's because you're an asshole."

Tony gave Val a punch in the shoulder and winked at Sydney.

"We need Liam for it to be the whole crew," Sydney said.

"I miss that skinny bastard. How is he doing?"

"He's great. Walks with a limp, but it's a miracle he walks at all. He's transitioned to an operational support role."

After Egypt, Liam surprised his friends by joining Special Activities, the CIA's covert paramilitary unit. He served tours in both Afghanistan and Iraq before being severely wounded outside Fallujah in December 2004. A 7.62-millimeter round shattered his left femur. Had it not been for the heroism of nearby marines, Liam would have bled out and died.

"Good to hear," Val said. Tony nodded.

"But, seriously," Sydney said, shaking her head, "what are you guys doing here?"

"Running HUMINT teams," Tony said. "I'm in al-Aqaba. Max is in Ramadi."

"Who the hell thought it would be a good idea to send you both here at the same time?" Sydney asked, only half joking.

This time around, Val and Tony had rotated to Iraq within weeks of each other. JSOC is a small community, and they had known for several months prior to deploying that their time downrange would overlap, and therefore started talking about collaborating before they set foot in Iraq.

Each lead a nine-man HUMINT team consisting of two Farm-trained case officers, three field control officers (army-trained case officers that could do some of what a Farm-certified case officer could do), two battlefield interpreters, and two targeters. When they got on the ground, they immediately began coordinating and comparing notes from their operations.

They were constantly pitching out-of-the-box combined initiatives that leveraged both teams and their integrated view of the situation. Few of their concepts had gotten as far as the one they were pitching today.

They were both increasingly alarmed by the number of arms and fighters coming across the Syrian border into Iraq and wanted to do something about it. "We've got to get on fucking offense," Tony groused to Val repeatedly. They formed a plan over the past few weeks and sent it up to Balad, expecting it to get rejected quickly. Instead, they were summoned.

"And what are you guys doing in the JOC today?" Sydney asked.

"Pitching the old man in…" Tony looked at his watch, "eight minutes. That's why I came to find him." Tony gestured at Val.

"Pitching the old man?"

"McStone."

"I know who the old man is. What are you pitching?"

"We want to reactivate an asset," Tony answered. "It's gone all the way to the old man's desk."

"Not Haskell?" Sydney asked.

"Yeah," Tony said with surprise. "Haskell."

"Oh shit." Sydney chuckled, looking at her watch.

"What?"

"I'm also in that meeting."

"Really?"

Val's eyebrows arched in surprise.

"Yep. I am." Sydney's smile widened. "No way we let you guys do that. I'm shooting it down."

CHAPTER 36

"As everyone in this room knows, sir, Akmal Abdul Razzaq is one of the most active foreign fighter facilitators in Iraq," Val began. He stood on one side of the wide-screen TV facing General McStone. Tony stood on the other.

McStone sat, hands folded together on the table in front of him, flanked by his operations officer, a former Delta squadron commander named Colonel Welch, and his intelligence officer, also a Delta officer, Lieutenant Colonel Nickels. The three CIA representatives, including Sydney, sat on the other side of Nickels. An NSA representative sat next to Colonel Welch, and there were several other people seated against the wall behind the table.

Val and Tony focused on McStone.

"We believe he is based in Syria and conducts his border-crossing operations through the small villages along the Iraqi border," Tony added. "He has orchestrated the entry of thousands of armed foreign fighters into Iraq and is responsible for hundreds of American and Iraqi military and civilian deaths in-country.

"After Zarqawi's death in June, it seems Abu al-Masri has taken the helm of al-Qaeda in Iraq and has been increasingly focusing on al-Anbar. We've certainly seen an increase in al-Qaeda forces in the western part of al-Anbar near al-Qaim." Val advanced the slide on the display to show a map of Iraq as he spoke. "This is Abdul Razzaq's doing and represents a genuine threat to our operations out of al-Asad Air Base and in the area in general. If unchecked, this buildup could threaten our recent progress in the region with the Awakening.

"Intel on Razzaq is close to nonexistent. There is just one published picture of him as a teenager, and our efforts to pinpoint and deal with him have been frustrated to date."

"And you two guys here to change all that for us, Major?" asked one of the CIA reps sitting next to Sydney.

She sat with her arms crossed, a neutral expression on her face so far.

"Not really," Val said flatly. "We've got nothing new for you today."

Val let his statement hang before continuing.

"We've been studying everything we have on Razzaq, like they taught us to do back at the Farm," Val began again, laying down an obvious marker. CIA operations officers didn't like the army's Cobra Snare program. They viewed the military knuckle draggers as wannabe spies that played at the profession in the cracks of their military job. Val wanted to double down on the condescension with the standard Cobra Snare response, *Yeah…Tony and I can do your job and ours, asshole.* But he didn't want to blow up the meeting before it started.

"We have been through the files backward and forward, sir." Val aimed his eyes and comments back at McStone. "It's about the only thing Sergeant First Class Chase and I do these days when we're not running missions outside the wire."

"Yet somehow you two still find time to send up harebrained operations for approval," Colonel Welch deadpanned.

Val thought he saw the hint of a smile on the colonel's face, though.

"If wanting to take the fight to the enemy is a crime," Val said with a mock bow, "we are guilty, sir."

"So, what do you have?" General McStone asked. He shifted his gaze back and forth from Val to Tony.

"Masudi Kader, sir. Code name Haskell." Val advanced the slide to show the photo and file summary of Masudi Kader. The picture was of a handsome man, probably in his early sixties. Thick silver-gray hair topped his head and blended into a white beard and mustache that framed his tanned, symmetrical face. His brow was furrowed, but in a way that might have been troubled by the horror of war or a hard choice between bottles of wine. It was hard to tell.

"Haskell has been a valuable source for us in the past, sir," Tony said. "Until about two years ago, he was back and forth between Syria and Ramadi and was the sole source of all of our information on Razzaq. The problem is that we have not had contact with him in a while because Syrian counterintelligence detained Haskell two years ago. He spent most of that time in a Syrian prison. He was just released about six weeks ago."

Val gave the group a moment to read through Haskell's summary before continuing.

"Twenty-seven days ago, the HOC got a text message from the cell phone that Haskell's former case officer had given him."

The HOC was the human intelligence operations center in the JOC, there in Balad. It was rolled up under Lieutenant Colonel Nickels and controlled all military HUMINT in theater.

"The HOC responded with the appropriate coded challenge, according to Haskell's file."

General McStone turned to look at Nickels.

Nickels nodded and said, "It checked out, sir. He's got one of the older models, but the phone is encrypted and secure. The signal guys gave it the thumbs-up." Nickels gestured at the NSA representative, who nodded in agreement. "Furthermore, he initiated contact with the correct code word, and responded correctly to our coded challenge per the handling protocol in his file."

"At that point, Colonel Nickel's team reached out to me seeking further guidance," Val said. "Sergeant First Class Chase and I discussed it and decided to issue a few more challenges to Haskell to further establish his bona fides. So we—"

"Excuse me, Major," Sydney interrupted. "At any point did you bring the agency in?"

"I'm doing that now."

"I'm sorry, General." Sydney turned in her chair to face McStone. "This is not something we can support."

Shit. She is in charge of their team, Val realized. *This isn't going to be easy.*

"After so long a break in contact," Sydney continued, "and after almost two years in the hands of Syrian counterintelligence, we don't know who is on the other end of that cell phone and should not be engaging at all."

"As I said," Val interjected, "the source responded correctly to every challenge. It's definitely Haskell."

"I'm sure he did." Sydney chuckled derisively. "And it may be Haskell on the other end. Probably is. But if you don't think his eggs and loyalty are properly scrambled after being in the hands of the Syrians for that long, you're living in a fantasy world. Syrian counterintelligence was looking over his shoulder for every response, no doubt."

Sydney looked from Val to Lieutenant Colonel Nickels. "We should've been consulted on this one, sir."

Nickels, a career special operator that served with the Rangers in Mogadishu and had been at McStone's side for more than a decade, looked at Sydney. "If I'm not mistaken. That's exactly what we're doing now."

"Yes, sir. Right," Sydney said, meeting his glare. She made a show of looking around the room and counting attendees. "Just saying, next time, if you can work us into the process earlier, my team and I can save you and the dozen other folks in the room from across the theater some time."

Nickels turned back to the front. "Please continue, Major."

Val nodded, happy to have Sydney's ire focused on someone else.

Val looked over his shoulder at the photo of the handsome Syrian. "Bottom line is this, we want to bring him in and revalidate him. We want to determine whether we can work with him or not. If we cannot, fine. But if we can, then let's use him to get to Razzaq."

"We have no reason to believe Haskell's relationship with Razzaq doesn't still exist in some form," Tony added. "We can use it to target Razzaq and finally take him out."

One of the CIA officers shook his head.

"You know why we gave him the code name Haskell? Because he is a slick, obsequious bastard that will tell you whatever he thinks you want to hear."

"We're aware," Val said. Haskell was well-known in the Iraqi human intelligence circuit for being a polished and intelligent source that was difficult to manage.

"And that was before they turned his ass in a Syrian prison," the other male CIA officer next to Sydney added.

Sydney maintained her poker face.

McStone looked skeptical.

"Sir, we know this isn't a layup," Val said. "But we drove some very successful operations off this source in the not-so-distant past. We may be able to do that again. At a minimum, we believe it's worth your consideration."

General McStone turned to look at Sydney.

"I've flown these two out here to hear them out. Colonel Welch is right. We get a lot of harebrained schemes from them. But I appreciate they're out there on the wire, being creative and trying to win. And they have a good track record of executing successfully on these Hail Mary hunches of theirs."

General McStone nodded toward Val and Tony without looking in their direction.

"And I want Razzaq," he continued. "You guys haven't given us anything to go on. So we're going to hear them out and then we'll decide."

Sydney nodded. "Understood, sir."

"All right then, gentlemen." McStone leaned back in his chair. "Proceed."

Almost two hours later, Val and Tony finally got a moment to sit down. They had started first with a detailed review of the value of Haskell's prior reporting before outlining risk mitigation steps and concluding with a high-level outline of his plan for running Haskell against Razzaq if they were to proceed.

The two male CIA officers had fought him the whole way, and it was a robust discussion with McStone and his staff peppering both sides of the argument with questions. Val was tired and could not read which way McStone was leaning.

He wanted a decision.

"So that's all we've got, sir," Val said as he took his seat at the far end of the table next to the NSA representative. Tony sat beside him. "Do we have your approval?"

Val looked across the room at McStone. The general was impossible to read.

McStone leaned forward onto his elbows and clasped his hands together. He looked at Colonel Nickels.

"I don't like it, sir," his intelligence officer said. "Haskell was a good source in the past. No doubt about that. But I think he's burned now. And, even if he isn't, I don't know how we validate him sufficiently to justify operations. I don't think it's worth the risk."

McStone turned to Welch.

Welch nodded. "I want Razzaq. If this slimy bastard Haskell can get us to him. I think it's worth a shot."

McStone then looked at Sydney.

"We all want Razzaq, sir," she said. "But we can't let that desire taint our judgment. CIA can't support this. Given the long break in contact and the time in Syrian captivity, we must assume Haskell has been compromised. It's simply too risky."

McStone sighed and leaned back in his chair.

Val and Tony sensed they were losing the moment.

"A 40 percent increase in cross-border arms smuggling in just the past month, sir," Tony said, repeating one of the most alarming facts from their briefing. "Each one of those weapons used against our forces and Iraqi civilians. And I'm not aware of any effective actions being taken to stem that flow."

Val waited half a tick to let Tony's statement sink in and then said, "And, sir, we're not asking to marry the guy. Just let us go out there and talk to the son of a bitch."

Val then swiveled his gaze to Sydney. "Send your best polygrapher with us. Let's base our decision on what they determine, firsthand, about the source. Not on rumor and urban legend."

Val turned back to McStone.

He and Tony didn't have to wait long.

"Okay, gentlemen. Go get him."

Sydney opened her mouth to protest, but McStone cut her off.

"Send your polygrapher. When you have a recommendation that's based on direct interaction with the source, we'll reconvene."

McStone stood up, showing his decision was final, and the meeting was over. Everyone else got to their feet and collected their things. Tony punched Val's leg under the table in excitement.

"Very well, sir," Sydney said. "I'll send our two best polygraphers, and I'll attend the interrogation personally. We can leave tomorrow night."

"I appreciate that," General McStone said before striding out of the room.

Val stared at Sydney, surprised by her declaration.

Sydney glared back at Val while everyone else left the room.

"Damn, Sydney," Tony said with a smile as soon as it was just the three of them left in the room. "Slumming it with us field types? Mighty egalitarian of you."

"Oh bullshit, Vinnie. I know how luxuriously you JSOC types roll. I'm not worried about it. Besides, I can't let Max's adventurism drive us all into a big mistake. Someone needs to be the adult in the room."

CHAPTER 37

30 November 2006

Camp Korean Village, Iraq

The Black Hawk helicopter leapt into the air, its engines howling under the strain of the max-performance takeoff. The pilot popped a full round of flares and chaff to throw off anyone targeting their lone ship as she leveled the aircraft fifty feet above the desert floor. Shots rang out left and right as door gunners checked the readiness of their miniguns. Satisfied, the crewmen settled into their stations, maintaining a vigilant scan of the desert.

Val, Sydney, Tony, Omar and another of Val's interpreters, and two CIA polygraphers sat in the aircraft as it sprinted at 120 knots toward Camp Korea. Sydney sat outboard on the last row of forward-facing seats. The large aircraft doors were closed against the winter desert chill, but cold air still grabbed at her pant legs.

After several deployments, Sydney found night helicopter lifts soothing. The rotors beat the air, sending a rhythmic pulse through the aircraft. The cabin was dark, every light doused to not interfere with the crew's night vision, leaving only a soft glow emanating from the cockpit. The lulling vibration, darkness, and expanse of desert below would combine to put Sydney in a relaxed, contemplative frame of mind.

Not tonight. Her mind was cycling, unable to relax. Val Rafter had returned.

Sydney looked out the window at the darkness and chuckled to herself and life's ability to catch one off guard. She should've seen it coming.

Just a few weeks ago, Sydney was in the JOC watching a mission take place. It was a sweep of a few houses suspected of harboring al-Qaeda operatives. Sydney's team had identified and prioritized the targets and was on standby to confirm identities should the team on the ground need assistance.

An hour into the mission, it was going well. Sydney's head was down as she reviewed her notes when Val's voice came over the radio, jolting her upright.

Sydney had stared intently at the screens, searching the overhead drone footage for signs of Val. Had she really heard him? But all the foreshortened helmets and shoulders moving around looked the same.

Then she heard him again.

It was Val. Without question.

The last time she'd heard his voice was his phone call to her from Garmisch. He was coming to see her. She couldn't wait. She'd floated through the next few days in anticipation. Right up until 9/11.

It seemed so long ago. Longer than five years. So much had changed. She'd looked around the massive JOC, full of Americans, Brits, and Aussies. What had they each been doing on the tenth of September 2001? Would any of them have imagined they would be among the tens of thousands fighting in Iraq today?

"Right, Sydney?" a CIA colleague had said that night, snapping her back into that moment in the JOC.

"What?"

"I said, that's a big fucking grab, right?" He'd gestured at the action on the screen, where Rangers had captured a high-value target.

"Yes," she'd answered, feigning a confirming glance at her notes to hide her befuddlement. "Big fucking grab."

After that, she spent days arguing with herself. *Should I try to find him? What would I even say? Would he care?*

After three days of angst, she told herself to relax. She had another month left in her deployment, after all. Plenty of time to give it some serious thought and decide what she wanted to do. No need to rush things, and, besides, Val was in a combat zone and needed to stay focused on staying alive, not on their dysfunctional relationship. She would reach out to him after she gained some clarity and perspective. Or not. Maybe she would just rotate back to Eastern Europe without talking to him at all. It was up to her.

Until Val Rafter walked into their office in Balad.

His sudden appearance had nearly overwhelmed her, the old Val Rafter intensity and crackle emanating from his eyes. He looked older. Gray had infiltrated his thick hair. His face and arms were weathered. But he looked good. Like a warrior. She'd felt the old familiar warmth well within her.

Sydney shook her head in the darkness. *Get ahold of yourself, Knox.* She tried again to tune into the rhythmic vibrations of the Black Hawk and looked out at the blackness beyond the window.

After about an hour, one of the door gunners passed the "six minutes" notification to the passengers. The group fidgeted in their seats as the aircraft decelerated.

The pilot brought the helicopter in for a smooth landing on the dirt helipad. The group hurried off the helicopter. Tony made sure everyone was on the ground and out from under the rotor disc before giving the crew chief the thumbs-up. When he did, the Black Hawk surged into the air and accelerated away. In just a few moments, they were standing in silence inside their home for the indeterminate future—Camp Korea.

Camp Korea was originally called Camp Korean Village and was named after Korean laborers who worked on the Amman-Baghdad highway years ago. It sits in the middle of a remote expanse of desert close to the Syrian border and has served as a Marine Corps facility ever since it was captured during the invasion of early 2003.

When the sun rose in the morning, it became obvious Camp Korea was not one of the Joint Special Operations Command facilities.

"What a shithole," Tony mumbled as they walked through the camp.

A deserted, failed-frontier-town ambiance lay on the camp. Its occupancy ebbed and flowed depending on the Marine Corps' operational needs, and the current need was low. The minimal staff seemed resigned to their forgotten plight of supporting marine outposts and firebases in the area.

Dirty, squatty cinder-block buildings sat in the sand, interspersed with GP medium tents. Large random piles of junk added to the derelict atmosphere. Sydney gawked at a twenty-foot pile of burned vehicle axles next to the small building the marines had converted into their headquarters.

"This was not what I had in mind when I pictured a plush JSOC facility."

"Write your congressman," Tony said.

Omar laughed at the comment.

There was no running water. The smell of porta-potties wafted back and forth through the small camp as the desert wind shifted direction.

"Lovely," Tony said when they walked into their assigned building. It was an empty one-story cinder-block bunkhouse with a low ceiling. A cinder-block wall divided the interior of the building into two bay-like rooms, each with a separate door to the outside on opposite ends.

The group spent an hour scrounging wooden pallets and a few cots. They put the cots in one room to sleep in and stacked the wooden pallets to use as chairs and tables in the other room for the interrogation. Tony surveyed their efforts with irritation.

"This is bullshit." Tony grabbed his rifle, which leaned against the wall with the rest of the group's weapons.

"Where are you going?" Sydney asked.

"I'm going to talk to the jarhead captain that runs this shithole. A table and chairs are not too much to fucking ask, for chrissake."

"Good luck."

"We're counting on you," Val added, conveying zero hope.

Tony came back an hour later. Behind him, four marine privates carried a small table and six folding chairs.

"Great job, Vinnie!" Sydney said. She'd drilled Val's and Tony's pseudo names into her head. She referred to them by those names only unless she was absolutely sure no one else was around. Even then, best practices were to maintain the pseudo-name. She was also in pseudo for this mission as "Tracy Croft" since she would be in contact with Haskell, and no one was certain of his loyalties.

"Yeah, sergeant," Omar said as they all stood in the interrogation room, staring at the stark setup. "Really pulls the room together."

Val and Sydney snickered at Omar's comment.

"You're all fucking welcome," Tony said as he glared at Omar.

"What about a vehicle for tonight?" Val asked Omar.

"Yes, Sir. Found us one. It's a shitty old Mercedes sedan. But it runs. The motor pool sergeant promised me it was reliable."

"Good. Haskell accepted the invitation to meet. We'll pick him up tonight."

"What's the plan for that?" Sydney asked.

"For what?"

"To pick up Haskell."

"It's pretty simple. Vinnie and I will drive out and pick him up."

"I'm coming with you," Sydney said.

"No fucking chance of that."

A smile of anticipation broke across Tony's face. Omar glanced at Val. The two polygraphers looked at their feet nervously.

"I'm not asking you for permission," Sydney said.

"Good. Because you're not getting it."

"I'm the ranking officer here." Sydney's hands clenched into fists. "I'm coming with you."

Tony raised his eyebrows. He made eye contact with Omar and gestured with his head toward the door. Omar nodded, already moving. The polygraphers and other interpreter leapt at the chance to leave and followed them out.

"Did you really just try to pull rank on me?" Val growled at Sydney.

"I didn't try. I'm the OIC here." She jabbed at the ground with a finger as she continued. "I'll be going with you to pick up Haskell. And you can like it or not. I don't really give a shit."

"You're out of your fucking mind."

"Oh, am I?"

"Yes!" Val shouted, surprising her.

But Sydney didn't flinch.

"You're out of your mind and way outside the wire!" he continued yelling. "Look around! We're in the fucking jungle now. This isn't Langley or Balad. We're fucking nowhere. And we have no idea what is going to happen tonight. As you have been harping on to anybody that will listen, Haskell may be a Syrian plant at this point. He may be rounding up all his buddies as we speak for an ambush. Or getting fitted for a suicide vest to go out in a blaze of fire and shrapnel and glory when we pick him up, or any number of other nasty things. There is only one way tonight goes well, and that's the boring scenario where Vinnie and I pick him up and bring him in.

"Vinnie and I have done this hundreds of times" Val's volume decreased, but veins bulged in his forehead. "How many times have you done it?"

"Fuck you." Sydney shook her head. She was not in the mood for a tough-guy lecture.

"Exactly." Val sneered and nodded. "This isn't Moscow, or Kyiv, where you do meets in front of pretty old fountains. This is the front end of the intel pipeline in Iraq. And the front end is nasty. I know because that's where Tony and I live in this shitshow of a country. Our job is to be jammed up the ass end of the world and to feel around in the dark for the right source, or indicator, or confirmation, or whatever else it is that the machine is demanding. We find it, yank it out of the hole it's in, and try not to get killed in the process."

"Oh right. How could I forget? You guys are just two regular working-class military heroes. Thank you for your service."

Val turned and walked over to grab his weapon. "This conversation is over."

"This conversation is not over, Major!" Now Sydney was the one shouting. "I'm the OIC, and I'll be going with you, so just get your fucking head around it!"

Sydney was technically right. The CIA ran strategic human intelligence collection in Iraq and the rest of the world. The Defense Intelligence Agency contributed case officers, like Val, who were under the operational control of JSOC and ran human intelligence missions in military contexts where they were better suited or placed for the specific activity. But human intelligence was the CIA's kingdom. Always had been. Always would be. Val and Sydney's specific mission was being conducted by the CIA at the request of JSOC. On paper, back in Balad, Sydney was the officer in charge of the mission.

Val walked out.

Sydney stood alone in the middle of the cinder-block room, clenching her fists and jaw. She almost swayed as rage swept through her in waves. She got control of her breathing and walked out into the desert night.

"Hey," Tony said.

He was leaning against the wall outside, waiting for her.

"Just like old times, huh?" he added.

Sydney resisted, but a chuckle escaped her.

"I guess."

Tony pulled out a pack of cigarettes. He put one in his mouth and held out the pack to Sydney.

"I don't smoke," she said.

"I don't either. Unless I'm in a combat zone."

Sydney took a cigarette from Tony. Each lit their own.

"I have to tell you, though," Sydney said after they had each had a deep first drag. "That didn't feel like old times."

"Didn't sound like it either."

"What's he so mad about?"

"Why didn't you ever call him?"

"Are you kidding me?"

Tony shrugged.

"Look, I don't know shit. But you asked me. Way I heard it, you guys had some kind of rendezvous planned. He was really looking forward to it. Then he got deployed to Afghanistan right off the jump. Six months later, he is back in the States and realizes, *Shit. She never reached out. Never checked in on me. What the hell?*"

Tony took another drag from his cigarette and leaned back against the cinderblock wall. "He acts all tough, but Val is a softie. Besides, you know how it is… Most of America doesn't fucking care about all this."

Tony swept his arms around at the war.

"I don't know about you," he continued, "but I get madder and madder about it every year. Fucking spoiled, unexamined lot, Americans are. But your friends? Your comrades?"

Tony gestured with his cigarette at Sydney.

"They're supposed to give a shit. Supposed to understand. Supposed to check in."

Sydney thought about Kyiv and what happened. Her shoulders sagged. She took a final, long pull from her cigarette and then dropped it on the ground, less than half smoked. She placed her boot heel on it and ground it into the sand.

"Well, I never checked on you either," Sydney said. "You don't seem to be all bent out of shape about it like a high school girl."

"I'm not sweet on you." Tony dropped the butt of his cigarette and stepped on it. He'd smoked his down to the filter.

"You think he is sweet on me?" Sydney asked before she could stop herself.

"Now this conversation has crossed into the ridiculous." Tony shook his head as he stepped forward from the wall. "You're both my friends, but that doesn't mean I have to take part in your incompetence. And I certainly won't pass notes for you at recess. I'm done. You guys should talk shit out like old friends and be done with it."

"Fine. What time are we going to get Haskell?"

Tony laughed.

"It's actually a really simple operation," Tony said. "Should be over in minutes. Why the hell do you want to go so bad?"

"If it's so simple, what's the big deal?"

"Seriously. Why so bad?"

"It's Haskell. I've only read about him in the files and briefing books. He's a big deal. I want to start taking the measure of him from the very beginning. I want to read his face as he walks up. Watch how he interacts."

Tony nodded.

"I get it. I feel the same. None of us have met the guy. I've been reading about him for more than a year now, I think. Puts butterflies in my stomach."

"Thanks."

"Oh, you're not going," he said in a voice that was friendly and final.

She started to protest, but Tony held up a finger.

"Too dangerous. Not necessary. The OIC has no business going on a meet like this. Simple or not. Use your head."

Tony walked away.

Sydney looked at the ground, wishing she hadn't thrown half a cigarette away.

CHAPTER 38

Val and Tony checked each other over as they stood next to the beat-up Mercedes sedan. It was almost midnight. Innumerable stars hung in the cloudless sky, and a waxing crescent moon was rising in the east.

It was a short operation, and they were going light. Dressed in their unmarked khaki clothes, each carried their M4 rifle, sidearm, and several magazines. Far less than the standard load they would pack for a mission where they expected heavy contact.

The two battlefield interpreters approached, M4s in hand.

"You guys ready?" Val asked.

"Yes, sir," Omar answered.

"Good." Val put his radio earpiece into his right ear. Tony did the same. "Stay sharp."

"Roger that." Omar and the other interpreter turned to walk toward the building they had scoped out earlier in the day. It was on the western edge of the camp, and its roof afforded a sweeping, unobstructed view of the desert. The two interpreters would set up overwatch there and would have their weapons trained on Val and Tony the entire time. They were packing night-vision goggles and could see for miles in the clear desert night.

They passed Sydney, who emerged from the shadows. Val gritted his teeth as she stepped up to the car.

"Don't worry." Her hands up in a surrender gesture. "I won't try to jump in the car with you guys."

Tony smiled. Val looked at her evenly.

"Just wanted to see you off," she said. She shuffled her feet and then jammed her hands in her pockets. "So, good luck. Please be careful."

"Thanks," Tony said. "We will."

Val got in the front passenger side of the car without saying a word.

A few minutes later, Tony got into the driver's side seat. Val looked past Tony at Sydney, who was walking away, back into the shadows.

Tony looked at Val and shook his head. "You know—"

"Overwatch set," Omar's radio call interrupted Tony, indicating the interpreters were on the roof, rifles trained, night vision in use.

"Roger that," Val said over the radio. Then he looked at Tony. "Drive."

Tony drove two hundred meters out from the edge of Camp Korea. He stopped the car and turned off the engine. Val keyed his mic and spoke into his radio.

"Set."

Val looked at his watch.

They had about half an hour until the linkup time given to Haskell. Val and Tony sat in the car in silence, each scanning their assigned sector with their helmet-mounted night-vision goggles. Val pictured the two interpreters doing the same from their rooftop position. Val felt good about Omar in overwatch. The new sergeant was a deadly shot.

The illumination was good that night. Nothing could creep up on them undetected.

Tony flipped his goggles up and looked at Val.

"Sydney talked to me about you guys. When are you going to clear the air with her, man?"

"Not any fucking time soon." Val did not raise his night vision goggles, keeping his eyes glued to the monochrome desert. "Do you mind if we focus on successfully picking up the high-value source that the JSOC commander sent us out here to get?"

"Yeah, fine. You guys can work that shit out on your own. I don't know why I let myself get pulled into it. It was a pain in the ass at the Farm, and it's a pain in the ass here. If you really—"

"Tony! Please!"

Tony faced the front and flipped his goggles down without speaking.

Twenty-six minutes later, a radio call from Omar broke the silence.

"Person on foot approaching from the west. Your eleven o'clock. Approximately five hundred meters."

"Roger that," Val responded. "I got him."

The walking figure was still a long way off, and Val could only see his top half from his ground-level vantage point. But he appeared to be alone.

"Me too," Tony said.

They both got out of the vehicle and raised their rifles toward the approaching figure. They used their NVGs to alternate between watching the lone man and scanning the area.

It was impossible to make out many details about the approaching figure at night under night vision. Val got excited, nonetheless.

"So much time talking about this guy," Val whispered. "And here he comes, walking out of the night."

"Yeah. Can't wait to get my hands on the bastard."

They had given Haskell a GPS coordinate via the secure cell phone. He was told to come alone, and to be on time, or the meeting would be canceled.

Tony and Val continued to watch as the lone person approached. At about two hundred meters, it was clear he fit Haskell's description—male, more than six feet tall, somewhat thin. He wore a small satchel slung across his body.

The figure stopped and pulled something out of the satchel. Val and Tony both instinctively crouched, tightening their grips on their M4s. The distant man turned on a flashlight and traced an X on the desert ground with the light.

"Bingo," Tony said. It was the signal they had instructed Haskell to give, to show it was him.

The figure started walking again.

"Overwatch," Val said softly into his radio.

"Nothing," came Omar's voice in his earpiece. "It's clear for miles. Just desert. He's alone."

Val keyed his mic twice to let Omar know he copied.

Shifting his weight on his feet, Val took a deep, even breath. He hated this part.

Tony looked at Val.

"Easy, peasey, partner. You'll see."

"Let's hope so," Val said with a nod before walking about twenty meters away from Tony.

They both kneeled, peering through their rifle night scopes, aiming at the approaching man.

Now about fifty meters away, the man stopped again. He could see the dark shapes of Val and Tony at this point. He raised his hands slowly, still holding the flashlight.

Val blinked his red-lensed flashlight twice.

The man blinked his three times, per the linkup instructions.

"Overwatch?" Val transmitted.

"Still nothing. You're clear."

Val keyed his mic twice.

"No further!" Tony barked as he turned on the bright-white light flashlight on his rifle. Val did the same. The man was well illuminated now and squinted in the intense light.

"You should not be out alone on a night like this, friend," Val said, extending the verbal challenge that only Haskell should know. "It's darker than West Texas tonight."

"Yes. But I must find the archeologist."

That confirmed it. It was Haskell.

"Raise your robe and slowly turn around," Tony ordered.

The man complied, lifting his dishdasha to show that he was not wearing a suicide vest. He shuffled his feet, turning his tall body all the way around.

"On the ground," Tony said. "Face down. Hands behind your head."

The man complied. Tony sprinted forward, while Val covered him with his M4. Tony kneeled with his knee on the man's back and patted him down, searching for weapons.

Tony sprang back up, bringing his rifle back to bear on the prone man. "He's clean."

"Overwatch?" Val prompted on the radio.

"Clear."

Tony grabbed the man by the arm and lifted him up. "Let's go, buddy."

The man lifted himself from the ground with Tony's help, and they all hurried back to the car.

Val shook his head. Even now, Haskell was living up to his reputation. He'd been a cool customer throughout what was typically the highest-stress portion of the meeting. Val's blood had been pumping, and he was sure Tony's was as well.

But Haskell had seemed no more stressed than if he were kicking off his boots at the end of a long day.

Tony put Haskell in the back seat. Val climbed in back as well. Tony got in the driver's seat, started the car, and drove them back to Camp Korea.

CHAPTER 39

ydney, Val, and Tony sat in the dimly lit cinder-block bay with Haskell at the small table that Tony had scrounged up earlier. They each had a cup of the tea that Val had brought along for this moment. He found, in the past, it helped to start to build the all-important rapport with his source. He and Tony and Sydney would try to build a relationship with this man, all while looking for signs of a lack of veracity. Could they trust him?

"Masudi Kader," Val said with a friendly smile. "Thank you for making the trip. We know it was dangerous for you as well as inconvenient."

Masudi nodded appreciatively at Val's comment, and Val could not help but notice that this was a very handsome man. His trim, tanned face was topped with thick, wavy salt-and-pepper hair that flowed into sideburns and then a neatly trimmed beard. At six foot two, his slender, athletic frame provided ample space for the fabric of his robe to flow. Val was always amused by shorter, chunkier men in their robes, which ended up making them look like a pile of laundry. Not Haskell. In every sense, he was well put together.

For chrissake. Do I smell cologne?

Suddenly, Val felt frumpy in his surplus-store military khakis. He pushed the thought from his head and continued.

"My name is Max," Val began before introducing Tony and Sydney. "This is Vinnie and Tracy. We're with the US Army."

Haskell smiled. "It is okay to use your real names with me. I am trustworthy."

"I'm sure you had expenses along the way," Val said, not acknowledging the comment. "That you had to pay someone at some point. We would like to give you this to cover those expenses, and any you might incur on your return journey."

Val pushed five one-hundred-US-dollar bills across the table.

"Thank you," Masudi said without reaching for the money. "But this is unnecessary."

Damn, his English is perfect. He still lives up to his code name, "Haskell."

"Please. As a token of our appreciation."

Masudi dipped his head again in an elegant nod of acceptance. He reached out and grabbed the money from the table. As he did, Val noticed the scars and discoloration around his fingertips. Most of his fingernails had been pulled out at some point.

"Thank you, Max," Masudi said, hesitating slightly before saying the name "Max" to make the point one last time that he knew how things worked.

"Masudi, the first thing I'd like to say is how much we appreciate what you have done for us in the past," Sydney said, leaning forward as she spoke. "You personally made big contributions to the war effort and to the people of Syria and Iraq. Your information and collaboration with us greatly reduced the violence. It's very much appreciated and has established your reputation as one of our best partners in the region."

Again, Masudi gave his elegant nod in Sydney's direction. Val suppressed a respectful chuckle. *This dude is the definition of chill. He gives off the air of being in total control. If you didn't know better, and were watching this meeting, you would think he had us dragged in under gunpoint to talk to him, not the other way around.*

"Is that why you left me in a Syrian prison for more than a year?" Masudi's eyes bored into Sydney.

"Masudi, that's not—"

"This enormous respect, I mean," he interrupted in a calm but direct voice. "This is why you didn't reach out to me when they finally released me? This is why I had to reach out to you?"

"Mr. Kader." Sydney made a point of using his last name as she crossed her arms and leaned back in her chair. "Are you kidding me with that?"

"I most certainly am not kidding you, Tracy."

Val thought he saw the faintest hint of anger on Haskell's face.

"You speak of my service and your appreciation, and yet you left me alone for almost two years." Masudi leaned slightly forward, placed a clenched fist on the table and stared at Sydney. "I doubt your sincerity."

"Disappointed," she said flatly.

"Indeed, I was."

"No," Sydney said, arms still crossed, voice matter-of-fact. "I'm disappointed."

Kader leaned back in his chair slightly. Eyes narrow.

"I'm disappointed that someone of your intelligence and experience would fail to realize that we would've been condemning you to death if we had tried to reach out to you during your captivity. We wanted to. It would've felt good, perhaps, to send you a cheery message of thanks and support while you were there. And it would've gotten you a bullet in the head."

Sydney met Masudi's glare.

Val and Tony waited.

"All I mean to say—" Masudi began, raising a finger to make a point. But Sydney interrupted him now.

"Disappointed that you're unable to recognize the professional restraint that was required to keep you alive. That, despite our desire to get in touch when you were released, we had to assume that you were being observed every minute of every day by Syrian counterintelligence. To reach out to you at that point would be to throw away what you had accomplished by surviving, Mr. Kader. Because, again, we would've condemned you to death.

"Despite wanting to send you messages of support, we knew it was safer to wait. Knowing that you, if you wanted to continue working together, would reach out when you knew, for certain, that it was safe to do so."

Masudi took a sip of tea.

Sydney uncrossed her arms.

"And yet, sir, I regret that our caution, out of great concern for your safety, hurt your feelings. I hope you can see now that no offense was intended."

He set down his tea.

"And we're very excited to work together again," Sydney concluded.

"As am I, of course," Masudi said with an easygoing shrug.

Again, Val suppressed a chuckle. Sydney had handled that well, not allowing Haskell to set the tone of the relationship. *She's good,* he admitted to himself.

"Can we start with a little background, Masudi?" Tony asked as he pulled out his pack of cigarettes and reached them across the table in offering.

Masudi took a cigarette and leaned back in his seat.

"We've all read your file." Tony pushed a lighter across the table and pulled a small ashtray out of one of his cargo pockets. "And, as Max and Tracy have said, you have a terrific reputation." Tony placed the ashtray in the middle of the table. "But it would be great to hear it firsthand from you."

"I agree," Val said. "I'd appreciate that as well."

Masudi lit the cigarette and inhaled deeply. "Of course."

"My father was an engineer," he began. "He traveled a lot within the region for work. Growing up, my brothers and sisters and I spent a lot of time in Kuwait with my mother while my father traveled. We were educated there and, as a result, were Western leaning in our perspective. We all supported the US liberation of Kuwait in the early nineties.

"At some point, I don't remember why, and my father never explained it to me, my family faced increasing pressure and scrutiny from the Assad regime. When this scrutiny turned to persecution, and several of our extended family members were imprisoned, my father moved the family to Iraq.

"Things were not much better. We faced persecution there as well. I had become an engineer like my father and tried to make a living for my family and keep my eye on my mother and sisters. We still traveled back to Syria for work and to see family and friends, and met Abdul Razzaq and his family during this period. We moved in the same circles. We began to share dinners and spend social time together. He invited my family and me frequently to Damascus, where Abdul Razzaq's family had a large home. One of my sisters, in fact, married one of Abdul Razzaq's brothers. In those early days, he and I were friends."

Masudi shifted in his chair. He took a long pull from his cigarette and held his sad gaze on the ceiling.

"And you're not friends now?" Tony asked.

"No." Masudi lowered his eyes back to the table.

"Why not?" Sydney asked.

Masudi looked at Sydney with a face that was cloaked in weariness. "He is part of the machine of suffering now. The machine that is grinding my family and my people into dust."

Val stifled a smile. *Confident and grandiose. Just like his file says. I like him. I just don't know if we can trust him.*

"He did not create the situation, of course," Masudi said with a shrug. "Indeed, I remember back in 2002, America had not invaded yet. But we all knew it was coming. We were excited. We spoke of our hope that it would restore order to the region."

Masudi chuckled ruefully and took a drag from his cigarette, which had almost burned down to the filter. "We hoped you would go after the radical Sunni factions that had killed so many," he said, gesturing at the Americans sitting across from him. "But things went to shit, as you say. And at some point, Abdul Razzaq decided to participate. To profit.

"He was always somewhat of a petty criminal. Even in our early days, he would brag of contraband of this sort or another that he'd managed to sneak into Syria. He always knew a guy. Always had an angle. But now? Now, it's not an amusing hobby. His trafficking causes so much suffering. The foreign fighters. The weapons. For you and yours, and for me and mine. They are a curse. It must end. I cannot look the other way."

Masudi leaned forward and ground out the cigarette in the ashtray. Then he leaned back in his chair, looked at Tony, and said, "That is my humble story," with a smile.

"Thank you."

"Oh. I forgot." Masudi raised a finger in the air. "I brought you something. May I have my satchel, please?"

Tony looked at Val.

Val nodded. He'd inspected it. It only held papers, some photos of Masudi and his family, and his flashlight.

Tony stepped away from the table to retrieve the satchel from the corner of the bare room.

As he did, Masudi leaned forward and took another cigarette from the pack at the center of the table.

Val and Sydney shared a quick glance at each other as Masudi lit his cigarette. Though they both wore expressionless masks on their faces, Val could tell she felt as he did. She wanted to compare notes.

"Here you go." Tony dropped the satchel in the middle of the table.

"Thank you, Vincent." Masudi grabbed the satchel and placed it in his lap. "I brought you these photos."

Terrific, now, we get to talk about Masudi's kids for an hour. Val was tired of trying to build rapport. He was ready to grill the man.

"This is Abdul Razzaq," Masudi said, pointing at a bearded man in the top photo of the small stack he'd placed on the table.

"Excuse me?" Sydney said.

"Akmal Abdul Razzaq?" Val clarified.

"What?" Tony asked.

"Yes. This is him." A proud smile spread across Masudi's his face. "These are all photos of him. I brought them with me in the hopes they would be useful to you."

Val raised his eyebrows for an instant before he caught himself. He fought the urge to glance at Tony or Sydney.

The entire American global intelligence organization had one old, grainy photo of Razzaq. It was taken decades ago when he was a teenager and was useless for identification purposes. This lack of identifying photographic intelligence contributed to Razzaq's near mythical reputation within the Joint Special Operations Command and the intelligence community. No one knew what he looked like today. It's very hard to kill someone when you don't know what they look like.

And Masudi was casually flipping through a stack of about two dozen clear and recent photographs of the man.

The photos were taken in various settings. Most were casual, with family and others smiling or eating with Razzaq. In all of them, it was clear that he was the center of gravity of whatever was happening. Most eyes in the photos clung to him. His gestures and postures were those of a man who regarded himself as important, and the others captured in the photos seemed to agree.

Val leaned forward to study one of photos. Razzaq looked nondescript to him. Ordinary. A little overweight, maybe. It was the image of someone who could easily be a shopkeeper or farmer, rather than the most wanted foreign fighter facilitator and arms smuggler in the world. Val smiled to himself. A decade into his intelligence career, and he still often relearned the maxim that looks could be deceiving.

"There are times, still, when I enjoy being around him," Masudi said, having caught Val's hint of a smile. Val looked up from the photo. Masudi was looking at him. They locked eyes.

"I listen to him telling one of his ridiculous stories about nothing. When he is in one of his moods. So indignant. Or so theatrical. Or just happy. I close my eyes, and it is twenty years ago. Before all of this. Before the world became so dark. And the peace seems real."

Val didn't know what to say. He still couldn't tell if Masudi was laying it on thick, or if he was really this reflective. Val just nodded and furrowed his brow as if he was in deep thought along with Masudi.

I just want to kill the man. Val shifted his eyes back to the images of Razzaq.

"These are fascinating," Sydney said. Val could tell from the tenor of her voice that she felt like he did. She was ready to grill him.

"I think what I'd like, if it's okay with you, Masudi, is for us all to call it a day," she said. "You traveled far to get here, and we just jumped right into all this. I'd like to let you shower and get some rest. We'll do the same and then we'll start fresh in the morning."

Masudi looked around the barren room. Aside from the table they sat at, the only other furniture was a cot at the far end in the shadows where the dim lights ran out of steam.

"This place isn't much, I know," Sydney said, tracking his gaze. "But you're safe here. And unobserved. I hope someday we can meet in a setting more befitting of your contribution."

"Oh," Masudi said, waving away her comment. "We are at war, Tracy. I am adaptable. And I am honored to be here." He stood and stretched his back. "And I appreciate the opportunity for a brief break."

"Good," Val said, "Let's all do that."

Val glanced at Sydney. Her look said, *Let's proceed.*

"And in the morning," Val said, in the most casual voice he could muster, "we'll do a quick polygraph and then get back to our discussion."

Masudi stood straighter, a hurt and surprised look on his face. It was a rare drop of his unflappable demeanor.

He caught himself quickly, though, and let his shoulders sag. He raised his hands slightly from his side in a sad, surrendering gesture and smiled. His eyes remained sad, though.

"You think the Syrians have sent me here."

"No. Of course not. It's a formality, I assure you," Val said, stepping around the table to get closer to Masudi, who was a couple of inches taller than him.

Masudi Kader cocked his head slightly at Val. His expression said, *Give me a fucking break*, but he did not verbally protest.

"We three believe you, Masudi." Val didn't look away from him but did gesture back toward Tony and Sydney. They nodded in agreement.

"And we're ready and excited to work together," Val continued. "But you know how this works. We will have to convince our superiors to let us do so. And they do not have the benefit of being here with us. We have to bring back to them not only our urgent conviction and judgment, but also data."

Val put his hand on Masudi's shoulder.

"Please, my friend," Val said. "Don't take offense."

Masudi looked at Val's hand and then back at Val.

"Are we friends?" he asked Val.

"You tell me."

Masudi smiled. "I believe we are on the path to being so."

"Good. Then let's move down that path together."

"Yes. Let's do that."

Val nodded and then stepped away.

"Thank you, Masudi," Sydney said. "We'll say good night. Sergeant Faisal will stay on this side with you tonight. If you need anything, don't hesitate to ask."

Masudi gave a knowing nod to Omar.

The two interpreters would split the duty of standing watch over Masudi until he departed. They would monitor him every minute. It was not uncommon for a source to change their mind and flee or even attack their handlers.

"In the morning, we'll do a quick polygraph session and then continue our conversation," Sydney said.

"As you wish, Tracy," Masudi said with a smile.

As Val left the room, he made eye contact with Omar.

Omar nodded to say, *No worries, boss.*

CHAPTER 40

"That's one slick son of a bitch," Tony said. He, Val, and Sydney were on their side of the cinder-block building, waiting for one of the polygraphers to finish his initial session with Haskell. They had met with Haskell at seven a.m. that morning while the polygrapher was setting up and talked through the pictures one more time.

"Too slick," Sydney responded to Tony. "It's obvious. The Syrians have extensively coached this guy. I'm tempted to call this off right now."

"Give me a break," Tony said, pointing at the wall between them and Haskell. "That ain't coaching. That's conviction. He's clearly still with us."

"He is clearly being run by the Syrians." Sydney shook her head.

"What about those photos?"

"What about them?"

"They're gold," Tony said. "We've got nothing like that on Razzaq. We can actually start looking for the motherfucker now. Why would the Syrians give up Razzaq like that?"

"Exactly," Sydney said.

"Ask yourself that question, Vinnie," Val said, rubbing his eyes. "Why would they do that? And how do we know that's really Razzaq in those photos?"

Tony's eyes narrowed as Val let the question hang.

Sydney nodded. "Exactly."

"They could easily have sent us photos of some poor, random bastard from Damascus," Val said.

"You don't know that," Tony said.

"Exactly."

Val and Tony both swung their heads to look at Sydney with irritation.

"Would you quit saying that, please?" Val said.

Sydney rolled her eyes. "I'm just pointing out the fact we don't know shit."

"We're aware of that, Tracy," Val said, irritation surfacing in his voice. "That's why we're here. To figure the shit out."

"You can't figure shit out if you're biased," Tony mumbled.

"Exactly," Sydney responded, her voice taut with anger.

"Hey," Val said, heading them off. "It's been a long couple of days. This place is a shithole. We're all tired. Let's take some time to clear our heads while the polygrapher works on him. He should be done in an hour. We can attack it with a fresh perspective then."

Tony and Sydney nodded.

Tony looked at his feet for a moment and then lifted his head and winked at Sydney.

Sydney smiled.

"Thank you. Now, if you two would get out of here for a while, I'll draw up the debriefing schedule."

"Come on," Tony said to Sydney. "I'll buy you a shitty cup of coffee."

For the next two days, Val, Tony, and Sydney worked in alternating pairs, spending hours debriefing Haskell. After each session, they would give him a brief break, and then a polygrapher would wire him and try to confirm or refute the veracity of his story, working off specifics from his most recent conversations. Following protocols and best practices, the polygraphers avoided each other. They pursued their goals separately to preserve their objectivity and independent judgment.

Val spent the second day focused on motive, and as the sun was setting over the Iraqi desert, he made one last run at it while Sydney sat next to him at the interview table.

"Okay, Masudi," Val said. "One more question, and we'll be done for the day."

Masudi smiled wearily and looked at his watch.

"This is it," Val said. "I promise."

"Yes. And then you go relax while I spend another hour with your lying detection experts."

Val heard the fatigue in Masudi's voice.

"No. This is it for the day. No polygraph."

Val kicked Sydney under the table in a warning not to contradict him. He pictured the polygraphers on the other side of the wall watching the live video feed and high-fiving each other. They were tired too.

"Also, we were going to surprise you, but I'm going to share it with you now because I can see you're tired, and I am too," Val said. "I called in a favor. That helicopter you heard about an hour ago brought us dinner. It was cooked this afternoon, and it's still hot."

"Bless you, Max. Your American MREs are hard on me." Masudi held a hand to his stomach.

"It was my pleasure."

"Okay, then? Before we feast, Max… What is your question?"

"Why give us Abdul Razzaq?"

"This again?" Masudi's tone was more amused than irritated. Val had asked this same question many ways over the course of the day.

"This again." Val offered a grin and a shrug as an apology. "Tell me again, please. Why betray your countryman? Such a long and good friend whose brother is married to your sister?"

"This question bothers you, doesn't it?"

"It doesn't bother me. I just would like to understand."

"You seek my motive," Masudi said, like a professor embarking on a lesson. "You believe, if you understand my true motive, then you will know if you can trust me. You will be able to determine whether I am working for the Syrians. Or if I am truly seeking to work with you."

Val returned Masudi's gaze and waited.

Both men smiled. But Val could not tell if Masudi's smile was that of a friend or a respectful adversary.

"Well, Max," Masudi finally broke the silence, "I do not envy you."

"Why's that?"

"A man's true motive is unknowable. Even to himself."

"That so?"

"I wish it were not."

"Then we're at an impasse."

"Perhaps." Masudi chuckled.

Val joined him in a weary laugh.

"But I will tell you again," Haskell said, "because, though I have not been able to convince you it is true, I want to work with you. I want to help your cause."

"Why?" Val asked, more insistence in his voice.

"Razzaq's border trafficking makes the violence and unrest worse. This has affected my family, my friends, and my country. I want it stopped. And I am not the kind of man that can sit idly by."

Val nodded. "Thank you for answering my question. I won't ask again."

"I also enjoy my relationship with you Americans," Masudi continued in a friendly voice. "And I appreciate the money."

CHAPTER 41

"Mind if I join you?" Sydney asked Val.

After eating dinner with Haskell, the team spent a few hours reviewing their notes and making a plan for the next day's sessions. Afterward, Omar and the polygraphers lay down on their cots to read and Tony fell asleep. Val stepped out. Sydney watched him leave, waited a few minutes, and then went to find him.

Val was sitting on the hood of a burned-out car, looking up at the clear desert sky.

"Sure. Pull up a chair."

"Thanks," Sydney said, smiling. "Does the waitress swing by here often?"

"Oh, yeah. She'll be by any minute. She's just grabbing me another glass of wine."

Sydney leaned over to peer at the hood of the car in the darkness, hesitant to hop up.

"It's actually more comfortable than it looks."

"That wouldn't be hard. I just don't want to slice my ass open on a rusty Opel tonight."

"Not up on your tetanus shots?" Val asked. He hesitated and then reached out his hand to Sydney.

"I wouldn't know," she said before noticing Val's outstretched hand. "They don't tell us what's in the needles."

Val nodded in understanding.

Sydney grabbed Val's hand to stabilize herself as she gingerly stepped on the crooked bumper. She lowered herself onto the hood and let go.

They sat in silence for a moment. Sydney rubbed her hand, recalling the feeling of his firm grip. She tried to remember the last time they had touched years ago and a world away in Garmisch.

She sat cross-legged. He rested his feet on the bumper. Sydney's left knee pressed against his. She thought of leaning into him, of resting her head on his shoulder. But resisted. She wondered what he was thinking.

She spoke to interrupt her thoughts.

"I can flag down the maître d'. Maybe he could find us another table."

"Please do. I'll take that slope-side table in the sun back at the Bayernhaus. Before the course at the Marshall Center started."

Sydney didn't answer. The images of white snow, blue skies, and a fleeting time when they seemed headed in a mutual direction washed over her.

"That would be nice," she managed to say.

Val nodded slowly and looked back up at the sky.

"You're not buying his bullshit, are you?" Sydney asked, veering back to work quickly to stave off her own memories and feelings.

"I don't know yet… I just don't know."

"Well, Tony is all in. He's swallowed it all. If it were up to him, we'd be tasking Predators tonight."

Val shook his head. "Tony is just tired."

"It has been a long day for everyone," Sydney conceded.

"That's not what I meant. He's tired of the whole thing. Running around the desert at night. Kicking in doors and killing people. Cleaning up gory kill sites after Razzaq's weapons or suicide bombers have done their work."

"I understand. You guys have been on the road a lot."

"We have. And Tony more than me. But don't worry. When it's time to make the call, he will be clear-eyed about it."

"I know."

She looked up at the sky. Deep in the dark western desert of Iraq, there was no man-made illumination to compete with. The stars and moon were bright.

They sat in silence. A dog barked in the distance.

Sydney wondered what to say. She looked at her hands in her lap. The moonlight gave a soft glow to her skin as she rubbed them together. She tried to remember what it was like when he'd grabbed her hand, only moments ago, but she could not.

Val chuckled.

"What?" Sydney asked.

"The two of us under a starlit sky, sitting on the hood of a car, no one around," Val said, a sad resignation in his voice. "There have been a lot of times in the past few years I'd have paid good money, crossed a big ocean, to get to this spot."

"I wish you had," she said, scared to look in his direction. She looked up at the stars.

"I wish I'd known you felt that way."

"I wish I didn't have to tell you."

"I guess wishing doesn't make it so." Val eased off the hood of the car onto his feet. "I'm going to turn in. See you in the morning."

Sydney, surprised by his abrupt departure, struggled to find something to say but failed. She nodded to herself.

"I miss you," she finally said softly into the darkness.

CHAPTER 42

By the end of their third day at Camp Korea, Val could sense the time had come. There was nothing more to be learned. They had combed through Haskell's head enough. It was time to make a call.

The two interpreters took Haskell to one of the shower facilities while Val assembled the team. He, Tony, and Sydney sat on their cots eating MREs for dinner while the two polygraphers made their cases.

"This guy is, without a doubt, the smartest asset I have ever tested," the first polygrapher began. "And while subtle, he is showing clear signs of deception. The call is easy for me. Not only do I not recommend working with this asset, but I'd kick his ass out of here tonight. He scares the shit out of me."

"Okay. That was easy," Sydney said. She turned to the second polygrapher. "And you?"

"It's not as clear to me. I didn't pick up the same signal. There were fluctuations in physiology, of course. But I'm not prepared to say they were clear indications of dishonesty. They were not what I'd call strong and unanimous indications, and could easily be explained by nerves, a desire to do well, and the poor conditions we're keeping the asset in. There are limits to a polygraph, of course. And while I agree he is highly intelligent and, at times, seems to play with us, I didn't pick up anything that indicates this asset is being dishonest."

Sydney sat with her mouth open.

Tony scratched his head.

Val rubbed his eyes.

This was the worst-case scenario. Inconclusive.

"You spent three days with that snake, and you didn't pick up anything that makes you distrust him?" Sydney finally said, incredulous, to the second polygrapher.

"How can you be so fucking sure he is lying?" Tony barked at the first polygrapher.

"All right, all right." Val stood and walked to the middle of the room before the two specialists could answer. "Let's work our way through this deliberately. It's been a long three days. We're all tired and ready to get out of this shithole. Let's not take it out on each other."

Val smiled wearily to show his camaraderie with everyone in the room.

Tony and Sydney both gave him a tired nod.

"Okay, Vinnie," Val said. "Can you rephrase your question?"

"Sure." Tony looked at the first polygrapher with a friendly face and said, "Can you give me an example, maybe? Walk us through one of the clearer instances where you believe the asset was lying?"

The polygrapher opened his notes.

But an hour and a half later, they were no closer to a consensus. Both of the polygraphers were adamant in their assessments, and neither Tony nor Sydney had moved a millimeter off their positions. Tony believed Haskell and was ready to work with him. Sydney didn't trust him and wanted him gone.

Val had been mostly quiet, soaking in both sides of the argument. He thanked the two polygraphers and dismissed them while he, Tony, and Sydney tried to finalize their decision.

The three of them stood in front of a section of wall where they'd taped the photos that Haskell had given them. The man who was supposedly Razzaq was laughing in a few of them, seeming to mock the three exhausted intelligence officers.

"Looks like you're the tiebreaker, buddy," Tony said. "What's it going to be?"

Sydney crossed her arms. "Tiebreaker?" she said in a disbelieving tone. "That how you guys do it in JSOC?"

Val and Tony looked at Sydney.

She smiled quickly to show it was a joke, uncrossing her arms and putting her hands in her pockets.

"I'm sorry," she said. "I know we're dog tired and our fuses are short. But, Vinnie, I just don't agree with you. Everything I have seen over the past seventy-two hours just confirmed my belief that Haskell is burned and cannot be trusted. I saw clear indications of Syrian coaching and prep, as well as a concerning level of ego and intelligence. Maybe I came into this with too strong a bias. I'm aware that could be clouding my judgment. But almost a decade after we all graduated from the Farm, I've learned to trust my gut."

"I appreciate that," Tony said. "I do. But I still come down on the other side. Is Haskell a wiseass? Yes. Arrogant and too smart for his own good? Absolutely. But if he were a normal fucking dude, he wouldn't be here with us after just getting out of a Syrian prison. A normal person would be cowering at home with his mommy. You gotta be an arrogant maniac to think you can get back at the Syrians and your former buddy, who is now an untouchable border trafficker in a war zone. And thank god, because I think his information is good, and we're not going to get it from anybody else. This is a closing window of opportunity. We should jump through it and fucking kill Razzaq."

Tony pointed at the pictures on the wall.

Sydney nodded respectfully to Tony.

"Well, I hate to have to say this, but I'm the OIC here," she said. "All joking aside, you guys know that we don't make important intelligence decisions by democratic vote."

Sydney looked down at her feet to avoid their angry glares.

"I feel strongly about my perspective on this," she continued slowly. "But I don't have total confidence in it. Our two best polygraphers are split, and I respect your judgment, Vinnie. I really do."

Sydney sighed and raised her head to look at Val.

"So, I'll back you a hundred percent. Whichever way you want to go on this, Max, I'll support. I trust you and I trust this team and I think we have done good work together on this. We've kicked over every stone I can think of. So you make the call, and we'll go back to McStone as a unified voice."

Tony smiled broadly.

Val's and Sydney's eyes were locked in on each other.

"Fucking A," Tony said, putting a hand on both of their shoulders.

Val took a deep breath.

He looked at the wall of photos and then back at Tony.

"I'm a no," Val said.

"What?" Tony gasped, dropping his arms to his sides.

"I'm sorry, buddy."

"Are you fucking kidding me?"

"I wish I were."

"You gotta be fucking kidding me."

"It's too high-risk, Vinnie. We've got an experienced polygrapher and an experienced case officer both saying don't do it."

"Yeah. And we've got an experienced polygrapher and an experienced case officer saying do it."

"Would you fly an aircraft that had a 50 percent chance of crashing?"

Tony shook his head in disgust.

"It's fifty-fifty." Val shrugged. "Heads, we win; tails, we lose. That good enough for you on this one?"

Val tried to make eye contact with Tony, who glared at the ceiling.

"Vinnie, let's say we do what you want. We take a chance at running Haskell. And let's say that coin comes up tails. We got it wrong."

Val paused.

Tony glared at him.

"The damage would be colossal," Val continued. "And the worst part is we wouldn't know where and when it was gonna hit us. What if the Syrians played the long game? What if they gave us Razzaq? Let us smoke him so that we fall head over heels in love with their double agent. So that Haskell can put some shit in our heads. Shit that makes bad things happen. And those bad things probably wouldn't happen to me and you. They'd happen to a bunch of soldiers or civilians who—"

"I know how the fucking game works!" Tony shouted, jabbing a finger in Val's face.

Sydney stood still, head hung low, letting it play out.

"I know you do. You're one of the best," Val said in a low voice. "That's how I know you know."

Tony's shoulders sagged.

"You know, deep down, we can't run Haskell. We gotta pass."

Tony walked out of the room.

Val and Sydney looked at each other, and then at the photos on the wall.

CHAPTER 43

"Good shower?" Val asked as he walked into Haskell's section of the cinder-block building. Haskell was sitting at the end of his bunk. Tony had gone on a sulking walk across Camp Korea, and Sydney was on the other side of the building, watching Val and Haskell on the video monitor.

"I have never had better, Max."

"I doubt that's true," Val said, chuckling. "Grab your things, please. Time to change locations."

Masudi sat straighter, an alarmed look on his face.

"Relax, Masudi," Val said in his most reassuring voice. "Standard procedure. We don't want anyone figuring out you're here. Time to rotate to a new safe house."

Masudi hesitated.

"What's wrong?" Val asked.

"I've come too far to be left in the desert with a bullet in my head, Max."

"Don't be ridiculous. We're not the Syrians."

Masudi stood slowly and gathered his few belongings. He followed Val out of the building, where the old Mercedes idled. Omar was in the driver's seat. Val got in the back with Masudi, and the car pulled away slowly.

"Where is the new location?" Masudi asked.

"Not too far," Val answered, avoiding eye contact.

They drove out of Camp Korea and headed west. They had only driven a few miles when Omar swerved off the road.

Masudi shook his head as the car came to a squeaking stop.

"I'm sorry," Val said. "We're not going to be able to work together at the moment."

Omar got out of the car quickly and came around to Masudi's side of the car, rifle at the ready. He jerked the door open, startling Masudi, who looked at Val with fear in his eyes.

"It's okay," Val said, holding a hand out, palm down, in a calming gesture. "No bullets. Just goodbye. I promise."

"Out of the car, please, sir," Omar said.

Masudi shook his head again and eased out of the back seat.

Val got out of the car and came around to stand next to Omar, who had pushed Masudi away from the car.

Val was startled to see tears streaming down Masudi's face.

"Why?" Masudi asked him. "After all I have been through?"

Masudi's breath quickened. He took a few steps back as if he'd been struck. Val thought he was going to start sobbing.

"We're not saying never." Val took a few steps forward. "Just not right now."

"Sir," Omar said, in a warning to Val. *Why the hell are you getting so close to him?* was what he meant.

Val ignored him. He stepped next to Masudi and put his hand on the crying man's shoulder.

"Masudi, please understand. It's for your protection. And just for the time being."

But his words rang hollow, and he knew it.

Val reached his other hand into his pocket and pulled out a cell phone.

"Take this. Keep it with you. When it's time, we'll use this to get back in touch with you."

Masudi looked at the phone with skepticism but put it in his robe pocket.

Val put his hand back into his pocket and pulled out a roll of US dollars. He extended it to Masudi.

"We value your time and appreciate you," he said, offering him the roll of money.

Masudi swatted Val's hand away.

The sudden motion caused Omar to shoulder his rifle. "Goddamn it, sir!"

"I do not want your money," Masudi said. "I did not survive a Syrian prison for money. After all this, you insult me."

"That's not my intention," Val said, still surprised by the emotional response.

He took his hand off Masudi's shoulder and shot an angry glance at Omar.

The interpreter got the message. He lowered his weapon but glared at Val.

"I came all this way to make a difference," Masudi said, almost to himself. "To fight for my country."

Masudi looked at Val.

"I could have done so much for you. For what I thought was our common cause."

Val had the awful realization that he believed him. *We fucked this up,* his gut screamed at him. *We should be working with him.*

Val looked at Omar but swallowed the urge to voice his feelings.

Omar, baffled, looked back at Val and gestured at the car. *Let's get the fuck out of here,* his expression screamed.

Masudi, seeming to regain his composure, wiped more tears away, adjusted his robe, and stood straight. He locked eyes with Val.

"Very well," Masudi said, raising his chin slightly in defiance.

Val gestured with the money again.

Masudi shook his head, a single tear running down his cheek.

Val placed the money on the ground.

"I hope you'll take it," Val said before nodding at the interpreter.

Masudi and Val stared at each other as Omar moved back to the driver's seat.

"I wish you safe travels," Val said.

"Three days of questions, and you never asked me about the Russian," Haskell said.

"Good luck." Val turned toward the car.

It was common at a moment like this for an asset to start making wild statements in a last-ditch effort to enhance their value. Val had heard some wild things when he was terminating an asset relationship. He'd learned not to take the bait.

"You want Abdul Razzaq so badly, it has blinded you," Masudi continued, anger in his voice now. "But he is just a mule. A pawn. A simple, greedy war profiteer."

Val opened the passenger door and got in the car.

"You are trying to stomp out an insect and ignoring the snake," Masudi continued.

Val slammed his car door.

Omar looked at him, waiting for the word.

"Together, we could have slain the wolf!" Masudi yelled.

"Drive," Val ordered.

Omar gunned the engine and pulled out onto the highway.

"What was all that shit about, sir?"

"Desperate nonsense," Val said.

CHAPTER 44

A bright sun in a cloudless sky shone on the airfield. Val and Tony sat on the C-130's ramp while the helicopter crew got their bird ready and the interpreters loaded their gear. A marine V-22 had ferried them back to Balad from Camp Korea a few hours ago. Now they were hitching a ride with some old buddies from the 160th. It would be a long ride for Val and his interpreters, since they would drop Tony off first, but he didn't mind. The Night Stalker Black Hawk was doing a milk run between a few JSOC locations tonight to give one of their lieutenant colonels some easy flight time. A droning, uneventful ride over a lot of empty desert fit Val's pensive mood well.

"What's bugging you, man?" Tony asked Val as he cleaned his sunglasses with his shirtsleeve and then put them back on.

"Huh?"

"I said, what's fucking bugging you, asshole?"

"I don't want to talk about it."

"Come on."

Val hesitated and then said, "I just can't shake the feeling that we might have fucked up with Haskell."

"Oh, we fucked up. I can assure you of that."

Val shook his head. "I can always count on you for a reflective and skeptical conversation. Thanks."

"You're fucking welcome."

"Like, maybe we should've taken another validation step of some kind," Val continued, eyes still on the horizon. "Maybe given him a hoop or two to jump through and see how he performed."

"Or just fucking killed Razzaq."

"But then I think, the Syrians are too good at this," Val continued, ignoring Tony, and working it through in his head for the hundredth time, only out loud this time. "And they're patient bastards. They'd have fed us small wins as long as they had to, just to position Haskell to do damage."

"Which wouldn't have mattered," Tony inserted. "Because Razzaq would be pink mist drifting out of a Hellfire missile crater."

Val looked at Tony. Tony glared back.

They took stock of each other from behind dark wraparound sunglasses. Their clothes were filthy, neither had shaven in more than a week, and their salt-and-pepper stubble was approaching beard length beneath dry, windburned cheeks. Their rifles, cross slung with barrels down, hung from their left shoulders, and they held their assault helmets in their right hands. Small packs hung from their right shoulders, holding the dirty clothes and essentials they had taken to Camp Korea. Other than Tony's slightly taller and stockier build, they were mirror images of each other.

Mirror images reflecting different perspectives on the past couple of days.

Val opened his mouth to speak, but Tony interrupted him.

"Sydney!" he yelled with an enormous smile. He came to his feet, raising his hand to wave.

Val stood, looking in the direction of Tony's gesture.

Sydney strode toward them, across the tarmac. She waved back at Tony.

"Ain't that cute," Tony said in a near whisper. "She came to see you off. When are you guys going to get it over with and just have sex?"

"Shut up," Val said, waving to Sydney.

"Hot, sweaty, desert sport sex."

"Shut up."

"Oh. Are you actually still mad at her? Grudge sex, then!"

"Shut up. I mean it."

"I'm so serious. Pickens owes me, man," Tony said, conspiratorial urgency slipping into his voice. He gestured with his head at the helicopter crew chief, who was pulling tie-downs from the rotor blades. "I pulled his ass out of a burning helicopter in Afghanistan back in '02. He will put that bird down for some maintenance bullshit if I ask him to. That would buy you at least an hour."

"Please shut up," Val said as Sydney neared their spot in the shade of the C-130's tail.

"Oh, like you need more than an hour?" Tony was enjoying himself now. "You would last five minutes with her."

Val shook his head in awkward frustration as Sydney stepped next to them into the shadow.

"Last five minutes with what?" Sydney asked.

"Disregard," Val grumbled. "Just Tony's normal babble."

"About sex, no doubt," Sydney said with a knowing smile.

Tony chuckled.

"Yeah. With his mom," Val said.

"Fuck you!" Tony shouted. "Not cool!"

Sydney belly laughed.

Val smiled, happy to have landed an insult.

Tony hesitated and then broke down as well.

The three friends shared a long laugh. Their common history splashed over them like water, washing away the tension of the past few days.

"Damn," Sydney said, catching her breath. "I'm gonna miss you guys."

The growl of a cranking auxiliary power unit interrupted her. They looked at the Black Hawk. The pilots were strapped in and starting their run-up.

Omar, standing next to the helicopter's open side door, looked their way. He pointed at his watch and then held up two fingers.

Tony gave Omar a thumbs-up and then turned back to Sydney.

"Two minutes," he said before extending his arms to Sydney. "Come here."

"Please be safe, Tony," Sydney said as they hugged.

"You too. I hope I see you soon."

"Me too."

"Last chance." Tony looked at Val with a mischievous smile.

"I'll be there shortly."

Tony turned and walked to the helicopter.

Val and Sydney looked at each other awkwardly.

"It was good to see you," Val said. "Even under the circumstances."

"You too. I used to think a lot about us rendezvousing somewhere. About us finally getting to spend time together. Camp Korea was not what I had in mind."

Val nodded. "Do you still think about it?"

"About what?"

"About us rendezvousing somewhere."

Sydney, surprised by the sudden question, stood motionless.

The first of the Black Hawk's two engines screamed to life.

Val took off his sunglasses and looked into Sydney's Ray-Ban aviators. "Because I do."

Sydney managed to nod.

"Good," Val said. "I rotate back at the end of this month. How about you?"

"Eight and a wake up."

The aircraft's number two engine started. The rotor blades accelerated, and the crew chief pointed at Val and then at the aircraft.

Val gave a thumbs-up and then turned back to Sydney.

He yelled so she could hear him over the roar of the helicopter. "Is it a date?"

She stepped forward and embraced him.

"It better be!" she shouted into his ear.

He squeezed her to him and kissed her neck.

She nuzzled against his ear.

They held on for as long as they thought they could get away with, then released each other. She wiped a tear from her cheek.

The helicopter was at full throttle. The shriek of its twin turbine engines and the hammering of its rotor blades were ear-splitting. Sydney and Val struggled to hear each other.

"Take care of yourself!" she yelled.

"I will!" Val put his hand on hers and held it tightly to his chest. He glanced toward the helicopter. The crew chief was pulling the chocks from the aircraft's wheels.

He looked at Sydney. "I'll see you soon!"

Then he turned and ran to the helicopter.

"I can't wait!" Sydney yelled into the wind.

CHAPTER 45

Two Black Hawks idled on the runway on Shark Base. Each helicopter had a full squad of irritated Rangers on board. Val and Omar were on the second aircraft. Also irritated.

"They are telling us to hold, sir," the pilot said to Val over the intercom.

"What the hell for?"

"Didn't say."

Sitting in the cramped, dark confines of a Black Hawk helicopter in full kit is an exercise in discomfort. The space is filled with the press of bodies, each special operator jammed shoulder-to-shoulder with their comrades. Lumpy radios and ammunition magazines hang from their body armor, digging into their neighbors with each slight shift or turbulent bump. Weapons are clenched between their legs, and the seats' stiff metal tubing bites into the backs of their thighs. Every breath feels heavy, constricted by chaffing body armor and equipment and weighed down by anticipation of the violence that lies ahead.

Val looked at his watch. They had been waiting for the launch command from the Ops Center for almost half an hour.

Val sat outboard on the left side of the helicopter, facing forward. Omar was to his right. Val could feel Omar shift his weight occasionally, but for the most part, the young sergeant was still. Val fidgeted more. His back, ten years older than Omar's, hurt.

The nightly helicopter raids were wearing on Val. The Task Force increasingly focused on interdicting foreign fighters trying to sneak across the Syrian border, bringing weapons and fresh bodies to the fight. The relentless pace was taking a toll on his team. The volume of nightly missions stretched them. And the focus on the Syrian border did nothing to ease Val's lingering doubts about how the Haskell mission ended.

As they often had over the past month, Val's thoughts drifted to Sydney. The idea of them being together overpowered the thrum of the rotor blades, the scream of the engines, and the ache of his back. He offered no resistance, allowing his eyes to close... They were in Paris, walking hand-in-hand, laughing. He could almost see the twinkling lights of the city, feel the luxury of the hotel. They were finally together, the rest of the world fading away.

He would be there in a week. His replacement had already arrived, a captain from Fort Belvoir that went through the Farm a few years after Val.

"Sir, Ops says you are off the mission," the pilot said over the intercom, interrupting Val's reverie. "They are sending someone to take your place."

"What? Why?"

"Didn't say."

Val shook his head. What a fucking goat screw.

"Tell them, no. I'm already loaded up. Let's fucking get going."

"Sorry, sir. They are insisting."

A pickup truck drove onto the airfield with no lights on. It stopped outside of the spinning rotor discs of the idling helicopters and a lone soldier hopped out of the passenger seat.

"Here is your replacement, sir," the pilot said.

Val took off the intercom headset and handed it to the crew chief seated in front of him. Omar watched as Val hopped out of the helicopter. Standing on the ground next to the open helicopter door, Val turned and made eye contact with Omar. The young sergeant looked at him with a what-now? Face. Val shrugged. He leaned into Omar and shouted over the slam of the rotor blades.

"Come find me when you guys get back."

Omar nodded and winked.

Val patted Omar's shoulder and then turned to jog to the pickup truck.

Sergeant First Class Amos, in full battle dress, was waiting for him.

"Sorry for the dick dance, sir," he shouted over the din of the helicopters. "But one of your sources showed up at the gate. He insists on talking to you. Says he has something hot."

"Which source?"

"I don't know, sir. They are bringing him to the meeting room now. But the colonel wants you to get what you can get ASAP in case it can drive additional targeting tonight."

Amos reached into the truck bed and pulled out his weapon.

"You briefed up on this mission?" Val asked him.

"Roger that. Bunch of assholes crossing the border. Kill or capture."

The helicopter rotor disks sliced through the night air with increasing urgency and the engines screamed louder as the pilots throttled up. The sudden change in tempo signaled they must have gotten the green light.

Amos held his rifle in one hand. With his other hand, he performed a rapid, instinctive gear check, his movements fluid and precise, honed by experience.

Val nodded, his voice now barely audible over the loud aircraft. "You're in chalk two with Omar."

"See you when we get back," Amos shouted.

Sergeant First Class Amos turned and jogged over to the trail aircraft. He pulled himself into the cabin and was swallowed by shadow. The crew chief leaned out over the barrel of his minigun as a vortex of dust and debris rose around the helicopters. Engines howled and wind buffeted the Toyota pickup. Val closed his eyes against the stinging sand as the Black Hawks rose into the night. In a minute, they were gone. The rhythmic thump of their rotors receding to the west.

Val hopped into the pickup truck.

"OK. Let's go see who showed up on our doorstep."

*

Val and his team conducted their source debriefings in a small room on the side of the Task Force headquarters palace. Whether the source was summoned or requested a meeting, each had to go through a security gauntlet to get to the meeting room on Shark Base - They were met off base somewhere in Ramadi, blindfolded, hooded, extensively searched and then thrown into the back of a civilian vehicle for passage through the conventional military base to Shark. There they were searched again and then placed in the meeting room where their hood and blindfold were finally removed.

Val's source had been through this gauntlet and was waiting for him in the meeting room, under the watchful eyes of an armed interpreter, when he walked into the Ops Center.

Walking along the edge of the great room turned operations center, Val stopped at the coffeepot to grab a cup. There were about three dozen soldiers and officers sitting around the horseshoe, working on their laptops while they monitored the border raid mission on the big monitor. The slowly tilting drone feed showed infrared footage of five men making their way across the desert on foot, nearing the Iraqi border. A large map inset on the screen showed the real time position of the two Black Hawks as they flew west toward the infiltrators. The aircraft would drop the Rangers off a few kilometers from the planned intercept point. Less than twenty minutes later, the infiltrator's evening would take a sudden violent turn for the worse.

"Major Santanna," one of Val's field control officers, Staff Sergeant Herrera, called as Val tasted the old coffee. "I'm glad they caught you in time, sir. Fastball says it is urgent."

Val's heart sank at the name Fastball. He turned from the coffeepot and looked at the staff sergeant.

"Fastball? Shit."

Fastball was the code name for Tariq al-Dulaimi, a young tribesman loyal to one of the more powerful Sheikhs in Ramadi. Val had been running Fastball for months. After some initial excitement about intelligence the young Iraqi could provide, Val had come to regard the source as ambitious and unreliable.

"Yes, sir. Fastball," the Herrera responded with a knowing nod.

Val tried to swallow his irritation with another sip of the awful coffee. He was frustrated, but there was nothing to be done about it. When a source shows up claiming to have important and urgent information, there was not much they could do other than take the meeting. And since Fastball was Val's source, it had to be him.

How much longer they would work with Fastball was a question for another time. But tonight, Val had to meet with his source and try to generate actionable intelligence.

"God, the coffee is bad tonight," Val muttered as he walked toward the corner of the palace and the meeting room.

Val knocked and stepped inside.

Tariq sat at the single table in the sparsely furnished room, his leg bouncing with nervous energy beneath his long, loose-fitting dishdasha. He wore a black leather jacket over the dark gray robe. Scuffed and worn thin in spots, the jacket provided an extra layer against the cool nights of winter in Ramadi and enhanced Tariq's air of edgy disquiet.

The interpreter, standing behind the Iraqi, shook his head at Val as if to say, "What an asshole this guy is."

"Good evening, Tariq." Val tried not to let his skepticism seep into his voice. "Good to see you again."

"And you, Max," Tariq said with a nod.

Over the past months, Tariq's face seemed to Val to alternate between youthful enthusiasm and a hardened, world-weary expression. Val noted tonight was the youthful version and wondered what that hinted at as he pulled a chair out from the small table and sat down.

"So, my friend. What is on your mind?"

*

Val emerged from the meeting room an hour later in a bad mood, carrying a piece of paper. Herrera caught up to him as he stalked across the Ops Center toward the NSA rep.

"You don't look happy, sir," Herrera said. "What did he say?"

"Nothing worth a damn," Val grumbled. He glanced at the big screen as he walked. The raid on the infiltrators was complete. The operation netted two prisoners and three KIA and the Black Hawks were on the LZ picking up the team. They would probably be back before Val was done with Fastball. Code word radio calls crackled over the Ops Center speakers as the pilots and assault team coordinated the mission wrap up before departure.

"Do me a favor, will ya?" Val said to the NSA rep as he handed him the sheet of paper. "See if you can get a fix on these cell phones?"

"Roger that," the rep said as he scanned the list.

"Thanks." Val turned toward the coffeepot.

Herrera followed Val across the room.

"I thought you said nothing good?"

Val lifted the coffeepot and gave it a sniff before pouring himself a cup.

"He said there is some kind of meeting tonight. He said al-Shammari was gonna be there."

"Shammari?" Herrera's eyes lit up. Al-Shammari was a well-known al-Qaeda leader the task force had been chasing for a long time. He had gone to ground in the past few months, all but vanishing from Val's human intelligence network.

Val shook his head.

"I don't believe it." He took a sip of coffee and winced at the sour taste. "I think he is throwing Shammari's name out there because he knows we will jump at the chance to take him out. I think he is trying to leverage the name to get us to eliminate a rival sheikh or two as collateral damage."

Herrera's eyes narrowed at the suggestion. It was a common a gambit by their Iraqi sources. Val's team had to be careful not to be manipulated into tribal rivalries.

Val glanced at the big screen. The drone footage of the LZ was no longer on display. The main feed was now of a new target, which would be hit in about an hour by a different team. The map displaying the returning Black Hawks' progress back to Shark Base was now relegated to a corner of the big screen. They were already clear of the LZ, accelerating toward home. Val looked at his watch.

Lucky bastards will definitely be done before I will tonight.

"Anyway." Val looked back at Herrera. "We'll see what NSA comes back with. My guess is most of the cell phones I gave them to look for are going to be all tucked into bed, not headed for this big meet. The only ones that will be moving are the ones Fastball and his tribe want eliminated."

Herrera nodded. "And no Shammari."

"And no Shammari," said over his shoulder as he walked back over to the NSA station.

The NSA rep saw Val coming. He lifted his eyes from his laptop and said, "Just give me five more minutes, sir. I should have them all located."

"Great. Knock on the meeting door when you have them?"

"Roger that, sir."

"Thanks." Val turned and headed back to the meeting room.

"Mayday! Mayday! Mayday!" a terrified pilot's voice came over the speakers. Every head in the Ops Center whipped around. Val stopped suddenly, spilling his coffee as he spun to look at the screen. "This is Atlas Two Five. Mayday! Mayday! Mayday!"

Warning tones and the sound of screaming filled the background of the pilot's transmission.

"Taking fire! In uncontrolled descent! Mayday! May—"

The transmission ended. Several officers gasped while others covered their mouths in shock.

The Ops Center was frozen, every set of eyes locked on the big screen.

Seconds ticked by in silence.

"This is Atlas One Five," the other Black Hawk came over the speakers, speaking quickly. "Atlas Two Five is down. Looked like a surface-to-air missile. Aircraft on the ground and burning. Request permission to secure the crash site."

Val stumbled forward.

Omar.

Amos

"Atlas One Five, this is Zeus Zero Three." It was the battle captain at Balad speaking calmly, as if the world had not just broken from its axis. "Establish site security ASAP. We are launching CSAR now, diverting a gunship your way and will have eyes over you shortly."

"Roger that," Atlas One Five responded. "On the ground now. Securing crash site."

Val spilled his coffee as he tried to pull out a chair and sit.

He made it into the chair.

The Ops Center's big screen flickered briefly and then the image split in two. One half was General McStone and several staffers in Balad. They were seated facing the camera, eyes fixed on the big screen above them. The other half of the screen was a distant overhead image of a burning helicopter. The glare from the heat signature washed out much of the drone's feed, but there was no mistaking - It was a Black Hawk. Broken and on fire.

Val put his head in his hands.

Omar.

Amos.

Colonel Wyatt, the task force commander, rushed into the Ops Center. He took a seat at the front row of tables. Two small cameras beneath the big screen swiveled to focus on him. His image would be on the screen in Balad, just as McStone's was here.

Val felt a hand on his shoulder. He looked up at Herrera.

The Staff Sergeant had tears in his eyes.

So did Val.

CHAPTER 46

A cold wind blew off the Euphrates and slid over the palace rooftop where Val and Tony stood leaning against the parapet at midnight. Looking down at the reflection of the moon on the dark river, they shared Tony's flask of bourbon. The dry wind carried the smell of smoke as it clutched at them before spilling off the other side of the palace.

Val was rotating out of Iraq in the morning. Tony hitched a ride on a Chinook down to Shark Base to say goodbye in person. They had not seen each other since the Haskell mission almost a month ago and spoke only briefly after the Black Hawk shoot down.

That night, the task force found and neutralized the small team that brought down Atlas Two Five. Located in a hide site ten kilometers east of the Syrian border, the three enemy fighters had used a late model SA-18 surface-to-air missile in what looked like either a brilliantly designed ambush or catastrophically good luck. The SA-18, a Russian infrared homing surface-to-air missile system, had been updated and perfected since the early eighties. SA-18's were deadly, easy to use, and ferociously regulated globally. It was exactly the kind of weapon that the intelligence community believed Razaq was trafficking across the Syrian border.

The question now haunting the task force was whether it was luck or a deadly new tactic. Was the enemy using its cross-border infiltrations as bait to lure American forces into ambushes? Or did they just get lucky that night?

Val was haunted by his own questions.

Why Omar?

Why Amos?

Why not me?

The day after the shoot down, Tony called to check on his friend. He hung up worried that Val had been deeply rattled by Omar's death.

Now, seeing him in person, Tony was sure of it. It looked to him like Val had aged a decade in the past month.

"Five years of this shit," Val said.

"What?"

"Five years since 9/11."

"Oh. Right."

"Feel like we're getting any closer? Feel like we're making progress?"

"I dunno." Tony glanced over his shoulder and snuck another shot of bourbon. Drinking alcohol while on deployment was strictly forbidden.

"I think we have a couple years left to go," he finally said, handing the flask back to Val. "Vietnam took ten years, right?"

"Terrific example."

"I don't mean that's how this ends. I just mean it takes time. Hell, we're still in Germany and Korea."

"God, I'd love to get back to Germany," Val said before swigging the bourbon. "You remember peacetime duty in Germany?"

Tony nodded.

"I told Omar that was where he needed to go for his next assignment," Val said. "He would have loved it."

Val shook his head and looked at Tony.

"I'm so sorry, brother," Tony said with a heavy sigh. "That kid was one of the good ones."

Tony watched as the corners of Val's mouth turned down and his eyebrows knotted together. Deep lines appeared around Val's eyes and mouth and his gaze passed through Tony, seeming to search for something in the distance.

Tony took a step forward and put his hand on Val's shoulder.

Val blinked rapidly and his lips pressed together in a thin line. His eyes met Tony's.

"I'm sorry," Val said.

"Nothing to be sorry about. That shit hurts."

Tony took the flask of bourbon from Val.

"To Sergeant Omar Faisal and the rest of Atlas Two Five," he said, before taking a large swig and handing the flask back to Val.

Val drank from the flask and handed it back to Tony with a nod that tried to persuade his old friend he was OK.

Tony was unconvinced. But thought it best to move on.

"So. Off to Paris, are we?"

"I'm headed to Germany tomorrow," Val said.

Tony nodded vigorously as Val continued, trying to pull his friend forward, away from grief.

"Gonna drop my shit with a buddy at Ramstein and take the train the next morning to Paris. Sydney is there for work. She's going to take a few days off, and we're going to hang out until the new year."

"New Year's Eve in Paris?" Tony asked lustily. "More like New Year's Eve in her pants, amirite?"

The hint of a smile flickered across Val's face.

Tony leapt at the sign of life.

"OK. What I want to know is how many different ways are you two gonna bump uglies?"

Val grinned and shook his head.

"This is nothing to be nervous about, buddy," Tony said, handing the flask back to his friend. "Think of it as just another military operation. It all comes down to planning and standard operating procedures."

Val grimaced, resigning himself to what was coming.

"Because objective Pound Town will not yield to a hasty attack." Tony winked at Val. "You gotta unleash the beast and storm that trench."

"Please..."

"No sir. Breaching and clearing the objective cannot be left to chance. How long has it been since you invaded her sovereign territory, anyway?"

"I'm done with this conversation," Val said, turning to look at the Euphrates.

"It's OK, Val. Just because it has been a while, it doesn't mean you are not still fully capable of a tactical insertion with your meat missile."

Tony could see Val fighting it, but laughter seeped out of him.

Tony's heart swelled at the sound.

"And remember, a well-timed assault to the rear can leave the enemy begging for a ceasefire. Just make sure you've got enough ammunition in your magazine for a sustained campaign on her landing strip."

Val bent over laughing, hands on his knees. Tony joined him. The sound of their guffaws tumbled off the palace roof into the night.

The two friends caught their breath and then each took another shot of whiskey.

"Truthfully," Val said, wiping his mouth with the back of his hand. "I just hope we have a good time. Feels sometimes like we are jinxed."

"Bullshit. You guys are great together. You're both just incompetent."

"Oh, really?"

"Yes. Really."

Tony handed Val the flask. Val took a swig, his eyes on the ancient river.

Tony studied him, worried his thoughts had drifted back to Omar and the rest of Atlas Two Five.

But Val surprised him.

"You ever think about Haskell?"

"Shit." Tony's face darkened. "Every day."

"Don't worry. I don't want to relive it either." He handed Tony the flask.

"What then?"

"He said something odd to me when I cut him loose. I've been turning it over in my head ever since."

"What was it?"

"He said, 'You never asked me about the Russian.'"

"So what?" Tony said. "The Russians have been pushing weapons into the region for decades. And we know they're trying to stir the pot from across the Syrian border."

"But he said, 'the Russian.'"

"And?"

"And he said something about the wolf."

"Oh no," Tony said in mock fear. "The wolf."

Val chuckled and took the flask from Tony.

"Assets say all kinds of shit when they see it ending, you know that," Tony said. "And Haskell was a colorful dude on a normal day. That sounds like some dramatic bullshit to me."

"I hope you're right."

"I'm right. Trust me… Now, back to how many times you guys are gonna shag in Paris."

CHAPTER 47

Sydney drove through the Parisian night as Tony and Val said goodbye on a rooftop in Ramadi. She changed lanes abruptly, scanning her rearview mirror for potential surveillance.

"Are you sure you were not followed?" Sydney asked Nicolae, who was riding in her passenger seat.

"Yes, of course," he said with a smile as they approached the Seine River. "Are you sure that you were not?"

Sydney rolled her eyes.

"You have the files?"

"Yes." He held up the small briefcase he'd brought with him. "Is all here. Everything the Moldovan government knows about Vasily Abakumov's operations in Transnistria. I have also included my own assessment of who is most likely to be taking bribes from him."

"Good, Nicolae. Really good."

Nicolae put the briefcase under his seat.

"So, what is going on?" Sydney asked, changing lanes again as they drove across the Grenelle Bridge over the Seine. "Why did this meet have to be in person?"

Nicolae was in Paris for the week for an OSCE meeting. Sydney was as well. This was a long-planned culmination of six months of work by Nicolae, and Sydney was eager to get her hands on his stolen intelligence. She was just as eager to get her hands on Val's body this coming weekend. But she kept those thoughts far from the center of her mind. Right now, she had to focus.

Nicolae had been working, at Sydney's direction, to gather comprehensive information on Vasily Abakumov and his activities in Transnistria. A Bulgarian arms dealer believed to be supplying weapons to foreign fighters in Iraq, Abakumov was infamous. He was known throughout the Western intelligence community as one of the untouchable whales of the business.

That made him Sydney's number one target. Taking Abakumov down would secure her name in the agency firmament forever.

It wouldn't be simple, though. Because of how many people Abakumov had bought off in Moldova and Transnistria, it would be easy to step unknowingly through one of his trip wires. And once alerted, the Bulgarian would contract his operations like an octopus withdrawing into its lair. It would take years to get another shot at him.

Sydney didn't want to risk any kind of traceable electronic exchange that might endanger her asset or alert an Abakumov mole in the Moldovan government, so she leveraged this widely attended OSCE meeting. Because of their official roles, they both would have cover for action to attend.

But the plan was to use a dead drop for the document exchange rather than risk physically getting together. Nicolae surprised Sydney when he used their pre-planned signal to request a face-to-face meeting. Something normally not done except in emergencies.

After a three-hour SDR through Paris to ensure she was clean, she was ready to know what the issue was.

"Daria is fourteen now."

Sydney tried not to scream. She knew where this was going. Instead of screaming, she concentrated on navigating the off-ramp from the bridge.

"I want her to go to school in America. We have not discussed this in a long time. I did not know when our next opportunity to meet in person would be."

"Nicolae, we have discussed this." Sydney worked hard to keep the irritation and impatience out of her voice. "We're going to help with that. Daria and Eniko will both get an American college education."

"My wife and I want to go to America when they do."

"You will be able to visit. We have talked about this also." Sydney shook her head, frustrated. This was not worth the risk of a face-to-face meeting. She scanned around their vehicle. They were not being followed as she drove along the river.

"Not visit. We want to emigrate. We want to become Americans."

"What?"

Nicolae looked at Sydney. His face lacked his usual smile. "You heard me correctly. When Daria goes to college, I want my family to go to America for good."

"What about your country? What about Moldova?"

"I have served Moldova well," Nicolae said, facing forward. "I have fought for her, been wounded for her, and continue to serve her. When Daria goes to college in a few years, you and I will have worked together for almost a decade. I have done my part. I have earned this. I want my family to go to America."

I didn't see this coming today, Sydney thought.

But it was not a surprise. This was not an uncommon ask by assets. Citizens of other countries that agree to work with the US government and pass on their own country's secrets tend to have a deep affinity for America. In countries where living conditions and opportunities for their families are not as good as in America, there is a natural pull to immigrate.

Sydney admired Nicolae's approach, though. He'd waited six years before bringing this up. Some assets got impatient and made this demand too early, before they had a track record. But Nicolae had proven his worth. He and Sydney had made good progress in Moldova and Transnistria.

"Wow," Sydney said, stalling. "I didn't realize you felt that way."

"This is why I wanted to tell you face-to-face. I want you to know that I'm very serious."

"Okay. Well, mission accomplished. I see it."

And she could. Nicolae's normal lighthearted and friendly air was absent. It reminded Sydney that, beneath his agreeable personae, there was a hardened, world-weary soldier, capable of killing.

Pride swelled within her again at having successfully recruited him.

"Nicolae, when the time is right, I want you to know that others and I will support you one hundred percent."

She turned her head from the road momentarily and looked him in the eyes and lied. "I've told you before that I will never promise anything that's not in my power to promise. But I feel confident I can get this done for you and your family. And I'll fight like hell to make it happen."

Sydney turned her head to the front as if to put her eyes back on the road, but she was really hiding her face from Nicolae. She hated this part of the job, and sometimes it was almost too much to bear. It was certainly too much to let Nicolae see. The guilt and doubt were nearly overwhelming. Guilt over her exploitation of Nicolae. Doubt whether it was worth it, whether it made her a bad person.

Times like this, she thought of the Farm and Mr. Wall. "We don't hire you to be caring, gentle people," he'd told them. "We hire you to be users. We hire you to manipulate other people to act against their own country's best interests. And we train you to be really good at it."

Sydney had chuckled with the rest of her side when Mr. Wall said that. It was cool to hear in the abstract. Cool to imagine herself as an intelligence officer out in the world, highly trained, impervious to doubt and feeling, making it happen, climbing the ranks.

It was not so cool to do it. Not to a good man like Nicolae.

"You have got to keep helping me build the case," she said, swallowing the doubt and putting herself back in mode. "We've got to maintain our momentum together so that when I step up to the plate for you, I'm swinging the biggest possible bat."

Sydney listened to herself and wished it were true, while the other side of her brain told her the hard reality. *He is a CIA asset. And he is only valuable as a CIA asset if he is in Moldova. He will be most productive and therefore most valuable to me right now if he feels like he is progressing toward his goal of American citizenship, and that I'm working with him toward that goal.*

"I will put an oak tree in your hands," Nicolae said, his smile returning.

"I believe you. But from now on, you must follow the protocol. Face-to-face meetings are risky. We'll meet face-to-face once or twice a year. But it cannot be a regular thing. And it can't be spur of the moment like this."

She turned her head and glared at him, her guilt at manipulating him morphing quickly to anger.

"You want to kill any chance of getting your family to America? Then get careless and let someone figure us out."

"This will not happen." Nicolae shook his head as if it were a ridiculous idea.

Sydney checked the road to her front and then turned back to face him angrily.

"I'm fucking serious, Nicolae!"

He started at the shift in her tone and volume.

"You get made, and your dream is fucking dead. You might be dead too if the wrong parties get wise to us. This isn't a fucking game. Do you understand me?"

"Yes," Nicolae said somberly. "You don't have to remind me of this. I am the one that will be shot as a spy. Not you."

"You're right. And everything I do starts with keeping you safe. You have to work with me on that. Not make it harder. This meeting here?" Sydney jabbed a finger into the seat between the two of them. "This is an unnecessary risk. You understand?"

"Yes."

They drove in silence for a moment. Sydney getting her temper back in check, while Nicolae stared straight ahead.

"I'm sorry," she finally said. "When it comes to your safety, I get passionate."

"Is okay. I appreciate it."

"It's not okay. I shouldn't have lost my temper. I apologize."

"I accept your unnecessary apology," he said, a slight smile sneaking across his face.

"Thank you." She allowed herself a smile in return.

"No. Thank you. Thank you in advance for going to bat for me and my family."

"Of course," she said, not wanting to talk about the topic again.

"I promise. I will give you the largest bat in the world."

"I know you will," she said curtly, pretending to focus on the traffic.

"And I know that, when the time comes, you will swing it with all your might."

Sydney nodded. She could picture Mr. Wall smiling at her with approval back at the Farm. She fought the urge to shiver.

"Together," Nicolae said, "how can we fail?"

Sydney nodded again. "We won't fail," she said, swallowing her feelings of guilt again, and speeding up to pass the car in front of her.

CHAPTER 48

The mercenaries finished cleaning Burian's blood and brains from the aft deck. They took the mop and hose below. Val watched them through the aft sliding glass door as they descended the staircase out of sight.

They're not going to shoot me out here. They could've shot me while they were holding me in that basement in Odesa. And this would've been a lot of trouble just to get me to a place where they could dump my body where it would never be found. There are much easier ways to make a body disappear. Alexei has something else planned.

The two mercenaries walked back up the aft stairs. They took one last look at their handiwork. Then, satisfied they had removed the evidence of Burian's murder, they slid open the door and walked back into the dining room. They closed the sliding glass door and returned to the bar.

Val looked at the bowl of bloody water on the table between him and Alexei. The switchblade sat on the other side of it. Agonizingly close.

Then what? Val asked himself for the hundredth time. *Fight off the machine-gun-toting mercenaries with a knife?*

"Hit me again," Val said to Alexei as he scooted his shot glass toward Alexei.

"What toast?" Alexei smiled as he poured.

"How about to our destination? Which is where, again?"

Alexei laughed. He poured them both more bourbon, then set the bottle down.

"Good try, Val!" he said, his laughter winding down. "Very good."

Val kept his eyes locked on Alexei as if expecting an answer to his question.

A sadness came over Alexei's face. "I'm sorry, Val. But you will find out soon enough. And will not be a happy ending like last time you were on the *Monarch*."

"That was a happy ending?"

"Happier than it might have been, my friend. Do you not remember?"

"Oh, I remember."

"I bet you do." Alexei nodded. A knowing smile broke across his face.

"And I remember that prick Abakumov," Val said in an angry voice.

"Yes. He was a prick."

Val nodded. "Such a prick."

"To that prick, then." Alexei, happy to have finally struck upon a toast and reason to drink, raised his glass to Val. "To that prick Abakumov."

"To that prick," Val said, not able to fight off a smile.

They tapped their glasses together and drank.

CHAPTER 49

Val studied Sydney's naked body as she walked back from the bathroom. Svelte and athletic, she had the look of a gymnast. The Sunday morning sun was weak, and only barely made it through to light Val's sparse bedroom. Uninterrupted by tan lines, her skin seemed luminescent in the dim morning light. Sydney's profession dressed her in either office or combat-zone attire, so she could seldom bare her arms or legs.

He reached out as she neared the bed, placing a hand on her thigh.

"Good morning," she said, leaning over to kiss his forehead.

"Good morning." Val angled his head back so she could kiss his lips. Her wet hair brushed his forehead.

"Shower's all yours," she said, standing up.

Val lay back on his pillow.

Sydney put a hand on her hip and waited.

"Come on, soldier. Mimosas and breakfast. Make it happen."

She walked away from the bed to her suitcase in the corner.

"Roger that," Val said with a groan. He threw the sheets aside and got up.

Sydney had arrived in Prague two days before. They were on a rare streak for their relationship and had seen each other at least once a month for almost a year. Val was posted to the embassy in Prague, and Sydney's counter-proliferation role afforded her the ability to travel.

It was a chilly fall day and the gray sky threatened rain. They held each other's gloved hands as they walked down the hill from Val's flat toward the Charles Bridge.

Sydney smiled at Val as they passed through the west tower onto the bridge.

"What?" he asked.

"You're such a tourist."

Val responded with a puzzled smile.

"You love it, don't you?"

"Love Prague? Yeah, I do." Val looked around and gestured at the bridge. "Come on. It's so cool."

"It's an old bridge over a dirty river. There's only, what? A million others like it in Europe?"

"There's no bridge like this anywhere," Val said.

Sydney rolled her eyes.

"This bridge had its beginnings in 1357." Val released her hand and pointed at the cobblestones as they walked over. "The first stone was set into place by Charles the Fourth himself. And for five hundred years, this bridge was the only way to cross the Vltava River, making Prague a center of trade between the East and West and the focus of centuries of conflict and espionage stretching through the rise and fall of the Holy Roman, Ottoman, and Soviet empires."

He finished with a flourish of his hands, gesturing around at the bridge and city. They were in the middle of the gently sloped span. Val gave her a knowing wink.

Sydney laughed. "Not bad."

"Thank you," Val said with a nod of his head. "I confess I've heard the tours a few times."

Sydney took his hand, and they started walking again.

"I think you do it the best."

"So do I."

They walked a few blocks away from the river to Val's favorite cafe. Inside, the smell of strong coffee and pastries filled the air. The hostess recognized Val with a smile and sat them by a street-side window. They ordered breakfast. Val got a coffee and Baileys while they waited. Sydney got her mimosa.

"Why do you love it here so much?" she asked him.

Val took a sip of coffee and looked out of the window at the passersby as he thought about her question. Just when Sydney decided he was ignoring her, he responded.

"I don't know that it's here I love. As much as places like here."

"Like here?"

"Old. I like places where I can feel the weight of history."

"Why's that?"

"I guess I feel more at home in an old city. It helps me to shift to the long view, to be less frustrated with the present."

Sydney smiled.

Val shrugged. "It works for me."

The server brought their breakfast, and they both dug in. The exertions of the past day and a half had made them hungry.

"Dammit." Val reached into his coat pocket. He pulled out his cell phone, grimacing as he recognized the number.

"I'm sorry," he said to Sydney. "I've got to take this."

Sydney, mouth full, gave him an *okay* gesture and kept eating.

"Rafter," Val said into the phone.

He rolled his eyes and shook his head.

"We've been through this, sir. I thought they signed off?"

Val's eyes narrowed and his face tightened in irritation.

"Fine, sir." He started to say more but was cut off by the speaker on the other end of the line. "Sir, I said, 'Fine.' But not tomorrow. I told you I was taking tomorrow off."

Val's mouth pressed thin, and he looked at the ceiling in exasperation.

"Roger that," he said grudgingly. "0700 Tuesday." After a moment, Val nodded and said, "Thank you. You too, sir."

Val jammed the phone back into his coat pocket and shoveled a large spoonful of eggs and sausage into his mouth.

"What's up?" Sydney asked him.

"Please tell me." He wiped a bit of egg from the corner of his mouth. "Why do agency leaders all have hummingbird balls?"

"It's the water," Sydney deadpanned before draining her mimosa. She waved at the waitress and gestured for another drink before adding, "Might also be why army clandestine officers have hummingbird brains."

When Val didn't smile at all, she asked, "What's up?"

"Finally, after almost a year of painstaking development, I pitched an asset. A Russian army colonel based at their embassy here in Prague. Was a pain in the ass to get it approved. Went all the way up to the director. But I got approval, and it went great. I've got him turned."

"So, what's the problem?"

"Well, I need to do a detailed debrief with him. You know the deal. A couple days of deep diving everything the guy knows."

Sydney nodded.

"But this guy is anxious. And with good reason," Val said gravely. "You know how those Russians are. Constantly watching each other. Everyone looking for the opportunity to bring the GRU counter-intel thugs the scalp of an intel officer who has betrayed Mother Russia."

"Total career-enhancing move." Sydney nodded.

"So, I want to get him out of Czech. Away from prying eyes for a few days."

Sydney stopped nodding.

"Cross the border with a brand-new asset?" Her eyebrows raised.

"Oh, for chrissake. Forget I mentioned it."

"Hey. Easy." Sydney chuckled. "I'm just saying, I can see how they'd be a little nervous. Cross-border operations are complex and risky enough without involving a new asset. Most folks wait until the asset is well vetted before doing something like that. Or they never do it."

"Like I said," Val grumbled, "hummingbird balls."

Sydney shook her head, grinning.

Val winked at her.

"Anyway. The station chief wants to go over it all again to soothe his case of agency testicular deficit."

They both ate their breakfast for a few minutes.

"What's the big deal about the colonel?" Sydney asked, wiping her mouth with a napkin.

"What do you mean?"

"What's he got? Why did you recruit him?"

Val hesitated. Talking shop was one thing. But sharing these kinds of operational details crossed the line. Everything in the intelligence community was compartmentalized and need-to-know. You didn't just share shit because you were having a frustrating day at work. But, lately, over the past few months, Sydney and Val had dropped their guards, and operational security, with each other. It felt good to talk to someone. To really vent and digest what was going on in their worlds. They each lived an isolated life of service and secrets and pressure. It felt good to share operational thoughts, concerns, and ideas with someone you could trust, particularly a beautiful someone you could trust.

It was also illegal. And sometimes their training gave them pause. They gave each other space when they needed it.

But they needed companionship more than space.

"Rosoboronexport," Val said, leaning forward across their table.

Sydney's leaned forward to meet him halfway.

"Yeah?"

"Yeah." Val nodded. "And there's more."

Sydney pursed her lips and nodded knowingly. Rosoboronexport was the sole intermediary between the modern Russian military-industrial complex and the world. Succeeding the state arms exporters that peddled Soviet military systems for the USSR, Rosoboronexport was a cocktail of Russian oligarchs, Putin's realpolitik, and profit motive. As a counter-proliferation intelligence officer, Sydney and her teams spent much of their time dealing with Rosoboronexport's moves around the world.

Rosoboronexport was aggressive, and it was not surprising to hear Val's colonel had ties there. Most Russian military embassy personnel were only once or twice removed from the ravenous weapons-selling goliath.

Val loved it when Sydney pursed her lips like that. He reached his hand out and touched her cheek.

She placed her hand on his, holding it against her face.

The waitress appeared at Val's side and placed Sydney's fresh drink on the table.

Sydney took her eyes off Val, smiling at her.

"Bring him another one too. He's earned it."

Val chuckled. He took his hand from her face and stood up.

"What are you doing?" she asked.

Val slid his chair closer to hers so that he could sit catty-corner to her, rather than across the small square table. He sat down and reached around her chair and slid it closer until it touched his.

Sydney giggled as her chair jostled and barked against the floor. She let the motion of the chair carry her into him. Val put his arm around her shoulder and squeezed. Sydney kissed his neck and placed her hand on his chest.

Val kissed her forehead.

"Don't leave tomorrow."

"I don't want to," she whispered.

"Then don't."

"You have your thing."

"I don't leave town until a week from Monday. Stay."

"You have meetings and prep," she said, slipping her fingers beneath his scarf and between the buttons on his shirt. "I know how all that is. I'll just be in the way."

"I'll cancel it."

Sydney laughed.

"And let the forces of evil advance, unchecked, against freedom?" She nuzzled her nose into his neck. "I couldn't live with myself."

Val placed a finger under her chin. "Let's do it. Let's walk away and let it all burn."

They kissed. Sydney pressed against him.

Later, they held hands as they walked back to Val's flat in silence. The narrow cobblestone streets rose from the river. Val took them on a detour that passed near the castle and offered his favorite view of the city. They leaned against the short wall between them and a drop to the switchback street below. Looking down past the red roofs that descended to the river, they could see the Charles Bridge spanning between its two defensive towers. In the distance, the dark towers of the Týn Church rose above the other spires and rooftops of Prague.

"I miss you already," Sydney said.

"Me too."

"When will we see each other again?"

Val took a deep breath. He'd been trying to figure that out but didn't want to mention what the calendar in his head said.

"When?" she asked him, sensing his hesitation.

"Two months." He let go of her hand and put his arm around her. "Maybe six weeks, if we're lucky."

He felt her sag into him.

"When have we ever been lucky?" she whispered into his coat collar.

"It will go fast."

"It won't."

"Come on," he said, tugging her hand.

"What?" she asked as she went with him.

"We've got about eighteen hours till you leave. I want us to be naked for most of them."

*

They spent the afternoon in bed, making love and dozing off in each other's arms. As the sun started to set, Sydney thought about food again.

"You hungry?"

"I'm thinking Italian." Val propped himself up to look at her.

"I'm game for whatever," she said, lying on her back, returning his gaze.

"Great. I'm going to take a quick shower."

"I'll jump in after you."

He leaned in to kiss her before swinging his legs off his mattress and walking to the bathroom. Sydney watched him as he walked away. A quick flame of attraction flared within her as she studied his muscular back and legs.

My lord, she thought. *Get ahold of yourself, Knox.*

Sydney shook her head and sat up.

*

The restaurant was on Val's side of the river and only a short walk from his flat. Sydney smiled when the hostess sat them at the best table next to a window overlooking the river several city blocks below them.

"What?" Val asked.

"Somehow, we seem to keep getting tables by the window."

Val shrugged.

"I may have coordinated some of this ahead of time."

"Impressive fieldcraft." She reached across the table and took his hand. "And appreciated."

Sydney let him order for her. Soon, they had a basket of bread and glasses of wine.

Sydney tore off a piece of bread. She dragged it through the olive oil sitting in front of her in a small dish and devoured it.

"Damn, girl."

"A lady gets hungry," Sydney said, wiping olive oil from her chin.

Val nodded as he reached for the bread.

"What was the 'there's more' from earlier?" she asked him.

"The what?"

"Earlier. When you were telling me about your Russian colonel, you said 'there's more.'"

"Oh yeah." Val took a sip of wine and then leaned forward, placing his elbows on the table.

"There's this guy," he began, speaking in a low voice. "A Bulgarian. Not a full-fledged oligarch type. But definitely one of the chosen ones. He runs gray and black deals for the Rosoboronexport puppet masters. He's fucking filthy, behind a lot of arms deals that have gotten Americans killed in Iraq and Afghanistan. Small arms, surface-to-air shit, IED shit, the works. I was introduced to him here by a crooked member of the Czech parliament—who is a great guy, by the way. Ton of fun."

Val sopped another piece of bread into the small plate of olive oil and shoved it into his mouth as he kept talking. "Anyway, this Bulgarian arms dealer has been working the shit out of me, thinking with a little attention and flattery, he'll be able to leverage me to expedite the approval of his end-user certificates through the US embassy."

Sydney nodded knowingly. Val's cover as the defense attaché in Prague gave him line of sight to every legitimate, and not-so-legitimate, arms dealer in the region. Both types congregated around the robust and lucrative flow of arms from the region to American fighting partners in both Iraq and Afghanistan. Since the US government was the benevolent bill payer, picking up the tab for all these arms transactions, the US embassy was the munition's point of origin and had to approve each deal, validating the buyer and seller with end-user certificates and thereby signifying Uncle Sam's official stamp of approval.

This "cover for action" afforded Val a perfect vantage point into shady arms deals the Russians were cooking up via their gray arms partners. From the other side of the equation, Val being the official power broker at the center of these murky transactions made him an enticing intelligence and old-fashioned bribery target. And, of course, being such a juicy target gave Val opportunities to conduct his own intelligence and old-fashioned bribery operations. He was having a blast in Prague.

"So, I've been doubling down on my cover as a benign, somewhat gullible US officer enjoying the trappings of the arms community in Eastern Europe. Long lunches, vodka-filled afternoons. You get the picture."

"Hard duty," Sydney said with a crooked smile. "God bless you."

"Freedom ain't free, baby." Val took another sip of wine.

Sydney shook her head in mock disgust but smiled.

"Anyway. This Bulgarian and I have been circling each other like boxers for a few months now. For a while, the guy was playing the legit, politically connected, uber-friendly arms dealer."

"And one who has a genuine respect and soft spot in his heart for the scrappy, democracy-loving Afghanis and Iraqis, no doubt," Sydney said with a falsely furrowed brow, hand clutching her chest, bread in her mouth.

Val chuckled. "Oh yes. He has made his solidarity achingly clear."

Val sat back in his chair and scanned the restaurant quickly. It was only about six p.m., so they were early, and the place was less than half full. Italian cafe music played, and no one was sitting next to them.

"So, a few weeks ago, this guy started talking to me about 'partnership payments' he could provide if I was able to help seal a few lucrative deals for him. Big offshore accounts I could access when I left the army."

"Wow." Sydney smiled. "He really went for it."

"Didn't stop there," Val said, beaming. "When I deferred, he started bringing a couple of his 'office ladies' with him to our lunches and made it clear they were available if I'd like some afternoon companionship in a hotel room he'd just happened to rent next door."

"Gross."

"The world is thus." Val shrugged.

The waitress brought their food. Val leaned back from the table as she set it down.

"Oh, this is perfect," Sydney said in an appreciative voice, taking in the spread of thin-crusted mushroom pizza, a large bowl of salad, prosciutto-wrapped asparagus, and, of course, more bread and olive oil.

Val served Sydney a slice of pizza as he continued. "So, obviously, this guy is going for kompromat on me."

"Gee...what was your first clue?"

"And I keep denying him the opportunity."

"And the lunch invitations dried up," Sydney said, recognizing the pattern well.

"No. We kept meeting." Val pulled a piece of pizza onto his own plate. "You're going to laugh, but I like the guy. I think he likes me."

Sydney did laugh, holding her napkin over her mouth to keep from spitting food.

"I think we have a genuine friendship."

"Oh god," Sydney said, managing to swallow and clear her airway. "Of course, you do."

"What does that mean?"

"Come on, Val. It's just the way you are. You think you can befriend anyone. That you can form a real connection."

Val winced when she put insincere emphasis on the word "real."

Sydney smiled. "I'm not saying you're not a charismatic guy. I'm just saying it's not as foolproof as you believe."

"Whatever. I'm not saying we're best friends, or anything," Val grinned sheepishly. "It's a strange balance of easy friendship mixed with a perceptible sense of suspicion and superficiality."

Sydney laughed and shook her head.

"I know. But I kind of like the guy."

"You kill me," she said, taking a sip of wine. "The confidence you go through life with. I alternate between awe and terror."

Val leaned back in his chair and took a sip of wine.

"It's a great story so far." Sydney placed her glass of wine on the table and leaned forward on her elbows. "Where are you taking it?"

Val took another sip, hesitating.

"Never mind. Don't answer. I respect our pseudo-Chinese-wall here." She gestured at an imaginary barrier between them and leaned back in her chair. "It's just such a good story. Maybe you can tell me about it one day when it's all said and done."

Val took another sip of wine and leaned forward, wearing a conspiratorial smile.

Sydney made a clapping gesture in front of her chest and leaned forward again.

Val looked around the room and then said, "Now that I have flipped the colonel, I'm going to get dirt on the Bulgarian arms dealer. Put that fucker away."

"I like it. But won't that be hard to do to a 'friend'?" Her pronunciation of "friend" was saccharine, and she held up air quotes to ensure he knew she was poking fun at him.

"No." Val's face darkened. A flash of anger surged in his voice. "He makes money shipping weapons to our enemies into war zones. Enemies that then use his weapons to kill Americans. If I could kill him right now, at this moment, at this table, I would. So getting him arrested, shutting down his pipeline, and making him personae non grata in Europe is letting him off easy."

Val leaned back and took a few deep breaths.

The anger on his face faded to sadness as he looked out the window onto a darkened Prague. Sydney studied him. He looked so tired. Deep, fatigued crow's feet extended from his eyes.

She didn't know what to say, so she took another sip of wine.

"Sorry," Val finally said, reaching to grab his own glass. "I'm not mad at you. You know that. It's just been a long war."

He took a long pull of wine.

"And gonna be longer," she said.

Val nodded and put his glass down.

Sydney reached across the table and took his hand from the stem of his glass. "You never have to apologize to me, Val. I understand."

He looked at her.

"What?" she asked.

"Nothing."

"You can tell me," she said softly, placing her other hand on top of his. She gently squeezed his hand between both of hers. "It's okay."

"It's just that… I don't think you understand. Not totally. How could you?"

She waited. She would not let him draw her into a fight.

"You been next to someone when they were killed?" he asked her.

"No."

"You kill anybody?"

"No," she said, holding his gaze.

"You been spared for no reason? By a fucking whim?"

Here it comes, she thought. *Here comes the speech about us CIA officers being genteel white-collar types. Never getting our hands dirty.*

Sydney resisted the urge to let go of his hand and grab her glass to take a big swig of wine.

I'm not going to fight with him, she promised herself.

"No, Val. I've been through none of those things." She squeezed his hand again.

"Well, it sucks," Val said, taking his eyes from her and looking out the window. "Changes your perspective."

Sydney nodded, relieved and saddened.

"I can't imagine," she said. "I truly can't. And I hate it."

"Hate what?"

"I feel in some ways like I know you better than anyone in the world ever could. Like no one could ever get you as well as I get you."

"I feel that way too," he said, nodding, a smile breaking across his face.

She smiled back.

"But, still, sometimes I feel like I'll never really know you. Ever. That I'll never know what you go through. What you endure."

"I feel that way too," he said, his voice catching slightly.

Val's words pierced Sydney. Her eyes welled up. She'd thought about it before, of course. All those hours in the JOC, watching combat unfold on the big screens on the wall. She saw the violence and death unfold in monochromatic scenes accompanied by urgent, sometimes agonizing, audio. But she'd never been there. Really been there.

Val reached a hand across the table and held it to her cheek.

"Hey," he whispered.

She tilted her head into his hand and closed her eyes. A tear broke free and ran down her cheek into his fingers.

"You're it for me, Sydney," he said. "You and me. Together. The rest is all bullshit."

She opened her eyes. A sad smile spread across her face.

"I feel the same."

"Do you ever think about quitting?" Val asked, taking his hand from her cheek.

"Quitting what?"

"The shit we do."

"And do what?"

"I don't know."

"No. You?"

"Yeah. A lot."

"What would you do?"

"Well, that's the problem," he said, sitting back in his chair and lifting his wineglass to drink. "I have no fucking idea."

Sydney chuckled and said, "I don't see you quitting."

"Not now," Val said, putting his glass down and leaning across the table and grabbing her hands again. "And maybe not soon. But there's going to be a day when I do. And on that day, I'm going to call you and beg you to join me."

Sydney laughed.

"And what will we do?"

"Whatever you want," he said, "Maybe move here. To Prague."

Sydney laughed again.

*

Later that night, after they made love again, they lay in bed holding hands and talking. The night sky had cleared, and moonlight poured in from the open balcony.

Val got up.

"Where are you going?"

"To get a glass of water," he said over his shoulder as he walked to the kitchen. "Want one?"

"Yes, please."

Sydney looked at her watch. It was almost one in the morning.

"Seven hours," she said when Val returned.

"Don't," he said. "No sad countdowns. Let's talk about something else."

They both took long drinks of water and then placed their glasses on opposite side tables.

Val got back under the covers and embraced Sydney.

"Tell me how it's going to go down," she said as she wrapped her arms around him.

"How is what going to go down?"

"Your debrief of the Russian colonel."

"We're going to link up in Bulgaria."

"Bulgaria?"

"Yes. It's an easily explained cover for his trip. Russian colonel visiting arms suppliers. There are a ton of those guys in Bulgaria. We're going to meet in a little town called Veliko Tarnovo."

"Never heard of it."

"You'd love it," Val said with enthusiasm. "It's a small town that's spread across three rolling hills that intersect a meandering stretch of the Yantra river. It was the capital of the Bulgarian empire almost a thousand years ago. It's pretty. They call it the City of the Tsars. Just a couple hours' drive from the Black Sea."

"Sounds romantic. Why have you never taken me to the Black Sea?"

"I'll take you next week." Val squeezed her to him. "Don't leave tomorrow. I'll quit the army. You quit the CIA. We'll go live on the Black Sea."

"Stop," she whispered. "Please stop talking like that."

She held herself tightly to him, teetering on the edge of saying yes. Of quitting and staying with him.

"Okay," he whispered into her ear. "No more pleading. I promise."

For an instant, she fought the urge to change her mind. To issue her own plea: "Yes. Let's quit. Let's run away together and never come back."

Val sat up and drank more water. And the moment was gone.

"Fine," he said, turning to look at her. "I'll just go to the Black Sea with my ugly Russian colonel and then use him to get to Mr. Vegas."

"Mr. Vegas?" Sydney asked, her voice suddenly sharp.

"That's the arms dealer," Val said, replacing the glass of water and lying back down beside her. "It's a nickname of his. One he seems to really enjoy, to be honest. I guess it's because he dresses flashy and often has a young woman on his side. To be honest, I don't know why. I think it's pretty cheesy. But you know how those Eastern Europeans are."

Sydney sat up.

"Tattoo of a dagger on his right forearm?"

"Um…yes."

"Oh my god," she said, blinking. "I can't believe it."

"What is it?"

"Is his name Vasily?"

Val sat up.

"Yes."

"Abakumov?" she asked slowly.

"Yes," Val said, hesitation in his voice. They were smashing the Chinese wall now. "I don't like where this is going."

"I can't believe it." Sydney shook her head. "Vasily Abakumov. Mr. Vegas. What are the fucking odds?"

"How do you know his name?"

"He works for us."

"He works for you?"

"Val, I don't have to tell you, but we're way off the reservation now. This is top-secret, compartmentalized, need-to-know stuff. This could end our careers. Worse. This could put us in jail."

"Yeah," Val said impatiently. "Yeah, I know. This is just you and me here. What the hell are you talking about? He works for you?"

"Not solely for us. I'm not sure he has any real loyalties. But to the extent he does, they lean to Russia, not to us. We just use him from time to time to get arms shipments to…to certain entities that would be difficult for most of our other partners to pull off."

"He works for the fucking Russians," Val said.

"Abakumov works for whoever pays him. We're under no illusions about his double and triple dealings. But sometimes he is the best way to get stuff to folks when we don't have a good way to get them stuff."

"Well, I'm taking the fucker out."

"Val, look—"

"He's a fucking arms dealer," Val said, cutting her off as he got out of bed. "He kills American soldiers. And I'm shutting him down."

He turned to walk to the bathroom.

"Val, listen—"

"How many troops get killed while you guys fiddlefuck around?" Val said over his shoulder as he stepped into the bathroom.

"We're not fiddling around," she called after him. "We're running a plan. The plan has a timeline."

Val slammed the door to the bathroom behind him.

"Well, I'm on a timeline too," he shouted through the door as he pissed. "And I bet mine is a lot faster than yours!"

Sydney got out of bed and walked toward the bathroom.

Val flushed the toilet and stepped back into the bedroom.

"Val, his next big shipment into the war zone isn't for six or seven months at the earliest," Sydney said, meeting him halfway in a pool of moonlight. "We're going to shut him down before that. But between now and then, we're going to work him for his network. His connections are deep. Expansive. We're going to leverage them and do some actual damage."

They stood naked, facing each other in the moonlight.

Val shook his head.

"Val," Sydney took a step closer to him and put her hand on his chest. "Please don't do anything crazy. We've been working this guy for years now. If you go charging in there, you're going to spook him, or tip our hand, or—"

"Sydney," Val said in a calm voice. He took her hand in his. "You've never even met this guy, have you?"

"No," she said in a tone that assessed his question as ridiculous. "He is one of a dozen operations we've got going right now."

"Well, I have a relationship with him. He's not just a PowerPoint slide or dossier from the field. I know this guy, and I know what I'm doing."

"Oh, do you?" Sydney said, stepping closer to him and putting her hands on her hips.

"Yeah, I fucking do," Val said, not giving any ground. He crossed his arms. When he did, the skin of his forearms brushed against her as their pale, toned bodies leaned toward each other.

"And I know I'm the dumb army guy, and that I'm not doing any complex agency algebra here," he continued. "But for me, it's a simple equation. Abakumov kills Americans. The longer he is allowed to operate, the more soldiers die. I'm going to end his operation as soon as possible."

Sydney shook her head. "I'm sorry, Val. This one is bigger than you. You have to stand down."

"Excuse me?"

"You heard me."

"I shouldn't have talked about any of it in the first place," Val said. "But when I did, I was talking to you as Sydney, my friend. Not Sydney, the agency counter-proliferation high command."

"Fuck you," she said wearily, turning from him.

"What?"

"I see where this is going, and I won't let you make me the bad guy here," she said, walking to her bag.

Val turned to face Sydney but didn't follow her.

She jerked a pair of jeans out of her bag.

"You're going to do what you want anyway." she jammed one leg into her pants. "You always fucking do."

She jammed her other leg in and zipped up the jeans.

"What are you doing?" Val asked.

"Getting dressed," she said, bending down to fish out a bra.

"Why?"

"Not sleepy anymore." She stood and put on the bra. "I'll head to the train station and give you some space."

"It's the middle of the night, Sydney."

Sydney bent down again to find a T-shirt.

"Sydney."

She didn't respond. She yanked a few articles of clothing out of the bag, frustrated.

Val walked to her. He knelt down on the other side of her bag and grabbed her flailing hands.

"Don't," she said. But she left her hands in his.

"I'm sorry."

"No, you're not."

"I am."

"But you've got to do what you've got to do," she said in an angry voice that mimicked his. "I've heard it before, Val. Please let me go."

She tried to pull her hands back, but he gripped them tightly.

She stopped pulling, but kept her eyes down, staring into her duffel bag.

"Listen to me, Sydney," he said. "I'm sorry. I'm sorry I got mad. I'm sorry for the high-command cheap shot. And I'm going to leave Abakumov alone."

She looked at him, a mix of surprise and skepticism on her face.

"I promise."

He stood up, pulling her with him by the hand.

"I meant it when I said I'd walk away with you and let it all burn down. I'm going to prove it to you."

He touched her cheek and then let his hands fall to his sides.

"I love you, Sydney. Please don't leave."

"Oh, Val. Please don't say things you don't mean."

"I mean every word."

She reached out to him, and they embraced.

"I love you too."

CHAPTER 50

16 October 2007

Sofia, Bulgaria

Val walked into the lobby of the InterContinental hotel in Sofia. Large black-and-white marble floor tiles formed chevrons that pointed toward reception. To his right, an enormous fireplace cast a warm glow onto a stylish seating area, where several guests sat with drinks and chatted. Val shook his head in envy. It would be a long time before he could relax with a cocktail tonight.

"Welcome to the InterContinental Sofia, sir," one of the attractive receptionists said to Val. "Checking in?"

"Yes." Val stepped up to the black marble counter. "Thank you."

"Passport and credit card, please, sir," she said with a warm smile.

Val pulled his visa out of his pocket and handed it, as well as his passport, to the receptionist. She was beautiful. Long black hair ran over her shoulders, outlining high cheekbones and full lips.

"What brings you to Sofia, Mr. Rafter?" Her dark, playful eyes glanced up to see his as she checked his passport. "Pleasure, I hope."

"Yes. Some much-needed rest and diversion." Val looked back at the group relaxing by the fireplace.

"Good. Have you been to Sofia before, sir?"

"Once." Val turned back to her. "Just enough to whet my appetite."

"Excellent!" she said, with what seemed like genuine excitement. "Still checking in today and leaving Monday morning?"

"That's the plan."

"Well, that sounds fun. Will you need one key or two?"

"Just one, thanks."

She nodded as she entered a few final keystrokes and gathered his things.

"Very well, then, Mr. Rafter. We have you in a lovely room on the fourth floor with a brilliant view of Nevsky Cathedral. The elevator is just to your left there."

"Thank you."

"Can I offer you a glass of champagne to begin your weekend, sir?"

"No, thank you. I have a few things to wrap up before this evening."

The receptionist gave a faint pout and knowing nod.

"Well, I do hope you can relax soon. If there is anything we can do to make your stay more enjoyable, do not hesitate to ask. My name is Martina."

"Thank you, Martina."

Val sighed heavily when the elevator doors closed. The thought of cocktails by the fire in that posh lobby and being waited on by the attentive and attractive staff while he flirted with other guests was much more enticing than the long night ahead of him.

Once in his room, he set down his bag and looked around.

It was a nice room, with a single king-size bed and a wide floor-to-ceiling window facing the Nevsky Cathedral. The neo-Byzantine church sat on a small rise only a couple of hundred meters to the north of the hotel.

Val gazed at the gold domes of the cathedral for a moment before getting to work.

He placed his bag on the bed and unpacked, hanging a few casual shirts in the closet, and setting underwear and socks on the bureau against the wall. He took a used toothbrush and toothpaste out of a toiletry bag and placed it next to the bathroom sink and left the toiletry bag on top of the small desk by the window.

Val took an empty leather satchel out of his bag and packed it with a change of clothes and a second toiletry bag. He also shoved his laptop and a notepad into the satchel, as well as a couple of other items. The leather satchel bulged as Val yanked on the zipper. He cross slung the satchel over his shoulder and tossed the now empty duffel on the floor of the small closet before walking to the head of the bed. Val yanked the covers down about halfway and jostled the pillows and then walked back to the bathroom.

Val splashed water on his face. He dried off with a hand towel, which he left lying across the sink. Grabbing one of the large towels, he placed it on the side of the tub before picking up one of the upside-down empty glasses next to the sink. He drew water from the faucet and then walked back to the bed to place the half full glass of water on the bedside table.

Val looked around.

Satisfied, he adjusted the satchel shoulder strap and walked out of the room.

Val looked at his watch as he rode the elevator down to the first floor. He had almost two hours until the meet.

Val gave the pretty receptionist a wave as he walked off the elevator and through the lobby.

"Taxi, sir?" the doorman asked as Val walked out.

"Yes. Thank you."

The bellman raised his hand at the group of taxis across the street. "And where will you be going, sir?"

"The airport, please."

"Leaving us so soon?"

"No. Fortunately not. I left something there and need to to retrieve it."

The taxi pulled to a stop in front of the doorman, who opened the door for Val.

"I'm glad to hear it, sir," he said as Val handed him a five-dollar bill and got into the back of the cab, placing the leather satchel in his lap.

The doorman leaned into the cab and told the driver, "Please take this gentleman to the airport," in Bulgarian. Val smiled at the similarity between the Bulgarian and Russian languages. He could make out a lot of what the Bulgarians were saying.

Val scanned the area as they pulled away from the hotel. No obvious surveillance in pursuit.

A good start.

He noted the time. It was 1715 hours. The sun would set in less than an hour, making surveillance gradually more difficult. Val kept a careful but discreet watch on the road behind him, looking for signs of anyone following.

Twenty minutes later, Val handed the driver cash and hopped out quickly when they pulled up to Terminal Two. He looked around for a moment as if lost, pretending to read signs and get his bearings as he scanned the area for surveillance. He knelt down to tie his shoes, stood, turning slightly to throw something into the trash, and then helped an older woman maneuver her bag over the curb. All of these movements were intended to appear mundane while affording him a 360-degree visual scan of the area. No sign of surveillance. Val went inside.

Terminal Two was only a couple of years old. The exposed trusses supporting the vaulted ceiling were still a pristine white, and the large aluminum-clad columns gleamed. Travelers surged through the large open space, eager to either catch their flight or get home for dinner.

Val approached the information desk.

"Where can I find the lost and found?"

"Go down one level and walk directly here, sir," the young lady said, pointing at the terminal map behind her.

"Thank you."

Val turned and departed quickly, as if he were late for something important, providing little reaction time to anyone following him.

No one obvious, he noted as he left the desk behind.

Val already knew where the lost and found was. He'd memorized the layout of Sofia's international airport during mission prep. He walked to the stairs and descended quickly to the lower level. At the bottom, he made a show of looking confused and trying to read signs to figure out where he was. This gave him a chance to check the top of the stairs for anyone trying to tail him, but only a couple of tired-looking business travelers followed behind.

Val hurried along the length of the bottom level, passing the many luggage turnstiles along the way. When he was almost halfway across, he doubled back as if suddenly deciding to use the bathroom he'd just walked by. He scanned the area behind him as he walked to the bathroom. Nothing.

He stepped up to a urinal, monitoring the door he'd just walked in. Val pissed quickly and then washed his hands before walking back out into the terminal. He looked about as if to orient himself and headed toward the lost and found.

Still clear.

Pausing at the glass door to the lost and found, Val glanced around as if trying to confirm his navigation. People clustered around the luggage turnstiles, occasionally stepping forward to drag a bag or two off the conveyor, oblivious to his existence. Just the way he liked it.

Val opened the door and stepped inside. He spent some time trying to find a jacket that he knew was not there. Val made sure to be very nice to the attendant and left the number of the InterContinental in case the fictional jacket showed up later.

Val left the lost and found and walked out of the terminal, stifling a smile. If anyone were to ask the attendant what the American gentleman had been up to, "looking for his jacket" was sure to be the report.

He doubled back to the information desk, following the same route, a move that gave him the opportunity to crash through any tailing surveillance that was lingering behind him. He spent a few minutes with the information attendant, confirming that there was, in fact, only one lost and found.

After thanking her, Val turned from the desk in defeat. He rubbed his eyes and looked around as if resigning himself to the loss of a jacket before walking toward the taxi sign at the far end of the terminal.

Val slowed down as he neared the terminal exit beneath the taxi sign. It worked, and he was approached by one of the lurking private car drivers that was dodging airport taxes.

"Sir, sir," the driver said as he looked around for the police. "You need ride?"

"Yes. How much to the city center?"

"You pay US? Twenty dollars."

"Deal. Let's go."

"Yes. Let's go." The driver smiled and held the door open for Val.

Val walked quickly out of the terminal, pleased with how this was going. He'd spent hours planning this phase of the operation last week at the station in Prague. What looked like a hasty bounce back to the airport to find a lost jacket was actually the meticulously planned anchor point of a multimode SDR. Val had used the airport as an intrusion point, which is any building with multiple entrances and exits that forces a surveillance team to enter for fear of breaking contact with their target. For the operator conducting the SDR, an intrusion point allows them to sift surveillants from the background by compelling them to break from their disguised activities. Surveillants don't like intrusion points.

Though he looked distracted and half lost at each turn, every footstep Val took in the airport was pre-planned and allowed him to change direction and force surveillance to highlight themselves. So far, he'd been clear all the way from the hotel and then through the airport. Now, his sudden departure, rather than waiting in the taxi line, would make it nearly impossible for anyone to follow him gracefully. They'd have to decide between burning their cover and letting him go.

"You have bags?" the driver asked.

"No. Was saying goodbye to someone."

The driver nodded and gestured at Val to follow him. Within minutes, they were in his car and leaving the airport. Val scanned behind them. No scrambling foot-borne surveillance or accelerating vehicles.

He smiled and looked at his watch. An hour to go till the meet, and it was dark now.

Val had the driver drop him off a few blocks east of the City Garden near a coffee shop. He scanned the area as the cab pulled away.

No activity.

Val turned and walked into the coffee shop. It was a cozy place with only one visible entrance, the main door. He stepped up to the counter and ordered a cup of coffee, waiting for it in a dark corner by the end of the counter.

Val chose this coffee shop to provide justifiable cover for action on the SDR, allowing him to execute a change in direction for the subsequent leg of the route. Anyone following Val wouldn't chance following him into a cover stop but would have to maintain visibility on the front door. They would then have to depart in the same new direction with Val, highlighting themselves. The process is tedious and time-consuming, but an effective way to further sift surveillance while appearing ordinary.

Val dropped a rock of brown sugar into his coffee, enjoyed the last swallow, and stepped back into the night. No signs of vehicles he'd seen earlier on the route, and no semblance of surveillance springing to action to follow him on the final leg. It was all to script, and uneventful. A textbook SDR.

That last leg of the route confirmed he was in the black and clear for the mission. He spent the next hour confidently, yet discreetly, circumnavigating the City Garden before working his way toward the fountains at its center. Well before nearing a man sitting on a bench near a fountain, Val was absolutely confident he was clean. He hoped his meet had done him the same courtesy.

The man on the bench was dressed in blue jeans and a sweater beneath an overcoat and wore a baseball cap pulled low over his brow. His hands rested on a folded newspaper in his lap. He watched as Val approached slowly from the side.

"I enjoy sitting on these benches at night," Val said, issuing the pre-planned challenge.

"Yes," the man said casually. "There are fewer pigeons and no bears."

Val nodded, acknowledging the correct response.

The man gestured at the bench, inviting Val to sit next to him.

"I bet you've had a long day," the man said as Val sat down.

"And it ain't over yet."

"I'm sure."

Val leaned back on the bench as a feeling of fatigue settled over him. He pushed it out of his mind. He had a long way to go before he could rest this evening.

Both men looked at the fountain for a moment.

"How do you like Sofia?" Val asked.

"Love it. Beautiful city. Nice people. Wife likes it more than I do, I think. So, you know, that's a plus."

Val chuckled.

"Seriously," the man said. "Great place. If you can get back here on leave or with some spare time, visit the botanical gardens of Vitosha and sip some wonderful rakia. Really nice."

"I'll do that."

The man scanned the area quickly and then said, "Here you go," as he handed Val the folded newspaper.

Val unfolded the newspaper and grabbed the passport, driver's license, and credit cards that rested inside. He shoved the new identity into his left-hand coat pocket. He reached into his right-hand coat pocket and pulled out his true name documents. A small rubber band bound his passport, driver's license, and credit cards together in a small bundle. He placed them on the newspaper, folded it, and handed it back to the man.

"We'll meet back here in seventy-two hours," Val said.

"Roger that. Something holds you up, I'll be here exactly one, four, and then twenty-four hours after that."

"I won't be late." Val stood up.

"Good luck," the man said with sincerity.

"Thanks." Val turned and walked off into the shadows.

The man sat on the park bench for another twenty minutes, then he stood and walked away in the opposite direction.

Val spent the next hour executing another walking SDR to ensure that he hadn't picked up a tail during the meet. When he was confident that he was clean, he stepped into a gas station to use the restroom and grab another cup of coffee.

When he was alone in the bathroom, Val reviewed his new documents. "Shane McDevitt," he read out loud from the passport. He repeated the name to himself several times as he stood at the urinal and pissed.

Biometrics had changed the nature of cross-border operations over the past decade. Fingerprints and retinas cannot be spoofed, no matter how extensively identity documents are backstopped. Databases and the internet made sharing that kind of biometric information effortless and instantaneous. And getting caught crossing a border with documents that don't match your biometric profile was the surest way to get tagged.

That's why Val had crossed the border and checked into the InterContinental with his real name. His biometric and financial signature had been digitally broadcast across the internet instantaneously. But an American military embassy staff member vacationing in Sofia was a happens-every-day-around-the-world kind of event that would draw no one's attention. Val's hotel check-in and credit card activity would establish that he spent a couple days in the city and not cut through the noise of the millions of data points that flooded modern intel analysts.

Shane McDevitt, though, rented a car in Sofia and then paid for everything else, including his hotel, in cash, making most of his activities much more difficult to trace. Not that anyone would care what this onetime-use, burner pseudo-identity did.

This was all critical to protecting the colonel. Val didn't want to leave any evidence of himself being in the same location as the Russian. The colonel had cover for his actions as well. An officer of his rank, in his role, would not draw any curiosity if he spent a few days inspecting weapons facilities in Bulgaria and treated himself to nice accommodation while he did so. But if a hotel registration or credit card receipt put Val Rafter in the same place at the same time? That was the kind of slipup that got agents killed. And the Russians made examples of turncoats. It would not be pleasant.

Val would not let that happen.

CHAPTER 51

The drive to Veliko Tarnovo took more than three hours. It was well after midnight when Val pulled up to the Yantra Grand Hotel. Newly opened, the large and modern hotel sat on the east side of the city as the Yantra river wrapped around it, tracing a haphazard dogleg between the hills before continuing south. The hotel's position afforded it a view of the Tsarevets fortress on the hilltops farther east. Before falling to the Ottomans in 1393, the medieval fortress served as the capital stronghold of the Second Bulgarian Empire for centuries. The massive stone complex was a dramatic sight above the forested hills.

Val would not be taking in the sights on this visit, though. He and Colonel Liev Sidorov would spend the next two days debriefing in the colonel's hotel room.

Val spread his folders and other materials on one of the twin beds and sat at the small writing desk against the wall. He took the old TV and lamp off the table to make room for his laptop and notebook. The colonel alternated between pacing the room with a cigarette and sitting in one of the dingy purple club chairs with a cigarette.

A small table sat between the two club chairs. Val had laid some snacks on the table to fuel their long sessions—mostly cheese and sausage sliced into chunks with his 13th Tactical switchblade that lay on the table. The colonel placed the room's ashtray next to the switchblade.

They rarely left, and if they did, they did so separately.

They could never be seen together.

This was the only time they would meet face-to-face unless there was an unforeseen emergency, so there was a lot to cover. In addition to having the colonel lay out details about the Russian embassy staff in Bulgaria and their operations in the region, he and Val had to establish all of their communications plan elements.

The "Commo plan" is the standard operating procedure for the clandestine relationship. It covers discreet messaging protocols for information exchange, procedures for missed meetings and emergency situations, and methods of transferring information and operational funds. Tailored to the specific handler-asset pair, commo plans are designed to keep the relationship under the radar and both handler and asset safe.

It was a detailed, painstaking process, but it was made easier by the fact that Sidorov knew the drill. He'd been an intelligence officer for most of his twenty-five-year career, and the fact is, the tactics, techniques, and procedures are, for the most part, common from one intelligence service to the next, regardless of nation. That's why there are little chalk marks all over the world's capitals and every good intelligence officer still has a stupid wig and fake moustache in their trunk. It's an old-fashioned game of deception and misdirection. There are only so many ways to keep and exchange state secrets.

Sidorov's seniority and experience were also a source of friction.

"I'm just trying to make sure you're safe," Val said when Sidorov chaffed at his coaching. "You have to do the cleansing route after every drop-off."

"Cleansing route?" The colonel scoffed. "Please tell me that is not really what you guys call it."

Val sighed and got up from the table. He walked to the window and stretched his back before walking to the room's small coffee pot. Sidorov lit another cigarette.

"I appreciate your concern, Valentine," the colonel said. He'd insisted on knowing Val's full name when he'd first accepted payment to spy for the United States a month ago and had used the full name ever since. Not even Sydney used "Valentine."

"But I have been doing this for twenty-five years," the colonel continued as Val returned to his chair with lukewarm coffee. "You have been in the game for, what? Ten at most?"

Val almost corrected him by saying, "Eleven." But he thought better of it. He took a sip of coffee and sat down.

"I promise you, I have no desire to face a firing squad," the colonel said, noting the consternation on Val's face. "I will be careful."

"I hope so." Val put his cup down and pulled his laptop nearer. He scanned his notes and tried to decide what to cover next.

Colonel Sidorov took a long drag from his cigarette as he observed Val.

"Do you enjoy this work, Val? Intelligence, I mean."

Val looked up from his laptop at the colonel. Sidorov's hair was nearly entirely gray, making him look older than his fifty-six years, and his face was weary and yellowed from a life of cigarette smoking. But his eyebrows, which were still black, hovered over his eyes in exaggerated arches. They gave the old colonel a skeptical, mischievous air.

The right eyebrow was raised even higher at the moment, as Sidorov met Val's gaze.

Val tried to stifle a smile. It was not a question one usually got from a newly recruited agent. But it was exactly the question Sidorov would ask him. A fondness for the old warrior swelled within Val.

"What?" the colonel demanded.

"Nothing." Val took another sip of coffee.

"Is serious question."

"Please, Liev." Val rubbed his eyes. "We've got a lot more to cover."

"There will always be more to cover, Valentine," Sidorov responded in a disappointed voice. "But we will not always have time like this. Together."

Sidorov gestured at Val and himself and then jammed his spent cigarette into the full ashtray. He reached for another, raised an eyebrow, and said, "Is called 'rapport building,' no?"

Val smiled.

"You cannot be in such a rush all the time, Valentine." Sidorov pointed at Val with the fresh cigarette. "Some things take time."

"For chrissake," Val muttered. He took another sip of coffee and leaned back in his chair with a sigh.

Sidorov lit up, inhaled deeply, and waited for Val to continue.

"Yeah," Val said. "I like it."

"What did you do before intelligence?"

"I was an armor officer. I drove tanks."

Sidorov nodded, as if Val had confirmed something he'd suspected.

"I think I would have liked to be armor officer," the colonel said.

"There is nothing quite like hauling ass across the countryside in an M1 Abrams main battle tank. I loved being a tanker."

"So, why the change? Why did you leave the tanks?"

"I was bored."

The colonel raised both of his dark eyebrows.

"It was the nineties," Val said added. "Post–Cold War, pre–Kosovo Europe."

"Sounds nice."

"Yes." Val chuckled. "In retrospect, it really was. My friends and I had a good time exploring Europe."

"And the women, I presume."

"Yes, sir," Val agreed with a smile.

"And yet, bored."

"I realize now it was the times," Val said, sadness in his voice. "But at the moment, I didn't know it was the last couple years before 9/11 and all the madness that would follow."

"None of us did."

Val nodded.

"Back then, to me, the army just seemed like bullshit. Like a lot of dress-up and comic opera. And it seemed like it always would be. So, when offered the chance, I switched to intelligence because it looked like it would be more real."

"And you like it? Intelligence?"

"Sure."

"What do you like about it?"

"I like that it's equal parts balls and homework."

Sidorov smiled. His yellow smoke-stained teeth and narrowed, crinkled eyes made Val smile back.

"Having balls big enough for the mission, and doing sufficient homework to succeed," Val explained. "It takes both. That's what I love about it. Sometimes homework counts more than balls. Sometimes it's the other way around. But you must have both. Always"

"Yes." Colonel Sidorov said, in solemn agreement. "You must have both."

Val took a sip of coffee, and Sidorov a long drag from his cigarette.

Val set his cup down and reached for his laptop.

"Speaking of homework. Let's get back to it."

Sidorov groaned but gave Val two hours of solid concentration.

Val drove him hard as he defined their contingency plans. He'd tried to plan an out for the colonel for every plausible scenario. The colonel listened intently. Written notes were not allowed on his part. He could not take any potential evidence of his betrayal of Mother Russia with him when he left the hotel. Val went over each contingency several times, quizzing Sidorov to make sure he was retaining every detail.

"Enough homework, Valentine," the colonel finally declared. "Is two in the morning. I will sleep now."

Val looked at his watch, surprised that it was so late.

"Okay. You're right. We'll take a break and pick back up again in a few hours. I'll be back at six a.m."

Sidorov sighed and reached for another cigarette.

Val stood and stretched. The colonel took a long drag from his cigarette and watched Val as he gathered his laptop and other things and put them into his backpack.

"All right, then," Val muttered, looking around to be sure he had everything.

"I appreciate your hard homework for me, Valentine. For my safety," Sidorov said. "I know how much work it is. And you have been very thorough. I want you to know I appreciate it."

Val nodded and smiled. Coming from an old cold warrior like Sidorov, it was a big compliment.

"Of course. We're a team now, me and you. I'll see you in a few hours."

"What is left to cover?" Sidorov rubbed his forehead.

"Just a couple ankle biters, really, that won't take any time. And then one major topic."

"What is the major topic?"

"Mr. Vegas."

"Of course," Sidorov said with a chuckle. "Abakumov."

*

When Val returned to the colonel's room at six a.m. the next day, there was already a thin haze of cigarette smoke floating in the air. There was also a fresh pot of coffee and a plate of pastries and fruit on the small table.

"Thank you," Val said, pouring himself a cup of coffee.

"You are welcome." The colonel sat in one of the club chairs.

Val surveyed the plate and grabbed a kifla and took a big bite. He devoured the crescent roll and then used his switchblade to slice and eat a pear as he set up his laptop.

"I am sorry," the colonel said, noting Val's appetite. "The kitchen would not give me anything more substantial at this hour."

"No problem." Val took another big bite. "This will do. I appreciate it. Let's get started."

"Always the homework."

Val ignored the comment and they got to work.

For the first hour, Val cleaned up a few loose ends in his notes. Then he turned the conversation to the final topic.

"All right, Liev. Last topic. Your friend Vasily Abakumov."

"He is no friend of mine."

The sudden venom in Sidorov's voice surprised Val. He looked up from his laptop. The colonel's face was dark. He glared at the floor. His eyebrows slanted down in anger.

"Damn parasites."

"I'm sorry?" Val asked, not following.

"These gray arms dealers." The colonel expelled a cloud of smoke as he stubbed out the butt of his cigarette. He grabbed another as he stood from his chair.

Sidorov walked to the window. The curtains were drawn closed, as they had been from the moment they'd arrived. He placed a finger between them and pulled open a gap no wider than a single eye. He leaned forward and cautiously looked out into the Bulgarian morning, the unlit cigarette clenched in his lips.

For the first time in their secret meeting, the old colonel looked nervous to Val.

That made Val nervous.

Sidorov dropped his hand to his side, letting the curtains close, and stepped back into the middle of the room.

"They work with the SVR pricks who operate toward their own agenda," the colonel said as he paced around the small room.

Val nodded. SVR is Russia's external intelligence service, like the US's CIA. It succeeded the first directorate of the KGB and other Soviet-era agencies in 1991 but traces its DNA back to the 1920s and the early days of the Soviet Union.

"So, Abakumov is their guy?"

"No," the colonel said with a rueful chuckle. "Abakumov is no one's guy. It is true that SVR helped make him who he is. But they do not control him. They do not care to. He alternates between doing their bidding and sowing chaos, all to enrich himself. Always. The SVR gets what they want sometimes. The rest of the time, I think they laugh at the chaos and consternation he generates. What else can they do? All the while, his actions bring heat down on the military. It is we who are blamed when surface-to-air missiles show up somewhere they should not be."

"What do you know about him? His past?"

"The basics." The colonel shrugged. "The same your government already knows."

Val smiled at Sidorov's coyness. "Tell me. Just to be sure."

"He was born in Bulgaria," the colonel began with a tired sigh. "His family was poor. Somehow, he got into the Soviet Army when he was eighteen. I have heard that perhaps his father was Russian. But I do not believe it. My guess is he talked his way in, rather than serve in the Bulgarian military.

"What is undeniably true is that he had a gift for languages. He went to the Military Institute of Foreign Languages, which is where I think he got his start in intelligence. That school's ties to the KGB were deep then and are deeper now. It remains a starting point for many intelligence officers."

Sidorov grabbed another cigarette and lit it without sitting down. He was burning through them faster than usual.

Val looked round the room and winced at the thickening smoke. He stood and walked to the window. Without opening the curtains, Val cracked windows at the top to provide some ventilation.

Sidorov seemed not to notice as Val walked back to his desk. The old colonel was rubbing his chin, staring at his shoes.

"What do you know about his service?" Val asked.

"I have heard he did a tour of duty in Afghanistan in the mid-eighties. That is where he got his tattoo. You know the one? The long black dagger on his forearm?"

"Yeah. I know it."

"And then Africa. Angola, I think, before he left the military. Africa is where he got his start. The legend is that he had a good friend who understood logistics. This friend set up an air cargo company. I believe they had two or three shitty Antonov AN-8 aircraft in the beginning. And Vasily had the links to Bulgaria that afforded him access to weapons."

"So, they had product and a way to move it around," Val said.

"Yes. They were in business. And Africa was their playground. They worked all over. Liberia, Sierra Leone, the Congo. Vasily and his crew would fly UN personnel and food and medical supplies around during the day, and then run those planes full of weapons at night."

"Where did they get the money for the aircraft? I didn't think a Soviet junior officer's salary was so good."

Sidorov gave a tired shrug. "A rich uncle, maybe?"

Val smiled.

"Clearly, they were set up by Russian intelligence to be a workaround. At the time, the Soviet Union was still playing the empire game on the continent. They needed a discreet, deniable way to get weapons to groups they sponsored. Well, they created a monster. Vasily was a quick study. He was charismatic and bold. I doubt they counted on him learning and moving so fast.

"He was also a ruthless bastard who did not like sharing. By the mid-nineties, his founding partner was dead. His yacht in Cape Town mysteriously caught fire with him on it. No one has ever figured out what really happened, and certainly not proven Abakumov did it. Shit, I have seen him tear up when talking about his old partner, swearing vengeance on the many enemies he has made around the world. But it was the beginning of a pattern. Those who work with him have a way of dying. Some in accidents. Though most simply vanish.

"One would have thought the end of the Cold War might have been bad for Vasily's business. Not so. The chaos of the past few decades has been big money for him. We think he helped al-Qaeda move gold and cash out of Afghanistan in the early days, even while supplying arms to the Northern Alliance for the CIA."

Val smiled at the boldness. "Full of cargo in both directions, eh?"

"No one plays both sides better than Vasily Abakumov."

"How has he not been caught yet?"

"He makes it very difficult." Sidorov nodded with grudging respect. "Always moving location. Always owning many companies and setting up new ones. Aircraft and ships that are registered and re-registered all over the world. Living in many places. Belgium, Lebanon, Rwanda, South Africa, Syria, and the UAE."

Val nodded and rubbed the back of his neck.

"Always coming back to his beloved Bulgaria, though. He has a place here on the Black Sea. He is there now, I think. Besides, Val, who wants to catch this man, really?"

"I do," Val said.

Sidorov smiled and shook his head. "You might be the only one. Men like Vasily know how to be useful. There is always someone who needs something taken somewhere for somebody that they do not want others to know about. Vasily has mastered this game of temporary favor and friendship. He has been doing it for a long time, Val. Think about it. The KGB and CIA were all over Africa in the nineties. Many of the men he met and did favors for at that time are now high-ranking in those organizations."

"You think they're looking out for him? Helping him?"

"No. But the web Vasily has spun around the world enables him to sense a shift in the wind from across the ocean. He is never where you thought he was. He cannot be caught."

The colonel sat down and let out a tired sigh.

"What do you get out of the relationship with him?" Val asked. "What are you working him for?"

"Ha," Sidorov laughed. "I do not get much."

Val waited.

"He is a good vantage point into the world of gray arms here in Bulgaria. He is too smart to give me anything of real importance. But he knows the kind of information I find useful, and he rations it out to me."

"So he is working you."

"He is working everybody."

Val leaned back from his laptop. "What's in Bulgaria that he keeps coming back to?" he asked, rubbing his eyes. He wished the colonel would stop smoking for just a few minutes. But he did not want to ask as long as the intel was flowing.

"Relationships. He has gotten most of his arms here for a very long time. Besides, is his home country. And his dacha on the Black Sea, of course. He spends a lot of time there."

"I'm surprised we let him do that," Val mused. "Why hasn't someone grabbed him from there?"

Colonel Sidorov laughed so loudly, it startled Val.

"You are very funny," the colonel said between guffaws.

Val crossed his arms and scowled.

"Oh, Valentine," Sidorov said, catching his breath. "You must realize there is no one in the Bulgarian government who has not taken money from Vasily. No one. Not even the lowest dog catcher in the smallest town. He owns them all. To move on Vasily in Bulgaria would be the most futile of gestures."

"I was just thinking out loud," Val said, looking back at his laptop.

"And that is to say nothing of the SVR and Putin himself," Sidorov added, his voice losing all mirth. "They would never allow Abakumov to be captured or extradited. That would be a bloody, bloody day."

"I get it," Val said, irritated. "I get it." He looked back down, glared at his laptop, and banged out some notes with angry fingers.

The colonel chuckled.

"Is nice place, though." The colonel lit another cigarette. "Vasily's Black Sea dacha, I mean."

"I'm sure. The bastard has invited me a few times."

"You should go."

"Right. I should go. Just step right into his kompromat machine."

"You don't have to partake. Is worth seeing."

"No, thanks."

Sidorov nodded. "I would not go if I were you either. But this tired old Russian enjoys the water. Is nice place to visit."

"Well, you've earned it as far as I'm concerned."

"Thank you."

"Now, tell me about this big shipment coming up. The one Vasily is working on."

One of Sidorov's bushy eyebrows arched involuntarily.

Val stifled a smile. A basic handling techniques was to give agents the sense that you knew more than they did—that they were useful, but in very narrow, verifiable niche of information—so that the agent never knew if what they were being asked for at that moment was new intelligence or a validation test.

The colonel would be familiar with this method. But it would disconcert, nonetheless. Val could see from Sidorov's reaction he'd surprised the old colonel. Sidorov didn't expect Val to know about the shipment.

Val's urge to smile dissolved at the thought of Sydney, and how mad she would be if she knew Val used information she told him in confidence—while naked. He pushed the thought of her, incandescent with rage, out of his head and looked evenly at the colonel.

Sidorov drew a long drag from his cigarette and gave Val a slow nod of respect.

"Yes. He sends two or three shipments a year. It is a good example of how he works. His shipments go to Syria, then the foreign fighter network infiltrates with the weapons into Iraq. Were he sitting here with us, he would argue it is not his fault that the weapons are used against Americans in Iraq. All he did was ship them to Syria. Where they go from there is not his business."

"What's in the shipment?"

"All the usual small arms and ammunition. And materials to make improvised explosive devices, of course."

Val nodded gravely.

"Tomorrow's shipment includes surface-to-air missiles, I believe," the colonel added. "These are an increasing request from the Iraqi insurgency. He is sending them SA-18s."

"What?" Val straightened in his chair.

The image of a burning Black Hawk helicopter on the big video monitor in the Ops Center on Shark base flashed through Val's mind at the mention of SA-18s. He was back there for an instant. Almost a year ago. He had spilled his coffee. Sergeant Herrera had tears in his eyes.

Omar.

Amos.

"Surface-to-air missiles, they—"

"I know SA-18s," Val snapped, coming back to the present. "But you said, 'tomorrow's shipment.'"

The colonel hesitated, realizing that the timing was new information to Val. Sidorov arched an eyebrow slightly as he said, "Yes. Tomorrow."

Val nodded, trying to maintain a mask of indifference as his mind raced. Sydney had clearly said it would be months before the next shipment, and that they would interdict it. Had she lied to him? Did they have bad information? Were they actually interdicting this shipment? He had to talk to her. Now.

Fucking SA-18s!

Val stood and stretched, still trying to convey a sense of indifference.

Sidorov wasn't buying it. "Valentine," he said as he pulled another cigarette out of the carton. "I thought you knew about this shipment. You seem troubled all of a sudden."

"No," Val said, grabbing his cell phone. "Not at all. I just remembered I need to check in with the embassy. Will you excuse me for a few minutes?"

"Of course."

Val stepped out of the colonel's room and walked hurriedly to the end of the hallway and the stairwell. He sped down the stairs to the ground floor, where he assumed a more reasonable pace.

He strode out of the lobby into the street and walked toward a fountain he'd scouted out during mission planning. It would mask his conversation from electronic eavesdroppers. Not that he suspected any. But this was going to be a very sensitive conversation with Sydney. There was a lot to do if there was any hope of interdicting the shipment on such short notice.

Val dialed Sydney's number as he stepped up to the fountain. He looked at his watch. It was about 8:30 in the morning. It would be about 1:30 a.m. for Sydney in DC.

Val scanned the area as the phone rang. The fountain sat in a small, cobblestoned roundabout surrounded by old mid-rise buildings.

Her voice mail picked up.

"Dammit!"

He hung up and dialed her number again.

Voice mail again.

"Come on!" Val said, hanging up.

He dialed her again.

He got voice mail again.

This time, he left a message.

"Sydney. It's Val. Important you call me back. About a mutual friend over here and his timeline. You've got it wrong. The party is tomorrow. Call me back."

Val glared at his phone as he assessed his situation. He knew that, even if he got through to Sydney in time, and even if she believed him, the bureaucratic slowness of the US intelligence community would not be able to react to his intelligence quickly enough. And he knew that his source, an unproven and freshly recruited asset, would not be trusted at this point. Certainly not enough to launch a risky last-minute interdiction of an international shipment by one of the world's most connected arms dealers.

"Fuck me," Val mumbled as he shoved his phone into his pocket, turned, and walked back to the hotel.

Colonel Sidorov sat smoking in one of the oversized chairs facing the windows when Val returned.

"Check-in went okay?"

"Yeah," Val said, walking back to the desk. He sat down and looked at the map of Bulgaria. "What was the street address of Vasily's dacha again?"

"I did not say."

"Well, what is it?" Val said as nonchalantly as he could while opening his laptop.

Sidorov chuckled.

Val looked at him evenly. "Don't hold out on me, Liev. What's the street number?"

"I am sure that the CIA knows this."

"Then it's no big deal for you to tell me," Val said, his voice tinged slightly by impatience.

Sidorov shook his head, a disapproving scowl settling onto his face.

"What are you planning, Valentine?"

"Planning? Nothing. I'm trying to wrap up this debrief so you and I can relax."

Sidorov nodded, but the scowl continued to cloud his face.

"To relax would be nice," the colonel said. "Tell you what, give me a list of information that you want as a result of all of our debriefing. I think you call them 'follows-up'? And you shall have them by the end of the week using the procedures you have given me. Deal?"

"Follow-ups," Val said.

"Sorry?" the colonel asked.

"They're called 'follow-ups. Not 'follows-up.'"

Sidorov waved a dismissive hand at Val's nitpicking.

"And no deal," Val continued.

"Please, Valentine."

"Come on, Liev. You know how this works. I need a few pieces of intel to start validating you."

The colonel's scowl softened. Sidorov did know, of course, how the validation process worked and how long it would take. He worked his agents the same way. In the initial stages of the relationship, he rarely asked a question he didn't already know the answer to so that he could validate what he got back. Only after a long period of validation would a source's intelligence be taken as truthful. And it would never be taken as gospel.

"I have no problem with the process, Valentine."

"Good. So, what's the issue?"

"I don't think your request is really about the process. And that concerns me."

Sidorov and Val looked at each other for a long moment.

The colonel's face became sad.

Val opened his mouth to ask the colonel what was wrong, but Sidorov stood from his chair suddenly.

He walked over to Val at the desk, leaned over, and grabbed the pen from in front of Val. Sidorov wrote an address on the corner of the map and then placed the pen on the desk back in front of Val.

"Thank you," Val said. "This will—"

"I think I will go for walk now," the colonel said. "I could use some fresh air."

Sidorov walked to the small table and picked up the pack of cigarettes. He placed them in his shirt pocket and then grabbed his cell phone. He walked to the hallway door but stopped before leaving.

"You have made me very nervous, Valentine," the colonel said, turning to face Val. "Nervous and sad. This is not how to begin a relationship with a new agent."

"What are you talking about?"

The colonel shook his head in fatherly disapproval and held up a finger in a shushing gesture.

"I need some time to think. And I believe you do as well. I'll be back in an hour or two. I hope you will also be here."

Val sat motionless.

Sidorov opened the door to leave.

"Liev!" Val called to him.

The door swung shut.

*

It was a sunny morning in the Bulgarian countryside as Val drove toward a confrontation with Vasily Abakumov. He looked at his watch again. He should be at Abakumov's dacha in about three hours.

Good.

He needed time to come up with a plan.

Problem is, I've got no weapon, no alias, no authorization, no nothing.

Val looked at his watch again. It would be about two in the morning in DC. He thought about trying Sydney again.

No. She'll just be pissed and try to talk me out of it.

Val rubbed his forehead.

God is she going to be pissed.

Val checked his rearview mirror and swerved off to the side of the road, coming to an abrupt halt on the shoulder. He turned off the motor, released the steering wheel, and closed his eyes.

What the hell are you doing? He asked himself the valid question that Sydney or the colonel or anyone else would ask.

Val looked at his watch again. He had less than twelve hours before he was supposed to be back in Sofia for the meet in the City Garden to get his true docs back.

Well, that ain't happening.

"And why not?" Val said out loud, alone in his car. "Why not go back to say goodbye to the colonel, drive to Sofia, get your true docs, and get the fuck back to Prague? It's been a productive two-day debriefing of the colonel. You've started something that will probably yield intelligence results for years to come. Turning the colonel was a big get. General Bryson is happy with you, and you're going to have some professional momentum coming out of this if you play it cool.

"Whereas, if you go through with this stupid bum rush at Abakumov, you're going to betray Sydney," he said, continuing his private debate. He counted off the impacts on his right hand. "Screw up whatever operation she has going on with him at the moment, potentially burn the colonel, and probably get yourself thrown out of Bulgaria, and then PNG'd out of Czech, royally piss off General Bryson, and probably be assigned to shovel shit in Louisiana until retirement if you're not drummed out of the army."

Val looked at the six fingers he held up in front of himself.

He leaned his head forward and rubbed his eyes.

Omar.

Amos.

Atlas Two Five.

Val shook his head, trying to dislodge the image of the burning helicopter.

He looked around at the Bulgarian countryside. He was still heading south, through the mountains. Soon, his route would bend to the east and follow the wide river valley toward the Black Sea. There was still a lot of green in the rolling countryside, but November would be here soon, and the vibrant green would fade before the snow came.

Sydney's operation may get Abakumov... eventually.

And the colonel and I may make sweet music together, creating some valuable intelligence...eventually.

But this shipment is going to kill Americans.

For certain.

Val took a deep breath and closed his eyes again.

Omar.

Amos.

Atlas Two Five.

What if you could have saved them? How far would you have gone? Is there anything you would not have done?

Val opened his eyes and started the car.

He pulled back onto the road and gunned the engine.

Still need a plan, though.

CHAPTER 52

19 October 2007

Nessebar, Bulgaria

V al arrived in Nessebar shortly after noon. The ancient sea town was not as busy as it would have been in the summer, but the cloudless October day had brought out many tourists. Nessebar's active history went back thousands of years to early Greece. Since then, the small seaside village had endured many conquerors. Romans, Byzantines, Bulgarians, Crusaders, Ottomans, and Communists. In modern times, it faced a happier annual invasion of beachgoers.

Admiring the low, red-roofed buildings on the small peninsula, Val continued north along the coast. Abakumov's dacha was a few miles north of Nessebar on Cape Emine, a prominent, sparsely populated headland that jutted east into the Black Sea like a defiant chin. Abakumov had built it about ten years ago on a dramatic piece of terrain that rose sharply, several hundred feet above the ocean.

The ruins of a medieval fortress lay nearby, as well as the small village of Emona, but Abakumov effectively controlled several square miles around his dacha. There was no way to approach the compound among the short, scrubby vegetation without being seen long in advance. If Vasily was home, his helicopter was always sitting at the ready, able to take off at a moment's notice, and his yacht was always moored a mile off the shore.

He'd never needed to activate his getaway contingencies, though. Not once.

The notoriety of his ever-present personal security detail, combined with the tactically daunting physical terrain, had deterred any unwanted surprises for Vasily.

Until Val Rafter.

Today.

Val drove through the one-intersection town of Emona and then toward Abakumov's dacha. The single-lane road worked its way east up a seaside hill and, because of the shape of the terrain, seemed to fall off a cliff into the ocean in the distance. There was nothing to indicate the presence of a grand Black Sea dacha in the area. Just brown and gray cows grazing on the steep, undulating green terrain in front of a windy seascape.

To his front, Val noted a simple wire and post farm fence that intersected the road and extended far off into the distance in both directions. A solitary small, old house stood at the intersection of the fence and road. Val slowed down as he approached the house, noting that a heavy-duty vehicle barrier, like the ones he was accustomed to seeing at embassies, was erected next to the house.

Two men stepped out of the house and motioned for Val to stop.

They were dressed in jeans and dark canvas field jackets. The man in front, gesturing at the ground to show Val where to stop, appeared unarmed. The man behind him carried a customized AR-15 that was, Val noted with chagrin, better than anything he ever carried in special operations.

The guard didn't aim the weapon at Val but carried it at the ready position as he glared from behind dark sunglasses.

Val stopped where the guard demanded and put his hands at the ten- and two-o'clock positions on the steering wheel. He had a sudden urge to call somebody. Liam, perhaps. Just so that someone knew where he was in case he vanished.

Too late, dumbass.

Now that he was closer, Val could see that the small, old house had been converted into a discreet and robust guard post. The glow from security monitors bathed the faces of two more guards seated inside. Camouflaged stone and steel structural reinforcements encrusted the old building on the outside. A large black Suburban sat behind the house alongside two BMW all-terrain motorcycles.

The long farm fence was also more than it seemed. The posts were metal and the barbed wire was heavy-gauged, much more than required for constraining cows. Also, sensors hung from each post that Val could see. Some had cameras, some had acoustic, and some had vibration sensors.

And me without even a green squirt gun.

The lead guard stepped beside the vehicle and tapped on Val's window. The other guard stepped in front of the vehicle.

Here we go.

Val smiled at the guard and rolled down his window.

"Hey there," Val said in his most friendly American voice. "Beautiful day, huh?"

"How can I help you, sir?" the guard said in a thick accent. Chechen, Val guessed.

"I'm Major Val Rafter, US Army." Val maintained his smile and extended his hand through the car window to the guard. "Here to see Vasily Abakumov, if possible."

"There is no one here by that name, sir," the guard said, ignoring the offer of Val's hand. "Please turn around and leave."

"Oh, come on!" Val said, louder and as if he'd just heard a ridiculous joke. "Vasily and I are friends. He has invited me here before. I was in the neighborhood and thought, *Hey, why not today? Why not stop on by and take Vasily up on all those invitations?* Right?"

The guard stood over Val's open window, motionless.

Val held his smile and tried to look as friendly as possible as he stared at the man's impenetrable sunglasses.

The silence got awkward quickly.

"Gosh," Val said, trying to think of a way to unstick the situation. "Maybe I'm mistaken. Where did I write that address?"

Val grabbed the map off the passenger seat and held it up to the guard, pointing at the spot where Sidorov had written Abakumov's address.

"Is this where I am?" Val asked, feigning bewilderment. "I'm so sorry. Maybe I'm lost. Or maybe I wrote it down wrong. But I swear that's the address Vasily gave me."

The guard took the map from Val's hand and walked back into the guardhouse.

"Good idea," Val said cheerily after him. "Ask your buddies. Maybe someone will know where I can find Mr. Abakumov."

Val nodded in approval and turned to smile at the second guard, who maintained his position in front of Val's car.

A moment later, the guard returned, this time followed by another guard.

Ah, management. Now, we're getting somewhere.

"Who are you looking for, sir?" The new guard's accent was less thick, but still likely Chechen.

"A friend of mine. His name is Vasily Abakumov. He and I know each other from work. I'm sorry to be a trouble. I thought he lived here. I'm hoping you can point me in the right direction."

The third guard was not wearing sunglasses. He scanned the area before looking back at Val.

"There is no one here by that name, sir."

For fuck's sake.

"But perhaps one of my colleagues knows this person you are seeking," he added.

"That would be terrific," Val said.

The guard turned to go back to the guardhouse.

"Because the truth is," Val added, deciding now was the time to up the ante, "I actually have some information for him. Some things I need to speak with him about. It's kind of urgent. So I really appreciate your help."

The third guard turned back to face Val.

"I see. And what was your name again, sir?"

"Major Val Rafter. US Army."

The guard smiled as if he'd heard something funny. He nodded slowly to Val and walked back to the guardhouse.

"Great guy," Val said to the remaining guards, gesturing at the departing man. "All you guys are great. So helpful. Really appreciate it."

Val looked at his watch. It was almost one p.m. In five hours, his contact in Sofia would be sitting on the bench by the fountains in the City Garden.

Val would not be there.

And Sydney would be awake by now or soon. She would get his message and probably freak out.

He checked his phone. No calls. Yet.

He put the phone down and put Sydney and her wrath out of his mind.

Val looked at the two video cameras pointed at him. One hung from the eave of the guardhouse, and one sat on a gatepost directly in front of him. He pictured Vasily Abakumov looking at him and wondering, *What the hell is that dumbass American army officer doing here?*

I'm wondering the same thing myself.

The guard leader exited the guardhouse and walked toward Val's car. "Sir, will you please pull your car around behind this building?"

Val noticed the guard in front of his car adjust his grip on his rifle.

"Sorry? I don't understand."

A fourth guard exited the building holding an assault rifle. He hastened to take a position behind Val's car.

Are you kidding me? Val checked his rearview mirror. *I will so fucking back over your Chechen ass.*

"Sir?" The guard leader, now standing over Val, put his hand on Val's car windowsill.

"You know what?" Val said, suddenly full of second thoughts about where he was and what he was doing. "I just remembered I'm expected at a meeting soon. I should really be going."

"I thought you wanted to speak to the boss?" the guard said. Val detected a taunting tone beneath the Chechen accent.

"And I thought you said he wasn't here?" Val answered, allowing a hint of a taunt in return.

The guard leader shrugged. He removed his hand from Val's car and straightened up. "Have a nice day, then, sir," he said as he gestured at the other guards.

The three guards relaxed, turned, and walked toward the guardhouse. The guard leader followed them.

Val chuckled and shook his head.

We gonna do this or not, Rafter?

"Okay," Val said, just before the guard leader stepped inside. "Where do you want me to park?"

*

Val sat in the middle of the middle row of the Suburban. Guards sat on both sides, in front of, and behind him.

Their vehicle followed the single-lane road up a large, steeply inclined hillside that threatened to drop off a sudden cliff side at any moment, hurtling them into the sea. They passed a few groups of idle cows that seemed to stare at them, waiting to see what would happen next.

Val leaned to his right to see around the thick neck of the large guard that sat in front of him to see where they were going. Just as he thought that he'd been duped, that there was no ocean-side dacha, the Suburban crested the hill, and it came into view.

Val smiled in admiration of the tactical competence.

Vasily's dacha was placed perfectly on the military crest of the ocean-side terrain. Anyone approaching overland from the west could not see it until, like Val, they got to the peak of the large hill. And at that point, they would be silhouetted against the horizon and at a huge tactical disadvantage.

The last hundred meters of the driveway descended from the hilltop and ended in a cul-de-sac in front of the dacha. Another black Suburban was parked to one side.

Three more security personnel met the vehicle as it came to a stop in front of the dacha.

Val looked at the dacha, surprised by its understated appearance. The modern single-story building exuded none of Abakumov's lethal reputation. It looked more like the quiet cliffside San Francisco home of a nerdy technology entrepreneur than the headquarters of one of the most notorious arms dealers in the world.

"Okay," the guard leader said, turning around to look back at Val from the front seat. His face expressed no goodwill as he said, "Good luck."

Val stepped out of the vehicle and watched as the guard that had escorted him handed his cell phone to the guards receiving him. Val had hidden his wallet and passport in his rental car, which he was sure was being thoroughly searched at the moment.

"Come with me," one of the guards said to Val.

Val tried to mask his reaction when he entered the dacha. It was spectacular.

What looked like a modest one-story building on the approach from the west revealed itself to be a towering multistory building embedded in the hillside and overlooking the Black Sea. Floor-to-ceiling windows that stretched the full width of the large room afforded Val an expansive view of the ocean and a perspective on the lower stories of the dacha that stairstepped below him toward the water. Val could not tell if there were five or six stories below them, and the terrain steepened, so he could not see where the plummeting hillside met the rocky beach a few hundred feet below. It felt to Val like the house erupted right from the ocean.

The noonday sun was nearly directly overhead in the clear sky, giving the Black Sea's choppy waters a sparkling surface. Abakumov's sleek white yacht sat about a mile out in the water.

Val got his bearings on the interior of the dacha as he followed his escorts. The top level was a sparsely furnished loft that served only as a foyer. It was suspended like a large balcony over the next level below. A single staircase descended in front of a massive window that stretched from wall to wall and from the ceiling to the floor below.

Smart. Val followed his escorts down the stairs. Any unwanted visitors that gain access to the "top" level would be isolated and easily neutralized.

The stairs landed in a large living room space that was oriented toward the massive window. Large brown leather chairs faced the ocean. There was a bar on one side of the room and a large TV surrounded by plush furniture on the other side. There was also an office set up against the "hillside wall" with a large desk in front of a long, full bookshelf.

Val noted two hallways, one on each side of the large room, which he could not quite see the ends of.

Damn. He has tunneled himself into the hillside.

"Major Rafter!"

Val recognized Abakumov's voice. He turned to see the Bulgarian walking up a stairway on the other side of the room wearing blue jeans and a dark-green patrol sweater over a white-collared shirt. The sweater sleeves were pushed up almost to his elbows above the rolled white shirt cuffs, exposing the long dagger tattoo on his right forearm.

Vasily looked as tan and happy as ever as he walked toward Val and extended his hand.

Val shook it.

"Mr. Vegas," Val said.

Vasily smiled and bowed his head at the nickname.

"So sorry to barge in on you like this."

"No, no, no," Vasily said, releasing Val's hand and waving in the air as if swatting a fly. "Don't be ridiculous. Is great to see you. I'm honored you finally accept my invitation. Would you like a drink?"

"Yes. Thank you."

Vasily waved the three guards away as he walked toward the bar. They turned without even a nod and left the two men alone.

"Bear, wine, whiskey?"

"Beer would be nice, thank you," Val said as he walked closer to the large plate glass window. This level afforded a better view of the next level below, which extended farther out toward the ocean. It was a larger floor that Val guessed housed actual living spaces.

"Here you are," the Bulgarian said, walking toward Val with two beers.

"Thank you, Vasily."

"*Nazdrave.*"

"*Nazdrave,*" Val responded, locking eyes with Vasily as they clinked their beers together.

They each took a large swallow as Val tried to figure out what to do next. He'd only given himself fifty-fifty odds of making it this far. He thought it more likely that the guards would deny him access and send him away.

"This place is incredible." Val was not ready for the confrontation yet. He made a gesture of looking around. "Did you build it, or was it already here?"

"There was nothing but rocky hillside when I got here. We worked for two years on the plans and design. Construction took another two years. But it was a labor of love for me. I love my homeland and I love the sea. I am glad that you like it."

"It's very impressive."

"Thank you."

Abakumov smiled, but Val could tell that the man was assessing him, trying to figure out what he was up to.

Good. The only advantage I have here is the initiative. So here goes.

"Vasily," Val said, in a low voice. "I hate to talk business, but—"

"Please. I did not think your dropping in was merely good fortune or happy coincidence. Say what you came here to say, my friend."

Val smiled and nodded.

"You're in danger and need to call off the shipment."

Abakumov betrayed nothing of his internal reaction. His face was a mask of tanned and happy serenity. Val waited for him to respond in some way.

Nothing.

"The weapons shipment, I mean."

"I'm sorry," Vasily finally responded. "I do not know what you are talking about."

Val nodded. "Good." He decided to take Vasily's misdirection and run with it. "Then my information is wrong, and I don't have to be worried about you."

Val smiled and took a large swig of beer. "Big relief."

Vasily put his beer down on the small table nearby.

"What information was that?"

"Oh, it doesn't matter. Forget I said anything."

"I'm curious. Tell me, please."

Val detected a change in Abakumov's tone of voice. It was less carefree. Maybe slightly annoyed or angry.

Good.

Val shrugged. "It seems silly now. But the word was that you were sending a large shipment of weapons to insurgents in Iraq. Via Syria. And that, in addition to small arms, ammunition, and explosive device material, this shipment would include SA-18s."

Val paused, but Vasily just looked at him.

The two men locked eyes.

For a long, awkward moment, they stared at each other in silence.

"I know," Val finally said in a friendly voice. "It was the SA-18s that really had people worked up, I think. Those things are really deadly, and the thought of American helicopters falling from the sky really focuses people, you know?"

Val locked eyes with Vasily again and took another swig of beer.

"So, anyway," Val said after swallowing. "Can't tell you how relieved I am that it was bad information."

"I can imagine."

A faint buzz emanated from the Bulgarian's jeans pocket. He took out his phone and looked at it.

"Would you excuse me for just a moment?"

"Sure."

Vasily walked to a far corner of the room to take the call. It was a quick one. When he returned, the chilliness of the recent exchange was gone. Vasily was warm again.

"Another beer?"

"Maybe in a moment," Val said, suddenly on edge. He'd learned not to like sudden mood swings in people. It usually meant information had been gained, a card had been turned over, an advantage was perceived.

"Do you want to see my yacht?" Vasily asked, grinning.

Val's gut screamed, *Fuck no!*

No one knows you're here. You've clearly pissed him off. Don't get on that boat.

"Oh god, Vasily," Val said, making a show of looking at his watch. "Shit. I'd love to. But I should probably get going. Expected at a meeting, you see."

"Oh, come on, Val." Vasily stepped closer and put his hand on Val's shoulder. "You've come all this way. And all the while thinking of my safety and well-being."

Vasily put his other hand on his heart in a gesture of appreciation.

"This dacha is nice," he continued. "But she is my one true love."

Vasily turned his head and looked out of the expansive window at the yacht in the distance. It was a mile away and below them on the horizon. The water shimmered around it.

The white vessel seemed to Val to be a million miles away. A distant point of no return he was not willing to go to.

Val opened his mouth to speak but stopped at the sound of footsteps coming down the stairs.

Four of Vasily's guards, including the leader from the gatehouse, descended, two carrying assault rifles.

Vasily smiled, his hand still on Val's shoulder.

The four guards walked up, two standing behind Vasily and two behind Val.

"Let's go now, Val," Vasily said, gesturing toward one of the hallways. "I won't take no for an answer."

Val's mind raced. His gut continued to scream, *Don't get on the boat.* But as he stared back at Vasily, he thought he saw hesitation, uncertainty, in the Bulgarian.

I can work with that.

CHAPTER 53

Val gripped the speedboat's handrail as they cut across the swells toward Abakumov's yacht. The powerful craft rose and fell rhythmically, spraying water far to each side.

Abakumov's yacht, which had seemed so small and remote when viewed from the dacha, now filled Val with unease. It grew as they approached until it loomed out of the sea like a white floating fortress.

"The *Monarch*," Vasily yelled to Val over the roaring speedboat engine. "I had her custom built in the Netherlands. A hundred and one meters!"

"Impressive!" Val answered, swallowing the sense of foreboding welling within him.

Fucking stupid to get on this thing. He looked around the speedboat. There was nothing in sight he could use as a weapon. His eyes met one of the guard's in the rear of the boat, seated with one hand on a handrail and one on his assault rifle.

Val smiled.

The guard did not.

They approached the *Monarch* from her front. Her prow rose straight out of the water, the lack of angle giving the ship a defiant, muscular appearance. Val thought he could count four levels, though he was not a yacht expert, and the expanses of dark glass intersected as they wove around the ship, making it hard to be sure.

It was a gorgeous ship.

Val wondered if he would ever get off it.

The speedboat settled lower in the water as the pilot eased the throttle back. The scream of the engine faded, replaced by a rumble. Shadow engulfed the small craft as it passed by the *Monarch*'s prow and floated aft by the tall port side of the yacht.

Val looked back to land a little more than a mile away. Abakumov's dacha, small in the distance, stood above the water in the middle of the rough and rocky Bulgarian hillside.

The pilot goosed the engine to swing the speedboat around as they approached the *Monarch*'s stern.

Two crewmen stood on the yacht's aft platform waiting for them, water splashing over their white tennis shoes.

The crewmen caught lines thrown to them and then pulled the speedboat to the *Monarch*.

"Here we are," Vasily said to Val as the small craft was secured. He stood and gestured to Val with a welcoming sweep of his arm.

Val, still seated, looked at his watch. "She is amazing, Vasily. I'm just worried about getting to my meeting. How long do you think we'll be here?"

"Oh, that's up to you," Vasily said with cheer. "Please, Val. Come aboard."

Val looked over his shoulder as two of the guards stepped closer to him.

"Why not?" Val stood and smiled at Vasily. "I came all this way, right?"

"You did!" Vasily laughed. "You really did!"

Val stepped off the speedboat and walked along the small plank the crew had placed between the two vessels. He followed Vasily up three flights of steps that ran along the side of the yacht. At the top of each flight, Val got a glimpse into different well-appointed sections of the yacht.

The top of the steps landed in a circular seating area. The deck was teak and the semicircular sofas were white leather. A small table sat in the middle.

Vasily gestured for Val to sit.

Val hesitated.

"Please, Val," Vasily said. "We'll have a quick conversation, and then I show you around, okay?"

"Do you have a phone I can use?" Val asked. "Maybe I'll just call my colleagues and let them know where I am."

"Oh, I'm sorry. Our phones are not working out here at the moment. Damnedest thing."

Val nodded at the "bad luck."

A reflective sliding glass door forward of the seating area opened, and a female crew member emerged. She wore the same white tennis shoes as the male crew members, but with a khaki skirt instead of chinos. Behind her, past the open glass door, Val glimpsed a dining area.

The female crew member walked over and stood by the table.

"Something to drink, Val?" Vasily asked as he sat down. "Beer, water, champagne?"

"I guess another beer wouldn't hurt."

"And I'll have a water," Vasily said to the crew member.

She nodded and turned to leave. The rest of the guards went with her.

Vasily and Val sat on opposite sides of the seating area, looking at each other. The sun was not as high now, and its shimmering effect on the water was gone. The Black Sea looked like an endless expanse of dark water stretching away forever over Vasily's shoulder.

The Bulgarian studied Val.

Val stared back in silence as he berated himself. The plan he'd concocted during his drive to Vasily's dacha was thin. He was just going to spook the shit out of the Bulgarian. He couldn't kill Vasily or take any other type of direct action. So he was going to bluff him, cause enough angst and doubt that the Bulgarian would not follow through with his shipment.

Stupid fucking plan.

The female crew member returned carrying a tray with two empty glasses, a bottle of beer, and a bottle of sparkling water. Vasily didn't take his eyes off Val as she set the tray on the table between them and left.

Vasily remained still.

Fuck it. I need a beer.

He leaned forward and grabbed the beer from the table. Leaving the clean glass alone, he took a sip from the bottle.

Vasily chuckled as if he approved.

"Who told you about the shipment?" Vasily asked as he leaned forward to grab the bottle of sparkling water and poured it into a glass.

"What shipment?"

"The one you came to warn me about."

"And that you said didn't exist?"

"Yes," Vasily said, a broad smile taking over his face. "That one."

"Nobody."

Vasily nodded as if he expected that answer.

"Was it Shane McDevitt?"

Val willed his face blank. He took another swig of beer from his bottle and then said, "Who?"

Vasily reached into his pants pocket and pulled something out. He tossed it onto the table between them.

Val glanced down at the American passport. He didn't need to open it to see that it was his burner ID. Val took another sip of beer, set the drink down on the table, and leaned back on the plush white sofa.

"I see how this would be addictive." Val took in a deep breath and let it out slowly as he gestured around at the *Monarch*. "I bet you've had some sick parties out here."

Vasily smiled and nodded. "I would invite you to the next one, but you would not come. And then you will appear randomly with accusatory rumors."

Val laughed.

Vasily picked up the glass of water and took a drink. He held the glass in his hands in his lap as he said to Val, "The shipment, Major Rafter, or Shane McDevitt, or whoever the hell you are. Who told you about it?"

"I thought we had settled on how this was going to go, Vasily. You're going to deny the shipment exists, and I'm not going to tell you how I know about it. We'll enjoy each other's company for a bit. Then I'll leave and you'll wonder if you should really call off the shipment."

Val leaned forward to take another sip of beer. As he did, he locked eyes with Vasily and said in a low, conspiratorial voice, "Trust me, you should really call it off." Val winked and leaned back on the sofa. "Then we'll see each other around town back in Prague."

"You have this all figured out, don't you?" Vasily said, a hint of amusement in his voice.

Val shrugged.

"Will you excuse me for just a moment?" Vasily stood up.

"Sure."

Vasily walked forward through the open sliding glass door and closed it behind him. Val grabbed his beer. He took a long pull and stifled a smile. Vasily was clearly concerned about how Val knew what he knew. His bluff was working. Val pictured the Bulgarian madly trying to get word to the various parties involved in the shipment tonight, trying to wave them off. International arms shipments were difficult to arrange and, once in motion, difficult to call off.

A vibration passed through the ship.

Val sat straight.

A rumble emanated from deep in the *Monarch*'s interior, and the ship inched forward.

Val stood and looked aft. Water churned behind the yacht.

Shit, we're moving.

The rumble increased to a higher frequency, and the ship began to accelerate until it was moving through the water at the speed of a fast-paced walk.

The *Monarch* turned slowly. The dacha and the large hill it sat on, which had been across from Val off the starboard side of the ship, swung around until it was directly aft.

The area behind the *Monarch* turned to seething whitewater as the ship's powerful twin propellers spun faster, and Val took a half step aft to maintain his balance as the ship sped up again.

Wind flowed over the seating area as the yacht settled into a steady cruise out to sea. Vasily's dacha on the hill receded.

"May I get you another beer, sir?"

Val turned to see the female crew member standing behind him.

"Where are we going?"

"I do not know, sir."

Val turned and looked back at the dacha. It already seemed smaller.

"Major Rafter," a voice said behind him.

Val turned. The guard leader now stood next to the female crew member. Behind him stood another guard, holding an assault rifle.

"Mr. Abakumov has some business he must attend to," the guard leader said. "He will rejoin you shortly."

Val heard footsteps climbing the stairs behind him. He looked aft over his shoulder as two more armed guards appeared.

"In the meantime, he asks that you remain here," the guard leader added.

For a brief moment, Val thought about jumping overboard. But it would be futile. They were a couple miles out at this point, and the water was not warm. And they would probably just shoot or run over him.

Val shook his head at his stupidity and looked at the female crew member. "Got any whiskey?"

*

Val sipped whiskey on the aft deck seating area while he waited for Vasily to return. The *Monarch* moved steadily through the water, carrying Val farther and farther from land.

Val reviewed his situation for the hundredth time. *No one knows I'm here, and Vasily regards me as a threat to his business.*

He took another sip of whiskey.

He glanced at his watch. It was after two in the afternoon.

He'd been waiting for Vasily for almost an hour.

I'm so fucking dead.

"I apologize," Vasily said, emerging from the cabin forward of the seating area. A guard closed the sliding glass door behind Abakumov. "But there were several phone calls I had to make." He sat across from Val.

"No problem. But I really need to get back. My colleagues will wonder where I am. Would you please turn us around and take me back now?"

"I'm sorry, Val. I can't do that until I know how you know about the shipment."

Val and the Bulgarian stared at each other across the small table.

The thrum of the *Monarch*'s engines rumbled through the seat and floor under Val. He felt the big yacht cutting through the water and the distance between him and the land increasing by the second. He wanted to scream. But he just returned Vasily's gaze.

"No?" Vasily said politely, without any hint of anger. He shrugged and smiled as if perplexed.

Val stayed quiet.

"The problem is no one can tell me what you are up to or who you are working for," Vasily said, with genuine disappointment. "Neither my SVR nor my CIA guys are any help. I've even got an FBI source. He knows nothing either."

A chill ran down Val's spine. Suddenly, Vasily was being very open about very sensitive information. Now Val was certain he was going to be killed.

He was also certain that Vasily's CIA and FBI sources would never be able to connect the dots. Cobra Snare was too secret, too compartmentalized.

For a brief second, the thought of giving up Colonel Sidorov crossed Val's mind.

But instead, he drained his glass of whiskey and said, "But, really, I'm probably stuck here even if I tell you, right?"

Vasily winced as if an embarrassing truth had been revealed.

Val nodded. "Well. I still would call off that shipment if I were you. It's gonna get rolled up."

Vasily chuckled.

"You are quite something, Val Rafter. I like you. I wish you had not waited so long to visit me. I think we would have had fun together."

"Can I get another whiskey?"

"Of course." Vasily stood up and gestured at the closed reflective sliding glass doors forward of the seating area.

The female crew member came out with the bottle of whiskey and refilled Val's glass.

As she did, Vasily pulled out his cell phone and took a picture of Val.

Val gave Vasily a puzzled look, which Vasily ignored. "Please excuse me for a moment," the Bulgarian said.

The female crew member followed Abakumov back into the cabin.

Val downed the whiskey in one swallow. He sat alone in the seating area and wondered if he was about to be tortured.

*

Vasily came back with four guards. Two of them carried long lengths of heavy chains. They were on Val before he could get up from his seat. Abakumov sat down and spoke to Val in a conversational tone as the four men held him down, arms behind his back, and wrapped the heavy chains around him.

"So, Val, I don't know if you know this, but the Black Sea is more than two thousand meters deep at its deepest point. Things that go to the bottom stay there, my friend. Forever."

Val struggled to get free, but it was hopeless. There were too many of the guards, and they were too strong. They tightened one of the lengths of chain around his legs. The other chain was wrapped around his waist, pinning his arms behind his back. Both chains were tight and uncomfortable.

"It's only a few hundred meters deep where we are at the moment," Vasily continued from the white leather sofa. "But in about forty minutes, we'll be past the shelf and it will be quite deep. Not the full two thousand meters. But sufficient."

The guards fastened the constricting chains with a large padlock and stepped back from Val, who lay on his side facing Vasily. The chains were cinched tight around him, pinching his flesh and pressing painfully against his bones. Several links of the chain poked him in the ribs as he lay on them, and his arms were pulled back at awkward angles.

The Bulgarian looked down at Val. "That is more than a forty kilos of steel chain. You'll be on the bottom very quickly."

Vasily sat quietly for a moment. The only sound was the *Monarch*'s engines and Val's heavy breathing.

Val's heart raced and he was close to hyperventilating. He'd resisted the guards with his full strength and was out of breath from the struggle, and now he was starting to panic.

"Tell me who gave you the information about the shipment, and it will be an easy send-off, Val," Vasily finally said. "If you don't tell me, it will not be easy at all."

Val tried to think of something to say.

He swallowed hard.

He had no ideas.

I'm going to die.

Vasily shook his head. "As you wish." He looked at the guard leader and said something to him in Bulgarian. Val thought he made out the words, "Show him example."

"Wait a minute, please!" Val protested.

Val felt the guards take his right hand in a firm grip. He tried to jerk it free, but the chains held him fast. A tearing, burning pain engulfed his right index finger.

Val screamed.

The pain was blinding.

Val gasped for air.

The guard leader shoved a pair of pliers in Val's face, a bloody fingernail clenched in its jaws.

"Do you really want to do this for forty minutes?" Vasily asked. "Or do you want to drink more whiskey?"

The guard leader loosened his grip on the pliers and shook them, flinging the bloody fingernail toward Val's cheek.

Val panted at the Bulgarian's feet, his face contorted in pain. The bloody fingernail slid into his mouth. He spat it onto the ship's deck. He felt lightheaded and wondered if he was going to pass out. He hoped he would.

Vasily nodded to the guard leader, who bent back down to Val's hand. Val flinched and tried to get away, but a soothing, numbing sensation replaced the flaming pain.

Vasily chuckled at Val's confused reaction.

The guard held a bottle of ointment in Val's face.

"You see?" Vasily said. "We can make this super easy for you, or super hard. What is it going to be?"

"Vasily, please," Val said between ragged, shallow breaths. "Let's…talk about this."

"No!" Impatience seeped into Vasily's voice for the first time. "There is nothing to talk about. It is time. You tell me right now—who told you about the shipment? Or you are going to experience hell."

Panic descended on Val.

He was going to die.

Loneliness and doubt smothered him. He didn't think he had the strength to endure the pain he was about to face.

Colonel Liev Sidorov.

All he had to do was say the name.

What do I do? What do I do? What do I do? I don't want to die like this! Shit. Shit. Shit.

"I am talking to you, Major Rafter!" Vasily shouted, interrupting Val's racing mind.

The words "Major Rafter" struck Val, penetrating his panic.

Major Rafter. Val latched onto the words like a life jacket. *I am Major Val fucking Rafter! United States Army officer. I don't squeal!*

"Fuck you!" Val yelled. "Fuck you and your Chechen fucking muscle, you cheesy fucking Bulgarian!"

Abakumov had witnessed many men's last moments. He'd sensed Val breaking and had thought he was on the verge of learning what he wanted to know. This reversal of spirit surprised him.

"I'll never tell you shit!" Val yelled. "You're fucked, Vasily! I came here to help you, but it's all about to come crashing down on you! You dumb motherfucker!"

Vasily stood up.

Val tried to catch his breath. The yelling hadn't helped his hypoxia. But it had helped his spirit.

Abakumov said something like, "Work him hard, I am going to try to call the Russian one more time," in Bulgarian to the guards. He walked forward, back into the cabin.

Val felt a knee in his back and hands gripping his left hand.

He cursed them.

Then the pain came again.

Val screamed.

His left index finger that time.

Laughing, the guard leader again held the pliers in front of Val's face. A piece of flesh clung to the bloody fingernail. He flicked it onto Val's face.

Val screamed in rage.

Rage at Vasily and his men.

Rage at his own arrogance.

Rage at dying.

The pain came again. On his right hand this time.

Val clung to the rage. It helped him deal with the fear.

He screamed at them, "Got to hell, you dumb motherfuckers!"

"Fuck this," Val heard one of them say in Bulgarian. "Let's cut his balls off."

"No! Fuck you. No! No! No!"

Val kicked and thrashed against the chains that bound him as they grabbed him and rolled him over. To no avail. One of the men standing over Val pulled out a large combat knife and kneeled over him, jamming his knee into the inner thigh of Val's right leg. One of the other guards held Val's left leg, prying it to the side.

The knife-wielding guard smiled as he brandished the long blade in front of Val's face.

"Let's see how you like this, fucking cowboy," the guard said as he used the blade to cut open Val's blue jeans, leaving a deep gash in Val's abdomen as he did so.

Val screamed when the blade cut into him.

The guards laughed.

"I not even get there yet, cowboy!" the man with the knife said, chuckling at Val's terror.

Val felt the warm blood dampen his pants.

I can't believe this! I can't believe it's ending like this!

One guard ripped open Val's pants the rest of the way.

Exposed now, Val screamed in a bestial mix of terror and anger.

The guards laughed as the knife man adjusted his weight and moved forward to get to work.

"Stop."

The guards froze and looked forward toward Vasily, who had just emerged from the cabin.

"Unchain him."

The guards hesitated for a moment. Unsure if it was a serious command.

"I mean it," Vasily said in a voice that acknowledged his own surprise as well. "Unchain him."

The guard with the knife stood and stepped away from Val as another bent over and unlocked the padlock. Another guard then helped the other unwrap the heavy chains from around Val.

Val thrashed and kicked free as the chains loosened. The guards stepped back. Val leapt to a crouched fighting stance. His pants fell to the deck. Val stepped out of them deliberately as his eyes darted around for something to use as a weapon. Blood ran down his right leg from the cut to his abdomen.

"Val!" Vasily said. "Val, it is over. I promise."

Val stepped back toward the rear of the boat. He looked at his bloody hands and the blood on the deck and then over the side rail at the water.

"Val, no!" Vasily said in a calm and reassuring voice. "Listen to me. It's over. Take this."

Vasily offered his cell phone to Val.

"He wants to talk to you," Vasily said.

Val stood motionless, still crouched, eyes darting around the group of Bulgarians to spot the one that would come after him first.

"Leave us," Vasily told the guards, trying to de-escalate the situation. They vanished forward into the cabin.

Vasily shook his head in seeming embarrassment. He held his hands up and took a couple of slow steps forward until he was standing in front of the small table in the seating area. He smiled at Val to show he was no threat as he bent over and placed his cell phone on the table before taking several steps back, almost all the way to the cabin door.

Val's breathing was still ragged. Blood trickled out of his clenched fists. He thought about lunging at Vasily. Could he choke him to death before the guards pulled him off?

"Val?"

Val flinched at someone calling his name.

"Val?"

His head swiveled back and forth, scanning the area.

Vasily slowly lowered a hand and pointed at the phone on the small table. He'd set it to speakerphone.

"Val, you crazy son of bitch, are you there?"

Val's head cocked involuntarily to one side. "Alexei?" he asked in barely more than a whisper.

"What?" the distinctive voice answered. "Val, was that you?"

Val leaned forward until his head was over the phone.

"Alexei?" he said, not taking his eyes off Vasily, who was now nodding, hands in his pockets.

"Val! I cannot believe it's really you!" Alexei answered with enthusiasm, techno music blaring in the background. "If Vasily had not texted me that photo of you, I would never even answered his call. You would be so dead, then, my friend. I am so happy to hear your voice. How are you?"

"I've fucking been better," Val growled, his eyes meeting Vasily's.

"Yes, I believe you!" Alexei laughed. "As usual, you have only yourself to blame for that! You are still a crazy son of bitch!"

Val looked at the phone with anger.

"Val, listen to me," Alexei said in a serious tone of voice. The music in the background was muffled now as if Alexei had walked to a new location or placed his hand over the phone. "I told Vasily he cannot kill you. No more questions, and they will take you back to his dacha and you can leave. But you must go directly back to Prague, okay?"

Val looked at the phone in bewilderment.

"Val, do you hear me?"

"Yes."

"Val, you promise me?" Alexei asked, some doubt in his voice.

"Yes."

"Because I cannot do this again. Ever. You know that, right?"

"Yes."

"Okay!" Alexei said, happiness in his voice. "Is Vasily still there?"

"I am here," Vasily said, stepping closer to the phone.

"You fucking do what I said, Vasily!"

"Of course. You know that I will. You are my best customer, buddy!"

"Okay!" Alexei said. "Good. Good."

Vasily and Val stood awkwardly over the phone for a moment.

"Well, gentlemen," Alexei said. "I leave you to it, then."

"Very good, Alexei," Vasily said. "Thank you."

"And Val!" Alexei said suddenly.

"What?"

"Tell Sydney that I say hello. I have not seen her in years. Since Kyiv."

CHAPTER 54

Val fidgeted in a chair outside the director's office. The stitches in his abdomen itched, and he couldn't get comfortable. The only time they didn't itch was when they pulled and threatened to tear.

He was also dreading this meeting.

It had been a long couple of travel days getting back to the States, and then the CIA and DIA had debriefed him for three solid days. At the end of the debriefing session last night, his interviewer, a longtime DIA clandestine operations veteran, told him gruffly, "You have a meeting with the director at 0730 hours tomorrow. Don't be late."

Val didn't sleep well, worrying about the meeting. When he did sleep, the dreams woke him up. The chains digging into him, his fingernails ripping off, the blade gouging his abdomen, and a straitjacket of fear squeezing the breath out of him.

He adjusted his weight in the chair again and looked at his hands. A little blood had seeped through the bandages on the tips of three fingers.

"Rafter," the general's aide called as he opened the door and poked his head out. "The director will see you now."

Val eased himself out of his chair and walked into Lieutenant General Bryson's office.

The director met Val in front of his desk.

"Good to see you, Val," the general said, reaching out to shake Val his hand.

Val grimaced and raised his right hand so that the general could see his bandaged fingers. Shaking hands would be agony.

"Christ, son," Bryson said in a not so sympathetic voice.

Val sat in one of the oversized chairs that was arranged around a large coffee table next to a window. He looked out at the picturesque view of changing leaves and rolling Virginia hills.

"Give us a few minutes, please," General Bryson said to his aide. "I'd like to speak to Major Rafter alone."

"Roger that, sir," the lieutenant colonel said as he left.

Bryson sat down opposite Val and looked at him for a long moment.

"How are you feeling?" the general finally asked.

"Good."

"Bullshit. I read the entire file this morning. That fucker Abakumov put you through the ringer. I'll ask you again, soldier, how are you?"

Val thought about the dreams.

"I'm good, sir. I mean it."

Bryson shook his head. His expression was a mix of irritation and sympathy.

"Well, look, Val," he said, sympathy winning out over the irritation. "We've got folks you can talk to, you know. Don't underestimate this shit. Being seconds away from ball removal and death is a hell of a thing. I want you to take care of yourself, you hear me?"

"Yes, sir. Thank you. I appreciate it."

The general nodded. Val thought he saw sadness in his face.

"Now. That said, you dumb son of a bitch, what the hell were you thinking?"

Here it comes.

"I'm sorry, sir. All I was trying to do was stop an imminent arms shipment into the sandbox that would've killed Americans and American allies."

"On your fucking own?"

"Time was of the essence, sir."

"So you decided to lone wolf your way into Vasily Abakumov's dacha. To, what? Talk him out of it?"

It seemed spectacularly stupid now. Val just nodded slowly.

Bryson shook his head.

"In more than twenty years of intelligence work, I have never seen one impulsive individual do so much damage so quickly." Anger surged in the general's voice. "That prick Abakumov broadcast your photo globally. It got picked up by the goddamn press here, in Europe, and in Russia. You're the most widely burned intelligence agent in the world. Probably ever. You're worthless to me now!

"Worse than that, every source, every agent, every partner you've ever worked with is now less secure! Colonel Sidorov, by the way, has gone colder than ice—won't let anyone close or respond to anything we send. The CIA station chiefs in Czech and Bulgaria are so fucking mad, they have requested the immediate removal of all DIA personnel. Even the goddamned administrative assistants.

"I've got the entire clandestine operations community at the agency crawling up my ass, demanding to know the name of every Cobra Snare officer, where they're stationed at the moment, and what their missions are. They insist on knowing this so that they can anticipate what we'll screw up next. They're making a case to the director of national intelligence for ending the entire program completely."

Bryson, a vein bulging in his forehead, leaned forward in his chair toward Val.

"They hate the Cobra Snare program, Major!" He pointed at Val as he yelled. "They always have. You know that! And you served up the perfect fucking crisis for them to leverage to finally kill it!"

Val sat motionless.

General Bryson lowered his hand and voice as he leaned back in his chair and rubbed his forehead.

"And, my god, the task force that has been working on taking Vasily Abakumov down over there at CIA is apo-fucking-plectic about this. They want your scalp. Especially the hotshot they have running the operation."

The director paused for a moment.

"I forget her name. But she is good. Harder than woodpecker lips, that one. Which doesn't help our case."

Val winced. That was Sydney. He'd called her a few times, but she hadn't picked up. He finally left a simple voice mail: "I'm back and I'm sorry. Please call me."

The director stood up. He glared at Val, sighed, and then walked to the other side of the room to the coffeepot.

"Coffee?" he barked at Val as he poured himself a cup.

"Yes, sir. Thank you."

The general walked back, handed Val a coffee, and sat down with his own.

"I heard the shipment didn't go," Val said. "Has that been confirmed?"

"Yes." The general took a sip of coffee and leaned back in his chair. "He called it off. SIGINT picked up all kinds of pissed off chatter, and HUMINT indicates it disrupted some big plans over in the sandbox."

Val nodded once and looked out of the window.

"I hope it was worth it, son."

"So do I, sir," Val said, looking back at the general.

"Why do you think Volkov got you off the hook?"

Val sighed, exhausted by the topic.

"The Russians had an opportunity for an arm's length rubout of one of our intelligence officers," the general continued. "An American intelligence officer that had confirmed meaningful insights into one of their illegal arms trading resources and was interfering in a major transaction."

Bryson stared at Val.

Val sat in silence, looking back at the general.

"You'd be rotting at the bottom of the Black Sea, out of Abakumov's and the Russians' way. We would've never known what happened to you. You would've vanished."

Bryson leaned forward and set his coffee cup down on the table in front of him.

"And all Volkov had to do was not do anything. Can you explain that to me?"

Val's shoulders sagged in irritation.

"Sir, I've been through this with the debriefers a dozen times."

"Yeah. I've read it all. Now I want to hear you say it. Why?"

"I think Alexei considers us friends," Val said with a shrug.

"Friends?"

"Yes, sir."

Bryson regarded Val for a moment and then chuckled to himself.

"You're one of a kind, Rafter. I'll give you that. It's just a damn shame."

"A shame, sir?" Val detected a shift in the general's tone.

"You're out of the program, Val."

Val didn't react. He was expecting this. He took another sip of coffee, held the cup in his lap, and looked back out of the window.

"Am I still in the army?"

"Barely."

Val didn't take his eyes off the window.

After a moment, the general asked him, "Do you still want to be in the army?"

"Depends."

"On what?"

"What you're about to tell me."

"You mean where you go from here?"

"Exactly."

"Well, lucky for you, you made a good impression on a few folks when you were in Iraq," Bryson said. "Special Operations Command said they would take you if you were game."

"The Activity?"

"Yep."

Tony. Always looking out for me.

Val turned back toward the window. Bryson looked at him for a long moment.

"What is it, son?" the general asked. "What makes you do this stupid shit?"

Val didn't answer. He kept looking out of the window.

"Are you trying to prove something?"

The sun was higher now, striking the changing leaves more directly. The colors of fall asserted themselves above the green fields.

General Bryson sighed.

"I don't know what goes on in that head of yours," he said in a voice tinged with concern. "But you seem incapable of playing the long game. Of being patient. Of balancing risk and reward. You need to figure that shit out, son. Get control of whatever it is. Because I think that episode on the yacht with Abakumov was it. You're well and truly out of luck now. The next time will kill you and maybe the folks around you."

Val nodded slowly, without looking back at the general.

Bryson shook his head wearily.

CHAPTER 55

"Watch this, Val!" Will said with a mischievous smile.

Val was sitting on a towel on the sandy beach of Echo Lake. He watched as his older brother dashed into the water, followed by two friends. The three young men lifted their knees high, running as long as they could, before diving forward and swimming for the rocky far side.

"What's he up to now?" Val's mother asked in a voice that really said, *Look at your older brother. Isn't he amazing?*

Val smiled and shrugged.

William Rafter Jr. was sixteen years old and was the bright sun around which his entire family revolved. Three years older than Val, Will was his younger brother's hero. His mother saw in Will the confirmation that her marriage was special—surely, she and William Sr. were brought together to bring forth this amazing young man. To her, Will was a Covington in all the best ways. A young man who could drive a pickup truck way too fast down a dirt road, hunt with a bow, sink a three-pointer, and sweep girls off their feet. All that and the smarts of a Rafter. He was magic.

Jessica Covington was a North Carolina girl, born and raised. The Covingtons were not rich and powerful like some other Carolina families, but they were respected and took great pride in being able to trace their history in Raleigh and North Carolina back to the mid-seventeen hundreds. Jessica and her older brother, David, grew up consistent with the expectations of their bloodline.

They were the sixth generation of their family to attend the University of North Carolina at Chapel Hill. David was the honor graduate of his ROTC battalion and was commissioned into the infantry. A year later, he was fighting in Vietnam. Jessica majored in marketing and was recruited by IBM before she graduated, which was uncommon for women in the late sixties. It was a family scandal when Jessica, back in Raleigh with IBM for only six months, eloped with a Yankee named William Rafter.

They met by chance in the IBM cafeteria. He fell for the beautiful brown-haired marketing manager in the five steps between the main course and desert stations. It took Jessica longer. But over time, the erudite gentleman from Massachusetts charmed her. He was so unlike the Carolina country boys that she'd gone to high school and college with. He was smart, cautious, and responsible, and provided well for their family. She loved him.

For his part, William Rafter Sr. was in awe of the young human that walked around bearing his name and kicking ass. William was a vice president in product engineering at IBM. He'd moved to Raleigh after graduating from MIT, where he double majored in electrical and computer science. William was smart. He was not athletic. So, as he watched his eldest son leap up and dash into the lake with grace and power, he was reminded again, as he was daily, of the miracle that occurred between him and his wife. Already the star of his high school's basketball team as a sophomore, William Jr. had a statewide reputation that belied his father's pocket protector aesthetic.

Val watched his brother's strong, precise strokes as he led the group of three swimmers across Echo Lake. Half an hour from Raleigh, the lake was a popular place for families to escape the heat on summer days like today. Parents sat on the shore discreetly drinking beer while the younger kids paddled around in the water and the older kids flirted and showed off. Officially, the state didn't condone the swimming and other activities at Echo Lake, but it also didn't try to stop them. Usually, one of the high school swim team seniors acted as lifeguard.

The principal venue for showing off was a rock face across from the small lake's beach. With a drop of almost fifty feet, "the cliffs" of Echo Lake offered a satisfying sense of acceleration and sufficient fall time to ham it up for the tamer folks lounging on the small rocky beach on the other side of the lake. Will and his basketball buddies, Jeff and Sanjay, had been perfecting a ridiculous grab-ass leap that had become a real crowd-pleaser with the rising junior girls. Will had recently updated it with a backflip and was excited to show his little brother.

Val smiled as he watched his brother climb from the water and quickly scale the rocks. Jeff and Sanjay followed behind. Will was always in the lead.

Will stepped to the edge of the drop-off and waved across the lake. A couple of girls waved back, but Val knew that Will was waving at him.

Val gave Will a thumbs-up.

Will gave one back.

Jeff and Sanjay stepped next to Will, and the threesome conferred for a moment. Will nodded at something that Jeff said, and then the three of them turned and walked back from the edge.

Val watched as the three boys crouched and sprung forward, sprinting toward the edge. Jeff and Will bumped each other slightly at the edge, and Val thought he saw Will's ankle turn over as he leapt from the rock.

Jeff and Will were tangled as they fell.

The three boys hit the water with a big splash.

Val stood up.

It looked wrong. Will seemed only to make it halfway through his backflip, and Jeff landed too close to Will's head.

Val searched the water.

Sanjay surfaced. Then Jeff.

Val looked at his mom. She was sitting next to him, reading a magazine. His father sat in a folding beach chair next to her, reading a book.

Val turned back to the water. Jeff and Sanjay were paddling and slashing around, smiles on their faces.

No Will.

Val took a few quick sidesteps to get a better line of sight. Still no Will.

"What is it, honey?" his mom asked.

"Will. I don't see Will."

"He's out there with Jeff and Sanjay," his mom said, lowering her eyes back to her magazine.

"I know! But he should be up by now."

"What?" his mom said with a hint of irritation.

"He hasn't come up yet! He is still underwater!"

Jeff and Sanjay now looked alarmed. They paddled around, peering down into the lake. Sanjay dove underwater, but Val could see he was far off from their point of impact with the water.

Val turned and looked back at the unofficial lifeguard's chair. It was empty. Seth, the supposed lifeguard for the day, was standing at the base of the tall chair, fully engrossed in his flirtations with two girls.

Val looked back at the water.

Still no Will.

Val lunged forward, eyes locked on the spot where Will had gone under. Val was going to get him.

A firm hand grabbed Val's arm and stopped him.

"Whoa, Val," his father said. "Hold up. What's going on?"

"Let me go! Will is under the water!"

His father, taken aback by Val's emotion, and not yet grasping the situation, gripped his son by both shoulders.

"Val!" he shouted. "Listen to me. What's going on?"

People sitting nearby turned and looked at their commotion.

"He hasn't come up yet!" Val screamed, tears running down his face now. "He's under the water. Let me go!"

Val's father held on to him. He waved at the empty lifeguard's chair.

"They were jumping off the rock!" Val's mother said to her husband, urgency in her voice.

"Let me go!" Val screamed. "I know where he is! Let me go!"

Val's father maintained his tight grip on his son while turning his head back toward the lifeguard's station and yelling, "Lifeguard!"

Seth's head jerked around. He saw Val's father holding on to his struggling son. He looked out at the water where Jeff and Sanjay had started waving frantically. A few people on the beach were pointing in their direction.

Seth grabbed his rescue buoy and ran into the water. He took three long strides and then dove in. When he surfaced, he was pulling hard toward Jeff and Sanjay.

"Oh god," Val's mother yelled. "Oh god. Hurry!"

Val looked at Jeff and Sanjay. They had drifted away from their landing point by at least twenty feet. Seth was swimming toward them. He would be there in minutes. But he would be in the wrong spot.

"Let me go!" Val shrieked. "They're looking in the wrong place! Let me go! I know where he is!"

"Son!" his father yelled. "Listen to me. Seth is a lifeguard. He will get Will. It's going to be okay."

"Val, listen to your father!" his mom pleaded. "Let the lifeguard take care of it."

But Val could see it clearly. They would be looking in the wrong place. It would take too long. It was up to him.

Val thrashed his legs and swung his arms. He landed blows to his father's shins and gut. His father grunted in pain, losing his grip on Val.

Val was loose. But as he turned to dash into the water, his mother screamed.

"No! Val! No! Stay right here!"

Val hesitated.

He glanced over his shoulder at her to tell her it was okay. That he knew what he was doing. That he would save her eldest son.

Then his father had him again. Strong hands held his closest arm.

"Let me go! Please!"

"The lifeguard is going out there!" his mother said to him. "It's better you stay out of his way."

Val felt the seconds slipping away. There was no time to explain.

He would get loose. He would save Will. It was up to him. He started to thrash again.

Val's father slapped him hard in the face. Val saw stars for an instant.

"Val Rafter!" his father yelled, his face inches from Val's. "Calm down! The lifeguard is on it. He will take care of it. I promise."

Val held his smarting cheek, tears running over his hand. He looked up at his father. Val wanted to believe him. But he was terrified for his older brother.

His father maintained a forceful grip on Val's arm.

"It's going to be fine, son. I promise."

Val looked back out at the water. Seth was almost at Jeff and Sanjay. Val tried to look back to where he thought Will was. But his father's slap had disoriented him. Panic surged within Val as he realized he wasn't sure where the spot was anymore. His legs gave out. He sagged to the ground, sobbing.

Thirty minutes later, Will Rafter's body lay lifeless under a towel beneath a tree by Echo Lake.

The coroner's report said later that Will had been knocked unconscious upon impact with the water and a blow to the head from one of the other jumpers as they hit the lake's surface. The coroner also surmised that Will's breath had been knocked out of him by the uncontrolled impact, contributing to the relatively quick and complete starvation of oxygen to the brain. And it had taken too long for the lifeguard to locate Will's submerged body.

The funeral was held a week later. It was well attended by the community, none of whom could get their heads around how suddenly so promising a life had been cut short. Casseroles and prayer groups stacked up in the Rafter house as people tried to support the grieving family. But within weeks, Val and his parents were alone as a glacier of grief and sadness crawled into their home and began to grind it down. Val reeled as what had once been a place of love and togetherness was reduced to a flattened emotional debris field. Val walked through it every day, trying desperately not to touch the wrong thing and cause the next outburst of tears, anger, or drunkenness. The chaotic emotional grinding was exhausting.

Grief began to asphyxiate Jessica and William's marriage, and Val's home dissolved. A system of emotional walls replaced it. His father's system was simply distance. Unable to live with himself and his failure to save his eldest son, he could not abide his wife and living son's company. He left. He went back to Boston and never came back. His mother fell into drinking and a succession of men. And though Jessica would dress them up and take them to church, they never fooled anyone and never lasted.

Val developed an ability to insulate himself from the waves of sadness and emotional self-destruction emanating from his mother. He struggled, though, to defuse the rage and anger within before it radiated off him and smashed into her.

His parents had promised. They had stopped him from saving Will, and they had promised he would be alright. But Will had died just like Val thought he would. Val was convinced he could have saved him. He felt guilty that, in that one terrible moment on which everything had tilted, the moment he could still remember with piercing, awful clarity, he'd hesitated. Confused for an instant by his mother's voice. Then the window closed. His father grabbed him, and his brother had died. If he wasn't careful, his rage and judgment would leap from him. And he knew that his mother could not withstand it. She was broken now.

Barely held together. Val promised himself he would not be the thing that finally knocked her apart. He did love her.

Jessica's drinking got worse as time went on. Almost two years later, her friends, unable to continue looking the other way, abandoned Southern politeness and demanded she get help. Jessica crumbled in the first minutes of the intervention and agreed to enter a discreet rehab program at a quiet mountain retreat in Western North Carolina.

It was a three-month program, though, and Jessica had no options for Val, who was almost done with his sophomore year in high school. She hadn't spoken to her ex-husband in more than a year, and she knew how Val felt about his father. She couldn't do that to him. So, she called her brother, who was at Fort Bragg.

At the time, David Covington was a forty-one-year-old infantry colonel. Val didn't know his uncle very well since he'd been in Germany, Korea, and South America for most of Val's life. Colonel Covington had only recently returned to the States for a staff tour at Fort Bragg. When his sister called, he got in his car and drove an hour and a half from Fort Bragg to his sister's place.

His mother answered the door. Colonel Covington walked over to Val. He kneeled down and put his hand on Val's shoulder. "Hello, Val. Let's pack up some of your things and get out of here for a while. What do you say?"

Val fought the urge to cry.

Just David's touch. Just the strong hand on Val's shoulder. It was like an anchor thrown into a rough sea. It stabilized Val immediately. It was not the fragile, angry, heartbroken touch of his parents that Val had gotten used to over the past two years. This was stronger, more certain, grounding. It said, *I've got you now. Come with me and be safe again. Heal. Move forward.*

Half an hour later, Val sat in the passenger seat of his uncle's pickup truck as they drove south to Fort Bragg.

Val had to fight back tears for a second time that day when he walked into his uncle's house on colonels' row. He felt a sense of calm the moment he stepped through the door, as if he had been held underwater for the past two years and could finally breathe.

And there was his uncle's dog. The four-year-old chocolate lab greeted them at the door. He circled Val, sniffing and wagging.

"That's Charlie," his uncle said. "He's a good boy."

Val's parents had never let them have a dog. His father was allergic, and his mother claimed they were a lot of work. Val leaned over to pet Charlie.

Colonel Covington smiled as the dog rolled over on his back. "He is normally a little more standoffish, to be honest."

Val got down on one knee and rubbed Charlie's belly.

"Come on," Val's uncle said after a moment. "Let me show you around."

Val stood and followed his uncle, Charlie at his side.

The modest brick house sat in one of the old housing sections on Fort Bragg that now served as field-grade officer quarters. It was a warm place. Not decorated so much as organized around the colonel's bachelor life in the military. The furniture was sparse and didn't go together, exactly, but was a collage of high-quality appointments acquired from a lifetime spent living around the world. Asian, South American, and European influences wove through the space, fascinating Val and beckoning him to stay.

"This will be your room." The colonel opened the door to the spare bedroom. It was plain with a single bed. But it already felt warmer to Val than his room in Raleigh. Charlie squirted by and hopped on the bed.

"I'll let you two work out your own rules," Val's uncle said, nodding at Charlie. The dog rolled onto his side and looked at Val as if to say, *This is cool, right?*

"I can assure you, he doesn't do that shit in my room," the colonel said, turning to leave.

Charlie slept with Val every night after that.

Months later, when his mother got out of rehab and returned to Raleigh, she called Val and asked him to come home.

Val refused.

He couldn't bear the thought of going back to Raleigh, to living in the sad mausoleum his home had become with his mother. Val stood in the kitchen on the phone and tried to explain it to her, stumbling through a conversation that left them both in tears. Charlie whined at his feet.

Uncle David, who had been listening from the den, walked over and gently took the phone from Val. He motioned toward the den and waited for Val to leave the kitchen, Charlie just a step behind.

Forty-five minutes later, Uncle David walked into the den and told Val he could stay as long as he wanted.

Colonel Covington spoke to the base commander, whom he knew from one of his tours in Vietnam, and somehow got Val enrolled in the Fort Bragg High School. The two of them drove to Raleigh the next weekend and piled the rest of Val's stuff into his uncle's pickup truck. Val's mother put on a brave face, but Val spied her crying a few times. His uncle spent time talking with her while Val made trips back and forth to the pickup truck. She hugged him for a long time while Uncle David waited in the idling vehicle when it was time to go. When she finally released him, Val got into the pickup truck and went back to Fort Bragg with his uncle.

Colonel Covington served on the division commander's staff, which meant he didn't travel much and had a predictable, mostly nine-to-five schedule. This worked well for him and Val and allowed the colonel to be near his doctor on Bragg, who was, as he explained to Val, "Helping clear up some shit I got in 'Nam."

Val thrived on Fort Bragg. The structure provided by the military rhythms of his uncle's lifestyle was the opposite of the emotional instability he'd lived in after his brother died. The persistent overflight of military aircraft and regular comings and goings of Colonel Covington's army buddies provided Val with constant hints and examples of lives of purpose, decisiveness, and adventure. The wrestling coach recruited Val the day he saw him in gym class. Val took to the sport immediately, setting himself on a course to a state championship his senior year.

Val made good friends. And, unlike his friends in Raleigh, who had regarded him with pity, Val's Fort Bragg friends had only vague impressions of his past. It seemed perfectly natural to them, members of military families who hopscotched around the world taking care of each other as their parents served, that Val would live with his uncle. After a while, it seemed perfectly natural to Val as well.

Charlie was Val's constant companion. If Val was not at school or at wrestling practice, he and Charlie were together.

Two years later, his uncle and mother beamed as Val accepted his high school diploma. That August, he drove his uncle's old pickup truck across the state to Boone, North Carolina, to start his freshman year at Appalachian State. Val hadn't even applied to UNC, a great disappointment to his mother.

If living with his uncle had been the safe harbor that saved Val, App State was the open sea where his independence and conviction took sail. It was a good time for him. Val did well academically, and he excelled at wrestling and ROTC. His charisma and confidence attracted friends and attention, and, though he didn't take part in fraternity life, he was immediately an informal leader among his classmates. The only thing lacking was Charlie, whom Val saw whenever he went home to visit his uncle.

During wrestling season, Colonel Covington would drive to Raleigh to pick up Val's mom and bring her to home matches in Boone. The pair embarrassed Val, cheering wildly, his mother ringing an obnoxious cowbell. But he could tell she loved it, so he never said anything.

The colonel would also pop into Val's ROTC events from time to time. The App State professor of military science, Lieutenant Colonel Gates, had served under Val's uncle in Vietnam and extended an open invitation to his old mentor. One evening during Val's sophomore year, Colonel Covington was the guest speaker at a dining in for his ROTC battalion. Val's uncle spoke of leadership and his time in Vietnam.

The cadets listened closely as the old colonel in his dress blues, chest full of medals, told stories from his two combat tours, one as a rifle platoon leader, and one as a rifle company commander. The cadet battalion gave Colonel Covington a standing ovation at the end of his remarks. A swell of warm pride filled Val.

The first Gulf War kicked off in January of Val's junior year, after a long windup over the previous summer. On weekends home, Val sat in front of the TV with his uncle, watching American tanks roll across the desert and complained that he was missing it.

"Don't worry, son," his uncle said, trying to suppress his persistent cough. "There will be more fights. Trust me."

By December of their senior year, Val and his fellow ROTC cadets were nearly hovering from anxiety. They would find out their branch assignments any day now. Val wanted armor badly. Though his uncle was infantry, and Val had spent two years, plus a few summers, living on Fort Bragg with C-130s and helicopters flying overhead at all times of the day and night, tanks had become his obsession. Their mobility and firepower captured his imagination.

His uncle feigned disappointment when he heard his nephew's professional aspirations.

"Tanks?" he would exclaim in a raspy voice. "You really want to spend your career in the motor pool fixing those rolling coffins? Are you kidding me?"

Val would always smile at the friendly barbs. It felt good to have a professional rivalry with his uncle. At the end of each of their jousts, Colonel Covington would lean in and put his hand on Val's shoulder. "Truthfully, I don't give a damn what you do in the army, son," he would say, locking eyes with his nephew. "Just be all in. Make a difference."

Val looked forward to sharing the experience and burdens of the profession of arms with his uncle and worked hard for four years to set himself up to get tanks. He consistently ranked in the top three of his battalion's order of merit. He felt confident but knew the whims of the army's personnel command had screwed up the careers of better candidates than he. The thought of serving in some REMF branch like quartermaster scared and disgusted him. He didn't know what he would do. He tried not to think about it.

Finally, the day arrived. Lieutenant Colonel Gates told the cadet battalion to rally at the High Country Tavern at 1800 that evening.

The Tavern was one of the local drinking establishments in Boone. Frequented by students, faculty, and locals, it was a fun spot with many beers on tap and tasty pub food. Gates booked the back room, which offered plenty of seating and a private bar.

Gates tortured Val and his two dozen senior classmates, making them sit and listen to twenty minutes of rambling commentary, which he seemed to extend for his own evil pleasure. Val fidgeted in his seat.

Finally, Gates passed out sealed envelopes to each of the seniors.

"Don't open them until I say," Gates commanded to groans of impatience.

Val squeezed the envelope in his hands, feeling the metal insignia inside. He tried to guess at its contours. Was it what he hoped for?

When everyone had their envelopes, Gates looked around the room one more time and then said, "Okay. Open 'em up."

Val tore open his envelope to find crossed sabers with a Pershing tank superimposed on top. He raised his hand over his hands and let out a victorious whoop, joining the others who had gotten their desired branch in celebration. Hugs and high fives rippled through the loud room as those who found disappointment in their envelopes put on brave faces.

As Val spun around from hugs and celebration to grab his beer, his eyes fell on the corner of the room, where Gates stood with his uncle. Colonel Covington was smiling as he gave Val a thumbs-up. Val learned later that Gates had been filibustering earlier to delay the moment of truth so that the colonel would make it.

Val crossed the room and hugged his uncle.

"Congratulations, son!" Colonel Covington said, holding his nephew tight. "I'm so proud of you."

It was the best feeling of Val's life.

Colonel David Covington succumbed to lung cancer the next year, while Val was at Fort Knox for the Armor Officer Basic Course. One of the tens of thousands of service members exposed to Agent Orange while serving in Vietnam, the colonel battled the disease for years. Colonel David Covington was laid to rest in Arlington just a few months shy of his fiftieth birthday.

Val's mother held on to his arm to steady herself as they stood graveside at the funeral. Six months later, after graduating from Ranger School, Val reported to his first unit in Germany.

CHAPTER 56

Val opened the door to his quarters, walked in, and set the pizza on the small kitchen table. He turned the oven to 350 degrees to warm the pizza after he showered. He was walking to the bathroom when his cell phone rang.

"Rafter," he answered, without looking at the number.

"Hello, Val," Sydney said.

Val froze.

A long moment passed.

"Val? You there?"

"Yeah. I'm just surprised to hear from you."

"I know. I'm sorry."

"I called you more than a month ago when I got back," Val said, getting angry again.

"I know, Val," Sydney answered, getting angry again herself. "I was pretty pissed off. And we were scrambling to react to the bomb you threw into our task force. After I asked you, and you promised me!"

Sydney caught herself.

Val held his tongue.

The seconds ticked by, as did all the things that they each wanted to say.

"Where are you?" Val finally asked, unable to take the silence any longer.

"Budapest."

"Oh. It's late there."

"Been a lot of late nights lately. Like I said. We're in reactive mode at the moment. You got Abakumov running silent and deep."

Sydney managed to say it without an edge. Val appreciated it.

"I'm sorry, Sydney," he said, sadness in his voice. "I'm damn sorry."

They were both quiet again as Val waited and Sydney tried to find a way forward through her anger and hurt.

"We can talk about all that later. We need to. I need to. I just don't understand… why you do the things you do. What goes through your head sometimes."

She paused. Val could almost hear her fighting with herself, trying not to yell at him.

"What I'm saying is we have so much to work through. I don't know if we ever will—"

"We have to, Sydney," Val said. "I still love you. Nothing has changed for me."

"That's the problem, Val. You haven't changed at all."

Silence expanded between them again.

"I just wanted you to know, Val," she tried continuing again, "that I read your debrief."

Val rubbed his eyes.

"What happened to you on that ship. It must have been terrifying. I'm so sorry."

Val leaned against the wall.

"I just…" Her voice faltered. "I don't know what to say. I just wanted you to know that I read it. And I wish I had been there for you somehow. Even as mad as you made me. And I'm really mad. I'm just so sorry, and I hope you're okay."

Val thought he heard Sydney sniffle.

He was fighting a wave of emotion himself.

"I wish you were closer," he said.

"Oh, Val." He was sure he heard her sniffle that time. "I just don't know."

Val tried to think of something to say, but a swirl of emotion clouded his thoughts.

"I'm out of the program, Sydney," came out of his mouth suddenly. "They kicked me out."

"I'm not surprised."

"Neither am I."

"I'm sorry," she said, genuine sympathy in her voice.

"Yeah. Me too."

"What do they have you doing now?"

"General Bryson assigned me to his headquarters temporarily. Made me go to one of his counselors here. For…you know. PTSD stuff."

"I think that's good. I'm glad."

The concern in her voice warmed Val.

"Me too. But a little of that stuff goes a long way."

He thought he heard her chuckle.

"I'm here for another few days and then headed to Belvoir."

"Tony's unit?"

"I think it was the only unit that would take me…after all the drama. I'm pretty sure he went to bat for me. Hard."

Sydney definitely chuckled at that. The sound made Val smile.

"He's in Iraq now. He's coming back for Christmas. Then he heads back in late January. I'll be going with him."

"God help them," Sydney said.

"You will be in Budapest then?"

"That's how it looks right now."

"Meet me in Germany when I head over?"

Sydney didn't answer.

"Or I could come to Budapest. Or we could meet somewhere else. Either way. I just want to see you."

"I don't think so, Val," Sydney whispered, choking back emotion.

Val waited.

"I'm really glad we talked," she finally said.

"Can we talk again this weekend?"

"No. I don't know. Let me—"

"Sydney," Val said, interrupting her. He couldn't hold it back anymore. "There was something I didn't tell them in the debrief. I didn't tell anybody."

"What was it?" Sydney asked, uncertainty in her voice.

"Alexei. When he called Abakumov on the boat and stopped it. He told me to tell you hello."

Sydney was quiet.

The silence extended. Val let it go on for a long moment before telling her, "He said, 'Tell Sydney that I say hello.'"

Val wished he could see her face when he drove it home.

"He used your true name."

CHAPTER 57

"Peskov," Alexei said without turning to look at the junior intelligence officer. "Open the curtains. Is lovely night out."

Peskov stole an *are you kidding me* glance at the bartender, who met his eyes but did not dare to shrug.

Val glanced at Alexei.

Alexei winked and said so only Val could hear, "Is good to give him bullshit tasks. Otherwise, he gets ego. What do you call it? Honing?"

"Hazing," Val said. "We call it hazing."

"Hazing. Yes. Is good to hazing."

Val smiled as he watched Peskov go window to window, tying back the curtains.

It was black beyond the windows. All Val could see was a reflection of the room he sat in. He tried to picture the expanse of water surrounding the *Monarch* as she made her way wherever they were going. The ship was barely rising and falling at all. The sea must be smooth. Swimmable. Perhaps the coast was not too far away.

Maybe I could make it, could swim to the coast. Val tried to look through the glare of the window's reflection into the night.

"What are you thinking, Val?"

Val turned his head from the window and looked at Alexei.

"Wondering if I could make the swim to the coast from here."

Alexei shook his head.

"You could not. The water temperature tonight is less than twenty degrees Celsius. Maybe as low as fifteen degrees where we are now. And you are like me, Val. Bad swimmer. You would tire and freeze and sink to the bottom."

Val nodded. "You're probably right. But it would be fun stabbing you on the way out."

Val gave an exaggerated glance toward the switchblade lying on the table in front of Alexei.

Alexei laughed. His reaction made Val chuckle.

"Okay," Val said. "Maybe not you." Val swung his attention to his right. He pointed at Zakir, leaning against the bar. "But that motherfucker would die, for sure."

Zakir scowled.

Alexei laughed.

Val smiled.

"I must tell you, Val. Zakir is not easy to kill."

Val, still staring at Zakir, shrugged a *whatever* shrug.

Zakir crossed his arms and jutted his chin forward, maintaining his level glare at Val.

"How many times have you almost died, Val? It must be many."

Val swiveled his head from Zakir and looked at Alexei. He smiled at the sincerity of the question. "Not sure."

"Was that day on the *Monarch* with Abakumov the closest?" Alexei reached across the table with the bourbon to fill Val's glass.

Val watched Alexei pour.

"I sort of doubt it."

Alexei put the bottle down and leaned back in his chair.

"Really?" Alexei said, surprised.

"Oh, that was a close one, for sure. But Afghanistan and Iraq?" Val's eyes dropped from Alexei's, settling into an unfocused gaze at the middle of the table. "So many missions. So many firefights. I think about how many bullets, most I don't even know about, got close to the mark. But I just happened to turn the right way, or ducked at the right time, or tripped and fell in the right spot…or…"

Or they took me off the helicopter.

Alexei's eyes narrowed as he regarded Val.

Val shook his head to clear his mind.

"Dumb luck," Val said. "It plays a role we don't always see."

Alexei shrugged and raised his glass. "To dumb luck."

"Better than no luck at all."

CHAPTER 58

17 April 2008

Mosul, Iraq

"So, what do you think?" Tony asked as he and Val walked toward the tactical operations center. "Is she still fucking him?"

Val took a sip of coffee rather than respond. A C-17 filled the silence between them as it labored off Mosul's runway and departed to the southeast.

Tony took Val's lack of response to his question about Sydney as a no.

"So, what's the problem?" He said impatiently as the loud rumble of the C-17's four engines receded to the point that he could continue his interrogation.

They made their way through the JSOC compound to the ops center, a path they both could have walked with their eyes closed. Three months of the grinding daily JSOC battle rhythm does that, distilling the days down to a sequence of rituals, actions, and operating procedures that repeat over and over, every day, every night.

Val and Tony's first order of business each day was a visit to the operations center.

After a couple hours of sleep in their C-huts, the two friends would usually wake up around noon, dress, grab coffee out of the pot in their HUMINT hooch, and walk across the JSOC compound to the ops center to see if anything big was being tracked on ISR or SIGINT. This visit usually gave them a feel for the day and night ahead of them.

"Seriously," Tony pressed as they walked into the dusty open space that served as the compound's courtyard and main traffic area. "What's the problem?"

Val continued to ignore the interrogation as they approached the ever-present row of armored Stryker vehicles lined up on the right side of the courtyard. Based on the Canadian LAV III, the US Army began fielding the infantry fighting vehicle shortly before the invasion of Iraq. They were soon a ubiquitous element of the US presence. Val found the eight-wheeled vehicle vaguely reminiscent of the Soviet BTR he'd spent so much time in back in Kosovo years ago.

Tony was undeterred by Val's refusal to acknowledge his questions. He wasn't waiting for an answer as they walked past the Strykers.

"Because the way I see it, neither of you guys is freaking perfect by a long shot. So why are you holding this against her?"

Tony knew Val was quiet at the start of his day. Val knew Tony was talkative. All day.

The result was that, for the first hour or so, Val was silent as Tony ran his mouth. The stream-of-consciousness monologue spilled out of Tony without a response from Val, usually until after they had hit the small free-weight gym in one of the shipping containers on the JSOC compound and emerged from the showers.

"It would be one thing if either of you was, like, an angel," Tony said as they stepped up to the operations center.

Val grabbed the door and held it open as Tony walked through, talking every step of the way.

"Well, I can vouch that neither of you is angelic in the fucking least." Tony walked a step ahead of Val into the operations center. "So, I'll ask you again, what's the problem?"

The center of activity of the JSOC compound was a couple of long, narrow buildings. One of which served as the operations center, while another housed the area where teams met and got kitted up before missions.

The ops center was a much smaller and less shiny version of Balad. Three large, wide-screen displays hung on one of the long walls, displaying ISR and mission feeds twenty-four seven. A horseshoe-shaped arrangement of tables and chairs encircled the displays. The last few rows of the horseshoe sat on risers, affording the rearmost rows unobstructed views of the displays. During missions, the ops center could get crowded with all the cross-functional elements in attendance to support and observe. At a time like now, though, during the rhythmic lull in operations before the furious pace of nighttime, only a handful of enlisted and officers worked the room.

Val and Tony split the horseshoe, walking up the center aisle. A lone officer stood silhouetted in front of the center screen. Arms folded across his chest, one hand rubbing his chin, the officer stood motionless, studying the slowly moving image.

"Morning, Mac," Val said, to interrupt Tony. "Got anything good cooking?"

"Afternoon, sir. Afternoon, Vinnie." The captain didn't bother to look away from the ISR feed he was studying. He knew the guys' voices and ritual well. "Not sure yet."

Like on their last trip to Iraq, Tony and Val were in pseudo for this assignment. Same theater. Same pseudos.

Tony and Val looked at the video image beamed from a Predator drone circling above Mosul. A beat-up sedan sat in front of a dilapidated building somewhere in town. There was nothing special about the image. It looked like tens of thousands of other images of other beat-up sedans in front of other dilapidated buildings they had studied. But they had learned to trust Mac's gut.

Pete MacNamara was a captain with the Ranger component of the JSOC task force at Mosul. A military intelligence officer, he was assigned to the operations cell, and spent most of his time in the ops center, monitoring the HUMINT, SIGINT, and ISR feeds.

Mac was on the nerdy side. He wore army-issue black eyeglasses with thick lenses. But he wore them with black retention straps instead of frames. The retention strap was a modification to keep eyeglasses in place when jumping out of airplanes, scuba diving, or in combat. Not for standing in front of large monitors all day with a cup of coffee in your hand. Mac wore his hair in a severe high and tight, with closely shaven skin above his ears. The black straps contrasted with Mac's pale, shaven skin as they wrapped around his head. None of the Rangers, though, usually a biting, sarcastic bunch, made fun of Mac. They respected him too much.

Mac had a reputation for pulling targets out of the ether. Solid targets that no one else had discerned within the volume and swirl of disparate information being fed to the ops center. A few months ago, the task force started launching operations against high-value targets based solely on Mac's analysis of strange activities that he found on ISR. The entire task force now called these "Mac Attacks." And his knack for picking out anomalies in traffic patterns had proven as good as any algorithm or team of resources at higher headquarters.

Val and Tony stood in silence behind Mac for a moment. The image on the screen rotated slowly as the Predator circled, but otherwise didn't change. Nothing was happening.

Mac pulled his glasses up onto his forehead and rubbed his eyes. "Slippery motherfucker."

"Who's that, Mac?" Tony asked. "Kzem Moussa?"

Mac turned and faced Val and Tony.

"Yeah," he said, now rubbing his neck. "Slippery motherfucker."

Val and Tony nodded. The task force had been chasing Kzem Moussa for months. One of Abdul Razzaq's main facilitators for his cross-border network, the name Moussa came up everywhere in HUMINT/SIGINT reporting. But no one knew what he looked like, or where he was.

"You think he's in that building?" Tony asked.

"No," Mac said flatly, turning back to the screen and pulling his glasses back down. "But I was hoping he was."

Mac stared at the screen.

"Slippery motherfucker," he said to himself.

The image continued to rotate slowly, the beat-up sedan seeming to circle the building.

Tony looked at Val and shrugged.

"All right, then, Mac. We'll see you after our meetings," Val said.

"Yeah… After your meetings, sir."

Val and Tony left the operations center, pulling down their wraparound sunglasses to thwart the blazing sunlight. They turned and walked toward the shitty little workout area as the daily JSOC rhythm and grind exerted itself.

After a quick workout and shower, Val and Tony met their translators and hopped into a Humvee. They drove south through the barriers ringing the JSOC compound out onto the main road. Still on the base, they followed the road around the southern end of the airstrip. It was an old one, dating back to before World War I when it was used by the Royal Air Force. It went on to host Iraqi Air Force MiGs for many years until being captured by coalition forces in 2003. Val and Tony would jog around it sometimes for exercise. Weeds grew through cracks in the concrete, and large, dilapidated navigational aids sat idle and rusting, giving that part of the base an uneasy, derelict feeling.

On the western side of the airfield, the road turned north and headed onto the main base, which was full of regular army units and activity. Val and Tony and their teams used the regular army gate exiting to the north to bring in their sources for meetings. There were several small cinder-block buildings just inside the gate reserved for this purpose. Val hated these grimy little buildings. The gritty concrete floor, one small window, and a handful of old folding metal chairs seemed specifically designed to insult him. He would sit in the uncomfortable chairs, waiting for his source to arrive, look around, and stew over what he'd lost when they'd kicked him out of the Cobra Snare program.

Running a source out of a European embassy differed greatly from the military intelligence process in Iraq. It was hard and often grinding work. But executing a surveillance detection route, no matter how late and long, through a European capital, was sexy compared to his life now. Running an asset in Europe was a solitary, high-pressure job. Military intelligence operations in theater were a team effort, much riskier, and potentially deadly.

Only one person from the embassy ever comes in contact with a source in traditional, embassy-based spy craft. In the desert, several people are in contact with the source at every meeting.

The process started with the Ranger special tactics team, who recruited and trained the approved Iraqi drivers who went outside the wire to pick up the source. Extensive background checks and validation procedures were applied to every driver candidate. Only a small percentage made it through the process. Once accepted and trained, the Tigernaich, as the pickup drivers were code-named, conducted the dangerous and critical mission of clandestine source pickup and drop-off.

The Tigernaich went off the base in ordinary-looking civilian vehicles. They would drive to a prearranged spot that provided a reasonable expectation of an unobserved pickup of the source. That the driver was just another ordinary-looking Iraqi provided an additional level of cover. The Tigernaich handed the source a hood, which the source put on so that they could see nothing. The Tigernaich then patted them down to ensure that they were not carrying an explosive vest or other lethal device.

Once cleared, the Tigernaich would drive the source through security, onto the base, and come to a stop next to the assigned meeting building. When the vehicle pulled up, Val and an interpreter would yank the source out of the car, patting them down aggressively to recheck for a vest. Trust in the vetted Tigernaich only went so far.

Over time, though, Val and Tony did develop high trust in one of the Tigernaichs. An Iraqi Kurd named Mazar. "That guy just thinks right," Tony declared after working a few sources with Mazar. Val and Tony always felt a little better when Mazar was working their source pickups. Fluent in English, Mazar also occasionally served as interpreter during source meetings. Val and Tony went out of their way to sneak Mazar contraband, such as cigarettes and mess hall food, whenever they could. Mazar was a particular fan of the mess hall soft-serve ice cream.

Mazar was married. Val was not sure where Mazar's wife and two-year-old son lived, but he knew it was not in Mosul. That would have been far too dangerous at the moment for the collaborating Kurd's family. But Val could tell they were never far from Mazar's mind. When Val learned Mazar's son had taken ill with pneumonia, he spoke with the task force doctor and secured a large quantity of medicine for the kid. Mazar accepted the medicine in silence, but Val could see the grateful emotion in his eyes.

Finally, once the source had been picked up, brought on base, and cleared, Val would enter the small cinder-block building with his interpreter and the source to conduct the meeting.

The meetings, depending on the source and the purpose, could last anywhere from just a couple of minutes to a couple of hours. On a good day, Val would crank through three or four meetings, all the while triangulating what he'd learned with the current intelligence situation and any requests Mac had given him that day. With luck, Val or Tony would uncover a piece of intelligence that would either validate a Mac theory or otherwise inform their operations that evening. On bad days, they learned nothing important, and Val daydreamed about the spires of Prague.

And Sydney.

By 1500 hours, Tony and Val were usually making their way south around the runway, back to the JSOC compound, where they would check in with Mac. Today was no different.

"Okay, so if she's not still fucking him," Tony continued as soon as they were out of earshot of the interpreters and walking back to the ops center to check in on Mac. "When do you plan on seeing her again?"

"I don't know," Val grumbled as he stepped up to the long operations building and pulled open the door.

"That's a problem." Tony jabbed Val in the chest as he stepped through the doorway into the ops center.

Val walked into the ops center as Tony came to a stop to continue his interrogation.

"Why the hell don't you know?" Tony asked as Val strode past him.

"It's complicated," Val said in a low voice so that no one else would hear him.

Val turned and gave Tony a *not now* gesture as he continued walking toward Mac and the big screens.

"You cannot leave things the way you guys did in Vienna!" Tony whispered forcefully.

Val ignored Tony and hoped no one else had heard him. He walked up to Mac, who was staring at a house on the middle screen.

"Hey, Mac," Val said. "Nothing good today, I'm afraid."

"Who did you leave in Vienna, sir?" Mac asked, taking his eyes off the screens for the first time in hours. He looked at Val through his strapped-on eyeglasses with curiosity.

"Vinnie's mom."

"Fuck you," Tony said. "That's uncalled for."

"That was actually pretty rude, sir," Mac said matter-of-factly.

"You've never met Vinnie's mom," Val responded with a shrug.

"True."

"Fuck you both, gentlemen." Tony shook his head in disgust.

"What's the word, Mac?" Val asked. "You find Moussa?"

"No, sir. But I think I have a couple of known associates teed up for you. Hopefully, they'll give us Moussa after you guys wine and dine them a bit."

The three men turned and looked back at the screen.

"I'm narrowing down the target list," Mac said. He picked up the display controller and panned back on the screen they were all looking at. It flashed from a tight view of one house back to a view of the entire neighborhood. A cluster of about two dozen houses slowly rotated on the screen. Mac clicked the controller, and the zoom level decreased again. More than fifty houses were now captured in the high-resolution video.

"Is that northeast Mosul?" Tony asked.

"Yep."

Val looked at his watch. It was almost 1700 hours.

"Let's go," he said to Tony. "I'm hungry."

"Roger that."

They had about an hour and a half before the standard cycle of pre-mission briefs began. They left the operations center and walked to the dining facility.

Val could feel the day's pitch getting steeper, the rhythm speeding up. The whole Joint Special Operations Command machine had tooled and refined itself for years, focused on the precise repetition of lethal operations in Iraq. There were times in the day when he could feel, almost physically, the gears of that deadly machine shift into a higher RPM as a mission approached.

Val sometimes felt like he lived on a continuous sine wave. When he and Tony woke up, they were at the top of the curve, the start of a new period. The slope beneath their feet was imperceptible. Almost flat. As the day progressed, he could feel the slope beneath his feet increasing, leaning him forward. The slope increased. Gradually. Predictably. Every second. And he could feel himself, and Tony, and the rest of the unit accelerating. Until late at night, every night, when it became vertical. That was when he, and everyone around him, fell into violence in a way that was impossible to stop. There would be blood, and screams, and bullets, and dog bites, and explosions, and death.

If he thought about it too much, he would get anxious. So he embraced the ritual instead.

After dinner, Val and Tony went back to their C-huts to get dressed and then returned to the ops center to begin the mission pre-briefings.

The energy in the ops center had shifted in the hour they had been eating and dressing. There were more people and more activity in the building as the interagency groups moved quickly to complete their supporting actions for the mission. The National Geospatial-Intelligence Agency rep was printing off imagery of the route, targets, and operational area. The National Security Agency rep was monitoring cell phone signatures and signals to further refine the targets for the night and to identify any other high-value targets that may be in the area of operations. The Central Intelligence Agency augmentee was checking for any updates on strategic HUMINT reports they were tracking.

During all this, the task force operators made their way around the building, executing responsibilities and engaged in rituals. Like most of the missions that stayed inside Mosul, the Rangers were taking this one. They double-checked routes, scanned ISR feeds of target areas, printed off their own configurations of grids or pictures of the objective, and bullshitted. Anything to better prepare for the mission and to fill idle time prior to the "Go" order.

Everyone could feel the steepening slope beneath their feet.

*

The Rangers had almost sixty soldiers assigned to the task force in Mosul and could take down a bigger objective and hold ground longer than the Delta Force contingent. Delta numbered about twenty-five and was primarily used on helicopter-supported raids on high-value targets outside of Mosul.

This evening was shaping up to be a standard mission profile. Besides the Rangers, the assault element would include two dog teams, two interrogators, two translators, and two medics, as well as Tony and Val. The entire force would be carried in and out on six Stryker vehicles.

Before the final mission huddle, the operators gathered in one of the buildings next door to the operations center to kit up. The long building was cleared out except for a row of tables in the center, where soldiers loaded magazines and put the final touches on their equipment like last-minute tape to prevent any unwanted noises and light reflection. Hooks lined the walls all around the building. Weapons and load-bearing equipment hung on the hooks until the last moment before the final huddle. No one wanted to lug that heavy stuff around until they had to.

One side of the building had been converted into a small kennel to house the canines selected for the mission prior to launch. Tonight would be Chico and Rip, both Belgian Malinois. The pair, sensing the energy in the air, paced back and forth. Their cameras and armor hung on hooks just outside the kennel. They would be kitted up by their handlers immediately after the last mission huddle.

"Final briefing in five minutes!" the mission commander announced as he walked into the room. Lieutenant Colonel Brandon Ramos was a veteran of several tours with JSOC in both Afghanistan and Iraq. A six-foot-three Black Arizonan—Ranger Ramos, as he was known—had served with the regiment off and on between Joint Special Operations Command assignments for ten years. Competent and decisive, Ranger Ramos evoked strong loyalty from his Rangers and the rest of his task force. He would get them through.

The large room was awash in the sounds of bags slinging over shoulders, body armor sliding into place, belts clicking, magazines seating into weapons, and Velcro ripping. Operators spoke to each other in hushed, reassuring tones as they checked each other's equipment.

"You're good to go," Val said to Tony after he'd done a quick check of his buddy.

Tony nodded and scanned Val. They didn't always go on missions together. In fact, Ramos hated it when they did. "You two are too important to our mission," he'd bellowed one night when they returned from a mission where a Stryker had been flipped upside down by an IED.

Several Rangers were severely wounded, and the rest of the vehicles had to assume a defensive ring formation around it. The team had to hunker down for five hours in a hostile area, under intermittent sniper fire, until the sun came up and a relief force was launched to retrieve them.

"I don't want you both outside the wire on the same mission ever again!" Ramos declared.

The prohibition lasted about a week. There was no way around it—some missions needed them both on the objective.

Val and Tony's role was critical to the machine. They knew the HVT priorities better than any of the operators and were best equipped to identify the targets, correlate the interrogation storylines, and assess the opportunities for follow-on targets. And it was the follow-on targeting that made the machine so lethal.

Without Tony or Val and their teams, the operational commander would be sitting inside the objective post-breach, trying to coordinate the team's security posture and make sense of the stories coming from the battlefield interrogation teams. He would have to juggle all that while trying to determine whether the individual was being truthful, assess if they had the right target, find out who else this person knew, and establish how they were connected to higher-level targets.

It was too much, and the operators were not trained for it.

Val and Tony were trained for it. But on some missions, there were too many targets and too much coming at them post-breach. They could get it done. But it took time. And the JSOC machine was built to compress time. So, rather than hold up lethal progress, Ramos relented and let them roll as a team.

Tony and Val had been on many missions together. Each knew how the other kitted out. They knew how to check each other over quickly and without error. They looked out for each other. Always.

"You're good to go." Tony gave Val a thumbs-up. "Other than being a fucking dumbass douchebag."

"Oh, for fuck's sake."

"Seriously," Tony leaned in close enough that their body armor touched. "That Vienna goodbye was bullshit."

"Briefing room!" Ramos said loudly.

Everyone, fully kitted up now, gathered in the briefing room next door for a final operations huddle. Intelligence was tweaked, targets confirmed, and important details were reviewed. Each person felt it now. The slope beneath their feet was steep. They were leaning toward a fight, toward violence and death.

After the final mission huddle was complete, the force loaded into the six Strykers and headed around the airfield to the gate. As they left the base and rolled out the gates into Mosul, a pair of OH-58 attack helicopters flew overhead, just above the rooftops. The aircraft circled the Strykers once before departing. The 58s were running the task force's ingress route, looking for indicators of ambush or IEDs.

The Strykers barreled down the streets of Mosul. They drove in formation so tight they would bump against each other. The drivers always tried to maintain as little separation as possible between the vehicles so that their RF jammers could interlock and provide a protective ring around the convoy, preventing remote IED detonations. The technology didn't always work, but it was better than nothing.

The ingress part of the missions was usually calm for Val. The sound of the Stryker's engine blended with the banter and reflection of the operators to weave a blanket of sound that Val found strangely peaceful. Chico and Rip went from person to person in the closely confined crew compartment. They sat in laps, nudged to be scratched, licked hands, and vied for attention, as dogs do.

Tonight, Val was grateful that Tony had to ride in a different vehicle, per Ramos's amended edict. It was just about the only time that day that he was spared Tony's incessant questions and commentary about him and Sydney.

Sydney.

Then he pushed her out of his mind. He leaned his head back and tried to sink his mind back into the banter, reflection, and Caterpillar diesel engine at work.

After about ten minutes of droning, Val was pulled back to reality by the five-minute call.

The Stryker commander would always give a five-, two-, and one-minute call. At the five-minute mark, the banter would decrease, and some of the younger Rangers on their first tour would glance around nervously. The two-minute call ended all conversation. And even the dogs would quiet down and focus when "One minute" was called.

When the back doors dropped, the dogs, like every other soldier, were singularly focused.

The task force was usually dropped several kilometers from the objective to preserve surprise. After taking a quick head count, they started a slow, methodical movement through the city toward Sparkle.

Also known as the IR God of Light, Sparkle was often used to light up an objective. The infrared beam of light was projected down from a UAV circling overhead and was so big that it would blind everyone's night-vision goggles the closer they got to it. The Iraqi insurgency, mostly, didn't have night-vision capabilities, and the average Iraqi certainly didn't either. So, a target-designating stab of IR light was only visible to coalition forces. It made navigating to a specific target house several kilometers distant in the chaotic sprawl of Mosul much easier.

Chico and Rip pulled at their leads throughout the march through the dusty and dark streets and alleyways. They anticipated the conflict ahead and the opportunity to chase and catch a target. The human team members moved in silence, taking turns painting every window, door, and alley with the IR targeting spots from their weapon scopes. Using IR in this manner made it possible to ensure that every potential vulnerability was covered, and that every target has at least one person ready to engage it immediately. The spots, visible only with night-vision goggles, zipped silently around the area surrounding their column, never resting in one place very long as the shooter moved forward and covered the next area.

Val much preferred these night raids to daytime operations. At night, there were not as many people on the streets, and even though sometimes things did go haywire, Val felt like there were fewer variables that he could not control. Operations during the day were invariably chaotic and unnerving because of the mass of people that had to be contended with in an urban area. Nighttime operations were calm for the most part until the shooting started.

Just a few blocks from the objective now, Ramos made a radio call to extinguish Sparkle. Like a banished demon, the God of Light disappeared.

"Snipers, peel off," Ramos transmitted a few minutes later.

The sniper teams broke away. They were always the first to separate from the main force. Two sniper teams would get into pre-selected positions on rooftops to cover the objective and any ingress and egress routes.

The column of soldiers paused, each soldier continuing to scan for threats. A few minutes later, the snipers called on the radio: "Snipers set. Ingress and egress covered."

The Rangers continued to the objective area.

"Roof team, break off," Ramos transmitted minutes later.

Assigned to go in through the roof if the objective structure permitted, the roof team took Rip with them. Rip would be carried in his harness as his handler climbed the ladder to access the top of the building.

The remaining three squads of Rangers; Chico; as well as Val and Tony, with their teams, waited about a block away from the objective while the roof team got set.

"Roof team set," came the quiet radio call.

The breach team moved quickly through the shadows to the objective. Led by a long-serving Ranger master sergeant named Boozier, the breach team always went one to two minutes ahead of the assault teams. They would set an explosive charge on the door if the assault was going in heavy or pick the lock to open the door if the intent was to sneak up on the target. Surprise was preferred, and until signs of life and activity indicated a compromise, the task force would usually follow this methodical and clandestine manner of gaining access to the objective. If lights came on or movement was detected, though, all timelines were discarded and the breach would kick off immediately.

Booze, as he was known throughout the regiment, was a legend. He'd been with the Rangers since he was a private twenty years before, making him one of the longest-tenured members of the unit and an informal leader and mentor to many. Delta had recruited him several times, but Booze politely declined every time. "Can't," he'd tell them. "I just love the regiment too much." Despite his nickname, he was a quiet, reserved, and precise man who didn't drink. Never had. Booze had led the special tactics platoon for years, and approached breaching operations like a surgeon, trying in most instances to be as delicate and quiet as possible, and keeping noise signatures and damage to a minimum. He prized the element of surprise.

Tonight, though, was going to be a heavy breach. Intel put the number of military-aged men, or MAMs, in task force speak, on the objective at eight to ten, which was enough to do damage if given the chance. So Ramos wanted to knock everyone in the house onto their heels.

That was fine with Booze. He did loud as well as he did quiet.

The team worked quickly. Once the charge was set and the team was in a protective posture, Booze gave the call over the radio.

"Breach team set."

Ramos waited a moment.

Val could feel the slope beneath his feet snap to vertical. The hungry machine, which coiled all the way back to Langley and Bragg and other secret locations in the States, could hold back no longer.

It was time for blood.

"Breach. Breach. Breach," Ramos transmitted calmly.

A deafening blast shattered the serenity of the night as the door splintered to pieces.

The dogs howled, overcome with excitement. Their handlers released them.

Though Ramos was reasonably sure how many people were inside the objective building, and he didn't believe enemy sentries had observed their ingress, he still had the dogs go in first. Chico leapt through the smoking door fragments as Rip dove into a hole blasted through the ceiling.

The dogs cut an efficient path through the dark house. The cameras on their harnesses captured the action and beamed it back, in real time, to the ops center as well as Ramos and his senior leaders on-site.

The dogs were trained to latch onto anyone in the house who was moving or demonstrated a threatening demeanor. As good as the dogs were, many times, they seized women who were often the first to react as their house got blown apart. They were very good this time, only attacking two MAMs who had grabbed weapons.

Satisfied by what he was seeing, Ramos transmitted, "Breach team, go," over the net.

Booze and his men surged into the house.

Women and children in the house screamed. A few MAMs shouted curses in Arabic.

A burst of gunfire cut down the MAM who was fighting with Chico before he could get his gun to bear on the dog. Chico continued to chew on the dead body until his handler arrived a moment later and gave the release command.

The breach team exercised restraint otherwise, physically subduing the rest of the occupants rather than shooting them. Sometimes, because of the tactical situation, the breach team would go in hot, shooting military-aged males on sight. But tonight, as on most nights, the task force was trying to keep the folks on the objective alive for questioning to work the ever-present list of higher-level bad guys they were trying to get to.

The three other Ranger squads, with Tony's and Val's teams in tow, poured into the structure. Fanning out with weapons drawn, they worked quickly to secure the objective.

This breach had gone by the book, and they secured the house within minutes. The team shifted to working the objective for intelligence.

The MAMs were separated from the women and children. Val's and Tony's battlefield interrogation teams started work. Val stood in the middle of the BIT teams, and each interrogator reported back on what they were hearing. Tony did the same with his teams.

As usual, the task force went on to the objective with a good idea of what they were looking for and expecting to find, so the line of questioning was focused on confirming the captured MAM's affiliation with higher-level targets, and then identifying where those higher-level targets were.

While Val and Tony ran the interrogations, a team of operators looked through the objective in an exercise called "sensitive site exploitation." They collected all cell phones, SIM cards, computers, thumb drives, loose documents, and anything else that looked interesting. It was all cataloged and packaged for transport back to the ops center.

"Sir, this one is full of shit," Sergeant Greer, a member of Val's BIT team, said to him.

Val stepped over to the male being interrogated. His hands were flex-cuffed behind his back. He had a scrape on his cheek but had otherwise been unharmed by the assault. He was sweaty and breathing rapidly, but his eyes were defiant. This was common, and the protocol was to bring in Val or Tony, who had been trained on how to dial up the heat.

Val strode toward the defiant captive and delivered a hard chop to the side of his neck. If possible, the task force tried to avoid broken noses or other wounds that might draw attention during in-processing back on base.

The force of the blow knocked the prisoner to the ground. Sergeant Greer and the interpreter yanked the man back to his feet as Val launched into an angry, spitting tirade so close to the man's face that their noses touched.

It was a well-rehearsed speech that Val had given, in precisely this manner, at least a hundred times now. Val glared at the prisoner as he listed all the ways that they were going to fuck him up unless he told them what he did for Abu Somebody and exactly where Abu Somebody was at that precise moment in time.

The captive, swaying from the strike to his neck, shirt drenched in stress-induced perspiration, and eyes wide in fear, hesitated. He wasn't ready to crack yet.

Val took a step back and nodded at the interpreter and interrogator. They heaved the shaking prisoner until he was barely on his toes while Val started rolling up his sleeves.

"Fuck you," Val hissed. "We've got other prisoners."

Val gestured over his shoulder at the group of three MAMs being interrogated by Tony and his team as the interpreter translated his words to the prisoner in a hushed voice.

Val loosened his arms and shoulders as if getting ready for exercise.

"I'm going to kill you so they know we're serious." He jabbed the terrified man in the chest with his gloved hand.

Val made sure the interpreter had time to relay his words before punching the prisoner as hard as he could in the face.

The Iraqi's head snapped back and his knees buckled. The interpreter and interrogator held him by the arms; otherwise, he would have fallen to the floor.

Val grabbed the prisoner by the hair and jerked his head up. His nose was flat and already purple. Blood ran down his face onto his shirt.

Val held the prisoner's head close and screamed at him.

"Ready to talk? Or do you want more? I want to know who your boss is, and where they are sleeping tonight!"

The interpreter yelled Val's questions into the prisoner's ear.

The Iraqi blinked rapidly as he tried to focus. Then his eyes got wide and darted around.

He's close.

The first five minutes of the battlefield interrogation, termed the "golden five minutes" by JSOC, were crucial. This brief period of intense shock and uncertainty drove a wedge of vulnerability through the detained combatant's resolve. The fear and confusion of the moment, amplified by the interrogator's increasing force and focused questioning, eroded the individual's will to resist. When the right levers were pulled and the correct amount of hostility employed in those first few minutes, the detainee wondered if he would be killed on-site.

The US Army was not in the business of killing captured combatants. But the detainee didn't know that, and that uncertainty was the wedge of doubt that caused them to crack. Once those five minutes had passed, there was almost a universal recognition among detainees that they were going to live through the ordeal, and their willingness to rat out their fellow combatants would wane.

Val and Tony were uniquely trained to apply increasing pressure and pain to quickly ramp up the fear within the prisoner in those first minutes. The correct application of those methods left the detainee struggling to grasp to their situation, figure out the stakes, and decide what they were going to do. The key was to keep them off-balance and terrified of what might happen next so that there was only one palatable option for them: to talk.

The vast majority of prisoners broke in that first five minutes. In fact, only one had ever not cracked under Val's application of increasing pressure. Val thought about that tough Iraqi often. His face bore several scars, and his hair had been burned off just above his left ear. He took everything Val threw at him in silence. Sure, he screamed in pain more than once. He gasped for air and choked on his own blood. But he never talked. Even when Val shoved his pistol into his mouth and yelled that this was it. He was going to die unless he told Val what he wanted right then.

But he didn't.

Val took the pistol out of that prisoner's mouth. He hid his grudging respect for the tough Iraqi and told the interpreter to take him to the prisoner-collection area. He would be processed and sent to one of the prisoner camps. Who knew when he would ever be released. Val still remembered him, though. And, in some of his darkest hours, Val thought of his time in chains at the mercy of Abakumov and compared himself unfavorably to that nameless Iraqi.

The prisoner in front of Val at the moment was not that tough. As Val wound up for another punch, the prisoner panicked. He tried to wiggle out of his captor's hands, but the two soldiers held him tight. He screamed and began to stammer, looking urgently at the interpreter.

The interpreter nodded to the prisoner and then looked at Val.

"Sir, turns out this young man knows where his boss is sleeping tonight."

In less than an hour, Chico and Rip were chewing on humans in the next target house as the breach team charged in through a shattered door.

As long as the task force was not having to shoot it out on one of the objectives and their intelligence prep was on the mark, they could execute this standard breaching raid four or five times a night until the sun was coming up and the sound of morning prayer rose above the city.

The morning prayer was always an ominous sound. The task force knew upon hearing the prayer that it was only minutes before they would be getting shot at.

"Something about that morning prayer," Tony would say. "The morning prayer and a fresh night of sleep put the extremists in a mood to mix it up."

At times, it seemed like the whole neighborhood was standing on rooftops, taking potshots at the task force. That was always the sign that it was time to get the hell out of Mosul and back to base.

CHAPTER 59

"Seriously," Tony said as he put a spoonful of soft-serve ice cream into his mouth. "Why did you leave it like that in Vienna?"

"Dude, wipe your mouth." Val shook his head in disgust. Vanilla ice cream clung to Tony's beard. A lone drip struggled down his chin before being absorbed in the curly salt-and-pepper hair beneath.

Tony took another large bite, releasing another ice cream drip.

"Seriously." Tony said, dragging his spoon through the paper cup of ice cream, assembling the last mouthful.

"I didn't plan it that way, asshole."

"Sure." Tony held the final spoonful in front of his mouth. "I didn't say you planned it that way. But you let it end that way."

Tony swallowed the last of the ice cream, then put the plastic spoon into the paper cup. Finally, he wiped his face with a napkin.

Val and Tony sat alone at a table in the Mosul dining facility. On a hill just north of the JSOC compound, the DFAC was a large fabric structure that fed thousands of American and coalition soldiers and contractors every day. It was a strange place to Val, full of regular army soldiers who were experiencing a very different war than he and his JSOC comrades were. Tired and bearded, the operators always stood out in the DFAC next to the younger and cleaner-shaven regular army types.

Today was a rare occasion for Val and Tony. It was an off day. So they treated themselves to a sit-down meal. Usually when they visited the DFAC, it was to grab a tray of chow quickly and hurry back to the compound so they could eat during a mission brief. Today, they had savored the bland DFAC fare and hit the soft-serve ice cream machine. Val liked the stuff okay. Tony loved it and went back three times.

Tony balled up his soiled napkin, dropped it into the empty paper cup, and waited for Val to continue.

Val took a sip from his coffee cup and sighed.

"It was just a mess, man. She was so fucking mad. And rightfully so. Then I got mad, and she stayed mad, and it just kind of spiraled."

Tony rolled his eyes.

Val shrugged.

They sat across from each other in silence, as if pondering a complex puzzle. The noise of the DFAC, always open and always slinging greasy food, surrounded them.

Gradually, over the past few months in Iraq, Val had told Tony everything. It felt good to do so.

Val trusted Tony. More than he trusted anyone in the world. More than he trusted Sydney. After the Farm, they spent little time together. Just one other combat tour besides this one and a couple of quick TDY missions over the years. And in some ways, they were an odd couple, the officer and the enlisted soldier. The major and the master sergeant. The educated and the crafty streetwise. The lifelong bachelor and the dedicated family man.

But they were tight. It wasn't just that they had dodged the same bullets together or gone through the same foundational training together. They fit together. And then, when put under unique pressures, they were sealed together.

And Val had to tell somebody. Had to. Navigating it alone over the past years had not gotten him and Sydney anywhere. So, he told Tony. Told him everything. From the very beginning. Even the parts that would get her, and him, thrown in jail.

"You want to know what I think?" Tony asked in a sincere voice.

"Major Santanna!" a voice called before Val could answer.

Val and Tony both turned to see a Ranger sergeant weaving his way quickly through tables full of eating soldiers.

"Major Santanna, Captain MacNamara would like to speak to you in the ops center," the soldier said, walking up to their table.

"It's our day off," Tony said.

"Roger that, Master Sergeant," the nervous buck sergeant responded.

"It's okay," Val said to Tony before standing and saying, "I'm coming."

"I'll go with you. But this is bullshit."

Val and Tony disposed of their trash and left the DFAC with the sergeant. The trio walked south, down the hill and through the large concrete barriers that separated the JSOC compound from the rest of the base.

The ops center was a lot more active than normal for this early in the day. Mac stood at his well-worn spot in front of the big screens. Ramos stood next to him, a full six inches taller.

The center screen showed UAV footage zoomed in on what looked to Val like some sort of market square. A couple of cars propped up on cinder blocks sat in front of a wide, single-story building. A throng of people milled about in front.

"Gentlemen!" Mac said when he saw Val and Tony walk in.

"It's our fucking day off, sir," Tony barked.

"I know, Vinnie. But I think he's in there."

Mac turned back around and gestured at the center screen.

"Moussa?" Val asked.

"Yes, sir. One of the cell phones we believe to be associated with him, as well as a few others we know are used by the insurgent network, just lit up in that building. NSA has been all over it."

"'Believed to be associated with'?" Tony asked skeptically.

"It's him," Mac declared. "And this is the best shot at him we've had in months."

Ramos, who had been listening to their conversation, leaned in. "We're going after him. Wheels up as soon as we're ready. I need you and your team with us on this one."

"You're going now, sir?" Tony asked.

"In the middle of the day?" Val looked back at the building on the center screen, surrounded by people and activity.

"Well, I guess we could wait around till it's dark and hope he's still there," Ramos said, some irritation in his voice.

"Which he won't be." Mac's eyes were glued to the screen.

"My guys are kitting up right now. All of them. We're going in heavy, ASAP, and we're going to get him."

"If he's there," Tony said.

"He's there," Mac said over his shoulder.

Val pictured the Rangers, still groggy from being woken up, throwing on their equipment and getting ready for a fight.

"Roger that," Val said. "If you guys are going, I'm going."

Ramos smiled. "I thought you'd feel that way."

"I'll get the guys and get ready." Val turned to leave.

"And I need you to hurry," Ramos said, still smiling.

"Be careful," Tony called after him.

Val hustled out of the ops center back to the intel hooch and alerted one of the battlefield interrogation teams. The three of them kitted up quickly and jogged back to the ops center. They joined the Rangers prepping in the long building.

The mood in the room was anxious and dark. Daytime raids in Mosul, or anywhere, were anathema to special operators. Daylight canceled out so many of JSOC's advantages. There were always more civilians in the mix, and an enemy that tried to use both factors against the Americans. It had to be a really valuable target to lure JSOC off their compound during the day. Val hoped this Mac Attack proved worth it.

Val quickly loaded half a dozen magazines and threw on his body armor. The dogs, Chico and Blaze this time, sensed the extra layer of anxiety in their pack. They paced around and barked loudly in their kennel.

"At ease!" Ramos bellowed. The tall Ranger put his hands on his hips and waited as the kitting room fell silent.

When he had the full room's attention, he smiled and nodded with respect before beginning.

"We have a shot at Kzem Moussa." He spoke loud enough that his voice carried to all fifty soldiers in the long room. "What we don't have is a lot of time to talk about it. We can't let him get away. When I'm done talking here, we're going to load the Strykers and go get him."

Ramos paused and scanned the room.

"Standard. Operating. Procedures," Ramos said, emphasizing each word. "Do your job. Shoot. Move. And communicate."

Ramos scanned the room, looking at his men, and then said, "Hooah?"

"Hooah!" the room of soldiers shouted back.

Ramos nodded with pride, then turned to head to the Strykers.

Val walked out, weapon in hand. His interpreter and interrogator followed him to one of the vehicles.

Two minutes later, six Strykers were rolling.

Val sat back and closed his eyes. There was not as much banter in the vehicle. The hasty daylight raid had everyone more on edge.

A weight landed on Val's lap. He opened his eyes to see Chico balancing on his knees. Chico looked at Val and licked his face quickly. Val rubbed Chico's neck just above his combat harness. The dog was still trying to assess what the hell was going on and why his humans were so on edge.

Their Stryker took a hard turn. Chico tried to lean into it, but then hopped across the vehicle onto another soldier's lap.

Val closed his eyes again and took deep breaths. He thought about what they were about to do. The danger. The complexity. The unknown. He was anxious, but also felt tremendous pride at being part of this team. A team whose commander could say simply, "Standard operating procedure," and fifty operators with dozens of different responsibilities knew exactly what they needed to do. And, just as importantly, knew exactly what everyone else was going to do. He wondered if so competent, lethal, and large a group of military professionals had ever existed before. He bet not. And was just proud to be part of it.

All of that pride and perspective vanished when the Stryker's doors lowered.

Val and the rest of his Stryker jumped out into a throng of people in a busy market square.

They had studied the objective in the ops center and had taken the printouts given to them by the NGA rep. But now that they were there, injected into the crowded reality of the place, it was a confusing mess. The objective, the single-story tire store, was not visible because of the crowd. Nor were the other members of the task force.

Val could see the fifty-caliber machine guns on top of a few of the other Strykers above the heads of the teeming crowd, but not much else. Though they had come with a force of fifty heavily armed operators, Val suddenly felt alone and vulnerable.

Scanning the faces of his team and the Rangers around him, Val could see the confusion and stress on their faces.

Val and the rest of the task force were accustomed to getting out of the vehicles in the calm and silence of night several kilometers from the objective and any expected hostile contact. The sudden stimulus of being ejected from the Stryker into the midst of hundreds of military-age male potential fighters was jarring. Val's mind, like every other operator's, amped immediately up to a high-speed threat-sorting mode with fingers on triggers.

"Objective is due east," Ramos's voice said in Val's radio earpiece. "Move east to the objective now!"

Val and a few of the Rangers checked their compasses quickly and then lunged to the east.

The crowd was thick. Stunned by the sudden arrival of half a dozen large, armored vehicles and dozens of commandos, the Iraqi crowd was frozen in place.

The Rangers shoved them out of the way. This agitated the crowd, who shouted and jeered at the Americans.

By the time the task force made it through the crowd to the tire store, it was clear that something was wrong.

The structure was a burned-out, unoccupied shell.

"Goddamn it!" Val heard Ramos yell.

The Rangers formed a perimeter as the crowd gained a little more confidence and started pointing at the Americans.

Val moved toward Ramos, who was screaming into his radio.

"We went exactly where you told us to, Mac! Give me the right location now or we're packing up! Our ass is in the wind out here!"

Val looked around to make sure his BIT team was by his side. He gave the interpreter a nod. The young NCO looked anxious but managed to nod back. The interrogator, a staff sergeant that Val had worked with in Iraq two years ago, gave him a thumbs-up.

Val scanned the Rangers. Everyone was sweaty and stressed out. The younger Rangers were bug-eyed as their heads darted one direction and then the other, searching for threats in the crowd of Iraqis. But, overall, the team was holding up.

Booze stood in a ready position on the other side of Ramos, about twenty feet from Val. The two made eye contact. Booze shook his head with calm resignation and smiled. *Whattaya gonna do?* he seemed to say. Val shrugged.

Mac, back in the ops center, looked at the overhead imagery beamed to him from the UAV orbiting over the task force. He realized they had arrived one building south of the objective. Easy for him to see with the god's-eye view of the drone. Impossible for Ramos and the rest of the task force to discern, surrounded by hundreds of Iraqi market goers.

"Sir, objective is due north, fifty meters."

"Roger that," Ramos said before transmitting to his unit: "Due north. Fifty meters."

Mac exhaled and watched on the video screens as the force of fifty surged through the crowd toward the objective.

Val charged forward with the rest of the unit. Booze and the breach team hit the building first, blowing down the doors and charging inside, Chico by their side. The rest of the Rangers poured into the breech as the roof team leaned a ladder against the wall and climbed up.

Three minutes later, the Rangers stood in the middle of the building with Ramos. The colonel was cursing into his radio.

"Fucking empty, Mac! The tire store is fucking empty."

"Roger that, sir. Stand by."

"Stand by?" Ramos was incredulous. "Stand by? We're in the middle of fucking Mosul, Mac! We're out of here. Aborting."

Ramos took his hand off his radio handset and looked around at the soldiers closest to him. He made eye contact with Val and said, "What a goat screw, huh?"

Val smiled and shook his head.

Ramos had just put his hand back on his radio handset to give the abort command when Mac's transmission came.

"Sir! We've picked up the cell phones again. They're hot in a building two blocks due west of you!"

"You sure, Mac?"

"Dead nuts, sir!" The enthusiasm in his voice carried through the radio.

Ramos winked at Val.

"Roger that! I copy, objective is two blocks due west."

"Affirmative," Mac transmitted back. "I've got eyes on you and the objective. I'll vector you in."

"Rangers, this is Ramos," the tall Ranger transmitted over his command frequency. "Objective is two blocks west. We're going on foot. Strykers, move to support as able. Move out!"

The crowded market, surprised by the midday interruption of six armored vehicles, was now startled again as fifty bearded, armed marauders burst out of the burned-out tire shop and sprinted off down a residential street.

Iraqis stood casually by as the task force charged through the neighborhood. It felt good to be out of the crowded marketplace, even though they were in no less jeopardy.

Ramos and his men ran down the middle of the road, taking no time to cover windows or avenues of approach on their route. They didn't know where the hell they were going, so how could the enemy at this point? The confusion and chaos the Rangers were stumbling through cloaked their actions in surprise to the enemy.

Val and his battlefield interrogation team ran at the tail end of the loose formation. Booze and his breach team ran up front.

"At the next intersection, look to your three o'clock, and that's the objective," Mac said over the radio. "It's a single-story house bounded by a small garden wall."

"Roger that."

Val and the rest of the task force were missing Sparkle badly.

"There it is!" Mac shouted over the radio as Booze and his team ran into the intersection. "Look to your three o'clock!"

Booze, still sprinting, turned in that direction and pointed at the building with his left hand, holding his weapon in his right.

"Yes!" Mac yelled on the radio. "That's it!"

The breach team didn't break stride. They sprinted to the front door and blew it off its hinges in a well-rehearsed economy of motion that took less than thirty seconds. Pieces of the door were still in the air as Chico leapt into the house, followed by the breach team.

Blaze was on the other side of the house with a squad of Rangers as they took positions on the "back side" of the target area. They're encircling the structure to prevent anyone from getting away, or "squirting," in JSOC speak.

A Ranger sergeant carrying a cell phone direction finder entered the house immediately after the breach team. His job was to find the designated cell phone signal using sophisticated handheld equipment that could parse a signal through walls and was very accurate. A Ranger followed him closely, providing cover and overwatch for his comrade, who was absorbed in his task and oblivious to threats.

The breach team had the situation in control two minutes after their forced entry, when Val entered the structure. Three women and two young children sat crying in the corner of the living room. No MAMs had been found.

"Dry hole," Booze said to Val.

"Rangers, shift one house east, move!" Ramos yelled on the radio.

Again, the force of fifty moved as one. The breach team dashed out through the broken doorway. Val followed.

They sprinted to the next house.

They didn't need to blow up the front door this time, as a hard kick from Booze knocked it off its rickety hinges.

The breach team fanned out, weapons up, fingers on triggers. Chico and Blaze dashed from room to room.

A scream rang out through the house as Blaze latched onto a MAM who made an ill-advised move.

Val entered the house with his team and started counting.

This house had seventeen Iraqi individuals inside. A mix of women, children, and a few MAMs cowered against the walls. Blaze, whose handler had detached him from his victim, barked ferociously at the bloodied young man who lay on the floor in front of the terrified group.

Val and his team got to work, starting with MAMs. There were four. The one who Blaze had attacked, two other able-bodied young men, and then a crippled man standing with the help of a leg brace and crutches. A middle-aged woman had her arms wrapped protectively around the swaying, broken man.

An hour later, Val and his team had interrogated all the MAMs with no luck. The three able-bodied men had cracked quickly but knew nothing. The crippled man seemed to also be mentally disabled and didn't follow most of Val's questioning.

Val walked over to the middle-aged woman who had been helping the disabled man stand.

"Ask her what his problem is," Val told his interpreter.

The interpreter spoke with the woman for a few minutes.

"She says her name is Zhala. She says she is a teacher. Says this guy has been this way since birth." The interpreter gestured at the disabled MAM. "Says he is also mentally slow. Kind of an idiot. I guess she takes care of him."

Val looked at the old woman. Her brow was furrowed with worry, and her eyes bore into him, trying to determine what was going to happen to them next. A child clung to her legs, crying.

"Fuck this," Val muttered to himself. These were the times he hated the job. He looked around the house at the terrified Iraqis, the broken furniture, the blood on the floor from Blaze's handiwork, the bitten man sobbing as a medic bound the wounds on his leg and arm, the crippled man leaning against the wall, and this terrified woman trying to comfort traumatized children and look out for her mentally ill, physically damaged ward.

"Bulldog six, this is Max," Val said over the radio. "Another dry hole."

"Roger that, Max. Stand by."

The radio went quiet.

Val stood motionless, waiting for the next radio call. Would they hit another target? Or pack it in? The rest of the Rangers wondered the same thing. So far, the afternoon had been stressful, but no one had been hurt. How many times could they pull off a hasty raid and not have something go wrong?

Val pictured Mac back in the operations center, madly searching for a clue and yelling at the NSA team so that he could put them onto the right spot.

"Max, Bulldog 6," Ramos said over the radio. "Ops is asking if you're certain. Confirm dry hole."

Val looked again at the pitiful sight of bleeding, crying, and scared Iraqis around him and shook his head in irritation. He understood Mac's intent and knew how disappointed and even embarrassed he must be about having sent the force outside the wire on a risky daytime raid that had turned into a fruitless clusterfuck.

But he resented being second-guessed.

"Bulldog 6, Max." Val tried to speak as unemotionally as possible. "Dry hole confirmed. We got nothing here."

"Roger that. Stand by."

Val, his team, and the Rangers stood in the house, listening to the sobs of children and the whimpering injured man, waiting for Ramos's next command.

"Rangers, this is Ramos. New objective. Three blocks to the east. We will move on foot. Strykers follow."

*

The task force hit three more houses before returning to base. They were tired and pissed off when the Strykers pulled back onto the JSOC compound. It had been a long, hard, dangerous day. Remarkably, though, no soldiers were hurt.

The team went to the kit building to stow their gear. As Val was dropping his magazines and getting out of his body armor, the same operations sergeant that had found him that morning in the DFAC approached.

"Major Santanna?"

"What's up, Sergeant?" Val answered, unstrapping his kneepads.

"Lieutenant Colonel Ramos and Captain MacNamara would like to speak with you in the ops center."

"I'll be there shortly."

Val could tell something was wrong the moment he stepped into the ops center. MacNamara and Ramos sat opposite each other at one of the inner-ring tables, reading.

They looked up when Val walked in and then at each other when they saw it was him.

"What's up?"

"Max," Ramos said in a serious tone of voice. "Have some bad news, I'm afraid."

MacNamara looked at Val with a strange expression.

What the hell is going on?

Ramos nodded to MacNamara. "Tell him."

"About an hour ago, we started getting al-Qaeda cell phone intercepts," MacNamara said, voice trembling.

Uh-oh. He's really mad.

"Most of the chatter is a bunch of back-and-forth reporting on today's events. The most interesting intercept was a female al-Qaeda member," MacNamara paused to look at one of the printouts in front of him. "A woman named Zhala."

He looked at Val and continued. "She described their house being searched and goes on to say that Kzem Moussa was questioned but released after she and he convinced the Americans that he was mentally underdeveloped and physically handicapped."

MacNamara looked back at the notes.

"Oh yeah. This transcript says she was laughing as she told the story."

Val nodded as the realization washed over him.

"That's enough, Captain," Ramos interjected. He looked at Val.

"Look, Max. This shit happens."

Val nodded, unable to speak.

MacNamara didn't look at him, keeping his eyes fixed on the papers in front of him.

"Get some rest," Ramos said. "Both of you. We'll get the bastard."

Val turned and walked out of the ops center into the Iraqi night.

CHAPTER 60

"I'm giving you one more night to be a pussy about this, and then we're done with it," Tony said as he handed Val another whiskey.

Val took the mess hall coffee cup from Tony and took a sip. He gave his friend a nod.

Val and Tony were sitting in the HUMINT hooch, a special section of the human intelligence operations building. The HUMINT ops building was Val's domain as the leader of human intelligence operations for the Mosul task force. It was configured like most of the buildings on the JSOC compound. Long and narrow, with a tin exterior that gave it a flimsy feel. The first section of the building held the team's desks, where they typed their reports and conducted the team's administrative activities. The middle of the building was the HUMINT hooch, and the last section was the place where the HUMINT team conducted their trusted source meetings.

Trusted sources were ones that had been extensively vetted and had proven their loyalty through their actions over an extended period of time. They would be picked up by a Tigernaich and forced to wear a hood, just like the less trusted sources. But they were driven through the post onto the JSCO compound. The Tigernaich would remove their hood and walk them to the back side of the HUMINT operations building.

The back section was outfitted with old couches and a couple of beat-up, comfortable leather chairs arranged around a wide-screen television. Behind the TV area was a simple table with four chairs where the meeting would take place. These were the "made men" of the source network. Not only was there a high level of trust, there was also an appreciation that these sources were placing themselves in grave and extended danger by working so closely with the United States. Every precaution was taken to protect their identities, and when they were on the JSOC compound for meetings, they were treated well. For these guys, that meant access to alcohol and porn. They would sit in the TV area, drinking and watching porn while they waited for their meeting to begin.

The HUMINT hooch section in the middle of the building was a sacred space. When Val and Tony arrived, they invested time with some of their sources collecting ridiculous and comfortable furniture. They outfitted the room with orange velvet couches, recliners, and a couple of very nice coffee tables that must have come from one of the palaces in Mosul.

The HUMINT hooch also had the only stocked bar in all of Mosul—one of the benefits of running source operations. Alcohol was of high value to many Iraqis and a good way to loosen up a nervous source. Val was authorized to procure and maintain a stock of it. In this effort, Liam proved to be a reliable friend, sending cases of contraband to Val and Tony through various means. He always put in a special bottle for Val. A new craft bourbon, or occasionally a rye whiskey, with a note attached designating it as "For Santanna's use only."

Made of plywood and two-by-fours painted black, the bar always had a bowl of figs, apples, pears, or whatever else the team could get their hands on. Val's 13th Tactical switchblade was always lying next to the bowl. Everyone admired it when they used it to slice fruit.

When no one was around, Val would let Mazar into the hooch to decompress. Tigernaichs had stressful jobs. Val and Tony valued Mazar's partnership. Access to the hooch was the highest form of respect they could pay him.

Occasionally, after a hard mission, operators that Val and Tony had entrusted with the knowledge would come over to the HUMINT hooch and partake in the stockpile of beverages. At those times, the HUMINT hooch reminded Val of a speakeasy. They would roll down the shades, lock the doors, and crack a few libations that were, throughout the rest of Iraq, strictly forbidden for American personnel to drink.

On longer speakeasy sessions, they let a few of the mission dogs in. The canines would jump off the couches chasing treats while Tony had the video from the cameras around their necks synched to the big-screen TVs. Chico, in particular, loved it, as did the humans. It was one of their favorite pastimes.

Tonight, though, it was just Val and Tony. A front had moved through northern Iraq, kicking up sandstorms that lay across Mosul and stretched almost all the way to Bagdad. The UAVs were in the hangar, and just about all missions were scrubbed. With no reason to be crisp when the day started tomorrow, Val and Tony were allowing themselves to withdraw from the HUMINT hooch's alcohol stash.

"I fucking had him, Tony," Val said for the hundredth time in the past forty-eight hours. "Had him in my hands."

Val held his right hand out and clenched his fist as he remembered holding Moussa by the shirt collar to steady what he thought was a feeble, unfortunate man. He shook his head and let his hand drop.

"Like I said, tonight is your last night to go on about it. That guy's days are numbered. You can take my word for it."

"I know," Val looked at the bourbon in his coffee cup. "But the task force is going to have to go outside the wire after him again, now, how many times? On missions, that would not have to happen if I had been smarter, had seen through the fucking guise and held those two."

"Oh, stop it. That math doesn't work."

"How the hell does it not work? We still have to find and go get that motherfucker. And people might get hurt when we do. And that would not be the case if I had not let him go."

"True." Tony shrugged. "But there will always be another mission, brother. We're always going to have to go outside the wire again and again, no matter who you catch or who you let go. This is a war. And it ain't gonna end anytime soon. You didn't start it. I didn't start it. Hell, Moussa didn't start it. And the three of us can't end it either. So taking on all this guilt and shit is actually pretty arrogant and self-centered. Seriously, dude, you give yourself too much credit. You can't take this shit so personally."

Tony took the last swig of rye whiskey from his coffee cup and wiped his beard. After he put the cup down on the coffee table, he lifted his eyes to see Val staring at him.

"Was all that supposed to make me feel better or worse?" Val asked.

"Up to you, bro," Tony said cheerily. "But tomorrow—"

"Tomorrow I'm done with it, I know!" Val interrupted with mock frustration.

Tony's brief speech on the futility of it all actually helped. More so because of their bond and friendship.

"Good." Tony got up to refill his cup.

"Here." Val handed over his cup as well.

"Let's talk about more important shit," Tony said from the bar across the room.

"With pleasure."

"Sydney."

"Oh, for fuck's sake," Val growled, shaking his head and throwing his hands up in exasperation.

"Fuck you," Tony said, walking back to the orange couch with two coffee cups full of whiskey. One bourbon, one rye. "I listened to your bullshit for almost an hour. Now I want to talk about what I want to talk about."

Tony gave Val his cup of bourbon and then walked to one of the orange recliners. He grunted as he lowered his body onto it. He took a long pull of rye whiskey and then shoved the recliner's side lever forward, laying his body out nearly flat.

Val sighed, suddenly exhausted.

"I really don't know what to tell you. I don't know what to do about it."

"Well, you can't just leave it where it is."

Val took another swig of bourbon.

"You two," Tony said. "You fucking amaze me. You're like the anti–Romeo and Juliet."

"Oh really?" A smile broke across Val's face despite his irritation at the topic of him and Sydney. "Well, against my better judgment, this I gotta hear. Tell me, wise one, how are we the anti–Romeo and Juliet." Val punctuated his final words with a two-handed air quotes gesture to emphasize his skepticism.

"I'll tell you why, asshole. Because Romeo and Juliet fought to be together. Fought against family, fought against friends, and fought against the forces of their day to be together.

"You two dumbasses fight to stay apart," Tony pointed at Val. "You know you're great together. You share an uncommon background and profession. And you love each other. But you fight against it. You both use the events of the day as an excuse for your own inaction and unwillingness to risk. To try. You especially."

"Me especially?"

"Yes, you." Tony took a swig of whiskey.

"Whatever. Nice speech, Shakespeare."

"I mean, look at you," Tony said. "You're the boldest motherfucker I have ever known. Professionally, you're ballsy to the point of foolishness. I'll never forget that damn green squirt gun stunt back at the Farm. I've seen you run through breeched doors here, ten strides ahead of Chico. For chrissake, Val! You single-handedly bum-rushed Vasily Abakumov and lived!"

Tony shook his head, appreciating Val's pyrrhic, solo attack on the most notorious arms dealer in the world all over again.

"But you won't risk anything when it comes to Sydney." An edge crept into Tony's voice. "You're so fucking timid. So gummed up. I don't even recognize you when I think about it."

Val didn't respond. He took another sip of bourbon and tried to pretend that the words had not struck home.

"Look, Val, I just want you two to be happy. I can't imagine life without my wife. I want you guys to have that."

The two friends sat in silence for a few minutes. Val, not sure what to say, turned Tony's words over in his head. Tony didn't have anything further to add.

"Shit, man," Tony finally said, looking at his watch. "I'm beat."

He pulled back on the recliner's side lever and then leaned forward to put his coffee cup on the table.

"I'm gonna hit the rack." Tony stood up stiffly.

"Okay. I'm going to have one more."

"All right, brother. Good night."

"Thanks, Tony."

Tony nodded and left.

Val got up and refilled his glass from one of the bottles Liam had sent him. He turned off the light and went back to the orange sofa. He sat in the dark and drank for another hour, thinking about Sydney and Vienna.

CHAPTER 61

Val's phone rang at four in the morning. Disoriented, he grabbed at it but missed. It fell off his bedside table onto the floor and continued to buzz. "Dammit." he rolled halfway off the bed and groped for it.

"What's that?" Samantha mumbled, clutching at him and the covers. Val met the army lieutenant two weeks ago the day he reported to Fort Belvoir.

The phone was just out of reach and still buzzing.

"Please…" Samantha begged.

Val got out of bed and grabbed the phone.

"This is Rafter. What is it?" he said in a quiet but angry voice.

"Nice," Sydney said with a chuckle.

Val straightened. It had been less than three weeks since she called last. He had not expected to hear from her again so soon.

"I'm sorry. I know it's early there."

Val walked out of the bedroom and shut the door. Naked, he stood in the middle of his small apartment's living room.

"Sydney?" Val asked in a whisper.

"Yep. It's me."

"Where are you?"

"Budapest, still."

"Everything okay?"

"Yeah. Everything is fine."

She paused.

"I know I should've waited till a decent hour there. But…I just…"

Val waited.

"I want to see you," she said.

Val blinked a few times.

"I know we have a lot to work out. And I'm still really mad…"

Val scratched his head.

"But I miss you," Sydney said, voice trembling. "I miss you a lot."

Val leaned back in the chair.

"Are you there?" Sydney asked.

"Okay."

"Okay?"

"I miss you too," he said. "Let's do it. When will you be back in the states? I Leave for Iraq in mid-January."

"I was actually thinking sooner…like, in about ten days."

"Really?" Val snuck a look at his bedroom door. He and Samantha had planned to take a few days of leave around then to visit some of her friends in Florida. "Okay. I can try to make that work. I'll just need to…Well, rearrange a few things. But I think —"

"In Vienna."

"Vienna?"

"Yeah," she said apologetically. "Things are still nuts with Abakumov having gone to ground."

Val held his breath. Was she going to get mad again?

"No one has seen or heard from the guy in about a week," she said, with no hint of anger. "I can't remember him ever going this dark. It's got people really spooked."

"I'm sure you guys will find him," Val said, wanting to turn the page quickly.

"I hope so. But I don't think I can get away before you go to Iraq. I have to be in Vienna for an OSCE conference from the 18th to 21st. My schedule should be pretty light and the conference wraps up on a Thursday. I thought it would be nice to be there together. Me and you."

Val's heart leapt at the prospect. But he was quiet, thinking it through.

"I know it's last minute and I don't know what your schedule is these days, but… You could fly in Tuesday or Wednesday and we could stay in Vienna through the weekend after the conference. Well, I thought it wouldn't hurt to ask? You've just been on my mind. I know you can't just drop everything and fly around the world. I'm—"

"Sydney. I'll be there."

"You will?"

"Yes." He glanced back at the bedroom door, then turned and took a few steps away toward one of the living room windows. "Give me a day to work on it. But yeah… I can make it."

"Only if you want to."

"I want to. I want to see you."

Sydney smiled.

A warmth welled within each of them, and the old pull tugged at both.

"When do you get to Vienna?" Val asked.

"Monday. The seventeenth."

"Okay. I'll talk to my commander today. Then I'll get to work on a Space A flight out of Dover. Then a train from Ramstein to Vienna, I guess."

Val shook his head, interrupting himself.

"Doesn't matter," he said. "Bottom line is I'll be there. I'll meet you in Vienna."

"Val?" Samantha called.

Val turned to see her poking her head out of the bedroom door.

"Everything, okay?" Samantha asked.

"Yeah. Yeah. Everything's fine. It's an old buddy. Overseas."

Samantha hesitated for a moment and then smiled. She closed the door and went back to bed.

"I'll let you go," Sydney said. "Sorry I called so early."

"It's okay. I'm glad you did. I'll see you in Vienna."

∗

Sydney sat and stared at her cell phone for a long time after they hung up. It was a grey, snowy morning in Budapest, cloaking her and her apartment in gloom. She could hear the occasional car drive by on the wet streets six floors below.

Sydney stewed a three-part cocktail of emotions, a whirlpool that swirled around Val Rafter.

She missed him every time she took a breath. So weary of the dangerous long distance that always separated them, she longed to be with him. She didn't begrudge him finding companionship, but it still hurt. They had long since earned their happily ever after, she thought. But she couldn't see when it might start. It was too far over the horizon.

And she was angrier at him than she'd ever been at anyone else in the world. When she thought about Val's selfish, impetuous solo assault on Abakumov, she couldn't think or even see straight, her outrage was so consuming, her sense of disappointment and betrayal so strong.

Sydney shook her head. She didn't want to get angry and worked up about it again. There would be plenty of that in Vienna.

Last, there was Alexei. She'd been foolish and tired in Kyiv. It was forbidden. It would be catastrophic to her career were anyone to find out. She was thrilled, still, by the memory that dissolved into intense regret whenever it played out in her mind. She was disappointed in herself. But years on from Garmisch, more experienced, worldly and at ease in the system, she hadn't reported it to anyone and sailed through the polygraph like a well-piloted corvette. It was years ago, and she thought she'd gotten away with it, that the danger had passed.

But Alexei gave Val a hint of their transgression.

And a hint was all that Val would need. That's why he'd mentioned it to her at the end of their phone call last week. He hadn't pressed. Just mentioned it and hung up.

Sydney had to know. What did Val know? And what did he think about what he knew? What was he going to do about it? What did it mean for them? And what should she do about it?

CHAPTER 62

Sydney tightened her scarf with a gloved hand and leaned against the snow-bearing gusts as she walked through Liberty Square toward the US embassy. Hungarian winters were tame compared to Russia's. And Sydney had lived through two in Moscow, so she knew how to endure the cold. But she didn't like it.

She was warm today, though. Anticipation of meeting with Val in Vienna had grown each day since they spoke almost a week ago, lifting her mood even in the freezing temperatures and wind.

Sydney skipped up the steps to the embassy.

As soon as she made her way through security and into the "back office," where the CIA station operated, her boss called her into his office.

"Knox!" Joe Kovack, the chief of station, yelled across the large meeting area outside his office. "Can I get a word, please?"

"Sure," Sydney said, glancing at Kovack's assistant for a clue as she walked by.

His assistant shrugged.

Kovack had been the chief of station in Budapest for a little more than a year. He was young for the role in the Central Eurasia Division, a traditional organization within the CIA known for its formal and excruciatingly long path for career succession. Tall, handsome, and intelligent, he and Sydney had butted heads from his first day. They were each ambitious overachievers, but it was not a simple case of like repelling like. On the contrary, they were both acutely aware of what made them different.

Somehow Kovack had rocketed through the ranks without having served in Iraq or Afghanistan, spending most of his time stationed in European capitals instead.

Not only had Sydney served tours in both theaters, but she'd spent her formative first case-office tour in Moscow. She viewed Kovack's nearly fifteen years in NATO or NATO-friendly countries with disdain. *He's like the captain of the JV team,* she thought. *Who really gives a shit?*

Kovack resented the boulder-size chip on Sydney's shoulder.

Their first six months working together were rough on everyone in the station. Tension lay across the office like a scratchy blanket. But after a few mutual wins, they settled into an uneasy, unspoken understanding. *As long as you don't fuck up my career momentum, we'll be fine.*

The understanding was tested at times.

"Good morning, sir." Sydney walked into Kovack's office.

"Morning." He gestured at her to close the door.

Kovack stood behind his desk. He picked up a folder and held it out to Sydney. "Vasily Abakumov turned up dead."

"What?" Sydney grabbed the file.

Abakumov had gone quiet after Val's visit to his dacha almost two months ago. It was not unexpected. After such a brazen intrusion into his operations, it was logical that Abakumov would take some time to assess his situation and security. But the pause had lasted longer than Sydney had expected.

Sydney had gained a reputation of expertise regarding Abakumov; she had a deep understanding of his operations and could sometimes predict his actions. She enjoyed fielding questions from across the agency regarding his next moves.

When Abakumov went dark, though, that reputation became an albatross. Sydney was hit with a wave of questions. She hated admitting to her colleagues and superiors that she didn't know where the mysterious arms dealer was or what he was up to. With each passing day, she could almost physically feel the patina of her reputation dulling. She threw herself into finding Abakumov, working her agents and team hard. But the man had ghosted himself. He'd vanished.

The only thing that made her smile over the past week was the promise of a visit from Val. She missed him badly. His visit would be a welcome respite from everything going on at the agency. She longed for him to hug her.

And she was furious with him. Everything going on with her at the agency was his fault.

She hadn't known it was possible for such strongly opposing feelings to coexist in one heart.

"The station in Sofia cabled late last night," Kovack said as Sydney sat in a chair in front of his desk. She flipped quickly through the file, her eyes racing over words and photos.

"His body was found in a trash pile in a back alley in Sofia," Kovack continued, not sitting down. "Police estimate he's been dead for about a week. His face was beaten to a pulp. His jaw was broken, and he was missing teeth. Six of his fingers had been broken, and he was missing several fingernails. The back of his head was missing from what they believed was a single gunshot. Entry point, as you can see, was his left eye."

Sydney looked at the glossy 8.5-by-11 photo. Vasily Abakumov had been brutalized. His face was unrecognizable.

Her mind raced. She shook her head.

"Bad way to go," Kovack said.

"And strange. Only the Russians would be this bold," she said, not looking up from the file. "But Abakumov was their guy. Untouchable except by them. And not by many of them."

"So you think it was the Russians? Rubbing out their own guy?"

"Problem is this isn't their way." Sydney studied the photo. "They like to make it look like suicide. So much so that the term being 'suicided' is an accepted phrase in the Russian language."

"That does not look like suicide. Even a pretend one."

No shit, Sherlock, Sydney thought.

"No. This looks like someone was pissed," she said. "Like they were making some kind of statement."

Sydney closed the file and rubbed her eyes. Her mind raced. *What now?*

"Aren't you supposed to be the expert on this guy?" Kovack asked in a voice that didn't hide his enjoyment.

Sydney looked up.

Kovack was still standing behind his desk, hands in his pockets.

"Not good, Knox." He shook his head. "How the hell did you not see this coming?"

Sydney stood from the chair and placed the file on Kovack's desk.

"Is that all, sir?"

"The questions are already pouring in," Kovack said, his voice sterner. "This isn't a good look. You better get your shit together, and fast. What the hell happened?"

Sydney turned and left.

Fucking paper tiger, Sydney fumed to herself as he stalked back to her office. *Val would hate him. He is the perfect fucking personification of what Val hates about the agency. And, god, Val would intimidate him.*

Sydney shook her head, remembering that this whole mess was Val's fault.

He barged in there like some over-testicled brute, nearly got himself killed, and spooked Abakumov into doing something stupid enough that someone finally took him out.

She walked into her office and slammed the door.

I could fucking strangle him.

Sydney shook her head.

Focus.

Sydney walked to the large window behind her desk. It looked west over Szabados Square. A gray sky hung over the bare trees, and the fountains were boarded up to protect them from the freezing weather.

Sydney took a few deep breaths and calmed her mind.

She knew what she had to do next.

CHAPTER 63

14 December 2007

Chișinău, Moldova—

The earliest records of Chișinău date back to the year 1436. The town became the capital of Moldova nearly four hundred years later, after the Russo-Turkish War. Russia, the victor, took the eastern half of Moldova as one of its prizes and named the former monastery village the capital. The Russian Imperial period was good for Chișinău. Its population grew rapidly, and it received generous investment in infrastructure and architecture.

When the revolution ended Imperial Russia in 1917, Chișinău and its surrounding areas declared independence, forming the Moldovian Democratic Republic. Shortly thereafter, the small country joined the Kingdom of Romania.

Chișinău was the second-largest city in the kingdom and once again enjoyed a period of robust investment.

In the summer of 1940, Chișinău's and Moldova's fortunes turned. As the Second World War approached, the Molotov-Ribbentrop Pact gave a large part of Moldova, including Chișinău, to the Soviet Union. The Soviets initiated a cruel and aggressive deportation strategy, dispersing native Moldovans deep into Russia to diffuse their influence and make the territory easier to assimilate. Then, on the tenth of November, an earthquake struck Moldova, killing scores and damaging thousands of buildings.

On June 22, 1941, Germany invaded Russia, negating the nonaggression pact, which had lasted just a year. Romania wanted Moldova back and entered the war under Wehrmacht command.

Romania recaptured Chişinău in less than a month, after intense air and artillery bombardment. The city also suffered under Soviet destruction battalions as they retreated, leaving rubble behind.

Three years later, after a violent Nazi occupation, Chişinău was the scene of heavy fighting yet again as the Soviets surged west. German forces were expelled from Chişinău on the twenty-fourth of August, 1944. The city's Soviet era had begun.

Another round of forced native deportations ensued while Russian city planners were flown in to plot Chişinău's resurgence. Stalinist architecture rose from the city's rubble, accelerating in the 1950s as the population increased. Development continued through the 1970s and 1980s. Massive high-rise apartment building complexes, encompassing entire city blocks, began to dominate the skyline. By the time the Soviet Union fell in 1991 and Moldova regained its independence, nearly three-quarters of the residences in Chişinău were housed in Soviet-era buildings.

Nicolae Muntenau woke up on the morning of December 14 at home in one of these large high-rise apartment buildings. He'd lived there with his wife and two daughters for about five years. The building manager had reached out to Nicolae after one of his promotions, offering him the nice unit on the northeast corner on a high floor. Despite its market reforms, a deeply ingrained system of favors still pervaded Chişinău, and respected junior government officials were sought-after tenants.

Nicolae rose at 5:30 a.m. as he always did, careful not to wake his wife, Sasha, as he made his way to the bathroom.

After showering, Nicolae dressed for work and then made a pot of coffee. He always enjoyed a solitary cup in the morning before the chaos unleashed by his two daughters.

Nicolae would step out onto their tiny balcony, no matter the weather, and lean against the railing while he enjoyed his coffee and looked east. When the weather was good, he loved to watch the horizon brighten over the distant rolling terrain. In those early-morning moments, as the sun rose, he would think about the Dniester River, Transnistria, and Ukraine beyond, and shake his head at the intractable mess history had made.

He usually had finished his coffee and returned to the kitchen before the flush of the toilet signaled that Eniko, his youngest daughter, was awake and getting ready for school. At thirteen years old, she already took after him, rising early and excelling at sports. He could picture her playing soccer or volleyball at a big American university. He liked the thought.

Daria, his oldest, was fifteen now. She favored her mother. She was intelligent, pensive, and enjoyed reading above all else. Nicolae liked to imagine Daria at Harvard. It excited him to think of her forging a new path for the family. One of education and accomplishment.

Daria was like her mom, slow to rise in the mornings. Nicolae waited a few minutes after Eniko left the bathroom, listening for the next telltale flush. When it didn't come, he stood from the kitchen table and walked down to the room that Daria and Eniko shared.

Eniko was nearly fully dressed. She looked at her father and said, "I tried, Pappa," with a shrug toward Daria.

Nicolae nodded and smiled as he walked across the small room. Daria had pulled the covers over her head.

"Daria," Nicolae said loudly, giving her warning. "It's time to get ready for school, sweetheart."

"Mm-hmm," Daria protested without moving.

Nicolae leaned over her and grabbed the covers. "Last chance."

"Just two more minutes."

"I'm sorry, sweetheart." Nicolae yanked the covers off her.

"So mean!" Daria said, coiling her body into a tight, pajama-clad ball and covering her eyes with her hands.

"The world is a mean place," Nicolae said with a shrug. "Education helps one cope."

"I get straight A's, Pappa." Daria rolled off the bed and scowled at her father. She stomped off to the bathroom.

"And it makes me so proud, sweetheart," Nicolae called after her. He tossed the covers back onto her bed and walked back to the kitchen.

Sasha stood in the kitchen in her robe with a cup of coffee.

Nicolae grabbed his briefcase and then walked over to her.

"I did the dirty work," he said as he kissed her on the forehead. "They should both be moving in the right direction."

"Thank you. Have a good day."

"I will." Nicolae put on his overcoat at the door. "Shouldn't be a late one."

"I'm glad. I'll see you this evening, love."

"Love you," Nicolae said, winking at her as he closed the door behind him.

He walked down the hall to the stairwell.

Nicolae always took the stairs. Both up and down. The elevator, like most from the Soviet era, was slow and unreliable. Also, walking was better for his leg, to keep it active and strong. The Russian bullet that struck it sixteen years ago had been successfully removed. It must have been a ricochet, the doctor told him. Usually, a Russian 12.7-millimeter round takes a leg off.

His leg ached in the morning but walking quickly down the stairs seemed to warm it up. By the time he exited the massive Soviet high-rise apartment complex, the ache faded.

Nicolae stepped out into the frosty morning air, mindful of the few ice spots on the wide landing that seemed to last all winter, every winter. He turned to his left and steeled himself against the wind. He had to walk a short distance through an alleyway to the main street where he caught the trolleybus each morning.

The hulking apartment building he lived in formed an alleyway with a warehouse just to the south. In the winter, the two buildings set a choke point, accelerating the frigid wind. Nicolae hunched his shoulders and leaned forward. There was a small shop on the corner just past the warehouse, where the wind slackened. It only took a moment to get through the gale, but he hated every step.

The shoppette was a new building, constructed in the late nineties. It was an attractive single-story brick building that seemed out of place amid the gargantuan Stalinist scale that surrounded it. Nicolae would stop in occasionally for a cup of coffee. But it was too cold today. He just wanted to get onto his trolleybus.

The wind slowed and then died as he made his way out of the alley. He relaxed his shoulders and straightened his back. Nicolae looked to his left to scan the street corner. No trolleybus yet.

Maybe I'll grab a coffee. He looked toward the shoppette.

Nicolae stared at the sight and almost came to a stop.

His heart raced. He had to remind himself to keep walking.

There was a blue flowerpot on the outside ledge of the corner window of the shoppette.

Act normal! he told himself.

Nicolae's feet shuffled and stutter-stepped as his head tried to calibrate to the unexpected development. He felt exposed, as if enemy eyes were watching him.

To hell with it. It would be normal to get a cup of coffee. Do that and make a plan.

Nicolae walked into the shoppette. He glanced a few times at the window as he ordered and then waited for a cup of coffee, confirming for himself that the blue flowerpot was there.

It was definitely there.

He took his coffee from the counter and walked to the tall tables on the opposite side of the shoppette from the blue flowerpot.

He took a sip of coffee and got out his cell phone. He noted the time: almost 7:30. A little early to call his assistant. But that couldn't be avoided.

"Hello?" Martina, his assistant, answered.

"Good morning, Martina." Nicolae hoped his voice sounded normal. "I'm so sorry to call you this early. But Eniko and Daria woke up sick this morning, I am afraid. I am going to have to help around the house this morning, and it might be wiser if I not come in until I am certain this is a simple flu bug. So you might not see me until after lunch. Can you please cancel my morning meetings? I don't think I had anything important."

"Of course, sir. No problem. I hope everyone feels better soon."

"Thank you. I'm sure they will."

Nicolae hung up. He placed his cell phone on the small high-top table and took another sip of coffee. He glanced around the shoppette.

It was a normal, bustling Friday morning. Several people, bundled against the cold, waited for their coffee near the counter, but there was no one in Nicolae's immediate area.

Satisfied that no one was paying him any attention, Nicolae grabbed his phone and held it beneath the table. He turned it off and then quickly removed the battery before placing the phone in one coat pocket and the battery in the other.

Nicolae took another sip of coffee and scanned the other occupants again. Nothing registered still.

His eyes came to rest on the blue flowerpot. He could just see the top of it through the corner window on the opposite side of the shoppette.

Nicolae's heart was not racing anymore, but a sense of dread and anxiety had settled over him. He wanted to tell Sasha. But he knew he could not. Not until he knew what it meant.

What does it mean? Are we in danger?

He took a last sip of coffee and walked out, throwing his coffee cup in the trash as he left.

Time to find out.

The blue flowerpot was a covert signaling trigger from Sydney. They had talked about it in detail years ago, when he first started working with her. But she'd never activated it in seven years. Until this morning.

Covert signaling methods, such as a flowerpot on a balcony, a chalk mark on a wall, or a certain number of candles burning in a window, enable case officers like Sydney to initiate preplanned actions outlined in the commo plan a handler trains their asset on shortly after recruitment.

Fortunately for Nicolae, Sydney was a good case officer. For years, she'd dedicated time to drilling Nicolae in tradecraft. He'd memorized the communication protocols and was comfortable with SDRs and other techniques. His knowledge and skill set were nowhere near those of someone who had graduated from the Farm. But Nicolae knew the basics. He ran through all those procedures in his head now as he walked to the trolleybus stop.

The blue flowerpot meant Nicolae was to go to a predesignated dead drop in Stephen the Great Central Park. Until he got there and retrieved the message, he wouldn't know why Sydney had initiated this alert.

The park was only a couple kilometers away. About ten minutes by car.

But Nicolae would not be going directly. As the trolleybus pulled up and he climbed aboard, Nicolae remembered Sydney's warning.

"Don't fuck around, Nicolae," she'd said, pointing at him. "If we initiate an emergency signaling, it's serious. Either you need our help fast, or we need your help fast. Either way, it's a big deal. The only thing that matters at that point is you safely and securely getting the message as quickly as possible. The minute you see that blue flowerpot, you start a surveillance detection route. Then, only when you're sure you're clean, you retrieve the message. Got it?"

Nicolae nodded to himself on the trolleybus. *Got it.*

Stephen the Great Park is the oldest park in Chișinău, seventeen acres of wide, tree-lined pedestrian avenues, fountains, statues, and green space sitting in the center of the city. In the spring and summer, the benches that line the avenues are always occupied by Chişinău's residents enjoying their lunch or just soaking up the sun. The park is not so active in the winter, but even then, Chişinăuers walk beneath the bare trees, stretching their legs and looking forward to warmer days.

Nicolae walked into the park after a two-and-a-half-hour multimode SDR. After multiple trolleybuses, taxis, and walking stints, he was sure he was not dragging surveillance. He was still anxious, though. And the closer he got to the dead drop, the more anxious he got about what it would reveal.

He scanned the area, moving only his eyes, as he walked toward the center of the park.

The park was mostly empty. Only a few other pedestrians moved through it. Their shoulders hunched against the cold, their head and eyes focused on the ground in front of them.

Nicolae walked through the center of the park and turned down one of the smaller pathways. About halfway down the pathway, he feigned dropping a glove. Bending over to pick it up afforded him one last cautious scan of the area. Certain he was still clear, he stepped over to one of the park benches that lined the pathway. A crumpled and folded newspaper lay against one of its legs.

Nicolae leaned over to grab the discarded newspaper. It was secured discreetly to the leg with a small piece of string so that it would not blow away. Nicolae pulled on the string sharply, and it broke. He jammed the newspaper into a coat pocket and walked out of the park.

An hour later, Nicolae walked by his assistant toward his office.

"Good morning, Martina."

"Good morning, sir."

"We managed to get things under control," he said, stopping at the door to his office. "Did I miss anything?"

"No, sir. A slow morning."

He nodded. "Good. I like them that way."

Nicolae closed his office door behind him. He took the crumpled newspaper out of his coat pocket and hung his coat on the back of his door.

Sitting down at his desk, Nicolae reached into the top drawer for what appeared to be a pair of ordinary bifocal reading glasses. Known only to him, though, these glasses came with a nearly invisible modification. Near the bottom of the lens was a focal magnification area that enabled the wearer to detect micro-writing embedded in a letter, advertisement, or picture. This method of passing information in the open, using an almost undistinguishable message body or image, was called steganography.

Like many techniques still widely used in clandestine tradecraft, steganography has been around for centuries. Hiding messages in open mediums provides great flexibility for discreet communications. In fact, the clandestine community is not the only practitioner of steganography. This simple and reliable covert communications method has been mastered by criminal enterprises, drug cartels, and cybercriminals alike.

In this case, hidden in the folded newspaper print, down in the corner, were the words, "Vienna University Christmas Market—1830HRS19DEC."

Nicolae leaned back in his chair and rubbed his eyes with both hands as relief washed over him. A meeting next week in Vienna suggested Sydney had an urgent intelligence need. Had he been in danger, the instructions would have been much different. Sydney had warned him that emergency extractions could be immediate and there was no guarantee that his family would be included.

Nicolae slumped in his chair. The tension he'd held inside for the past four hours was draining away, leaving exhaustion in its wake. He put his elbows on his desk and held his head in his hands.

How much longer can I do this?

He'd been an American agent for more than seven years now.

A knock on his door interrupted Nicolae's self-reflection.

"Yes?"

"Sorry to interrupt, sir." Martina opened the door and leaned her head into the room. "I'm going to grab lunch now if you don't need me."

"Yes. No problem."

"Are you okay?"

"Me? Yes. Of course. Why?"

"You look exhausted, sir. Can I bring you a cup of coffee?"

Nicolae nodded slowly. "That would be nice, Martina. Thank you. Didn't sleep well."

"I understand. Give me one moment."

Martina returned a moment later with a cup of coffee and placed it on Nicolae's desk.

"Thank you. Please have a nice lunch."

"Shall I bring you anything?"

"No, thank you."

"Okay, sir. I'll be back shortly."

Martina closed the door as she left.

The coffee tasted good. Nicolae sipped from it, staring out of the window at the gloomy winter sky.

I have had it. When I meet with Sydney in Vienna next week, I will tell her I am done. I have done enough and I want out. I want to go to America with my family.

CHAPTER 64

18 December 2007

Vienna, Austria

"Ahhh…" Val smiled and closed his eyes as he swallowed the last of the bitter, sweet double espresso. He placed the empty demitasse cup back on its white saucer and leaned back against the tufted leather bench, putting his arm around Sydney. She leaned into him, her forehead to his cheek, her arm around the front of his waist.

Val kissed her forehead as he looked around the Kleines Cafe.

"I like this place."

"I thought you would," she said, lifting her head to kiss his cheek. "Probably my favorite cafe in Europe."

The Kleines Cafe might be the smallest cafe in all of Vienna. Just half a dozen small bistro tables sit snugly against leather benches that run along each short wall and face the center of the cafe. Dark bentwood chairs sit on the tile floor on the other side of the bistro tables. In the summer, the small cafe's capacity quintuples, as patrons sit at tables in the square, soaking up the sun as they enjoy their wine or coffee.

This time of year, though, the Kleines Cafe was a comfortable and intimate oasis from Austria's winter. Today, the cafe was full of its usual diverse mix of discreet lovers, midday revelers, introverted bookworms, and ordinary Viennese seeking camaraderie with each other. It was a motley array of humanity that appealed to both Val and Sydney.

Sydney had brought Val here directly from the train station. It was a miracle they'd gotten a table, and she took it as a good omen. Val shook his head at the chair opposite Sydney as she squeezed between the tables and sat on the leather bench. Instead, he followed her through the narrow pass, jostling their neighbor's table.

A disapproving look from the couple next to them melted as they watched Val sink onto the bench next to Sydney and put his arm around her.

Val glanced their way and said, "Please, pardon me," in German.

The man winked, and the woman nodded with a smile.

Who can be angry at a couple so in love?

Val and Sydney had agreed not to be angry today.

When Sydney met Val at the train station an hour earlier, she'd proposed no work talk.

"A cease-fire?" Val responded with a smile. "I'm happy to agree to that for the entirety of my visit."

Sydney laughed.

"I'm sure. And, truthfully, I am too. But at the very least, not today, not tonight. I just want to hang out like we used to in Prague."

Val reached out and pulled her in for a hug.

"Me too." He kissed her ear. "God, me too."

They hugged for a long time in the middle of the train platform. People swerved to get around them. It was getting close to four p.m. Soon, the station would be crowded with workday commuters.

"It's a deal, then," she said, holding him tightly to her. "No work talk today."

"Agreed. But part of the deal also needs to be feeding me soon."

"Oh, that's definitely part of the deal. Let's go."

They grabbed a taxi and went to the hotel to drop Val's bag. Sydney was staying at the Marriot for the conference and had talked the front desk into giving her a suite.

Ideally located in the old town center, Sydney stayed there often when she was in Vienna. The hotel overlooked the City Park, across the "ring road" to the east. A fixture of the old town, the City Park was loved by the Viennese and foreigners alike. At the main entrance to the park, a golden statue of Johann Strauss greeted visitors, who could then choose any of the numerous walking paths around small ponds or through wooded glades. It was also not uncommon to be greeted by classical music from a spontaneous, informal concert in the park.

Several blocks due west of the hotel, through the winding cobblestone roads and plazas of old Vienna, stood the Hofburg Palace, headquarters of the Organization for Security and Co-operation in Europe and the location of this week's conference. It was a picturesque place to work and enhanced the OSCE's reputation as a country club of a diplomatic organization, as ostentatious as it was ineffectual.

But today, for Sydney, there would be no formal work duties to attend to, and no feigning interest in the legalistic minutia of diplomatic agreements that would make little difference in the conflicts they sought to resolve. Today was all about being in Vienna with Val.

After dropping Val's bags at the hotel, the two bundled against the cold and walked through the old town to the Kleines Cafe. Initially, Sydney's happy energy was counterbalanced by Val's fatigued disposition. His flight to Ramstein had been delayed several hours because of a maintenance issue with the C-5.

Now, though, with a double espresso in his bloodstream and Sydney in his arms, he was energized and warming to the day.

"I'm hungry," he said to Sydney.

"There is a restaurant I really like around the corner."

"No." He kissed her forehead. "I like it here. I don't want to leave. I'll just order something easy here."

Val ordered Schnittlauchbrot, a dense farmer's bread with butter, chives, and tomatoes. When it arrived, he devoured it in minutes.

"My lord," Sydney said, always amused by how fast he could eat.

Val shrugged and leaned back against the bench. He put his arm around Sydney. Now that his body had sustenance, other appetites flared within him.

They sat in silence for a few minutes, watching the comfortable scene in the Kleines Cafe.

Sydney leaned into Val, interlacing her fingers in his. "I have a new suggestion for dinner."

"What's that?"

"I say we go back to the hotel and get naked," she said. She untangled her arm from Val and sat straight so that she could look him in the eyes. "We can just get room service if we don't wear ourselves out and fall asleep first."

Val smiled. He stood and offered Sydney his hand. They left the Kleines Cafe and walked back to the hotel.

They ended up not needing room service.

*

The next morning, Val and Sydney slept late. Sydney didn't have to be at the OSCE until one p.m., and Val had no obligations at all.

Sydney woke up first. She took a long shower, lingering beneath the warm water as she thought about the day ahead. She was nervous about her meet with Nicolae for all the normal reasons: Would the Moldovan execute his SDR well enough? Would they get away with a clean, unobserved meeting? What, if anything, would he be able to tell her about Abakumov?

Then there was Val. What had seemed like a great and romantic idea two weeks ago – having him in Vienna with her – was now a complication. Could she pull off the meeting with Nicolae without Val knowing about it?

Finally, she and Val had yet to deal with things. She was still angry about his interference with Abakumov. She blamed Val for the arms dealer's death. And he'd damn near gotten himself killed. If not for Alexei…

Alexei.

She would have to deal with the topic of Alexei. Val hadn't mentioned it yet. He didn't seem to be acting like someone who was about to turn her in to counterintelligence. But he would have questions. She would have to tell Val everything. It would be uncomfortable. He may never forgive her.

She wanted to just stay in the shower and not face any of it.

But Val interrupted.

"Hey, baby. I need to piss," he said through the door.

Sydney turned off the shower. "Sure," she said as she grabbed a towel. "Give me one minute."

Val kissed Sydney on the cheek as she left the bathroom.

She stood at the window looking out at the City Park. She heard the toilet flush and then the sound of the shower.

Sydney paced around the hotel room in a robe, rehearsing in her head the surveillance detection route she would take to the meet with Nicolae. It was easier to think about that than the conversation she needed to have with Val.

She was lost in thought on the other side of the room when Val stepped out of the bathroom.

"How about room service?"

"Sure," she said, turning to face him.

He was naked and smiling, the handset of the bedside phone in one hand, the other on his hip.

A pang of desire ran through Sydney. She welcomed it as it pushed away all other concerns.

Val leaned over and touched the number for room service. Sydney studied the way his oblique muscles flared and tightened, holding his upper body over the bedside table.

"Yes, good morning," he said, straightening and winking at Sydney. "I'd like to order some breakfast, please."

Sydney was drawn to him. She started toward Val, walking slowly as he ordered.

"Two of your Parisian omelets with roasted potatoes," he said, watching Sydney approach. "An order of croissants. No, make that a double order of croissants. Could you also bring extra butter and preserves? Oh, and some honey. Please tell me you guys have honey?" He paused. "Great, thank you. And we'll need some sparkling water and a pot of coffee."

Sydney smiled. Val knew she loved honey with her croissants. She untied her robe as she crossed the room in his direction.

"That's great," Val said into the phone as he watched Sydney's robe open. It swayed left and right as she approached him, offering glimpses of her. "We'll be here. Thank you."

Val hung up the phone and turned to Sydney, who was now standing in front of him.

She smiled at his arousal.

"They said about thirty minutes."

"Perfect," Sydney said, letting her robe fall to the floor.

*

After they had eaten and pushed the room service cart out into the hallway, they lay in bed. Sydney rested her head on Val's chest. She ran her finger along the scar on Val's abdomen.

About an inch and a half long, it was still pink and puffy, unlike the older scars scattered across Val's body, which had flattened and faded with time.

"Did it hurt?"

"Not really," he said, running his fingers through her hair. "Not in the moment. I was too full of adrenaline."

"Were you scared?"

"Yeah. I thought I was going to die."

"I'm so glad you didn't," Sydney said, taking her hand off Val's scar and hugging him.

"Me too."

Sydney kissed his chest.

They lay in silence for a few minutes.

Val sat up. Sydney propped herself up on an elbow and placed her hand on his.

"What is it?" she asked him.

"You know the clearest thought I had on the back of that boat?" Val looked down at their hands.

Sydney waited for him to continue.

"How the fuck did I get here?"

Sydney fought the urge to say, "By being an impetuous dumbass."

"I mean, I know how I got there, as a practical question. But I mean big picture. How did I end up in the army? How did I end up in intelligence?"

Val shook his head.

"If I'm honest with myself," he said, lifting his eyes to meet Sydney's concerned gaze, "I think I went into the army because of my uncle. I looked up to him so much, and he was in the army. So, you know? Maybe I should join the army."

Val shrugged.

Sydney nodded. She knew the basics of that time in Val's life. She knew he'd lived with his uncle and had admired him a great deal before he died.

"There was also a desire for adventure or challenge, I think. Then I got bored as a peacetime tanker and the program seemed like a cool thing to do. Then, after 9/11, it was about serving with my buddies, my comrades. Helping to win, saving lives. There is a part of me that is dedicated to the fight, a hundred percent. That was probably the part that got me stuck on the back of a yacht in the Black Sea with Chechen thugs about to cut my balls off. But then there is a part of me that feels like I got into all this by accident, because I loved my uncle. And now I keep going just out of… habit?"

There was a pleading in his eyes that saddened Sydney.

"Like its all really just habit?"

"All of what?"

"All of it."

Sydney smiled, not knowing what to say.

"Anyway." Val shifted his body to sit straight against the headboard. "It's just…"

"What?"

"I'm going on this rotation with Tony. Then I don't know what's going to happen. I don't know what I'm going to do."

"Why do you have to go back to Iraq? You've done enough. Seen enough. Why can't you get a safe, stateside banishment from the program?"

Val smiled at the comment.

"I could."

"So, why?" she asked, urgency in her voice. "If it's all just habit, why the hell go back to the meat grinder?"

"Tony," Val said with a weary smile.

"Tony?"

"He's my friend. He's going back for one last shot at Razzaq. I want to go help him."

Sydney shook her head, surprised by the emotion welling within her. She fought it back.

"We've both agreed it's our last tour," Val said. "He'll be close to twenty years when he gets back. He'll put in his retirement papers and ride off in the sunset."

"And you?"

Val shrugged again. "I'm not sure yet."

"You can't quit. You've only got about five years left to get your pension. Again, why can't you find a quiet bullshit job somewhere in the States and let the clock run out?"

"I might do that," Val said without conviction.

Sydney shook her head, frustrated.

"There is one thing I can tell you, with certainty, that I'd do when I got back. If it were possible."

"And what's that?"

"I'd run away with you," Val said, a smile breaking across his face. "Run away to Prague, maybe. Live there and let it all burn."

Sydney smiled also.

"I know you won't do it," Val said with sadness. "But I would. I just want you to know that I would. I mean it."

Sydney put her hand to his cheek rather than saying what she was thinking. Val said it for her.

"I know that you wouldn't do it."

"No," Sydney said, her hand still on Val's cheek. "Not yet."

"Not yet?"

Sydney smiled and put her hand down.

"What does 'not yet' mean?"

She shrugged. "I'm not done yet. I still have goals. Professional goals that are going to take me a while to achieve. And after that, when I'm done, I want to travel."

"Travel? All we do is travel."

"Yeah, but it's all work right now. I'm different from you. I can't really appreciate it while I'm working. You can. You see that damn bridge in Prague for what it is every time you walk over it. There are just so many places I want to go. To see. To really see."

She looked at him with sad eyes.

"I'm sorry. I'm just trying to be as honest as I can."

"It's okay. I'm just trying to be honest also. When I'm done, I'm gonna be done. I'm not shagging my ass around the world anymore. I'm going to get a dog and settle down and…"

Val hesitated.

"And what?"

"And wait for you to join me."

Sydney smiled.

"Well, I can't tell you when," she said, leaning in to kiss him, "but that day will come."

"I hope so."

Sydney got out of bed. "I've got to pee. Be right back."

Sydney took deep breaths in the bathroom. She felt the press of time. It was going to be a long day with lots of moving pieces. She'd been forcing herself to be focused on Val, but her impending meet with Nicolae and the SDR she had to execute to get there were weighing on her. *Ten more minutes in bed, then I've got to get moving,* she thought.

Sydney washed her hands and splashed water on her face before returning to bed.

She looked at Val as she got under the sheets. He had a faraway look on his face.

"What are you thinking about?"

Val didn't look at her. "What happened between you and Alexei in Kyiv?"

Sydney was caught off guard by the question. She knew they had to talk about it. She wanted to talk about it. But she wasn't ready for the sudden swerve into the topic.

Val waited for her to speak.

"What did he say happened?"

Val shook his head in disappointment.

"Please don't cat-and-mouse me, Sydney. Just tell me what's going on."

"He met me in Kyiv. During 9/11. I was coming out of the embassy after a forty-eight-hour shift, and he was there waiting."

Val was silent.

Sydney shrugged. "That's what happened."

"Why?"

"After 9/11, the Russians were trying to send the same 'we had nothing to do with it' message through every official and nonofficial channel they could find."

Val nodded skeptically.

"So, he surprised you, delivered the message, and left?" Val said, watching Sydney closely.

She met his gaze but didn't speak.

"Then you turned and went back to the station to report it, right?" he added, his eyes still locked on her.

Sydney hesitated.

Val nodded slowly.

Sydney looked at her hands.

"You never reported it," Val said flatly.

This was not going the way Sydney had wanted.

"I did not."

They sat motionless and naked on the bed. Sydney had pulled the sheets up to cover herself. Val sat with his arms crossed.

They both looked straight ahead at nothing.

"You fucked him."

Sydney didn't answer.

"Didn't you?"

"Yes. We had sex."

Val rubbed his eyes.

"It was six years ago." There was no pleading or apology in her voice. She was stating facts. "You and I were not," Sydney sighed, "whatever we are now."

She glanced at Val. He continued to stare straight ahead. There was a hardness in his face that made her uncomfortable.

"It was that one night. And we have not been in contact since. Nothing."

Val nodded.

"I guess you've gotten really good at beating the polygraph," he said, turning to look at her.

Val got out of bed before Sydney could respond.

"What are you doing?"

"I'm going for a walk," he said, pulling on his jeans.

"Please don't be like that."

Val yanked on his T-shirt.

"You promised me," he said, emotion creeping into his voice.

"What?" Sydney asked sharply.

"You promised me you'd never see him again."

"Oh, we're going to talk promises now?" She jumped out of bed.

Sydney stood naked, one fist clenched, one hand pointing at Val, who was across the room from her, pulling on his socks.

"You promised me!" she yelled.

The sudden rage in her voice startled Val. He looked up from his feet.

Sydney took several steps toward Val. "Or do you not remember?" she said through clenched teeth. "You looked me in the eye and promised me you wouldn't go after Abakumov."

Val stood, a single sock in his right hand.

"You're right. I did. But this is different."

"Oh, really?" Sydney put her hands on her hips.

"Yes! It is!"

Val threw the single sock to the floor.

"That was work," he said, his voice trembling with anger. "That was saving lives. Not screwing a foreign intelligence officer."

"Oh, fuck you." Sydney walked past Val to the bathroom. She grabbed a robe off the back of the door and jerked it on. When she'd tied the sash around her waist, she looked back at Val.

They held each other's gaze for a moment, each of them breathing heavily with anger.

"What I did was stupid," Val said. "I know that, but—"

"You promised me! You promised me you wouldn't mess with Abakumov."

"I did. And I'm sorry I had to break that promise."

"Had to break?" Sydney's voice rose. "Had to break?"

"The situation demanded something be done!" Val matched her volume. "Had I known what the future held, I wouldn't have made that promise."

"Got it. I see now. Next time you give me your word, I'll just have to remember it comes with your standard caveat. Depends on what the future holds."

"Like I said." Val's voice took on a low growl as he tried to control his emotions. "What I did was stupid. But it wasn't wrong. What you did..." His voice trailed off as he struggled to control his temper. He closed his eyes. "What you did was wrong."

"What I did was a onetime thing, years ago."

"But it wasn't a onetime thing, was it? That's the problem!"

"Fine," Sydney said, with a dismissive wave. "Even so. It was between two consenting adults. Done and forgotten. What you did blew up years of work by multiple governments and agencies to eliminate a global threat permanently. And for what? For the selfish gratification of Val Rafter."

Val shook his head and bent over to put on the last sock.

"You broke your promise to me for the same reason you do everything else,"

Sydney continued. "You're incapable of putting anyone else's point of view before your own. It always has to break your way, your cause, your worldview."

Val took her onslaught in silence. He straightened and met her angry stare with his own.

"I mean, seriously?" Her voice descended to a normal volume. "When have you ever put someone else before what you wanted to do?"

"Oh, I don't know. How about the first time you fucked a Russian intelligence agent?"

"Yeah." Her voice was low with hurt and anger. "Maybe you should've just turned me in. Would have made my life a lot simpler."

Val leaned over to grab his shoes. Sydney leaned against the bathroom doorway and watched as he walked over to a chair, sat down, and put them on.

Val stood from the chair.

"I'm going for a walk."

"I've got to go to work soon," Sydney said as she watched him cross the room to grab his jacket.

He didn't respond.

"Val?" she called as he opened the door to leave.

Val hesitated.

"I wanted to talk about these things. But not like this. Not so angry. I do love you. I'm looking forward to dinner tonight."

Val said nothing, his eyes fixed on the floor.

He'd made reservations for them for that evening at a small restaurant on the outer edge of the eleventh district. An agency friend who had spent a few years working out of the station in Vienna had recommended it. The friend had said it was the most romantic place for dinner in all of Vienna. Sydney and Val had been excited to go.

"I don't know," Val said.

"Well, I'll be there."

Val turned and left.

CHAPTER 65

Sydney walked beneath the snow-laden tree branches into the softly lit Christmas market in the University of Vienna's large courtyard. Snow flurries drifted down from the dark, cloudy sky while the smell of pastries and spiced wine filled the air. The closely set, temporary wooden stalls were decorated with white Christmas lights that hung like icicles from their roofs. Smiling vendors stood behind their wares: Christmas decorations, wooden crafts, winter mittens, hats, scarves, warm food and drink.

Sydney stopped at one of the stalls. She picked up a hand-carved nutcracker and pretended to examine it as she nonchalantly checked behind her.

No one.

Good.

That confirmed her long SDR had been successful. She'd arrived without surveillance. She put the nutcracker down and continued along the narrow row of market stalls for the final twenty meters until it opened into a small courtyard area. A dozen slim high-top tables sat in the middle of a small gathering area created by a ring of wooden stalls.

Sydney smiled for the first time since her fight with Val. The spot was ideal for a meet. For starters, it was a near-perfect intrusion point with several entry and exit points. Someone surveilling Sydney would have to enter the faux courtyard—impossible without her noticing. Next, the close quarters of the space offered the perfect hidden-in-plain-sight cover. Sitting at one of the centermost tables, the voices and laughter of the other folks in the courtyard would make electronic eavesdropping nearly impossible, and she and Nicolae would be unrecognizable in the throng of people, all bundled in coats and hats against the cold.

Sydney checked her watch. It was almost 1830 hours. Nicolae should be here momentarily. She purchased two glühweins from one of the vendor stalls and walked back to the center of the courtyard. Leaning against one of the high-top tables, she pushed a spiced wine to the other side in anticipation of Nicolae's arrival. Sydney then took a sip of her hot beverage and waited.

Made with red wine, oranges, cloves, and cinnamon, glühwein always struck Sydney as too sweet. This one tasted good, though. Probably because of its warmth. The SDR had been a cold slog of walking, taxis, and subways through Vienna.

The couple at the table next to her laughed. Sydney watched as they leaned into each other and kissed.

An ache ran through her as she thought of Val. The SDR, as long and tedious as it was, had been a respite from thinking of their fight. SDRs had always been like that for Sydney, disconnecting her from whatever was going on and staking her perceptions in the present. But seeing the couple embrace, lips pressed together, hands seeking and pulling, made Sydney sad.

Why is it so hard for us?

Sydney shook her head and took another sip of glühwein. There would be time to make peace or more war with Val later tonight.

It was time to focus. She ran through her questions for Nicolae in her head again.

Five minutes later, Sydney was still alone.

She was getting anxious. Nicolae should be here by now.

After another few minutes, Sydney grew angry. Steam no longer rose from the neglected glühwein she'd bought for Nicolae.

Where the hell is he?

At 1810 hours, Sydney took a swallow of her cooling spiced wine.

"Shit," she said under her breath. She tightened her scarf and walked out of the small courtyard.

Standing operating procedure dictated Sydney only wait for Nicolae for ten minutes. If he didn't show, the procedure was to leave the meeting site and return exactly one hour later.

She walked out of the Christmas market, cursing to herself.

Nicolae must have run into difficulty on his SDR or, worse, detected surveillance and aborted.

Sydney wouldn't know until an hour from now, after another SDR, when he either showed or did not.

There was no way to get in touch with Nicolae now to ask what the situation was. Both he and Sydney would be running "dark" with their cell phones off and batteries removed.

Sydney winced as she thought of Val.

She had no way of letting him know she would now be late for dinner.

She took a deep breath and pushed Val from her mind as she rounded the corner out of the market and put herself back into surveillance detection mode.

The snow fell harder as she turned the corner.

Perfect.

*

Sydney returned to the small market courtyard fifty-five minutes later. She scanned the area as she walked to the glühwein kiosk and purchased two more spiced wines.

No Nicolae.

Sydney tried not to get anxious or irritated. She was cold from walking the SDR and looked forward to the warm liquid, no matter how sweet.

She stepped through a few occupied high-top tables to the middle of the courtyard and sat at the last open table.

Sydney took a large sip of glühwein and let out a sigh as it warmed her from the inside. She was preparing to take another sip as Nicolae stepped into the courtyard.

He spotted Sydney immediately.

She nodded to him, and he wove through the other tables in her direction.

Sydney gestured at the glühwein as he stepped up to the table.

"Thank you," he said, wrapping his hands around the warm cup.

Sydney waited as Nicolae raised the glühwein and took a sip.

"What happened?" she asked as he set the cup down.

"I thought I was being followed," he said in a hushed voice.

"Were you?" Sydney asked, already knowing the answer. Had Nicolae determined he was being followed, he would have aborted the meet.

"I don't think so."

"What do you mean you don't *think* so?" Anger crept into her voice. "If you have any doubt, this meeting is over."

"No. I am certain. I did everything you trained me to do. I am clean."

Sydney held his gaze for a moment, looking for certainty in his eyes.

Satisfied, she nodded.

"What happened to Abakumov?"

Nicolae looked around the courtyard quickly before saying, "First we talk about me."

Sydney's eyebrows arched.

"What?"

"First, we talk about me. I'm done. I want to go to America with my wife."

Sydney fought the urge to scream.

"Nicolae," she said in a quiet and measured voice. "We'll discuss this another time, when we're not so pressed for—"

"No!" Nicolae leaned forward over the table. His eyes met Sydney's. "It's always later. This is my life. My family's life. I am telling you, I am done. We will discuss it now!"

The emotion in his voice forced Sydney to change her approach. Had they been meeting in a safer, more secluded location, she would have laid into him. But they could not cause a scene in the small market. She had to placate him, get the information she needed, and do both quickly. A meeting like this should last no more than ten to fifteen minutes. Any longer risked discovery, no matter how thorough the SDR.

"Okay. Let's discuss it."

"Is simple," Nicolae said, glaring at Sydney. "It has been seven years. I have done good work. Done everything asked of me. But I am finished now. I have earned passage to America. You must honor your promise to me. My family must be safe."

Sydney nodded slowly. She'd promised him more than once that she would help him get to America when the time was right.

"You have done good work, Nicolae. Great work, as a matter of fact. But I have always been honest with you. These things are never up to me alone. You must know that."

"Don't tell me that. You have done well in your career. I have watched you be promoted. You have authority. You must fight for me, Sydney!"

Sydney gestured at him to settle down.

"I do fight for you." She reached and took his hand in hers.

Sydney had trained Nicolae from the beginning that their opposite genders were an advantage, that people observing them together would be prone to interpret them as furtive lovers. This would give them plausible cover for their meetings, and they could likely get away with things that two males or two females would not. She trained him to use that dynamic, to foster the interpretation through appearances. They had to be affectionate when together.

Nicolae leaned in and put his hand on her cheek. The gesture seemed loving, but his eyes were narrow and accusatory. "You promise me?"

"Of course."

"No. Don't say it if you don't mean it. Do you promise me?"

"Yes, Nicolae. I promise. I'll make it happen." Sydney held his gaze, her voice steady and assured.

Nicolae studied her face.

Sydney looked back at him, trying not to let her anger and shame leak onto her face.

"Okay," Nicolae said, dropping his hand and taking a sip of glühwein. "Thank you."

Sydney looked at her watch. They were burning time in the open. Also, Val would be getting to the restaurant about now.

She would not.

She pushed the thought of Val away.

"Nicolae," she said, voice low. "What happened to Abakumov?"

Nicolae leaned in over the table and took Sydney's hands in his. He tilted his head forward as if beckoning to kiss her. She eased toward him until he kissed her gently on the cheek. He slid his lips to her ear and kissed her again.

"The Russians," he whispered.

"The Russians?"

"Yes."

"But he was their guy. Are you sure?"

"Without question," Nicolae said, still nuzzling against her cheek. "What we have heard is the Russians told him to cool off for a while after the incident with

Val and let the attention pass. But Abakumov was still trying to find a buyer for his arms shipment. We heard he was talking to Muslim buyers in Chechnya or Dagestan."

"Greedy son of a bitch." Sydney kissed Nicolae's cheek and they parted, cold air replacing the warmth of his skin. She shook her head at Abakumov's impudence.

Nicolae nodded.

The Russians were always concerned about the Muslim fundamentalist element smoldering in the southern republics of the Russian Federation, an area they viewed as a potential contagion of instability that had to be managed with an iron fist. If Abakumov had even glanced in that direction, it would have incensed his Russian partners. If he'd actually tried to sell arms to fundamentalist Muslims operating in the southern republics, Sydney could see the Russians killing him.

"Why the hell would he do that?" Sydney was exhausted by the thought of starting over. It had taken her years to orchestrate the constellation of sources and monitoring structures around Abakumov, and what she'd created was working. She knew almost every move he made and was gaining insight into the more distant strands of his global web. Even those that extended into Russia. With just six more months, she would have been able to make some aggressive moves. Moves that would have done real damage to Russia's illicit arms activity and set her already rising professional star on a course for greatness.

But it was all gone now.

Nicolae shrugged. "I have seen this before. Arms traffickers that live long enough travel one of two roads. The first is paranoia. They end up trusting no one, fearful of their own plotting shadow. This road leads to insanity. The other path is arrogance. They are lucky long enough to believe they are untouchable, that they are a master of the game and can get away with anything. This path leads to death. Every time."

Nicolae released Sydney's hands and picked up his glühwein.

"This arrogance was Abakumov's downfall." He raised his mug of spiced wine in a toasting gesture. "May he rot in hell now."

Sydney drank with Nicolae.

"Do you guys know anything about who ordered it?" she asked after putting her mug down.

"No. Nothing specific. But we know that they killed him in his home."

"But the reports I read said his body was discovered on the streets in Sofia."

"That is true. But I have sources in the Bulgarian police. They searched his house and found signs of a struggle and torture. His DNA was found in some of the blood. It looks like whoever got Abakumov went to his dacha, subdued and killed his guards, and then tortured and killed him before taking his body away from there."

Sydney nodded as she thought it through. "Makes sense. Abakumov would have let Russians in, not realizing what they were really there to do."

Nicolae nodded.

"What about Abakumov's businesses? Who will take over? The Russians will need an outlet to replace him."

"And they will find one, I am sure. There are dozens of arms dealers who would love to fill that niche in the market."

"Well, we're going to need to know who does."

Nicolae caught the edge creeping into Sydney's voice. He nodded. "Of course. I already have sources working on this. When the successor emerges, we will know."

"You better." Sydney looked at her watch.

Nicolae checked the time as well. He walked around the small table and put his arm around Sydney. He bent his head down toward her. "We have not talked about Val," he said, unable to suppress his smile.

Sydney tensed.

"What about him?" She forced himself to smile back.

"Did US government really send him in after Abakumov alone like that? Was big mistake."

"No!" Sydney said, with more force than she wanted. She corrected herself. "Truthfully, I don't know. But, come on, did that look like how we do business?"

Nicolae chuckled. "Well, certainly not how *you* do business."

The sudden mention of Val irritated her, reminding her how late she was going to be to their dinner.

She was also frustrated by Nicolae. The US government had, of course, responded to all the international chatter about Val with: "No comment." She would not add to her problems by providing an official confirmation regarding

Val. Nicolae was a good agent, though. And good agents worked their handlers as well.

"I don't know what Val was up to. But you remember how he is, don't you?" Nicolae chuckled.

"I do. I liked him very much. But I thought he was a little crazy."

"Well, you were wrong. He is totally crazy."

"Yes." Nicolae nodded, smiling. "I suppose he is." He reached across the table to grab his glühwein and took another sip, his face clouded with concern. "Val is okay, though? I heard that he had been hurt very badly."

"From what I know, yes. I heard he is okay."

"That is good. His photo is everywhere now, though. Russians, arms dealers, allies. Now everyone knows Val is spy."

"I don't know about all that," Sydney said with a shrug, trying not to give Nicolae anything.

Nicolae nodded. He took his arm from around Sydney and said, "Please tell him I said hello, if you get the chance."

"I don't think I'll get the chance. We're not really in touch."

Nicolae's head tilted at the comment. He studied Sydney's face for a moment. But he didn't pursue it.

Sydney looked at her watch. It was time.

"We've been here too long." She put her hand on Nicolae's shoulder and looked him in the eyes.

Nicolae put his hands on her waist.

They kissed and then hugged each other. Sydney nuzzled into Nicolae's scarf and whispered into his ear, "Make it a long SDR. Be double sure you're clear."

"I will." Sydney released him and tried to turn to leave, but Nicolae held on. He pulled her in tightly and whispered in her ear. "You promised me, Sydney. I want out. And you promised me. Do not forget. I will not. The clock starts now."

Sydney tried to respond. But Nicolae kissed her on the lips and turned abruptly to leave.

*

It took Sydney a little more than an hour to execute her surveillance detection route. She turned her cell phone back on just as she walked into the restaurant to meet Val. There were no voice mails or texts from him. Nothing.

Sydney looked at her watch. She was an hour and a half late. She scanned the restaurant, but already knew that Val wasn't there.

Sydney went back to their hotel. Val was not there either and all his stuff was gone.

Sighing heavily, she opened a bottle of wine and started the shower.

CHAPTER 66

"I appreciate the detailed report, Sydney," the deputy director said. He sat in a large meeting room in Langley with several senior members of the CIA's counter-proliferation team.

"Of course, sir. I wish I had better news."

Sydney was sitting alone in a secure briefing room in the Vienna CIA station the day after meeting with Nicolae. Three large monitors hung on the wall on the opposite side of the conference table from her. Two of the screens showed the deputy director and his team. On the other, Kovack sat in his secure conference room in Budapest. Sydney tried to ignore him.

"Me too," the deputy director said. "We were starting to really get close with Abakumov. Close to being able to do something meaningful."

Sydney tried to think of a good response, something other than "I'm sorry."

The deputy director shook his head as he stood up. He looked at the camera without smiling and said, "That will be all, Miss Knox."

Langley's screens went blank before she could answer.

Sydney sat motionless, stewing in frustration and anger.

"Why don't you take the rest of the week off?" Kovack said with genuine concern in his voice. "Get rested. Get some perspective. Start back fresh on Monday."

"No, thanks, sir." Sydney pushed back from the table and stood up. "I've got too much shit to do. I'll be back in the office tomorrow."

The expression of sympathy from Kovack enraged her. She took deep breaths and methodically shoved folders into her briefcase to settle her temper and avoided looking at the monitor with his image on it.

"What about your agent?" Kovack asked her after a moment.

"What about him?"

"His request to exit. To immigrate with his family to the US."

"Um, yeah. We'll see. Let's discuss that when I get back, sir."

Sydney killed the video call before Kovack could respond. She slumped back into her chair in the briefing room. The mention of Nicolae and his desire to be done, to leave Moldova, had struck her unexpectedly deep. From her perspective, Nicolae was right. He'd earned it. He should be allowed to quit the work and immigrate to the States. Sydney could not help but smile at the thought—the Muntenaus would make a terrific American family.

Her smile was short-lived. She leaned forward, elbows on the table, and put her head in her hands. Abakumov was dead and his demise put a stink on her inside the agency. She had to start over. Fast. Otherwise, her ascent through the CIA was finished. The thought exhausted and angered her.

She could do it. Of that, she had no doubt.

But a deep shiver of shame and guilt ran through her. She needed Nicolae more than ever now. She could not let him go. She would not help him.

Sydney sat alone in the dimly lit secure briefing room for an hour, laying out for herself all the reasons it was okay. Why she was not terrible. Why Mr. Wall and the rest of the CIA machine would approve. Hell, they would be proud of her.

She was not proud of herself.

CHAPTER 67

27 February 2014

2237 Hours

The Black Sea

"Excuse me for a moment, Val," Alexei said, standing from the table. "I need to speak with the ship's captain. I will be right back."

Val watched Alexei leave through the forward door to the left of the bar. Peskov, sitting on one of the barstools, avoided eye contact as Val scanned the bar. The bartender looked down at the glass he was cleaning.

Val looked back at Alexei's empty seat. The switchblade lay in front of the chair.

"Do it," Zakir said to Val.

Val turned his head to the right, away from the knife and locked eyes with Zakir.

"Hey, boss, I'm sorry, but he grabbed knife," Zakir said in a singsong voice with a shrug of the shoulders. "So I shot his fucking head off."

"You got it all figured out, Clausewitz," Val said, shaking his head.

"Will not be so long now, cowboy." Zakir traced a finger across his own neck.

The mercenary next to Zakir chuckled.

"Fuck you," Val said before looking away.

Staring out one of the dark windows, Val tried to estimate how long they had been underway. They had taken his watch when they captured him. But he thought it had been at least an hour. That would put them well on their way to Crimea, where Val guessed they were heading.

Alexei stepped back into the room, closing the door behind him.

Val watched as Alexei whispered to Peskov and then returned to their table.

"Did you think of another toast?" Alexei asked cheerfully.

"No. I'm over toasts. Where the hell are we going?"

Alexei's smile faded.

He shook his head, declining to comment on Val's question. Instead, he picked up the bottle and poured bourbon into each of their shot glasses.

"Seriously, Alexei," Val said. "What is going on? This is a hell of a lot of trouble to go through to settle a personal score."

Alexei shook his head in disappointment. "Personal? The only thing personal tonight is here at this table."

Alexei leaned back and spread his arms wide. "All of this? The work and effort that takes place tonight? This is all professional, Val. This is my job. This is Peskov's job. This is their job." He pointed at the junior intelligence officer and the mercenaries.

He leaned forward again, reaching across and jabbing his finger into the table in front of Val. "But this? This conversation and whiskey together at this table? This is personal. This is my gesture to you. To our friendship. Something that I, for one, still very much value!" Alexei's voice was rising.

"This table is brotherhood!" he yelled as he stood and pounded his fist on the table. "The rest is politics!" Standing over Val, Alexei waved his hands around at the *Monarch* and the rest of the world.

The mercenaries leaned forward, hands on their weapons, uncertain where this was going.

"I was in Prague minding my own fucking business!" Val yelled back, also coming to his feet. "I was done with all of it. I was out!"

"Yes! So I heard. And yet here you are." Alexei leaned across the table, pointing at Val's chest. "You don't get to choose when you are out! None of us do. You are not special. You cannot take this so personal. Why? Why do you do that?"

Val seethed. His breath came in angry heaves. He hauled back and punched Alexei hard in the face.

Alexei stumbled back, surprised by the strike.

Val lunged across the table, trying to get to the switchblade, but was intercepted by Zakir.

The two men crashed to the deck, Zakir on top.

Zakir drove his forearm into the back of Val's head.

Val's nose broke against the polished wooden deck. Blood gushed and spread onto the floor.

Zakir jammed his knee into Val's kidney. Val grunted in pain, air leaving his lungs.

Maintaining pressure on the back of Val's head with one arm, Zakir pulled a large combat knife from his belt with his other hand.

He raised the knife to drive it into the back of Val's neck.

"Stop!" Alexei shouted. He pulled his pistol as he moved to stand over Zakir and Val.

Zakir hesitated, taking his eyes off the back of Val's neck for an instant to make eye contact with Alexei.

"You kill him now, and I will kill you," Alexei said in a measured voice.

Zakir looked from Alexei's pistol to Val and back.

"I mean it," Alexei said.

Zakir cursed in Chechen. He put all his weight on Val's head as he lifted himself up. Val grimaced. More blood flowed from his nose.

Val lay on the floor, panting, as Zakir sheathed his knife and walked back to the bar.

Alexei holstered the pistol behind his back, righted the table and picked up the chairs. He snatched the red cloth from the floor and spread it back on the table. The bottle of bourbon and switchblade had bounced across the room in opposite directions. Alexei walked over to the knife first and then to the bottle of whiskey. The bottle was still intact. Cap secure. Alexei gestured at the bartender as he walked back to the table.

Alexei sat down, placing the bottle and knife on the table in front of him. He felt his left cheek, which had already begun to swell from Val's punch. Alexei glanced at Val and shook his head like an exasperated parent.

The bartender brought two fresh glasses. Alexei leaned back in his seat and gently prodded his bruised left eye.

"You see, Zakir?" Alexei said. "It's not just you. Anyone around Val long enough gets punched in the face."

Zakir didn't laugh.

Val picked himself up. Holding his nose and leaning his head back, he plodded to the table and sat opposite Alexei.

Alexei looked at the bartender and pointed at Val.

The bartender brought Val a clean white hand towel, which Val took and held to his nose.

Val looked at Alexei from behind the white hand towel he held against his nose. After a long moment, he said, "You're not the first person to tell me this."

"To tell you what?"

"That I should not take it all so personally."

"Whoever told you this was right. So, why do you?"

"At some point, it becomes personal or meaningless," Val said. "And I couldn't bear it if it was meaningless."

Alexei's eyes narrowed slightly.

"You make no sense to me," he said, shaking his head slowly. "Do you not see? If it all just becomes personal, then there is no meaning to any of it…and that I could not bear, my friend."

Val shrugged.

Alexei sat motionless, his shoulders slumped.

Peskov and the bartender looked at their boss with his downturned gaze and shared a quick troubled glance. What next tonight?

A long moment passed before Alexei sat straight. He shook his head as if shaking off the cold and then opened the bottle of bourbon. He poured two full shots. Placing the bottle in the middle of the table, he slid one shot glass across to Val.

"Okay, then," he said, picking up his glass of whiskey and raising it to Val. "To the shit we take personally."

Val lowered the white hand towel. A red stain bloomed from its center where he'd pressed it to his nose. He grabbed his shot glass and knocked it against Alexei's.

They both drank.

CHAPTER 68

29 April 2008

Mosul, Iraq

The task force was exhausted. They had gone outside the wire on missions to grab Kzem Moussa ten nights in a row with no success.

Val's anxiety ramped up with each mission. Every afternoon during the mission brief, he berated himself for letting Moussa go. Then, at night, outside the wire, when things got kinetic, he held his breath until the bullets stopped flying. He was terrified someone would get wounded, or worse, while chasing the high-value target he'd let go. Each day, Val woke up more tense than he had been the day before. And he went to bed more tense than when he woke up.

Some of the missions did net valuable targets, but never Moussa. They didn't even have any leads. At all. He had vanished.

Mac seemed not to have slept since the night they let Moussa go. Dark circles hung beneath his bloodshot eyes, and a rash had broken out beneath the straps of his glasses. Standing in the middle of the operations center, coffee cup in hand, staring at the big screens, Mac looked to Val as if he'd lost weight. Val avoided eye contact with the exhausted Ranger; his guilt and anger at letting Moussa go wouldn't let him look at the man.

Not comfortable with the signs of deep fatigue he saw throughout the team, Ramos told everyone to take a down day. Most in the task force embraced it, grateful for a chance to rest. Val, though, felt his anxiety rise. The op tempo for the past ten days had been brutal, but it monopolized his time and demanded his attention, helping him keep his mind off an idea that he'd been trying to push away almost since the moment he'd learned he let Moussa go. It festered within him, rising to the top each morning, and calling to him as he fell asleep each night.

Mac also had a problem with the down day. It never occurred to him that it might apply to him as well. When one of his ops sergeants suggested that it did, Mac ignored him.

When Ramos heard Mac was still on duty, he grabbed one of the military policemen assigned to the task force area and walked into the ops center.

"Come with me, Captain," Ramos said, in a voice that made it clear even to Mac's exhausted brain that negotiation was not possible.

Ramos and the MP escorted Mac to his quarters.

"Do not let this man leave his quarters for the next twenty-four hours except to go to the chow hall or latrine," Ramos told the MP as Mac hesitated at the door. "Do you understand me?"

The MP glanced at Mac and then nodded to Ramos.

"Yes, sir."

Ramos turned to Mac. "Listen," he said, putting his hand on the exhausted captain's shoulder. "Don't fuck with me on this. If you don't rest for twenty-four hours, your next stop is the hospital, where I'll have you sedated. We clear?"

Mac nodded.

"Say it," Ramos insisted.

"Clear, sir." He entered his room and shut the door behind him.

Val didn't have the ability to shut it out.

He and Tony slept late and went to the gym. Val hoped it would keep the thoughts at bay. It didn't work, though. Later that afternoon, preoccupation blanketed his face as he sat in the mess hall with Tony, enjoying a full cup of soft-serve chocolate ice cream.

"What the hell is up with you, man?" Tony asked him.

"What?"

"What the hell is up with you?" Tony repeated, irritation hardening his words.

"Nothing." Val shook his head. "Nothing. Just tired, is all."

"Bullshit. Are you cycling about Sydney again?"

"Yeah," Val lied. Not ready to share what he was really thinking, what he wanted to do. "Yeah. I'm sorry, man. Just can't shake it today."

"Dude." Tony put his head in his hands and then slowly rubbed his eyes. "I can't do this with you today. I've told you what I think. I'm just fucking sick of talking about it."

"I know," Val said, grateful for the out. He stood slowly. "You've been a good friend. I really appreciate it. I think I'm going to take a walk around the airfield. Clear my mind."

"Okay."

Val put his tray on the drop-off and walked out of the mess hall.

Piercing sunlight hit him in the face. It was early afternoon, there were no clouds in the sky, and it was hot. *Perfect.* Val set out walking. *Maybe the heat will burn this dumb idea away.*

An hour and a half later, soaked in sweat, Val had been unable to talk himself out of it. He hadn't been able to resolve all his doubts, either. Nonetheless, he walked into the little AAFES shoppette near the mess hall and bought a throwaway cell phone with sixty minutes of talk time in cash.

Stepping back into the hot sun, Val held the flip phone in his hand. He sat down on a plastic bench just outside the shoppette and leaned forward on his knees. Holding the small device in both hands, he typed in the phone number he'd memorized years ago. For some reason, it had stuck with him.

Perhaps, for this purpose, for this day.

Val started mashing numbers with his thumb, typing in the message. A few minutes later, it was done. Val sat straight and read it a few times to make sure he'd phrased it correctly.

He wiped the sweat from his forehead as he stared at the handful of words. Soldiers came and went from the mess hall and the shoppette, walking little more than an arm's length from Val as he sat, hesitating on the bench. What was he waiting for?

"Afternoon, sir," a voice called.

Val looked up. He recognized the two soldiers from the task force and gave them a wave. They were young Rangers, in their early twenties, Val guessed. One was tall with reddish hair, and the other was shorter, maybe five foot five, with black hair and a Hispanic influence. They were squad mates and friends and spent nearly every waking moment together. Combat or downtime like now, Val didn't remember ever seeing them apart. Even on missions.

"Enjoying your down day, sir?" the shorter one asked in a friendly voice as they walked by. He was the more sociable of the pair. The tall redhead gave Val a respectful nod.

"I am," Val answered. "You guys?"

"Just another day in paradise, sir," the shorter one said, as he gave Val a knowing wink.

As the pair disappeared into the shoppette, thoughts of Omar flooded Val. Guilt and anxiety surged within him. Those two young men were going outside the wire to find Moussa because of his mistake. Val knew what he had to do. It was never really in question.

Enough fiddlefucking around.

He hit send on the flip phone.

Val stood and glanced around as he put the phone in his pocket.

Now, I need to find Mazar ASAP. And I need to somehow avoid Tony for a few days.

He started walking back toward the task force's encampment to look for the trusty interpreter.

CHAPTER 69

Tony was pissed.

He stalked across the task force compound, fists clenched, jaw set, head swimming in a swirl of confused anger and concern. The setting sun cast a red glow over the area that matched Tony's mood as he walked in and out of long shadows, grumbling curse words as he went. Tony wanted to make sure Val was okay. And punch him in the face. Order to be determined.

For the past months, Tony and Val had been, if not inseparable, in very close orbits with one another. They were side by side while eating, interviewing sources, planning missions, or going outside the wire, or they knew exactly what the other was doing—like sleeping, eating, interviewing sources, or going outside the wire. But over the past two days, after Val went for a walk around the airfield on the task force's down day, Tony had barely seen him. At first, it seemed novel.

Then it seemed weird.

Today, despite looking constantly, he could not find Val anywhere.

Now Tony realized it was intentional.

He was definitely going to punch Val in the face.

There was only one place left to check.

Tony stomped up the short flight of wooden steps and threw open the HUMINT hooch door.

Val and Mazar looked up, startled by Tony's sudden appearance. They were sitting together at one of the small tables near the bar. A map lay between them.

Tony glared.

The surprise on Val's face melted into guilt.

Mazar's eyes shot from Tony to Val and back before finally settling on Val's face, seeking guidance.

Val took his eyes off Tony. He looked at Mazar and nodded toward the door.

Mazar stood and turned from Val. He walked slowly toward the exit, nervous at having to approach Tony, whose large body stood in the doorway, panting in anger.

Without taking his eyes off Val, Tony stepped into the HUMINT hooch and to one side so that Mazar could leave.

"I'll deal with you later," Tony growled at Mazar as the Kurd darted out of the building.

Tony slammed the door shut behind Mazar, put his hands on his hips, and said, "What the hell is going on?"

"What do you mean?" Val asked half-heartedly.

"Don't play fuck-fuck with me!" Tony shouted, crossing the HUMINT hooch toward Val in angry lunging strides.

Startled, Val stood from his chair and prepared for impact.

Tony pulled up short, though, and jabbed his finger into Val's chest.

"You have been sneaking around, avoiding me for two fucking days!"

Val opened his mouth to respond, but Tony cut him off.

"Don't!"

Val stood silent and motionless.

Tony stopped jabbing Val in the chest and lowered his hand slowly.

"At first I thought you might have finally cracked under your indulgent, self-imposed guilt and stress at letting Moussa go," Tony said, no longer shouting, but his voice rapid and angry. "I thought maybe you had gone to Ramos and asked for reassignment back to the States and just didn't want to tell me.

"I thought, gee, maybe I should give the guy some space," Tony continued in a self-mocking voice. "Imagine how surprised I was last night, then, when, as I was walking across the compound to get to the evening's mission briefing, I see you and fucking Mazar getting into a civilian duty vehicle." Tony raised his eyebrows in feigned shock.

Val kept still and quiet.

"It was odd when neither of you heard me call out," Tony said in a voice dripping with false wonder. "Can you believe that? You both just got in the beat-up Opal and drove off post."

Val looked at the floor to avoid Tony's glare.

"The next day, I figured you must have some kind of compartmentalized mission shit going on. I mean, this is SOCOM, right? Need-to-know, right?"

Anger was surging back into Tony's voice.

"So I go into the ops center and poke around when Mac wasn't paying attention. How stupid do you think I felt when I learned that you had actually requested a few days off the nightly mission rotations?" Tony raised his hands, stabbing quotes into the air as he said, "'In order to take care of some personal matters.'"

Tony's eyes bored into Val's guilty face like drill bits as he slowly lowered his hands. His chest rose and fell with rapid, angry breaths.

"I've been looking for you all day, brother. The mess hall, the gym, the showers, the shoppette, the operations center, the med station, the motor pool, and the kennels."

Tony paused. He glanced down at the map on the table between him and Val.

"And now I find you squirreled away in our hooch with Mazar whispering like schoolgirls over a map of Mosul."

Tony held eye contact with Val for a long moment and then leaned across the table, raising his right hand.

"I'm going to ask you one time, brother," Tony said, extending his index finger like a bayonet. "Just once."

Val shook his head. "I'm sorry, Tony. I can't tell you."

Tony lunged forward, shoving Val hard in the chest.

"Bullshit!" he yelled as Val stumbled backward over a small end table in front of the orange sofa.

Val landed on his back. Tony leapt around the table and put his knee in Val's chest.

"You don't get to cut me out, asshole!" Tony pointed at Val's face.

Val, caught off guard, didn't fight back. He lay still beneath Tony's knee.

"We're a fucking team!" Tony's face was red and pinched with anger. "We agreed from the beginning this was our last mission over here together. Together! I don't care how sad or guilty or butt-hurt you are about shit that goes down over here, you don't get to just quit the team! Not after everything we have been through together! The only way to quit this team is to die, you asshole!"

Tony paused, chest heaving as he caught his breath.

Val slowly swiveled his arms out to his sides, palms up, in a gesture of surrender.

Tony, not convinced, left his knee and weight on Val's chest. But the sharp angles and creases of rage in his face gradually dissolved. He shook his head, face slack and frowning.

"How can you be so long into this shit and not get that by now?" Tony said in a heartbroken voice as he stood off of Val. He turned away without helping his friend up.

"Tony," Val said as he sat up.

Tony ignored him. He crossed the HUMINT hooch toward the door to leave.

"Tony!"

Tony said nothing as he put his hand on the doorknob.

"I initiated contact with Haskell," Val said quickly, before Tony opened the door.

Tony froze.

Val stood slowly and brushed himself off. He looked at Tony, who didn't turn to face him, and spoke to his back.

"I've got two strikes with Razzaq now. Two times, I have made the wrong call and I have given him more time living on this earth. The first was out at Camp Korea. I should've listened to you. We should've worked with Haskell. The second was a few weeks ago, letting Moussa go. And because of my mistakes, we're all still trying to find him. And sooner or later, some young Ranger, or veteran Delta operator, or navy medic, is going to get killed on one of our nightly trips outside the wire on thin intel looking for the bastard in shitty neighborhoods surrounded by jihadis."

Tony turned around. Head cocked. Hands on his hips.

"I can't live with that anymore, brother." Val shook his head. "I can't just let it ride and hope it turns out okay. I had to do something."

Val rubbed his eyes.

"I haven't been able to get Haskell out of my mind since that night," Val added, dropping his hand to his side. "And I still remember the challenge and responses we gave him when we let him go two years ago."

When they turned Haskell loose in the desert outside of Camp Korea, they had followed the standard agent-release procedure, giving Haskell a phone and a coded challenge-and-response protocol should they need to reactivate him in the future. Consisting of a handful of innocuous phrases such as, "Hey, in the mood to meet and go shopping?" Haskell's coded response, just as innocuous, would signal his situation and willingness to work.

But reactivating an agent was not done lightly, or single-handedly, as Val had done. It was the result of intelligence need, analysis, and a rigorous process. The first time Tony and Val had interacted with Haskell, it had taken the approval of the theater commander himself.

Tony was rubbing his forehead, his breathing accelerating.

"He may know something useful," Val continued. "Something that could help us stop stumbling around in the dark, hitting dry holes every night. All I want to do is talk to him. And it would take too long if I went the official route. I'd have to go through a fucking bureaucratic gauntlet of bullshit. It would take months of getting lectured and resisted at every turn by a bunch of Agency counterintelligence dickheads. By the time I got permission to do what I have already done, the window of opportunity would be closed. And, in the meantime, who knows how many times the task force would have gone outside the wire, and how many soldiers would be wounded, or worse?"

Tony stood motionless. His face reddening.

"So, as you can see, I'm way off the reservation, brother," Val said. "So far off, I don't know how I get back. I'm gonna be dirty after this. And I didn't want you to be…"

Tony looked like he was about to explode.

Val shrugged in frustration.

"I was trying to keep you out of it. Keep you clean."

Val sighed wearily and his shoulders sagged. He looked at his feet.

Tony laughed.

Val looked up.

Tony bent over, held his stomach, and laughed.

Val stood still, puzzled, waiting for Tony to ignite with rage.

"You crazy fucking son of a bitch!" Tony lurched across the room.

Val tensed at his abrupt approach, ready or another confrontation.

"Now we're fucking talking!" Tony bellowed, wrapping his arms around Val in a bear hug. "I knew my guy was still in there!" He slapped Val's back.

Tony released Val and took a step back.

"You were wrong to do this behind my back," Tony said, seriousness flashing across his face. "Don't ever do that shit again. But I love this! What's the plan?"

"The plan?"

"Yeah!" Tony nodded enthusiastically. "The plan. What's next with Haskell?"

Val shook his head.

"There is no plan. Not for you. This is my thing. I'm walking the plank on this. You don't have to."

"No. Bullshit. Team, remember? Don't make me go through it again. What's the plan?"

"Tony, there is no coming back from this. We're going to have to step over some red lines. You'd never pass a poly again."

"Val, this is it for me. You know that. The only reason I came back again was for one more shot at that motherfucker. I'm done after this tour. Finished. I'm going home to my wife, and I'm going to be a fat, dumb, and happy civilian. I don't need any of this shit anymore—the badges and medals and access. All I want is to take that dude out and end with a win. I want to do this with you. Together."

Tony smiled.

"Now, will you please shut the hell up about all that and tell me the plan?"

CHAPTER 70

The gas station sat on the outskirts of Mosul on a two-lane road. It was a simple off-white building with one open garage. A disassembled car sat on cinder blocks in the garage, long forgotten by its mechanic, and there were two old, dust-covered gas pumps out front. A small chalkboard leaned against what looked like the building's office wall, listing prices for diesel and unleaded petrol. Prices were too volatile for more permanent signage.

Inside the office, an old, bearded man sat behind a counter. A random configuration of shelves encircled him. Motor oil, water bottles, cigarettes, old magazines, and snacks sat on the shelves. The smell of strong Arabic coffee competed with the dust and gasoline, and the sound of Arabic music played from a small radio.

The gas station was never busy. But it got just enough business to never die. Val liked it for a couple of reasons. First, the barren terrain that surrounded it, dotted by derelict buildings and occasional stands of palm trees, provided numerous options for concealed and effective overwatch. Tony picked a burned-out building about 150 meters north of the gas station. From the roof, he could scan both directions of the two-lane road, seeing potential trouble coming from a long way away. He would also be able to cover Val and Mazar, laying down effective suppressive fire on the gas station should he need to.

Second, the dual pump setup gave Val the perfect setting for a quick, no-bullshit meet with Haskell. Instructions to Haskell were to pull up on the inside side of the pumps at 0930 hours. He was to get out, walk to the front of his car, and lift the hood immediately, indicating that he was sure he hadn't been tailed. If the trunk went up, Tony would radio Val and the meet would go down. If the trunk didn't, the meet was off.

Finally, the gas station sat on a road that the US military transited often. It was unlikely, given the traffic and activity during the day, that there would be a lot of unfriendly eyes in the area. Particularly in the morning.

At 0915 hours, Mazar and Val sat in a civilian duty vehicle idling behind a derelict building a mile south of the gas station. Tony had been in his overwatch position for more than an hour. Val leaned his head back against the headrest, closed his eyes, and tried to relax. He'd been on edge all morning. He wanted to get this part over with, to see Haskell with his own eyes and assess if they could work with him.

Finally, Tony's voice came over the radio.

"Idaho."

Val straightened in his seat and took a deep breath. It was the code word for Haskell having arrived at the gas station. He and Mazar shared a glance. Val's hand moved to the pistol grip of his M14 between his legs. They waited for the next call from Tony.

They didn't have to wait long.

"Dakota."

Haskell had raised the hood of his car. He was clean.

Mazar pulled out onto the road and gunned the engine.

A few minutes later, as they approached the gas station, Val's eyes narrowed while he scanned the lone figure pumping gas in front.

The car was an old green Toyota sedan. Its trunk was propped open, and the gas nozzle hung in the receptacle in the rear quarter panel. The driver stood in a relaxed pose, leaning against the driver's side door, arms crossed, head down, wearing a dusty white robe over dark trousers and brown leather sandals. The robe was knee length and made of lightweight fabric, adorned with simple black and blue accent stitching along the cuffs of the long sleeves and open collar.

A frisson of recognition ran through Val as Mazar slowed down to turn into the gas station.

It was Haskell, no question, emanating the same calm and cool vibe he'd had at Camp Korea two years ago.

Val chuckled to himself and shook his head subtly at the sight.

Slick son of a bitch.

Mazar pulled alongside the gas pumps and put the car in Park but left the engine running. His car faced the opposite direction of Haskell's, the two gas pumps between them. Mazar keyed the radio handset on the seat between him and Val, breaking squelch one time.

Tony keyed his handset twice, indicating, "All clear," from his overwatch position. No questionable activity down either side of the road as far as he could see.

Val winked at Mazar and got out of the car.

Mazar pulled the nine-millimeter pistol from his leg holster and held it in his lap, pointing it through the car door at Haskell.

"Looks like it will be another hot day," Val said to Haskell as he walked around to the gas pumps. This was a final challenge phrase. A last chance for Haskell to indicate he'd been tailed or otherwise compromised. There was only one correct response.

"That is a safe bet," Haskell responded leisurely, indicating he was all clear.

Val nodded as he grabbed the nozzle from its cradle. He took a few steps away from the pump and put the nozzle into his car. He looked at the nozzle for a moment as if making sure it was pumping correctly and then turned as if to watch the numbers on the pump roll over as he filled his car. In reality, neither man was pumping gas; the nozzles sat inactive as they studied each other.

"It's good to see you, Masudi."

"You as well, Max," Haskell said, hesitating just a bit before saying the name "Max" as he used to do at Camp Korea, signaling he knew the name was bullshit.

The two men stood in silence for a long moment, Val searching for that certain indescribable gut feeling.

Can he be trusted?

Haskell looked like he'd lost a bit of weight to Val. There was an air of fatigue to the man that he didn't remember from before. But that didn't bother him.

The wily man looked back at Val.

I can only imagine how I look to him. This fucking war.

"I must admit," Haskell said, still leaning back against his car. "After you left me alone in the desert that night, I did not think I would ever hear from you again."

"Really?" Val worked hard to remove any sign of stress from his voice. "And

I left our last meeting thinking it was only a matter of time before we worked together."

"Perhaps I have become too skeptical in my old age."

"Too skeptical to work with us?"

Haskell chuckled.

"I am happy to be of service, if I can."

"I'm glad to hear it." Val reached into his pocket and took out a small picture of Moussa. He placed it on top of the gas pump between him and Haskell.

"Do you know this man?"

Still leaning back against the driver's side door of his car, Haskell looked at the gas pump and then at his feet. He casually leaned forward from the car and took the photo off the top of the gas pump. He looked at the photo before putting it, along with his hands, into his robe pockets and leaning back against his car.

Haskell looked at Val and said, "I know this man."

"I'd like to know where he is."

Haskell nodded, understanding the implications of Val's statement. Then he raised an eyebrow and cocked his head to one side.

"You want to know?"

Val held his gaze but said nothing.

The hint of a smile ran across Haskell's face and then was gone.

"Usually you guys say, 'we,' Max," he said with a shrug before looking back at his feet.

Val ignored the comment. He pulled an envelope and a new burner phone out of one of his pockets and placed them both on the gas pump. The envelope contained a thousand dollars. He and Tony had both withdrawn five hundred dollars from the ATM on base earlier. It was an important part of the bluff. They needed Haskell to believe this was official and that there was more where this came from.

"What is this?"

"A new phone for our communications," Val said. "A number that we monitor is saved on it. Use text messages only. Keep it brief."

Val took the gas nozzle out of the car and returned it to the pump, placing himself closer to Haskell. Val looked at him, making eye contact.

"The envelope is a token of our appreciation. There will be more if you help us find our friend."

"This envelope is not necessary, Max," Haskell protested unconvincingly.

"I understand. But we appreciate your time and partnership."

Val turned from Haskell and walked back to the passenger side of the car. He opened the door and paused for a moment.

"It's good to see you, Masudi. Be safe."

"You also, Max."

CHAPTER 71

The next three days passed slowly for Val and Tony. Val kept the Haskell cell phone on vibrate in his pocket during the day and set it next to his head when he slept. The task force went outside the wire each night on missions looking for Moussa, yielding only firefights and dry holes. Mac operated on just a couple of hours of sleep each night. Ramos stalked back and forth in the operations center, fuming. Task force morale was low. Why couldn't they find this guy?

Finally, in the afternoon on day four, while Val was interviewing a source with Mazar in one of the cinder-block meeting rooms, the Haskell phone vibrated in his pocket. Val nearly jumped out of his chair to get at it, startling the source, an Iraqi man in his mid-thirties.

Val stood and gave Mazar a look before stepping away from the small table.

Mazar engaged the source, continuing questioning as Val read the message from Haskell.

"Your friend will be staying in Tanak tonight. I'm sure he would love to see you."

Val blinked as he stared at his phone. There was a house address at the end of the text. He didn't recognize it right away, but he knew the neighborhood of Tanak well.

"Thanks for your time today," Val said to the source as he shoved the phone back in his pocket. "I've been called to another meeting. Mazar will take you back."

Val shot Mazar a look, which the Kurd understood immediately, and left the meeting room.

Val walked to the cinder-block building where Tony was meeting with a source and knocked on the door. Protocol dictated he not barge in, potentially spooking the source or learning an identity he didn't need to know.

Val heard the scrape of a metal chair on the floor and Tony's heavy steps approaching before the door popped open. Tony stuck his head out.

"What?".

"Haskell," Val said.

"Gimme a minute," Tony said before stepping back and closing the door.

A few minutes later, Val and Tony stood in the midday Iraqi sun, talking in hushed voices.

"I was starting to think we were not going to hear back from the bastard," Tony said.

"Me too."

"But he came through," Tony said with a broad smile. "Have you checked out the address yet?"

"I gave it a quick look. I know the neighborhood. We prepped for an operation there a while ago, but it never went off. Shitty little spot in the western outskirts of town called Tanak. Not too developed. Lots of old beat-up houses and empty lots."

Tony looked at his friend. "What's bugging you?"

"What to do next. How to handle it."

"We talked about this. Do you want me to do it?"

"No. I own this. I'll do it."

"We own this together, brother."

Val nodded slightly.

"I'm going to go talk to Mazar," he said. "Then we'll run the play."

Val could not just run into the operations center and say, "Hey, so I decided to reactivate Haskell on my own, and he told me that Moussa was going to be in this location tonight, so let's mobilize the task force and go after him." He had to integrate the priceless, ill-gotten nugget into the intelligence stream in a way that would appear to be the normal course of operations.

This was the part of their plan that had given Val and Tony the most pause. Now they would cross over the line, leaving the fuzzy gray cloud that obscured right and wrong in war, and commit a clear legal and ethical violation. They were breaking the foundational rule of conduct of human intelligence: to convey only what the legitimate source revealed. They were going to lie, to plant intelligence and manipulate the machine.

*

Val and Tony walked into the operations center early that afternoon. Mac looked away from the big screens as they approached, hopeful they'd brought something useful.

"Whatcha got, gentlemen?"

"Nada," Tony said. "Seven source meetings. Nothing good."

"I actually think I got something," Val said, casting an irritated glance Tony's way before continuing. "Young Iraqi male who has been working with us for about six months says he overheard where Moussa would be tonight."

"No shit?" Mac's eyebrows raised hopefully.

"I don't buy it," Tony said.

Val shrugged at Tony's comment, maintaining eye contact with Mac.

"It's a little thin," Val admitted. "Our source does not have a direct relationship with Moussa. But he claims to know him by reputation and says a friend of his is actually Moussa's cousin. Recently he has heard the cousin talking about the effort to keep moving Moussa around so we don't pinch him."

"I don't think he is in Mosul anymore," Tony interjected.

"It sounds like it's become kind of a social status thing out there to have Moussa or one of the other wanted people stay at your place for a night," Val said, trying to ignore Tony. "It's the same old story. They're bouncing around each night, living off the generosity and spirit of adventure of others."

"I'm telling you, it's thin," Tony said. "Dry hole."

Val gave Mac a roll of the eyes at Tony's comment.

"Nonetheless. Our source gave us an address. Says Moussa will be there tonight."

Val handed Mac a three-by-five card with an address written on it.

Mac read it and then looked at Val.

"Who was your interpreter on this meet, sir?"

"Mazar," Val said. "He is solid."

It was not uncommon, with important intelligence like this, for the interpreter to be questioned. Their role was so important in the intelligence chain of custody, sometimes they were regarded as a risk.

Mazar's reputation was beyond reproach, though. That was why it was important he be on board.

Mac nodded in approval and read the address again.

"This is in the Tanak neighborhood," he said, almost to himself. "Far west corner of Mosul. Lotta strange shit goes down in that area, though recently it's been kinda quiet. We got reports months ago about a weapons shipment moving through Tanak. It's a known landing spot in western Mosul for shit being piped in from Syria. Never got solid targeting, but I've been watching that part of town ever since." Mac's eyes narrowed. "What did your source say?"

"The source is from the same neighborhood as Moussa's cousin. Grew up with him. Runs into him a lot. The cousin was stocking up on food and other supplies this week, and let our source know he had a bunch of family coming into town and would be busy for the next few days. When the source poked around about whether certain family members he knew would be there, the cousin listed several names, one of which was Moussa. The source knew Moussa was from Tal Afar but threw out a red herring. He asked the cousin if that was his relative Moussa from Tikrit. The cousin replied no, that Moussa was from Tal Afar."

"Nice work with the red herring," Mac said.

Val nodded. "We train 'em right."

Mac looked at the three-by-five card and then back at Val.

"You worked with this source before, sir?"

"Yeah. Many times."

"Reliable?"

"Yep. He was the brother of one of our Tigernaichs that was killed a while back. Volunteered right after. He passed his validation tests easily. Since then, we've even used him on several reconnaissance missions where we have watched him from a distance. He executed flawlessly. He's solid."

Val spoke confidently because he was thinking of a real source. Just not the one that the intel had actually come from. That was Haskell. If Mac knew that Val was trying to sell him on intel from an unauthorized communication with an unvalidated source that had failed the vetting process in the past, he would have thrown him out of the building and reported him to Ramos.

But Mac didn't know.

He scratched his head in thought and looked at Val.

Val returned his gaze. This was the moment that he'd been dreading. He and Mac had worked together for a while. Mac had relied on Val's HUMINT to launch high-profile, successful missions at least a dozen times in the past. Despite the mistake of letting Moussa go, Val knew that Mac trusted him, trusted his experience and judgment.

And Val was taking advantage of that trust in this moment.

Mac held up the three-by-five card and stared at it for a moment.

"Fuck it, Mac," Tony said. "I admit, like the major said, the source is solid. One of our best. Even if the intel is thin."

Tony shrugged.

"Maybe task a drone to watch the house," he added. "Who knows? It could be more than I think it is. And, besides, I got nothing for you today."

Mac nodded.

"Yeah… Yeah. I'll put eyes on it. Thanks, guys."

"Roger that," Val said. He and Tony turned and left.

*

Mac tasked an ISR line on the address. Soon, he had a live feed from an overhead drone. The site didn't look like much. A typical-looking house for Mosul surrounded by a large walled garden in the back.

Mac took his glasses off. He pulled a handkerchief out of his BDU chest pocket and cleaned their lenses before putting them back on and pulling the strap around his pale head. Folding the handkerchief and putting it away, Mac settled back in his chair. He took a sip of coffee and prepared for an afternoon of watching uneventful ISR feeds.

Val and Tony stopped at the operations center on their way to the mess hall for an early dinner.

"Anything?" Val asked.

"Nope." Mac stood from his chair. "All I've seen is a woman step out to throw out some trash. No vehicles have come or gone."

Val looked at the screen and grimaced in frustration.

"Anything else for us tonight, sir?" Tony asked.

"Not yet. Slow day."

Tony nodded. "Might as well watch this shithole some more, then," he said, looking at the big screen.

"Yeah," Mac said. "Might as well."

Val and Tony left the operations center troubled, wondering if Haskell had given them a dry hole.

By the time they had eaten and returned, though, things had started to develop.

"Three cars arrived," Mac said, pointing at the big screen. "A total of seven military-aged males entered the house and have not come out yet."

"Kinda promising," Tony said.

"I dunno…" Mac rubbed his forehead.

Val and Tony shared a look.

Mac stared at the screen.

Val and Tony left the operations center and walked back toward their quarters.

"Don't worry," Tony said as they walked. "By the time we get back for the mission brief and planning, that house will be crawling with MAMs. Mac is going to be begging Ramos to hit it."

Val said nothing. His face was troubled.

"I'm telling you." Tony's voice was calm and confident. "We're hitting that house tonight, and we're getting Moussa. Without question."

Val nodded half-heartedly. "I hope so."

"Gonna happen. Now I need to hit the latrine. See you at the ops center later."

*

An hour later, Val and Tony stood next to Colonel Ramos as Mac gave him the update, referring to the notes in his small notebook as he spoke. Ramos stood with his feet spread wide, arms crossed, rubbing his chin as he listened intently to Mac.

"For the first couple of hours after Major Santanna gave us the target, nothing really happened, sir. But he was clear from the beginning it was thin intel."

Ramos looked at Val.

Val nodded.

"Totally fucking thin," Tony mumbled.

"But the plot has thickened in the past hour," Mac continued. "Five cars have come and gone. Three arrived and are still on-site. And we believe there are a total of eleven military-aged men now on-site."

Overhead imagery of the target house rotated slowly on the big screen behind Mac. The Ranger captain shifted on his feet as if he were about to make a fastball pitch.

"And fifteen minutes ago, NSA was able to co-locate one of the priority cell phones from our list at this house. It's one we believe to be associated with Moussa."

Ramos uncrossed his arms.

Tony's eyebrows arched and his mouth fell open.

Val took a step forward.

"Are you shitting me, Mac?"

"It's one of the older numbers, sir." Mac tried to moderate the enthusiasm in the room. "But yeah…it's a number on our target list, and they have confirmed it."

Mac gestured at the NSA rep, standing to his side.

Ramos, Val, and Tony all swiveled their heads toward the civilian at once. The sudden, focused attention flustered the khaki-clad NSA rep. He was a technician and good at his job, but even after four months in-country, he still felt uncomfortable around the battle-hardened warriors he worked for.

"You sure about this?" Ramos asked him in a sharp voice.

"Yes, sir. I've triple-checked. It's a positive ID."

"I want to emphasize it's an old number, sir," Mac interjected.

"Yeah, you said that. You got anything else?"

Mac checked his notes, even though he knew the answer.

"No, sir. That's it."

"Okay. Good work, Mac," Ramos said before addressing the entire operations center. "Mission briefing in half an hour!"

Everyone nodded, and the energy level in the room ratcheted up. Ramos turned to Val and Tony.

"Looks like this will be a big party. A lot of MAMs on the objective to sort through. We're going to go in heavy. I hate it, but I want both of you on this one tonight."

"Roger that, sir," Val said.

Ramos turned to leave and then stopped. He swiveled back around and pointed at Val.

"And good work, Max."

Then he left the ops center to get his gear.

Tony winked at Val.

CHAPTER 72

The task force dismounted one kilometer from the objective and began their ingress.

The column rounded an intersection about two hundred meters from the target. Just as Val, who was in the middle of the task force, stepped through the small intersection and got eyes on the objective, a light came on in the house.

That's not good.

The next second, a "Compromised" call came over the radio. They were made. There was no use trying to keep the element of surprise.

Every operator broke into a sprint.

Each element of the assault force scrambled to put their piece of the operation into play.

The snipers climbed the first available buildings to get eyes on the objective.

The roof team had no chance to get set. They fell in behind the breach team, Rip running at their side.

Booze, running at the front of the entire task force, rolled a grenade ahead into the front door.

"Grenade!" he yelled.

The lead element of the task force ducked and took cover.

The grenade exploded.

Booze led the breach team, guns firing, through the hanging fragments of the front door. Chico followed, with a squad of Rangers right behind him.

Val entered the objective with the next squad.

He turned into the first room on the right. A dead elderly Iraqi lay on the floor in a large pool of blood. Ten dirty bedrolls were scattered around the floor.

Tony ran into the objective with the next squad. He met Val as he was coming out of the room with the dead man.

"Anything?"

"One dead guy," Val said. "A lot of bedrolls."

Tony nodded.

The task force continued to search for the objective. "Clear!" calls were ticked off room by room as the Rangers worked quickly through the structure.

Val kept waiting to hear the quick burst of gunfire that would indicate another MAM had chosen to fight rather than surrender.

But it never came.

Nor did the ferocious snarl followed by a scream that would accompany one of the dogs encountering resistance.

The sound of crying women, however, filled the house.

Val looked across the main living room and saw Rangers corralling a small group of women into a corner to organize them for interrogation.

He shot a glance at Tony, who returned a look that said he shared Val's unease.

"Sir," a Ranger sergeant said as he walked over to Val, hand outstretched.

He handed Val a couple of IDs and driver's licenses.

"Found these in that room with all the bedrolls, sir," he said to Val.

"No other MAMs in the house?" Val asked, looking at the IDs.

"No, sir."

The sergeant walked back to his squad.

Tony shook his head at Val.

"I know," Val said. "Something isn't right. Mac said they tracked eleven MAMs in, none out. And that many bedrolls? Where the hell are the MAMs?"

Val had learned that the men always slept together in one room, separate from the women and children. He looked over at the group of scared women. He counted at least half a dozen.

Val walked over to one of the translators who was helping manage the women. Tony followed him.

"Ask them where these men are," Val told the interpreter.

Val held up the handful of IDs as the translator asked the question. One of the older women responded, and the translator told Val, "She says they were in the room with the bedrolls."

"Fuck me," Tony whispered.

Val grabbed his radio.

"Ramos, this is Max."

"Go ahead."

"I think there are up to eleven MAMs unaccounted for on the objective."

Tony raised his rifle to a more ready position.

"Roger that, Max."

A current of electricity seemed to flow through the task force as they listened to Val and Ramos's radio exchange. Every operator tensed and then crouched a little lower toward a fighting stance wherever they were in the house.

A moment ago, it seemed like this was going to be one of those easier-than-expected objectives.

Now, it felt like a trap.

Val continued to work with the interpreter to question the women about the whereabouts of their men.

A moment later, an urgent radio call came over the net.

"We have what appears to be a trapdoor in the bathroom here near the shower."

Val felt the sensation of momentum building. He raised his rifle.

"We've got one here in the male bedroom also," another Ranger said on the radio.

Val and Tony made eye contact.

AK-47 gunshots rang out through the house.

Rangers stumbled backward out of the bathroom into the main room, where Val and Tony were with the women. The Rangers tried to put distance and cover between themselves and the enemy as rounds impacted the ceiling and walls around them.

One Ranger dragged another by the back of his load-bearing equipment, smearing blood across the floor. The wounded Ranger had taken a round to the shoulder as he'd opened the trapdoor in the bathroom.

"Allah Akbar!" yelled an Iraqi insurgent as he leapt out of the bathroom, shooting wildly. He was cut down by fire from several directions, his body landing in a crumpled pile just outside the bathroom.

A live grenade rolled out of his bloody, dead hand.

"Grenade!" shouted the closest Ranger.

Everyone dove to the ground and behind the furniture. Val and Tony shoved the women to the ground and shielded them with their bodies.

The grenade exploded, spraying the room with shrapnel, dousing it in smoke.

Another MAM charged from the bathroom, sweeping the room with AK-47 fire.

A Ranger screamed out in pain as a round struck his leg.

A well-placed burst from one of the other Rangers struck the Iraqi in the gut. He doubled over and fell forward, another live grenade tumbling to the floor.

As the grenade struck the floor and rolled, two Iraqi insurgents stormed out of the bedroom. They were met by a wall of lead and fell backward.

The grenade cooked off. Shrapnel and debris flew through the room.

Another MAM charged out of the bathroom as two grenades exploded in the bedroom.

The attacking Iraqi was shot just as he reached his dead comrade. He fell, lifeless, on top of the other body. A second later, a grenade exploded between the two dead Iraqis, throwing blood and body parts through the room.

The Ranger squad leader motioned to Tony and Val to get the women out of the house as he directed fire into the bathroom and bedroom doorways.

Tony and Val sprung up and began corralling the women in front of them out toward the back of the house.

Val scanned the room as he shoved women forward toward safety. It was a bloody mess. The ceiling sagged in places, and a large fallen beam had opened a hole through which Val could see the sky. He wasn't sure how many more grenade blasts the structure could take before the roof fell in.

Val and Tony exited into the rear courtyard of the house as the volume of gunfire behind them increased.

A shoulder-high wall surrounded the house and its large courtyard. Tony and Val led the women to a corner of the courtyard that was out of the direct line of fire of what was now a raging gunfight in the house. Judging by the intensity and volume of fire, Val thought there could be twenty MAMs pouring out of the basement bunker.

Another grenade went off inside the structure.

Val crouched in front of the women with Tony. As he looked to his left, he saw a group of children huddling on the ground at the base of the wall about fifty meters away at the other corner of the courtyard wall.

They were terrified.

Val sprinted over to them.

There were five children who Val estimated to be between the ages of six and ten years old. They were wide-eyed and crying.

They were initially terrified of Val. But as he gathered the closest in a protective gesture, they all saw in him a savior and clustered around his legs as he crouched.

"I've got a group of children here," Val said over the radio.

"Headed your way shortly," Tony answered quickly.

Val looked back at Tony, who was helping the women over the wall. Tony lifted them quickly, one at a time, favoring speed over grace. A few of the women tumbled ass-over-teakettle onto the ground on the other side. Then Tony jumped over the wall.

"On the way," Tony transmitted.

Half a minute later, Tony transmitted again.

"I'm on the opposite side. Ready when you are."

Val grabbed the youngest child. He tried to give the kid a comforting smile and then said, "Now!"

Val and Tony stood at the same time. Val hoisted the screaming child over to Tony. Then they both crouched back down. AK-47 rounds struck the wall just above Val's head.

"Dammit!" Val looked at the house. A MAM was firing at him from a window.

Val let loose at the window, emptying a full magazine to make the shooter duck.

The children at his feet winced and screamed at the sudden loud noise above their ears. Val grabbed the two smallest and motioned to the other two to follow him. He ran with the little group to the opposite corner of the courtyard, hoping that the new location would prevent the shooter from getting a good angle on them.

"Fuckers are shooting at their own children. I had to move. Other corner," he transmitted.

"Roger. Moving," Tony responded.

"This is Max at the southeast corner of the courtyard," Val transmitted to the larger task force. "Need covering fire. Trying to get kids clear."

Another round struck the wall next to Val, narrowly missing him and one of the children.

I'm running out of time. Sorry, kids!

Val grabbed the oldest kid, smiled at him. And threw him over the wall. More rounds impacted the wall as he did. He felt the pressure snap of a narrow miss just behind his back.

"Jesus, Max!" Tony said as he watched the kid bounce off the ground, safely on his side of the wall. "I'm almost there."

"No time!" Val grabbed the next oldest and tossed him over.

A bullet struck Val in the chest, knocking him down. The two remaining children bawled and stared at him in horror.

Val coughed and forced a smile at them.

"No worries," he said to the kids, grimacing at the pain. "Vest."

Val made a fist and punched his chest to indicate he was fine. The two children stared in wonder at the Superman before them.

"Trying to get someone to you, Max," one of the Ranger squad leaders transmitted. "Give me a couple more minutes."

Val didn't respond. He grabbed the nearest kid and said, "Now!" over the radio to Tony.

He and Tony leapt up at the same time. Val handed the child to Tony and ducked back down. Bullets peppered the wall.

Val changed his magazine and fired a few bursts into the house, hoping to rattle whoever was taking potshots at him. He grabbed the last child with one hand.

"Last one," he said over the radio. "Now!"

Tony and Val stood up.

The child jerked in Val's hand, and blood sprayed across his face.

Val looked at the dead child, then at Tony.

Tony met Val's eyes an instant before his throat exploded in red mist. Tony fell over backward, a geyser of blood spraying from beneath his chin.

Val leapt over the wall.

Tony was on his back, writhing, his hands on his throat. Blood ran out of him like out of a faucet.

The children shrieked and cried at the sight.

"Tony!" Val dropped his rifle and kneeled next to his friend. "Tony! Shit! Shit! Shit! Tony! It's gonna be okay.

"Medic!" Val yelled into the radio.

His voice startled the children, they turned and ran into the night.

"Medic! Need a medic here, just over the wall to the southeast of the objective."

"Moving!" the medic responded.

Val looked at Tony.

"Medic's on the way, brother." Val put one hand on Tony's chest and one hand on Tony's hands, which were wrapped around his own throat.

Tony and Val locked eyes.

Tony's eyes were wide with fear.

Then they were vacant.

"Tony?"

Tony's hands slackened, and a gurgling noise emanated from his throat.

"Tony?"

Tony's hands fell away from his neck, revealing the gaping wound. A softball-size chunk of Tony's throat, just below his jawbone, had been blown away. The shattered tubular cartilage of Tony's esophagus rose from the gaping neck cavity. Bits of bone from Tony's neck swam in the blood and gore.

"I've got him, sir," the Ranger medic said as he ran up.

Val fell back as the medic leaned over Tony.

"Shit!" the medic said.

Val sat cross-legged on the ground, looking at his hands and arms, slick with Tony's blood.

The medic stood up. He sighed heavily and shook his head.

"I'm sorry, sir. Wound like that? He didn't have a chance."

Val sat motionless.

The medic looked at Val.

"You okay, sir? You hit anywhere?"

Val didn't respond.

"Medic!" one of the Ranger squad leaders called over the radio. "We need a medic! Northeast of the objective. Hurry!"

"Sir, unless you're wounded, I gotta go," the medic said, already stepping away.

Val said nothing. The medic left.

Val sat at Tony's feet and stared at the bloody body.

The gun battle on the objective was de-escalating. There hadn't been a grenade explosion in a few minutes.

Ten minutes later, Ramos's voice came over the radio.

"Objective secure."

Val rubbed his eyes, trying to get his head around what had just happened, smearing blood on his face.

"Max, Ramos."

The radio call didn't register in Val's brain. He continued to stare at Tony.

"Max. This is Ramos. Need you on the objective. We're secure and have some prisoners to process."

Another moment ticked by.

"Vinnie," Ramos tried, impatience in his voice. "Vinnie. Ramos. You with Max? I need one of you on my objective ASAP. Acknowledge."

Hearing Tony's alias snapped Val back. He stood up.

"Ramos, Max. On the way," he said into his radio.

Val picked up his rifle, scrambled over the wall, and walked into the objective.

"Jesus Christ," Ramos said as Val walked into the main living room. Blood was smeared across his face, hands, arms, and chest. "You okay?"

"Yeah. It's not mine."

Ramos nodded.

"It's Vinnie's."

"Oh shit. He okay?"

"He's dead."

Ramos put his hand to his forehead. "Oh shit. Not Vinnie."

Ramos stood in the middle of the main living room with his first sergeant. Val could hear women crying in the next room where the bedrolls were.

"I'm sorry, Max," Ramos said, in a low voice. "I know you guys were close."

"Let's just get this shit wrapped up." Val didn't make eye contact with Ramos. "I got a lot of folks I need to call when we get back."

"Yeah," the first sergeant said. "What a fucking night. Turns out this house basically sits on a bunker. We're secure now. But have six wounded and two KIA, including Vinnie."

Ramos rubbed his eyes. Those were staggering casualties for the task force on a single operation. They went for weeks at a time with no wounded. Longer without a friendly KIA. It was a horrible night.

"We went into murder mode there for a bit. But still managed to get some MAM prisoners and a few women as well. They're under guard in there."

Ramos gestured toward the big bedroom.

Val looked over his shoulder. He could see the group of women through the open door. One of them, at first glance, seemed to be a special-needs individual. Her face was contorted, and she didn't seem to understand the BIT sergeant talking to her.

A lightning bolt of recognition ran through Val's body.

It was Zhala.

Val turned from Ramos and walked toward the large bedroom, his hands clenched in fists.

Zhala saw him come through the door and dropped her act immediately. Her face smoothed into a mask of tension, and she looked at the floor.

Zhala's transformation was so sudden, it confused the BIT sergeant talking to her, and he didn't notice Val approaching.

Val didn't break stride as he punched Zhala in the face as hard as he could.

Zhala's nose was crushed, and she flew several feet back before landing hard on her back, unconscious.

"What the fuck, sir?" the BIT sergeant yelled at Val.

Chico, behind Val, barked and strained at his leash, excited by Val's sudden attack. His handler jerked him back and tried to maintain control.

Val ignored the stunned BIT sergeant and Rangers in the room and walked over to the group of four MAMs who were flex-cuffed and seated in the room's corner with hoods over their heads.

Val started yanking hoods up, one by one, looking for a face he recognized.

"Sir?" the BIT sergeant said hesitantly. He had never seen Val like this.

When Val lifted the fourth hood, he let out a terrifying, rage-filled scream.

It was Kzem Moussa.

Val snapped.

He dragged Abu Moussa to the middle of the room and went to work on him.

The BIT sergeant and Rangers stood by, frozen by Val's violence.

Val punched Moussa in the face. Then hauled back and punched him again.

Then again.

And again.

Moussa's blood sprayed on the ground and mixed with Tony's blood on Val's fists.

Tony's death, and the stress of feeling personally accountable for letting Moussa go the first time, combined and ignited within Val.

Rage consumed him.

Val picked Moussa up by the shoulders. Moussa's head lolled left and right as he passed in and out of consciousness. Val heaved him into the wall.

Moussa struck the wall headfirst and landed in a limp pile on the floor.

Val kicked the listless body hard in the ribs with the toe of his combat boot several times, feeling the satisfying crunch of ribs.

Val leaned over to pick the man up to continue beating him.

Chico could not watch anymore. He lunged suddenly, escaping his handler's grip, and joined Val. Chico sank his teeth into one of Moussa's legs and thrashed.

Chico's attack startled the Rangers in the room into action.

"Sir!" The BIT sergeant tried to catch Val's arm in midswing.

Val kept striking Moussa, unfettered.

"Goddamn it!" yelled Booze. He ran across the room and tackled Val.

Val and Booze slammed into the nearby wall. Booze made sure Val took the brunt of their momentum.

The collision stunned Val, partly knocking the breath out of him.

The handler grabbed Chico by the harness and tried to pull him off the unconscious Moussa as the medic knelt to take his vitals.

"I need help here!" the handler yelled.

Three Rangers leapt to his side and tried to pry Chico's jaws off Moussa.

"He's flatlining!" the medic yelled.

Booze held Val against the wall. "Goddamn it, Max! Calm the fuck down!"

"What the hell is going on?" Ramos yelled as he entered the room and saw four soldiers trying to get the snarling Chico off Moussa's leg, a medic trying to stick the Iraqi with an IV, and Booze pinning Val against the wall.

"Max was trying to kill this one, sir," the medic said, not looking up from the IV needle he was taping to Moussa's arm.

The four Rangers finally pried Chico's jaws open, and the handler jerked the dog back and out of the room.

Blood oozed from deep bite wounds in Moussa's leg.

Ramos walked over to Booze and Val.

"You cool, sir?" Booze asked him.

Val, panting, head pinned against the wall by Booze's strong right forearm, said nothing.

"I can't let you go till you promise me, bro," Booze said in a quieter voice, trying to get through to Val.

Val said nothing.

Ramos leaned over and whispered into Booze's ear, "They got Vinnie."

Booze nodded. A knowing look came over his face, but he kept his full weight against Val.

"Sir, I'm losing him!" the medic said.

"Dammit. Does he matter?" Ramos asked the BIT team sergeant, who stood in stunned silence next to the other prisoners.

"I don't know, Sir. We haven't processed any of them."

"He matters," Val said.

"What's that?" Booze asked, maintaining the pressure on Val's head with his forearm.

"It's Moussa."

"That's fucking Moussa?" Ramos shouted, stepping back over to Booze and Val.

"His heart has stopped!" the medic said.

"Yes," Val said.

Booze shook his head.

"Shit, Max." Ramos stepped away in disgust and spoke hurriedly into his radio.

"Help me!" the medic said to the BIT sergeant, yanking the breathing bag from his kit and handing it to him.

The BIT sergeant kneeled over Moussa's bloody head. He wiped away tooth fragments from Moussa's lips, pressed down to get a good seal, and then started squeezing the bag to assist Moussa's breathing.

"Rhino Zero One Seven, this is Bulldog Zero Six, we need a medevac ASAP," Ramos yelled into his radio.

Ramos stood over Moussa. The medic was on top of the Iraqi, performing chest compressions. The BIT sergeant sat at his head with the bag.

"Bulldog Zero Six. Rhino One Seven. Roger. Copy medevac. On the way. Send PZ location ASAP."

"Roger that, Rhino. Will do."

A Black Hawk helicopter spun up back on the airfield at Mosul. Part of the 160th, the aircraft had been sitting on the tarmac, auxiliary power unit running, monitoring the mission on its radios. It would be airborne in two minutes. It would be at the LZ in seven.

Ramos yelled, "First Sergeant!" as he walked out of the large bedroom toward the front of the house.

"Sir?" Val heard the first sergeant answer.

"We got Moussa." Ramos spoke quickly. "But he's dying. Medevac is on the way. We need an LZ."

"There is a small playground space about two blocks away."

"Can it take a Black Hawk?"

"Yes, sir."

"Okay. Give me the lat/long and get moving."

"Roger that."

Ramos came back into the bedroom as the first sergeant started barking orders. "How is he?" Ramos asked the medic, who was still bobbing up and down on Moussa's chest.

"Still dead."

"Keep at it. Medevac is on the way."

"Yes, sir."

Moving a casualty to an LZ was always hairy. If you were lucky enough to have a nearby area suitable to take a helicopter, the landing zone had to be checked for obstacles and hazards like hard-to-see wires or towers, and then secured. Then it was usually a running gunfight to get the casualty to the LZ.

Helicopters were big, juicy, high-value targets for the enemy. When one got shot down, it made the news both in America and within the insurgency. When they detected a medevac effort kicking off, the enemy usually went all in.

And during all this, the patient had to be kept alive.

"Three squads securing the route and LZ," the first sergeant said over the radio. "Rhino has the LZ coordinates now."

"Roger that, Top," Ramos said.

He walked over to Booze and Val.

"Max, Booze is going to let you go now because we need help moving Moussa, the high-value target that you just tried to murder, to the LZ. You need to keep your shit together and help us clean up your fucking mess."

"Can you handle that, sir?" Booze asked, leaning his head next to Val's ear.

"Yeah. I'm good now."

"All right, then," Ramos said to the room as Booze stepped back from Val. "Let's go."

Booze put his hand on Val's shoulder and said, "I'm so sorry, brother. We all loved Vinnie."

Val managed a nod.

"I still don't have a pulse!" the medic said. "We're gonna have to do CPR on the way."

Two Rangers ran into the room with a makeshift stretcher they had assembled from a metal bed frame, some ceiling beams, and duct tape. They laid the stretcher down next to Moussa.

The medic hopped off Moussa, and the group lifted him onto the stretcher.

The medic jumped back onto Moussa, straddling him at the waist and resuming the chest compressions. The BIT sergeant continued to work the breathing bag.

The two Rangers, Val, and Booze each took a corner of the makeshift stretcher and lifted it, holding their weapons in one hand, the stretcher in the other.

"Goddamn it!" the medic yelled as he nearly tumbled off the unsteady stretcher. "Hold it fucking level!"

"Give me your weapons," Ramos said.

Each man on the stretcher team handed Ramos his rifle. Val didn't like the feeling of giving away his weapon. Booze gave Ramos a hard look.

"This will be over in a few minutes, Booze," Ramos said with a look that said, *Don't give me any shit.* "You guys focus on holding it level so he can work."

Ramos pointed at the medic, who was engrossed in the chest compressions. Sweat poured from his forehead as he bobbed up and down on Moussa's chest."

"Rhino two minutes out," the first sergeant said over the radio. "LZ secure."

"How is the route?" Ramos asked.

"Sporty. I sent a fire team back to escort. They should be there now."

Four Rangers burst into the room. "You ready, sir?" their sergeant said.

"Roger that," Ramos said both into his radio and to the Ranger sergeant. "We're on the move."

The stretcher team moved out of the battered house and into the night, with the fire team forming a loose cordon around them. The awkward formation moved through the street at a clumsy jog as the medic tried to continue chest compressions and the BIT sergeant worked the breathing bag.

The stretcher team felt naked with no weapons in their hands. Val tried not to notice all the windows and alleyways that didn't have a red laser dot covering them.

The Ranger fire team escort swiveled and pivoted as they ran alongside, doing their best to cover as many vulnerabilities as possible.

Ramos ran in trail, four rifles slung over his shoulder and one in his hands.

Val heard the helicopter approaching.

A burst of fire rang out at the front of the formation as one of the Ranger escorts addressed a threat.

The medic moved up and down like a slow diesel piston, trying to keep Moussa's blood flowing.

A second burst of fire rang out, this time right behind Val.

The stretcher bearers kept their heads down, focused on maintaining a stable platform for the medic as they moved through the street toward the LZ.

Two more Rangers joined the group from the shadows, taking positions in the running cordon.

The sound of the helicopter got louder as they neared the LZ, and the bird maneuvered to land, demanding more power from its engines.

An Apache gunship thundered over the street, moving perpendicular to the group. It was in view only briefly before zooming past the buildings on the other side of the street.

Val felt better. Good to see that kind of friendly muscle in the air.

The group rounded the next intersection, and the LZ came into view. More Rangers were visible now, crouched in fighting positions to secure the LZ. Val knew the snipers would be overwatching as well.

The helicopter, flying blacked out, was a dark, loud, thrashing shape approaching the LZ.

The team sped up, sensing the end of their footrace.

The helicopter landed a hundred meters away.

This would be the most dangerous phase of the operation, while the helicopter was on the ground. Val tried not to think about it.

The Apache shrieked over the LZ as the stretcher team closed the final fifty meters to the medevac bird. The gunship's thirty-millimeter chain gun fired at an unseen enemy.

As the team ran under the Black Hawk's rotor disc, one of the crew chiefs jumped out to help with the stretcher. The medic stayed on Moussa, compressing all the while, as the team maneuvered the stretcher onto the helicopter. The BIT sergeant handed the breathing bag to the helicopter's waiting medic.

Transfer complete, Ramos led the team just outside the rotor disc, where they all crouched and shielded their eyes.

A scream of turbine engines and a blast of sand and dust engulfed the area as the pilot pulled maximum power and the helicopter left the ground. Wind whipped the huddled group and then dissipated as the aircraft accelerated away. Within seconds, it was nearly silent again.

"Alright, Rangers," Ramos said over the radio as he straightened up. "Back to the objective."

Ramos handed the rifles back to the stretcher team, saving Val's for last.

"I hope, for your sake, he doesn't die." Ramos put his hand on his shoulder and gave him his rifle. "Now let's go get Vinnie."

CHAPTER 73

Tony had been with the Activity for so long and had survived so much that his death sent tremors through the special operations community. Upon hearing the news, his commander on Fort Belvoir immediately dispatched one of the unit's Gulfstreams. It arrived the next day with two Farm-trained senior enlisted case officers to replace Tony, and orders to bring his body home.

Val's HUMINT team got to work briefing the two new case officers, getting them ready for missions outside the wire as soon as possible.

In the afternoon, after he was certain the official notification chain had gotten through to her, Val called Tony's wife.

She and Val were not close, but they had met a few times and had each heard Tony talk fondly about the other for more than a decade. Val worked to get himself into a mental place where he could make it through the conversation without breaking down. He told her it had been quick, that he didn't think Tony had suffered, and that Tony had been saving children when he died. He told her he'd loved Tony and would escort his body back to the States. If it was okay with her, he would like to attend the funeral.

She didn't answer. She just cried.

General Bryson called Val. "I heard about Tony. Goddamn, son. I'm so sorry."

"Thank you, sir. I appreciate that."

They talked for a few more minutes, the old general trying to determine how his officer was really doing. Val was in robot mode, though, and didn't betray much. He was still digesting his call with Tony's wife.

"Sir, they're going to take Tony back on the Activity aircraft that brought their case officers over," Val told Bryson. "I'd like to go, to escort him, if I could."

"Of course, son. Take as much time as you need."

Ramos approved also.

"Roger that," Ramos said when Val found him in the ops center. "And you should take some time, Max. I know you have a pile of leave built up. Use some of it."

"I'll think about it, sir." Val looked past the lieutenant colonel at the large video screens. "Any word on Moussa?"

"Still in a coma. Doctors say it's fifty-fifty."

Val nodded.

Ramos looked at Val for a moment and then said, "I'm serious. Take some time before you come back. You look like shit."

The next morning, Tony was placed in an aluminum transfer case packed with ice and loaded onto the aircraft. Val boarded behind it, and they started their journey back to the States.

The aircraft stopped at Ramstein Air Base to fuel up before crossing the ocean. Val told the crew he was going to grab some things from the little shoppette near flight ops. He looked at his watch as he walked across the tarmac. It was ten a.m.

It had been almost forty-eight hours since Tony was killed. He didn't want Sydney to find out from somebody else. So, he knew he had to call her before they took off. Vienna was in the same time zone as Germany. Hopefully, she would be at her desk.

Val found a quiet corner in the lounge and pulled out his cell phone.

Sydney's phone went to voice mail on the first call.

Val stood in the corner, facing the window. He took a deep breath and called again.

She answered before the second ring.

"This is Knox."

Val tried to speak. But his throat clenched. Tears ran down his face.

"This is Knox," she said with impatience. "Who is this?"

Val struggled to get his breathing under control. He wiped the tears from his eyes and clenched his fist.

"Val," he managed to say in a choked whisper.

"Val?" The emotion in his voice frightened her. "Are you okay?"

Val sobbed. He had held it in for two days. Through the site exploitation process, interrogating the rest of the prisoners, overseeing the transportation of Tony's body to the morgue, telling the HUMINT team, talking to Tony's wife, talking to Bryson.

But he lost it now.

He bent over, one hand on a knee.

Sydney straightened in her chair. She clutched her heart, listening to Val in pain.

"Val! What is it? Where are you?"

Val stood up and got control of himself long enough to say one word.

"Tony."

"Oh god," Sydney put her head in her hand. "Oh no. Not Tony."

Val hung up.

CHAPTER 74

Val rode in the back of the aircraft with Tony. He spent most of the flight lying on his back on the floor next to the cold metal container, unable to sleep.

A mortuary affairs team met the aircraft when it landed at Dover. Val rode along as the transfer case was moved by van to the Dover Port Mortuary, where Tony's identification was verified by DNA and dental analysis.

"We'll take him from here, sir," the lead technician said gently to Val, who was unable to take his hand off the cold metal container.

She put her hand on his shoulder.

"Okay," was all he could say.

The lead tech stayed by Val while two men wheeled Tony away, down the hall.

"Are you accompanying him to the service, sir?"

"Yeah," he answered, looking at her only after Tony had been wheeled out of sight into a side room.

She nodded knowingly as she looked him over.

"Do you need a dress uniform, sir?"

Val blinked. Suddenly conscious of the dirty digital camos and beat-up desert boots he was wearing. He also hadn't shaved in a long time. He hadn't even remembered to pack toiletries.

"Oh shit. I didn't…"

"It's okay, sir. Not a problem at all. I'll get you a shower kit, and we'll get a uniform together for you before you leave in the morning."

"Thanks, um…" Val stammered, a lack of confidence on his face.

"Sir, we have every type of uniform." She pulled him by the elbow down the hall with her. "Every badge, every insignia, every ribbon. Everything. We'll get you squared away."

Val took a long shower and shaved before checking into the transient barracks for the night.

The next morning, when Val went back to the mortuary, the female tech met him with a dress uniform.

"Here you go, sir. Try it on and let me know if there are any issues."

There weren't. It fit perfectly and was badged correctly. Val hadn't worn dress blues in a long time. Probably since Germany. He stood in the bathroom and looked at himself for a few silent minutes, not sure if he liked what he saw.

"Thank you," Val said when he stepped out of the latrine into the hallway.

"You're very welcome, sir."

"Well, look at you," a voice said behind Val.

Val spun on his heels, not quite believing his ears.

"Liam! What the hell are you doing here?"

"Couldn't let you do this on your own," Liam said, closing the last few steps to Val. The two men hugged.

"God, it's good to see you. How did you know I was here?"

"Sydney."

Val nodded.

"Gentlemen," the female tech said, reluctantly interrupting their reunion. "He's ready."

She gestured down the hall.

Val's and Liam's smiles dissolved.

"I'd like to see him before we load him on the aircraft," Val said softly.

"Of course, sir."

She led Val and Liam a short way down the hall to a small room where Tony lay in an open casket on a wheeled device. She waited at the door as the two men walked cautiously to the casket. They stood motionless and looked at the body.

"They did really good," Val said to Liam, not taking his eyes off Tony. "He was… He was…"

Val's throat tightened. Liam put his hand on Val's shoulder.

There was scant evidence of the ragged, gaping hole in Tony's neck. Disguised by the reconstruction and makeup, Tony's now peaceful face lay still above a pristine dress-blue uniform.

Val gave an *I'm okay* nod to Liam and then leaned forward over Tony. He inspected each button, badge, and insignia. Finally, in a soft whisper, he said, "You look good, brother."

Once Tony was loaded back on the Gulfstream, it took off for the short flight to New Jersey. Liam rode along with Val.

Tony's family lived outside of Trenton. His commander had arranged for one of the hangars on McGuire Air Force Base to be emptied for Tony's arrival. The family would receive the casket there and then proceed to their small hometown church, where the funeral would be held the next day.

It was a cold, overcast day, and the aircraft didn't drop out of the thick gray clouds until they were less than a thousand feet over the airfield. Val placed his hand on Tony's casket as they touched down and left it there as the aircraft taxied to the last hangar on the northwest side of the field.

Liam cleaned his glasses and looked out the window as they approached.

"Little bit of a crowd in the hangar," he said.

Val leaned over to look out one of the aircraft windows.

The hangar door was raised. A group of about fifty people stood against the far wall, waiting.

"I don't see Tony's wife."

"I'm sure she's there," Liam said.

The plane stopped just short of the hangar, and the pilot quickly killed the engines. Val gave Tony's casket a pat and followed one of the crew chiefs out the forward door and down to the tarmac. Liam stayed on the aircraft, waiting for Tony's body to be off-loaded.

Val remained by the nose of the plane as the crew chief stood below the oversized cargo door, preparing to off-load the casket. Two uniformed soldiers wheeled a special metal gurney out from the hangar and came to a stop next to the crew chief. At his direction, they centered the gurney on the cargo door.

Val snuck a look at the crowd in the hangar and was suddenly grateful for the dress uniform.

The oversized cargo door on the side of the Gulfstream opened, and the crowd saw the flag-covered coffin for the first time.

Sobs emanated from the gathering.

The two soldiers raised the telescoping gurney until it was level with the floor of the aircraft. The second crew chief carefully pushed the casket onto the raised gurney.

A woman separated from the crowd, walking toward the aircraft and lowering the casket. One hand held a white handkerchief. Two men in civilian clothes followed her.

Tony's wife.

One man behind her reached for her elbow. She jerked it away and walked faster.

The casket was almost all the way down now.

Tears ran down her face as she stepped up to the casket, startling the two soldiers who had been focused on lowering it without incident.

Tony's wife put both hands on the casket and hung her head. The two men that had followed her hesitated.

The whole operation paused as Tony's wife leaned onto the casket, placing her cheek on the cold metal. She sobbed quietly. One soldier took an unconscious step backward, pushed away by the pain emanating from the sad, intimate moment. The other soldier fixed him with a glare.

Liam stood in the aircraft, looking out of the cargo door, not knowing what to do.

The widow's quiet sobs went on for a long, heartbreaking moment.

The soldiers, worried she would pull the casket over onto herself, stepped forward to steady it.

The two men who had followed her were paralyzed, not sure what to do.

Val moved toward her without thinking. He stepped behind her and put a hand on her back. "Vanessa, let me help you back to the hangar. They will follow us with Tony."

Tony's widow lifted her head. She looked around before finding Val. After a moment, as if trying to place exactly who he was, she stood slowly and nodded.

"Okay," she said, wiping her eyes with the white handkerchief.

Val took Vanessa's elbow, and together they walked toward the hangar. The two men in civilian clothes fell in behind them, and the soldiers set to the task of rolling the casket into the hangar.

It seemed to Val as if there were ten miles of tarmac to cross to get to the hangar. The crowd of attendees watched as he and Tony's widow slowly closed the distance. Vanessa hung on to his arm as if she would fall if she let go. Val tried not to walk too fast.

As they finally walked into the large hangar, a woman stepped forward from the crowd and took Vanessa's other hand. The woman shot Val a quick look that said, *I can take her from here. Thank you.*

Val gave the woman a quick nod and held still as he felt Vanessa's hand slide from his forearm.

The woman put her arm around Vanessa's shoulder. "Let's go to the car now," she said in a gentle voice. "They will bring him to the church."

Tony's widow nodded and took a step with her, but then stopped and turned around.

The woman, startled by Vanessa's sudden move, dropped her arm from her shoulder.

"You're Val, aren't you?" Tony's widow said, as if she'd only just now realized it.

The eyes of the crowd fell on Val.

"Yes. Yes, I am."

Vanessa studied Val's face as she slowly walked back to him. She stopped less than a step away, in front of him, and said, "He loved you so much."

"I…"

She leaned in closer.

"Please tell me it was worth it," she said in a whisper. "Please."

"It… It…"

Val struggled to form the words. He wanted to tell her it was. He wanted to believe it, too.

"We did a lot of good together," he finally managed. "He and I… We did our best together."

Tears welled in Vanessa's eyes again, and her shoulders sagged. She looked at Val as she took a step back and then hesitated. Val felt like he was sinking. A wave of shock and sadness crashed over him as if he were witnessing Tony's death for the first time. Vanessa finally turned and walked away into the crowd, leaving Val standing alone.

Val felt unsteady. He leaned over and put his hands on his knees and struggled to catch his breath. Dizziness washed over him. He went down to one knee. Rubbing his eyes, Val tried to clear his head, but was smothered by a penetrating blanket of fatigue. He wasn't sure he could stand back up. The sadness had him now.

Someone took his hand.

They put their other hand on his upper arm and pulled him up.

"I've got you," Sydney said to him.

Sydney led him to the side of the hangar.

They found a water fountain, and Val splashed his face, clearing his vision. Sydney took his hand and led him out to her rental car.

Sydney held his hand through the next twenty-four hours. Val tried to stay in the background through the viewing and ceremony the next day. Sydney and Liam stayed by his side. When it was over, they rode together back to the airfield.

Sydney held Val's hand while they waited in the small flight operations lobby on McGuire. He and Liam were hitching rides on the Activity's Gulfstream to Dover Air Force Base. From there, Val would get on a larger transport back to Iraq, and Liam would drive back to Langley.

They didn't talk. They had talked little the past day.

"Gentlemen," the crew chief said, walking into the flight ops lobby. "We're ready. Wheels up as soon as you board."

"Roger that," Val said.

"I'll head on to the aircraft and let you guys say goodbye," Liam said. He hugged Sydney, nodded at Val, and left.

Val looked at Sydney.

"Thanks for coming. I don't know what I'd have done without you here."

Sydney nodded, fighting back tears.

Val hugged her and then walked out to the waiting aircraft.

Sydney sat in the flight operations lobby and watched as the small jet taxied to the runway and took off into the evening sky.

She sat there for another hour, watching military aircraft take off and land in the night.

CHAPTER 75

6 May 2008

Mosul, Iraq

"Didn't know you were coming back so soon, Max," Lieutenant Colonel Ramos said when Val walked back into the operations center.

"Well, I'm back, sir."

Val stepped next to MacNamara who was standing in his standard spot, staring at the screens.

"Hello, Mac."

Mac turned from the screens to look at Val. He stared at him for a moment and then adjusted his strapped-on glasses. "You look like shit, sir."

Val shrugged, not taking his eyes off the screens.

Mac glanced at Ramos and then turned back to the screens.

"I thought you had two months of leave built up?" Ramos asked Val.

"What's Moussa's status?" Val asked, ignoring the colonel's question.

Ramos and Mac shared another sidelong glance.

"He's alive," Ramos said. He thought he saw Val's shoulders sag in relief.

"He spent three days in a coma, but on the fourth day, he woke up. He'll be eating soup for a few months, but he's alive. And singing."

Val looked at Ramos.

Ramos smiled.

"On day five, he started talking." Ramos nodded to Val. "He talked and talked and talked. He's still talking."

Val smiled for the first time since Tony died.

"Anything good?"

"Oh yeah. He's given us details on the foreign fighter network in Iraq. We've already used some of it operationally."

"To lethal effect," Mac chimed in.

"Best part, though, he gave us several cell phone numbers. Numbers he claims belongs to Abdul Razzaq himself."

"No shit?" Val asked, not wanting to get his hopes up.

"Razzaq probably tossed them the moment he heard we got Moussa," Mac mumbled to no one in particular.

"You don't know that, Mac!" Ramos glared at the captain for a moment and then turned back to Val.

"That's all good news, sir," Val said. "I'm going to grab some lunch and I'll be back."

"Okay, Max." Ramos watched Val walk out of the ops center and then went to call General Bryson.

Bryson called Val later that day.

"You know how pissed off I get when another officer fucking surprises me with your location?"

Val didn't respond. Technically, he was not in General Bryson's chain of command. But he knew the old man still thought of him as one of his. In many ways, he was. And org charts aside, a three-star general could still make Val do what he wanted.

"I told you to take some time off, Major!"

"You told me to take all the time I needed, sir," Val said flatly. "I did that."

"Don't quibble with me, dammit. It's time for you to come back," Bryson said, stopping just short of ordering Val to return. "You were already on an extension before the shit with your buddy went down. I'm sorry, but I'm concerned about you. And not just about you, Rafter. I'm worried about the soldiers you're working with. Your state of mind, reliability, and performance are shit, son. You're coming home."

"No, sir. Not yet."

"No, sir? I wasn't asking you a question, Major."

"I know. But I need to finish it with Razzaq, sir."

Bryson was silent.

"Look, sir. I'm toast. I'm not denying that. I need to get home. I want to get home." Val was trying to avoid an edict he couldn't wiggle out of. "But I need to see the Razzaq thing through to the end."

He didn't say, "For Tony."

He didn't have to.

"Some of what Moussa gave up was actionable," Val continued, thinking of the cell phone numbers. "I can't leave until we have exhausted those leads."

Bryson was quiet.

Val closed his eyes, fighting back emotion. "Please, sir."

Bryson wavered.

"Okay, goddamn it. But this isn't an open-ended blank check. I'll give you four weeks. That's it."

Val opened his mouth to protest.

"Don't argue with me, Major," Bryson said, cutting him off. "Four weeks. Period."

"Four weeks. Thank you, sir."

"Don't thank me. Just get the bastard and then get your ass home. You've earned it, son."

"Roger that, sir."

General Bryson hung up. *The kid was going to disobey me if I told him to come home, anyway.*

CHAPTER 76

Mac and Ramos pestered the NSA rep almost hourly for an update on the cell phone numbers Moussa had given up.

"Sir, I promise," the harried GS-12 would say. "I promise I'll tell you the moment we get anything."

"This is our chance, goddamn it!" Ramos would bellow. "You guys better have every freaking device in-country listening out for the son of a bitch. Who knows how much longer he will use those cell phones. We've gotta get him now!"

Ramos pushed the HUMINT team just as hard. Every source, every lead, every hint of Razzaq's shadow got followed up. The two case officers from Belvoir were pros, enabling the HUMINT team to respond. Ramos also leveraged their presence to take the heat off Val.

"I'd like you to back up McNamara in the ops center for a bit, Max. Help him connect the dots coming at him. Help us get Razzaq."

Val knew what Ramos was doing and couldn't blame him. He went with it.

Over the next week, Ramos and his task force killed or captured a large component of Abdul Razzaq's operation in northern Iraq. Razzaq had to be feeling the pressure.

But he hadn't turned one of those phones on.

*

"He's moving!" the NSA rep yelled from across the ops center. He ran up to Mac and Val, panting.

"What?" Val asked. "Who's moving? Calm down! Talk to us."

The NSA rep caught his breath and then said as deliberately as he could, "One of the Razzaq cell phones that Moussa gave us, sir. It just went hot. It's in a vehicle northwest of Mosul, headed west toward Syria."

Mac spun around to the operations sergeant. "Find Colonel Ramos. Bring him here. Now!"

"Yes, sir!" the Ranger said, already running for the door.

Val checked his watch. It was 2115 hours.

Twelve minutes later, Lieutenant Colonel Ramos, along with a host of other people, stared intently at the center screen in the ops center.

"How sure are you guys?" Ramos asked the NSA rep. "We gotta be sure on this one."

"Hundred percent, sir."

"How long has the phone been hot?"

"About fifteen minutes, sir."

"He'll brick his phone any minute now," Mac mumbled.

Ramos nodded. "Good work getting the ISR on him so fast," he said to Mac and the NSA rep as he looked at the overhead drone footage on the center screen. A sedan drove west across the desert on Highway 1.

Ramos looked at his watch.

"So, how long till he gets to the border?"

"Maybe half an hour."

"Shit," Ramos said. "Not much time."

"Sir, I've got a field control officer with three Rangers on the Syrian border meeting with an asset," Val said. "If we get them moving now, they will have time to set up an ambush before Razzaq crosses the border."

"Good," Ramos said. "They're our backstop. Get them moving."

Val nodded and moved to a radio to call his team.

"Mac, get a Delta platoon moving," Ramos ordered. "I want them airborne ASAP."

"They'll never make it in time, sir. Razzaq is less than half an hour from the border."

"We don't know shit yet, Mac," Ramos said, irritation in his voice. "I want optionality. Get 'em in the fucking air."

"Roger that, sir."

"We lost it!" the NSA rep said, stepping back into the group in front of the center screen.

"Lost what?" Ramos demanded.

"The cell phone. It's gone completely cold. He must have turned it off and removed the battery. Hell, he might have destroyed it, I don't know. But we're no longer receiving a signal from it, that I can tell you."

"Was bound to happen." Ramos stared at the vehicle on the center screen. "But we still have visual."

Ramos turned to face the group.

"We won't let this opportunity slip away," he said in a loud voice. "The next hour or two might be the most important time in your entire career. So, everyone, get your mind right. Right fucking now!"

There were already a couple more people than usual in the operations center. Important intel and missions exerted their own gravity on the task force, drawing people in. There was an elevated energy level in the room. They all nodded earnestly at Ranger Ramos.

"Team is moving," Val said to Ramos. "When they're set up and Razzaq gets closer, we'll start counting them down."

"Thank you. But I'm really hoping we get lucky and can drop a Delta platoon on his ass."

Val nodded. He felt the same.

"Max, get someone to the hospital to talk to Moussa," Ramos said. "See if he can give us any details that might be helpful. Does he know where Razzaq is going? Who is he meeting with? Does he take a piss before the border? Anything we might use to understand our timeline and what to expect."

"On it." Val turned to walk to the telephone. He called the HUMINT operations center and dispatched one of the recently arrived case officers to the hospital.

"Delta is wheels up, sir," Mac told Ramos.

"Damn," Ramos said with respect. "That was fast."

"When they heard it was Razzaq, they jumped through their ass," Mac said with a smile. "The Night Stalker pilots were drooling, too. I hope they get a shot at him."

"Me too. How long till they get there?"

"About thirty minutes."

Ramos looked at the vehicle on the center screen. "It's gonna be tight. He'll get to the border in about twenty minutes."

Once Razzaq got to the border, he would vanish. The task force had, on very few occasions, pursued targets into Syria, but only in remote areas. They went across unobserved, killed a bunch of people, and then returned. This area was not unobserved. There was a checkpoint with official personnel on both sides and a lot of civilians. The task force would not have the option of a quick, stealthy incursion.

The ambush, if it came to that, would not be a layup. It was nighttime, and the darkness would make a positive identification of the car difficult for the team on the ground. There was a hesitance to use Sparkle, since there was a good chance there would be friendly and non-friendly elements with night vision near the border. There was also a strong desire to hit Razzaq before he got too close to the actual border itself, where there would be more civilians and other actors.

The ops center was engulfed in activity. Val communicated via radio with his field control officer, sending updated intelligence as they prepared to ambush the vehicle if Delta didn't make it in time. Mac pushed hard on the NSA, NGA, and other reps to get the Delta platoon team as much information as possible as their Black Hawks flew west. All the while, the center screen glowed with the infrared image of a car making its way across the desert on Highway 1 toward Syria.

There was cautious excitement in the ops center. Maybe tonight was the night. Maybe they would finally kill Razzaq, a deadly foreign fighter coordinator that had eluded the Joint Special Operations Command machine for years.

Val's phone rang. It was the case officer Val had sent to the hospital to see if Moussa could provide any helpful last-minute intelligence. "Steve," as the task force knew him, was excited.

"Moussa says he knows where Razzaq is going," Steve told Val. "He says Razzaq will turn off the highway before getting to the border. Says there is a small town a few kilometers south called Masif, or something like that. He doesn't think Razzaq will risk crossing the border, rather one of his foreign facilitators will meet him there."

Ramos, Val, and Mac huddled in front of the large display. In the center of the large screen, a lone vehicle moved west on a mostly empty highway, its headlights lancing feebly into the dark.

"I don't trust Moussa," Mac said.

"I sure as hell don't trust Moussa either," Val said. "But he has no reason to lie to us about this."

"Well, if he is telling the truth, this is going to be a big night," Ramos said.

The three men looked at the map spread out on the table in front of them.

Highway 1 runs from Baghdad to Mosul and then continues to the northwest. The road crosses into Syria at a small border town called Rabiah. Masif, a village of not much more than a single crossroad, sits about five kilometers to the south of Rabiah, on a road that parallels the Syrian border. The turnoff to Masif is just prior to Rabiah, about two kilometers from the border crossing.

"Too bad we can't get to him before he gets to that intersection," Mac said. "We could hit him before he had the option to turn off."

"True," Val said. "But if we did that, we'd lose any chance at intel from letting him meet his contact."

"It would be the surest way to make sure we got him, though"

Val nodded.

"Mac, get on the radio to the pilots," Ramos said. "Give them the update. They need to be prepared to divert to Masif if he heads that way."

Mac stepped away to the radio.

"This is going to be messy," Val said to Ramos. "That stretch of road through Rabiah and the border checkpoint is a nightmare. There is always a lot of traffic and congestion, even at night. And we're going to be relaying instructions to the team, trying to help them positively ID the right vehicle, while they contend with all the bullshit around them."

"It's Delta," Ramos said. "They'll cope."

Ramos looked at his watch and grimaced. He wished they had more time. He also wished time would go faster. But there was nothing to do. He paced back and forth in front of the big screen. Everyone in the operations center gave Ramos space as they went about their duties.

"Can we zoom out here?" Ramos pointed at the middle screen as he asked the drone operator. "Can we get the intersection in frame as well?"

The operator nodded, reducing the zoom on the drone's image. The intersection lay on the far left edge of the frame. Razzaq's vehicle was on the far right.

The car drove west. The ambush team waited. The helicopters sprinted.

After long minutes of silence in the ops center, Ramos said, "All right, heads up. He's less than a minute from the intersection."

Everyone froze. All eyes focused on the center screen.

The drone operator had zoomed in so that the car and intersection both loomed large on the screen.

Mac stood by the radios, ready to call the helicopters and ambush team as soon as Razzaq's route was known.

Val stood next to Ramos, directly in front of the screen.

The two men stood in silence as the vehicle's brake lights flared and it turned south, off Highway One, toward Masif.

"Fuck me," Val said. "We gotta chance."

"Mac! Divert the helicopters to Masif," Ramos yelled.

Mac gave a thumbs-up as he held the radio handset to his ear with his other hand. He was already talking to the pilots.

"Zoom out the imagery, please," Ramos said. "How long we got till he gets to Masif?"

"Probably about seven minutes, sir," one of the operations sergeants answered.

"How far out are the helicopters?"

"About fifteen minutes, sir."

"Mac, let the pilots know they're assaulting on the X," Ramos said. "We'll send coordinates as soon as Razzaq gets there."

A wave of anxiety swept through the operations center. Hearing Ramos say "assaulting on the X" drove home what everyone knew but hadn't yet been acknowledged.

This was going to be a high-risk operation.

The room grew quiet as everyone watched the car on the center screen work its way to the south on the desolate road.

For several minutes, no one spoke.

Ramos paced back and forth.

Val sat at one of the inner ring tables.

Mac stood near the radios.

The room was nearly full. Word had gotten out that this may be a big one.

"He's approaching Massif," Mac said. "Helicopters are nine minutes out."

"We better get a visual on him before the birds get there," Ramos said. "We cannot hit the house without visual confirmation it's him. I do not want to make CNN tonight."

The car slowed as it entered the small village. It turned off the main road down one of the small side streets.

"He's going there" Val gestured at the large screen. Near the top of the image, at the end of the side street, was a small house with four vehicles parked in front of it. "That's where the party is."

"I think you're right," Ramos said. He stopped pacing and watched the vehicle proceed to that house and come to a stop. "That's it, Mac! Give the pilots the lat/long! That's the target."

"Sending!" Mac said loudly before transmitting the information to the helicopters.

"Zoom in," Ramos ordered. "We've got to ID him. Zoom in!"

"Helicopters six minutes out," Mac said.

The image on the large center screen zoomed in, tightening around the vehicle as the operator magnified the image. In seconds, the vehicle and stone walkway to the house filled the scene. A bright light above the front door of the house illuminated the area in a large, clear cone of light.

Two men got out of the parked car, the driver and a passenger from the front seat. They walked toward the house along a stone pathway into the bright light.

A man emerged from the house and walked out to greet them.

"Damn this viewing angle," Ramos said. "I can't tell if that's him. Can you, Max?"

Val stared intently at the screen.

"Max, this is your call," Ramos said. "You make the ID."

It made sense. Val was the high-value target expert. He'd studied Razzaq's face for years.

But when Ramos passed that baton, Val felt the weight of the entire operation and all of his past mistakes land on him. Years ago, he'd let Haskell walk. A month ago, when Tony was still alive, he'd let Moussa go. Anxiety tightened his throat. He had to make the right call this time.

The drone's point of view was from behind the two men that had just exited the vehicle. It swiveled to the right slowly as the drone executed its circling loiter pattern.

Val thought it was Razzaq, but he waited for the man's profile to come into better view.

"Five minutes," Mac said.

"Max?" Ramos asked.

Val's entire awareness focused on the image in front of him. He felt confident it was Razzaq, but he had to be certain. He couldn't fuck this up.

The man who had come from the house closed the distance to the other two.

"Max!" Ramos barked. "What's the call?"

Val ignored Ramos. He narrowed his eyes. He had to get this right. People were going to live or die based on his next words.

On the screen, the three men in the pool of light in front of the house shook hands and laughed.

A jolt of recognition ran through Val as if he'd stuck his finger into a wall socket.

Val fought a sensation of disbelief.

"Max!" Ramos yelled. "Talk to me!"

The drone's viewing angle had shifted about forty-five degrees, giving Val a perfect image of each of the men.

It was Razzaq. Beyond all doubt. They had him.

But that was not who Val focused on.

"Zoom in!" Val shouted as he bolted from his seat and lunged at the screen. "Zoom in! Give me all the zoom you have!"

"Do it, goddamn it!" Ramos shouted.

"Sir, we are—"

"Shut the fuck up!" Ramos yelled, interrupting Mac. He turned to Val.

"Max," Ramos said, in a voice that was suddenly calm and measured. "It's now or never, brother."

"It's him," Val said, not taking his eyes from the screen.

"We're a go!" Ramos announced to the ops center. He pointed at Mac. The Ranger captain gave Ramos a thumbs-up as he spoke to the pilots on the radio.

"Three minutes to target!"

"They'll hear the helicopters approaching soon," Ramos said, stepping next to Val. "I have a feeling this is going to be a hell of a shootout."

Val didn't respond.

He was staring at the large screen, transfixed by the image of the man who had emerged from the house.

He was staring at Alexei Volkov.

CHAPTER 77

Val studied the dead body as the sun neared the horizon. A searing yellow-orange ribbon blazed to the east, stars were still visible to the west.

Val looked at his watch, impatient for the sunrise. Ordinarily, this was his favorite time in the desert. The nautical twilights at the beginning and end of each day when the sun was still just below the horizon, and the world seemed to hang between night and day. Color and light to one side, darkness to the other.

Now, though, as he worked to positively ID bodies, he wanted visual acuity.

He pulled out his flashlight and shined it on the dead man's face. The right half had been mangled by a well-placed bullet to the forehead, just above the eye.

Val shook his head in grim appreciation of Delta. No matter how many times he worked with them, he came away impressed every time.

Most of that side of the man's skull was gone, including the eyeball. Even so, Val could see right away it was not him.

Not Razzaq. He moved to the next one. *Not Alexei either.*

Ramos had been right. It was a hell of a shootout.

Val had watched it unfold with the rest of the team in the operations center.

Razzaq, his driver, and Alexei had heard the helicopters approaching only a minute or two before they arrived. They ran into the house to give warning, and armed men started pouring out of the house and taking up defensive positions. Val and Ramos tried to keep count.

"Shit," Ramos said when he reached ten and more kept spilling out.

Val didn't respond. He was trying to scan the faces as they emerged from the house, looking for Alexei.

The helicopters came in hot. The pilots maintaining their airspeed until the last possible moment in order to minimize the time between them being heard and the assault.

They decelerated aggressively, putting the Black Hawks nearly vertical to shed airspeed.

The door gunners opened up. Miniguns spat fire down on the hastily assumed fighting positions around the house.

One pilot flew to the ground, touching down tailwheel first. He held the aircraft nose high, letting the rotor disc slow them further before slamming it down on its main landing gear. The pilot stood on the brakes as the aircraft slid fifty meters across the sand before coming to a halt, miniguns blazing throughout.

The Delta commandos were off the helicopters in an instant. And the aircraft was off the ground seconds later.

The other aircraft decelerated just as aggressively and terminated to a hover above the objective as the crew chiefs kicked thick fast ropes out of each open door. The door gunners swept the area with 7.62s as the operators plunged down the ropes into the darkness. Seconds later, the helicopter was accelerating away, and the Delta commandos were on the roof.

"Okay," Ramos whispered to himself, relieved to have one of the most vulnerable phases of the mission, the helicopter-borne insertion, behind them with no casualties. There were ten Delta operators on the roof, twelve on the ground. "Now give 'em hell."

Less than twenty minutes later, the firefight was over.

Two Delta operators had been wounded, and both of the helicopters had suffered minor battle damage. But the hasty, chaotic assault had been successful. Twelve enemy had been killed. Five wounded and captured.

A single ground vehicle had escaped with an estimated three men on board before Delta had secured the area. The four-wheel-drive vehicle had left the melee driving in a straight line for the border, a little more than a mile away. Within minutes, it had crossed into Syria, and Ramos elected not to pursue. With wounded Americans on the objective and both aircraft already damaged, he didn't have the stomach for more unquantifiable risk.

When the ground commander called, "Objective secure," over the radio, Ramos launched the site exploitation team with a platoon of Rangers in two Night Stalker Chinooks. He stayed in the operations center and waited with all of his fingers crossed, hoping they had gotten Razzaq.

Val went with the site exploitation team on one of the Chinooks.

When he arrived, Delta had already dragged the bodies out of the battered house and fighting positions where they had died. They had lined the dozen dead men up in a neat row to the side of the house.

Val started the identification task immediately. One of his BIT team sergeants followed him to take pictures of the dead men and tissue samples to be used later for DNA analysis, if possible.

He stepped next to the second body, illuminating his face with the large flashlight.

"Shit." Val looked away quickly. The dead man had taken a round to the throat. Thoughts of Tony flooded Val's mind. He could feel his pulse quickening.

"You okay, sir?" the BIT sergeant asked.

"Yeah." Val rubbed his eyes. "Little sand in my eyes, is all. I'm good."

Val moved to the next body.

Not Razzaq.

Not Alexei.

After six negative IDs, Val was anxious. Had Razzaq escaped?

Recognition shot through Val as he stepped over the seventh body.

Haskell.

Masudi Kader had taken several rounds to the chest, and his robe was soaked in blood. His head, though, was untouched. Masudi's handsome and distinguished face with its eyes closed as if in thought could have been resting before a dinner party. His tousled and dusty hair was the only indication of the earlier violence.

I should've fucking known. Anger surged within Val. Anger at himself. Anger at Tony for going along with his stupid idea. Anger at Haskell. Razzaq. Alexei.

Val took a few steps away from the bodies. He shook his head and looked at the darkness in the west.

"Sir? You okay?" the BIT sergeant asked.

Val's anger dissolved into regret as he stood with his hands on his hips, looking at the shadows on the western horizon. *If you hadn't vouched for me, brother, I wouldn't be here, and you'd be alive. I'm so sorry.*

"Major Santanna?"

Val closed his eyes. He wanted to cry and scream.

"Sir? You good?"

"I'm fine, damn it," Val said, walking back to the row of dead men. Val avoided looking at Haskell as he walked to the eighth body. "Don't ask me that again."

The eighth was much younger, maybe in his twenties. The victim of a grenade or similar explosive device, his body was burned and covered in deep puncture wounds.

Val stepped over to the ninth body and illuminated its face with his flashlight. An involuntary sigh of relief escaped him. He turned off his flashlight and stepped away from the body. Val stood still for a moment and let his eyes rest on the horizon to the east. The yellow and orange glow burned brighter now. The stars were fading. It wouldn't be long before the sun was up.

Val closed his eyes.

We got him, Tony. We got Razzaq. You can rest a little easier now.

The BIT sergeant looked at him with concern but was afraid to ask him if he was okay.

Val opened his eyes. He caught the concerned sergeant looking. "I'm good, Sergeant. Just getting my head around the moment."

He walked back to the body and stood over it. The dead man had taken several rounds to the legs and torso. His head was angled slightly back, and there was a deep laceration across his forehead. His eyes were still open, and his mouth gaped as if he were trying to take one last breath.

"That him?" the sergeant asked with excitement.

Val smiled. Rather than answer directly, he grabbed his radio and called Ramos, smiling at the sergeant as he did.

"Ramos, Max."

"Go ahead, Max."

"We got him." Val winked at the sergeant.

"You sure?" Ramos asked as the sergeant pumped his fists next to Val.

"Yeah. I'm sure. We'll get the tissue samples so we can confirm."

Val looked down at Razzaq's body.

"But I'm telling you, we got him."

CHAPTER 78

1 Jun 2008

DIA Headquarters, Bolling Air Force Base

Val and General Bryson sat across from each other in a secure conference room. Photos and files were strewn across the table.

Val sat with his hands folded in his lap, looking at the general, who was studying a photo.

"You were right," Bryson said. "It's Alexei Volkov."

Val nodded slowly.

"I've had the image analysis team go over it three times just to be sure," the general said, putting down the photo, a freeze frame of the drone image of the men outside the small house that night in Massif.

"That assessment is corroborated by the interrogations of the prisoners we got during the raid," Bryson continued. "They said Razzaq was there to meet with 'the Russian,' whose identity they didn't know.

"The vehicle that escaped the raid made it across the border," the general gestured at a different stack of printed photos. "Satellite imagery of the area determined that the vehicle drove to a remote airstrip, where one of the passengers was transferred to a helicopter that then flew north into Turkey, where we lost it."

General Bryson pointed at another photo on the table.

"And that dead son of a bitch is Masudi Kader. The infamous Haskell."

Val looked down at the photo.

Bryson waited until Val raised his eyes from the bloody image. "He was the one you vetted but then passed on in Iraq a few years ago, wasn't he?"

"Yes, sir."

The general nodded slowly.

"Did it surprise you to find him there?"

"Yes, sir. It did."

Bryson studied Val for a long, tense moment. Val met his gaze evenly.

"Kader, Razzaq, and Volkov all at the same place," the general finally said, shaking his head and leaning back in his chair. "Fucking Russians. You didn't tell anyone in the task force? Not even the commander?"

"No."

"Why not?"

"Didn't seem like the right thing to do. To begin with, I could have been wrong. I haven't seen the guy in almost ten years."

"The Marshall Center?"

"That's right." Val nodded. "And second, I didn't think it was relevant to the mission at hand, which was going to be hairy enough. If I had thought it was important for the operators to know, I'd have spoken up. But…"

Val's voice trailed off as he relived the event.

"I think you did the right thing," General Bryson said. "This is highly sensitive, need-to-know-only intelligence."

Val's face was pensive. Bryson didn't like it.

"More than the right thing, Val," the general said, leaning forward in his chair, "you did good work. Really good work. You helped put Razzaq in the ground and confirmed Russian involvement in the foreign fighter network operating in Iraq. We've suspected it for years, but you just gave us the intelligence to prove it. Hell of a job, son."

Val nodded slowly, as if thinking of something else.

"Stop it!" General Bryson said sharply.

Val's eyes darted from his hands to meet Bryson's gaze.

"What, sir?"

"Stop thinking what you're thinking."

"Sir?"

"Don't fuck with me! I've known you a long time."

Val took a deep breath and let it out slowly, trying to get control of his emotions.

"Alexei Volkov isn't your problem."

Val tried to focus on the breathing techniques he'd learned in his PTSD counseling.

"Listen to me, Major," the general said in a voice that was friendlier than Val expected. "I get it. You want to kill him. You want to get up from that chair, leave this office, chase that Russian around the world, and kill him."

Val looked at General Bryson. He had to say it.

"I do," Val said through clenched teeth. "And I will."

Bryson shook his head sadly.

"No. You won't."

Val shifted in his chair. The rage was close to getting the better of him.

"Val, listen to me," the general said in a gentle voice. "There are about one-point-three million active-duty American military personnel. Only about 10 percent of them see actual combat. Less than half of those who see combat actually fire their weapon. Essentially, none of them actually know the enemy. They rarely even see their face.

"You have done everything we have asked you to do. And done it well. You've seen combat, and you have seen the enemy. Up close.

"Worse, though… you know the enemy. You befriended one of them. And you did so because we made it your mission more than ten years ago.

"And it has burdened you. Affected your perception. It has twisted what was just your duty, and Tony's duty, and Zyph's duty, and, yes, Volkov's duty, into something personal."

General Bryson paused. It pained him to see the emotion on Val's face.

"You have to put down this personal lens you're viewing the world through. If you don't, it will continue to twist and torture you."

"I'll never let it go," Val said.

"You have to. Trust me on this, Val. There is no satisfaction at the end of the road you're on. None."

"Well, I'm going to bloody well walk it, anyway."

"No, you're not," Bryson said. "I'm taking you off it."

Val looked at the general. "What the hell are you talking about, sir?"

"You need a break. You need distance and perspective."

Val shook his head. "Don't you fucking dare, sir."

"We're reassigning you, Major."

"I won't do it," Val's voice shook with anger. "I'm not going to the Pentagon or anyone's candy-ass staff."

"Oh, Val." The general chuckled ruefully and shifted his weight in his chair, getting ready for Val's reaction. "That would be too close to the fight, son. I said you need a total break. A complete change of pace. Some perspective."

"What the hell are you talking about? I have unfinished business." Val jabbed his finger on the conference table. "And I'm going to finish it."

"Son, I'm doing this because I love you," General Bryson said with a smile that was genuine. "Someday you will thank me. I'm putting you as far from the fight as I possibly can."

Val was shaking his head vigorously.

"No, no, no. I won't do it. I'll quit, sir. I'll leave the military. I'll go get him myself."

"Not without a goddamn passport, you won't."

Val's head cocked at the comment.

"Who do you think you're dealing with here, Major?" Bryson was incredulous. "You don't think I can shut your ass down with the snap of a finger? And let's remember, you're still the single most famously burned intelligence officer in the fucking world! You better get your head around this, or you won't even be able to cross county lines without appealing to me."

Val glared.

Bryson took a breath.

"Val, I'm thinking of your well-being here. No one has been through more than you. This doesn't have to be the end. But it's going to be a pause. Whether or not you quit is up to you, of course. But I think that would be a waste and a damn shame."

The two men sat in silence for a moment.

"Well, let's hear it," Val finally said. "Where do you think you're sending me?"

"You're going to West Point."

Val started yelling all over again.

CHAPTER 79

It looked like the world was burning behind the mountains on the far side of the Hudson River. Val paused for a moment, appreciating the crisp morning air, before hefting his backpack and locking his car. He looked at the spreading glow of the sunrise to the east for another moment and then started walking.

Val adopted the custom of parking as far from his office as possible early in his West Point assignment. He made the walk from Buffalo Soldiers Field to Washington Hall, a little more than a mile, no matter the weather. The mountains rising on all sides reminded him of North Carolina. They were the same mountains, after all. The Appalachians.

The Hudson runs almost due south as it threads its way to New York Bay. The United States Military Academy sits on high ground above the river about fifty miles north of the city. Thayer Road runs from the main gate to the barracks and academic buildings, tracing the west side of the river and offering spectacular views of the mountains to the east and the river below.

Besides the dramatic views, the walk gave Val's mind some meditative space. By the time he walked into the academic area, with its hulking gray stone buildings squatting on either side of Thayer Road, his body and mind were both warm.

Val would step into one of the various academic departments before continuing on to Washington Hall in the center of the cadet area. He walked the halls and dropped in on fellow officers and professors to say hello and chat.

Since arriving almost four years ago, Val had worked West Point as if he'd been working a foreign government. He didn't suffer from the sentimental fog that affected the perspective of officers who were alumni. The place fascinated his intelligence officer mind. It was a target. He studied it objectively.

Val's colleagues soon referred to his morning custom as his "mayoral walks," and ribbed him for the way he worked the hallways. But Val couldn't help himself. After fifteen years as an intelligence officer, the muscle memory was too strong. It was as if he were stationed at a foreign embassy. He was building a network of relationships and a mental template for how the place worked.

He concluded early on it was like no organization he'd ever studied.

"Twenty-three separate pirate ships flying under the same black flag," was how Val now described West Point to newly reporting officers. "The twenty-three academic departments here operate under the dean's command," he advised. "But they are not allies. They raid each other, competing for budget, resources, visibility, and the most valuable coin of the realm—cadet time."

Time with cadets was the ultimate measure of relevancy. Academic department members competed fiercely for it, all searching for the unique alchemy that would gain them favor among the Corps of Cadets. Favor that could bring fortune to field-grade military careers, sending them out of West Point at the end of their tour with new professional momentum.

Val was assigned to the geography department, led by Colonel Hugh Baum. He learned later that Baum had taken him on as a favor to an old friend, General Bryson. Baum was an intelligence officer by training and an academic by inclination. He and Bryson had gone through the Farm together and served in the same unit in Berlin in the early eighties.

Their careers had diverged, though. When Captain Baum toured at West Point as a professor, he was hooked. He loved teaching cadets and the academy. Baum found his home in academia and took over the geography department in 1998. He hoped to never leave. In his words, it was going to take a truckload of C-4 to get him out of his seat.

Despite their professional divergence, Baum and Bryson had remained close friends. Baum stayed connected to the intelligence community. He was an expert in human and physical geography, and Special Operations Command sought his expertise as the War on Terror became a global undertaking. General Bryson appointed him to a special board of advisors that assisted the US Army intelligence community's leadership. When Bryson asked Baum to find a place for Val, the colonel professor did so without hesitation.

"He's a pain in the ass," Bryson warned Baum. "But he's a hell of a human intelligence officer and combat leader. And he has been through some shit. He needs to heal up. I don't know what else to do with him."

"Say no more," Baum said. "I'll find him a spot."

"Thanks, Hugh. But if he becomes too much of a pain in the ass, you call me. I'll come grab the knucklehead."

Val spent his first year at West Point in a haze of rage and mourning. Thoughts of Tony, Omar, Haskell, Abakumov, and Alexei were never far from his mind. Sydney also. Everything seemed unfinished. Unfair. Unavenged.

He was angry.

At everyone.

Colonel Baum kept him busy, assigning Val numerous additional duties that were time-consuming and forced him to interact with cadets often.

Over time, the grounding power of West Point's natural setting and the regenerative, naïve energy of the Corps of Cadets began to work on Val's spirit.

Sitting astride the Hudson River and beneath mountains on every side, there is no place further from the desert than West Point. Each season there declares its arrival in a change of colors, weather patterns, and hours of sunlight. It lingers for months and is then replaced by the next. The natural rhythm prodded Val's mind forward, out of its agonizing paralysis.

And the corps embraced him.

Val didn't have a geography degree. But as an intelligence offer and combat veteran, he had an appreciation and respect for natural and human geography. He didn't teach "by the book." Instead, he tried to organize his classes to be valuable to cadets' future army careers. He provided them with a way to think about deployments to foreign lands, fighting in different terrains, and interacting with different cultures.

Val was not embraced by West Point's small PhD community or by the curriculum or accreditation committees. But the corps loved him. His classes were in high demand. And he therefore held sway in the realm.

The pain never went away. The agonizing memories were always walking by his side, ready to leap forward in his mind. Gradually, though, the distance between those experiences and the life he was leading increased. He found his enthusiasm for instructing and mentoring cadets distracted him from the pain. And he let it do so.

Val was surprised to be promoted to lieutenant colonel in the fall of 2011, after three years at West Point. He'd been certain his spectacular run-in with Abakumov and ejection from the program had eliminated him from consideration for higher rank.

But Bryson worked the situation harder than Val knew. The wily general spun the positive, the interruption of the arms shipment, and made the story sexy for the promotion board.

"Fucking promotion boards." The general had chuckled when Val called him to express surprise at making light colonel. "So easy to play those vanilla army wannabes."

Val laughed.

"Not that you don't deserve it, son," Bryson added quickly. "You do."

"I do. But I'm still grateful. You just materially increased my pension."

"Well, you know my favorite beer."

"I do, sir. I'll work on Herr Dorn to increase your allocation and let me pay for it."

"Well, I appreciate it. But unless someone dies, you won't be able to."

Val laughed.

"Besides, I was just doing my job. The army has sunk too much money into you to let you go too soon. You never know when I may need a few more laps out of you."

"I'm radioactive, sir," Val said without sadness. "Burned beyond all usefulness."

"You're done sneaking up on people. That's for sure. But there is plenty of overt shit I could use help with."

Val looked out of his office window at the Hudson Valley fall.

A moment passed.

"Well. I'll be damned," the general said.

"What's that, sir?"

"There was a time you wouldn't leave me alone about getting out of there," the general said in a voice that betrayed his smile. "You remember your demands to let you go to South Ossetia?"

Val couldn't resist smiling to himself as well. It was true. He'd called the general a few times a week during those first few months at the academy. He hated it. He was angry. It didn't help when Russia invaded Georgia. Val wanted a rifle and a plane ticket back to the fight. He'd wanted to find Alexei. He'd yelled at anyone who answered.

Bryson's staff stopped transferring the calls to the general. Which enraged Val even more.

"Back then, if I had cracked open the door of possibility for you, like I did just now, you'd have knocked me over charging through it."

"Yeah," Val said, not taking his eyes off the colors of the changing leaves across the river. "Maybe I'll feel that way again. But…"

General Bryson waited in silence.

After a full minute of thought, Val said, "I don't know why I like it so much here. I'm not a grad. I'm not an academic. I don't buy all the 'duty, honor, country' bullshit."

"I can see why they like you so much," Bryson said with a sigh.

"Oh, come on, sir. You know it's all bullshit. It starts off as duty, honor, country for all of us. But it ends up, decades later, just…"

Val's voice trailed off again.

Again, Bryson waited for him to finish the thought.

"Habit…Or something like it."

The general didn't respond.

"Hell, I don't know, sir. But I guess being around these ignorant kids makes me remember what it was like when it was still duty, honor, country for me."

Silence filled the line again.

"Anyway. I really appreciate your help with the promotion."

"Like I said, son, you earned it."

"Thank you, sir," Val said, finally taking his eyes off the mountains to the east.

"If you ever do feel the itch. Just raise your hand."

"I will, sir. I promise."

"No need to be in a rush. This goddamn war will sure as hell be here if you ever want back in."

It had been a year since that phone call, and Val had still not raised his hand.

He thought about it from time to time, often during his morning walks, like today's.

The sun crested the mountains as Val neared the academic area. The Hudson, hundreds of feet below Val as he walked along Thayer Road, was silver now. A blaze of orange lit the sky to the northeast. Purple smudges of cirrus clouds spread high above, radiating into the distance.

Hulking gray stone buildings rose on both sides as Val walked into the academic area. He entered Mahan Hall on his right. The mechanical engineering department always had coffee and good donuts on Fridays.

Val worked in the mechanical engineering department for about half an hour, spending most of his time with a young artillery captain, Seth Weber. Weber was trying to put together summer experience for cadets and sought Val's advice on how to get approved and funded.

"Some of the best examples of turn-of-the-century bridging projects are right down the road in New York City and the surrounding area," Weber said with excitement.

"Uh-huh," Val said, grabbing another donut.

"In just a week, a cadet could be immersed in suspension, cantilever, and cable-stay constructions."

Val smiled as he chewed. He loved the enthusiasm.

"I think I could put together a one-week experiential curriculum that would be as good as a semester-long forty-hour class," Weber continued. "One week touring and studying actual structures around the island of Manhattan, then each cadet would pick a structure to write a report about. You know, demonstrate what they learned. I've already got three or four cadets that have expressed interest. What do you think, Colonel?"

Val took a swig of coffee and then said, "I like it."

Captain Weber beamed.

"But it won't fly."

Weber sagged.

"I'm not saying you can't make something of it," Val said, unable to suppress a chuckle at the crestfallen officer.

He placed his hand on the captain's shoulder.

"You've got the bones of a good cadet experience there. But remember, you're up against the history department and all their damn staff ride trips. How do you make it compete against touring the beaches of Normandy during the day, and guzzling French wine and chasing members of the opposite sex at night?"

A major who was familiar with Val smiled and leaned in. She loved to hear him preach.

"And you need at least a few dozen cadets to be interested. A handful won't get you funding to walk off post into Highland Falls."

Val took his hand from the captain's shoulder and moved across the room to the coffeepot.

Captain Weber looked at his shoes in defeat.

"Tell you what I'd do," Val said, not looking up from topping off his coffee.

Weber stepped closer. The major followed. Another captain did as well.

"Add a public service component to the trip." Val turned from the coffeepot to face Weber. Five other officers clustered around to hear his thoughts. "Set up meetings with the municipal departments that are tasked with maintaining the bridges. How do they do it? What are the challenges? How do they fund it? Blah-blah-blah. See if you can get the mayor's office to respond. See if Bloomberg will meet with the kids. Even for five minutes. Then see if you can get someone from the mayor's office to send a note to the administration here about how excited His Honor is to meet with the future leaders of America." Val leaned toward Weber conspiratorially. "That shit will get you funded."

Weber nodded as if suddenly understanding the world.

"But you gotta get your numbers up," Val said. "Remember, in a cadet's mind, a big part of these trips is about escaping this place." Val pointed at where they were standing. "Getting away from the academy and its suffocating grip.

"You gotta ramp up the social component. Couple nice dinners in town. See if you can get a cool hotel to give you a screaming rate to have uniformed cadets in the building. And organize some kind of mixer with schools in the city. You know, give 'em a target-rich environment. That always lines 'em up," Val said with a wink.

"Roger that, sir," Captain Weber said, nodding.

Val looked at his watch.

"I've got to run. Great seeing you guys."

"Sir," Weber said. "Just one more thing. Can I—"

"I'm sorry, Captain." Val walked toward the door. "I let time get away from me. Shoot me an email."

"I will, sir."

Val grabbed his backpack and hustled out into the cool air. He walked quickly through the central area, dodging cadets as he hurried to make his standing 0800 hours appointment. It was a meeting he'd started attending on his first day at West Point. One that he made it to without fail every day.

His morning solo time in the Washington Hall SCIF.

A SCIF is a sensitive compartmented information facility. It's a secure area that's used to review information or communicate without danger of compromise or unauthorized access. Most US military facilities have one. Typically, SCIFs sit deep in a basement, wrapped in a faraday cage and other electronic eavesdrop-defeating measures and are accessed only by a very few with the proper clearance.

West Point's SCIF, sitting in its ivory academic tower far from the fight, rarely saw a lot of use. Until Val arrived.

Washington Hall was the central building in the cadet area, containing both the cadet mess hall and extensive academic facilities. The six-story gray stone building rises at the intersection of several long barracks buildings and looms over the center of the Plain, where cadets march in their parades.

Some professors disliked working in Washington Hall. The fact that the academic facilities sat on top of the mess hall meant that there were always cadets in the building three times a day. Many professors preferred the shadowy corridors of the more remote academic buildings where cadets seldom wandered.

But Val liked Washington Hall. He enjoyed being close to the energy of the corps.

Val's office and the classrooms he taught in were on the sixth floor. He also liked the fact that Washington was rich in lecture halls, big and small. He could always get one when the need arose, whether it was to review material with cadets or host impromptu strategy sessions with colleagues.

The SCIF was embedded in the upper floors of Washington Hall, at the end of an obscure hallway near the dean's office. Behind the key-card-restricted SCIF door lay a top-secret access terminal, a secure telephone, a safe, and a large paper shredder.

Every morning before class, Val would scan the cables and materials. His interest was general, but by the end of each season, his reviews were focused. Russian foreign fighter activity in the Middle East and elsewhere.

He held his 13th Tactical switchblade, turning the closed knife over in his hand, as he scanned the material with a cool, emotionless eye. He was not driven into the SCIF by passion. The balm of West Point was real. It permeated Val and had brought him some measure of happiness.

But he'd promised himself.

Someday, he would find and kill Alexei.

He didn't know how. And in reasonable moments, he knew it was a vow he made to make himself feel better. To assuage his guilt. It was a vow destined to be left unfulfilled.

But it was probably the only reason that he would leave West Point.

During his first year at the academy, Val spent all his free time in the SCIF. Russia's invasion of Georgia in August of 2008, only a month after Val arrived, taunted him. Surely Alexei was there. Pouring over intelligence cables and assessments, photos, foreign press reports—anything he could access - Val searched for signs of Alexei.

He found none.

He was more systematic now. Less passionate and wild-eyed.

But, after four years, not even a fleeting glimpse.

It made sense to Val. They had gotten close to Alexei that night. They had imagery of the Russian officer in Iraq with known insurgents and foreign fighter facilitators. They had narrowly missed killing or capturing him during the raid that ended Razzaq and Haskell. Val didn't know how that message had been delivered to Russia. But he was sure it had been.

The Russians would want to preserve Alexei's ability to operate globally as much as possible and would make him sit on the sidelines for a while. Get him back within Russian borders and let things cool off before putting him back in play.

It had been four years since that night in the desert. Val had expected to uncover Alexei's trail a while ago. But he'd found nothing.

So he came to the SCIF every day and kept looking.

Today was the same as every other day, though. Nothing.

He shoved his switchblade in his pocket, left the SCIF, and climbed the stairs to his office.

Val sat down to grade cadet papers but was interrupted by his cell phone ringing.

"Colonel Rafter," he answered.

"Colonel?" Sydney asked.

Val leaned back in his chair.

"Yeah. For about a year now."

"Belated congratulations."

They hadn't spoken in years. It was strange to hear her voice. Strange and good.

"Thanks."

"How are you?" Sydney asked.

"No complaints. And no one to listen to them if I had any. How about yourself?"

"Same."

"What do they have you doing these days?"

"Oh, you know," Sydney said playfully. "Keeping the world safe for democracy."

"Uh-huh."

"How about you? Still molding the military minds of tomorrow?"

"One at a time."

Sydney smiled.

"You sound good. The professorial life must agree with you."

"Parts of it certainly do. I won't deny it."

Pleasantries exhausted, an awkward silence expanded between them. Val held the phone to his ear and fought the urge to ask her where she was.

"I'm sorry to barge in on your morning like this. I'm sure you have a class to get to," Sydney said. "But I wanted to let you know that I'm in New York City this week for the UN counter-proliferation meetings. You'll never guess who is in town as well."

Sydney paused for a moment but didn't make Val guess.

"Nicolae! From the Marshall Center, remember?"

"Oh, yeah?" A smile broke across Val's face as fond memories flashed by, followed by tangled emotions. Relief? Regret? Nostalgia?

"He is attending the conference also and, get this, dropping off one of his girls at college. Can you believe that? We are old.

"Anyway," Sydney continued, confidence wavering. "We ran into each other yesterday and started talking about old times. Your ski parties and whatnot. I told him I thought you were still at West Point and that I'd give you a call. See if I could talk you into meeting us for dinner tonight."

Val thought of the Marshall Center. The brilliant sun on the mountain. Nights at the Local Cure.

And Alexei.

"If you're busy, I totally get it," Sydney said quickly. "I told Nicolae I didn't know what your—"

"I'd love to. I'll be there."

"Really?"

"Yeah… Yeah, really."

"Okay, then. I'll text you when we figure out where we're going to eat. Could you get down here around six thirty?"

"Yep." Val stood and walked to the window. "I can do that."

"Great. You know, he has done really well since the Marshall Center. He is a deputy director now."

"I'm not surprised. Nicolae is a good man."

"He is. And he is going to be so excited to see you…and…and I am too, Val."

"It will be good to see you, Sydney. It's been a while."

"Four years, right?"

"That's right."

"It was…"

Val couldn't tell if emotion choked Sydney's words or if she just decided not to finish the sentence. But he knew what she was going to say.

It was Tony's funeral when they'd seen each other last.

"So…I'll text you the address when we figure out which restaurant," Sydney said. "And we'll see you tonight."

"Perfect."

"Great. Bye."

Val lowered the cell phone from his ear but remained in front of the window.

He stood motionless. Though he thought of Tony every day, he tried not to remember the funeral. Ever.

The call from Sydney exhumed it, and it crashed forward in his mind. Val stood at the window as the memories tore through him.

CHAPTER 80

Sydney sighed and stood from the chair in her hotel room. Her memories of Tony's funeral were hard, and she rarely let herself dwell on them. But it was impossible to think of Val and not remember Tony. She smiled as she put away her cell phone. It would be good to see Val tonight.

Sydney hoped having him there would put Nicolae in a better mood. Last night had been a rough meeting with her Moldovan agent.

The United Nations Arms Counter-Proliferation Summit in New York City provided the perfect cover for Nicolae and Sydney to conduct a face-to-face meeting.

After they had each performed a long SDR to eliminate the possibility of surveillance, they met in a CIA safe house across the Hudson River in New Jersey late that night.

The timing of the meeting was good for Nicolae. He and his wife had come to the States a week earlier to drop their youngest, Eniko, off at college.

The three of them flew into Boston, and spent a weekend visiting with Daria, who was going to be a junior at Harvard this year. Nicolae and Sasha then rented a car and took Eniko on a road trip down to Charlottesville, VA. She would be starting at UVA in the fall. Nicolae's wife held herself together well as they said goodbye to Eniko. Then, unable to hold back the tears any longer, Sasha cried most of the day-long drive from Charlottesville to New York City.

Nicolae drove Sasha to LaGuardia on Sunday morning before the conference began the next day. Embracing in front of the terminal, Sasha kissed Nicolae before holding him by the shoulders.

"You tell her, Nicolae," she said in a stern voice. "You tell her we're done."

"I will."

"I want our daughters to live in America. And I want to be near them."

So when Nicolae sat down with Sydney in the sparsely furnished apartment in Rutherford, New Jersey, he was determined.

"I'm finished," he told Sydney as he glared across the small table.

Sydney regarded him in silence for a moment. She'd been expecting this. Dreading it. For the past few years, even as Nicolae's intelligence output became better and better, more and more valued by the machine, Sydney felt worse and worse. She hated manipulating him, holding the carrot just in front of his nose and jerking it away at the last instant as he got close. She hated that she loved the professional recognition and advancement. Most of all, she hated that she didn't know, deep down, what she would really choose if she had the power: Set Nicolae and his family free? Or continue to ride him? She knew what Mr. Wall and the machine would choose. What would she choose?

At times like this, her self-reproach transmuted into anger. She could feel it coming on now.

Don't lose your temper, she told herself.

"Okay," she said to Nicolae. "I understand."

"Okay?"

"Okay. I'm disappointed. We could have done a lot more together. Especially with you in the new role. But I understand."

Nicolae had recently been appointed as deputy director of the Moldovan Security and Intelligence Service. Functioning much like America's CIA, the Security and Intelligence Service worked to ensure Moldovan national security through intelligence and other means. A deputy director seat would afford Nicolae line of sight into many of the shadowy corners of the international gray and black markets that eluded Sydney and the rest of the CIA. It would also give him greater access to his government's efforts against and in collaboration with the Russians.

Sydney wanted Nicolae to stay in that seat.

"If you really want out," she said, injecting a note of resignation into her voice. "I can make that happen."

"I want out. It is time."

Sydney sighed and then nodded.

"What will you do?" she asked, already knowing the answer. "Without me in your life?"

Nicolae chuckled.

"I will find a way to carry on."

"I'm sure you will."

"Sasha and I will move to America. Both our daughters are here now."

"How will you do that?" Sydney asked, playing confused.

Nicolae's mouth tightened.

"You promised you would help us."

"And I'll do all I can. But you're not making it easy on me, quitting like you are."

"Quitting?" Nicolae voice raised. "I have worked for you for twelve years! Quitting is not how I would describe it."

"Easy. I'm not describing it that way, either." Sydney gestured at Nicolae with her palms down. "I'm just telling you, you're taking away my leverage."

"Leverage?"

"With my bosses. They are not in the business of doing favors. They are in the business of intelligence."

"Favors? After twelve years of dangerous service, I must beg for favors?" Nicolae's eyes were wide with frustration.

"You have to realize that—"

"No!" Nicolae slammed his fist on the table. "You must realize!"

Sydney arched her eyebrows. Then her eyes narrowed to slits.

Nicolae missed the cue as his rant continued.

"I have lived in fear of discovery and execution for more than a decade," he said in a loud voice as he rose to his feet. "All the while doing whatever you asked. Finding whatever information you needed. Spreading whatever lies you told me to spread."

Nicolae pointed down at Sydney. "Everything you ever asked me to do, I did, no matter how dangerous. And the entire time, you have dangled false promises in front of me, always out of reach.

"We'll talk about it later, Nicolae," he said in a mocking, singsong voice. "If you do this one last thing, we'll be able to help you, Nicolae. Perhaps if you take the role with the Security and Intelligence Service, Nicolae.

"Well, I am done dancing to your tune! You owe me the—"

"Enough!" Sydney yelled, slamming her own fist on the table as she stood up. Her chair skidded away and fell over on the floor behind her.

"Don't forget who you're talking to!"

The transmutation was complete. She was pissed.

Sydney pinned Nicolae with her angry glare.

"I have been with you every step of the way. And I'm the one person in the world who knows exactly how you have benefited from our arrangement. Do you know how much we have paid you over the years?"

She didn't wait for him to answer.

"Over half a million dollars," she said, holding up one finger between them.

"Access to information that has placed you ahead of your peers in consideration for promotion," she continued, extending a second finger.

"And let's not forget, two fully funded scholarships at prestigious American colleges." Sydney held up a third finger, her eyes locked on Nicolae.

Nicolae opened his mouth to talk, but Sydney intercepted him, crossing her arms and shaking her head vigorously.

"Don't act like you didn't know."

Nicolae sank into his chair.

"Oh, for chrissake." Sydney's arms dropped to her side. She worked hard to keep sympathy from creeping into her voice.

"Are you kidding me?" she said in an incredulous tone. "Nicolae Muntenau, famed Moldovan intelligence officer? You're just now figuring it out?"

Nicolae stared at the middle of the table.

"They are so proud," he whispered. "They can never know."

Now Sydney really wanted to scream. There was an aspect to Nicolae she never understood. Here was a man who had seen the really ugly side of his fellow man. Citizen of a country that had been shit on for centuries. Wounded in combat against the Russians. Waist deep in one of the nastiest counterintelligence theaters in the world. He'd personally ordered the execution of foreign spies. And, yet, when it came to his family, to his daughters, all of that perspective and skepticism vanished. He was as naïve as a schoolboy.

And, truthfully, that worked to her advantage.

He never suspected.

Never suspected that Sydney had orchestrated Daria's and Eniko's college acceptances and scholarships.

It felt to Nicolae that his family was getting closer to its dream. That he could almost touch it. All that was left was to get him and his wife to America for good.

He never suspected that Sydney was aligning everything against him. That she was conjuring a mirage. A mirage that he would walk through the desert to reach. That would always be just out of reach. Just over the next sand dune. Forever.

She felt sorry for him. She hated this part. She hated that she was good at it. She wished it were over.

But she had to continue.

She had to extinguish his rebellion.

"What you do next is up to you, Nicolae," Sydney said sternly. "If you want out, I can get you out."

She let the statement hang in the air. Nicolae didn't lift his eyes from the table.

"But you and your wife will never get to America. And I don't just mean immigrate. I mean ever. Not even for a weekend. You already pop up red on every 'Known Russian Associates' list out there.

"Do you even realize that every time you want to come over here, it's an extra week of work for me running around the State Department and the CIA getting your visa unstuck? I won't be able to do that if you quit. Your girls too. It's not a sure thing that they would even get to finish college."

Nicolae put his head in his hands.

Sydney let him sit in it as she walked over and picked up her chair.

"I understand the desire to be done." she finally said as she walked the chair back to the table. "Trust me, I do."

She sat down and looked at Nicolae.

"You have to decide what is best for you and your family."

He rubbed his eyes, leaned back in his chair, and looked over at her.

"What will it take?" he asked her.

"Take to what?"

"For Sasha and me to immigrate."

Sydney took a deep breath and let it out slowly.

"I honestly don't know."

"Is it really possible?"

"Yes. But not if—"

"Not if I quit. I know this."

Sydney nodded.

"Not if you quit."

"And in the meantime. My daughters stay in school? And my wife and I can continue to visit?"

"Of course."

"You promise this?

"I promise."

Nicolae sat in silence for a moment. Sydney did also.

"It seems so long ago, doesn't it?" Nicolae asked her.

"What does?"

"Our time in Germany. At the Marshall Center."

Sydney chuckled. "Like a million years."

They both smiled.

"You, me, Val, Alexei, and the others."

Sydney swallowed at the mention of Alexei. She did not have the energy to deal with those memories.

"That was a good time," Nicolae said. "So much has happened since then."

Sydney smiled.

"What?" he asked her.

She leaned forward.

"I just had an idea. Probably a bad one, though."

There was something about her smile, Nicolae noticed. Something wistful.

"Tell me."

"Val," Sydney said, listening to his name as she said it.

"Yes?"

"He's right up the road at the military academy," she said hesitantly. "We could see if he would meet us for dinner tomorrow."

Nicolae hesitated, but Sydney spotted the flicker of interest in his eyes.

"What do you say?" she pressed gently. "Might be a nice break from…All this shit." Sydney gestured around at the world that had bound the two of them together like this.

Nicolae resisted, his eyes searching Sydney's face for any sign of an agenda. But slowly, a smile spread across his face.

Sydney smiled too.

"I'll call him in the morning."

CHAPTER 81

The Italian restaurant was tucked into the bottom floor of one of the converted warehouses in the lower east side of the city. Sydney got there early and talked the hostess into letting them have the table at the street-side window of the shoebox-shaped establishment. The hundred-dollar bill helped her case.

She ordered a glass of Nebbiolo and sat at the table looking out through the window at the hip passersby. She checked her watch, wondering if Val would really show.

Nicolae arrived half an hour later. He sat down at the end of the table with his back to the restaurant's entrance. He told the waitress, "I will have what the lady is having."

They sat together in silence, sipping their wine, looking out of the large window as night fell over Manhattan. They ignored each other like a couple locked in a loveless marriage, waiting for the night's diversion. Sydney checked her watch again.

"Are you sure you don't want to go ahead and order?" the waitress asked them on her third pass by their table.

"No. We'll wait. He's almost here."

The waitress nodded curtly and left.

Val walked in a minute later.

Sydney saw him first. She stood, smiling widely.

Nicolae turned to face the door.

Val and Sydney hugged.

"Thanks for coming," she said, stepping aside for him and Nicolae.

"I wouldn't have missed it," Val said, beaming as he extended his hand to Nicolae.

The Moldovan was slow to react, his eyes locked onto Val.

The two men shook hands.

"You okay, Nicolae?" Val asked.

"I am. Is good to see you."

"Get in here, you crazy old Moldovan," he said, pulling Nicolae into his arms.

The two men hugged and slapped each other's backs.

Sydney smiled.

"So this is your third?" the waitress asked, appearing behind the two embracing men.

"Yes." Sydney gestured for everyone to sit down.

"We ran into Burian today," Nicolae told Val excitedly. "We laughed, remembering our good times in Garmisch. We invited him to dinner, but he could not join us. He said to tell you hello."

Val smiled. "How is Burian?"

"He is well," Sydney said. "Seems happy."

"Yes," Nicolae said. "He seems heavier and happier."

Val chuckled. "That's great. If you see him tomorrow, tell him I said hello."

"I will."

"I'm going to hit the men's room," Val said. "Go ahead and order for me."

"Okay." Sydney picked up the menu.

Nicolae leaned over to her after she'd ordered and the waitress left.

"Val looks terrible," he said, sadness in his eyes.

Sydney, caught off guard, said nothing.

"He seems so tired. So sad."

Sydney, an ache welling within her, nodded. "He's been through a lot, you know."

"Yes, but…"

Val returned to the table. Sydney poured each of them a glass of wine from the bottle the waitress had brought. She raised her glass.

"To old friendships."

Nicolae and Val talked rapidly through the dinner. Nicolae showed Val many pictures of his wife and girls, which Val studied intently.

"Beautiful, Nicolae. You're a lucky man."

Nicolae asked Val about his time in Iraq and, of course, the incident in Bulgaria.

"When I saw your picture and heard what little I did about the incident, I was both surprised and, at the same time, said, 'That is the Val I know.'"

Val smiled sheepishly and tried to avoid glancing at Sydney, who, surprising even herself, smiled at the comment.

"We all did, Nicolae," she said.

Val looked at her with a face that seemed to apologize all over again. But she met his gaze with a wide smile. She put a hand on his shoulder and said, "And none of us would have it any other way."

"A toast to that," Nicolae said. "To Val Rafter!"

"Yes!" Sydney said.

Reluctantly, Val clinked his glass with theirs.

"What will you do next, Val?" Nicolae asked with genuine excitement.

"Not much. I'm quite boring now. And have realized I like things that way."

"You like being a professor, then?"

"I do. Young minds to corrupt. No bullets to dodge. It's nice."

Nicolae nodded. "That sounds very nice."

"And you? How is work?"

Nicolae shrugged. "It is work."

"Still in government?"

"Yes."

"Come on," Val said, sensing the walls go up. "Give me a little bit. I don't want to talk shop. I'm just curious about what my good friend is doing with his life."

Nicolae smiled.

"I am deputy director now. Security and Intelligence Service."

Val raised his eyebrows.

"Well, congratulations! That's a proper fucking job."

Nicolae chuckled and nodded with pride.

"Thank you, Val. It is indeed. And I take command of our special actions team next month."

"Special actions team? What is that?"

"Well, it is not so big. Maybe one of your platoons. But is a special operations strike force we use from time to time to interrupt illegal arms activities within our borders. Our little country still has so many problems, you know."

Val nodded, sensing Nicolae's humility taking hold. Val reached across the table and put his arm on Nicolae's shoulder.

"As we say over here, it's not the size of the dog in the fight that matters, it's the size of the fight in the dog."

Nicolae smiled.

"Your country is lucky to have you, friend. Congratulations," Val said. He squeezed Nicolae's shoulder.

Nicolae smiled widely.

Sydney could not help but smile as well.

The waitress stepped up. "May I take these?" she asked, gesturing at the empty dishes.

"Yes, please."

"Excuse me," Nicolae said. "I go to restroom."

Val stared at Sydney, smiling, as Nicolae walked away.

"What?" she asked.

"All this time," Val said, shaking his head. "I should've guessed."

"What?"

"I can't believe I missed it back then."

Sydney said nothing.

Val leaned in, his smile melting away. He raised one eyebrow and tilted his head slightly forward at her.

Sydney sat motionless, hands in her lap.

The two of them matched gazes, neither moving for a dozen heartbeats.

Then, in a gesture no one else in the restaurant could detect, Sydney gave Val a single nod.

Val's face softened. He leaned back in his chair and picked up his wineglass. He extended his arm across the table and held his drink in front of Sydney, a heartfelt smile on his face.

She hesitated. Then smiled and raised her own glass to his.

They both drank and then set their wine back on the table.

"Really nice move," Val said. "As a Moldovan government official, he sits on key terrain not only in the illicit arms market but Russian adventurism as well.

And a deputy director in the intelligence apparatus now?"

Sydney shrugged. It felt good to have Val acknowledge her like this.

"I don't want any specifics," Val said. "But tell me the truth. They must know all kinds of shit about what the Russians are up to?"

Sydney leaned forward. "No specifics. But I'll tell you this, I get shit on the Russians long before the Moscow station, or anyone else, for that matter."

"Really?"

"Really."

"Well. I'll say it again. Well done."

"Thank you."

Nicolae returned to the table.

"You know what would be really fun?" Val said.

"What?" Nicolae said.

"If Alexei were here."

Sydney's eyes narrowed, and her jaw clenched.

Nicolae laughed ruefully and shook his head.

"I don't think so, my friend."

"What do you mean?"

Sydney took another drink. *Surely he won't. Not tonight.*

"Oh," Nicolae said, his face a mask of concern. "Is difficult to say."

"Guys. We said we would not talk shop," Sydney said.

"Nonsense." Val ignored Sydney's glare. "We're talking about a friend here. Not about work."

"Well. In that spirit, then," Nicolae said. "I will just say that Alexei is not someone I think you would still be a friend of."

"What makes you say that?"

Nicolae shifted in his chair.

"Val, please," Sydney said, forcing herself to laugh as she said it.

"I'm sorry. I just haven't seen the guy since we were all together in Germany. I wonder how he is doing, that is all."

"We come across his handiwork from time to time," Nicolae said in a low voice. His face was dark.

Sydney tried to shoot Val a *shut the fuck up* look, but his eyes were locked on Nicolae.

"He is a monster now, I am afraid," Nicolae said. "Or, at least, works for the monster."

Sydney could see from Val's reaction that he wanted to press for more information. She had to shut this conversation down now.

"Do you know where Alexei is?" Val asked.

Goddamn it. I should've never put these two together.

Sydney turned and looked at Val.

Nicolae nodded.

"Where is he?" Val asked, leaning in toward the Moldovan.

"Okay, guys," Sydney said. "Let's back off."

"Syria," Nicolae said.

Syria?

Sydney looked back and forth between the two men.

Val took a deep breath and let it out slowly.

"You're certain?"

Nicolae nodded.

"Thank you."

Nicolae nodded again.

Sydney raged inside. She wanted to pound on the table and punch Val in the face. Instead, she took another sip of wine and waved at the waitress.

"Can I get the check, please?" Sydney asked when she came to the table.

"No desert?" Val asked as the waitress walked off.

"No."

Later, outside the restaurant, Val and Nicolae shook hands as they said goodbye.

"Thank you for meeting us tonight, Val," Nicolae said as Sydney stood off to the side. "It means very much to me."

"It meant a lot to me also. I hope we see each other again soon."

"Me too. I will make a point of it."

Nicolae held on to Val's hand, looking him in the eyes for an awkward moment.

"What is it?" Val asked.

"I hope you will remain a professor for a long time. You have earned your rest."

Val chuckled, not knowing how to respond.

"And you look like you need that rest."

"Well, Nicolae. That's the most polite way anyone has ever told me I look like shit."

"I only say it because I care about you," Nicolae said, smiling and letting go of Val's hand.

"Do you want us to call you a cab?" Sydney asked.

"No. It is nice night. I will walk a bit."

"Okay. See you tomorrow."

Nicolae waved and walked off into the night.

Val and Sydney watched him walk away. When he turned the corner, Sydney spun and said, "I don't believe you!"

Val stood in silence on the sidewalk.

"After all this time? After all the iterations of all the fights and all the bullshit, you're still obsessing over Alexei? You have worn me out, Val. Worn me out."

"It's not what you think," Val said.

"Oh, I'm sure. It never was. I'll tell you the most ridiculous part," she continued, voice quavering. "I actually thought that someday we would get past it. That you and I were something to each other that was going to win out in the end. What a fool I am!"

Val began to speak, but Sydney cut him off.

"You know, I've never begrudged you any of your girlfriends. I've never kept a tally of who you're fucking. I respected your space. I guess I thought you'd earned your privacy. And that it might help you get over it. Was I jealous? Of course! But that's the difference between you and me, Val. I can keep the big picture in mind. I can get over shit. And I thought you and I were the big picture. I guess I was wrong."

Val looked at the ground and then back at Sydney.

"Do you have anything to say?" she asked him.

"He killed Tony."

Sydney blinked several times.

"What?"

"Alexei. He killed Tony."

"What are you talking about?"

"He was working with Abdul Razzaq. In Iraq."

"That's bullshit," Sydney whispered.

"I saw it with my own eyes. We almost got him when we got Razzaq. But he got away. Got across the border."

Sydney shook her head.

"It was confirmed. Validated. It went all the way up. You've got access. Liam can probably find it. Go look it up if you don't believe me."

"Val—"

"I know," Val said, holding up a hand. "It wasn't personal. Alexei didn't know Tony. Didn't know I was there. Alexei was just doing his duty. But…"

Old emotions tightened his chest.

Sydney said nothing.

"He didn't pull the trigger." Val looked Sydney in the eyes. "But he was pulling the strings."

Sydney looked at the ground between her and Val, trying to stop her world from spinning.

"I can't get over it," Val said quietly. "I never will."

A taxi pulled up to the restaurant. Two couples got out, smiling and talking as they walked between Val and Sydney. One of the men trailed behind the group after paying the driver. Sensing they had interrupted something, he gave Val a nod as he walked by. Val waited for the door to close behind them.

"I'm sorry," Val said. "I didn't know how to tell you before. Without it getting all mixed up in…in all our bullshit."

Sydney turned from Val. She rubbed her forehead and took a few steps away from the restaurant.

Val put his hands in his pockets. He waited for Sydney to turn back around, but she stood with her back to him.

"I've been trying to figure out where he is for years," Val finally said to her back. "Now, after tonight, I've finally got a good lead on him. I know the country, at least. Just have to figure out exactly where."

Val waited. But Sydney stood, head bowed, back to Val.

"I love you, Sydney," he said. "But that's what I am going to do."

Sydney turned around with small, hesitating steps, her fists clenched, the streetlight reflecting off the tears running down her face.

Val was gone.

CHAPTER 82

The blood from Val's crushed nose had dried on his right cheek and upper lip. A purple bruise flared in the middle of his face, spreading from his nose, which was out of joint, skewing to the right. His hands, resting on the table in front of him, were also covered with flakes of dried blood. His wrists were swollen, circled by deep lacerations from the zip tie bindings. The lacerations wept blood and clear liquid, as every time Val moved his hands, it reopened the wounds. His clothes were matted with sweat, blood, and other stains.

At least I'm half drunk.

"You look terrible, my friend," Alexei said.

"Yes, well, the service on this ship is a bit…rough," Val said with a strained smile.

"Is your own fault. You make everything harder than it needs to be, Val. Everything."

"Yes," Val said with a gracious nod. "Especially kidnappings. I really need to be more accepting when kidnapped."

Alexei chuckled at the comment. His face softened.

Val looked at the bottle of bourbon.

Alexei looked at Val, looking at the bottle.

"Yes. Not much left to go."

Val leaned back in his chair. "What do you think? We got two more toasts in there?"

Alexei looked at the bottle and then at his watch. He nodded and then said, "Seems about right."

Val leaned forward, grabbed the bottle, and poured two more shots. He picked up his glass and hesitated, waiting for Alexei to pick up his.

Alexei looked at his glass and sighed.

Val rolled his eyes.

"Is sad, asshole," Alexei said.

"Some of it is," Val said, an edge to his voice.

Alexei picked up the glass. He looked at Val and waited.

Val hesitated, lost in memories. His eyes narrowed.

"Perhaps to Masudi Kader?" Val wondered aloud.

Alexei's head tilted slightly.

"You knew this man?" he asked, surprised.

"Yeah…" Val nodded slowly. "And I killed him. Or helped kill him."

Alexei lowered his glass slowly.

Val did the same.

Alexei leaned back in his chair. He rubbed his chin as he held eye contact with Val. After a moment, he dropped his hand back on the table and turned his head from Val.

The bartender looked at Alexei and then at Peskov. The two shared a troubled glance and then put their eyes back on their boss. Alexei's lips were pursed as he gazed out of the dark windows over Val's shoulder. From his face, though, Val could tell that their boss was looking back into his past, not out at the Black Sea.

The *Monarch*'s engines droned beneath them. Val could feel the prow of the ship slowly rise and fall as it pushed through the cold water.

Alexei's head turned suddenly back to Val. His lips were pressed thin, and his jaw muscles twitched.

Zakir, sensing the sudden increase in tension, moved his hand moving to his weapon's pistol grip.

Alexei leaned forward.

"You were there that night? In Iraq?"

"No. Not on the ground. I was in our operations center. But I was there the next day. Before the sun came up."

Alexei took a deep breath. He shot a look at Zakir that said, *Sit the fuck down.* He glared at the mercenary until he sat back on his stool and then looked at Val.

"I stood over Kader's dead body," Val said. "Then I stood over Razzaq's."

Alexei frowned and crossed his arms.

"I was disappointed not to find yours," Val said.

Alexei shook his head.

"I bet you were. It would have saved you some trouble later, my friend. Am I right?"

Val nodded slowly. He blinked a few times and his eyes welled up. His lower lip trembled. He looked down as a tear broke free and ran down his bruised cheek. It was still too much. It had been six years, but the regret and heartbreak burned like fresh, hot coals. He missed Tony.

"I lost a comrade there," Val said, staring down at the table. "A brother."

Alexei watched Val wipe the tear away. The blood on his cheek smeared onto the back of his hand.

"Because of Razzaq," Alexei said, almost in a whisper. "Because of our mission together."

Val sat motionless, head bent low.

"Yes," Val said, choking on the word.

Alexei's eyes narrowed.

"I remember. I told Razzaq he was being careless. Dangling this man like he did. I forget his name."

"Moussa," Val said, not raising his head.

"Yes. This was the name. But Razzaq was stubborn. He wanted a bloody ambush. Wanted chaos and to kill as many American soldiers as possible that night. He snuck many fighters into that house before telling Kader to give you the address. He was certain the Americans would kill everyone…including this Moussa. Erasing the path back to him."

Alexei's face softened slightly. "You were lucky you did not kill this man."

"It was not…" Val fought the crush of sadness. "It was not a lucky night."

Alexei's face drooped, and his shoulders sagged as if a weight had suddenly settled over him.

"I think I finally understand Syria now, Val." Alexei's eyes grew wet and shiny.

"I am sorry for your brother. But was my mission. That is all."

Val shook his head slowly. He sighed heavily and looked up.

"To Syria," he said, grabbing his glass and lifting it up.

"Fine," Alexei said in a sad and weary voice. "To Syria."

"Had I only shot straighter."

Val threw back his bourbon.

Alexei did the same.

CHAPTER 83

"I said left, goddamn it!" Val yelled.

The old Toyota pickup truck careened through the dusty intersection. Its fifty-caliber machine gun, mounted in the truck bed, shook the entire vehicle as it fired. The gunner gripped the swiveling weapon tight, trying not to fall out of the hurtling truck and aim at the same time.

Mazar shouted at the driver in Arabic.

The driver barked back.

"What did he say?" Val demanded.

"He say we should retreat with the others!" Mazar yelled over the screaming truck engine. "He is right!"

"I'm not paying you bastards to retreat!" Val screamed at Mazar while glaring at the driver. "He better take the next fucking left!"

Mazar shouted at the driver again.

The driver gave Val a murderous look.

Val looked rearward, past the legs of the gunner.

Good! No Syrian Army on our tail.

This was the best shot he had had at Alexei in three months in Syria. He didn't want it to go to waste.

Val had four armed men, real-time intel, and a satellite phone connection to Liam in the JOC in Turkey. And, most importantly, cover for action.

The Assad regime was executing an offensive in northwest Syria with the goal of taking back the small towns and outposts it had lost to the rebels over the past months. Maarat al-Numan, a small city less than twenty-five miles from the border with Turkey, occupied strategic terrain astride highway M5, the north–south running artery between Damascus and Aleppo.

The Free Syrian Army had captured the town six months before and, despite ongoing efforts, the regime hadn't been able to retake it.

Making things more interesting and sporty, a small Syrian Army base sat just outside Maarat al-Numan on the other side of the M5, not even a kilometer away from the outskirts of the small town. Called Wadi Deif, the small base was important to the Syrian Army, hosting a large barracks, an armored regiment, and a fuel depot. The rebels were determined to capture the base, but Wadi Deif repulsed the initial assault in October and withstood the siege that followed.

For months, the Syrian Army sent armed convoys north to try to relieve Wadi Deif. The rebels thwarted each assault but were unable to capture the base despite numerous attempts.

This ongoing dynamic made Maarat al-Numan particularly chaotic and strife-ridden, even for Syria. Frequent government assaults from the south and attacks from the air harried the city as the rebels tried to cling to their position and dislodge the army from Wadi Deif.

A vigorous regime offensive had kicked off the day before and was having more success than past operations. The Syrian Army overwhelmed rebel checkpoints on the M5 and pushed into the outskirts of Maarat al-Numan. Though not losing control of the city entirely, the rebels were forced to fall back, giving up city blocks they had controlled for months.

Most importantly, regime units recaptured two key hilltops along the M5, enabling them to break the rebel blockade of Wadi Deif and deliver critical supplies to troops trapped there.

Since the siege began in October, the only meager resupply of the base was via airdrop.

Val and his small team had taken advantage of the chaos and the fact that neither side in this fight was very well coordinated. Separating from the rebel retreat, the team hid in their vehicle in a garage on the southern outskirts of the city and let the attacking elements advance past their position.

Now behind enemy lines, with Liam's help, Val would finally get his shot.

If he could stay alive long enough to take it.

Val checked his GPS again. A little more than a kilometer to go. He returned his attention to the driver as they approached the next intersection.

Mazar said something to the driver.

The driver shook his head in disgust but took his foot off the gas as they approached the intersection.

The pickup truck skidded through the turn. The gunner in back clung to his pedestal-mounted weapon, trying not to fly out of the truck bed. Capture, at this point, meant torture and death.

"Good!" Val yelled as the truck straightened out. "Good! Okay. Keep it straight till I tell you."

"How far?" Mazar asked.

"Till I fucking tell you!"

Mazar muttered to the driver again, who yelled back in Arabic.

Val recognized the curse words but ignored them.

His goal was a small neighborhood on the southern side of Maarat al-Numan. Val planned on the cluster of two dozen buildings giving him and the team several options for concealed firing positions. If they could get there in time, they would have excellent broadsiding fields of fire on the target vehicles. If they were late, all was for naught, and they would have to evade their way north back to rebel positions without a scalp.

"Lancer Two Six, this is Viper," a voice called over the radio.

Mazar looked at the radio and then at Val.

Val shook his head.

"Lancer Two Six, this is Viper," the voice repeated urgently.

Val checked the GPS again.

Mazar gave Val a disapproving look.

"Lancer Two Six, this is Viper."

"Dammit," Val muttered as he reached for the radio handset. "Keep fucking straight!" he yelled at the driver before keying the handset.

"Viper. This is Lancer Two Six."

"Lancer, what's your status?" the radio said.

"We're good. But it got crazy back there. We got separated from the main element."

Mazar rolled his eyes.

Viper was the call sign for Alex McDaniel, the one-star army general in command of American advisory elements in Syria. Based on an airfield in Turkey with the Syrian Free Army command elements, McDaniel's command authority went beyond the handful of military advisors across the border in Syria. His logistics team ran the small airfield into which the US and other aligned nations poured small arms, medical, and other supplies bound for the rebels. They also ran the cross-border operation to get them those supplies as well. The in-theater intelligence-gathering operations also reported to McDaniel, including all drone activity.

The general had been in this role for more than a year now. Long enough to see the rising tide and spirit of the Free Syrian Army peak and then dissolve as they realized America was not going to get involved in a meaningful way. He watched as the high-quality Syrian Army leaders who risked their lives to defect early and fight Assad quietly left and sought refuge in Switzerland and other places. The FSA was a lot different now than in 2011 and early 2012. McDaniel tried not to dwell on what might have been. He focused on the twin beacons that had guided his entire career: execute the mission, bring his soldiers back.

McDaniel was commissioned infantry before going into the Special Forces. A Green Beret for fifteen years, he led troops through countless deployments in Afghanistan and Iraq. He was a combat veteran with a master's degree in systems engineering and a keen sense for risk mitigation in complex operations.

And Val was the thing he worried most about.

McDaniel was, of course, aware of Val's infamous flameout in Bulgaria. He also knew of Val's reputation as a unique double threat—an outstanding combat leader with a proven ability to recruit and run sources in a war zone. Some days, the general was glad Bryson had sent him the maverick lieutenant colonel. Syria was a mess. McDaniel needed advisors who could react to crazy on their own and not make things worse. And, if things went to hell, could get themselves out of a scrape without any help. Val could do that.

It was the "cowboy shit" that worried McDaniel. He'd made that clear to Val as Val and his team were getting ready to leave the airfield and cross the border into Syria with a Free Syrian Army contingent months ago.

"Advise and observe, Rafter," the general said to Val as the two men stood near the rear of the old Toyota pickup truck. Val's team of three men loaded ammunition and MREs into the truck bed. "That's all you're there to do. No recruiting assets, no engaging the enemy, no cowboy shit. Advise and observe."

Val nodded, handing Mazar a medical bag.

"Read back for possible correction," the general said.

"Sir?" Val asked, facing the general. Mazar glanced at McDaniel. Sensing the tension, he turned back to the truck.

"I said, 'Read back for possible correction,'" McDaniel said slowly, closing the distance between him and Val and locking eyes with him. "I want there to be no ambiguity between you and me."

"Advise, sir… Advise and observe. That's all I'm here to do."

McDaniel scanned Val's face for an awkward moment. Mazar fidgeted behind Val, and the other two FSA soldiers glanced at each other, wondering what was happening.

"All right, then," McDaniel finally said. "Good."

The general looked at the old pickup truck and then back at Val. "Watch your ass over there, Rafter."

"I will, sir. Thank you."

The general turned and walked away. Mazar waited until McDaniel was gone before saying, "I guess is good thing he not know our special deal?"

"Shut the fuck up," Val said.

Val had sought out Mazar for this rotation, calling in several favors from special operations buddies to help find the Kurd who had performed so well as a Tigernaich in Iraq.

After more than a decade of war, Val had learned, over and over, that vetted, dependable comrades were invaluable in combat. And particularly to special operations of a personal nature like the one Val was trying to pull off. Liam and Val had pooled some of their money to be able to offer Mazar a healthy bounty for their off-book operation. It didn't take much, given the relative poverty of the Kurds.

For Mazar's part, the opportunity to kill Syrians was attractive. But, of more personal importance to him, Mazar had fond memories of Tony. So, when Val said he was going after the Russian who had caused his death, Mazar was all in.

Now, speeding south of Maarat al-Numan, his goal almost within reach, Val tried to hide his excitement and convey a businesslike calm as he responded to General McDaniel.

"We're trying to avoid contact. Evading north to rejoin."

"Roger that, Lancer. Do you need help?"

"Negative," Val said quickly.

"Good. Don't have any to give you, anyway. Hurry your ass up. Won't be long before enemy air gets involved."

The interpreter glanced at Val at the mention of aircraft.

Val shook his head dismissively.

"Roger that, Viper."

Val put the radio handset back and pulled his sat phone out of his tactical vest. He pressed a button and jammed the sat phone handset to his ear. "Sitrep!"

"No change," came Liam's voice. "Still proceeding north on M5. Ground speed, approximately forty miles per hour. You've got maybe seven minutes to get set up."

"Roger! We'll make it!"

"Doesn't look like it to me," Liam said, looking nervously at the drone footage on the big monitor. Located in the joint operations center on Incirlik Air Base in Turkey, Liam was a willing coconspirator in Val's quest for vengeance for Tony.

Val had looked up Liam as soon as he'd landed in Incirlik. He had a few days before a helicopter would ferry him south to the corner of Turkey, where McDaniel's task force headquarters was located. Val spent those days putting the finishing touches on his personal operation. Talking to Liam was the last piece. Val wanted to be as tight as possible before the conversation.

Liam had just started a six-month rotation in JSOC operations center. Val had expected Liam to reject the idea, and Val would have understood. Instead, Liam had jumped on board.

"Yes," Liam had interrupted as Val pitched his idea. "I'll do it."

"You're sure?"

"Yeah. I'm sure. Why would you ask me that?"

"We'll be coloring way outside the lines here," Val said with a shrug. "I just…"

"Fuck you. You think you're the only one that loved Tony?"

"No, I know I wasn't."

"Besides, those bastards almost took my leg off."

"Okay, then. Let's get to work."

It was a simple plan that relied on a fair bit of luck. First, they used their access and connections to confirm that Alexei was in-country. Val and Liam assumed that Alexei, or those around him, would demonstrate the customary Russian lack of signal discipline. They were constantly making unscrambled calls in the open, not even using code words. And their officers tended to carry the same cell phones for long stretches. And why wouldn't they? The enemy, in Syria in particular, didn't have cell phone tracking and targeting capabilities. Only the US did.

And the US would not be crazy enough to target a Russian officer… Right?

Liam used his relationships back at Langley to get the list of potential phones tied to Alexei. Then he put those numbers into the targeting set for Syria—an easy task, given his role and access in the JSOC operations center. If Liam got a ping, he would let Val know, and Val would figure out how to get to a location to ambush or attack. Liam would also feed Val relevant intel and situational awareness from the drone feeds in the Incirlik joint operations center.

They counted on the chaos and friction in Syria to mask their actions from any internal scrutiny.

It didn't take long to ID Alexei's phone in Syria. But it was never in a location Val could get to. For months, Liam traced the Russian officer's phone all over Syria. It was agonizing.

Would they ever get their shot?

When the Syrian government started preparing for its northwestern offensive and Alexei's phone started moving in concert with those preparations, Val and Liam got excited. When the offensive kicked off and the phone traveled north, Val and Liam got serious.

Now Liam was concerned for Val as he looked at the big monitor in the operations center. The rebels had managed to slow the Syrian Army's advance, but more government troops were headed up the M5, and every minute that ticked by meant Val and his team would have to evade farther north to get back to friendly lines, and more consolidated enemy positions to weave between.

Then came the alert of Syrian Air Force activity.

"Val!" Liam tried to keep his voice low enough that others in the operations center would not notice him but also trying to convey the seriousness of the situation. "There are two Frogfoots inbound. You need to pull out."

Val glanced at Mazar, whose attention was forward, through the windshield, as they careened down the narrow, rutted village road.

Frogfoots were Su-25s, Russian-made close-air-support aircraft. Though smaller and less heavily armed than the American A-10, the Frogfoot nonetheless had a well-earned, fearsome reputation. In the right pilot's hands, it could shred a ground position. Val hoped the Syrian pilots were as bad as he'd heard.

"Val, head north!" Liam said with as much urgency as he could risk. "We'll get another shot."

"No. It's today. It's now."

"Then you'd better hurry up."

Liam looked back at the big monitor and shook his head in resignation. Two vehicles moved north on the M5. He believed Alexei was in the second vehicle. He also believed Val would not get there in time.

"Left! Left!" Val yelled.

Mazar repeated the command in Arabic. He didn't need to. The driver knew "left" and "right" from hearing Val bark the commands repeatedly over the past months.

The vehicle skidded off the asphalt and onto the dirt road that cut across a dusty orchard of old, gnarled olive trees.

"Okay, follow the road around to the right!"

Olive trees whizzed by. Branches struck the truck's mirrors.

The driver braked to make the upcoming turn.

The gunner in the back lost his grip and slammed into the floor of the truck cab. He fell onto the ammo boxes as the vehicle lurched to the right.

"There!" Val pointed at a small shed on the edge of the neighborhood. "Park there!"

The truck slid to a stop next to the shed.

"Move! Move! Move!" Val yelled as he hopped out of the truck.

He cross slung his AK-47 as he dashed to the rear of the truck. The gunner lowered the tailgate and handed Val an AT4.

Val threw the tube-shaped, recoilless anti-tank weapon's carrying strap over his shoulder as the gunner handed the driver an RPG-7.

The driver quickly looked over the rocket-propelled grenade launcher to ensure it hadn't been damaged during his evasive driving.

The gunner hopped off the vehicle. He reached back into the truck bed and grabbed the other AT4 as Mazar reached in and took the last RPG-7.

"Follow me!" Val turned toward the small neighborhood and ran south.

The weapons-laden team sprinted almost a hundred meters to a squat one-story house. Val thought about running deeper into the neighborhood to afford them more cover and concealment. He didn't like being on the more easily targeted edge.

But they were out of time.

Val ran to the base of the wall and pointed up. He set down the AT4, turned, and joined his hands below his waist.

Mazar handed his RPG to the driver and stepped into Val's hands.

Val hoisted him up. Mazar scrambled onto the roof.

The driver passed the RPG-7 and the rest of the weapons up to Mazar, who stretched down to grab them.

Val was the last up.

On the roof of the building, Val scanned the southern horizon.

The team was panting after the sprint and climb. Sounds of the battle boomed and popped a kilometer to their north.

Their rooftop perch was only about fifty meters from the road. Looking south, to their right, they could see almost three hundred meters of road before it bent behind the buildings of the rest of the neighborhood.

Val gritted his teeth. This was not optimal. They wouldn't have much notice of the target vehicles' approach, and their shot was perpendicular to the line of travel. Tricky.

The road was empty.

Tense seconds ticked away.

Val stood as the other three men unslung their AK-47s and leaned them against the knee-high wall that encircled the rooftop. Then they got down into prone firing positions, rocket launchers resting on the parapet.

Val got nervous.

Did we miss them?

Val kept his eyes on the road to the south as he unslung his AK-47 and set it down. He stood back up and reached for the sat phone in his vest to call Liam for a sitrep.

Then he saw the vehicles emerge, rounding the bend from behind the buildings of the small neighborhood.

"Shit!" he said in a low, urgent voice, as if the two approaching cars might hear them. "There they are!"

Val dove to a prone position behind the wall as the rest of the team craned their necks to the right to acquire the target.

An extended cab pickup truck traveled in front of what looked like an old VW sedan.

"You two take the first vehicle. The pickup truck," Val said to Mazar and the gunner. "We'll take the second vehicle. The sedan."

Mazar nodded and repeated the instructions quickly. The vehicles had already closed a third of the distance.

"This is a broadside shot. You gotta lead 'em. Probably ten to twenty meters."

Mazar repeated a shortened version of Val's unneeded coaching. They had been fighting in Iraq and Syria for more than a decade. They were pros.

The vehicles were two-thirds of the way to the kill box.

Val steadied his breath.

He peered through the AT4's scope. In addition to a crosshair aiming point, it had tick marks left and right to assist the gunner in estimating left and right offsets. Val wished he'd paid more attention when he was trained on these things years ago.

He didn't have time to dwell, however. The vehicles moved into the kill box.

Val held his breath and focused on his aim.

His entire world and awareness narrowed down to the tunnel-visioned view through the scope.

The vehicles were less than a hundred meters away now.

Val saw three silhouetted passengers in the sedan.

For a long second, he waited for some hint of recognition to swell within him. He felt certain he would recognize Alexei in any circumstance. The front passenger…was he—

Boom.

Swoosh.

The backblast from the two RPGs and other AT4 blew a cloud of dust and smoke over the rooftop. Rocket exhaust obscured Val's vision of the vehicles. He cursed his slowness and squeezed the trigger.

Boom.

Swoosh.

Val's AT4 rocket departed two seconds later than the others.

The pickup truck disappeared in twin explosions as both rockets scored direct hits. The hood of the truck spiraled into the air, and flames erupted from the cabin as the fuel tank combusted.

The other rocket-propelled grenade struck the VW in the rear wheel. The explosion shoved the vehicle up and forward, nearly flipping it end over end.

The sedan collided with the rear of the crumpled and burning pickup truck, a flailing body crashing through the VW's windshield, disappearing into the flames.

The VW's rear end slammed back to the ground as the rocket from Val's AT4 struck the road twenty meters short of the vehicle. Shrapnel and chunks of asphalt peppered the VW.

Val and his team transitioned to their AK-47s and opened fire.

Each man emptied two full magazines at the vehicles.

Val lowered his weapon and scanned the target area. The front half of the sedan was crumpled into the flames of the pickup truck. There was no movement other than the black smoke rising from the fire, alternately obscuring and revealing the bullet-riddled vehicles.

"Let's go," Val said.

Leaving the spent rocket launchers on the roof, the team lowered itself back to the ground. Val came down last.

When his feet hit the ground, Val started running toward the vehicles.

"Where are you going?" Mazar shouted as the other two began moving back to the vehicle.

"I gotta be sure!" Val called over his shoulder.

"There is no time!"

Val didn't respond.

"You damn fool!" Mazar called after him before turning to run toward their vehicle.

Val sprinted toward the burning, tangled vehicles.

His cell phone buzzed in his vest. Probably Liam calling to warn him of fast movers, he thought. He ignored it.

But he glanced south.

Shit!

Two aircraft, low to the ground, flew toward him, a smudge of sooty exhaust trailing behind them.

Val recognized the high-winged silhouette of Su-25s.

Still running, he scanned the ambushed vehicles for signs of life.

Smoke and flames obscured his vision.

He glanced back to the south. The airborne silhouettes were bigger, their exhaust darker, full ordinance loads visible.

Val was less than fifty meters from the VW when the rear door opposite him opened. He saw a man's head and shoulders briefly before the person threw himself out of the car and onto the ground.

Val raised his AK-47 and fired at the vehicle as he continued to run. The bullets sprayed in an erratic pattern, disrupted by his strides.

He was twenty-five meters from the smoldering sedan when the man on the other side lurched up. He took an awkward, limping step away from the vehicle and then turned to look at Val.

It was Alexei.

Val came to an abrupt stop, shoes scrapping across the dusty ground.

Alexei's face was warped with pain, confusion… and recognition.

Val raised his AK-47 to sight in on Alexei's head. An easy shot for Val at this distance.

An explosion knocked Val into the air and tore the rifle from his hands. Searing heat wrapped around him and stole his breath. His vision went red and then faded to black.

CHAPTER 84

Val became aware of the pain. His head ached. And his right arm was throbbing.

He blinked.

The right side of his head itched. He reached to scratch it, but something tugged at his wrist.

"Don't do that. You'll pull out your IV," Liam said from across the room.

Why is Liam here? Val wondered. He felt so fuzzy. It was hard to think.

And where am I, anyway?

"My head itches."

"It should," Liam said, leaning over Val. "It's got a hole in it."

"Very funny."

Val and Liam locked eyes. Val saw the concern on his face.

I must be really hurt.

"Did we get him?"

Liam took a deep breath and took his glasses off. He shrugged as he cleaned the lenses on his shirt and said, "Probably."

"Dammit," Val whispered.

"I studied all the imagery I could discreetly get my hands on," Liam said, replacing his glasses. "And we intercepted a lot of chatter about an ambush and Russian fatalities. But I cannot tell you for certain."

Val lay in silence for a moment.

"Where am I?" he finally asked.

"Landstuhl."

"Germany?" Val said with surprise. "How long was I out?"

"Until just now. You were unconscious for about a week. Most of that was because they kept you out. You've suffered a pretty bad traumatic brain injury. They had to drill a hole in your head to reduce the pressure on your brain."

"You were serious about that hole in my head, then?" Val asked wearily. He lifted his other hand to his head and felt the bandage. "Shit," he mumbled.

"Yeah. A five-hundred-pound Russian bomb will do that to a person."

Val tried to lift his head but couldn't.

"Will you help me sit up?"

Liam pressed the bed's incline button until Val's upper body was raised halfway vertically.

"Tell me what happened. Who got me out?"

"Mazar. Don't ask me how he did it. But he showed up at the border the next day with you laid out in the back seat of a shot-up car. I could only talk to him briefly. But he said he went back for your body after the Su-25s dropped their bombs on you. He was shocked to find you still breathing.

"Taking that tough son of a bitch with you to Syria saved your life." Liam shook his head in disbelief.

Val smiled at the thought of Mazar.

"He also told me he thought they captured the other two."

Val closed his eyes and cursed.

Liam waited until Val opened his eyes again.

"The medic called for a medevac bird the instant he saw you," Liam said. "Just dumb luck that there was a Chinook on the helipad at that moment, delivering the weekly supply run.

"They threw you on the back of that thing, and it flew you to Incirlik. You were on a plane to here less than half an hour after the Chinook landed."

A grim smile spread across Liam's face.

"Seriously, Val. No one has your luck. No one."

"You sound disappointed."

Liam chuckled. He turned from Val's bed and walked back to the chair he'd slept in while waiting for Val's condition to improve. He sat down and rubbed his eyes with both hands.

"Did we get away with it?" Val asked. "Anyone on to us?"

Liam dropped his hands to his lap. "We're clean. Far as I can tell. No one is the wiser. General McDaniel bought the 'separated during combat' story, and you know Mazar won't say shit. The other two…"

Liam hesitated.

Val nodded. If they were really captured, then the Syrians had gotten the truth out of them. Val tried to put the thought out of his head.

"When did you get here?" Val asked.

"Two days ago."

"How much longer can you stay?"

"I'm headed back to Turkey later in the day."

"What time is it, anyway?"

"A little after three in the morning."

"I'm suddenly exhausted."

"I bet you are."

"Will you lower me back down?"

Liam got up from his chair and returned to Val's side. He pressed the button and stood next to Val as it flattened out.

"Thanks," Val said.

Liam walked back to his chair and sat down.

Val was asleep within minutes. Liam dozed in his chair until he had to leave a couple of hours later.

CHAPTER 85

28 April 2013

DIA Headquarters, Bolling Air Force Base

"The general will see you now," Bryson's aide said, leaning his head out of the door to Bryson's office.

Val nodded and stood up, evoking a wince from Bryson's aide. An artillery major, he disapproved of Val's attire. Dressed in jeans, a white T-shirt, and an App State baseball hat, Val didn't look like General Bryson's typical visitor as he approached the door.

"Would you remove your cover, sir?" the major said, disapproval rising from his voice like steam as he glared at Val's baseball hat.

"No." Val winked at the irritated army major as he walked through the door. The major followed.

"Val! Goddamn good to see you!" Bryson boomed, getting up from his desk.

Val and the general shook hands.

"Let me see," Bryson said, tilting his head at Val's cap.

Val took his baseball hat off to reveal a shaven head with a long scar running over the top from his right ear to his left. His hair had just begun to grow back. The fine, dark stubble highlighted the puffy pink scar.

The general's aide looked at his feet.

"Impressive," the general said, grimacing.

Val shrugged. "They had to crack open my skull to drain off the fluid pressure."

"At least, in your case, there are no vital organs in there."

Val smiled.

"Major, I'm going to step out with Colonel Rafter for a moment," General Bryson said to his aide.

"Roger that, sir."

Bryson gestured at Val and strode out of his office.

Val followed the general through the labyrinth of corridors, elevators, and stairways until they exited the DIA headquarters building and stepped out into the courtyard between several of the large buildings.

The general walked toward the 9/11 memorial, dedicated to DIA personnel who were killed in the attack on the Pentagon. Seven muted stained-glass panes, one for each DIA employee killed in the pentagon that day, were mounted in a stainless-steel sculpture.

The general looked around. It was still early, and he and Val were the only ones in the courtyard.

Val wondered if the general had brought him here so he could speak freely, away from audio recording and listening devices.

"So," Bryson said with sadness. "Two old intelligence officers at the end of their roads."

Val nodded. "One a legend. One infamous."

"Both did their best," the general said in a tired voice.

Val nodded again.

"What's your official date?" the general asked him.

"First of June. That will be my twenty-year mark. You?"

"July first. My thirty-fifth."

Val made an exaggerated, wide-eyed expression.

"I know," Bryson said. "I can't believe it either."

"Hell of a thing, sir. Congratulations."

"Thank you, son. But don't sell yourself short. I think you packed at least thirty-five years of service into your twenty years in uniform."

"Thank you, sir. You saying that means a lot to me."

"I still wish you'd let me conduct your retirement ceremony. We'd do it up right. Hold it down here at the memorial and—"

"I appreciate it, sir. I really do. But I'm just…I'm just not in the mood."

The general held up his hands in a surrender gesture. "Okay, okay…had to try one more time. I won't mention it again."

"Who is conducting yours, sir?" Val asked, pivoting the conversation.

"Admiral Mullen."

"The chairman, himself. Fitting."

"I guess. After a certain rank, these things are no longer for you. They're for the larger organization."

Val nodded and looked at the expanse of manicured grass behind the memorial and surrounding the DIA headquarters. After months in Syria, it seemed unreasonably lush. A low-flying gray cloud cover extending past the horizon.

"I know what you did, son," General Bryson said.

"Sir?"

"I want us to conclude our professional relationship with an understanding."

Val sighed and squared up to the general. The discreet outdoor setting made sense now.

"Before you open your mouth and try to fucking deny it, let me remind you who you're talking to. I've known you for a long time. I know what I'm dealing with."

Val fought the urge to roll his eyes.

"When I got the report that your team had been separated from the main Free Syrian Army element, I was concerned. Then I read signal intercepts indicating Russian officer casualties, including a high-level advisor, getting smoked in an ambush. *Damn,* I think to myself. *FSA got lucky on that one and landed a punch. Good for them.*

"Then I get this weird feeling. Like I have been here before. Like one of my officers went off the fucking reservation again. I made a few inquiries.

"While I'm waiting to hear back, you miraculously show up back in Turkey, nearly dead. They get you to Landstuhl just in time, and I am, once again, astounded at how you repeatedly survive your own stupidity.

"Right about then, I hear back from a couple of sources. And, you know what? Turns out Alexei Volkov was in Syria at that time also."

Bryson paused, as if he had just placed a chess piece well.

Val's head tilted as he regarded his mentor.

"Sir, I thought you wanted to end our professional relationship with an understanding?" he said, crossing his arms. "Are you really going to stand there and tell me that was when you first found out Alexei was in Syria?"

The general's gaze did not waver. He studied Val's face.

"How long had you known Volkov was in Syria, sir?" Val asked, studying him right back. "And why did you never tell me like you promised you would?"

After a moment, the general sighed.

Val looked south past the memorial at the gray clouds.

"How do you feel now, sir?" he asked without looking away from the horizon. "Here at the end, I mean."

Bryson turned his gaze south as well, past the memorial on the horizon. "Part of me isn't ready. If I close my eyes, I can get the feeling back, that feeling of being a dumbass second lieutenant walking onto Fort Benning in 1978 for the Basic Course. So long ago. But feels like yesterday sometimes."

The general stood quietly for a moment.

"Truthfully, that feeling doesn't last that long, though," the general finally continued. "And then I just feel tired. I'm ready. I'm proud of my service. But I'm ready."

"Does it feel worth it, though?"

The general looked at Val. The younger officer's face was a knot of emotion.

"It was for me, son."

A tear ran down Val's cheek. He wiped it away quickly.

"Goddamn it. The doc said getting my bell rung like that might make me more emotional for a while."

"It's going to get better, Val."

Val just nodded, not wanting his emotions to get away from him again.

The general put his hand on Val's shoulder.

"I don't know if you got the bastard or not. My guess is you will find out in a year or two. Either way, my heartfelt wish for you, Val, is that you can walk away now. Find a little peace. You have earned it. It has been a long war, and we asked a lot of you."

Val did not take his eyes off the horizon.

"Time is a powerful thing," the general said. "The pain stays with you. But it will dim. It will become tolerable. But you have to want it to. You have to accept that none of it was personal."

Val looked at the general.

"But if it's not personal, then it all feels meaningless."

"The meaning comes and goes, son," Bryson said with a sighing breath. He dropped his hand from Val's shoulder.

The general wasn't sure if he'd gotten through or not. He couldn't tell if his words had been helpful or had worsened things.

"Still bound for Prague?"

"Yes, sir," Val said, turning back to Bryson and forcing a smile. "Leaving in a week."

"Good. You've earned your rest. Go enjoy it."

Val smiled.

"You too, sir."

CHAPTER 86

"I thought you were joking." Sydney stared in disbelief at the three large vats of water on the Prague sidewalk. It was an odd Christmas Eve sight for an American. The vats were made of strong plastic and stood about waist high. Live carp swam in the water, their dark, scaly backs rippling the surface as they jostled each other. Two men in rain gear smiled and smoked cigarettes as they milled around the vats and waved at passersby.

"This is a great tradition," Val said. "I couldn't make this up."

Val put his arm around Sydney and squeezed her shoulder as he kissed her forehead.

"Okay. Let's get dinner." He tugged her gently forward to the edge of one of the vats.

The two men in rain gear smiled at Val and Sydney. Val nodded and gestured at the vat of carp.

"Yes! Good!" one of the men said in a thick Slavic accent. He dropped his spent cigarette to the ground and stepped on it before bending over to grab a handheld fishing net. He walked over to the vat and scooped out a large carp.

The fish gaped at Sydney as the man held it up in the net for inspection.

"Is good?"

"Good!" Val said, offering a thumbs-up.

"Good." The nodded as if a solemn understanding had been reached. He scooped the fish out of the net with one of his gloved hands and put it on the scale. After noting the fish's weight, he stepped over to a small table between the vats. He gripped the fish on the table with one hand, dropped the net out of the other, and picked up a simple wooden club.

"Wait!" Sydney gasped as the man raised the club.

The man hesitated, club above his head, ready to strike. He shot Val a *what's it gonna be, buddy* glare.

"It's up to you," Val said in a sweet voice. "But tradition says if we don't have the fish butchered here, we can take it home and put it in the bathtub for a few days before eating him."

"Now you're definitely joking" Sydney's eyes narrowed.

"I'm not. Folks do that when they buy the carp a few days before Christmas. And, sometimes, they actually end up putting the fish back in the river after the holiday rather than eating it. Usually when there is a child in the household who makes a convincing appeal for the fish's life after getting attached."

Sydney hesitated.

"Let me remind you that my flat only has one bathroom," Val said.

"Do what you must."

Val nodded to the man.

A wet thud rang out as the club crushed the fish's skull. The man released the dead fish and exchanged the club for a large cleaver. He severed the fish's head from its body in a single stroke.

"He gave his life for a good cause," Val said to Sydney as the man wrapped the decapitated fish in a newspaper.

"I'll take your word for it," Sydney muttered.

The man grabbed the fish's head and placed it in the rolled-up newspaper. Val paid him and took the fish.

The pair walked back toward the river. Val held the fish in one hand and Sydney's hand in the other. Sydney grasped Val's upper arm and pulled herself in close to him as they walked.

They crossed Charles Bridge and started up the hill. The sun, already below the horizon, threw dark-orange light onto the clouds behind the castle looming above them.

Back at Val's apartment, Sydney left her coat on and went to the balcony as Val took the fish to the kitchen. Molly, a brown wire-haired mutt, followed him, nose twitching, as she sniffed rapidly at the newspaper-wrapped treasure.

"Back off, Molly," Val said sweetly as he pushed her away from the refrigerator. He placed the fish on the top shelf and grabbed the bottle of wine.

Molly looked at the refrigerator for a moment. Accepting her defeat, she walked out to the balcony to join Sydney.

"Merry Christmas." Val walked onto the balcony with two glasses of wine. Sydney was leaning over, rubbing Molly's ears.

"Merry Christmas." Sydney straightened and took a wine from Val.

They clinked their glasses together above Molly and drank.

"I still can't believe you got a dog."

"What's not to believe?" Val squatted to pet Molly.

"I don't know," Sydney said, suddenly stumped by the question.

Val stood and shrugged. "Maybe I'm just becoming more domesticated. You know, nesting."

"Uh-huh."

"Besides, I like dogs. And she is a good one."

"She is." Sydney looked down at the forty-pound mutt leaning against Val's legs. "And she is smitten with you."

Val smiled at the comment.

"Where did you get her?"

"She lived in one of the parks nearby. At least, I think she lived in the park. I used to give her treats when I walked through. One day, she followed me home. I told her to go back to the park, but a couple hours later when I stepped out onto this balcony, I looked down and she was still there, sleeping next to the door."

Val gestured down toward the door to his building three floors below.

"It kind of reminded me of another stray I knew once. So…"

Sydney waited for him to go on. A flash of emotion passed across Val's face and then was gone.

"So, I said, let's try it." He took a sip of wine. "That was almost six months ago."

"I'd say it's working out."

"I would too." Val smiled at Molly, who had stepped onto a thick sheepskin he'd placed on the balcony for her and curled up.

Sydney turned back to the view of Prague. The spires of Old Town, now doused in shadow, stood below on the other side of the Charles Bridge. It was a cloudy Christmas Eve, and the dark surface of the Vltava River shimmered, reflecting the lights of the far bank.

"Tell me again how you found this apartment?"

"I did a favor for a Czech buddy back when I was stationed here. This apartment belongs to his father, I think."

"A favor?" Sydney tilted her head Val's way.

Val gave her his best blank-faced spy look.

Sydney shook her head.

"Anyway. He graciously said I could stay here while I figured out a more permanent situation."

"It must have been a hell of a favor."

Val shrugged.

"You enjoy the view. I'm going to cook dinner."

"I think I'll do just that." Sydney leaned in to kiss Val before he turned to go to the kitchen.

Molly followed him in.

Sydney wrapped herself in a blanket and sat in one of the rocking chairs on the small balcony. She lit a cigarette and leaned back in the chair, resting her feet on the iron railing. It was still early evening, and festive sounds emanated from Old Town. Music, laughter, and the comings and goings of loud, happy gatherings.

She took a sip of the red wine and a long pull on the cigarette. It was nice to be here. To spend time with Val. She tried not to think about saying goodbye tomorrow.

Sydney was leaving in the morning, Christmas Day, headed for Langley and a series of urgent meetings on the situation in Ukraine.

In November, protests had erupted across Ukraine when President Viktor Yanukovych rejected an agreement to increase ties with the European Union. Despite widespread public support and nearly unanimous parliamentary approval of the agreement, Yanukovych defied the will of Ukrainians and moved to increase ties with Russia.

In Kyiv, protestors established a camp in Independence Square, determined to outlast Yanukovych and attract the world's attention. Independence Square became the scene of regular conflicts between the protestors and police as the government ratcheted up the pressure and violence. By the end of 2013, both sides sensed the conflict was existential. So did the CIA. Ukraine was at a tipping point. The agency wanted to be sure it fell in the right direction.

Demonstrations and civil unrest, combined with the Kremlin's determination to keep Ukraine out of the EU and their puppet Yanukovych in power, created a high probability of violence and worsening instability...and opportunity. The director had requested Sydney's participation by name. Her experience and expertise in Russia generally and the gray arms market specifically made her a sought-after advisor in this situation. Sydney was excited. More than fifteen years in the agency, and it finally felt like her career was gaining altitude. She also felt more at risk than ever.

Posted to Sofia, Bulgaria, Sydney was the senior counterproliferation intelligence officer in Eastern Europe. Her boss, Madison Jackson, was a long-time agency veteran stationed in Vienna. "Maddi," as everyone is the agency knew her, was a renown former case officer that had started her nearly three decades of service as an Army officer before being recruited by the CIA. Possessing high levels of both intelligence and attractiveness, she was widely respected even though no one really knew the details of her service - In an organization built on secrecy, this was the ultimate sign she was the real deal.

Sydney viewed Maddi as a mentor. Jackson liked Sydney, had confidence in her and stayed out of her way. "Keep doing what you're doing," Maddi told Sydney when she was promoted to the role. "I'll let you know when you screw up."

Sydney's charge ranged from Russia in the east to the Czech Republic in the west. The countries of Ukraine and Moldova, hotbeds of Russian gray and black arms activity, fell squarely in her area of responsibility. Just as the situation in Ukraine presented the US with opportunity and risk, Sydney could sense that she stood at an inflection point. She would emerge from the crisis in Ukraine strengthened, her career trajectory elevated, or she would be diminished.

Now, though, sitting on Val's balcony overlooking the city and its river on Christmas Eve with a glass of wine in her hand and a warm blanket on her lap, the thought of staying had a pull.

But so did her professional opportunity.

Situations like the one in Ukraine came around only once in a career. Maybe.

"My lady?" Val leaned his head out onto the balcony. "Dinner is served."

Sydney crushed out her cigarette and stood up.

"Lead the way, sir."

It was a modestly sized apartment. One bedroom, a small kitchen that flowed into a dining and living room, one bathroom, and the balcony. But it exuded the solid charm of the revival architecture buildings built in the late 1800s. Dark hardwood floors, solid plaster walls, and tall arched windows. Prague was spared much of the destruction of the Second World War, leaving many buildings like this one untouched.

Val had dimmed the lights, and soft music played in the background. Molly lay sleeping on her dog bed in the corner of the living room.

"My goodness," Sydney said, approaching the dinner table. "This smells and looks lovely."

Val smiled.

"I did my best." He pulled her chair out.

Sydney took her seat.

She leaned in and smelled her food as Val walked to his chair.

"It's the traditional Christmas preparation," Val said, pouring her more wine and then refilling his own glass. "The filets are covered in flour, breadcrumbs, and egg and then pan-fried. The potato salad has peas, onions, carrots, parsley, eggs, and mayonnaise."

Val raised his glass.

"Merry Christmas, Sydney."

"Merry Christmas."

Val set his glass down and waited as Sydney picked up her fork and knife to try the fish.

A smile broke across her face as she chewed.

"Wonderful," she said after swallowing the first bite. "If I didn't know that this fish was bludgeoned to death on a street corner only a few hours ago, I would never guess." Sydney picked up her wineglass. "My compliments to the chef."

Val bowed his head slightly at the praise.

"Really. It's fantastic." Sydney put another forkful of fish into her mouth. "

Val didn't respond as he chewed on a crispy bite. He was pleased.

The door to the balcony was still open, affording them a clear view of the night sky. Festive sounds wafted up from the town below.

They both saw the snowflakes outside beyond the balcony at the same time.

"Did you arrange for those as well?" Sydney asked Val, as if discovering a surprise gift.

"I did. Nothing like making love while it snows outside."

"That so?"

Val leaned back in his chair, wined and took a sip of wine.

Sydney smiled and took another bite of fish.

They ate without speaking. It had been a long day of walking and enjoying the holiday sights around Prague. They were hungry.

After a few moments, Val set his knife and fork down. He looked at Sydney. "I love having you here."

"I love being here."

"Stay."

Sydney looked up from her plate at Val. He sat across from her with a hopeful smile.

"Don't leave tomorrow. Stay with me here."

Sydney put her silverware down.

"Val…I…"

"We had a deal, remember?" Val's smile acknowledged how ridiculous he sounded, but his voice was sincere. "You said you'd join me if I quit and moved to Prague."

"No," Sydney said, loving tolerance in her voice. "You said you'd move to Prague and then beg me to join you."

"Well, I'm begging." Val reached across the table and took her hand. "Come live with me here. Please."

Sydney blushed at the directness of the question.

"And then what?"

"Who cares? Then we're together. We made it."

Sydney shook her head and pulled her hand back.

"Just ask for Prague as your next assignment," Val said as if a brilliant idea had occurred to him. "Get posted here and then coast."

"I'm sorry, Val. But I'm not done yet."

Val's smile melted away.

"I'm not ready to just coast."

Val nodded.

"There is more I want to do. Besides, I've got about eight years to go before I can retire with benefits. Walking away now would be a waste."

Sydney reached across the table and took Val's hand.

"You make it tempting, though."

"What gets it done? What would convince you?"

She smiled patiently.

"Time."

"How will you know when it's time?" Val asked.

"I'll know."

Val stared at his food. Thoughts of Tony swept over him. Their time in Iraq. Tony's wishes for him and Sydney.

I'm trying, brother. I really am.

Sydney squeezed his hand. "Hey."

Val looked up, his eyes welling with tears.

"I'm sorry. I don't know why I'm getting so emotional. I think that knock on my head in Syria loosened my emotions more than my brains. I just—"

"Hey… I'm not saying no."

Val tried to smile.

"I'm saying *not now.*"

Val nodded half-heartedly.

"There will be a day," she said, squeezing his hand again. "I'll come walking across that old bridge of yours with a bag on my shoulder. And that will be that. We'll be together."

Val's smile surfaced. He was sad. But didn't want it to spoil the rest of their time together. He picked up his wineglass.

"I'll be here. Please don't make me wait too long."

"I promise I won't."

They each drank and then set their glasses down.

"What's this?" Sydney asked, tilting her head to the side as she looked at her plate. She lifted one side of the dish and peered underneath. "Are these fish scales?"

"Yep," Val picked his plate up. "I put them under mine as well."

Sydney poked at one of the large scales with her finger.

"Um…Why?"

"They're supposed to be good luck," Val said, putting his plate back down on the scattering of fish scales. "I guess I didn't use enough tonight."

He smiled to let her know he was kidding.

"Some men here even carry a few scales from their Christmas dinner in their wallet during the year. For good luck."

"Gross. Will you?"

"I'd carry that fish's head in my pocket all year, if I thought it would help get you here for good."

Sydney didn't laugh. She could see from Val's face that he was serious.

"Sometimes it seems like you and I need all the luck we can get, doesn't it?" she said.

*

Val took it easy on Sydney on Christmas Day. He'd made his case over the previous days and nights and decided to let it rest that morning. Opting instead for a long hug under the Terminal Two departure sign at the Václav Havel Airport, he said, "I love you," into her ear.

"I love you too. God help me, but I do."

Val stepped back and said, "You know where to find me."

"I do."

"I'll be watching the bridge." Val smiled sheepishly.

"I'll be easy to spot," she said as she leaned in and kissed him on the cheek.

After a breath's hesitation, she turned and walked into the terminal. Val waited until she'd vanished in the throng before leaving.

*

The last week of December passed slowly. Val took Molly on long walks and visited old friends from his embassy days to pass the time. New Year's came and went. January crawled by.

Val was obsessed by the worsening situation in Ukraine. Molly lay on her bed, her eyes on Val as he spent most days in his apartment watching the news and calling old friends still "in the game" to beg for information.

"Tell me, Liam," Val pleaded, nearly yelling into his cell phone. "Please tell me what we're doing."

"You're supposed to be retired. Relax. Go have fun."

"The Russians are all over this!" Val pointed at his TV. "I guarantee you that.

We need to smash them in the mouth. It's the only thing that will make them back off."

"You know how this works, Val." Liam's voice betrayed his irritation. "This isn't a secure line, and you're not need-to-know."

"Don't give me that bullshit! Tell me what the hell is going on. I earned that much. I—"

"You earned your retirement. You truly did. And now you need to enjoy it. You don't need to know shit. Now I've got to go."

"Liam, please…"

"I've got to go, Val."

Liam hung up.

CHAPTER 87

January flew by for Sydney. It was the most exciting time of her career. As the emergency meetings at Langley concluded, the director made a point of coming over to thank her. "I'm glad you're on the team, Miss Knox," he told her, shaking her hand.

Sydney clenched her fists in excitement as she left the room. She wanted to scream and pump her fist. This was what she'd been working toward for so long. To be in the inner circle. To personally move the needle of history.

Back in Sophia, her excitement mixed with anxiety. She was on the big stage now, monitoring and attempting to disrupt Russian efforts to funnel weapons into Ukraine. Her reports and assessments were read by the director, National Security Council staff, and probably the president himself. Her boss coached her from Vienna.

"Stay focused on what's important, Sydney," Maddi told her. "And what's important is the intelligence. Don't worry about who is reading what. Just get your part right."

It was clear the Russians would not allow Ukraine to escape their sphere of influence without a fight. What was not clear was how overt their efforts would be, how "hot" things would get. The unthinkable, a shooting war in Ukraine, was increasingly thinkable.

Sydney rarely left the embassy. Living on coffee and cigarette breaks, she pushed her staff hard and herself harder. Somehow, to her relief, they were making it work. Through a special cocktail of human assets, signal intelligence, and Sydney's strong foreign intelligence community relationships in the region, they were making an impact. Multiple Russian arms shipments into Ukraine had been seized or disrupted, including several originating out of Moldova.

Nicolae continued to be her secret weapon. Not only was his network of agents producing actionable intelligence, but his small strike force also proved to be lethal and competent. The small team gave Sydney a direct action capability cloaked in plausible deniability. She took advantage of it, striking targets in Transnistria as well as the coast of Ukraine. It was sensitive, in-and-out-quickly stuff that Moscow could not trace to the US. And the Moldovans were motivated. Better to stop Russia in Ukraine than face the juggernaut on its own soil.

Despite the international cooperation, Transnistria remained opaque and porous, leaking weapons into Ukraine via circuitous routes. And Ukraine itself was riddled with Russian supporters, agents, and unacknowledged military personnel. Sydney didn't want to guess how it was going to play out, but her gut told her badly.

CHAPTER 88

Val seethed in his apartment as he watched the twenty-four-seven coverage of the violence in Kyiv. Protestors and police fought in the streets from the eighteenth until the twentieth of February. Almost a hundred protestors were killed, as well as many police. Val studied the conflict in real time, pestering his agency and military contacts for insight. Liam would no longer take his calls.

On the twenty-first of February, Yanukovych agreed to the transition to an interim government, which would be followed by elections and constitutional reforms. The next day, Saturday, in the darkness of early morning, Yanukovych fled the capital, seeking refuge in the Russia-leaning Crimea. Hopeful developments, but Val was certain Putin had a fistful of cards left to play.

Val took Molly and left his apartment on Saturday evening. After three days of little sleep watching TV and working his phone, he needed to stretch his legs, clear his head, and have a few beers. Molly did too.

He and Molly walked downhill through the narrow cobblestone alleys toward the river. Molly darted in and out of the shadows after city rats, enjoying speed and pursuit after seventy-two hours locked in an apartment with her grumpy father. The sound of muted, throbbing music reached them as they crossed the Charles Bridge. The dance clubs in Old Town, deeply embedded in the tangle of stone buildings, had already come to life. Val stopped in the middle of the bridge at the feet of the statue of Saint John of Nepomuk, as he always did. Molly trotted over and sat next to him. She was accustomed to his cover stops.

Saint John was still his favorite statue, and he loved the view past it to the north. And, after more than fifteen years as a spy, he couldn't go anywhere without conducting an SDR.

Saint John was his standard cover stop. Val would stop and gaze up at the statue of the doomed martyr. Head encircled in gold stars, the green oxidized-bronze face looked back down at him. Then, under the guise of taking in the unique riverscape around him, Val would use his peripheral vision to clear the bridge behind him to be sure no one was following. Molly provided excellent, ever-present cover for his scans. He would kneel and give her a treat or pet her while clearing in all directions.

No one was following him tonight, of course. He was out of the game now. Of no use or importance to anyone.

"Still," he said quietly to Molly, "I have the strangest feeling we're being watched."

Molly looked back at him, unperturbed.

"Maybe you've finally pissed off too many rats."

He shrugged, and they continued across the bridge.

Their destination was the Stunt Bar. Situated on the edge of Old Town, the place served several dozen beers on tap and good pub food and had become a hangout for expats living in Prague. Though not one of the hard-core regulars, Val went there often enough to be recognized and to know exactly what he wanted without needing a menu. They were cool about letting Molly in, who would sleep beneath Val's table.

He was hoping the laid-back atmosphere, multiple TVs set to the world's sporting events, and attractive waitstaff would help him relax and dislodge his headspace from events in Ukraine. But after an American-style cheeseburger and three beers, he was still thinking of car fires and hasty barricades in Kyiv. Dead protestors lying in the street. And the Russians.

"Fuck me," he muttered.

Val paid and pulled his jacket on.

"Let's go, girl," he said to Molly.

As they crossed the bridge on the way back, he got the feeling again. He called

Molly to his side and dropped to one knee. He pretended to check one of her paws while he did a full 360-degree scan.

Nothing.

Molly pulled her paw out of Val's hand. She tilted her head and looked him in the eyes.

"I'm sorry," he said in a sad voice. "I think your dad is losing it."

They continued on, passing through the bridge's north tower and then up the hill to his apartment.

Val came to an abrupt stop as they rounded the last corner to his place. Molly, locked on his hip, growled.

A man stood in the doorway to their building.

Backlit by the streetlight, shadow obscured the man's face. Slightly overweight, the man had jammed his hands into his coat pockets and turned up his collar against the cold. He turned to face Val and Molly.

Certain now that he was being surveilled earlier, anger surged within Val. It combined with his pent-up frustration of the past few days, and he strode, hands in fists, toward the man.

Molly broke from his side, sprinting toward the stranger.

"Who the fuck are you?" Val shouted as Molly cornered him in the doorway, barking like she wanted to kill him.

The man tried to take his hands out of his coat pockets as Val approached.

"Stop!" Val drew his concealed pistol from behind his back in a smooth motion and pointing it at the man's head. Molly crouched, preparing to attack.

The man froze, hands still in his coat pockets.

"Val," the man said with a Ukrainian accent. "Please don't shoot me."

Val's eyebrows raised.

"Burian?"

"Yes! Please don't shoot me."

"You have gained weight."

"Fine," Burian said with a huff. "Can you please lower gun?"

"Why are you here?"

"I need to talk to you."

"About what?"

"Perhaps you have been watching the news lately?"

Val scanned the area. They seemed to be alone.

Molly, aggression defused by Val's demeanor, growled at the man's feet.

"Val, please." Burian tilted his head toward the raised pistol.

"Shit," Val said, lowering the pistol. "I'm sorry, Burian."

"Thank you."

"Molly, come," Val said. Molly trotted to his side. "But you can't ambush someone like that."

"I did not ambush you," Burian said, offended at the accusation.

"You might as well have." Val stepped closer, Molly at close heel. "Showing up unexpected like that."

"I am sorry. But it is urgent we speak. Can we go inside?"

Val looked around again and stuffed his pistol behind his back. "Sure."

Burian followed Val and Molly into the building and up the stairs.

"Beer?" Val asked as they entered his apartment. "I've got whiskey too."

"A beer would be nice, thank you." Burian took off his coat and laid it on a chair.

Val took the pistol from behind his back and placed it back in the kitchen drawer he kept it in before grabbing two beers from the fridge. Molly went to her bed but didn't lie down. She sat upright, eyes locked on Burian.

"Well?" Val asked after they were seated in the living room and had each taken a sip of beer. "What are you doing here, Burian?"

"We need help."

"'We' who? Help with what?"

"We the Ukrainians," Burian said, indignant. "We are under attack. Have you not seen the news?"

"Of course, I have."

"And you, of all people, know what we are facing. We need help, Val."

"What the hell do you think I can do about it?"

"Tell your leadership! Tell them there is no time for hesitation. The Russians are already in Ukraine. It is time to join the fight. We need help."

"Oh, is that all?" Val took a sip of beer.

The Ukrainian looked at Val with wounded puzzlement.

"Burian, you know I am retired, right?" Val put his beer down. "I'm done.

Out. No longer in the game. I have no authority and no access. There is nothing I can do."

Burian chuckled and shook his head.

"Please, Val," he said, as if taking offense. "I am longtime friend. We heard about your retirement." Burian rolled his eyes.

Val glared back at him.

"We saw it for what it was," Burian said.

"What do you mean?"

"Is cover story, of course," Burian said quietly, as if he were sharing a secret.

Val leaned back in his chair, a mixture of amusement and irritation washing over him. He looked at Molly, who had laid down, but still held her head up, eyes on Burian.

"Why would they let you retire?" Burian shrugged. "You are too good."

"Because I'm burned, that's why. Everyone on the fucking planet knows I worked in intelligence."

"Oh yes, Bulgaria." Burian chuckled. "I always knew you were crazy."

"Well, it caught up to me."

"Being burned like that can be an advantage. You know this. They know this."

"Who knows this?"

"The people you work for."

Val shook his head with fatigue.

"The CIA," Burian said with certainty.

Val leaned forward and grabbed his beer. He took a long pull on it and slouched back into his chair.

"And the truth is, I'm fucking tired, Burian." Val rubbed the scar on his head. His hair had grown back, and the scar was no longer visible unless you knew where to look. It was puffy and soft beneath his fingers. "I'm tired and beat-up."

"Pretend if you must. But please help us."

"How?"

"Show the world that Russia has already invaded," Burian said, emotion creeping into his voice. "We cannot hold them off on our own. It is not the time for your president to be restrained. We need help and action."

Val stood up, frustrated.

"The president? Let me just give him a ring right now. Set him straight. Get him headed in the right fucking direction."

Burian looked at Val, surprised at the sarcasm.

"You're still intelligence, right?" Val asked. "Talk to the fucking CIA yourself."

"We are, Val!" Burian stood up. "We talk to them every day."

"Then why the hell are you here talking to me?"

"Because you are man of action! We need action! All they do is talk. I am asking you to help us get action."

Molly growled.

Burian paused, realizing that he'd raised his voice.

Val sighed.

"I'm sorry, Burian. I truly am. But I'm out. For real. I'm of no help to you."

Val walked away from Burian toward the balcony. The Ukrainian stood still, absorbing Val's words as if he finally understood.

Val slid open the glass door and stepped out into the cold air. He took a sip of beer and stared into the dark void where the river flowed. Molly trotted out and sat on her sheepskin.

After a moment, Burian walked over to stand behind Val.

"I understand, Val. I am sorry I bothered you."

"It's okay. I'm sorry I have let you down," Val said, turning back to Burian. "But we all have to walk away from it at some point."

Burian chuckled ruefully and looked at the ground. "I wish that were true."

Val's head cocked at the comment.

"What do you mean?" Val asked as Burian turned to leave.

Burian turned around slowly. "Alexei. I wish he would walk away from it."

The name struck Val like a slap.

"Alexei?"

Burian nodded.

"But I thought he was…" Val's voice trailed off.

"He was what?"

"Nothing," Val said, shaking his head and stepping back into the apartment. "Why did you mention him?"

"Because he is in Ukraine. Because we think he is important. Maybe running the whole thing for them."

"Are you sure?"

Burian reached into his pocket and pulled out his phone. He fiddled with it for a minute and then held it up for Val to see.

There was Alexei's face. The photo showed him getting out of the back seat of a dark vehicle.

"This was him last week in Kyiv," Burian said. He turned his hand and looked at the photo. His face grew somber. "Is sad to think of us all together, almost fifteen years ago, at the Marshall Center."

"Is he still in Kyiv?" Val asked, almost whispering.

"The parties and the skiing," Burian said in a faraway voice, still focused on the photo of Alexei. "Was good time."

"Burian," Val said sharply.

Burian looked up from his phone as if waking from a nap.

"Is Alexei still in Kyiv?"

"We don't think so." He put his phone back in his pocket. "We think he is in Illichivsk now, coordinating the smuggling of arms to Russian sympathizers in Crimea. We need help stopping him. Is why I came. I thought your bosses would listen to you. If you came to see for yourself that Alexei is there. You could have told them. You could have…done something."

Burian paused. He looked at Val and shrugged.

Val blinked a few times before turning and walking back out onto the balcony.

He lived. I can't believe it.

Val gripped the railing. Hands wide, head bowed as if preparing to lift a massive weight.

And now I've got one more shot at him. One more chance to end it.

Burian stood in the apartment.

Val raised his head and looked out at the river. He stood motionless, hands still wide on the railing for a moment to be sure. He took a few deep, long breaths and a sad smile broke across his face.

After all this time. And all that has happened. To have this last shot at Alexei… And not want it. I'm done. I'm not at peace yet. Not by a long shot. But I'm done. It's not my fight anymore. I don't need it anymore.

Val looked down at Molly, who peered up at him from her sheepskin.

"I think Tony would understand, don't you?" Val said to her.

"What was that, Val?" Burian said, approaching the porch. He paused in the doorway.

"Nothing. Just talking to Molly."

Burian looked down at the dog quickly and then back at Val.

"So, still no? You are sure?"

"Yes. I am. I'm sorry."

"I understand. Of course." Burian turned and walked toward the door.

Val followed him in.

Burian paused and took out his phone. He sent a quick text and then smiled at Val.

"Thank you for the beer," Burian said. He walked slowly over to his jacket and then turned back to Val. "It was good to see you, my friend."

"You too, Burian."

Burian looked at his watch and put on his coat. He walked to the door, unlocked it, and then turned to look at Val, one hand on the doorknob.

His face was sad as he opened the door and stepped out of the way. Six men charged into the apartment. They were on Val in an instant, knocking him to the floor. Val heard Molly barking viciously as he felt the needle plunge into his neck. Molly yelped in pain.

They better not hurt my dog.

Val lost consciousness.

CHAPTER 89

Val tried to open his eyes, but they wouldn't obey. *Why am I so damn tired? I know there's something really important I should be doing. But I don't remember what it is.*

He spent a few minutes slipping back and forth between sleep and almost being awake. A steady rushing noise surrounded him, and he wondered what it was.

Val tried his eyes again. They opened slowly. His vision was blurry. He was in a chair. He thought the fuzzy, dark blob shape in front of him was another seated person. It seemed like he should know who it was.

There is definitely something important I should be doing right now.

He blinked his eyes rapidly.

"I think he wakes up now," the fuzzy blob seated in front of him said.

I know that voice!

Val blinked a few times. He was sitting inside a tube of some kind, and the blob was definitely a person.

"How do you feel, Val?" the blob said.

Burian!

Val narrowed his eyes, and the fuzzy blob came into better focus. It *was* Burian, seated across from him.

I remember now! I'm supposed to be beating the shit out of him!

Val tried to leap onto Burian, but all he managed to do was slide out of his chair onto the floor.

The small tube filled with laughter.

Oh yeah. He had a bunch of goons grab me…and my hands are tied. Terrific.

"Pick him up," Burian said.

Strong hands grabbed Val and placed him back in his seat. His vision was rapidly improving now. He looked around.

I'm on an airplane.

He looked across at Burian.

"Where…" Val croaked as he tried to speak. His throat was dry. He worked his tongue around to no effect.

Burian handed him a bottle of water.

Val, wrists bound together with a large black zip tie, fumbled trying to open it.

Burian took it back and twisted the top off. He handed the open bottle back to Val.

Val drank half the bottle and then asked Burian, "Where are you taking me?"

"Ukraine. To see your buddy."

"My buddy?"

"Alexei."

"Why?"

"I am not sure. But he said it was important."

Val sat straighter in his chair. Whatever they hit him with was burning off quickly now. He looked around the aircraft. It was small. Only ten seats. The men who had assaulted him took up six places. Looking out the window, Val saw only blackness.

"We will be there around one in morning," Burian said.

Val looked at his wrist. They had taken his watch.

"Maybe half an hour," Burian added.

Val raised his hands.

"I'm not going anywhere. And these things are killing me."

Burian's brow furrowed.

"Please?"

"Okay. But if you are asshole…"

Val nodded. "I know. I know."

Burian leaned across with a knife. He cut the bindings from Val's wrists and then sat back into his seat.

Val rubbed his wrists.

"Thank you."

Burian nodded.

"And fuck you," Val added.

He turned and started out the dark window.

After the aircraft landed, Val looked out the window while it taxied the entire length of the runway toward the dark south side of the airfield. The plane came to a stop next to a large, unlit hangar. The hangar doors opened, and a tug drove out of the light, hooked the aircraft's nosewheel, and pulled it into the hangar.

Val saw two cars in the hangar. Half a dozen armed men milled around next to the automobiles. As the plane got closer, they tightened and fidgeted with their weapons.

The men were dressed in dark-green camouflage fatigues and carried modified AK-74s. They had the look of mercenaries.

The plane came to a stop.

Burian looked at Val.

"Please do not do anything stupid, Val. Those men do not work for me. I won't be able to control them."

Val looked back out the window.

The pilot opened the door.

"Follow me," Burian said as he stood up. He waited for Val, who shook his head with resolve and then stood up. Burian stepped out of the aircraft first. Val followed him down the steps to the concrete floor of the hangar.

Burian walked quickly from the aircraft toward the vehicles and armed men.

Val hesitated. He stood at the bottom of the aircraft steps and glanced at the tug operator standing at the nose of the aircraft. The tug operator looked at his feet.

"You are dismissed, asshole," Burian shouted in Ukrainian at the tug operator. "Get the fuck out of here."

The tug operator nodded and hurried out of the hangar.

"What's going on, Burian?" Val asked, still not moving.

Burian didn't respond.

Five of the mercenaries trained their weapons at Val's head as the sixth approached him with plastic flex-cuffs and a mean smile.

Burian turned his back to Val and leaned against one of the cars, bringing his cell phone to his ear.

"What the hell, Burian?" Val yelled.

The tall mercenary with flex-cuffs stepped in front of Val. He chuckled and said something to him in Chechen.

"Fuck you," Val said as he punched the tall mercenary in the face.

The mercenary staggered back as the five others charged. Val was on the ground, several knees on his back, in seconds.

"Fuck all of you!" he screamed, unable to get up. "I'm gonna kill you, Burian! I swear to God. I will kill you!"

The men rolled Val over onto his back and restrained each of his limbs. The tall mercenary appeared over Val, his left eye and cheek already swelling from Val's punch. He slapped Val hard across the face.

"Enough!" the mercenary bellowed.

Val glared at the man standing over him. The mercenary's eyes were narrowed in anger.

"You are lucky the boss said, 'Not a scratch on him,'" he said, looking down at Val. "For now."

Val realized the man standing over him was the leader of the mercenary team.

The leader barked an order to the other five. Val fought in vain as they bound his hands behind his back and tied his knees and feet together.

Two of the men hoisted him and carried him toward the vehicles.

"Fuck you!" Val screamed. He thrashed and kicked, but the two men carried him easily to one of the sedans. They opened the trunk and threw him in.

The mercenary leader leaned over Val in the vehicle's trunk. "But the boss did not say I had to make you comfortable, asshole."

He leaned over and jerked a hood over Val's head.

"Burian!" Val yelled. "Goddamn it! I'm gonna kill—"

The trunk slammed shut.

CHAPTER 90

Nicolae stood in by the Zodiac Fountain at the front entrance to Carol Park in Bucharest. The large bowl-shaped structure, ringed with mosaics of the twelve zodiac signs, stood in an empty circular pool. The fountain had been drained for the winter. Water would not flow again until late April.

Darkness settled over the park as the sun sank lower beneath the horizon. The streetlights behind Nicolae were already lit, their pale-yellow glow ineffective against the lingering twilight. The evening was quiet, with only intermittent cars passing by on the on the street that approached the fountain and then curved away.

The dry fountain was silent, so he heard her approach from a long way away. He smiled as the rhythmic scrape and click of her shoes on the sidewalk grew louder. She was angry. Her choice of shoes was a giveaway. Loud and ill-suited to an SDR, they said, *Fuck you*, with every step.

Good, I'm angry too.

He didn't turn around as she got closer. He stood motionless, hands in his coat pockets, staring at the sign of Taurus on the curved underside of the fountain.

"Follow me," Sydney said as she walked by him.

Nicolae scanned the empty park and street corner and then turned to follow Sydney.

They walked out of the park and across the street into the residential neighborhood to the northwest. Sydney led him around a corner, where a black BMW sedan waited for them. They got in the back seat of the vehicle, and the car accelerated out of the upscale neighborhood and onto the main street.

Sydney looked at Nicolae and shook her head slightly, telling him to stay quiet, and then locked her head and eyes to the front. Nicolae did the same.

After a twenty-minute vehicle-borne SDR, the driver turned off the street into an underground parking deck. He stopped the car in front of the elevator, where Sydney got out. Nicolae followed. The car exited the parking deck and drove away.

They took the elevator to the third floor, where it opened onto a hallway. Nicolae followed Sydney to one of the doors, which she unlocked before stepping inside. She locked the door behind them.

"We're good here," she said, gesturing at the table and chairs in the middle of the plain room. "This is one of our safe houses."

Nicolae unbuttoned his jacket and sat down.

"So, tell me," Sydney said, taking a seat opposite him. "What's so important I had to drag my ass to Romania?"

Yesterday, Nicolae activated the emergency communications protocol to request a meeting with Sydney. The reverse of the blue flowerpot in Chișinău that told him Sydney needed to get in touch, Nicolae called a phone number Sydney had made him memorize when she'd first recruited him. After a few circuit handovers to mask the origin of the transmission, the call rang in Langley, where a desk officer answered, "Ray's Pizza, may I help you?"

"I'd like a pepperoni pizza, please," Nicolae responded.

After a few verbal challenges, to which Nicolae responded correctly, confirming his identity beyond all doubt, the voice on the other end of the line in Virginia answered, "I see that it is six fifteen p.m. We'll get that right out to you."

Nicolae looked at his watch. The protocol was to meet at the Zodiac Fountain in Bucharest exactly twenty-four hours later. He went home and told his wife he had to go on a business day trip the next day. He left by car early the next morning.

In the embassy in Sophia, Sydney was getting ready to go home for the day when the operations officer pulled her aside.

"Lightfoot activated their protocol," he said in a low voice. "We just got it."

Perfect, Sydney thought. *Ukraine is facing the greatest existential crisis of its brief independence, and now this.*

Then a pang of guilt traveled through Sydney's body.

He's my agent. My responsibility. I must ensure his safety.

"Thank you," Sydney said, mentally clearing her schedule for the next day. She walked back to her office and accessed the classified cable.

Actions in case of an urgent need to communicate or to be extracted had been part of Sydney's drills and discussions with Nicolae since the day she'd recruited him. She kept the plan updated based on their situation and assignments so that it always remained as practical and effective as possible. In all those years, though, this was the first time he'd activated the protocol.

Bucharest lay somewhat in between Moldova and Sydney's current posting in Sofia and offered the additional benefits of being inside a friendly NATO partner country that was a member of the EU. Sydney took the agency jet assigned to her the next day to coordinate the use of the safe house and agency driver.

As the agency's ranking counter-proliferation officer in Europe, Sydney's portfolio was "at large" throughout the region, and the director was trying to leverage it.

"I'm assigning an aircraft to you for the duration of this crisis," he told Sydney as she left DC in January. "I want you out there helping to drive our response in Ukraine, Miss Knox. Work with the station chiefs and everyone else. Go where you need to go. Be where you need to be."

Sydney was anxious during the flight to Bucharest, anticipating the bad news. Her mind raced as the old C-20—the military variant of the Gulfstream IV regional business jet—flew from Sofia to Bucharest. Had Nicolae been compromised? Had he discovered a Russian initiative? Was there something she'd missed?

Finally, sitting across from him in the safe house, she was blindsided by what he asked her.

"What is Val doing in Ukraine?"

Sydney blinked.

Her head tilted.

"Say again?" was all she could manage.

"What is Val doing in Ukraine?" he repeated, an insistent tone creeping into his voice.

"Val isn't in Ukraine." Sydney shook her head.

Nicolae glared at her.

"He is retired and living in Prague. He even has a dog."

"Oh yes," Nicolae said in a mocking voice. "We have all heard how he has retired. Even so…"

Nicolae held his phone up for Sydney to see.

Sydney leaned forward, eyes fixed on the image.

"And what am I looking at?" she asked, hoping it was not what she thought.

"Security camera image taken two nights ago."

"Where?" Sydney asked.

"Odesa."

Sydney took a deep breath and let go of a long, sad exhale. It was Val, without question.

It was a blurry photo, obviously taken in haste. Val was walking down the steps from a small jet aircraft. In the second photo, he was at the bottom of those steps, looking toward someone off out of frame.

The old feeling surged within her. *Dumb, arrogant, selfish son of a bitch.*

"Two nights ago?"

"Yes."

"In Odesa?"

"Yes."

Sydney rubbed her eyes.

"What is that speech you always give me? We must work together?" Nicolae said, lowering his phone. "I am tasking every agent and relationship I have in Ukraine to deal with the Russian situation there. It is not helpful when your government acts on its own. Tell me what he is doing. What is his mission?"

"I told you. He is retired. I have no fucking idea what he's doing, and neither does CIA."

Nicolae sat motionless regarding Sydney.

"I'm telling you the truth," she said.

Nicolae sighed.

"I believe you."

Sydney closed her eyes and shook her head.

"Where is he now?" she asked, snapping into action mode. "I'll have him arrested and on a plane to the US within the hour."

"We don't know."

"What do you mean? You have this footage. You didn't have him followed?"

"I got this from my source yesterday. They have standing orders to let me know when anything unusual happens. But they do not know Val, do not know the significance, and were not equipped to do anything, even if they did. It is solely because of their judgment and courage that we have anything at all."

"Damn it," Sydney muttered.

"You're welcome," Nicolae said angrily.

"Hey," Sydney said quickly, palms raised. "I'm sorry. I appreciate what you have done here. Sincerely. I'm just frustrated… Not with you."

Nicolae nodded with understanding.

"Can your sources help us find him?"

"We will try. But I fear it will not be easy."

"I'm sure it won't be."

Sydney sat motionless as Nicolae fiddled with his phone.

"Finally," he said in a sad voice. "There is this."

Nicolae held his phone up for Sydney again.

She leaned forward to look at the new image. Taken just as the jet's door had opened, Burian's head was clearly recognizable, emerging from the dark aircraft cabin.

Sydney's face was frozen in thought as Nicolae withdrew the phone and put it back in his pocket.

"Burian," she said finally as she leaned back in her chair.

"When is the last time you saw him?"

"Last year when we were in New York City."

"Same for me."

The two intelligence officers sat silently, troubled by questions and unknowns.

CHAPTER 91

"Well, Val Rafter is fucked," Tyler Ray, Ukraine chief of station, said flatly.

Sydney nodded in agreement as she sat in the embassy SCIF in Kyiv with Ray. Printouts of Nicolae's photos of Val and Burian lay on the table between them, as well as a large map of Odesa.

Sydney had arrived in Kyiv that morning. After meeting with Nicolae yesterday, she'd flown back to Sophia, slept for a few hours, and packed a large bag of gear and clothes. She had the feeling she was going to be bouncing around the region for a few weeks.

She briefed Ray on Val's situation immediately upon her arrival, sharing with him the photos of both Val and Burian. It didn't take long for him to confirm that Val was not in-country at the invitation of the Foreign Intelligence Service of Ukraine. The Ukrainians were clear that they were not aware Val had crossed their borders. It was also clear that they didn't much give a shit at the moment.

"So, what are you going to do?" Sydney asked.

"Nothing." Ray rubbed his eyes.

Sydney didn't respond. She leaned back in her chair.

She knew Tyler Ray by reputation only. He was ten years older than her and had just been made chief of station a year ago. He was known as a solid intelligence professional and had done his time in both Iraq and Afghanistan. Sydney could see by his tight jaw and crossed arms that Ray was irritated. She didn't blame him. She would not like it either if some cross-border agency muckety-muck flew in on her private jet, walked into her station, and presented her with a bullshit distraction.

Ray leaned back in his chair and looked at Sydney.

She looked down at the photo of Val. The swirling tangle of anger and concern over Val burned in her gut. She worried Ray could sense it.

"I'll keep Mr. Rafter's situation in mind," Ray finally said, leaning forward and folding his hands together.

Sydney raised her eyes to meet his gaze across the table.

"But, I have to say, his timing could not be any shittier. Ukraine dodged the bullet here in Kyiv last week, but things are getting worse by the hour. As you and I sit here, Russian sympathizers are protesting in front of the Crimean parliament. The country is crawling with Russians and Russian sympathizers, and our ability to counter the bastards is muted by the fact that probably half the Ukrainian government has been bought by the Russians. Your guy Burian, here?" Ray gestured dismissively at the photo of Burian on the table between them. "Wouldn't surprise me if he is working for the Russians.

"Langley is pounding on me, demanding to know what Putin is up to, even though it's obvious," Ray continued, resignation in his voice. "He is about to run the same play he ran in Georgia six years ago. But, even though it's obvious, I can't find any concrete proof. And, even if I did find proof, I don't think Langley would want it because they're not prepared to do anything. Neither is the administration. Just like Georgia, Ukraine isn't part of NATO yet. So, at the end of the day, all my team and I can do is try to keep our agents safe while we all wait for Putin to make his next move. And, judging by all the little green men running around, I'll put my money on him seizing Crimea."

Ray leaned back in his chair and shook his head.

"Putin took the Soviet playbook from the 1960s and updated it while we've been fucking off in Iraq and Afghanistan," he said with a rueful chuckle.

Sydney nodded slowly in agreement.

The two intelligence officers sat in silence for a moment, eyes resting on the large map of Odesa, feeling the press of world events just outside the windowless SCIF.

Sydney stood up.

"Thanks for your time, Tyler." She placed the photos back into their folder and then into her briefcase. "I'm sorry for the interruption. I know you're busier than hell, so I'll get out of your hair and back to Sophia."

Tyler stood and walked around to meet Sydney at the door. He offered her his hand as she came around.

"It's no problem, Sydney. We'll do what we can to find Rafter, I promise. I'll let you know immediately if we get a lead, no matter how thin."

"Thank you," she said as they shook hands.

A CIA driver took Sydney back to the airport. She sat in the back seat in silence, fighting the urge to scream. She closed her eyes and took deep breaths. No one else in the world could make her feel like this, could evoke the caustic cocktail of emotions. Only Val.

It would be a blessing if he were already dead. It really would. And yet, even as she acknowledged that, her pulse quickened. Worried for him. Running scenarios of how she might help him.

"Ma'am," the driver said.

"Yes?"

"We are here, ma'am. That's your aircraft."

"Oh. Right. Sorry."

"No problem, ma'am," the driver said. He'd carried enough distracted intelligence officers to recognize the troubled, thousand-yard stare.

Sydney made no move to open her door and get out. She sat and looked out at the jet that had brought her here. The forward aircraft door was lowered, a crewman standing by at the bottom of the steps, waiting.

The driver glanced at her in the rearview mirror and then fixed his eyes to the front.

Sydney thought about telling the pilot to take her back to the States instead of Sophia. Or somewhere entirely new. The Caribbean, maybe. She thought about just asking him to pick.

Just somewhere away from this dilemma.

"Thanks for the ride," she said to the driver as she got out of the car.

She walked to the idling aircraft and jogged up the steps into the cabin.

"Afternoon, ma'am," the pilot said, standing in the companionway to greet her. "Ready to go?"

"Yes. Let's get the hell out of here."

CHAPTER 92

27 February 2014

Sophia, Bulgaria

Sydney and the rest of the world woke up to more bad news the next day. Early morning, before the sun rose, two dozen masked and heavily armed men stormed the Crimean parliament building in Simferopol. They raised the Russian flag above the building and demanded succession from Ukraine. The men brandished modern Russian weapons, and though they wore unmarked uniforms, there were no doubts who they worked for. Putin's boldness had surprised the world again.

Cables and secure phone calls ricocheted around the agency in the early hours of the twenty-seventh, followed by secure video meetings. By the afternoon, Sydney was sick of talking about it. Like the rest of the agency, she wanted to take action. And, like the rest of the agency, she had no idea what to do.

Sydney was fuming as she read cables from Kyiv when one of her secure cell phones buzzed. Lying on her desk with several others, arm's length away from her computer keyboard, the small phone alternated between buzzing for a few seconds and sitting silent. Sydney leaned back in her chair and regarded it with dread.

Now What?

The only person who had this number was Nicolae. She'd given him several secure burner phones when she'd met with him in Bucharest a few days before.

"These are secure for one call only. Use them once, then destroy them."

Nicolae had nodded as he'd taken the five phones from Sydney.

"They each have one phone number in their memory," Sydney had said. "Mom."

Nicolae rolled his eyes. "Nice touch."

"They will encrypt our conversation," Sydney said, ignoring his comment. "Let me know the second you learn anything about Val."

"I will."

Now, as the phone buzzed on her desktop, Sydney wasn't sure what she wanted to hear. That Nicolae had found Val? That he'd found Val's dead body? That it was a false alarm?

She reached over and grabbed the phone.

"Yes?"

"I have news." Nicolae got right to the point. Sydney noted that he hadn't integrated their alert word, "static," into his greeting. If he had, she would have known that Nicolae was compromised and not alone.

"What is it?"

"I have a source working the port in Illichivsk. The *Monarch* arrived this afternoon and docked."

Sydney recognized the name of Abakumov's yacht. She leaned forward and rubbed her eyes. "And?"

"I sent a two-man team to Illichivsk. I told them to get eyes on the *Monarch* and to maintain constant surveillance. A moment ago, they reported that they spotted Alexei on board."

Sydney froze.

"Are you there?" Nicolae asked after a moment of silence.

"Yes."

More silence.

Sydney had chosen to believe that Alexei died in Syria. Val had told her everything. About chasing Alexei for months, never getting close enough, about Liam, Mazar, the Frogfoots bearing down on him, the last thing he saw. Everything. Val made it clear that they could not be certain. But they thought they got him. Liam had his eyes out for signs of the Russian resurfacing in cables or other information sources. But now, nearly twelve months later, there was still no indication of life anywhere.

Sure, she had moments of doubt when she thought, *That would just be too clean. Too easy. Karma has more in store for me.* But she was always able to push those thoughts aside, get busy in life, and forget about it for a few weeks.

There was no brushing this off.

"Are you there?"

"Yes, goddamn it," Sydney said, standing from her desk. "I'm here." She paced around in her office as she talked. "You're certain it's Alexei?"

"Yes."

"On the yacht?"

"Yes."

"And you're sure it's the *Monarch*?"

"Quite sure."

"What the hell is he doing in Illichivsk?" Sydney mumbled, thinking out loud.

"I don't know. He has not left the yacht. And they only catch glimpses of him from time to time."

"And nothing on Val? His location or anything?"

"No. Nothing."

"Okay. Well, look, we know the Russians are crawling all over Ukraine," Sydney said, speaking fast. "The fact that Alexei is there is consistent with that. That it's him is just a particular, not a contradiction or insight into anything we didn't already know or surmise."

"Uh-huh."

"Good work, Nicolae," Sydney continued. "Really good work. Keep eyes on the *Monarch* and let me know the moment anything changes."

"I will."

"And destroy that phone after we hang up."

"I know. I will."

Sydney hung up. She stood motionless for a moment. It was too much: Russia was infiltrating Crimea, Val was being held somewhere in Ukraine, and Alexei had just shown up on Abakumov's yacht. She had to do something.

Only one thing came to mind. It didn't matter that her motivations were mixed and conflicted. It was action.

"I'm going to head to Chișinău, ma'am," she told her boss. "I can do more good there than here at the moment. Moldova is one of the primary sources of arms for Putin's manufactured liberation movement in Crimea, and I can work my network much more effectively out of the embassy there. I'll be closer to the situation."

And to Val, wherever the hell he is.

"Sounds good," Maddi said. "But keep me in the loop on everything."

"Will do, ma'am."

Sydney had been to Chişinău many times while running Nicolae. Her role gave her the cover for action and, really, the necessity to do so. Moldova was the epicenter of her regional counter-proliferation role.

She and Nicolae had strict protocols for her visits. They avoided one-on-one meetings, never spent time together socially, and only met alone when it was absolutely necessary, and only after long SDRs, far outside of the city.

Sydney did have access to a CIA safe house in Chişinău but reserved that only for time-urgent meetings. Its code name was Hickory, but the entire time they worked together, they had yet to use it.

Nicolae and Sydney had devised a network of dead drops across Chişinău that enabled the efficient and secure exchange of documents when she was in town, and they mostly limited themselves to that system for detailed communication. Their in-office interactions were friendly but business focused, bordering on bland. An observer, and there were many, would never guess they were witnessing one of the most successful active agent-handler relationships in the CIA at work.

So, it was not new or risky for Sydney to fly to Chişinău. And there was truth to what she told Jackson. She was very effective operating out of the embassy there. The embassy in Chişinău also afforded her more immediate access to Nicolae, his network, and, if needed, his special actions team.

By the time Sydney's flight landed in Chişinău, the armed takeover of the parliament had produced a new Crimean prime minister. Sergei Aksyonov—a politician of Moldovan descent, rumored organized crime lieutenant, and long-time Russian separatist—had been elected. Somehow, despite barricades in front of the building and the lack of any media presence, a majority of the one hundred parliament members had managed to physically cast votes in favor of Aksyonov, whose party had barely won 4 percent of the vote in the last parliamentary election.

Perhaps more troubling, there were reports that Russian armed forces had shut down the Simferopol and Belbek airports and were blocking land routes into Crimea from Kherson.

Events were accelerating away from the West.

As her aircraft's wheels touched down on the runway, Sydney wondered if Val was already out of reach.

CHAPTER 93

It was almost eight p.m. when a phone buzzed in Sydney's briefcase on the drive from the airport to the embassy. She looked. It was the line to Nicolae.

"Can you pull over, please?" she asked the driver. He was a vetted contractor. Still, she didn't want to take any chances.

The driver nodded and put on his blinker. They were in the city, and he had to let a few cars pass on his right before being able to swerve to the sidewalk.

Sydney pressed the call button on the phone and said, "Stand by," to Nicolae.

The car came to a stop. Sydney hopped out and walked a few meters away.

"What is it?" she asked after looking around to clear her immediate surroundings.

"It's Val."

The tone in his voice told her it was not good.

"What happened? Did you find him?"

"My guy just saw him being taken on board the *Monarch*."

"What?"

"He saw Val being taken on board the *Monarch*," Nicolae repeated with irritation in his voice.

"Are you sure it was Val?"

"Yes."

"You have photos?"

"Not yet. I will soon."

Sydney stood motionless, phone pressed to her ear, palm to her forehead, mind racing.

"If the *Monarch* leaves the port, Val will be gone," Nicolae said. "We'll never find him."

"I know."

"Or his body."

"I know!" she shouted, startling a passerby.

Sydney grimaced to herself, embarrassed by her outburst. She shook her head, turned, and walked back to the car.

"What do you want me to do?" Nicolae asked in an apologetic voice.

"Where are you?" she asked, now standing by the car's rear passenger door.

"Outside, walking near my office."

"Okay. Hickory. One hour."

"Roger that."

"And have the photos!"

"Understood."

Sydney jerked open the car door.

"I'm going to walk from here," she said as she leaned in to grab her briefcase. "Please take my bags to the hotel. I'll be there later."

"Ma'am?"

"I said take my bags to the hotel, please."

"But, ma'am, the hotel is on the other side of town."

Sydney shut the car door and started her surveillance detection route.

*

Sydney held Nicolae's phone and stared at the photo. A yacht sat in the dark water tied to its berth. The photo focused midship, where a gangway was laid from the dock. A group of men crossed the gangway toward the yacht. The man in the middle was hooded.

The next photo was zoomed into one of the ship's aft decks, where the same group of men stood. The man in the middle of the group was no longer hooded.

It was Val.

Sydney studied the image.

Val looked haggard. Tired. But unharmed, from what she could see.

She nodded wearily and handed the phone back to Nicolae.

"If the *Monarch* leaves that port—" Nicolae began.

"He's gone! I know."

Nicolae looked at Sydney as he put his phone back in his jacket pocket.

Sydney leaned back in her chair.

It's worse than Nicolae knows, she thought. *Alexei came here for Val. He was involved in getting Val here. Burian must be working for him.*

"Do you think that—"

"Nicolae, please. Let me think for a second."

Alexei used Burian to lure Val to Ukraine somehow. Then Alexei went there to get Val. Now Alexei is going to kill him.

Val said he and Alexei locked eyes in Syria, that there was a moment of recognition before the bombs hit. If Alexei survived, I'm not sure he would ever let that go.

Sydney closed her eyes.

This was not an abduction for leverage.

Sydney stood up. She had to move to keep her mind from running away. She started pacing the room.

Nicolae regarded her for a moment.

"Sydney, is there something here, something that is going on, that you are not telling me?"

"What are you talking about?" Sydney snapped. "I'm worried about a missing American and a land war in Europe. Does there really need to be something else going on?"

She kept pacing.

"No… Sorry… I just…"

"Just help me think!"

"Okay. So, how do we stop the *Monarch* from leaving?" Nicolae asked, more as a problem statement than a real question.

"How long do you think we have?" Sydney asked.

Nicolae shrugged. "Val has been on board for almost two hours now. They could pull out of there in a few minutes. Or in a few hours? A few days? I do not know."

"Damn it," Sydney muttered.

"My source will let me know the moment the situation changes. If they start her engines or untie her, we will know immediately."

"Okay, good," Sydney said, still pacing. "Well, Kyiv is a shit show. They're trying to repel a quiet Russian invasion at the moment."

"And they have no dependable resources in Illichivsk. I can tell you that."

"And the *Monarch* is more than three hundred miles from Kyiv, anyway."

"What about your agency?" Nicolae asked. "Can you not tell them what has happened? They have special military teams, no?"

"Oh sure, we do. And I could run this up the flagpole. But it would take weeks, even if I could get priority. Our teams are good. But too few. They can't help on the time frame we're talking about."

"Special Operations Command?"

"Same problem," Sydney said. "There are more of them. But they're stretched beyond thin these days. And they're already tracking a dozen American hostages around the world. Even if there was a team in a location that would enable them to respond in less than seventy-two hours, they're not going to let Val cut in line just because you and I are his friends."

Or just because I love him.

I mean, hate him.

Both.

Whichever it is, right now, I just want to kill him.

After I rescue him.

Then I—

Nicolae's phone buzzed.

He pulled it from his pocket and read the text message.

He grimaced and shook his head.

"What is it?" Sydney asked.

"The *Monarch*. She is leaving port."

Sydney slumped into her chair. She looked at the floor. Events were getting away from her.

It can't end like this.

"I am sorry, Sydney," Nicolae said in a consoling voice.

"It's not over yet!" She stood up and started pacing again.

Nicolae put his phone back in his pocket as his eyes tracked Sydney walking back and forth.

"I think the best thing we can do now is tell the Russians that we know they have Val. Demand his safe return."

"You don't understand!" Sydney stopped pacing. "He is going to kill Val!"

"You do not know this for certain. Letting the Russians know we are aware of their actions will make them more cautious."

"No. There has to be another option."

"Sydney, the *Monarch's* departure makes things much more difficult," Nicolae said slowly, like a doctor delivering a terminal diagnosis. "Assaulting a ship while it is underway at sea is very complex. Rescuing a hostage in the process makes it more so. Very dangerous."

Sydney stopped pacing and faced the table.

"What about your team?" she asked.

"Team? I have no team in Illichivsk. Just an informant."

"I mean your special actions team," Sydney said, looking down at Nicolae.

"My team here in Chişinău?"

"Yes."

Nicolae laughed at the ridiculous suggestion.

Sydney held his gaze.

Nicolae's smile faded.

"I thought you had two helicopters under your command."

"Yes," Nicolae said, shaking his head. "Again, here in Chişinău, Moldova. Ukraine is another country, you know."

Sydney leaned down, hands on the table, her gaze leveled at Nicolae.

He kept shaking his head.

"I have just one platoon. Not enough for such an operation."

Sydney's face was a mask of intensity.

"Will take too long," Nicolae said, still shaking his head.

Sydney pulled a chair out from the table and sat down.

"Why?"

"Because we are same as you!" Nicolae said, voice raising as he stood from his chair and started pacing. "Our fighting force is controlled by a slow-moving bureaucracy. It will take days to launch a mission after we get the request."

"But you are the commander."

"Yes," Nicolae said with impatience in his voice. "But is not my personal resource."

She leaned forward. "You could do it."

"Sydney, you do not know what you are asking." Nicolae rubbed his forehead as he walked back and forth. "This is a very dangerous operation. Even with weeks of planning and triple the resources."

"You could do it."

"This is simple." Nicolae stopped pacing. He pointed at Sydney. "If your country wants our assistance, it must request it through the proper channels and process. My team's authority comes from the president of Ukraine."

"But we just agreed there was no time for that."

"Then we need to think of another way to help Val."

Nicolae started pacing again.

"This is the way!" Sydney brought her fist down on the table. "You are the way."

Nicolae stopped. He looked down at her fist. He was getting angry.

"No! This is ridiculous. You are not being reasonable."

"You could alert your team and launch within the next hour, and no one would stop you," Sydney said. "No one on your team would question it."

"Yes. No one on the team would," Nicolae said, raising his voice and leaning forward across the table.

"But when we return, If I survive, I will be relieved and arrested," he shouted, pointing at himself. "Probably shot."

Sydney leaned back in her chair. She felt a cold swell of panic in her gut.

"It's over, then," she said, almost in a whisper.

She was frozen. She didn't know what to do. Val was going to die.

Sydney leaned her head into her hands.

Nicolae looked at her for a long moment and then looked down at his feet.

Long seconds ticked by.

Nicolae rubbed his forehead and then lifted his eyes.

"If I do this… "

Sydney raised her head slowly.

Nicolae's face was stern, chin raised. His eyes narrowed.

"If I rescue Val, there is one condition."

Sydney sat back in her chair, eyes locked on Nicolae.

He held one finger in the air between them.

"It is not negotiable."

"What?"

"Permanent visas," he said.

Sydney smiled a sad smile.

"For my family."

"So, it comes to this," she said.

"And we go to America. Tonight." He lowered his finger, leaned over, and jabbed it into the tabletop. "When I get back with Val."

Sydney chuckled and rubbed her eyes. She pushed back from the table and stood up. Turning, she took a few steps away from the table.

Nicolae crossed his arms and stared at her back.

Sydney ran the play in her mind a few times.

A long shot.

But not impossible.

"Okay." She turned back to him. "You do it, and I'll get the visas."

Nicolae dropped his arms to his side.

"Are you serious?"

She stood still.

Am I serious?

"Yes," she said.

"And we must leave tonight. Not tomorrow. Not next week. Tonight."

"I will do my best."

"Best is not good enough. It must happen tonight."

"After all that whining about how complex and dangerous this is going to be, you're going to stand here and promise me you'll get Val back safe?" Sydney said in a voice full of resignation.

Nicolae thought about his part. A hastily executed hostage-rescue operation on a yacht underway on the Black Sea.

He gave himself a fifty-fifty chance of success. Probably less.

"I will do my best."

Sydney nodded. "We both will."

They stood frozen for a moment, looking at each other. Each expecting the other to think better of the idea.

Instead, Sydney extended her hand to Nicolae.

He shook it.

"I need to get started on my part," Sydney said. "I expect you need to as well. How soon until you can launch?"

"I hope to be airborne in an hour."

"Good." Sydney pulled her jacket on as she walked to the door. "Then I'll be at your airfield in one hour to see you off."

"What did we use to say?" Nicolae asked. "Before we all went on Val's crazy suicide ski races in Garmisch?"

"Launch the fleet."

CHAPTER 94

Nicolae and Sydney stood in the shadows next to an aircraft hangar on a small military airfield ten kilometers to the east of the capital. The hangar's large door was open, and light spilled out into the night as a motor tug pulled a gray Mi-14 helicopter out onto the tarmac. Two of Nicolae's commandos, one on each side, walked beneath opposite rotor blade tips to ensure clearance. The helicopter's five rotors, each almost thirty-five feet long, sagged and bounced as the tug pulled the aircraft.

Dressed in all black, Nicolae held his armored helmet under his right arm. A modified AR-15 hung on a single-point sling on his right side and a large pistol was strapped to his right thigh. Ammunition and full cargo pockets bulged from his uniform.

Looking back into the hangar where his men were conducting final gear checks, Nicolae took deep slow breaths to try to calm himself.

It wasn't working.

As he watched the young men of his platoon prepare, memories of Transnistria flooded his mind. It had been twenty-two years since he fought the Russians there. Though he had taken many risks and faced danger since as a Moldovan intelligence officer and American agent, it was nothing like direct combat. Nothing like seeing men killed. Nothing like the day he almost died.

Nicolae shook his head, purging the memories. Combat was something he never wanted to experience again. Ever.

Tonight was different, though.

Earlier, when he saw how desperate Sydney was, when he realized she saw no other option, he knew that he would never have this much leverage again. If he wanted to escape a life of endangered servitude to the CIA, to secure the life his wife wanted, to keep his family close… he had to seize the opportunity.

Nicolae took a deep breath, filling his lungs with the cool night air.

No matter how dangerous. This was his chance.

Or was it?

Is Val even still alive?

Will Sydney do her part?

He glanced at her.

Sydney's face, one side lit by the light of the hangar, one side dark in shadow, was tense as she watched the tug pull the large helicopter further into the dark.

She better.

A squad of Nicolae's commandoes walked out of the hanger toward the towed helicopter. In full kit and carrying their weapons, each member of the squad made eye contact with Nicolae and nodded confidently. Pride welled within Nicolae as he nodded back. They were good unit. He was honored to lead them and enjoyed their full confidence.

Nicolae looked at the ground after they passed and tried to push down the surge of guilt.

I am using them.

He shook his head.

It is a good mission. We are fighting Russians. So what if my family benefits also?

"I need your wife's cell phone number and address," Sydney said in a low voice.

Nicolae nodded, thankful for the interruption.

The time for doubt is over.

He pulled a notepad from one of his cargo pockets. Thoughts of Sasha flooded him as he wrote down the information. She had no idea what was happening, how her family's fate hung now on the outcome of the next few hours. He had not had a free second to call her. There had been too much to do to get the operation moving and he could not spare the focus… And he had not wanted his resolve to waver.

Now his eyes rested on the address he had written.

Is this what she would want me to do?

I don't know.

"Hey," Sydney said, putting her hand on his shoulder. "You OK?"

Nicolae blinked and looked up at her.

He nodded.

The tug disconnected from the first helicopter and swung by Nicolae and Sydney on its way to hook up the other one.

Nicolae ripped the page out of his notepad and handed it to Sydney, watching as she folded it and put it into her pocket.

"But I must ask something of you," he said.

"What is it?"

A shrill whine filled the night as the first helicopter fired up its auxiliary power unit. Nicolae's pulse quickened. It would not be long now.

He leaned closer to Sydney so she could hear him clearly over the noise of the helicopter.

"She does not know what is going on tonight. I did not have time to talk to her."

"Just as well. I'll handle it."

Nicolae shook his head.

"That is not what I mean. If..."

His voice broke. He grabbed Sydney's arm and pulled her closer.

"If I do not come back. You must tell her what I tried to do and why. For her and our daughters."

"Don't talk like—"

"Promise me!"

Sydney put her hand on the back of Nicolae's neck and pulled his head next to hers. Speaking into his ear, she said, "I will make sure they know if it comes to that. I promise. But don't worry about them now. Focus. It is time for you to be a warrior, Nicolae."

She squeezed his neck gently and then let him go.

Nicolae nodded.

The tug pulling the second Mi-14 passed by them, the same two commandos walking beneath its rotor tips.

"What did you tell your team?" Sydney asked.

"The truth. Or part of it. A high-value American intelligence officer has been abducted and is being carried away on a yacht by the Russians for purposes we don't yet understand. We are the closest and best option, so have been asked to help."

"Sounds pretty good when you say it like that."

"Yes. The men are excited. They are eager to show what they can do."

Sydney glanced at her watch. "What is the timeline? How long before you are back?"

"Three and a half hours, give or take. Four at the most. We will be pushing the limits of our fuel endurance."

"Understood." Sydney looked at Nicolae, her expression a mix of concern and determination. "I'll be here when you get back."

The tug returned from the second helicopter. When it had passed them, Nicolae looked at Sydney. "So we are clear... If you don't have the visas when I get back, I will not give you Val."

Sydney smiled.

"If you don't have Val..." She started but then stopped. She didn't have it in her anymore. Sydney was done manipulating Nicolae. "Just... please... get him back."

He nodded.

"I should join my men now."

Sydney grabbed his hand.

"Good luck, Nicolae."

"Thank you."

Nicolae turned and walked into the dark toward the aircraft, his resolve increasing with every step.

Within minutes, the helicopters' large rotors were beating rhythmically, turbine engines howling. They lifted to a hover, each aircraft twenty feet in the air as the pilots conducted their last checks.

The two helicopters dipped their noses simultaneously. They accelerated forward and began to climb.

CHAPTER 95

Alexei looked at the nearly empty bottle of bourbon. He shook his head slowly and leaned back in his chair. Looking at Zakir, Alexei gestured at his lips with two fingers. The mercenary nodded and took a pack of cigarettes out of one of his cargo pockets as he walked over to Alexei. He gave Alexei a cigarette, lit it and then walked back to the bar, sneering at Val on the way.

Alexei took a deep drag and then let out a deep, smoky sigh. The gray smoke spread quickly through the room, the harsh smell clashing with the briny scent of the black sea.

Val watched as Alexei carefully poured the last of the bourbon into their glasses, making sure that each got an equal amount. A hollow thud filled the room as he set the empty bottle down and looked at Val with sad eyes.

"Oh, give me a break," Val said.

"Is sad, my friend." Alexei filled his lungs with the cigarette again.

"Sad?" Val raised an eyebrow. "Seems like you've won. The guy who supposedly doesn't take any of this personally won his personal vendetta."

Alexei shook his head. "You are idiot." He exhaled more cigarette smoke.

"Do tell."

"None of this is for me," Alexei said, gesturing around at the world in frustration. As he did, his cigarette traced a burning line through the air. "When

I heard you retired, I was happy for you. Even after Syria. You are my brother. I do not hold you responsible for the world. And I forgive you for being idiot in Syria."

Val rolled his eyes.

"So, what happened? Why the change of heart and the orchestration to get me to Ukraine?"

"I was given mission." Alexei took another slow drag.

"A mission to abduct a disgraced and retired mid-level American intelligence officer?" Val asked incredulously. "You're striking a real blow for the motherland, buddy."

Smoke spilled out of his mouth as Alexei chuckled and shook his head.

"We use you. To show Ukraine and world the truth."

"The truth?"

"The truth that only we, Russia, can protect Ukraine. That only we look out for their best interests. Without Russia, there is no Ukraine, not really."

Val raised his eyebrows as he processed Alexei's words.

Several heartbeats passed as the men stared at each other.

Holding his gaze on Val, Alexei raised his cigarette and took a pull, the tip glowing orange.

"You still underestimate yourself, Val." Smoke escaped the sides of Alexei's mouth in thin, vanishing streams. "You are the most infamous American intelligence officer in the world. Everyone knows you after Bulgaria. Everyone knows who you work for."

"Ah…" Val nodded as he recognized the play. "Put me somewhere in Ukraine. Capture me. Publicize it widely. Say I was running America's destabilization operations and fomenting discontent against Russian Ukrainians. Maybe throw in some accusations of ethnic cleansing, hints at murder and so forth."

"Yes," Alexei said.

Alexei leaned back in his chair, his face sad.

"We are going to put you north of the Dnieper River," Alexei continued in a tired voice. "Somewhere in the Kherson area. We will stage an attack on ethnic Russians, killing many. They will find you at the scene of the atrocity. You will be blamed. There will be outrage. Our tanks will roll through Crimea, seize the bridges across the Dnieper in Kherson, and drive on to Kyiv."

"Well, I guess the past few weeks have shown you guys it's definitely gonna take tanks, eh?"

Alexei glared at Val.

"I mean, the students and shopkeepers in Kyiv basically threw your asses out," Val added with a mocking smile.

"We were too soft. We won't make that mistake again."

Alexei took a long hard drag on the cigarette, burning it down almost to his fingers.

"And what if your tanks don't get it done? What then?"

Alexei jammed the butt of his cigarette into the red tablecloth.

"Ukraine and Europe should hope our tanks succeed." Smoke curled around Alexei's face. "For their sake."

Val rolled his eyes and shook his head at Alexei.

"You sound ridiculous. But I see the strength of your plan as it pertains to me. No one is going to believe me when I claim I was brought there against my will and am innocent."

Alexei looked at Val for a long moment.

Finally, he said, "You will not be able to make such claims."

Val returned his gaze in silence.

"Your dead body will provide your only testimony," Alexie added. "And your testimony will be written by us."

"I see."

"A small boat will meet us shortly. You will go with them. They will take you ashore at Stanislav and then travel inland to where the atrocity will occur, closer to Kherson."

"Why tell me all this? Why not just kill me?"

"Because you are my friend, Val. I wanted to spend this last bit of time together, and I think you deserve to know."

Val chuckled.

"Well, I know you Russians like your send-offs."

"Is true."

The forward door sprung open, and Peskov walked quickly to Alexei's side. He held up a hand and spoke into Alexei's ear.

"Already?" Alexei asked in Russian. He looked at his watch.

"Yes, sir."

"Is too soon."

"Yes, sir. But the captain said he is certain he sees the small boat approaching from the south."

"From the south?" Alexei said, irritation in his voice now. "That is from the wrong direction. Fucking idiots got lost."

Alexei shook his head and rubbed his eyes before saying to Peskov, "Prepare to receive them."

Peskov nodded. He walked past the dining table and left through the sliding glass door, taking two of the mercenaries with him. They proceeded aft and disappeared down the stairs as they headed to the lowest deck to help receive the motorboat.

"They are here early," Alexei said to Val. "I am sorry."

"You going to do it? Or are you just going to tell them to do it?"

Alexei didn't respond. He pushed a shot glass closer to Val and said, "Last toast."

"What's left?" Val asked without reaching for the whiskey.

"Friendship."

Gunshots rang out from the lower aft deck.

Alexei stood up, drawing his pistol. Zakir shouldered his rifle as he moved aft to the sliding glass door. Val crouched in his chair as the gunfire escalated into what sounded like a full-on firefight.

Peskov came running up the aft stairway, pistol in hand, as Zakir opened the sliding glass door.

"What the hell is going on?" Alexei yelled as he met Peskov at the open door.

"The boats! They are attacking!"

Alexei yanked Peskov into the dining room. "Watch him," he said, pointing at Val. "If he moves, kill him."

Peskov raised his pistol to cover Val and strode quickly over to the bistro table.

Alexei looked at Zakir and the bartender. "Come with me!"

The bartender bent over and grabbed a pump shotgun from behind the bar. He racked it, chambering a round, as he ran to join Alexei and Zakir.

The three men stepped through the sliding glass door onto the aft deck as a helicopter thundered across the ship, just a few feet above their heads. The sound was deafening.

They all dove for cover as large-caliber machine-gun fire rained down on the ship, splintering the wooden deck and tearing apart the leather furniture.

The bartender's head jerked back, fragmenting like a pumpkin hit by a hammer, and he toppled over the side of the ship.

Zakir screamed as 7.62 mm rounds tore into his back. His intestines splattered onto the deck, spraying Alexei with blood and gore.

The helicopter thundered into the darkness, the sound of its rotors receding as suddenly as it had appeared.

Alexei reached across Zakir's twitching body to grab his AK-74 from the bloody mess. As Alexei's hand closed on the rifle's pistol grip, he heard the signature hiss of activated CS grenades. A cloud of caustic white vapor engulfed him.

A loud hissing noise also filled the dining room, and white vapor spewed from a grenade that had skidded through the open doors, between the dining table legs and across the deck. Val immediately recognized the smell and pain of CS gas.

Alexei, blinded and choking in a crouch, struggled to orient himself. He dropped the weapon and fell to his hands and knees. He had to get to clear air. He fumbled on the blood-slicked deck in the direction he thought would take him to the aft stairs.

Peskov stood, mouth agape, eyes fixed on where the bloody mess of Zakir's body had been, obscured now by the dense cloud of CS gas. He didn't see Val coming.

*

"Bring us around, goddamn it!" Nicolae yelled into the helicopter's intercom.

He stared down at the *Monarch* from one of the windows. The scene was not good.

The assault boats had been caught out on the open water, a hundred meters before reaching the *Monarch*. He estimated they had lost half their combat power, shot dead as they sped toward the ship.

It was almost as if the *Monarch* had been expecting a boat assault.

The plan had been simple. Not easy. But simple. The two Mi-14 helicopters would fly to within five miles of the *Monarch* before setting down into the water to release their Zodiac assault boats. That distance would reduce the chance of anyone on the *Monarch* hearing the aircraft, and the small inflatable motorboats could close on the ship in about fifteen minutes.

Each Mi-14 carried two boat teams of five commandos each. Nicolae remained on board the lead helicopter with one boat team, which would serve as the reserve force. The three other boat teams would assault in their Zodiacs. After the boats were deployed, they would run to the target at top speed. Each had a designated assault point on the *Monarch*: bow, stern, and midship.

The most vulnerable point of the mission would be when the boat teams approached and boarded the ship. Packed into the Zodiacs like puppies in a box, a single burst of fire could take out an entire team. To mitigate this, Nicolae planned to use the aircraft.

The helicopters would loiter in the distance until the boats were almost on the *Monarch* and then dash at 140 miles an hour to arrive a moment prior to the boarding teams.

First, the noise of the aircraft would draw the defenders' eyes to the sky, distracting them from the imminent boat attack. Then the aircraft would strafe the ship at low altitude, dropping CS grenades as they passed over.

2-Chlorobenzalmalononitrile is the key component of CS gas. Exposure to it feels like breathing molten nails while red-hot steel wool scrapes across your eyes. Also known as tear gas, it's a debilitating crowd-control agent.

The assault teams would be masked. Nicolae was counting on the airborne machine-gun fire and cloud of CS gas to give them a window to get on board the *Monarch*.

Nicolae would deploy with the reserve at his command if needed. Otherwise, they would remain airborne and wait until the assault commander gave the all clear.

It was a simple mission structure similar to the innumerable training missions Nicolae and the team had conducted over the past few years.

And it had gone to shit almost immediately.

Minutes ago, Nicolae had peered through the cockpit window at the distant *Monarch* as the aircraft loitered miles to the south. The second hand on his watch ticked down. Just as Nicolae had been about to give the command for the helicopters to sprint north, he'd seen bright spotlights lance out from the *Monarch,* illuminating the assault boats. Then muzzle flashes up and down the ship.

"Under fire!" the assault commander transmitted over the radio. "Taking casualties! Expedite air assault!"

"Go! Go! Go!" Nicolae yelled at the pilots over the intercom.

The MI14's engines screamed as the pilot pulled max power and dove toward the water, trading what little altitude he could for airspeed.

Nicolae cursed as the aircraft tore through the air toward the target. Gunfire erupted all over and around the *Monarch.* The assault boats were caught in the open with no air cover.

The second helicopter followed at less than one rotor disc's separation. The flight of two was barely twenty feet above the ocean. Seawater sprayed the canopy windshield.

"Weapons free," Nicolae said to the flight of two over the radio. "Open fire on the target as soon as able and prepare to drop grenades."

Moving at 140 miles an hour, the helicopters closed the distance to the *Monarch* in less than two minutes.

Noise, smoke, and vibrations ran through Nicolae's helicopter as the door gunners opened fire. They were close enough now for Nicolae to see the aft section of the *Monarch* was a melee. A few commandos had made it to the lower aft deck and were firing at defenders. Their assault boat was half submerged, riddled with bullets.

Nicolae looked quickly at the *Monarch's* prow. The forward assault team had fared worse. Three dead commandos were still in their attack boat. The midship team fared just as badly. A pile of bodies lay in the bobbing, half-sunk Zodiac.

Nicolae was not sure how many commandos had survived and boarded the *Monarch.*

It didn't seem like enough.

The pilot had lifted the aircraft's nose slightly, gaining altitude just in time to avoid colliding with the *Monarch.* Nicolae caught sight of three men emerging onto the aft deck just as his helicopter passed over, both door guns firing, aircrew shoving a dozen CS grenades off the ramp.

*

Peskov was distracted by the helicopter and CS gas.

Val glanced at the switchblade. It was on the other side of the bistro table. Too far.

He punched Peskov hard in the throat. The young intelligence officer collapsed onto his back.

Val dropped all of his weight onto a knee on Peskov's neck to finish the job and felt a sickening crunch. He picked Peskov's pistol up from the deck as gurgling noises escaped the Russian's throat.

Peskov clutched his neck as he suffocated. What little air made it through his crushed larynx was laced with CS gas.

Val racked the pistol to make sure a round was chambered and raised the weapon.

Val tried to aim in the direction where he'd last seen Alexei, but his vision was obscured. Tears ran from his eyes, and he could not hold them open. The searing CS gas also burned his throat. He used his left hand to cover his nose and mouth with his shirt, but it was too late. His lungs were on fire. He had to get to clear air. The pistol fell from his hands. He felt his way across the floor in a direction he hoped would take him to a window he could break.

*

Nicolae craned his neck to maintain visual contact with the *Monarch* through a window as the pilot executed a steep turn. He was relieved by what he saw. His commandos, equipped with gas masks, were now advancing against the choking, blinded defenders. They weren't winning. But they were no longer being murdered.

The *Monarch*, though, had maintained her speed and was already starting to outrun the cloud of CS gas.

Intelligence on their target had been thin. Nicolae didn't know how many men they were up against. But his gut was that his commandos were outnumbered. And all this was for naught if they didn't get Val out alive. And, despite the mission briefing and extensive photos of Val he'd walked his men through, he didn't have confidence in their ability to recognize Val at night on a ship at sea in a firefight, and not shoot him.

"Put the ramp over the ship's forward deck," he told the pilot. "We're going in."

It was risky, but he had no alternative.

"Sir, there is still a lot of gunfire on that ship."

"That's why we are going in!" Nicolae yelled into the intercom. "Now, do what I say!"

The pilot grimaced and pointed the helicopter's nose at the ship's prow.

*

Val wretched and spat as he crawled. The air in the saloon was improving slowly, but he could not tell. He felt as if his eyes had melted out of their sockets and were dragging across the wooden deck. He could not see anything. His breaths came in painful gulps.

At the same time, Alexei pulled himself forward on his belly with his forearms, desperately seeking clear air. His eyes burned, and he dragged a trail of snot and mucus from his mouth and nose. He felt the doorjamb of the sliding glass door and realized he was crawling into the dining room rather than toward the aft stairway.

Val reached one side of the room. He felt the wall as he stood up. A window!

Val pulled his elbow back and then jammed it through the window. Glass shattered and spilled onto the floor. Val felt the rush of cold night air. He forced himself to take a deep breath and then felt his way to his left. When he got to the next window, he struck it with his elbow. More clean air.

The sound of beating rotor blades got louder. Val wondered if they were friend or foe. What would they do if they found him?

And will they find me dead or alive?

He shuffled once more to his left and broke the next window.

More clean air swept through the dining room, pushing the CS gas out through the open sliding glass doors.

Val faced the cold, blowing wind and blinked his eyes rapidly. It felt like rubbing a cheese grater over his eyes. But it helped. He began to make out colors and shapes.

He squeezed his eyes shut to clear them of tears and turned inward toward the center of the dining room. He leaned his back against the sill of the broken window and used his shirt to rub his eyes.

He blinked a few times as he regained his ability to focus.

I need a weapon.

He swept the area with blurred vision, looking for the pistol he'd dropped.

His gaze fell on a dark shape charging toward him.

He recognized the shape at the last instant.

It was Alexei.

*

Nicolae grasped at the side of the helicopter for balance as it bucked and shuddered. The pilot had dumped power and raised the nose almost vertically to decelerate as they approached the *Monarch*'s prow. Just as Nicolae regained his balance, the floor dropped out from under him as the pilot leveled the aircraft at the last possible second. The Mi-14's tail rotor, stretching more than fifty feet behind the pilot, lifted just in time to avoid striking the ship.

Nicolae regained his feet as the aircraft swayed and tilted while it slid into position, its open ramp over the ship's prow. The *Monarch* was still making fifteen knots, which the pilot had to account for in his hover. It was tricky.

"Ropes! Ropes! Ropes!" the pilot said over the intercom.

The crewman stationed at the ramp picked up the coiled length of thick nylon and threw it out. The other end was fastened to the cabin ceiling.

Nicolae and his team of five shuffled aft toward the open ramp.

The crewman checked his safety harness quickly and then leaned out over the end of the ramp. Confirming the rope landed on the *Monarch*'s prow, rather than dangled over the water, he pulled himself back in and said, "Ropes out!" over the intercom.

"Exit! Exit! Exit!" the pilot commanded.

Nicolae went first. He gripped the thick rope with his gloved hands and swung his body out into the air, letting himself drop toward the ship.

Heat built up rapidly in his gloves as he slid down the rope, but he maintained his grip. Fortunately, it was a quick drop.

His feet hit the deck.

He stepped quickly to the side just in time to get out from under the next commando, who landed on the deck with a heavy thud.

The first commando released the rope and took a position, weapon pointed aft, next to Nicolae. The second followed quickly.

Machine-gun fire erupted from the bridge of the *Monarch*, sweeping the ship's prow, as the third commando descended.

Nicolae heard a rapid succession of wet impacts, and the commando next to him grunted as bullets hit him in the head and chest. He slumped forward, dead.

Nicolae and his team returned fire at the *Monarch's* bridge. The helicopter's door gunner opened up, trying desperately to suppress enemy guns.

The pilot struggled to hold the aircraft steady as rounds tore through the fuselage. The fourth commando was still on the rope, and the fifth still standing on the ramp.

The helicopter started to drift.

The fast rope dangling beneath the aircraft began to slide off the ship.

Nicolae turned and sprinted after the end of the fast rope as the other commando continued firing on the bridge.

The fourth commando reached the bottom of the rope just before it left the ship's prow.

Nicolae grabbed the commando by the body armor as he landed with one foot on the ship and one foot off. Nicolae lunged backward, tugging the commando back onto the ship.

Nicolae fell to his back, grunting as the commando landed on top of him.

The commando sprung to his feet, firing his weapon and charging toward the bridge.

Nicolae lay on his back, looking at the helicopter twenty feet above him. Sparks and fire flared from the tail rotor as the persistent gunfire from the *Monarch's* bridge found its target. The fifth commando, unable to exit and still standing on the aircraft's ramp, clung to the helicopter with one hand and fired his weapon with the other.

The aircraft swung abruptly left and right.

That's not good, Nicolae thought.

Nicolae watched as the struggling aircraft's tail rotor disintegrated. Flaming parts sailed off the helicopter and the aircraft began to spin.

The pilot, out of options, pulled in power to get clear of the ship, worsening the uncontrolled spin. The fifth commando lost his grip. He flailed through the air and vanished into the black water.

The aircraft thrashed through the air, spinning on its vertical axis, smoking tail boom narrowly missing the yacht's bridge superstructure.

Two explosions rocked the ship and blew out the windows on the bridge. Nicolae's commandos had finally gotten grenades on target.

Glass rained down on Nicolae. He got to his feet as the stricken helicopter veered wildly away to the ship's ten o'clock.

The aircraft corkscrewed in a wide, flaming arc that brought it down into the ocean a hundred meters to the *Monarch*'s front. Water erupted into the air as the rotor blades beat into the ocean and disintegrated.

Nicolae looked at the aircraft in the water less than a hundred meters off the bow and said, "Shit."

The *Monarch* was headed for a direct hit.

*

Alexei smashed into Val.

Val bounced off the wall and fell to the floor on his back, Alexei on top of him.

Alexei punched Val in the face. Blood from Val's already broken nose sprayed onto the deck. Alexei reared back to punch again.

Val swung his right arm in a wide hook that struck Alexei in the ear, knocking the Russian's weight to one side.

Thrashing his legs, Val slipped from under Alexei.

The Russian rolled away into a barstool lying on the deck. He stood and grabbed it in a two-handed grip.

Val lunged from the ground, trying to cover the distance between him and Alexei quickly.

Alexei raised the barstool and swung it down hard on Val's head.

The barstool broke apart, and Val fell to the deck, stunned.

Alexei stood and kicked Val in the face, flopping him onto his back.

Alexei reached down for one of the broken barstool legs. He raised it over his head to cave Val's skull in.

*

Nicolae looked at the smoke pouring out of the ship's bridge. Thankfully, the machine gun had been silenced.

But no one is steering!

Nicolae looked back at the sinking helicopter.

The *Monarch* had already closed half the distance.

"This is Muntenau, is there anyone on the bridge?" he said urgently into the radio, looking aft.

"Sir, we have eliminated the enemy on the bridge. All clear on the bridge.

Moving to occupy," a commando transmitted.

"No, goddamn it!" Nicolae said, turning back to look at the helicopter. It was damn close now. "Is there anyone there who can steer this thing?"

No response.

Nicolae spun and ran aft, yelling, "Brace for impact!" into his radio. "Brace! Brace! Br—"

*

"I am sorry, my brother," Alexei said to Val.

The deck tilted suddenly. A loud crash and the sound of metal ripping filled the ship. Alexei, Val, and everything in the saloon flew forward.

Alexei and Val slammed into the base of the bar inches from each other. The tables, chairs, Peskov's body, books, and everything else crashed into them.

*

Nicolae made it to the ship's bridge just in time. Had he not, the collision would have thrown him forward into the sea to drown with the helicopter crew.

That didn't mean it felt good.

Nicolae and his two commandos slammed forward and were nearly crushed by flying and falling equipment.

Then the ship seemed to settle back into the water.

Nicolae lifted himself up.

The two commandos with him on the bridge stood and shouldered their weapons, ready to continue the fight.

Nicolae's warning had served his team well. Alexei's mercenaries, without the few seconds' notice to brace, had suffered badly.

"This is Muntenau," Nicolae called over the radio. "Press the attack while they are stunned by the collision. Attack now!"

Nicolae moved aft, descending the steps from the *Monarch*'s bridge and motioning for his two commandos to follow.

*

Val was lying on the deck, jammed between the bar and Peskov's body. There was debris everywhere. Staccato gunshots rang out on the ship, forward and aft.

Val pushed Peskov's body away and tried to stand. He was still groggy from the barstool blow to his head. He reached to the top of the bar and started to pull himself up.

He was halfway to his feet when Alexei slammed into him again.

Val fell to his back, Alexei's hands on his neck.

Alexei screamed in exertion as he put his full weight on Val and squeezed his hands tightly around his throat.

Val reached for Alexei's face to gouge an eye, but his arms couldn't quite reach. Alexei bit down hard on his fingers.

Val tried to scream in pain. But he couldn't breathe.

Val grabbed at Alexei's hands, getting a grip on one of his fingers. He bent Alexei's finger back until it snapped.

Alexei howled in pain. But maintained his grip. He leaned forward, putting all his weight on Val's throat.

Val's eyes bulged as his vision dimmed.

Alexei grunted through clenched teeth as he squeezed tighter and tighter.

Val tried but could not get a grip on another of Alexei's fingers. His strength was fading. He could feel the end coming.

Val thrashed and lashed out at Alexei.

To no avail.

Val's arms flailed, searching for leverage against Alexei's weight. To somehow tilt him off. His right hand felt something on the ground. It was a familiar shape. From a distant past, before he was dying.

His hand closed on it reflexively.

The switchblade.

He pressed the button, opening the long blade, and swung his arm hard, back and forth, across Alexei's body.

Blood sprayed over Val's face, stinging his eyes. Alexei's grip loosened.

Val drove the knife into Alexei, not seeing or caring where it landed.

A gurgling, growling noise erupted from Alexei. Val bucked and writhed. Alexei's weight fell away.

Val rolled over, gasping and coughing.

He filled his lungs with heaving, scratchy breaths. Through blurry vision, dark at the edges, he lunged away from Alexei.

He knew he had to get to his feet to keep fighting.

Val stood, wheezing, shaky and lost.

He spun around, looking for Alexei, fists clenched.

*

Nicolae worked aft through the ship. He and his commandos checked every compartment as they moved. They encountered two defenders with limbs broken in the collision who offered no resistance. The commandos zip-tied their hands and ankles and proceeded aft.

They encountered three defenders who offered resistance but did not last long.

"Aft is clear," came a radio call. "One enemy captured."

"Roger that," Nicolae responded. "We are midship. Moving aft."

A closed door at the end of the passage blocked their way.

The two commandos trained their weapons on it as Nicolae kicked it open.

Nicolae heard sobbing.

He crouched, rifle trained into the wrecked dining room.

Weapon at the ready, Nicolae stepped over a dead body into the saloon area, his commandos moving with him. They moved forward quickly to get clear of the large wooden bar on their left. Nicolae swung his weapon to cover the bar area as the commandos continued aft to the sliding glass door.

Val was on his hands and knees in a large pool of blood, weeping. Alexei lay next to him on his back, dead, his neck slashed open, a large switchblade knife in his chest.

CHAPTER 96

Sydney stood in the dark on the tarmac off the nose of her C-20, looking at her watch and waiting to hear the sound of approaching helicopters. She'd been standing there for an hour, her ears playing tricks on her in the silence of the abandoned airfield outside Chișinău. Her pulse quickened when she thought she heard the faint sound of beating rotor blades in the distance. Leaning forward, straining to hear the faraway sound getting stronger, she scanned the horizon.

Minutes later, though, she was still alone. Cursing. Worrying.

Then she would hear it again. Rotor blades. To the south.

She leaned forward.

Nothing.

It was almost two in the morning. They were late.

They must be out of fuel by now. If they survived the assault.

Nicolae had executed the mission as planned, in total radio silence, except during the assault. He and Sydney didn't want to tip off one of the Russian listening assets deployed all over the Black Sea. It was the right tactic. But she was regretting it now.

Where the hell are they?

Sydney shook her head and started pacing back and forth. The C-20's wings span almost seventy-eight feet. She walked briskly around the aircraft's nose, from one wing tip to the other. Over and over. On the left side of the aircraft, she looked at the two ambulances parked off the runway with their engines and lights off. The paramedics and drivers smoked cigarettes and talked in low voices while they waited. She had talked the Moldovan station chief into helping her get two crews from Chişinău's main hospital. She didn't tell him what it was for.

Sydney had talked a lot of people into a lot of things this evening. She tried not to think about the inevitable moment when she would have to answer for each of them.

On the right side of the airplane, she didn't allow herself to look up at the aircraft's round windows.

She didn't want to see Sasha, Nicolae's wife, who sat in a window seat in the front of the plane crying. Getting her to come along had been dicey. Sydney had allowed Nicolae to send Sasha one text before leaving that said simply, *Do what she says. I love you.*

Then, hours later, Sydney had shown up at their apartment. Introducing herself as "Nicolae's long-time American colleague," Sydney told Sasha to pack a small bag and come with her. She told Sasha she would not be coming back. Probably ever.

Sydney then drove to the small airfield ten miles south of Chişinău that she and Nicolae had selected for the post-assault linkup. It had a runway that was just long enough for the C-20 and was far enough outside of Chişinău that any negative official response would take time to get there. Her aircraft had arrived at midnight, as ordered.

The pilot had given Sydney a sideways look when she'd boarded with Sasha and told him to plan for a flight to Virginia.

"We'll need to refuel to get there, ma'am."

"Then fucking plan to refuel," she said before walking back down the aircraft steps to wait for the helicopters.

But the agreement was that if Nicolae didn't return four hours after they took off on the mission, Sydney would depart and take Sasha to the US without him. Four hours was more than enough time to be successful and return. The helicopters didn't carry more fuel than that, anyway. Sydney would leave with Sasha and figure out how to get Nicolae out later.

If he'd survived.

Sydney looked at her watch again.

They had been gone four hours and eleven minutes.

Sydney exhaled sharply.

"Fuck me," she mumbled as she contemplated what she had to do now.

Sydney stopped at the bottom of the aircraft steps, thinking, *Sasha is going to lose her shit when I tell her we're leaving without Nicolae.*

She paused.

Rotors blades in the distance?

No.

Wishful thinking.

She started up the ladder steps.

The sound got louder.

She spun on her heels and hopped off the steps. She walked south toward the noise.

There was no mistaking it now. The sound of beating rotors reverberated over the trees.

Sydney ran.

She knew the helicopters would land far from the jet so that their rotor wash didn't flip it over.

She ran to meet them.

Something was now visible to the south. Flying blacked out, with no lights, just over the trees, the dark, bulbous helicopter grew in size as the sound of its rotor blades got louder.

Just one? Sydney came to a stop. *Just one helicopter made it?*

The single Mi-14 flared as it decelerated. Sydney closed her eyes as the rotor wash struck her. Dirt and debris flew into her face and then subsided as the pilot dumped power and the big aircraft came to a rest.

Sydney stood just outside the spinning rotor disc as the pilot went through the shutdown procedure.

The aircraft's ramp came down, and a lone figure exited. Shoulders sagging and head held low, the man walked toward Sydney.

Nicolae.

She could see failure weighing him down as he walked. She thought he might collapse before he got to her.

"Nicolae!" she yelled over the scream of the helicopter's turbine engines. She reached out to steady him, holding him by the shoulders. "What happened?"

Nicolae shook his head without raising it to meet her eyes.

"Badly. It went badly. Like they knew we were coming."

Her heart sank.

"Fourteen of my men dead. A helicopter lost." He had tears in his eyes. "What have we done?"

Sydney could not wait any longer.

"Where's Val? Did you get him? Is he okay?"

A long wailing sound poured out from the helicopter as its engines suddenly died. The aircraft had run out of fuel before the pilot could shut her down. Silence spread across the airfield again.

"Yes," Nicolae said, sorrow in his voice. "Yes. We got him."

Sydney sagged into Nicolae. The two leaned into each other.

"Alexei also. We got him also."

Sydney looked up.

"Val killed him."

Sydney took a step back from Nicolae.

"A lot of death tonight, Sydney. We put a horrible thing in motion."

Sydney shook her head. "You and I didn't start all this."

The two ambulances started up, their headlights washing over the helicopter. Bathed in light, Sydney could see bullet holes in the machine.

The ambulances drove by Sydney and Nicolae toward the helicopter's ramp.

"The Russians were going to use Val as a provocation for war," Nicolae said in a voice that betrayed no satisfaction. "We have three prisoners and Alexei's body to prove it."

A figure stumbled off the helicopter's ramp as the ambulances pulled alongside. Sydney recognized him immediately.

It was Val. He put a hand on the helicopter's flank to steady himself.

Sydney stood still, looking at him. Illuminated by the ambulance headlights, even a hundred feet away, he looked like hell. His clothes were stained and ripped, his face smashed, and his hands dark with dried blood.

Val leaned on the helicopter, disoriented. Head down, he rubbed his eyes.

"Nicolae!"

Sydney turned. It was Sasha, running to her husband.

Val looked up and watched Nicolae and his wife embrace.

Sydney turned back to look at Val.

He recognized her.

Val and Sydney stared at each other, separated by the length of the helicopter.

Two commandos carried a body bag off the aircraft's ramp and placed it on the ground near Val. They walked back onto the helicopter.

Val looked down at the body bag. When he raised his eyes back to Sydney, she had turned away.

"Nicolae. We need to leave now," Sydney said. "Get on the plane."

"Okay. Let me say goodbye to my men."

"Are you out of your mind?" Sydney glared at him. "We've got to get out of the country."

Nicolae hesitated.

"Nicolae! I'm sorry. No time for goodbye. And if there were, it would only make things worse. It's time to go. Now."

Nicolae took his wife's hand and walked toward the plane.

Val watched Sydney walk away.

CHAPTER 97

"So, what's new in Prague?" Liam asked when Val answered his phone.

"Just tell me, Liam," Val said as he pulled a chair out and sat down at his dining room table. "Tell me what happened."

Val's anxiety had been ramping up each day for the past month as the CIA's investigation into the events in Moldova and on the Black Sea had progressed.

Moldovan security forces had shown up with a team from the CIA station shortly after Sydney's plane left. They swarmed over the Mi-14, took everyone into custody, and secured Alexei's body.

A week later, Val was on a plane back to Prague, having told his story, everything he knew, a dozen times. His CIA debriefers alternated between irate exasperation and borderline starstruck curiosity. How did this guy, Val Rafter, always end up in these situations? And how the hell did he always survive?

Val was kept isolated during the debriefing. He had no context or understanding of the bigger picture, of what the Moldovan commandos or Russian mercenary prisoners were saying. Worse, he didn't know where Sydney and Nicolae had gone. Were they in trouble? In jail? What?

All he knew was what they told him at the end of his debriefing. It wasn't informative.

"Go home," the Chişinău station chief told him. "And, if I were you, I wouldn't travel or make any headlines again. Ever. Everyone is sick of your bullshit, Rafter. All of us."

After that, the chief of station assigned a marine to escort Val onto his flight out of the Kyiv airport. The young sergeant kept his eyes on Val until the moment the aircraft door shut and then waited at the airport until he was sure the plane had departed Ukraine's airspace.

Liam refused to answer Val's calls for more than a month. When he finally picked up, Val said, "All I want to know is that she is okay."

"Oh, she's great, Val. She's under investigation for a bootleg operation to save your ass. Threw away the most promising career at the agency in the process. How the hell do you think she is?"

"Liam, I—"

But Liam had already hung up.

Ten days later, Liam called Val back.

"CIA is investigating the whole thing," he said, without saying hello. "Sydney's role in it. Alexei's role in it. What the Russians were up to. Who in Ukraine was working with them. All of it. I'll let you know what happens."

"Thank you," Val said as Liam hung up.

Liam called every week or two with a brief update. This morning was the last one. The investigation was complete.

"It's over," Liam said. "The matter is closed."

Val waited, cell phone to his ear.

Molly sensed the tension within him. She came and lay down at his feet.

"I think it worked out pretty well for her, all things considered."

Val exhaled in relief and put his head in his hand.

"Have to say," Liam said in an earnest voice, "what she did was ballsy. More ballsy than your stupid green squirt gun and your even stupider solo assault on Abakumov both put together. She buffaloed the Moldovan station, got a whole bunch of people there, and here in Langley, to jump through their asses to get her agent and his wife visas in just a couple of hours."

Val lifted his head and smiled. He'd wondered, when he saw Nicolae and his wife get on the jet with Sydney, what was going on.

"How did she do that?" Val asked.

"Some kind of bullshit about hypersonic missiles in Transnistria, I think."

"Are you kidding me?"

"No. They think she coached her agent on what to say. Of course, when he got to the States, it was clear he knew nothing about hypersonic missiles."

Val chuckled.

"It's weird," Liam said. "That guy would have been an international hero. Probably could have been president of Moldova some day after what he did. Successfully leading a platoon-size unit on a hasty assault on an underway surface vessel, saving an American citizen, exposing clandestine Russian destabilization ops, and averting an invasion of Ukraine. He would have been the toast of the Western national security community. But he traded it in for life in American suburbia."

Val smiled, picturing Nicolae visiting his daughters at college.

"Good for him."

"Yeah. I guess."

Val said nothing.

"I don't know what would be happening in the world right now if you guys hadn't stopped Alexei."

Val leaned back in his chair and looked down at Molly.

"I don't think any of us do," he said.

"Having Alexei's body was the key," Liam said. "Absent that, it would have been just a bunch of strange, inconclusive debriefings with just Sydney's word to tie it all together."

Liam hesitated and then said, "They sent his body back to Russia."

Val looked up from Molly.

"They attached a big 'fuck you' note to it, of course," Liam added. "Told them we knew everything. We'll be watching. Don't try it again, etcetera, etcetera."

Liam listened for a response. But Val was silent.

"So, Alexei's gone now, Val. All the way gone."

"And Sydney?" Val said, wanting to know and wanting to change the subject. "She's free and clear?"

Liam laughed.

"I guess you could say that."

"What do you mean?"

"She quit. She left CIA."

Val sat in silence, stunned.

"They offered her a choice: some bullshit administrative desk in counter-narcotics to ride out the last years of her career, or early retirement. She took the early retirement."

"But…" Val shook his head. "But she just stopped a land war in Eastern Europe. She should be a hero."

"Yeah. But that's not how she played it the night of the twenty-seventh. For about four hours, she raised hell trying to extract her agent. She promised he had actionable, strategic intelligence. She claimed the Russians had put a contract on him and he had to get out that night.

"Then, all hell broke loose on the Black Sea, and she is standing on an airfield in Moldova with a shot-up helicopter and the body of a dead Russian intelligence officer.

"And you, more than anyone in the world, know that bureaucracies do not appreciate being told, 'Well, you guys are too slow, so I took care of shit myself.'"

Val winced.

"I heard if it wasn't for her boss, she wouldn't have even gotten her retirement."

"What happened?"

"I know you don't know who Maddi Jackson is," Liam said. "But she is part of the old guard here. Grew up through the ranks with the Director. She flew back from Vienna to be in person for the meeting. I've got a buddy that works in Brennan's office. He said Maddi went off on the old man and everyone else in the meeting. The whole floor heard her yelling. Not defending Sydney, really. She was as mad as anyone. But she said Sydney deserved her retirement benefits. Said too many men have gotten away with incompetence and stupidity for too long for her to watch a woman get drummed out for the crime of having more balls than anyone else."

Val laughed.

Molly looked up at him.

Val looked down at her and let out a long, heavy sigh.

Liam was quiet, letting Val come to grips with it.

A moment passed. And then another.

"Where is she now?" Val finally asked.

"I don't know. I tried to talk to her when she left the building, but…she didn't say much."

"What did she say?"

"Something about finally getting to really travel," Liam said with a chuckle. "I woulda thought she'd be done with travel for a while. The way you guys crisscross the world. But she said she would be on a plane tonight. She just didn't know where yet."

"I've called her personal phone a few times. But she won't pick up."

"She's pretty mad."

"But I didn't..." Val started. Then he sat quietly, phone to his ear, looking out at the porch. It didn't matter.

"And sad too, I think," Liam added.

"I get it."

The two old friends sat in silence.

"If I send you something, will you get it to her?"

"Um…yeah. I'll try."

"Thanks."

Liam shook his head.

"What are you gonna do now?" he asked Val.

Val sighed. He looked down at Molly, curled up at his feet.

"I don't know."

Molly lifted her head and looked at Val. He leaned down to scratch her behind the ears.

"But right now, we're going to go for a walk."

"Okay," Liam said. "Talk next week?"

"Yeah. Give me a ring when you have time."

"I will."

"And thanks, Liam. For everything."

"What are friends for?

CHAPTER 98

Val and Molly walked uphill from his flat. The narrow and winding cobblestoned streets climbed from the river toward the castle. After a few steps, Val stole a glance at Molly to see how she was doing.

One of the men must have given her a hard kick during the assault with Burian. The widow who lived next door to Val heard Molly crying the next day as she walked by his flat. After knocking and calling Val's name a few times, she got nervous and summoned the maintenance supervisor. He let her in with the master key, and she found Molly lying on her side, whimpering in pain. The vet said she had two broken ribs. By the time Val finally returned home, she was doing better, but the ribs had been slow to heal. It wasn't until about a month ago that Molly seemed back to her old self. But Val's habit of checking on her persisted.

Molly ignored his concerned look and scampered ahead, darting from smell to smell.

A few blocks later, Val and Molly stepped into a small jewelry store. The faint tinkling of a bell tied to the doorknob announced their entry. The old man behind the counter nodded to him and disappeared into his workshop in the back.

Molly took a few sips from the water dish by the door as Val looked around the shop while they waited. The walls were covered in red velvet, punctuated by antique mirrors hung haphazardly between tall mahogany cabinets. Pieces of every kind sat behind the cabinet glass: delicate filigree, weighty gold, precious stones. Some of the jewelry was covered in dust, forgotten for decades, while others sparkled like new, as if placed there that morning.

The old man returned with a small box. He sat down and motioned Val over to the counter. An elderly woman, the man's wife, stepped out from the back. She smiled at Val and put her hand on her husband's shoulder.

"He is very proud of it."

Her husband, not understanding English, ignored her comment.

The man opened the little jewelry box and lifted a silver locket out by its chain. He gestured at Val, who offered his hand, and the man lowered the silver locket into it. The weight was solid but light. It felt good.

"Beautiful, yes?" the woman said.

Val smiled as he studied the little oval-shaped locket. An intricate fish-scale pattern covered its surface. The work was meticulous, each scale covering the next almost rhythmically, like an actual fish. A tiny but sturdy clasp held the closure shut. Val opened it to reveal two small compartments.

"Yes. Beautiful." Val smiled at the old man. "It's perfect, sir."

The wife translated Val's words, and the old man smiled and put his hand over his heart. "*Děkuji moc.*"

*

Later that evening, Val sat on his balcony and looked down at the river. The sun was below the horizon behind him and the castle, but still throwing light against the sky. The spires on the other side of the river seemed backlit by the blue-tinged clouds.

Val had his feet on the railing, a glass of whiskey sat on the side table next to him. Molly lay on her sheepskin nearby. He took a sip and then got up and went inside his flat.

Molly lifted her head, curious about what he was up to.

Val stepped back onto the balcony a few moments later, carrying the pocket-sized box from the old jeweler in one hand and something else in the other. Molly raised her nose and sniffed, trying to figure it out. Val sat back in his seat.

Lifting the silver locket from the box, Val smiled. He then placed it on his thigh and opened it, admiring the craftsmanship.

Molly watched as Val looked at something in the palm of one of his hands. Giving in to her curiosity, she got up from the sheepskin. She sat at his feet and looked up as he picked something small out of his open palm.

Val smiled at her. He held the small thing in front of her nose. She sniffed at it, and thoughts of fish flooded her brain.

"That's right." He winked at her.

He carefully dropped the carp scales into the locket's compartments.

"From our Christmas together."

The scales fit perfectly. He smiled, thinking of the elderly craftsman. Val had felt awkward a month ago, explaining what he wanted to the wife. But the old man had nailed it.

Val snapped the locket shut. He held the locket up for a moment, admiring it as it dangled from its sliver chain.

"I know…" He glanced at Molly. "It's a little ridiculous."

Val set the locket down on the side table.

"But I hope she'll like it."

Grabbing his whiskey, he leaned back in his chair and put his feet on the railing. He took a slow sip and then looked at Molly.

"I don't know when I'm gonna mail it."

Molly tilted her head.

"I'm hoping I'll know when the time is right. And then I'm hoping she'll get it when I send it. And then I hope…"

Val shrugged at Molly and lifted his gaze to the horizon.

Molly walked back to her sheepskin. She lay down and rested her head on her forepaws, looking at Val.

AUTHOR'S NOTE

This book is based on the experiences of an army buddy of mine. He and I served together back in the early 90s in Germany. We were aviation officers on our first operational assignment. After a few years there, we rotated back to the States and took different paths. I eventually went special operations aviation, and he went human intelligence—recruiting and running spies.

I got out of the army in 2000. My buddy, and many like him, stayed in, enduring the past two decades plus of conflict. The stories of his service told to me over whiskies, at Army Navy games, and during weekends with our wives fascinated and humbled me. I started writing *Duty's Cost*, inspired by him, in 2016.

The inciting spark was his time in Kosovo in 1999. Troubled as it was, it seems now to be the apogee of Russian/American cooperation on the international stage. The tales of his time there amused, intrigued, and disturbed me. They also reinforced my belief that military professionals from different countries, even the most adversarial, have more in common with each other than they do with their own respective civilian populations. Particularly in America, where the civil/military divide yawns ever wider.

So, the concept of a close friendship—formed during shared hardship, when Russian and American interests were, if not aligned, at least temporarily not openly antagonistic—bounced around in my head for a few years. How, with a slight nudge of fate, could their paths cross again after Kosovo? And then again? And then, perhaps...again? And how would that friendship fare as the arc of history and diverging national interests sparked off each other? Under Putin? After 9/11? Iraq? Afghanistan? Syria and then Ukraine? And what would it do to the two friends?

Striving for a realism, I researched extensively and interviewed former CIA, special operations, and State Department professionals. I also leaned on my own experience with the 160th SOAR (A).

The resulting narrative is accurate in terms of the training, tactics, techniques, procedures, and fieldcraft used at the time of the story. Big events, like Kosovo, 9/11, and the Iraq War, are also portrayed as accurately as possible. The same with places and settings. One of the most enjoyable aspects of writing *Duty's Cost* was the opportunity to write about many of the places my friends and I loved so much when we were stationed in Europe.

Using all of that, I wove as realistic a tapestry of fictional events as I could. And then dropped in a couple of characters that are entirely made up.

The three questions I hear a lot are, first: Who is this army buddy? Then: Did any of it really happen? And finally: Why did you end the story in 2014 before the war in Ukraine?

In response to the first: Not going to say. He is too modest, and the topics are too sensitive.

Regarding the second: Yes, some of the funniest, scariest, and most awful things in here are pretty close to shit that really happened.

And finally: The truth is that history accelerated past me. I had the story outlined for a couple of years before Russia invaded Ukraine. (And, yep, I'm an outliner. I can't just sit down and write. At least not very well.) I thought about adjusting the story arc but decided against it. Mostly because I don't think the story needed it. And, also, as flawed as they are, I like the characters too much to put them through that.

Stepping back now, I see the through line from *Spirit Mission* to *Duty's Cost*. I majored in philosophy at West Point and am interested in circumstances that put personal expectations at odds with institutional or national obligation, particularly that most excruciating and lonely of times—when the demands of duty, honor, and friendship come into direct conflict with each other. The characters of this story each have different perspectives on duty, but they all pay a cost.

The Global War on Terror has lasted for more than two decades now. I've steered clear of the national and institutional strategic and moral questions in *Duty's Cost*. The characters in this story, like those that have served in all conflicts, are trying to do their best during the time they served. I'm happy with how the book turned out and hope that the reader will find it interesting enough to finish. By the end of its writing, I had even more respect for my buddy, and all of my classmates and friends that stuck with it and served in this time of war. I hope that the reader will as well.

ACKNOWLEDGEMENTS

First, I must thank him. He knows who he is. But I am not sure he realizes what a gift he was to a writer. Not only was he the inciting spark that launched *Duty's Cost*, which would have been enough—more than a writer has a right to expect—he was also a faithful and generous resource along the way. Thank you, buddy.

Much of the subject matter in *Duty's Cost* was way outside of my experience and sensitive. I relied on a handful of intelligence and military professionals that I need to thank but refrain from naming. Thank you, guys.

Many others were generous with their time, either reading early drafts or providing valuable perspectives on places or events important to the story: James Aiken, Kirby Andrews, Amber Lilyquist, John Melkon, Ted Miller, Rob Rain, Dan Ruiz, Jen Ruiz, Mike Russ, Jean Russ, Mylinh Shattan, Kevin Virgil, Morgan Watson, and David Weinstein. I'm grateful to each of you.

Then there is the finishing crew. Every indie author has one. But the editors and book designer I work with are the best: Michelle Hope, Beth Dorward, and Mark Thomas. Thank you, team!

Finally, and always, my wife, Anna. None of it works without her. What are the odds, baby? I love you.

Ted Russ – June 2024

OTHER BOOKS
BY
TED RUSS

SPIRIT MISSION

To honor bonds forged twenty-five years ago at West Point, Lieutenant Colonel Sam Avery leads an illegal mission deep into ISIS-held territory.

An MH-47G Chinook helicopter departs formation in the Iraqi night. The mission is unauthorized. Success is unlikely. But to save a friend, Sam Avery and his crew of Night Stalkers have prepared for one last flight.

ISIS operatives in Tal Afar, Iraq, have captured American aid worker Henry Stillmont. Avery knows Stillmont as "the Guru," the West Point squad leader who taught him about brotherhood, loyalty, and when to break the rules as a young cadet twenty-five years ago. Sam will risk his career and his life to save him.

As they near their target, Sam reflects on his time in the crucible of the United States Military Academy. West Point made Sam the leader he is. But his fellow cadets made him the man that he is. The ideals of duty, honor, and country have echoed throughout his life and drive him and his comrades as they undertake their final and most audacious spirit mission.

Available now, in paperback and for Kindle®, from Amazon.

SPIRIT OF THE BAYONET

In a future where AI soldierbots do most of the fighting, a dwindling cadre of humans still bear the heavy burden of combat leadership. But even the most advanced military AI is no match for the insatiable appetites of the military-industrial complex. Paul Owens learns that the hard way, igniting a quest for vengeance that burns across the solar system.

Spirit of the Bayonet is a character-driven, thought-provoking hard sci-fi series filled with powered battle suits, derelict spacecraft, sexy synthetics, and ruthless space pirates. Set in a volatile near-future—and told with the same gripping realism and moral complexity readers loved in *Spirit Mission* and *Duty's Cost*—the series explores loyalty, humanity, and the brutal price of vengeance.

Available now, in paperback and for Kindle®, from Amazon.

ABOUT THE AUTHOR

Ted Russ is a writer living in the Carolina mountains with his wife, Anna, their dogs, Charlie and Ripple, and a bunch of chickens and bees.

In a distant prior life, he served as an army officer after graduating from West Point. Ted left the military in 2000 with experience as a special operations helicopter pilot and a philosophy degree.

Possessing no marketable skills, he went back to school and got an MBA. His 25 year journey through the business world was winding—from startups to fortune 500s, domestic to expat assignments, general management and sales to M&A.

He discovered writing late in life, publishing his first novel in 2016 and now tries to make a living writing full time.

Exploring themes of identity, loyalty, and the complexities of the human experience, Ted's works span contemporary fiction and thought provoking sci-fi. Readers praise his novels for their gripping narratives, authenticity, and moral depth.

For new stories, updates, and dispatches from the Ridge — sign up for Ted's newsletter at his website:

tedruss.com